THE COLLECTED STORIES OF
KATHERINE MANSFIELD

THE COLLECTED STORIES
of Katherine Mansfield

◆

with an Introduction by
STEPHEN ARKIN

WORDSWORTH CLASSICS

For my husband
ANTHONY JOHN RANSON
with love from your wife, the publisher.
Eternally grateful for your unconditional love.

Readers who are interested in other titles from
Wordsworth Editions are invited to visit our website at
www.wordsworth-editions.com

This edition published 2006 by Wordsworth Editions Limited
8B East Street, Ware, Hertfordshire SG12 9ET

ISBN 978 1 84022 265 4

Text © Wordsworth Editions Limited 2006
Introduction © Stephen Arkin

Wordsworth® is a registered trade mark of
Wordsworth Editions Limited

Wordsworth Editions
is the company founded in 1987 by
MICHAEL TRAYLER

Typeset in Great Britain by Antony Gray
Printed and bound by Clays Ltd, Elcograf S.p.A.

CONTENTS

IN A GERMAN PENSION

GENERAL INTRODUCTION

Wordsworth Classics are inexpensive editions designed to appeal to the general reader and students. We commissioned teachers and specialists to write wide ranging, jargon-free introductions and to provide notes that would assist the understanding of our readers rather than interpret the stories for them. In the same spirit, because the pleasures of reading are inseparable from the surprises, secrets and revelations that all narratives contain, we strongly advise you to enjoy this book before turning to the Introduction.

Editorial Adviser
KEITH CARABINE
Rutherford College
The University of Kent at Canterbury

INTRODUCTION

Katherine Mansfield's claim on our attention rests on the subtlety, emotional depth and originality of her gifts as a short-story writer. While it is easy to get distracted by the almost operatic drama of her life – her early years in New Zealand, her movements to and from London, her friends, lovers, enemies, her failed health and early death – it is important to remember that she worked tirelessly at her writing and saw in it the best and truest definition of what she had to offer the world. I begin with a brief sketch of her life and her career but would ask you to stay focused on the skill with which Katherine Mansfield brings her imaginitive gifts to bear on many kinds of lives in quite disparate settings with an artist's feeling for the angle and light that would bring her stories to life.

This edition of *The Collected Stories* brings together all the work that she had either published in her lifetime or was readying for publication.

Katherine Mansfield was born on 14 October 1888, in Wellington, New Zealand. Her father, Harold Beauchamp, was a very successful banker. Her mother, Annie Burnell Dyer Beauchamp, had already given birth to two other girls. When Katherine was a year old, her parents left the children to visit England. Her mother came home after six months and gave birth to a fourth daughter, who died. A fifth child, Jeanne, was born, and then in 1893 the family moved to Karori, outside the city, to a house called Chesney Wold that is fondly remembered in Mansfield's story 'Prelude'. It was here that the last Beauchamp child, a boy named Leslie, was born. Having given birth to six children in nine years, Mrs. Beauchamp bore no more.

The Beauchamps set off for England again in 1898, leaving the children with Annie's mother, the much-loved Granny Dyer. The parents were gone for nine months. When they returned, the family moved back to Wellingon, to an elaborate house on Timakori Road with a billiard parlour and a tennis court in the garden. (It was this sumptuous house that Mansfield remembered in 'The Garden Party', where the fictional Sheridan family live above but near the shabby houses of the poor.)

From 1903 to 1906, Katherine attended Queen's College, London. She published five sketches in the *Queen's College Magazine* and returned to New Zealand. Unhappy to be back in the stultifying world of her family, she pleaded to be allowed to go back to England and was permitted to do so with a modest allowance in 1908. Her life in London was bohemian, with a very brief marriage to George Bowden in 1909, and an affair that involved joining a light-opera company, a pregnancy, and a miscarriage in Bavaria, where her mother had arranged lodgings for her. She returned to London in 1910, lived for a short time with Bowden and began publishing the stories in the *New Age* that would be collected as *In a German Pension* in 1911. In December of 1911, she met John Middleton Murry, an editor and critic, and in April of 1912, Murry moved into Mansfield's flat. In 1912 and 1913, Mansfield and Murry co-edited a magazine called *Rhythm* which folded in March of 1913. She met D. H. and Frieda Lawrence in that year, worked as an extra in movies and met a Frenchman named Francis Carco with whom she began an affair.

In February of 1915, her brother Leslie came to London to join his regiment on the Western Front. On 7 October, Leslie Beauchamp was killed at Ploegsteert Wood in Belgium. Katherine was devastated by this death and began obsessively recalling their childhood in New Zealand in her diaries and letters.

In April of 1916, Mansfield and Murry moved to north Cornwall to be near the Lawrences in an attempt at utopian communal living that failed quite miserably. Mansfield returned to London and met Ottoline Morrell and the members of the Bloomsbury circle who were frequent guests at Garsington, the Morrell country house. (She was welcomed into this world; Murry wasn't.) In 1917 she rewrote her early story 'The Aloe' and renamed it 'Prelude'. In that same year she was diagnosed with tuberculosis.

Unable to stand the cold of English winters, Mansfield moved to Bandol in the South of France in January of 1918, and in February had her first tubercular haemorrhage. She returned to London, and in April was divorced by George Bowden. On 3 May she married Murry and in June 'Prelude' was published by the Hogarth Press, which had been created by Leonard and Virginia Woolf. Her mother, whom she had not seen since 1909, died in August 1918.

In 1919, John Middleton Murry became the editor of the *Athenaeum*, and Mansfield began publishing book reviews and poetry (under a pseudonym) in this journal.

In January 1920, Mansfield moved to Menton, France, returning to London in April, where *Bliss and Other Stories* was brought out by Constable at the end of the year. She went back to Menton in September of 1920 and lived with Ida Baker, a friend from her earliest years in London. She produced a steady stream of stories in 1920 and 1921, although her health was precarious. In May of 1921 she moved to Montana-sur-Sierre, Switzerland, where she wrote a great many more stories. In 1922 she went with Murry to Paris for radium treatment for TB and returned to Switzerland when it came to an end in June. She had a second course of radium treatment in September, and in a desperate search for a spiritual cure for her illness, she moved into the Gurdjieff Institute in Fontainebleau, France, in October 1922. On 9 January 1923, she suffered a severe haemorrhage and died. She was buried in the Protestant cemetery in Fontainebleau on 12 January.

What should be clear from this brief summary of Katherine Mansfield's life is that through all her tempestuous relationships (including a brief, intense friendship with Virginia Woolf and another with Bertrand Russell), dangerous travel to France during periods of heavy bombardment, the loss of her beloved brother, and her marriage to Murry, much of which was spent separated from him, she devoted herself to her work. The result is a body of stories remarkable for their range, accomplishment and profound importance to other writers. Elizabeth Bowen, Katherine Anne Porter and Frank O'Connor have all published essays acknowledging her influence as a writer who helped define the modern short story. (See 'Suggestions for Further Reading' on page XVI for references to these essays.)

This collection contains seventy-three stories that Mansfield considered finished (almost all of which were published in her lifetime), and fifteen stories that were unfinished at the time of her death. She was very reluctant to allow John Middleton Murry to republish *In a German Pension*, since she considered these stories to be apprentice work, not at the level of her subsequent fiction. (She had reluctantly agreed to a reprinting, and so the volume was included in the 1945 edition of her work published by Constable under Murry's supervision.)

This edition follows the format of the 1945 volume. Rather than encumber the text with footnotes, I have written a brief headnote for each group of stories.

STEPHEN ARKIN
San Francisco State University

HEADNOTES

A reader of Katherine Mansfield's stories quickly notices that her tone is often satirical and there is an almost fierce candour in the way she addresses family life, relations between men and women and social divisions. Whether she is looking at Germans in her earliest published stories (*In a German Pension*), or looking back at colonial life in New Zealand in such stories as 'The Woman at the Store' or 'Millie', or writing about people she has encountered in Bloomsbury or at Garsington in stories such as 'Bliss' or 'Psychology', there is a narrative perspective that seems to see the fictive worlds Mansfield presents from an angle that is outside and critical of what is being presented. It is as though the young woman who left New Zealand (where she was far from comfortable once childhood had passed) was never really comfortable anywhere else. A good deal of what defines Katherine Mansfield's fiction as modern is the edgy quality her stance as an outsider gives her work. You can hear this tone in this passage from 'A Woman at the Store': 'There is no twilight in our New Zealand days, but a curious half-hour when everything appears grotesque – it frightens – as though the savage spirit of the country walked abroad and sneered at what it saw.'

Bliss and Other Stories

Published by Constable in London in 1920. This was the second collection Mansfield produced (after *In a German Pension* in 1911) but the first she considered mature work. 'Prelude' was first published as a sixty-four-page book by Virginia and Leonard Woolf at the Hogarth Press in 1917. The story was first written as 'The Aloe' in 1915–16.

The setting for 'Prelude' is the New Zealand of Mansfield's childhood. The place names, flowers and wildlife refer to the South and North Islands that make up New Zealand, which was under a British governor-general living in Government House in Wellington.

In general, Mansfield's stories set in New Zealand tend to focus on a search for an authentic self in either a young person (Kezia, Laura) or an adult (Aunt Beryl, Mother), where the temptation is to perform a role expected by society or family. The sense of being an outside observer is strong in these stories and their satirical bite is also powerful. Note how the narrator of 'Je ne Parle pas Français' is allowed to reveal how deeply cynical and exploitative he is through his apparently meandering story.

The Garden Party and Other Stories

Published by Constable in London in 1922. This collection carries over some of the New Zealand settings so important to Mansfield after the death of her brother Leslie during the First World War and offers powerful stories such as 'The Daughters of the Late Colonel'. Alternating between stories set in New Zealand and in Europe was important to Mansfield's sense of who she was as a writer, someone who had moved from a colonial outpost to England, had lived on the Continent, and was always an outsider – even in New Zealand – looking in on people whose customs and speech were strangely fascinating. Notice how 'The Garden Party', 'The Young Girl', 'Her First Ball' and 'At the Bay' all deal with a very young woman facing a crisis in which she must choose between maturity or falling back into comfortable family assumptions.

The Doves' Nest

This collection was edited by J. M. Murry and appeared in London in 1923. In his 'Introductory Note' to the collection, Murry pointed out that Mansfield had died on 9 January 1923, and that the stories were written at about the same time as the stories in *The Garden Party and Other Stories*. These stories were written under great physical duress while Mansfield was in Switzerland and getting radiation treatment in France. There is more than a trace of the complexity of the writer's mood in 'The Fly', the last story she completed.

Unfinished Stories

The unfinished material left by Mansfield at her death offers a valuable insight into her writing process and the high standards she set herself. Murry listed fifteen stories as 'unfinished' in the Constable edition of 1945. Mansfield thought that the number was closer to thirty, but she was invariably severe in judging her own work.

Something Childish and Other Stories

This is the second posthumous collection edited by J. M. Murry, and it appeared in London in 1924. It contains material that Mansfield wrote between publishing *In a German Pension* in 1911 and *Bliss and Other Stories* in 1920. (One remarkable exception is 'The Tiredness of Rosabel' written in 1908 when Mansfield was nineteen.) Murry included 'Poison' in this collection, which Mansfield had rejected (along with 'Sixpence') from *The Garden Party and Other Stories*.

In a German Pension

This was Mansfield's first published collection, and it appeared in London in 1911. She subsequently felt the stories (which are fiercely satirical) were not worthy of her and only reluctantly agreed to have them reprinted. (She was, among other things, sensitive to the anti-German feelings in Britain during and after the First World War.) The setting is a boarding-house and the Bavarian town it is located in. There are quarrels over cultural superiority and a young writer's delight in recording speech found in unlikely places. Readers of the late Jean Rhys may find haunting echoes in her use of Mansfield's alienated young women waiting for some sort of salvation in their lonely rooms.

SUGGESTIONS FOR FURTHER READING

By Katherine Mansfield

The Collected Letters of Katherine Mansfield, Vols 1–4, edited by Vincent O'Sullivan and Margaret Scott, Clarendon Press, Oxford, 1984, 1987, 1993, 1996

The Critical Writings of Katherine Mansfield, edited by Clare Hanson, St Martin's Press, New York, 1987

Journal of Katherine Mansfield, edited by John Middleton Murry, Constable, London, 1954

Secondary sources

Alpers, Antony, *The Life of Katherine Mansfield*, London, 1982

Boddy, Gillian, *Katherine Mansfield: The Woman and the Writer*, Harmondsworth, 1988

Bowen, Elizabeth, 'A Living Writer', in *Collected Impressions*, New York, 1950

O'Connor, Frank, *The Lonely Voice: A Study of the Short Story*, London, 1963

O'Sullivan, Vincent, *Katherine Mansfield's New Zealand*, Auckland, NZ, 1974. (This is a splendid collection of contemporary photographs of the New Zealand in which Mansfield grew up.)

Porter, Katherine Anne, 'The Art of Katherine Mansfield', in *The Collected Essays*, New York, 1970

Tomalin, Claire, *Katherine Mansfield: A Secret Life*, London, 1987

Two useful websites

The Katherine Mansfield Birthplace Trust offers interesting material on the house Mansfield was born in and on her life in New Zealand.
www.katherinemansfield.com

The New Zealand Book Council has a large collection of scholarly material relating to Mansfield's life and work.
www.bookcouncil.org.nz/writers/mansfield.html

COLLECTED STORIES OF
KATHERINE MANSFIELD

BLISS
and other stories

To

JOHN MIDDLETON MURRY

First published 1920

Prelude

I

THERE WAS NOT an inch of room for Lottie and Kezia in the buggy. When Pat swung them on top of the luggage they wobbled; the grandmother's lap was full and Linda Burnell could not possibly have held a lump of a child on hers for any distance. Isabel, very superior, was perched beside the new handyman on the driver's seat. Holdalls, bags and boxes were piled upon the floor. 'These are absolute necessities that I will not let out of my sight for one instant,' said Linda Burnell, her voice trembling with fatigue and excitement.

Lottie and Kezia stood on the patch of lawn just inside the gate, all ready for the fray in their coats with brass anchor buttons and little round caps with battleship ribbons. Hand in hand, they stared with round solemn eyes first at the absolute necessities and then at their mother.

'We shall simply have to leave them. That is all. We shall simply have to cast them off,' said Linda Burnell. A strange little laugh flew from her lips; she leaned back against the buttoned leather cushions and shut her eyes, her lips trembling with laughter. Happily at that moment Mrs Samuel Josephs, who had been watching the scene from behind her drawing-room blind, waddled down the garden path.

'Why nod leave the chudren with be for the afterdoon, Brs Burnell? They could go on the dray with the storeban when he comes in the eveding. Those thigs on the path have to go, dod't they?'

'Yes, everything outside the house is supposed to go,' said Linda Burnell, and she waved a white hand at the tables and chairs standing on their heads on the front lawn. How absurd they looked! Either they ought to be the other way up, or Lottie and Kezia ought to stand on their heads, too. And she longed to say: 'Stand on your heads, children, and wait for the storeman.' It seemed to her that would be so exquisitely funny that she could not attend to Mrs Samuel Josephs.

The fat creaking body leaned across the gate, and the big jelly of a face smiled. 'Dod't you worry, Brs Burnell. Loddie and Kezia can have tea with by chudren in the dursery, and I'll see theb on the dray afterwards.'

The grandmother considered. 'Yes, it really is quite the best plan. We are very obliged to you, Mrs Samuel Josephs. Children, say "thank you" to Mrs Samuel Josephs.'

Two subdued chirrups: 'Thank you, Mrs Samuel Josephs.'

'And be good little girls, and – come closer – ', they advanced, 'don't forget to tell Mrs Samuel Josephs when you want to . . . '

'No, granma.'

'Dod't worry, Brs Burnell.'

At the last moment Kezia let go Lottie's hand and darted towards the buggy.

'I want to kiss my granma goodbye again.'

But she was too late. The buggy rolled off up the road, Isabel bursting with pride, her nose turned up at all the world, Linda Burnell prostrated, and the grandmother rummaging among the very curious oddments she had put in her black silk reticule at the last moment, for something to give her daughter. The buggy twinkled away in the sunlight and fine golden dust up the hill and over. Kezia bit her lip, but Lottie, carefully finding her handkerchief first, set up a wail.

'Mother! Granma!'

Mrs Samuel Josephs, like a huge warm black silk tea-cosy, enveloped her.

'It's all right, by dear. Be a brave child. You come and blay in the dursery!'

She put her arm round weeping Lottie and led her away. Kezia followed, making a face at Mrs Samuel Josephs' placket, which was undone as usual, with two long pink corset laces hanging out of it . . .

Lottie's weeping died down as she mounted the stairs, but the sight of her at the nursery door with swollen eyes and a blob of a nose gave great satisfaction to the S. J.s, who sat on two benches before a long table covered with American cloth and set out with immense plates of bread and dripping and two brown jugs that faintly steamed.

'Hallo! You've been crying!'

'Ooh! Your eyes have gone right in.'

'Doesn't her nose look funny.'

'You're all red-and-patchy.'

Lottie was quite a success. She felt it and swelled, smiling timidly.

'Go and sit by Zaidee, ducky,' said Mrs Samuel Josephs, 'and Kezia, you sid ad the end by Boses.'

Moses grinned and gave her a nip as she sat down; but she pretended not to notice. She did hate boys.

'Which will you have?' asked Stanley, leaning across the table very politely, and smiling at her. 'Which will you have to begin with – strawberries and cream or bread and dripping?'

'Strawberries and cream, please,' said she.

'Ah–h–h–h.' How they all laughed and beat the table with their teaspoons. Wasn't that a take in! Wasn't it now! Didn't he fox her! Good old Stan!

'Ma! She thought it was real.'

Even Mrs Samuel Josephs, pouring out the milk and water, could not help smiling. 'You bustn't tease theb on their last day,' she wheezed.

But Kezia bit a big piece out of her bread and dripping, and then stood the piece up on her plate. With the bite out it made a dear little sort of a gate. Pooh! She didn't care! A tear rolled down her cheek, but she wasn't crying. She couldn't have cried in front of those awful Samuel Josephs. She sat with her head bent, and as the tear dripped slowly down, she caught it with a neat little whisk of her tongue and ate it before any of them had seen.

2

After tea Kezia wandered back to their own house. Slowly she walked up the back steps, and through the scullery into the kitchen. Nothing was left in it but a lump of gritty yellow soap in one corner of the kitchen window-sill and a piece of flannel stained with a blue bag in another. The fireplace was choked up with rubbish. She poked among it but found nothing except a hair-tidy with a heart painted on it that had belonged to the servant girl. Even that she left lying, and she trailed through the narrow passage into the drawing-room. The Venetian blind was pulled down but not drawn close. Long pencil rays of sunlight shone through and the wavy shadow of a bush outside danced on the gold lines. Now it was still, now it began to flutter again, and now it came almost as far as her feet. Zoom! Zoom! A bluebottle knocked against the ceiling; the carpet-tacks had little bits of red fluff sticking to them.

The dining-room window had a square of coloured glass at each corner. One was blue and one was yellow. Kezia bent down to have one more look at a blue lawn with blue arum lilies growing at the gate, and then at a yellow lawn with yellow lilies and a yellow fence. As she looked a little Chinese Lottie came out on to the lawn and began to dust the tables and chairs with a corner of her pinafore. Was that really Lottie? Kezia was not quite sure until she had looked through the ordinary window.

Upstairs in her father's and mother's room she found a pillbox, black and shiny outside and red in, holding a blob of cotton wool.

'I could keep a bird's egg in that,' she decided.

In the servant girl's room there was a stay-button stuck in a crack of the floor, and in another crack some beads and a long needle. She knew there was nothing in her grandmother's room; she had watched her pack. She went over to the window and leaned against it, pressing her hands against the pane.

Kezia liked to stand so before the window. She liked the feeling of the cold shining glass against her hot palms, and she liked to watch the funny white tops that came on her fingers when she pressed them hard against the pane. As she stood there, the day flickered out and dark came. With the dark crept the wind, snuffling and howling. The windows of the empty house shook, a creaking came from the walls and floors, a piece of loose iron on the roof banged forlornly. Kezia was suddenly quite, quite still, with wide open eyes and knees pressed together. She was frightened. She wanted to call Lottie and to go on calling all the while she ran downstairs and out of the house. But IT was just behind her, waiting at the door, at the head of the stairs, at the bottom of the stairs, hiding in the passage, ready to dart out at the back door. But Lottie was at the back door, too.

'Kezia!' she called cheerfully. 'The storeman's here. Everything is on the dray and three horses, Kezia. Mrs Samuel Josephs has given us a big shawl to wear round us, and she says to button up your coat. She won't come out because of asthma.'

Lottie was very important.

'Now then, you kids,' called the storeman. He hooked his big thumbs under their arms and up they swung. Lottie arranged the shawl 'most beautifully' and the storeman tucked up their feet in a piece of old blanket.

'Lift up. Easy does it.'

They might have been a couple of young ponies. The storeman felt over the cords holding his load, unhooked the brake chain from the wheel, and whistling, he swung up beside them.

'Keep close to me,' said Lottie, 'because otherwise you pull the shawl away from my side, Kezia.'

But Kezia edged up to the storeman. He towered beside her big as a giant and he smelled of nuts and new wooden boxes.

3

It was the first time that Lottie and Kezia had ever been out so late. Everything looked different – the painted wooden houses far smaller than they did by day, the gardens far bigger and wilder. Bright stars speckled the sky and the moon hung over the harbour dabbling the waves with gold. They could see the lighthouse shining on Quarantine Island, and the green lights on the old coal hulks.

'There comes the Picton boat,' said the storeman, pointing to a little steamer all hung with bright beads.

But when they reached the top of the hill and began to go down the other side the harbour disappeared, and although they were still in the town they were quite lost. Other carts rattled past. Everybody knew the storeman.

'Night, Fred.'

'Night O,' he shouted.

Kezia liked very much to hear him. Whenever a cart appeared in the distance she looked up and waited for his voice. He was an old friend; and she and her grandmother had often been to his place to buy grapes. The storeman lived alone in a cottage that had a glasshouse against one wall built by himself. All the glasshouse was spanned and arched over with one beautiful vine. He took her brown basket from her, lined it with three large leaves, and then he felt in his belt for a little horn knife, reached up and snapped off a big blue cluster and laid it on the leaves so tenderly that Kezia held her breath to watch. He was a very big man. He wore brown velvet trousers, and he had a long brown beard. But he never wore a collar, not even on Sunday. The back of his neck was burnt bright red.

'Where are we now?' Every few minutes one of the children asked him the question.

'Why, this is Hawk Street, or Charlotte Crescent.'

'Of course it is,' Lottie pricked up her ears at the last name; she always felt that Charlotte Crescent belonged specially to her. Very few people had streets with the same name as theirs.

'Look, Kezia, there is Charlotte Crescent. Doesn't it look different?' Now everything familiar was left behind. Now the big dray rattled into unknown country, along new roads with high clay banks on either side, up steep, steep hills, down into bushy valleys, through wide shallow rivers. Further and further. Lottie's head wagged; she drooped, she slipped half into Kezia's lap and lay there. But Kezia could not open her eyes wide enough. The wind blew and she shivered; but her cheeks and ears burned.

'Do stars ever blow about?' she asked.

'Not to notice,' said the storeman.

'We've got a nuncle and a naunt living near our new house,' said Kezia. 'They have got two children, Pip, the eldest is called, and the youngest's name is Rags. He's got a ram. He has to feed it with a nenamuel teapot and a glove top over the spout. He's going to show us. What is the difference between a ram and a sheep?'

'Well, a ram has horns and runs for you.'

Kezia considered. 'I don't want to see it frightfully,' she said. 'I hate rushing animals like dogs and parrots. I often dream that animals rush at me – even camels – and while they are rushing, their heads swell e–enormous.'

The storeman said nothing. Kezia peered up at him, screwing up her eyes. Then she put her finger out and stroked his sleeve; it felt hairy. 'Are we near?' she asked.

'Not far off, now,' answered the storeman. 'Getting tired?'

'Well, I'm not an atom bit sleepy,' said Kezia. 'But my eyes keep curling up in such a funny sort of way.' She gave a long sigh, and to stop her eyes from curling she shut them . . . When she opened them again they were clanking through a drive that cut through the garden like a whiplash, looping suddenly an island of green, and behind the island, but out of sight until you came upon it, was the house. It was long and low built, with a pillared veranda and balcony all the way round. The soft white bulk of it lay stretched upon the green garden like a sleeping beast. And now one and now another of the windows leaped into light. Someone was walking through the empty rooms carrying a lamp. From a window downstairs the light of a fire flickered. A strange beautiful excitement seemed to stream from the house in quivering ripples.

'Where are we?' said Lottie, sitting up. Her reefer cap was all on one side and on her cheek there was the print of an anchor button she had pressed against while sleeping. Tenderly the storeman lifted her, set her cap straight, and pulled down her crumpled clothes. She stood blinking on the lowest veranda step watching Kezia who seemed to come flying through the air to her feet.

'Ooh!' cried Kezia, flinging up her arms. The grandmother came out of the dark hall carrying a little lamp. She was smiling.

'You found your way in the dark?' said she.

'Perfectly well.'

But Lottie staggered on the lowest veranda step like a bird fallen out of the nest. If she stood still for a moment she fell asleep, if she leaned against anything her eyes closed. She could not walk another step.

'Kezia,' said the grandmother, 'can I trust you to carry the lamp?'

'Yes, my granma.'

The old woman bent down and gave the bright breathing thing into her hands and then she caught up drunken Lottie. 'This way.'

Through a square hall filled with bales and hundreds of parrots (but the parrots were only on the wallpaper), down a narrow passage where the parrots persisted in flying past Kezia with her lamp.

'Be very quiet,' warned the grandmother, putting down Lottie and opening the dining-room door. 'Poor little mother has got such a headache.'

Linda Burnell, in a long cane chair, with her feet on a hassock, and a plaid over her knees, lay before a crackling fire. Burnell and Beryl sat at the table in the middle of the room eating a dish of fried chops and drinking tea out of a brown china teapot. Over the back of her mother's chair leaned Isabel. She had a comb in her fingers and in a gentle absorbed fashion she was combing the curls from her mother's forehead. Outside the pool of lamp and firelight the room stretched dark and bare to the hollow windows.

'Are those the children?' But Linda did not really care; she did not even open her eyes to see.

'Put down the lamp, Kezia,' said Aunt Beryl, 'or we shall have the house on fire before we are out of the packing-cases. More tea, Stanley?'

'Well, you might just give me five-eighths of a cup,' said Burnell, leaning across the table. 'Have another chop, Beryl. Tip-top meat, isn't it? Not too lean and not too fat.' He turned to his wife. 'You're sure you won't change your mind, Linda darling?'

'The very thought of it is enough.' She raised one eyebrow in the way she had. The grandmother brought the children bread and milk and they sat up to table, flushed and sleepy behind the wavy steam.

'I had meat for my supper,' said Isabel, still combing gently.

'I had a whole chop for my supper, the bone and all and Worcester sauce. Didn't I, father?'

'Oh, don't boast, Isabel,' said Aunt Beryl.

Isabel looked astounded. 'I wasn't boasting, was I, Mummy? I never thought of boasting. I thought they would like to know. I only meant to tell them.'

'Very well. That's enough,' said Burnell. He pushed back his plate, took a toothpick out of his pocket and began picking his strong white teeth.

'You might see that Fred has a bite of something in the kitchen before he goes, will you, mother?'

'Yes, Stanley.' The old woman turned to go.

'Oh, hold on half a jiffy. I suppose nobody knows where my slippers were put? I suppose I shall not be able to get at them for a month or two – what?'

'Yes,' came from Linda. 'In the top of the canvas holdall marked "urgent necessities".'

'Well you might get them for me will you, mother?'

'Yes, Stanley.'

Burnell got up, stretched himself, and going over to the fire he turned his back to it and lifted up his coat tails.

'By Jove, this is a pretty pickle. Eh, Beryl?'

Beryl, sipping tea, her elbows on the table, smiled over the cup at him. She wore an unfamiliar pink pinafore; the sleeves of her blouse were rolled up to her shoulders showing her lovely freckled arms, and she had let her hair fall down her back in a long pigtail.

'How long do you think it will take to get straight – couple of weeks – eh?' he chaffed.

'Good heavens, no,' said Beryl airily. 'The worst is over already. The servant girl and I have simply slaved all day, and ever since mother came she has worked like a horse, too. We have never sat down for a moment. We have had a day.'

Stanley scented a rebuke. 'Well, I suppose you did not expect me to rush away from the office and nail carpets – did you?'

'Certainly not,' laughed Beryl. She put down her cup and ran out of the dining-room.

'What the hell does she expect to do?' asked Stanley. 'Sit down and fan herself with a palm-leaf fan while I have a gang of professionals to do the job? By Jove, if she can't do a hand's turn occasionally without shouting about it in return for . . . '

And he gloomed as the chops began to fight the tea in his sensitive stomach. But Linda put up a hand and dragged him down to the side of her long chair.

'This is a wretched time for you, old boy,' she said. Her cheeks were very white but she smiled and curled her fingers into the big red hand she held. Burnell became quiet. Suddenly he began to whistle 'Pure as a lily, joyous and free' – a good sign.

'Think you're going to like it?' he asked.

'I don't want to tell you, but I think I ought to, mother,' said Isabel. 'Kezia is drinking tea out of Aunt Beryl's cup.'

4

They were taken off to bed by the grandmother. She went first with a candle; the stairs rang to their climbing feet. Isabel and Lottie lay in a room to themselves, Kezia curled in her grandmother's soft bed.

'Aren't there going to be any sheets, my granma?'

'No, not tonight.'

'It's tickly,' said Kezia, 'but it's like Indians.' She dragged her grandmother down to her and kissed her under the chin. 'Come to bed soon and be my Indian brave.'

'What a silly you are,' said the old woman, tucking her in as she loved to be tucked.

'Aren't you going to leave me a candle?'

'No. Sh–h. Go to sleep.'

'Well, can I have the door left open?'

She rolled herself up into a round but she did not go to sleep. From all over the house came the sound of steps. The house itself creaked and popped. Loud whispering voices came from downstairs. Once she heard Aunt Beryl's rush of high laughter, and once she heard a loud trumpeting from Burnell blowing his nose. Outside the window hundreds of black cats with yellow eyes sat in the sky watching her – but she was not frightened.

Lottie was saying to Isabel: 'I'm going to say my prayers in bed tonight.'

'No you can't, Lottie.' Isabel was very firm. 'God only excuses you saying your prayers in bed if you've got a temperature.' So Lottie yielded:

> Gentle Jesus meek anmile,
> Look pon a little chile.
> Pity me, simple Lizzie,
> Suffer me to come to thee.

And then they lay down back to back, their little behinds just touching, and fell asleep.

Standing in a pool of moonlight Beryl Fairfield undressed herself. She was tired, but she pretended to be more tired than she really was – letting her clothes fall, pushing back with a languid gesture her warm, heavy hair.

'Oh, how tired I am – very tired.'

She shut her eyes a moment, but her lips smiled. Her breath rose and fell in her breast like two fanning wings. The window was wide open; it was warm, and somewhere out there in the garden a young man, dark and slender, with mocking eyes, tiptoed among the bushes, and gathered the flowers into a big bouquet, and slipped under her window and held it up to her. She saw herself bending forward. He thrust his head among the bright waxy flowers, sly and laughing. 'No, no,' said Beryl. She turned from the window and dropped her nightgown over her head.

'How frightfully unreasonable Stanley is sometimes,' she thought, buttoning. And then, as she lay down, there came the old thought, the cruel thought – ah, if only she had money of her own.

A young man, immensely rich, has just arrived from England. He meets her quite by chance . . . The new governor is unmarried . . . There is a ball at Government house . . . Who is that exquisite creature in *eau de nil* satin? Beryl Fairfield . . .

'The thing that pleases me,' said Stanley, leaning against the side of the bed and giving himself a good scratch on his shoulders and back before turning in, 'is that I've got the place dirt cheap, Linda. I was talking about it to little Wally Bell today and he said he simply could not understand why they had accepted my figure. You see land about here is bound to become more and more valuable . . . in about ten years' time . . . of course we shall have to go very slow and cut down expenses as fine as possible. Not asleep – are you?'

'No, dear, I've heard every word,' said Linda.

He sprang into bed, leaned over her and blew out the candle.

'Good-night, Mr Business Man,' said she, and she took hold of his head by the ears and gave him a quick kiss. Her faint far-away voice seemed to come from a deep well.

'Good-night, darling.' He slipped his arm under her neck and drew her to him.

'Yes, clasp me,' said the faint voice from the deep well.

Pat the handyman sprawled in his little room behind the kitchen. His sponge-bag, coat and trousers hung from the door-peg like a hanged man. From the edge of the blanket his twisted toes protruded, and on the floor beside him there was an empty cane bird-cage. He looked like a comic picture.

'Honk, honk,' came from the servant girl. She had adenoids.

Last to go to bed was the grandmother.

'What. Not asleep yet?'

'No, I'm waiting for you,' said Kezia. The old woman sighed and lay down beside her. Kezia thrust her head under the grandmother's arm and gave a little squeak. But the old woman only pressed her faintly, and sighed again, took out her teeth, and put them in a glass of water beside her on the floor.

In the garden some tiny owls, perched on the branches of a lace-bark tree, called: 'More pork; more pork.' And far away in the bush there sounded a harsh rapid chatter: 'Ha-ha-ha . . . Ha-ha-ha.'

5

Dawn came sharp and chill with red clouds on a faint green sky and drops of water on every leaf and blade. A breeze blew over the garden, dropping dew and dropping petals, shivered over the drenched paddocks, and was lost in the sombre bush. In the sky some tiny stars floated for a moment and then they were gone – they were dissolved like bubbles. And plain to be heard in the early quiet was the sound of the creek in the paddock running over the brown stones, running in and out of the sandy hollows, hiding under clumps of dark berry bushes, spilling into a swamp of yellow water flowers and cresses.

And then at the first beam of sun the birds began. Big cheeky birds, starlings and mynahs, whistled on the lawns, the little birds, the gold-finches and linnets and fantails flicked from bough to bough. A lovely kingfisher perched on the paddock fence preening his rich beauty, and a tui sang his three notes and laughed and sang them again.

'How loud the birds are,' said Linda in her dream. She was walking with her father through a green paddock sprinkled with daisies. Suddenly he bent down and parted the grasses and showed her a tiny ball of fluff just at her feet. 'Oh, papa, the darling.' She made a cup of her hands and caught the tiny bird and stroked its head with her finger. It was quite tame. But a funny thing happened. As she stroked it began to swell, it ruffled and pouched, it grew bigger and bigger and its round eyes seemed to smile knowingly at her. Now her arms were hardly wide enough to hold it and she dropped it into her apron. It had become a baby with a big naked head and a gaping bird-mouth, opening and shutting. Her father broke into a loud clattering laugh and she woke to see Burnell standing by the windows rattling the Venetian blind up to the very top.

'Hallo,' he said. 'Didn't wake you, did I? Nothing much wrong with the weather this morning.'

He was enormously pleased. Weather like this set a final seal on his bargain. He felt, somehow, that he had bought the lovely day, too – got it chucked in dirt cheap with the house and ground. He dashed off to his bath and Linda turned over and raised herself on one elbow to see the room by daylight. All the furniture had found a place – all the old paraphernalia – as she expressed it. Even the photographs were on the mantelpiece and the medicine bottles on the shelf above the washstand. Her clothes lay across a chair – her outdoor things, a purple cape and a round hat with a plume in it. Looking at them she wished that she was going away from this house, too. And she saw herself driving away from them all in a little buggy, driving away from everybody and not even waving.

Back came Stanley girt with a towel, glowing and slapping his thighs. He pitched the wet towel on top of her hat and cape, and standing firm in the exact centre of a square of sunlight he began to do his exercises. Deep breathing, bending and squatting like a frog and shooting out his legs. He was so delighted with his firm, obedient body that he hit himself on the chest and gave a loud 'Ah'. But this amazing vigour seemed to set him worlds away from Linda. She lay on the white tumbled bed and watched him as if from the clouds.

'Oh, damn! Oh, blast!' said Stanley, who had butted into a crisp white shirt only to find that some idiot had fastened the neckband and he was caught. He stalked over to Linda waving his arms.

'You look like a big fat turkey,' said she.

'Fat. I like that,' said Stanley. 'I haven't a square inch of fat on me. Feel that.'

'It's rock – it's iron,' mocked she.

'You'd be surprised,' said Stanley, as though this were intensely interesting, 'at the number of chaps at the club who have got a corporation. Young chaps, you know – men of my age.' He began parting his bushy ginger hair, his blue eyes fixed and round in the glass, his knees bent, because the dressing-table was always – confound it – a bit too low for him. 'Little Wally Bell, for instance,' and he straightened, describing upon himself an enormous curve with the hairbrush. 'I must say I've a perfect horror . . . '

'My dear, don't worry. You'll never be fat. You are far too energetic.'

'Yes, yes, I suppose that's true,' said he, comforted for the hundredth time, and taking a pearl penknife out of his pocket he began to pare his nails.

'Breakfast, Stanley.' Beryl was at the door. 'Oh, Linda, mother says you are not to get up yet.' She popped her head in at the door. She had a big piece of syringa stuck through her hair.

'Everything we left on the veranda last night is simply sopping this morning. You should see poor dear mother wringing out the tables and the chairs. However, there is no harm done – ', this with the faintest glance at Stanley.

'Have you told Pat to have the buggy round in time? It's a good six and a half miles to the office.'

'I can imagine what this early start for the office will be like,' thought Linda. 'It will be very high pressure indeed.'

'Pat, Pat.' She heard the servant girl calling. But Pat was evidently hard to find; the silly voice went baa-baaing through the garden.

Linda did not rest again until the final slam of the front door told her that Stanley was really gone.

Later she heard her children playing in the garden. Lottie's stolid, compact little voice cried: 'Ke–zia. Isa–bel.' She was always getting lost or losing people only to find them again, to her great surprise, round the next tree or the next corner. 'Oh, there you are after all.' They had been turned out after breakfast and told not to come back to the house until they were called. Isabel wheeled a neat pramload of prim dolls and Lottie was allowed for a great treat to walk beside her holding the doll's parasol over the face of the wax one.

'Where are you going to, Kezia?' asked Isabel, who longed to find some light and menial duty that Kezia might perform and so be roped in under her government.

'Oh, just away,' said Kezia . . .

Then she did not hear them any more. What a glare there was in the room. She hated blinds pulled up to the top at any time, but in the morning it was intolerable. She turned over to the wall and idly, with one finger, she traced a poppy on the wallpaper with a leaf and a stem and a fat bursting bud. In the quiet, and under her tracing finger, the poppy seemed to come alive. She could feel the sticky, silky petals, the stem, hairy like a gooseberry skin, the rough leaf and the tight glazed bud. Things had a habit of coming alive like that. Not only large substantial things like furniture but curtains and the patterns of stuffs and the fringes of quilts and cushions. How often she had seen the tassel fringe of her quilt change into a funny procession of dancers with priests attending . . . For there were some tassels that did not dance at all but walked stately, bent forward as if praying or chanting. How often the medicine bottles had turned into a row of little men with brown top hats on; and the washstand jug had a way of sitting in the basin like a fat bird in a round nest.

'I dreamed about birds last night,' thought Linda. What was it? She had forgotten. But the strangest part of this coming alive of things was what they did. They listened, they seemed to swell out with some mysterious important content, and when they were full she felt that they smiled. But it was not for her, only, their sly secret smile; they were members of a secret society and they smiled among themselves. Sometimes, when she had fallen asleep in the daytime, she woke and could not lift a finger, could not even turn her eyes to left or right because THEY were there; sometimes when she went out of a room and left it empty, she knew as she clicked the door to that THEY were filling it. And there were times in the evenings when she was upstairs, perhaps, and everybody else was down, when she could hardly escape from them. Then she could not hurry, she could not hum a tune; if she tried to say ever so carelessly – 'Bother that old thimble' – THEY were not deceived. THEY knew how frightened she was; THEY saw how she turned her head away as she passed the mirror. What Linda always felt was that THEY wanted something of her, and she knew that if she gave herself up and was quiet, more than quiet, silent, motionless, something would really happen.

'It's very quiet now,' she thought. She opened her eyes wide, and she heard the silence spinning its soft endless web. How lightly she breathed; she scarcely had to breathe at all.

Yes, everything had come alive down to the minutest, tiniest particle, and she did not feel her bed, she floated, held up in the air. Only she seemed to be listening with her wide open watchful eyes, waiting for someone to come who just did not come, watching for something to happen that just did not happen.

6

In the kitchen at the long deal table under the two windows old Mrs Fairfield was washing the breakfast dishes. The kitchen window looked out on to a big grass patch that led down to the vegetable garden and the rhubarb beds. On one side the grass patch was bordered by the scullery and washhouse and over this whitewashed lean-to there grew a knotted vine. She had noticed yesterday that a few tiny corkscrew tendrils had come right through some cracks in the scullery ceiling and all the windows of the lean-to had a thick frill of ruffled green.

'I am very fond of a grape vine,' declared Mrs Fairfield, 'but I do not think that the grapes will ripen here. It takes Australian sun.' And she remembered how Beryl when she was a baby had been picking some white grapes from the vine on the back veranda of their Tasmanian house and she had been stung on the leg by a huge red ant. She saw Beryl in a little plaid dress with red ribbon tie-ups on the shoulders screaming so dreadfully that half the street rushed in. And how the child's leg had swelled! 'T–t–t–t!' Mrs Fairfield caught her breath remembering. 'Poor child, how terrifying it was.' And she set her lips tight and went over to the stove for some more hot water. The water frothed up in the big soapy bowl with pink and blue bubbles on top of the foam. Old Mrs Fairfield's arms were bare to the elbow and stained a bright pink. She wore a grey foulard dress patterned with large purple pansies, a white linen apron and a high cap shaped like a jelly mould of white muslin. At her throat there was a silver crescent moon with five little owls seated on it, and round her neck she wore a watchguard made of black beads.

It was hard to believe that she had not been in that kitchen for years; she was so much a part of it. She put the crocks away with a sure, precise touch, moving leisurely and ample from the stove to the dresser, looking into the pantry and the larder as though there were not an unfamiliar corner. When she had finished, everything in the kitchen had become part of a series of patterns. She stood in the middle of the room wiping her hands on a check cloth; a smile beamed on her lips; she thought it looked very nice, very satisfactory.

'Mother! Mother! Are you there?' called Beryl.

'Yes, dear. Do you want me?'

'No. I'm coming,' and Beryl rushed in, very flushed, dragging with her two big pictures.

'Mother, whatever can I do with these awful hideous Chinese paintings that Chung Wah gave Stanley when he went bankrupt? It's absurd to say that they are valuable, because they were hanging in Chung Wah's fruit shop for months before. I can't make out why Stanley wants them kept. I'm sure he thinks them just as hideous as we do, but it's because of the frames,' she said spitefully. 'I suppose he thinks the frames might fetch something someday or other.'

'Why don't you hang them in the passage?' suggested Mrs Fairfield; 'they would not be much seen there.'

'I can't. There is no room. I've hung all the photographs of his office there before and after building, and the signed photos of his business friends, and that awful enlargement of Isabel lying on the mat in her singlet.' Her angry glance swept the placid kitchen. 'I know what I'll do. I'll hang them here. I will tell Stanley they got a little damp in the moving so I have put them in here for the time being.'

She dragged a chair forward, jumped on it, took a hammer and a big nail out of her pinafore pocket and banged away.

'There! That is enough! Hand me the picture, mother.'

'One moment, child.' Her mother was wiping over the carved ebony frame.

'Oh, mother, really you need not dust them. It would take years to dust all those little holes.' And she frowned at the top of her mother's head and bit her lip with impatience. Mother's deliberate way of doing things was simply maddening. It was old age, she supposed, loftily.

At last the two pictures were hung side by side. She jumped off the chair, stowing away the little hammer.

'They don't look so bad there, do they?' said she. 'And at any rate nobody need gaze at them except Pat and the servant girl – have I got a spider's web on my face, mother? I've been poking into that cupboard under the stairs and now something keeps tickling my nose.'

But before Mrs Fairfield had time to look Beryl had turned away. Someone tapped on the window: Linda was there, nodding and smiling. They heard the latch of the scullery door lift and she came in. She had no hat on; her hair stood up on her head in curling rings and she was wrapped up in an old cashmere shawl.

'I'm so hungry,' said Linda: 'where can I get something to eat, mother? This is the first time I've been in the kitchen. It says "mother" all over; everything is in pairs.'

'I will make you some tea,' said Mrs Fairfield, spreading a clean napkin over a corner of the table, 'and Beryl can have a cup with you.'

'Beryl, do you want half my gingerbread?' Linda waved the knife at her. 'Beryl, do you like the house now that we are here?'

'Oh yes, I like the house immensely and the garden is beautiful, but it feels very far away from everything to me. I can't imagine people coming out from town to see us in that dreadful jolting bus, and I am sure there is not anyone here to come and call. Of course it does not matter to you because – '

'But there's the buggy,' said Linda. 'Pat can drive you into town whenever you like.'

That was a consolation, certainly, but there was something at the back of Beryl's mind, something she did not even put into words for herself.

'Oh, well, at any rate it won't kill us,' she said dryly, putting down her empty cup and standing up and stretching. 'I am going to hang curtains.' And she ran away singing:

> How many thousand birds I see
> That sing aloud from every tree . . .

' . . . birds I see That sing aloud from every tree . . . ' But when she reached the dining-room she stopped singing, her face changed; it became gloomy and sullen. 'One may as well rot here as anywhere else,' she muttered savagely, digging the stiff brass safety-pins into the red serge curtains.

The two left in the kitchen were quiet for a little. Linda leaned her cheek on her fingers and watched her mother. She thought her mother looked wonderfully beautiful with her back to the leafy window. There was something comforting in the sight of her that Linda felt she could never do without. She needed the sweet smell of her flesh, and the soft feel of her cheeks and her arms and shoulders still softer. She loved the way her hair curled, silver at her forehead, lighter at her neck, and bright brown still in the big coil under the muslin cap. Exquisite were her mother's hands, and the two rings she wore seemed to melt into her creamy skin. And she was always so fresh, so delicious. The old woman could bear nothing but linen next to her body and she bathed in cold water winter and summer.

'Isn't there anything for me to do?' asked Linda.

'No, darling. I wish you would go into the garden and give an eye to your children; but that I know you will not do.'

'Of course I will, but you know Isabel is much more grown up than any of us.'

'Yes, but Kezia is not,' said Mrs Fairfield.

'Oh, Kezia has been tossed by a bull hours ago,' said Linda, winding herself up in her shawl again.

But no, Kezia had seen a bull through a hole in a knot of wood in the paling that separated the tennis lawn from the paddock. But she had not liked the bull frightfully, so she had walked away back through the orchard, up the grassy slope, along the path by the lacebark tree and so into the spread tangled garden. She did not believe that she would ever not get lost in this garden. Twice she had found her way back to the big iron gates they had driven through the night before, and then had turned to walk up the drive that led to the house, but there were so many little paths on either side. On one side they all led into a tangle of tall dark trees and strange bushes with flat velvet leaves and feathery cream flowers that buzzed with flies when you shook them – this was the frightening side, and no garden at all. The little paths here were wet and clayey with tree roots spanned across them like the marks of big fowls' feet.

But on the other side of the drive there was a high box border and the paths had box edges and all of them led into a deeper and deeper tangle of flowers. The camellias were in bloom, white and crimson and pink and white striped with flashing leaves. You could not see a leaf on the syringa bushes for the white clusters. The roses were in flower – gentlemen's buttonhole roses, little white ones, but far too full of insects to hold under anyone's nose, pink monthly roses with a ring of fallen petals round the bushes, cabbage roses on thick stalks, moss roses, always in bud, pink smooth beauties opening curl on curl, red ones so dark they seemed to turn black as they fell, and a certain exquisite cream kind with a slender red stem and bright scarlet leaves.

There were clumps of fairy bells, and all kinds of geraniums, and there were little trees of verbena and bluish lavender bushes and a bed of pelargoniums with velvet eyes and leaves like moths' wings. There was a bed of nothing but mignonette and another of nothing but pansies – borders of double and single daisies and all kinds of little tufty plants she had never seen before.

The red-hot pokers were taller than she; the Japanese sunflowers grew in a tiny jungle. She sat down on one of the box borders. By pressing hard at first it made a nice seat. But how dusty it was inside! Kezia bent down to look and sneezed and rubbed her nose.

And then she found herself at the top of the rolling grassy slope that led down to the orchard . . . She looked down at the slope a moment; then she lay down on her back, gave a squeak and rolled over and over into the thick flowery orchard grass. As she lay waiting for things to stop spinning, she decided to go up to the house and ask the servant girl for an empty matchbox. She wanted to make a surprise for the grandmother . . . First she would put a leaf inside with a big violet lying on it, then she would put a very small white picotee, perhaps, on each side of the violet, and then she would sprinkle some lavender on the top, but not to cover their heads.

She often made these surprises for the grandmother, and they were always most successful.

'Do you want a match, my granny?'

'Why, yes, child, I believe a match is just what I'm looking for.'

The grandmother slowly opened the box and came upon the picture inside.

'Good gracious, child! How you astonished me!'

'I can make her one every day here,' she thought, scrambling up the grass on her slippery shoes.

But on her way back to the house she came to that island that lay in the middle of the drive, dividing the drive into two arms that met in front of the house. The island was made of grass banked up high. Nothing grew on the top except one huge plant with thick, grey-green, thorny leaves, and out of the middle there sprang up a tall stout stem. Some of the leaves of the plant were so old that they curled up in the air no longer; they turned back, they were split and broken; some of them lay flat and withered on the ground.

Whatever could it be? She had never seen anything like it before. She stood and stared. And then she saw her mother coming down the path.

'Mother, what is it?' asked Kezia.

Linda looked up at the fat swelling plant with its cruel leaves and fleshy stem. High above them, as though becalmed in the air, and yet holding so fast to the earth it grew from, it might have had claws instead of roots. The curving leaves seemed to be hiding something; the blind stem cut into the air as if no wind could ever shake it.

'That is an aloe, Kezia,' said her mother.

'Does it ever have any flowers?'

'Yes, Kezia,' and Linda smiled down at her, and half shut her eyes. 'Once every hundred years.'

7

On his way home from the office Stanley Burnell stopped the buggy at the Bodega, got out and bought a large bottle of oysters. At the Chinaman's shop next door he bought a pineapple in the pink of condition, and noticing a basket of fresh black cherries he told John to put him a pound of those as well. The oysters and the pine he stowed away in the box under the front seat, but the cherries he kept in his hand.

Pat, the handyman, leapt off the box and tucked him up again in the brown rug.

'Lift yer feet, Mr Burnell, while I give yer a fold under,' said he.

'Right! Right! First-rate!' said Stanley. 'You can make straight for home now.'

Pat gave the grey mare a touch and the buggy sprang forward.

'I believe this man is a first-rate chap,' thought Stanley. He liked the look of him sitting up there in his neat brown coat and brown bowler. He liked the way Pat had tucked him in, and he liked his eyes. There was nothing servile about him – and if there was one thing he hated more than another it was servility. And he looked as if he was pleased with his job – happy and contented already.

The grey mare went very well; Burnell was impatient to be out of the town. He wanted to be home. Ah, it was splendid to live in the country – to get right out of that hole of a town once the office was closed; and this drive in the fresh warm air, knowing all the while that his own house was at the other end, with its garden and paddocks, its three tip-top cows and enough fowls and ducks to keep them in poultry, was splendid too.

As they left the town finally and bowled away up the deserted road his heart beat hard for joy. He rooted in the bag and began to eat the cherries, three or four at a time, chucking the stones over the side of the buggy. They were delicious, so plump and cold, without a spot or a bruise on them.

Look at those two, now – black one side and white the other – perfect! A perfect little pair of Siamese twins. And he stuck them in his buttonhole . . . By Jove, he wouldn't mind giving that chap up there a handful – but no, better not. Better wait until he had been with him a bit longer.

He began to plan what he would do with his Saturday afternoons and his Sundays. He wouldn't go to the club for lunch on Saturday. No, cut away from the office as soon as possible and get them to give him a couple of slices of cold meat and half a lettuce when he got home. And then he'd get a few chaps out from town to play tennis in the afternoon. Not too many – three at most. Beryl was a good player, too . . . He stretched out his right arm and slowly bent it, feeling the muscle . . . A bath, a good rub-down, a cigar on the veranda after dinner . . .

On Sunday morning they would go to church – children and all. Which reminded him that he must hire a pew, in the sun if possible and well forward so as to be out of the draught from the door. In fancy he heard himself intoning extremely well: 'When thou did overcome the *Sharp*ness of Death Thou didst open the *King*dom of Heaven to *all* Believers.' And he saw the neat brass-edged card on the corner of the pew – Mr Stanley Burnell and family . . . The rest of the day he'd loaf about with Linda . . . Now they were walking about the garden; she was on his arm, and he was explaining to her at length what he intended doing at the office the week following. He heard her saying: 'My dear, I think that is most wise.' . . . Talking things over with Linda was a wonderful help even though they were apt to drift away from the point.

Hang it all! They weren't getting along very fast. Pat had put the brake on again. Ugh! What a brute of a thing it was. He could feel it in the pit of his stomach.

A sort of panic overtook Burnell whenever he approached near home. Before he was well inside the gate he would shout to anyone within sight: 'Is everything all right?' And then he did not believe it was until he heard Linda say: 'Hallo! Are you home again?' That was the worst of living in the country – it took the deuce of a long time to get back . . . But now they weren't far off. They were on the top of the last hill; it was a gentle slope all the way now and not more than half a mile.

Pat trailed the whip over the mare's back and he coaxed her: 'Goop now. Goop now.'

It wanted a few minutes to sunset. Everything stood motionless bathed in bright, metallic light and from the paddocks on either side there streamed the milky scent of ripe grass. The iron gates were open. They dashed through and up the drive and round the island, stopping at the exact middle of the veranda.

'Did she satisfy yer, sir?' said Pat, getting off the box and grinning at his master.

'Very well indeed, Pat,' said Stanley.

Linda came out of the glass door; her voice rang in the shadowy quiet. 'Hallo! Are you home again?'

At the sound of her his heart beat so hard that he could hardly stop himself dashing up the steps and catching her in his arms.

'Yes, I'm home again. Is everything all right?'

Pat began to lead the buggy round to the side gate that opened into the courtyard.

'Here, half a moment,' said Burnell. 'Hand me those two parcels.' And he said to Linda, 'I've brought you back a bottle of oysters and a pineapple,' as though he had brought her back all the harvest of the earth.

They went into the hall; Linda carried the oysters in one hand and the pineapple in the other. Burnell shut the glass door, threw his hat down, put his arms round her and strained her to him, kissing the top of her head, her ears, her lips, her eyes.

'Oh, dear! Oh, dear!' said she. 'Wait a moment. Let me put down these silly things,' and she put the bottle of oysters and the pine on a little carved chair. 'What have you got in your buttonhole – cherries?' She took them out and hung them over his ear.

'Don't do that, darling. They are for you.'

So she took them off his ear again. 'You don't mind if I save them. They'd spoil my appetite for dinner. Come and see your children. They are having tea.'

The lamp was lighted on the nursery table. Mrs Fairfield was cutting and spreading bread and butter. The three little girls sat up to table wearing large bibs embroidered with their names. They wiped their mouths as their father came in ready to be kissed. The windows were open; a jar of wild flowers stood on the mantelpiece, and the lamp made a big soft bubble of light on the ceiling.

'You seem pretty snug, mother,' said Burnell, blinking at the light. Isabel and Lottie sat one on either side of the table, Kezia at the bottom – the place at the top was empty.

'That's where my boy ought to sit,' thought Stanley. He tightened his arm round Linda's shoulder. By God, he was a perfect fool to feel as happy as this!

'We are, Stanley. We are very snug,' said Mrs Fairfield, cutting Kezia's bread into fingers.

'Like it better than town – eh, children?' asked Burnell.

'Oh, yes,' said the three little girls, and Isabel added as an after-thought: 'Thank you very much indeed, father dear.'

'Come upstairs,' said Linda. 'I'll bring your slippers.'

But the stairs were too narrow for them to go up arm in arm. It was quite dark in the room. He heard her ring tapping on the marble mantelpiece as she felt for the matches.

'I've got some, darling. I'll light the candles.'

But instead he came up behind her and again he put his arms round her and pressed her head into his shoulder.

'I'm so confoundedly happy,' he said.

'Are you?' She turned and put her hands on his breast and looked up at him.

'I don't know what has come over me,' he protested.

It was quite dark outside now and heavy dew was falling. When Linda shut the window the cold dew touched her fingertips. Far away a dog barked. 'I believe there is going to be a moon,' she said.

At the words, and with the cold wet dew on her fingers, she felt as though the moon had risen – that she was being strangely discovered in a flood of cold light. She shivered; she came away from the window and sat down upon the box ottoman beside Stanley.

* * *

In the dining-room, by the flicker of a wood fire, Beryl sat on a hassock playing the guitar. She had bathed and changed all her clothes. Now she wore a white muslin dress with black spots on it and in her hair she had pinned a black silk rose.

> Nature has gone to her rest, love,
>   See, we are alone.
> Give me your hand to press, love,
>   Lightly within my own.

She played and sang half to herself, for she was watching herself playing and singing. The firelight gleamed on her shoes, on the ruddy belly of the guitar, and on her white fingers . . .

'If I were outside the window and looked in and saw myself I really would be rather struck,' thought she. Still more softly she played the accompaniment – not singing now but listening.

' . . . The first time that I ever saw you, little girl – oh, you had no idea that you were not alone – you were sitting with your little feet upon a hassock, playing the guitar. God, I can never forget . . . ' Beryl flung up her head and began to sing again:

> Even the moon is aweary . . .

But there came a loud bang at the door. The servant girl's crimson face popped through.

'Please, Miss Beryl, I've got to come and lay.'

'Certainly, Alice,' said Beryl, in a voice of ice. She put the guitar in a corner. Alice lunged in with a heavy black iron tray.

'Well, I have had a job with that oving,' said she. 'I can't get nothing to brown.'

'Really!' said Beryl.

But no, she could not stand that fool of a girl. She ran into the dark drawing-room and began walking up and down . . . Oh, she was restless, restless. There was a mirror over the mantel. She leaned her arms along and looked at her pale shadow in it. How beautiful she looked, but there was nobody to see, nobody.

'Why must you suffer so?' said the face in the mirror. 'You were not made for suffering . . . Smile!'

Beryl smiled, and really her smile *was* so adorable that she smiled again – but this time because she could not help it.

8

'Good morning, Mrs Jones.'

'Oh, good morning, Mrs Smith. I'm so glad to see you. Have you brought your children?'

'Yes, I've brought both my twins. I have had another baby since I saw you last, but she came so suddenly that I haven't had time to make her any clothes, yet. So I left her . . . How is your husband?'

'Oh, he is very well, thank you. At least he had a nawful cold but Queen Victoria – she's my godmother, you know – sent him a case of pineapples and that cured it immediately. Is that your new servant?'

'Yes, her name's Gwen. I've only had her two days. Oh, Gwen, this is my friend, Mrs Smith.'

'Good morning, Mrs Smith. Dinner won't be ready for about ten minutes.'

'I don't think you ought to introduce me to the servant. I think I ought to just begin talking to her.'

'Well, she's more of a lady-help than a servant and you do introduce lady-helps, I know, because Mrs Samuel Josephs had one.'

'Oh, well, it doesn't matter,' said the servant, carelessly, beating up a chocolate custard with half a broken clothes peg. The dinner was baking beautifully on a concrete step. She began to lay the cloth on a pink garden seat. In front of each person she put two geranium-leaf plates, a pine-needle fork and a twig knife. There were three daisy heads on a laurel leaf for poached eggs, some slices of fuchsia-petal cold beef, some lovely little rissoles made of earth and water and dandelion seeds, and the chocolate custard which she had decided to serve in the pawa shell she had cooked it in.

'You needn't trouble about my children,' said Mrs Smith graciously. 'If you'll just take this bottle and fill it at the tap – I mean at the dairy.'

'Oh, all right,' said Gwen, and she whispered to Mrs Jones: 'Shall I go and ask Alice for a little bit of real milk?'

But someone called from the front of the house and the luncheon party melted away, leaving the charming table, leaving the rissoles and the poached eggs to the ants and to an old snail who pushed his quivering horns over the edge of the garden seat and began to nibble a geranium plate.

'Come round to the front, children. Pip and Rags have come.'

The Trout boys were the cousins Kezia had mentioned to the storeman. They lived about a mile away in a house called Monkey Tree Cottage. Pip was tall for his age, with lank black hair and a white face, but Rags was very small and so thin that when he was undressed his shoulder blades stuck out like two little wings. They had a mongrel dog with pale blue eyes and a long tail turned up at the end who followed them everywhere; he was called Snooker. They spent half their time combing and brushing Snooker and dosing him with various awful mixtures concocted by Pip, and kept secretly by him in a broken jug covered with an old kettle lid. Even faithful little Rags was not allowed to know the full secret of these mixtures . . . Take some carbolic tooth powder and a pinch of sulphur powdered up fine, and perhaps a bit of starch to stiffen up Snooker's coat . . . But that was not all; Rags privately thought that the rest was gunpowder . . . And he never was allowed to help with the mixing because of the danger . . . 'Why, if a spot of this flew in your eye, you would be blinded for life,' Pip would say, stirring the mixture with an iron spoon. 'And there's always the chance – just the chance, mind you – of it exploding if you whack it hard enough . . . Two spoons of this in a kerosene tin will be enough to kill thousands of fleas.' But Snooker spent all his spare time biting and snuffling, and he stank abominably.

'It's because he is such a grand fighting dog,' Pip would say. 'All fighting dogs smell.'

The Trout boys had often spent the day with the Burnells in town, but now that they lived in this fine house and boncer garden they were inclined to be very friendly. Besides, both of them liked playing with girls – Pip, because he could fox them so, and because Lottie was so easily frightened, and Rags for a shameful reason. He adored dolls. How he would look at a doll as it lay asleep, speaking in a whisper and smiling timidly, and what a treat it was to him to be allowed to hold one . . .

'Curve your arms round her. Don't keep them stiff like that. You'll drop her,' Isabel would say sternly.

Now they were standing on the veranda and holding back Snooker who wanted to go into the house but wasn't allowed to because Aunt Linda hated decent dogs.

'We came over in the bus with mum,' they said, 'and we're going to spend the afternoon with you. We brought over a batch of our gingerbread for Aunt Linda. Our Minnie made it. It's all over nuts.'

'I skinned the almonds,' said Pip. 'I just stuck my hand into a saucepan of boiling water and grabbed them out and gave them a kind of pinch and the nuts flew out of the skins, some of them as high as the ceiling. Didn't they, Rags?'

Rags nodded. 'When they make cakes at our place,' said Pip, 'we always stay in the kitchen, Rags and me, and I get the bowl and he gets the spoon and the egg beater. Sponge cake's best. It's all frothy stuff, then.'

He ran down the veranda steps to the lawn, planted his hands on the grass, bent forward, and just did not stand on his head.

'That lawn's all bumpy,' he said. 'You have to have a flat place for standing on your head. I can walk round the monkey tree on my head at our place. Can't I, Rags?'

'Nearly,' said Rags faintly.

'Stand on your head on the veranda. That's quite flat,' said Kezia.

'No, smarty,' said Pip. 'You have to do it on something soft. Because if you give a jerk and fall over, something in your neck goes click, and it breaks off. Dad told me.'

'Oh, do let's play something,' said Kezia.

'Very well,' said Isabel quickly, 'we'll play hospitals. I will be the nurse and Pip can be the doctor and you and Lottie and Rags can be the sick people.'

Lottie didn't want to play that, because last time Pip had squeezed something down her throat and it hurt awfully.

'Pooh,' scoffed Pip. 'It was only the juice out of a bit of mandarin peel.'

'Well, let's play ladies,' said Isabel. 'Pip can be the father and you can be all our dear little children.'

'I hate playing ladies,' said Kezia. 'You always make us go to church hand in hand and come home and go to bed.'

Suddenly Pip took a filthy handkerchief out of his pocket. 'Snooker! Here, sir,' he called. But Snooker, as usual, tried to sneak away, his tail between his legs. Pip leapt on top of him, and pressed him between his knees.

'Keep his head firm, Rags,' he said, and he tied the handkerchief round Snooker's head with a funny knot sticking up at the top.

'Whatever is that for?' asked Lottie.

'It's to train his ears to grow more close to his head – see?' said Pip.

'All fighting dogs have ears that lie back. But Snooker's ears are a bit too soft.'

'I know,' said Kezia. 'They are always turning inside out. I hate that.'

Snooker lay down, made one feeble effort with his paw to get the handkerchief off, but finding he could not, trailed after the children, shivering with misery.

9

Pat came swinging along; in his hand he held a little tomahawk that winked in the sun.

'Come with me,' he said to the children, 'and I'll show you how the kings of Ireland chop the head off a duck.'

They drew back – they didn't believe him, and besides, the Trout boys had never seen Pat before.

'Come on now,' he coaxed, smiling and holding out his hand to Kezia.

'Is it a real duck's head? One from the paddock?'

'It is,' said Pat. She put her hand in his hard dry one, and he stuck the tomahawk in his belt and held out the other to Rags. He loved little children.

'I'd better keep hold of Snooker's head if there's going to be any blood about,' said Pip, 'because the sight of blood makes him awfully wild.' He ran ahead dragging Snooker by the handkerchief.

'Do you think we ought to go?' whispered Isabel. 'We haven't asked or anything. Have we?'

At the bottom of the orchard a gate was set in the paling fence. On the other side a steep bank led down to a bridge that spanned the creek, and once up the bank on the other side you were on the fringe of the paddocks. A little old stable in the first paddock had been turned into a fowl-house. The fowls had strayed far away across the paddock down to a dumping ground in a hollow, but the ducks kept close to that part of the creek that flowed under the bridge.

Tall bushes overhung the stream with red leaves and yellow flowers and clusters of blackberries. At some places the stream was wide and shallow, but at others it tumbled into deep little pools with foam at the edges and quivering bubbles. It was in these pools that the big white ducks had made themselves at home, swimming and guzzling along the weedy banks.

Up and down they swam, preening their dazzling breasts, and

other ducks with the same dazzling breasts and yellow bills swam upside down with them.

'There is the little Irish navy,' said Pat, 'and look at the old admiral there with the green neck and the grand little flagstaff on his tail.'

He pulled a handful of grain from his pocket and began to walk towards the fowl-house, lazy, his straw hat with the broken crown pulled over his eyes.

'Lid. Lid–lid–lid–lid–' he called.

'Qua. Qua–qua–qua–qua– ' answered the ducks, making for land, and flapping and scrambling up the bank they streamed after him in a long waddling line. He coaxed them, pretending to throw the grain, shaking it in his hands and calling to them until they swept round him in a white ring.

From far away the fowls heard the clamour and they too came running across the paddock, their heads thrust forward, their wings spread, turning in their feet in the silly way fowls run and scolding as they came.

Then Pat scattered the grain and the greedy ducks began to gobble. Quickly he stooped, seized two, one under each arm, and strode across to the children. Their darting heads and round eyes frightened the children – all except Pip.

'Come on, sillies,' he cried, 'they can't bite. They haven't any teeth. They've only got those two little holes in their beaks for breathing through.'

'Will you hold one while I finish with the other?' asked Pat. Pip let go of Snooker. 'Won't I? Won't I? Give us one. I don't mind how much he kicks.'

He nearly sobbed with delight when Pat gave the white lump into his arms.

There was an old stump beside the door of the fowl-house. Pat grabbed the duck by the legs, laid it flat across the stump, and almost at the same moment down came the little tomahawk and the duck's head flew off the stump. Up the blood spurted over the white feathers and over his hand.

When the children saw the blood they were frightened no longer. They crowded round him and began to scream. Even Isabel leaped about crying: 'The blood! The blood!' Pip forgot all about his duck. He simply threw it away from him and shouted, 'I saw it. I saw it,' and jumped round the wood block.

Rags, with cheeks as white as paper, ran up to the little head, put out a finger as if he wanted to touch it, shrank back again and then again put out a finger. He was shivering all over.

Even Lottie, frightened little Lottie, began to laugh and pointed at the duck and shrieked: 'Look, Kezia, look.'

'Watch it!' shouted Pat. He put down the body and it began to waddle – with only a long spurt of blood where the head had been; it began to pad away without a sound towards the steep bank that led to the stream . . . That was the crowning wonder.

'Do you see that? Do you see that?' yelled Pip. He ran among the little girls tugging at their pinafores.

'It's like a little engine. It's like a funny little railway engine,' squealed Isabel.

But Kezia suddenly rushed at Pat and flung her arms round his legs and butted her head as hard as she could against his knees.

'Put head back! Put head back!' she screamed.

When he stooped to move her she would not let go or take her head away. She held on as hard as she could and sobbed: 'Head back! Head back!' until it sounded like a loud strange hiccup.

'It's stopped. It's tumbled over. It's dead,' said Pip.

Pat dragged Kezia up into his arms. Her sunbonnet had fallen back, but she would not let him look at her face. No, she pressed her face into a bone in his shoulder and clasped her arms round his neck.

The children stopped screaming as suddenly as they had begun. They stood round the dead duck. Rags was not frightened of the head any more. He knelt down and stroked it, now.

'I don't think the head is quite dead yet,' he said. 'Do you think it would keep alive if I gave it something to drink?'

But Pip got very cross: 'Bah! You baby.' He whistled to Snooker and went off.

When Isabel went up to Lottie, Lottie snatched away.

'What are you always touching me for, Isabel?'

'There now,' said Pat to Kezia. 'There's the grand little girl.'

She put up her hands and touched his ears. She felt something. Slowly she raised her quivering face and looked. Pat wore little round gold earrings. She never knew that men wore earrings. She was very much surprised.

'Do they come on and off?' she asked huskily.

10

Up in the house, in the warm tidy kitchen, Alice, the servant girl, was getting the afternoon tea. She was 'dressed'. She had on a black stuff dress that smelt under the arms, a white apron like a large sheet of paper, and a lace bow pinned on to her hair with two jetty pins. Also her comfortable carpet slippers were changed for a pair of black leather ones that pinched her corn on her little toe something dreadful . . .

It was warm in the kitchen. A blowfly buzzed, a fan of whitey steam came out of the kettle, and the lid kept up a rattling jig as the water bubbled. The clock ticked in the warm air, slow and deliberate, like the click of an old woman's knitting needle, and sometimes – for no reason at all, for there wasn't any breeze – the blind swung out and back, tapping the window.

Alice was making watercress sandwiches. She had a lump of butter on the table, a barracouta loaf, and the cresses tumbled in a white cloth.

But propped against the butter-dish there was a dirty, greasy little book, half unstitched, with curled edges, and while she mashed the butter she read:

To dream of black-beetles drawing a hearse is bad. Signifies death of one you hold near or dear, either father, husband, brother, son or intended. If beetles crawl backwards as you watch them it means death from fire or from great height such as flight of stairs, scaffolding, etc.'

'Spiders. To dream of spiders creeping over you is good. Signifies large sum of money in near future. Should party be in family way an easy confinement may be expected. But care should be taken in sixth month to avoid eating of probable present of shellfish . . .

How many thousand birds I see.

Oh, life. There was Miss Beryl. Alice dropped the knife and slipped the *Dream Book* under the butter-dish. But she hadn't time to hide it quite, for Beryl ran into the kitchen and up to the table, and the first thing her eye lighted on were those greasy edges. Alice saw Miss Beryl's meaning little smile and the way she raised her eyebrows and screwed up her eyes as though she were not quite sure what that could be. She decided to answer if Miss Beryl should ask her: 'Nothing as belongs to you, miss.' But she knew Miss Beryl would not ask her.

Alice was a mild creature in reality, but she had the most marvellous retorts ready for questions that she knew would never be put to her. The composing of them and the turning of them over and over in her mind comforted her just as much as if they'd been expressed. Really, they kept her alive in places where she'd been that chivvied she'd been afraid to go to bed at night with a box of matches on the chair in case she bit the tops off in her sleep, as you might say.

'Oh, Alice,' said Miss Beryl. 'There's one extra to tea, so heat a plate of yesterday's scones, please. And put on the Victoria sandwich as well as the coffee cake. And don't forget to put little doyleys under the plates – will you? You did yesterday, you know, and the tea looked so ugly and common. And, Alice, don't put that dreadful old pink and green cosy on the afternoon teapot again. That is only for the mornings. Really, I think it ought to be kept for the kitchen – it's so shabby, and quite smelly. Put on the Japanese one. You quite understand, don't you?'

Miss Beryl had finished.

        That sing aloud from every tree . . .

she sang as she left the kitchen, very pleased with her firm handling of Alice.

Oh, Alice was wild. She wasn't one to mind being told, but there was something in the way Miss Beryl had of speaking to her that she couldn't stand. Oh, that she couldn't. It made her curl up inside, as you might say, and she fair trembled. But what Alice really hated Miss Beryl for was that she made her feel low. She talked to Alice in a special voice as though she wasn't quite all there; and she never lost her temper with her – never. Even when Alice dropped anything or forgot anything important Miss Beryl seemed to have expected it to happen.

'If you please, Mrs Burnell,' said an imaginary Alice, as she buttered the scones, 'I'd rather not take my orders from Miss Beryl. I may be only a common servant girl as doesn't know how to play the guitar, but . . . '

This last thrust pleased her so much that she quite recovered her temper.

'The only thing to do,' she heard, at she opened the dining-room door, 'is to cut the sleeves out entirely and just have a broad band of black velvet over the shoulders instead . . . '

II

The white duck did not look as if it had ever had a head when Alice placed it in front of Stanley Burnell that night. It lay, in beautifully basted resignation, on a blue dish – its legs tied together with a piece of string and a wreath of little balls of stuffing round it.

It was hard to say which of the two, Alice or the duck, looked the better basted; they were both such a rich colour and they both had the same air of gloss and strain. But Alice was fiery red and the duck a Spanish mahogany.

Burnell ran his eye along the edge of the carving knife. He prided himself very much upon his carving, upon making a first-class job of it. He hated seeing a woman carve; they were always too slow and they never seemed to care what the meat looked like afterwards. Now he did; he took a real pride in cutting delicate shaves of cold beef, little wads of mutton, just the right thickness, and in dividing a chicken or a duck with nice precision . . .

'Is this the first of the home products?' he asked, knowing perfectly well that it was.

'Yes, the butcher did not come. We have found out that he only calls twice a week.'

But there was no need to apologise. It was a superb bird. It wasn't meat at all, but a kind of very superior jelly. 'My father would say,' said Burnell, 'this must have been one of those birds whose mother played to it in infancy upon the German flute. And the sweet strains of the dulcet instrument acted with such effect upon the infant mind . . . Have some more, Beryl? You and I are the only ones in this house with a real feeling for food. I'm perfectly willing to state, in a court of law, if necessary, that I love good food.'

Tea was served in the drawing-room, and Beryl, who for some reason had been very charming to Stanley ever since he came home, suggested a game of crib. They sat at a little table near one of the open windows. Mrs Fairfield disappeared, and Linda lay in a rocking-chair, her arms above her head, rocking to and fro.

'You don't want the light – do you, Linda?' said Beryl. She moved the tall lamp so that she sat under its soft light.

How remote they looked, those two, from where Linda sat and rocked. The green table, the polished cards, Stanley's big hands and Beryl's tiny ones, all seemed to be part of one mysterious movement. Stanley himself, big and solid, in his dark suit, took his ease, and Beryl tossed her bright head and pouted. Round her throat she wore an unfamiliar velvet ribbon. It changed her, some-how – altered the shape of her face – but it was charming, Linda decided. The room smelled of lilies; there were two big jars of arums in the fireplace.

'Fifteen two – fifteen four – and a pair is six and a run of three is nine,' said Stanley, so deliberately he might have been counting sheep.

'I've nothing but two pairs,' said Beryl, exaggerating her woe because she knew how he loved winning.

The cribbage pegs were like two little people going up the road together, turning round the sharp corner, and coming down the road again. They were pursuing each other. They did not so much want to get ahead as to keep near enough to talk – to keep near, perhaps that was all.

But no, there was always one who was impatient and hopped away as the other came up, and would not listen. Perhaps the white peg was frightened of the red one, or perhaps he was cruel and would not give the red one a chance to speak . . .

In the front of her dress Beryl wore a bunch of pansies, and once when the little pegs were side by side, she bent over and the pansies dropped out and covered them.

'What a shame,' said she, picking up the pansies. 'Just as they had a chance to fly into each other's arms.'

'Farewell, my girl,' laughed Stanley, and away the red peg hopped.

The drawing-room was long and narrow with glass doors that gave on to the veranda. It had a cream paper with a pattern of gilt roses, and the furniture, which had belonged to old Mrs Fairfield, was dark and plain. A little piano stood against the wall with yellow pleated silk let into the carved front. Above it hung an oil painting by Beryl of a large cluster of surprised looking clematis. Each flower was the size of a small saucer, with a centre like an astonished eye fringed in black. But the room was not finished yet. Stanley had set his heart on a Chesterfield and two decent chairs. Linda liked it best as it was . . .

Two big moths flew in through the window and round and round the circle of lamplight.

'Fly away before it is too late. Fly out again.'

Round and round they flew; they seemed to bring the silence and the moonlight in with them on their silent wings . . .

'I've two kings,' said Stanley. 'Any good?'

'Quite good,' said Beryl.

Linda stopped rocking and got up. Stanley looked across. 'Anything the matter, darling?'

'No, nothing. I'm going to find mother.'

She went out of the room and standing at the foot of the stairs she called, but her mother's voice answered her from the veranda.

The moon that Lottie and Kezia had seen from the storeman's wagon was full, and the house, the garden, the old woman and Linda – all were bathed in dazzling light.

'I have been looking at the aloe,' said Mrs Fairfield. 'I believe it is going to flower this year. Look at the top there. Are those buds, or is it only an effect of light?'

As they stood on the steps, the high grassy bank on which the aloe rested rose up like a wave, and the aloe seemed to ride upon it like a ship with the oars lifted. Bright moonlight hung upon the lifted oars like water, and on the green wave glittered the dew.

'Do you feel it, too,' said Linda, and she spoke to her mother with the special voice that women use at night to each other as though they spoke in their sleep or from some hollow cave – 'Don't you feel that it is coming towards us?'

She dreamed that she was caught up out of the cold water into the ship with the lifted oars and the budding mast. Now the oars fell striking quickly, quickly. They rowed far away over the top of the garden trees, the paddocks and the dark bush beyond. Ah, she heard herself cry: 'Faster! Faster!' to those who were rowing.

How much more real this dream was than that they should go back to the house where the sleeping children lay and where Stanley and Beryl played cribbage.

'I believe those are buds,' said she. 'Let us go down into the garden, mother. I like that aloe. I like it more than anything here. And I am sure I shall remember it long after I've forgotten all the other things.'

She put her hand on her mother's arm and they walked down the steps, round the island and on to the main drive that led to the front gates.

Looking at it from below she could see the long sharp thorns that edged the aloe leaves, and at the sight of them her heart grew hard . . . She particularly liked the long sharp thorns . . . Nobody would dare to come near the ship or to follow after.

'Not even my Newfoundland dog,' thought she, 'that I'm so fond of in the daytime.'

For she really was fond of him; she loved and admired and respected him tremendously. Oh, better than anyone else in the world. She knew him through and through. He was the soul of truth and decency, and for all his practical experience he was awfully simple, easily pleased and easily hurt . . .

If only he wouldn't jump at her so, and bark so loudly, and watch her with such eager, loving eyes. He was too strong for her; she had always hated things that rushed at her, from a child. There were times when he was frightening – really frightening – when she just had not screamed at the top of her voice: 'You are killing me.' And at those times she had longed to say the most coarse, hateful things . . . 'You know I'm very delicate. You know as well as I do that my heart is affected, and the doctor has told you I may die any moment. I have had three great lumps of children already . . . '

Yes, yes, it was true. Linda snatched her hand from her mother's arm. For all her love and respect and admiration she hated him. And how tender he always was after times like those, how submissive, how thoughtful. He would do anything for her; he longed to serve her . . . Linda heard herself saying in a weak voice: 'Stanley, would you light a candle?'

And she heard his joyful voice answer: 'Of course I will, my darling.' And he leapt out of bed as though he were going to leap at the moon for her.

It had never been so plain to her as it was at this moment. There were all her feelings for him, sharp and defined, one as true as the other. And there was this other, this hatred, just as real as the rest. She could have done her feelings up in little packets and given them to Stanley. She longed to hand him that last one, for a surprise. She could see his eyes as he opened that . . .

She hugged her folded arms and began to laugh silently. How absurd life was – it was laughable, simply laughable. And why this mania of hers to keep alive at all? For it really was a mania, she thought, mocking and laughing.

'What am I guarding myself for so preciously? I shall go on having children and Stanley will go on making money and the children and the gardens will grow bigger and bigger, with whole fleets of aloes in them for me to choose from.'

She had been walking with her head bent, looking at nothing. Now she looked up and about her. They were standing by the red and white camellia trees. Beautiful were the rich dark leaves spangled with light and the round flowers that perch among them like red and white birds. Linda pulled a piece of verbena and crumpled it, and held her hands to her mother.

'Delicious,' said the old woman. 'Are you cold, child? Are you trembling? Yes, your hands are cold. We had better go back to the house.'

'What have you been thinking about?' said Linda. 'Tell me.'

'I haven't really been thinking of anything. I wondered as we passed the orchard what the fruit trees were like and whether we should be able to make much jam this autumn. There are splendid

healthy currant bushes in the vegetable garden. I noticed them today.
I should like to see those pantry shelves thoroughly well stocked with
our own jam . . . '

1 2

My darling Nan

Don't think me a piggy wig because I haven't written before. I
haven't had a moment, dear, and even now I feel so exhausted that
I can hardly hold a pen.

Well, the dreadful deed is done. We have actually left the giddy
whirl of town, and I can't see how we shall ever go back again, for
my brother-in-law has bought this house 'lock, stock and barrel',
to use his own words.

In a way, of course, it is an awful relief, for he has been threatening to take a place in the country ever since I've lived with them –
and I must say the house and garden are awfully nice – a million
times better than that awful cubby-hole in town.

But buried, my dear. Buried isn't the word.

We have got neighbours, but they are only farmers – big louts of
boys who seem to be milking all day, and two dreadful females with
rabbit teeth who brought us some scones when we were moving
and said they would be pleased to help. But my sister who lives a
mile away doesn't know a soul here, so I am sure we never shall. It's
pretty certain nobody will ever come out from town to see us,
because though there is a bus it's an awful old rattling thing with
black leather sides that any decent person would rather die than
ride in for six miles.

Such is life. It's a sad ending for poor little B. I'll get to be a most
awful frump in a year or two and come and see you in a mackintosh
and a sailor hat tied on with a white china silk motor veil. So
pretty.

Stanley says that now we are settled – for after the most awful
week of my life we really are settled – he is going to bring out a
couple of men from the club on Saturday afternoons for tennis. In
fact, two are promised as a great treat today. But, my dear, if you
could see Stanley's men from the club . . . rather fattish, the type
who look frightfully indecent without waistcoats – always with toes
that turn in rather – so conspicuous when you are walking about a
court in white shoes. And they are pulling up their trousers every
minute – don't you know – and whacking at imaginary things with
their rackets.

I used to play with them at the club last summer, and I am sure you will know the type when I tell you that after I'd been there about three times they all called me Miss Beryl. It's a weary world. Of course mother simply loves the place, but then I suppose when I am mother's age I shall be content to sit in the sun and shell peas into a basin. But I'm not – not – not.

What Linda thinks about the whole affair, per usual, I haven't the slightest idea. Mysterious as ever.

My dear, you know that white satin dress of mine. I have taken the sleeves out entirely, put bands of black velvet across the shoulders and two big red poppies off my dear sister's *chapeau*. It is a great success, though when I shall wear it I do not know.

Beryl sat writing this letter at a little table in her room. In a way, of course, it was all perfectly true, but in another way it was all the greatest rubbish and she didn't believe a word of it. No, that wasn't true. She felt all those things, but she didn't really feel them like that.

It was her other self who had written that letter. It not only bored, it rather disgusted her real self.

'Flippant and silly,' said her real self. Yet she knew that she'd send it and she'd always write that kind of twaddle to Nan Pym. In fact, it was a very mild example of the kind of letter she generally wrote.

Beryl leaned her elbows on the table and read it through again. The voice of the letter seemed to come up to her from the page. It was faint already, like a voice heard over the telephone, high, gushing, with something bitter in the sound. Oh, she detested it today.

'You've always got so much animation,' said Nan Pym. 'That's why men are so keen on you.' And she had added, rather mournfully, for men were not at all keen on Nan, who was a solid kind of girl, with fat hips and a high colour – 'I can't understand how you can keep it up. But it is your nature, I suppose.'

What rot. What nonsense. It wasn't her nature at all. Good heavens, if she had ever been her real self with Nan Pym, Nannie would have jumped out of the window with surprise . . . My dear, you know that white satin of mine . . . Beryl slammed the letter-case to.

She jumped up and half unconsciously, half consciously she drifted over to the looking-glass.

There stood a slim girl in white – a white serge skirt, a white silk blouse, and a leather belt drawn in very tightly at her tiny waist.

Her face was heart-shaped, wide at the brows and with a pointed chin – but not too pointed. Her eyes, her eyes were perhaps her best feature; they were such a strange uncommon colour – greeny blue with little gold points in them.

She had fine black eyebrows and long lashes – so long, that when they lay on her cheeks you positively caught the light in them, someone or other had told her.

Her mouth was rather large. Too large? No, not really. Her underlip protruded a little; she had a way of sucking it in that somebody else had told her was awfully fascinating.

Her nose was her least satisfactory feature. Not that it was really ugly. But it was not half as fine as Linda's. Linda really had a perfect little nose. Hers spread rather – not badly. And in all probability she exaggerated the spreadiness of it just because it was her nose, and she was so awfully critical of herself. She pinched it with a thumb and first finger and made a little face . . .

Lovely, lovely hair. And such a mass of it. It had the colour of fresh fallen leaves, brown and red with a glint of yellow. When she did it in a long plait she felt it on her backbone like a long snake. She loved to feel the weight of it dragging her head back, and she loved to feel it loose, covering her bare arms. 'Yes, my dear, there is no doubt about it, you really are a lovely little thing.'

At the words her bosom lifted; she took a long breath of delight, half closing her eyes.

But even as she looked the smile faded from her lips and eyes. Oh God, there she was, back again, playing the same old game. False – false as ever. False as when she'd written to Nan Pym. False even when she was alone with herself, now.

What had that creature in the glass to do with her, and why was she staring? She dropped down to one side of her bed and buried her face in her arms.

'Oh,' she cried, 'I am so miserable – so frightfully miserable. I know that I'm silly and spiteful and vain; I'm always acting a part. I'm never my real self for a moment.' And plainly, plainly, she saw her false self running up and down the stairs, laughing a special trilling laugh if they had visitors, standing under the lamp if a man came to dinner, so that he should see the light on her hair, pouting and pretending to be a little girl when she was asked to play the guitar. Why? She even kept it up for Stanley's benefit. Only last night when he was reading the paper her false self had stood beside him and leaned against his shoulder on purpose. Hadn't she put her hand over his, pointing out something so that he should see how white her hand was beside his brown one.

How despicable! Despicable! Her heart was cold with rage. 'It's marvellous how you keep it up,' said she to the false self. But then it was only because she was so miserable – so miserable. If she had been happy and leading her own life, her false life would cease to be. She saw the real Beryl – a shadow . . . a shadow. Faint and unsubstantial she shone. What was there of her except the radiance? And for what tiny moments she was really she. Beryl could almost remember every one of them. At those times she had felt: 'Life is rich and mysterious, and good, and I am rich and mysterious and good, too.' Shall I ever be that Beryl for ever? Shall I? How can I? And was there ever a time when I did not have a false self? . . . But just as she had got that far she heard the sound of little steps running along the passage; the door handle rattled. Kezia came in.

'Aunt Beryl, mother says will you please come down? Father is home with a man and lunch is ready.'

Botheration! How she had crumpled her skirt, kneeling in that idiotic way.

'Very well, Kezia.' She went over to the dressing-table and powdered her nose.

Kezia crossed too, and unscrewed a little pot of cream and sniffed it. Under her arm she carried a very dirty calico cat.

When Aunt Beryl ran out of the room she sat the cat up on the dressing-table and stuck the top of the cream jar over its ear.

'Now look at yourself,' said she sternly.

The calico cat was so overcome by the sight that it toppled over backwards and bumped and bumped on to the floor. And the top of the cream jar flew through the air and rolled like a penny in a round on the linoleum – and did not break.

But for Kezia it had broken the moment it flew through the air, and she picked it up, hot all over, and put it back on the dressing-table.

Then she tiptoed away, far too quickly and airily . . .

Je Ne Parle Pas Français

I DO NOT KNOW why I have such a fancy for this little café. It's dirty and sad, sad. It's not as if it had anything to distinguish it from a hundred others – it hasn't; or as if the same strange types came here every day, whom one could watch from one's corner and recognise and more or less (with a strong accent on the less) get the hang of.

But pray don't imagine that those brackets are a confession of my humility before the mystery of the human soul. Not at all; I don't believe in the human soul. I never have. I believe that people are like portmanteaux – packed with certain things, started going, thrown about, tossed away, dumped down, lost and found, half emptied suddenly, or squeezed fatter than ever, until finally the Ultimate Porter swings them on to the Ultimate Train and away they rattle . . .

Not but what these portmanteaux can be very fascinating. Oh, but very! I see myself standing in front of them, don't you know, like a Customs official.

'Have you anything to declare? Any wines, spirits, cigars, perfumes, silks?'

And the moment of hesitation as to whether I am going to be fooled just before I chalk that squiggle, and then the other moment of hesitation just after, as to whether I have been, are perhaps the two most thrilling instants in life. Yes, they are, to me.

But before I started that long and rather far-fetched and not frightfully original digression, what I meant to say quite simply was that there are no portmanteaux to be examined here because the clientele of this café, ladies and gentlemen, does not sit down. No, it stands at the counter, and it consists of a handful of workmen who come up from the river, all powdered over with white flour, lime or something, and a few soldiers, bringing with them thin, dark girls with silver rings in their ears and market baskets on their arms.

Madame is thin and dark, too, with white cheeks and white hands. In certain lights she looks quite transparent, shining out of her black shawl with an extraordinary effect. When she is not serving she sits on a stool with her face turned, always, to the window. Her dark-ringed eyes search among and follow after the people passing, but not as if she was looking for somebody. Perhaps, fifteen years ago, she was; but now the pose has become a habit. You can tell from her air of fatigue and hopelessness that she must have given them up for the last ten years, at least . . .

And then there is the waiter. Not pathetic – decidedly not comic. Never making one of those perfectly insignificant remarks which amaze you so coming from a waiter (as though the poor wretch were a sort of cross between a coffee-pot and a wine bottle and not expected to hold so much as a drop of anything else). He is grey, flat-footed and withered, with long, brittle nails that set your nerves on edge while he scrapes up your two *sous*. When he is not smearing over the table or flicking at a dead fly or two, he stands with one hand on the back of a chair, in his far too long apron, and over his other arm the three-cornered dip of dirty napkin, waiting to be photographed in connection with some wretched murder. 'Interior of Café where Body was Found'. You've seen him hundreds of times.

Do you believe that every place has its hour of the day when it really does come alive? That's not exactly what I mean. It's more like this. There does seem to be a moment when you realise that, quite by accident, you happen to have come on to the stage at exactly the moment you were expected. Everything is arranged for you – waiting for you. Ah, master of the situation! You fill with important breath. And at the same time you smile, secretly, slyly, because Life seems to be opposed to granting you these entrances, seems indeed to be engaged in snatching them from you and making them impossible, keeping you in the wings until it is too late, in fact . . . Just for once you've beaten the old hag.

I enjoyed one of these moments the first time I ever came in here. That's why I keep coming back, I suppose. Revisiting the scene of my triumph, or the scene of the crime where I had the old bitch by the throat for once and did what I pleased with her.

Query: Why am I so bitter against Life? And why do I see her as a rag-picker on the American cinema, shuffling along wrapped in a filthy shawl with her old claws crooked over a stick?

Answer: The direct result of the American cinema acting upon a weak mind.

Anyhow, the 'short winter afternoon was drawing to a close', as they say, and I was drifting along, either going home or not going home, when I found myself in here, walking over to this seat in the corner.

I hung up my English overcoat and grey felt hat on that same peg behind me, and after I had allowed the waiter time for at least twenty photographers to snap their fill of him, I ordered a coffee.

He poured me out a glass of the familiar, purplish stuff with a green wandering light playing over it, and shuffled off, and I sat pressing my hands against the glass because it was bitterly cold outside.

Suddenly I realised that quite apart from myself, I was smiling. Slowly I raised my head and saw myself in the mirror opposite. Yes, there I sat, leaning on the table, smiling my deep, sly smile, the glass of coffee with its vague plume of steam before me and beside it the ring of white saucer with two pieces of sugar.

I opened my eyes very wide. There I had been for all eternity, as it were, and now at last I was coming to life . . .

It was very quiet in the café. Outside, one could just see through the dusk that it had begun to snow. One could just see the shapes of horses and carts and people, soft and white, moving through the feathery air. The waiter disappeared and reappeared with an armful of straw. He strewed it over the floor from the door to the counter and round about the stove with humble, almost adoring gestures. One would not have been surprised if the door had opened and the Virgin Mary had come in, riding upon an ass, her meek hands folded over her big belly . . .

That's rather nice, don't you think, that bit about the Virgin? It comes from the pen so gently; it has such a 'dying fall'. I thought so at the time and decided to make a note of it. One never knows when a little tag like that may come in useful to round off a paragraph. So, taking care to move as little as possible because the 'spell' was still unbroken (you know that?), I reached over to the next table for a writing-pad.

No paper or envelopes, of course. Only a morsel of pink blotting-paper, incredibly soft and limp and almost moist, like the tongue of a little dead kitten, which I've never felt.

I sat – but always underneath, in this state of expectation, rolling the little dead kitten's tongue round my finger and rolling the soft phrase round my mind while my eyes took in the girls' names and dirty jokes and drawings of bottles and cups that would not sit in the saucers, scattered over the writing-pad.

They are always the same, you know. The girls always have the same names; the cups never sit in the saucers; all the hearts are stuck and tied up with ribbons.

But then, quite suddenly, at the bottom of the page, written in green ink, I fell on to that stupid, stale little phrase: *Je ne parle pas français.*

There! it had come – the moment – the *geste*! And although I was so ready, it caught me, it tumbled me over; I was simply overwhelmed. And the physical feeling was so curious, so particular. It was as if all of me, except my head and arms, all over me that was under the table, had simply dissolved, melted, turned into water. Just my head remained and two sticks of arms pressing on to the table. But, ah! the agony of that moment! How can I describe it? I didn't think of anything. I didn't even cry out to myself. Just for one moment I was not. I was Agony, Agony, Agony.

Then it passed, and the very second after I was thinking: 'Good God! Am I capable of feeling as strongly as that? But I was absolutely unconscious! I hadn't a phrase to meet it with! I was overcome! I was swept off my feet! I didn't even try, in the dimmest way, to put it down!'

And up I puffed and puffed, blowing off finally with: 'After all I must be first-rate. No second-rate mind could have experienced such an intensity of feeling so . . . purely.'

The waiter has touched a spill at the red stove and lighted a bubble of gas under a spreading shade. It is no use looking out of the window, madame; it is quite dark now. Your white hands hover over your dark shawl. They are like two birds that have come home to roost. They are restless, restless . . . You tuck them, finally, under your warm little armpits.

Now the waiter has taken a long pole and clashed the curtains together. 'All gone,' as children say.

And besides, I've no patience with people who can't let go of things, who will follow after and cry out. When a thing's gone, it's gone. It's over and done with. Let it go then! Ignore it, and comfort yourself, if you do want comforting, with the thought that you never do recover the same thing that you lose. It's always a new thing. The moment it leaves you it's changed. Why, that's even true of a hat you chase after; and I don't mean superficially – I mean profoundly speaking . . . I have made it a rule of my life never to regret and never to look back. Regret is an appalling waste of energy, and no one who intends to be a writer can afford to indulge in it. You can't get it into shape; you can't build on it; it's only good for wallowing in. Looking back, of course, is equally fatal to Art. It's keeping yourself poor. Art can't and won't stand poverty.

Je ne parle pas français. Je ne parle pas français. All the while I wrote that last page my other self has been chasing up and down out in the dark there. It left me just when I began to analyse my grand moment, dashed off distracted, like a lost dog who thinks at last, at last, he hears the familiar step again.

'Mouse! Mouse! Where are you? Are you near? Is that you leaning from the high window and stretching out your arms for the wings of the shutters? Are you this soft bundle moving towards me through the feathery snow? Are you this little girl pressing through the swing-doors of the restaurant? Is that your dark shadow bending forward in the cab? Where are you? Where are you? Which way must I turn? Which way shall I run? And every moment I stand here hesitating you are farther away again. Mouse! Mouse!'

Now the poor dog has come back into the café, his tail between his legs, quite exhausted.

'It was a . . . false . . . alarm. She's nowhere . . . to . . . be seen.'

'Lie down then! Lie down! Lie down!'

My name is Raoul Duquette. I am twenty-six years old and a Parisian, a true Parisian. About my family – it really doesn't matter. I have no family; I don't want any. I never think about my childhood. I've forgotten it.

In fact, there's only one memory that stands out at all. That is rather interesting because it seems to me now so very significant as regards myself from the literary point of view. It is this.

When I was about ten our laundress was an African woman, very big, very dark, with a check handkerchief over her frizzy hair. When she came to our house she always took particular notice of me, and after the clothes had been taken out of the basket she would lift me up into it and give me a rock while I held tight to the handles and screamed for joy and fright. I was tiny for my age, and pale, with a lovely little half-open mouth – I feel sure of that.

One day when I was standing at the door, watching her go, she turned round and beckoned to me, nodding and smiling in a strange secret way. I never thought of not following. She took me into a little outhouse at the end of the passage, caught me up in her arms and began kissing me. Ah, those kisses! Especially those kisses inside my ears that nearly deafened me.

When she set me down she took from her pocket a little round fried cake covered with sugar, and I reeled along the passage back to our door.

As this performance was repeated once a week it is no wonder that I remember it so vividly. Besides, from that very first afternoon, my childhood was, to put it prettily, 'kissed away'. I became very languid, very caressing, and greedy beyond measure. And so quickened, so sharpened, I seemed to understand everybody and be able to do what I liked with everybody.

I suppose I was in a state of more or less physical excitement, and that was what appealed to them. For all Parisians are more than half – oh, well, enough of that. And enough of my childhood, too. Bury it under a laundry basket instead of a shower of roses and *passons outre*.

I date myself from the moment that I became the tenant of a small bachelor flat on the fifth floor of a tall, not too shabby house, in a street that might or might not be discreet. Very useful, that . . . There I emerged, came out into the light and put out my two horns with a study and a bedroom and a kitchen on my back. And real furniture planted in the rooms. In the bedroom a wardrobe with a long glass, a big bed covered with a yellow puffed-up quilt, a bed table with a marbled top and a toilet set sprinkled with tiny apples. In my study – English writing-table with drawers, writing-chair with leather cushions, books, armchair, side-table with paper-knife and lamp on it and some nude studies on the walls. I didn't use the kitchen except to throw old papers into.

Ah, I can see myself that first evening, after the furniture men had gone and I'd managed to get rid of my atrocious old concierge – walking about on tiptoe, arranging and standing in front of the glass with my hands in my pockets and saying to that radiant vision: 'I am a young man who has his own flat. I write for two newspapers. I am going in for serious literature. I am starting a career. The book that I shall bring out will simply stagger the critics. I am going to write about things that have never been touched on before. I am going to make a name for myself as a writer about the submerged world. But not as others have done before me. Oh, no! Very naïvely, with a sort of tender humour and from the inside, as though it were all quite simple, quite natural. I see my way quite perfectly. Nobody has ever done it as I shall do it because none of the others have lived my experiences. I'm rich – I'm rich.'

All the same I had no more money than I have now. It's extraordinary how one can live without money . . . I have quantities of good clothes, silk underwear, two evening suits, four pairs of patent leather boots with light uppers, all sorts of little things, like gloves and powder boxes and a manicure set, perfumes, very good soap, and nothing is paid for. If I find myself in need of right-down cash – well, there's always an African laundress and an outhouse, and I am very frank and *bon enfant* about plenty of sugar on the little fried cake afterwards . . .

And here I should like to put something on record. Not from any strutting conceit, but rather with a mild sense of wonder. I've never yet made the first advances to any woman. It isn't as though I've known only one class of woman – not by any means. But from little prostitutes and kept women and elderly widows and shop girls and wives of respectable men, and even advanced modern literary ladies at the most select dinners and soirées (I've been there), I've met invariably with not only the same readiness, but with the same positive invitation. It surprised me at first. I used to look across the table and think, 'Is that very distinguished young lady, discussing *le Kipling* with the gentleman with the brown beard, really pressing my foot?' And I was never really certain until I had pressed hers.

Curious, isn't it? I don't look at all like a maiden's dream.

I am little and light with an olive skin, black eyes with long lashes, black silky hair cut short, tiny square teeth that show when I smile. My hands are supple and small. A woman in a bread shop once said to me: 'You have the hands for making fine little pastries.' I confess, without my clothes I am rather charming. Plump, almost like a girl, with smooth shoulders, and I wear a thin gold bracelet above my left elbow.

But, wait! Isn't it strange I should have written all that about my body and so on? It's the result of my bad life, my submerged life. I am like a little woman in a café who has to introduce herself with a handful of photographs. 'Me in my chemise, coming out of an eggshell . . . Me upside down in a swing, with a frilly behind like a cauliflower . . . ' You know the things.

If you think what I've written is merely superficial and impudent and cheap you're wrong. I'll admit it does sound so, but then it is not all. If it were, how could I have experienced what I did when I read that stale little phrase written in green ink on the writing-pad? That proves there's more in me and that I really am important, doesn't it?

Anything a fraction less than that moment of anguish I might have put on. But no! That was real.

'Waiter, a whisky.'

I hate whisky. Every time I take it into my mouth my stomach rises against it, and the stuff they keep here is sure to be particularly vile. I only ordered it because I am going to write about an Englishman. We French are incredibly old-fashioned and out of date still in some ways. I wonder I didn't ask him at the same time for a pair of tweed knickerbockers, a pipe, some long teeth and a set of ginger whiskers.

'Thanks, *mon vieux*. You haven't got perhaps a set of ginger whiskers?'

'No, monsieur,' he answers sadly. 'We don't sell American drinks.'

And having smeared a corner of the table he goes back to have another couple of dozen taken by artificial light.

Ugh! The smell of it! And the sickly sensation when one's throat contracts.

'It's bad stuff to get drunk on,' says Dick Harmon, turning his little glass in his fingers and smiling his slow, dreaming smile. So he gets drunk on it slowly and dreamily and at a certain moment begins to sing very low, very low, about a man who walks up and down trying to find a place where he can get some dinner.

Ah! how I loved that song, and how I loved the way he sang it, slowly, slowly, in a dark, soft voice:

> There was a man
> Walked up and down
> To get a dinner in the town . . .

It seemed to hold, in its gravity and muffled measure, all those tall grey buildings, those fogs, those endless streets, those sharp shadows of policemen that mean England.

And then – the subject! The lean, starved creature walking up and down with every house barred against him because he had no 'home'. How extraordinarily English that is . . . I remember that it ended where he did at last 'find a place' and ordered a little cake of fish, but when he asked for bread the waiter cried contemptuously, in a loud voice: 'We don't serve bread with one fish ball.'

What more do you want? How profound those songs are! There is the whole psychology of a people; and how un-French – how un-French!

'Once more, Deeck, once more!' I would plead, clasping my hands and making a pretty mouth at him. He was perfectly content to sing it for ever.

There again. Even with Dick. It was he who made the first advances.

I met him at an evening party given by the editor of a new review. It was a very select, very fashionable affair. One or two of the older men were there and the ladies were extremely *comme il faut*. They sat on cubist sofas in full evening dress and allowed us to hand them thimbles of cherry brandy and to talk to them about their poetry. For, as far as I can remember, they were all poetesses.

It was impossible not to notice Dick. He was the only Englishman present, and instead of circulating gracefully round the room as we all did, he stayed in one place leaning against the wall, his hands in his pockets, that dreamy half smile on his lips, and replying in excellent French in his low, soft voice to anybody who spoke to him.

'Who is he?'

'An Englishman. From London. A writer. And he is making a special study of modern French literature.'

That was enough for me. My little book, *False Coins*, had just been published. I was a young, serious writer who was making a special study of modern English literature.

But I really had not time to fling my line before he said, giving himself a soft shake, coming right out of the water after the bait, as it were: 'Won't you come and see me at my hotel? Come about five o'clock and we can have a talk before going out to dinner.'

'Enchanted!'

I was so deeply, deeply flattered that I had to leave him then and there to preen and preen myself before the cubist sofas. What a catch! An Englishman, reserved, serious, making a special study of French literature . . .

That same night a copy of *False Coins* with a carefully cordial inscription was posted off, and a day or two later we did dine together and spent the evening talking.

Talking – but not only of literature. I discovered to my relief that it wasn't necessary to keep to the tendency of the modern novel, the need of a new form, or the reason why our young men appeared to be just missing it. Now and again, as if by accident, I threw in a card that seemed to have nothing to do with the game, just to see how he'd take it. But each time he gathered it into his hands with his dreamy look and smile unchanged. Perhaps he murmured: 'That's very curious.' But not as if it were curious at all.

That calm acceptance went to my head at last. It fascinated me. It led me on and on till I threw every card that I possessed at him and sat back and watched him arrange them in his hand.

'Very curious and interesting . . . '

By that time we were both fairly drunk, and he began to sing his song very soft, very low, about the man who walked up and down seeking his dinner.

But I was quite breathless at the thought of what I had done. I had shown somebody both sides of my life. Told him everything as sincerely and truthfully as I could. Taken immense pains to explain things about my submerged life that really were disgusting and never could possibly see the light of literary day. On the whole I had made myself out far worse than I was – more boastful, more cynical, more calculating.

And there sat the man I had confided in, singing to himself and smiling . . . It moved me so that real tears came into my eyes. I saw them glittering on my long silky lashes – so charming.

After that I took Dick about with me everywhere, and he came to my flat, and sat in the armchair, very indolent, playing with the paper-knife. I cannot think why his indolence and dreaminess always gave me the impression he had been to sea. And all his leisurely slow ways seemed to be allowing for the movement of the ship. This impression was so strong that often when we were together and he got up and left a little woman just when she did not expect him to get up and leave her, but quite the contrary, I would explain: 'He can't help it, baby. He has to go back to his ship.' And I believed it far more than she did.

All the while we were together Dick never went with a woman. I sometimes wondered whether he wasn't completely innocent. Why didn't I ask him? Because I never did ask him anything about himself. But late one night he took out his pocketbook and a photograph dropped out of it. I picked it up and glanced at it before I gave it to him. It was of a woman. Not quite young. Dark, handsome, wild-looking, but so full in every line of a kind of haggard pride that even if Dick had not stretched out so quickly I wouldn't have looked longer.

'Out of my sight, you little perfumed fox-terrier of a Frenchman,' said she.

(In my very worst moments my nose reminds me of a fox-terrier's.)

'That is my mother,' said Dick, putting up the pocket-book.

But if he had not been Dick I should have been tempted to cross myself, just for fun.

This is how we parted. As we stood outside his hotel one night waiting for the concierge to release the catch of the outer door, he said, looking up at the sky: 'I hope it will be fine tomorrow. I am leaving for England in the morning.'

'You're not serious.'

'Perfectly. I have to get back. I've some work to do that I can't manage here.'

'But – but have you made all your preparations?'

'Preparations?' He almost grinned. 'I've none to make.'

'But – *enfin*, Dick, England is not the other side of the boulevard.'

'It isn't much farther off,' said he. 'Only a few hours, you know.' The door cracked open.

'Ah, I wish I'd known at the beginning of the evening!'

I felt hurt. I felt as a woman must feel when a man takes out his watch and remembers an appointment that cannot possibly concern her, except that its claim is the stronger. 'Why didn't you tell me?'

He put out his hand and stood, lightly swaying upon the step as though the whole hotel were his ship, and the anchor weighed.

'I forgot. Truly I did. But you'll write, won't you? Good-night, old chap. I'll be over again one of these days.'

And then I stood on the shore alone, more like a little fox-terrier than ever . . .

'But after all it was you who whistled to me, you who asked me to come! What a spectacle I've cut wagging my tail and leaping round you, only to be left like this while the boat sails off in its slow, dreamy way . . . Curse these English! No, this is too insolent altogether. Who do you imagine I am? A little paid guide to the night pleasures of Paris? . . . No, monsieur. I am a young writer, very serious, and extremely interested in modern English literature. And I have been insulted – insulted.'

Two days after came a long, charming letter from him, written in French that was a shade too French, but saying how he missed me and counted on our friendship, on keeping in touch.

I read it standing in front of the (unpaid for) wardrobe mirror. It was early morning. I wore a blue kimono embroidered with white birds and my hair was still wet; it lay on my forehead, wet and gleaming.

'Portrait of Madame Butterfly,' said I, 'on hearing of the arrival of *ce cher Pinkerton*.'

According to the books I should have felt immensely relieved and delighted. ' . . . Going over to the window he drew apart the curtains and looked out at the Paris trees, just breaking into buds and green . . . Dick! Dick! My English friend!'

I didn't. I merely felt a little sick. Having been up for my first ride in an aeroplane I didn't want to go up again, just now.

That passed, and months after, in the winter, Dick wrote that he was coming back to Paris to stay indefinitely. Would I take rooms for him? He was bringing a woman friend with him.

Of course I would. Away the little fox-terrier flew. It happened most usefully, too; for I owed much money at the hotel where I took my meals, and two English people requiring rooms for an indefinite time was an excellent sum on account.

Perhaps I did rather wonder, as I stood in the larger of the two rooms with Madame, saying 'Admirable', what the woman friend would be like, but only vaguely. Either she would be very severe, flat back and front, or she would be tall, fair, dressed in mignonette green, name – Daisy, and smelling of rather sweetish lavender water.

You see, by this time, according to my rule of not looking back, I had almost forgotten Dick. I even got the tune of his song about the unfortunate man a little bit wrong when I tried to hum it . . .

I very nearly did not turn up at the station after all. I had arranged to, and had, in fact, dressed with particular care for the occasion. For I intended to take a new line with Dick this time. No more confidences and tears on eyelashes. No, thank you!

'Since you left Paris,' said I, knotting my black silver-spotted tie in the (also unpaid for) mirror over the mantelpiece, 'I have been very successful, you know. I have two more books in preparation, and then I have written a serial story, *Wrong Doors*, which is just on the point of publication and will bring me in a lot of money. And then my little book of poems,' I cried, seizing the clothes-brush and brushing the velvet collar of my new indigo-blue overcoat, 'my little book – *Left Umbrellas* – really did create,' and I laughed and waved the brush, 'an immense sensation!'

It was impossible not to believe this of the person who surveyed himself finally, from top to toe, drawing on his soft grey gloves. He was looking the part; he was the part.

That gave me an idea. I took out my notebook, and still in full view, jotted down a note or two . . . How can one look the part and not be the part? Or be the part and not look it? Isn't looking – being? Or being – looking? At any rate who is to say that it is not? . . .

This seemed to me extraordinarily profound at the time, and quite new. But I confess that something did whisper as, smiling, I put up the notebook: 'You – literary? you look as though you've taken down a bet on a racecourse!' But I didn't listen. I went out, shutting the door of the flat with a soft, quick pull so as not to warn the concierge of my departure, and ran down the stairs quick as a rabbit for the same reason.

But ah! the old spider. She was too quick for me. She let me run down the last little ladder of the web and then she pounced. 'One moment. One little moment, monsieur,' she whispered, odiously confidential. 'Come in. Come in.' And she beckoned with a dripping soup ladle. I went to the door, but that was not good enough. Right inside and the door shut before she would speak.

There are two ways of managing your concierge if you haven't any money. One is – to take the high hand, make her your enemy, bluster, refuse to discuss anything; the other is – to keep in with her, butter her up to the two knots of the black rag tying up her jaws, pretend to confide in her, and rely on her to arrange with the gas man and to put off the landlord.

I had tried the second. But both are equally detestable and unsuccessful. At any rate whichever you're trying is the worse, the impossible one.

It was the landlord this time . . . Imitation of the landlord by the concierge threatening to toss me out . . . Imitation of the concierge by the concierge taming the wild bull . . . Imitation of the landlord rampant again, breathing in the concierge's face. I was the concierge. No, it was too nauseous. And all the while the black pot on the gas ring bubbling away, stewing out the hearts and livers of every tenant in the place.

'Ah!' I cried, staring at the clock on the mantelpiece, and then, realising that it didn't go, striking my forehead as though the idea had nothing to do with it. 'Madame, I have a very important appointment with the director of my newspaper at nine-thirty. Perhaps tomorrow I shall be able to give you . . . '

Out, out. And down the métro and squeezed into a full carriage.

The more the better. Everybody was one bolster the more between me and the concierge. I was radiant.

'Ah! pardon, monsieur!' said the tall charming creature in black with a big full bosom and a great bunch of violets dropping from it. As the train swayed it thrust the bouquet right into my eyes. 'Ah! pardon, monsieur!'

But I looked up at her, smiling mischievously.

'There is nothing I love more, madame, than flowers on a balcony.'

At the very moment of speaking I caught sight of the huge man in a fur coat against whom my charmer was leaning. He poked his head over her shoulder and he went white to the nose; in fact his nose stood out a sort of cheese green.

'What was that you said to my wife?'

Gare St Lazare saved me. But you'll own that even as the author of *False Coins*, *Wrong Doors*, *Left Umbrellas*, and two in preparation, it was not too easy to go on my triumphant way.

At length, after countless trains had steamed into my mind, and countless Dick Harmons had come rolling towards me, the real train came. The little knot of us waiting at the barrier moved up close, craned forward, and broke into cries as though we were some kind of many-headed monster, and Paris behind us nothing but a great trap we had set to catch these sleepy innocents.

Into the trap they walked and were snatched and taken off to be devoured. Where was my prey?

'Good God!' My smile and my lifted hand fell together. For one terrible moment I thought this was the woman of the photograph, Dick's mother, walking towards me in Dick's coat and hat. In the effort – and you saw what an effort it was – to smile, his lips curled in just the same way and he made for me, haggard and wild and proud.

What had happened? What could have changed him like this? Should I mention it?

I waited for him and was even conscious of venturing a fox-terrier wag or two to see if he could possibly respond, in the way I said: 'Good evening, Dick! How are you, old chap? All right?'

'All right. All right.' He almost gasped. 'You've got the rooms?'

Twenty times, good God! I saw it all. Light broke on the dark waters and my sailor hadn't been drowned. I almost turned a somersault with amusement.

It was nervousness, of course. It was embarrassment. It was the famous English seriousness. What fun I was going to have! I could have hugged him.

'Yes, I've got the rooms,' I nearly shouted. 'But where is madame?'

'She's been looking after the luggage,' he panted. 'Here she comes, now.'

Not this baby walking beside the old porter as though he were her nurse and had just lifted her out of her ugly perambulator while he trundled the boxes on it.

'And she's not Madame,' said Dick, drawling suddenly.

At that moment she caught sight of him and hailed him with her minute muff. She broke away from her nurse and ran up and said something, very quick, in English; but he replied in French: 'Oh, very well. I'll manage.'

But before he turned to the porter he indicated me with a vague wave and muttered something. We were introduced. She held out her hand in that strange boyish way Englishwomen do, and standing very straight in front of me with her chin raised and making – she too – the effort of her life to control her preposterous excitement, she said, wringing my hand (I'm sure she didn't know it was mine), '*Je ne parle pas Français.*'

'But I'm sure you do,' I answered, so tender, so reassuring, I might have been a dentist about to draw her first little milk tooth.

'Of course she does.' Dick swerved back to us. 'Here, can't we get a cab or taxi or something? We don't want to stay in this cursed station all night. Do we?'

This was so rude that it took me a moment to recover; and he must have noticed, for he flung his arm round my shoulder in the old way, saying: 'Ah, forgive me, old chap. But we've had such a loathsome, hideous journey. We've taken years to come. Haven't we?' To her. But she did not answer. She bent her head and began stroking her grey muff; she walked beside us stroking her grey muff all the way.

'Have I been wrong?' thought I. 'Is this simply a case of frenzied impatience on their part? Are they merely "in need of a bed" as we say? Have they been suffering agonies on the journey? Sitting, perhaps, very close and warm under the same travelling rug?' and so on and so on while the driver strapped on the boxes. That done –

'Look here, Dick. I go home by métro. Here is the address of your hotel. Everything is arranged. Come and see me as soon as you can.'

Upon my life I thought he was going to faint. He went white to the lips.

'But you're coming back with us,' he cried. 'I thought it was all

settled. Of course you're coming back. You're not going to leave us.'
No, I gave it up. It was too difficult, too English for me.

'Certainly, certainly. Delighted. I only thought, perhaps . . . '

'You must come!' said Dick to the little fox-terrier. And again he made that big awkward turn towards her.

'Get in, Mouse.'

And Mouse got in the black hole and sat stroking Mouse II and not saying a word.

Away we jolted and rattled like three little dice that life had decided to have a fling with.

I had insisted on taking the flap seat facing them because I would not have missed for anything those occasional flashing glimpses I had as we broke through the white circles of lamplight.

They revealed Dick, sitting far back in his corner, his coat collar turned up, his hands thrust in his pockets, and his broad dark hat shading him as if it were a part of him – a sort of wing he hid under. They showed her, sitting up very straight, her lovely little face more like a drawing than a real face – every line was so full of meaning and so sharp cut against the swimming dark.

For Mouse was beautiful. She was exquisite, but so fragile and fine that each time I looked at her it was as if for the first time. She came upon you with the same kind of shock that you feel when you have been drinking tea out of a thin innocent cup and suddenly, at the bottom, you see a tiny creature, half butterfly, half woman, bowing to you with her hands in her sleeves.

As far as I could make out she had dark hair and blue or black eyes. Her long lashes and the two little feathers traced above were most important.

She wore a long dark cloak such as one sees in old-fashioned pictures of Englishwomen abroad. Where her arms came out of it there was grey fur – fur round her neck, too, and her close-fitting cap was furry.

'Carrying out the mouse idea,' I decided.

Ah, but how intriguing it was – how intriguing! Their excitement came nearer and nearer to me, while I ran out to meet it, bathed in it, flung myself far out of my depth, until at last I was as hard put to it to keep control as they.

But what I wanted to do was to behave in the most extraordinary fashion – like a clown. To start singing, with large extravagant gestures, to point out of the window and cry: 'We are now passing, ladies and gentlemen, one of the sights for which *notre Paris* is justly famous,' to jump out of the taxi while it was going, climb over the roof and dive in by another door; to hang out of the window and look for the hotel through the wrong end of a broken telescope, which was also a peculiarly ear-splitting trumpet.

I watched myself do all this, you understand, and even managed to applaud in a private way by putting my gloved hands gently together, while I said to Mouse: 'And is this your first visit to Paris?'

'Yes, I've not been here before.'

'Ah, then you have a great deal to see.'

And I was just going to touch lightly upon the objects of interest and the museums when we wrenched to a stop.

Do you know – it's very absurd – but as I pushed open the door for them and followed them up the stairs to the bureau on the landing I felt somehow that this hotel was mine.

There was a vase of flowers on the window-sill of the bureau and I even went so far as to rearrange a bud or two and to stand off and note the effect while the manageress welcomed them. And when she turned to me and handed me the keys (the *garçon* was hauling up the boxes) and said: 'Monsieur Duquette will show you your rooms' – I had a longing to tap Dick on the arm with a key and say, very confidentially: 'Look here, old chap. As a friend of mine I'll be only too willing to make a slight reduction . . . '

Up and up we climbed. Round and round. Past an occasional pair of boots (why is it one never sees an attractive pair of boots outside a door?). Higher and higher.

'I'm afraid they're rather high up,' I murmured idiotically. 'But I chose them because . . . '

They so obviously did not care why I chose them that I went no further. They accepted everything. They did not expect anything to be different. This was just part of what they were going through – that was how I analysed it.

'Arrived at last.' I ran from one side of the passage to the other, turning on the lights, explaining. 'This one I thought for you, Dick. The other is larger and it has a little dressing-room in the alcove.'

My 'proprietary' eye noted the clean towels and covers, and the bed linen embroidered in red cotton. I thought them rather charming rooms, sloping, full of angles, just the sort of rooms one would expect to find if one had not been to Paris before.

Dick dashed his hat down on the bed.

'Oughtn't I to help that chap with the boxes?' he asked – nobody.

'Yes, you ought,' replied Mouse, 'they're dreadfully heavy.'

And she turned to me with the first glimmer of a smile: 'Books, you know.' Oh, he darted such a strange look at her before he rushed out. And he not only helped, he must have torn the boxes off the *garçon*'s back, for he staggered back, carrying one, dumped it down and then fetched in the other.

'That's yours, Dick,' said she.

'Well, you don't mind it standing here for the present, do you?' he asked, breathless, breathing hard (the box must have been tremendously heavy). He pulled out a handful of money. 'I suppose I ought to pay this chap.'

The *garçon*, standing by, seemed to think so too.

'And will you require anything further, monsieur?'

'No! No!' said Dick impatiently.

But at that Mouse stepped forward. She said, too deliberately, not looking at Dick, with her quaint clipped English accent: 'Yes, I'd like some tea. Tea for three.'

And suddenly she raised her muff as though her hands were clasped inside it, and she was telling the pale, sweaty *garçon* by that action that she was at the end of her resources, that she cried out to him to save her with 'Tea. Immediately!'

This seemed to me so amazingly in the picture, so exactly the gesture and cry that one would expect (though I couldn't have imagined it) to be wrung out of an Englishwoman faced with a great crisis, that I was almost tempted to hold up my hand and protest.

'No! No! Enough. Enough. Let us leave off there. At the word – tea. For really, really, you've filled your greediest subscriber so full that he will burst if he has to swallow another word.'

It even pulled Dick up. Like someone who has been unconscious for a long long time he turned slowly to Mouse and slowly looked at her with his tired, haggard eyes, and murmured with the echo of his dreamy voice: 'Yes. That's a good idea.' And then: 'You must be tired, Mouse. Sit down.'

She sat down in a chair with lace tabs on the arms; he leaned against the bed, and I established myself on a straight-backed chair, crossed my legs and brushed some imaginary dust off the knees of my trousers. (The Parisian at his ease.)

There came a tiny pause. Then he said: 'Won't you take off your coat, Mouse?'

'No, thanks. Not just now.'

Were they going to ask me? Or should I hold up my hand and call out in a baby voice: 'It's my turn to be asked.'

No, I shouldn't. They didn't ask me.

The pause became a silence. A real silence.

' . . . Come, my Parisian fox-terrier! Amuse these sad English! It's no wonder they are such a nation for dogs.'

But, after all – why should I? It was not my 'job', as they would say. Nevertheless, I made a vivacious little bound at Mouse.

'What a pity it is that you did not arrive by daylight. There is such a charming view from these two windows. You know, the hotel is on a corner and each window looks down an immensely long, straight street.'

'Yes,' said she.

'Not that that sounds very charming,' I laughed. 'But there is so much animation – so many absurd little boys on bicycles and people hanging out of windows and – oh, well, you'll see for yourself in the morning . . . Very amusing. Very animated.'

'Oh, yes,' said she.

If the pale, sweaty *garçon* had not come in at that moment, carrying the tea-tray high on one hand as if the cups were cannonballs and he a heavyweight lifter on the cinema . . .

He managed to lower it on to a round table.

'Bring the table over here,' said Mouse. The waiter seemed to be the only person she cared to speak to. She took her hands out of her muff, drew off her gloves and flung back the old-fashioned cape.

'Do you take milk and sugar?'

'No milk, thank you, and no sugar.'

I went over for mine like a little gentleman. She poured out another cup.

'That's for Dick.'

And the faithful fox-terrier carried it across to him and laid it at his feet, as it were.

'Oh, thanks,' said Dick.

And then I went back to my chair and she sank back in hers.

But Dick was off again. He stared wildly at the cup of tea for a moment, glanced round him, put it down on the bed-table, caught up his hat and stammered at full gallop: 'Oh, by the way, do you mind posting a letter for me? I want to get it off by tonight's post. I

must. It's very urgent . . . ' Feeling her eyes on him, he flung: 'It's to
my mother.' To me: 'I won't be long. I've got everything I want. But
it must go off tonight. You don't mind? It . . . it won't take any time.'

'Of course I'll post it. Delighted.'

'Won't you drink your tea first?' suggested Mouse softly.

. . . Tea? Tea? Yes, of course. Tea . . .

A cup of tea on the bed-table . . . In his racing dream he flashed the
brightest, most charming smile at his little hostess.

'No, thanks. Not just now.'

And still hoping it would not be any trouble to me he went out of
the room and closed the door, and we heard him cross the passage.

I scalded myself with mine in my hurry to take the cup back to the
table and to say as I stood there: 'You must forgive me if I am
impertinent . . . if I am too frank. But Dick hasn't tried to disguise
it – has he? There is something the matter. Can I help?'

(Soft music. Mouse gets up, walks the stage for a moment or
so before she returns to her chair and pours him out, oh, such a
brimming, such a burning cup that the tears come into the friend's
eyes while he sips – while he drains it to the bitter dregs . . .)

I had time to do all this before she replied. First she looked in the
teapot, filled it with hot water, and stirred it with a spoon.

'Yes, there is something the matter. No, I'm afraid you can't help,
thank you.' Again I got that glimmer of a smile. 'I'm awfully sorry. It
must be horrid for you.'

Horrid, indeed! Ah, why couldn't I tell her that it was months and
months since I had been so entertained?

'But you are suffering,' I ventured softly, as though that was what I
could not bear to see.

She didn't deny it. She nodded and bit her underlip and I thought
I saw her chin tremble.

'And there is really nothing I can do?' More softly still.

She shook her head, pushed back the table and jumped up.

'Oh, it will be all right soon,' she breathed, walking over to the
dressing-table and standing with her back towards me. 'It will be all
right. It can't go on like this.'

'But of course it can't,' I agreed, wondering whether it would look
heartless if I lit a cigarette; I had a sudden longing to smoke.

In some way she saw my hand move to my breast pocket, half draw
out my cigarette case and put it back again, for the next thing she said
was: 'Matches . . . in . . . candlestick. I noticed them.'

And I heard from her voice that she was crying.

'Ah! thank you. Yes. Yes. I've found them.' I lighted my cigarette and walked up and down, smoking.

It was so quiet it might have been two o'clock in the morning. It was so quiet you heard the boards creak and pop as one does in a house in the country. I smoked the whole cigarette and stabbed the end into my saucer before Mouse turned round and came back to the table.

'Isn't Dick being rather a long time?'

'You are very tired. I expect you want to go to bed,' I said kindly. (And pray don't mind me if you do, said my mind.)

'But isn't he being a very long time?' she insisted.

I shrugged. 'He is, rather.'

Then I saw she looked at me strangely. She was listening.

'He's been gone ages,' she said, and she went with little light steps to the door, opened it, and crossed the passage into his room.

I waited. I listened too, now. I couldn't have borne to miss a word. She had left the door open. I stole across the room and looked after her. Dick's door was open, too. But – there wasn't a word to miss.

You know I had the mad idea that they were kissing in that quiet room – a long comfortable kiss. One of those kisses that not only puts one's grief to bed, but nurses it and warms it and tucks it up and keeps it fast enfolded until it is sleeping sound. Ah! how good that is.

It was over at last. I heard someone move and tiptoed away.

It was Mouse. She came back. She felt her way into the room carrying the letter for me. But it wasn't in an envelope; it was just a sheet of paper and she held it by the corner as though it was still wet.

Her head was bent so low – so tucked in her furry collar that I hadn't a notion – until she let the paper fall and almost fell herself on to the floor by the side of the bed, leaned her cheek against it, flung out her hands as though the last of her poor little weapons was gone and now she let herself be carried away, washed out into the deep water.

Flash! went my mind. Dick has shot himself, and then a succession of flashes while I rushed in, saw the body, head unharmed, small blue hole over temple, roused hotel, arranged funeral, attended funeral, closed cab, new morning coat . . .

I stooped down and picked up the paper and would you believe it – so ingrained is my Parisian sense of *comme il faut* – I murmured '*pardon*' before I read it.

MOUSE, MY LITTLE MOUSE,

It's no good. It's impossible. I can't see it through. Oh, I do love you. I do love you, Mouse, but I can't hurt her. People have been hurting her all her life. I simply dare not give her this final blow. You see, though she's stronger than both of us, she's so frail and proud. It would kill her – kill her, Mouse. And, oh God, I can't kill my mother! Not even for you. Not even for us. You do see that – don't you.

It all seemed so possible when we talked and planned, but the very moment the train started it was all over. I felt her drag me back to her – calling. I can hear her now as I write. And she's alone and she doesn't know. A man would have to be a devil to tell her and I'm not a devil, Mouse. She mustn't know. Oh, Mouse, somewhere, somewhere in you don't you agree? It's all so unspeakably awful that I don't know if I want to go or not. Do I? Or is mother just dragging me? I don't know. My head is too tired. Mouse, Mouse – what will you do? But I can't think of that, either. I dare not. I'd break down. And I must not break down. All I've got to do is – just to tell you this and go. I couldn't have gone off without telling you. You'd have been frightened. And you must not be frightened. You won't – will you? I can't bear – but no more of that. And don't write. I should not have the courage to answer your letters and the sight of your spidery handwriting –

Forgive me. Don't love me any more. Yes. Love me. Love me.

DICK

What do you think of that? Wasn't that a rare find? My relief at his not having shot himself was mixed with a wonderful sense of elation. I was even – more than even with my 'that's very curious and interesting' Englishman . . .

She wept so strangely. With her eyes shut, with her face quite calm except for the quivering eyelids. The tears pearled down her cheeks and she let them fall.

But feeling my glance upon her she opened her eyes and saw me holding the letter.

'You've read it?'

Her voice was quite calm, but it was not her voice any more. It was like the voice you might imagine coming out of a tiny, cold sea shell swept high and dry at last by the salt tide . . .

I nodded, quite overcome, you understand, and laid the letter down.

'It's incredible! incredible!' I whispered.

At that she got up from the floor, walked over to the washstand, dipped her handkerchief into the jug and sponged her eyes, saying: 'Oh, no. It's not incredible at all.' And still pressing the wet ball to her eyes she came back to me, to her chair with the lace tabs, and sank into it.

'I knew all along, of course,' said the cold, salty little voice. 'From the very moment that we started. I felt it all through me, but I still went on hoping – ' and here she took the handkerchief down and gave me a final glimmer – 'as one so stupidly does, you know.'

'As one does.'

Silence.

'But what will you do? You'll go back? You'll see him?'

That made her sit right up and stare across at me.

'What an extraordinary idea!' she said, more coldly than ever. 'Of course I shall not dream of seeing him. As for going back – that is quite out of the question. I can't go back.'

'But . . . '

'It's impossible. For one thing all my friends think I am married.'

I put out my hand – 'Ah, my poor little friend.'

But she shrank away. (False move.)

Of course there was one question that had been at the back of my mind all this time. I hated it.

'Have you any money?'

'Yes, I have twenty pounds – here,' and she put her hand on her breast. I bowed. It was a great deal more than I had expected.

'And what are your plans?'

Yes, I know. My question was the most clumsy, the most idiotic one I could have put. She had been so tame, so confiding, letting me, at any rate spiritually speaking, hold her tiny quivering body in one hand and stroke her furry head – and now, I'd thrown her away. Oh, I could have kicked myself.

She stood up. 'I have no plans. But – it's very late. You must go now, please.'

How could I get her back? I wanted her back. I swear I was not acting then.

'Do feel that I am your friend,' I cried. 'You will let me come tomorrow, early? You will let me look after you a little – take care of you a little? You'll use me just as you think fit?'

I succeeded. She came out of her hole . . . timid . . . but she came out.

'Yes, you're very kind. Yes. Do come tomorrow. I shall be glad. It makes things rather difficult because – ' and again I clasped her boyish hand – '*je ne parle pas français.*'

Not until I was half-way down the boulevard did it come over me – the full force of it.

Why, they were suffering . . . those two . . . really suffering. I have seen two people suffer as I don't suppose I ever shall again . . .

Of course you know what to expect. You anticipate, fully, what I am going to write. It wouldn't be me, otherwise.

I never went near the place again.

Yes, I still owe that considerable amount for lunches and dinners, but that's beside the mark. It's vulgar to mention it in the same breath with the fact that I never saw Mouse again.

Naturally, I intended to. Started out – got to the door – wrote and tore up letters – did all those things. But I simply could not make the final effort.

Even now I don't fully understand why. Of course I knew that I couldn't have kept it up. That had a great deal to do with it. But you would have thought, putting it at its lowest, curiosity couldn't have kept my fox-terrier nose away .

Je ne parle pas français. That was her swan-song for me.

But how she makes me break my rule. Oh, you've seen for yourself, but I could give you countless examples.

. . . Evenings, when I sit in some gloomy café, and an automatic piano starts playing a 'mouse' tune (there are dozens of tunes that evoke just her), I begin to dream things like . . .

A little house on the edge of the sea, somewhere far, far away. A girl outside in a frock rather like Red Indian women wear, hailing a light, barefoot boy who runs up from the beach.

'What have you got?'

'A fish.' I smile and give it to her.

. . . The same girl, the same boy, different costumes – sitting at an open window, eating fruit and leaning out and laughing.

'All the wild strawberries are for you, Mouse. I won't touch one.'

. . . A wet night. They are going home together under an umbrella. They stop on the door to press their wet cheeks together.

And so on and so on until some dirty old gallant comes up to my table and sits opposite and begins to grimace and yap. Until I hear myself saying: 'But I've got the little girl for you, *mon vieux*. So little . . . so tiny.' I kiss the tips of my fingers and lay them upon my heart. 'I give you my word of honour as a gentleman, a writer, serious, young, and extremely interested in modern English literature.'

I must go. I must go. I reach down my coat and hat. Madame knows me. 'You haven't dined yet?' she smiles.

'No, not yet, madame.'

Bliss

ALTHOUGH BERTHA YOUNG was thirty she still had moments like this when she wanted to run instead of walk, to take dancing steps on and off the pavement, to bowl a hoop, to throw something up in the air and catch it again, or to stand still and laugh at – nothing – at nothing, simply.

What can you do if you are thirty and, turning the corner of your own street, you are overcome, suddenly, by a feeling of bliss – absolute bliss! – as though you'd suddenly swallowed a bright piece of that late afternoon sun and it burned in your bosom, sending out a little shower of sparks into every particle, into every finger and toe? . . .

Oh, is there no way you can express it without being 'drunk and disorderly'? How idiotic civilisation is! Why be given a body if you have to keep it shut up in a case like a rare, rare fiddle?

'No, that about the fiddle is not quite what I mean,' she thought, running up the steps and feeling in her bag for the key – she'd forgotten it, as usual – and rattling the letter-box. 'It's not what I mean, because – Thank you, Mary' – she went into the hall. 'Is nurse back?'

'Yes, m'm.'

'And has the fruit come?'

'Yes, m'm. Everything's come.'

'Bring the fruit up to the dining-room, will you? I'll arrange it before I go upstairs.'

It was dusky in the dining-room and quite chilly. But all the same Bertha threw off her coat; she could not bear the tight clasp of it another moment, and the cold air fell on her arms.

But in her bosom there was still that bright glowing place – that shower of little sparks coming from it. It was almost unbearable. She hardly dared to breathe for fear of fanning it higher, and yet she breathed deeply, deeply. She hardly dared to look into the cold mirror – but she did look, and it gave her back a woman, radiant, with smiling, trembling lips, with big, dark eyes and an air of listening, waiting for something . . . divine to happen . . . that she knew must happen . . . infallibly.

Mary brought in the fruit on a tray and with it a glass bowl, and a blue dish, very lovely, with a strange sheen on it as though it had been dipped in milk.

'Shall I turn on the light, m'm?'

'No, thank you. I can see quite well.'

There were tangerines and apples stained with strawberry pink. Some yellow pears, smooth as silk, some white grapes covered with a silver bloom and a big cluster of purple ones. These last she had bought to tone in with the new dining-room carpet. Yes, that did sound rather far-fetched and absurd, but it was really why she had bought them. She had thought in the shop: 'I must have some purple ones to bring the carpet up to the table.' And it had seemed quite sense at the time.

When she had finished with them and had made two pyramids of these bright round shapes, she stood away from the table to get the effect – and it really was most curious. For the dark table seemed to melt into the dusky light and the glass dish and the blue bowl to float in the air. This, of course in her present mood, was so incredibly beautiful . . . She began to laugh.

'No, no. I'm getting hysterical.' And she seized her bag and coat and ran upstairs to the nursery.

Nurse sat at a low table giving Little B her supper after her bath. The baby had on a white flannel gown and a blue woollen jacket, and her dark, fine hair was brushed up into a funny little peak. She looked up when she saw her mother and began to jump.

'Now, my lovey, eat it up like a good girl,' said nurse, setting her lips in a way that Bertha knew, and that meant she had come into the nursery at another wrong moment.

'Has she been good, nanny?'

'She's been a little sweet all the afternoon,' whispered nanny. 'We went to the park and I sat down on a chair and took her out of the pram and a big dog came along and put its head on my knee and she clutched its ear, tugged it. Oh, you should have seen her.'

Bertha wanted to ask if it wasn't rather dangerous to let her clutch at a strange dog's ear. But she did not dare to. She stood watching them, her hands by her side, like the poor little girl in front of the rich little girl with the doll.

The baby looked up at her again, stared, and then smiled so

charmingly that Bertha couldn't help crying: 'Oh, nanny, do let me finish giving her her supper while you put the bath things away.'

'Well, m'm, she oughtn't to be changed hands while she's eating,' said nanny, still whispering. 'It unsettles her; it's very likely to upset her.'

How absurd it was. Why have a baby if it has to be kept – not in a case like a rare, rare fiddle – but in another woman's arms?

'Oh, I must!' said she.

Very offended, nanny handed her over.

'Now, don't excite her after her supper. You know you do, m'm. And I have such a time with her after!'

Thank heaven! Nanny went out of the room with the bath towels.

'Now I've got you to myself, my little precious,' said Bertha, as the baby leaned against her.

She ate delightfully, holding up her lips for the spoon and then waving her hands. Sometimes she wouldn't let the spoon go; and sometimes, just as Bertha had filled it, she waved it away to the four winds.

When the soup was finished Bertha turned round to the fire.

'You're nice – you're very nice!' said she, kissing her warm baby. 'I'm fond of you. I like you.'

And, indeed, she loved Little B so much – her neck as she bent forward, her exquisite toes as they shone transparent in the firelight – that all her feeling of bliss came back again, and again she didn't know how to express it – what to do with it.

'You're wanted on the telephone,' said nanny, coming back in triumph and seizing *her* Little B.

Down she flew. It was Harry.

'Oh, is that you, Ber? Look here. I'll be late. I'll take a taxi and come along as quickly as I can, but get dinner put back ten minutes – will you? All right?'

'Yes, perfectly. Oh, Harry!'

'Yes?'

What had she to say? She'd nothing to say. She only wanted to get in touch with him for a moment. She couldn't absurdly cry: 'Hasn't it been a divine day!'

'What is it?' rapped out the little voice.

'Nothing. *Entendu*,' said Bertha, and hung up the receiver, thinking how more than idiotic civilisation was.

They had people coming to dinner. The Norman Knights – a very sound couple – he was about to start a theatre, and she was awfully keen on interior decoration; a young man, Eddie Warren, who had just published a little book of poems and whom everybody was asking to dine; and a 'find' of Bertha's called Pearl Fulton. What Miss Fulton did, Bertha didn't know. They had met at the club and Bertha had fallen in love with her, as she always did fall in love with beautiful women who had something strange about them.

The provoking thing was that, though they had been about together and met a number of times and really talked, Bertha couldn't yet make her out. Up to a certain point Miss Fulton was rarely, wonderfully frank, but the certain point was there, and beyond that she would not go.

Was there anything beyond it? Harry said 'No.' Voted her dullish, and 'cold like all blonde women, with a touch, perhaps, of anaemia of the brain'. But Bertha wouldn't agree with him; not yet, at any rate.

'No, the way she has of sitting with her head a little on one side, and smiling, has something behind it, Harry, and I must find out what that something is.'

'Most likely it's a good stomach,' answered Harry.

He made a point of catching Bertha's heels with replies of that kind . . . 'liver frozen, my dear girl', or 'pure flatulence', or 'kidney disease' . . . and so on. For some strange reason Bertha liked this, and almost admired it in him very much.

She went into the drawing-room and lighted the fire; then, picking up the cushions, one by one, that Mary had disposed so carefully, she threw them back on to the chairs and the couches. That made all the difference; the room came alive at once. As she was about to throw the last one she surprised herself by suddenly hugging it to her, passionately, passionately. But it did not put out the fire in her bosom. Oh, on the contrary!

The windows of the drawing-room opened on to a balcony overlooking the garden. At the far end, against the wall, there was a tall, slender pear tree in fullest, richest bloom; it stood perfect, as though becalmed against the jade-green sky. Bertha couldn't help feeling, even from this distance, that it had not a single bud or a faded petal. Down below, in the garden beds, the red and yellow tulips, heavy with flowers, seemed to lean upon the dusk. A grey cat, dragging its belly, crept across the lawn, and a black one, its shadow, trailed after. The sight of them, so intent and so quick, gave Bertha a curious shiver.

'What creepy things cats are!' she stammered, and she turned away from the window and began walking up and down . . .

How strong the jonquils smelled in the warm room. Too strong? Oh, no. And yet, as though overcome, she flung down on a couch and pressed her hands to her eyes.

'I'm too happy – too happy!' she murmured.

And she seemed to see on her eyelids the lovely pear tree with its wide open blossoms as a symbol of her own life.

Really – really – she had everything. She was young. Harry and she were as much in love as ever, and they got on together splendidly and were really good pals. She had an adorable baby. They didn't have to worry about money. They had this absolutely satisfactory house and garden. And friends – modern, thrilling friends, writers and painters and poets or people keen on social questions – just the kind of friends they wanted. And then there were books, and there was music, and she had found a wonderful little dressmaker, and they were going abroad in the summer, and their new cook made the most superb omelettes . . .

'I'm absurd. Absurd!' She sat up; but she felt quite dizzy, quite drunk. It must have been the spring.

Yes, it was the spring. Now she was so tired she could not drag herself upstairs to dress.

A white dress, a string of jade beads, green shoes and stockings. It wasn't intentional. She had thought of this scheme hours before she stood at the drawing-room window.

Her petals rustled softly into the hall, and she kissed Mrs Norman Knight, who was taking off the most amusing orange coat with a procession of black monkeys round the hem and up the fronts.

' . . . Why! Why! Why is the middle-class so stodgy – so utterly without a sense of humour! My dear, it's only by a fluke that I am here at all – Norman being the protective fluke. For my darling monkeys so upset the train that it rose to a man and simply ate me with its eyes. Didn't laugh – wasn't amused – that I should have loved. No, just stared – and bored me through and through.'

'But the cream of it was,' said Norman, pressing a large tortoise-shell-rimmed monocle into his eye, 'you don't mind me telling this, Face, do you?' (In their home and among their friends they called each other Face and Mug.) 'The cream of it was when she, being full fed, turned to the woman beside her and said: "Haven't you ever seen a monkey before?" '

'Oh, yes!' Mrs Norman Knight joined in the laughter. 'Wasn't that too absolutely creamy?'

And a funnier thing still was that now her coat was off she did look like a very intelligent monkey – who had even made that yellow silk dress out of scraped banana skins. And her amber earrings; they were like little dangling nuts.

'This is a sad, sad fall!' said Mug, pausing in front of Little B's perambulator. 'When the perambulator comes into the hall – ' and he waved the rest of the quotation away.

The bell rang. It was lean, pale Eddie Warren (as usual) in a state of acute distress.

'It *is* the right house, *isn't* it?' he pleaded.

'Oh, I think so – I hope so,' said Bertha brightly.

'I have had such a *dreadful* experience with a taxi-man; he was *most* sinister. I couldn't get him to *stop*. The *more* I knocked and called the *faster* he went. And *in* the moonlight this *bizarre* figure with the *flattened* head *crouching* over the *lit–tle* wheel . . .'

He shuddered, taking off an immense white silk scarf. Bertha noticed that his socks were white, too – most charming.

'But how dreadful!' she cried.

'Yes, it really was,' said Eddie, following her into the drawing-room. 'I saw myself *driving* through Eternity in a *timeless* taxi.'

He knew the Norman Knights. In fact, he was going to write a play for N. K. when the theatre scheme came off.

'Well, Warren, how's the play?' said Norman Knight, dropping his monocle and giving his eye a moment in which to rise to the surface before it was screwed down again.

And Mrs Norman Knight: 'Oh, Mr Warren, what happy socks!'

'I *am* so glad you like them,' said he, staring at his feet. 'They seem to have got so *much* whiter since the moon rose.' And he turned his lean sorrowful young face to Bertha. 'There *is* a moon, you know.'

She wanted to cry: 'I am sure there is – often – often!'

He really was a most attractive person. But so was Face, crouched before the fire in her banana skins, and so was Mug, smoking a cigarette and saying as he flicked the ash: 'Why doth the bridegroom tarry?'

'There he is, now.'

Bang went the front door open and shut. Harry shouted: 'Hallo, you people. Down in five minutes.' And they heard him swarm up the stairs. Bertha couldn't help smiling; she knew how he loved doing things at high pressure. What, after all, did an extra five minutes matter? But he would pretend to himself that they mattered beyond measure. And then he would make a great point of coming into the drawing-room, extravagantly cool and collected.

Harry had such a zest for life. Oh, how she appreciated it in him. And his passion for fighting – for seeking in everything that came up against him another test of his power and of his courage – that, too, she understood. Even when it made him just occasionally, to other people, who didn't know him well, a little ridiculous perhaps . . . For there were moments when he rushed into battle where no battle was . . . She talked and laughed and positively forgot until he had come in (just as she had imagined) that Pearl Fulton had not turned up.

'I wonder if Miss Fulton has forgotten?'

'I expect so,' said Harry. 'Is she on the phone?'

'Ah! There's a taxi, now.' And Bertha smiled with that little air of proprietorship that she always assumed while her women finds were new and mysterious. 'She lives in taxis.'

'She'll run to fat if she does,' said Harry coolly, ringing the bell for dinner. 'Frightful danger for blonde women.'

'Harry – don't,' warned Bertha, laughing up at him.

Came another tiny moment, while they waited, laughing and talking, just a trifle too much at their ease, a trifle too unaware. And then Miss Fulton, all in silver, with a silver fillet binding her pale blonde hair, came in smiling, her head a little on one side.

'Am I late?'

'No, not at all,' said Bertha. 'Come along.' And she took her arm and they moved into the dining-room.

What was there in the touch of that cool arm that could fan – fan – start blazing – blazing the fire of bliss that Bertha did not know what to do with?

Miss Fulton did not look at her; but then she seldom did look at people directly. Her heavy eyelids lay upon her eyes and the strange half-smile came and went upon her lips as though she lived by listening rather than seeing. But Bertha knew, suddenly, as if the longest, most intimate look had passed between them – as if they had said to each other: 'You, too?' – that Pearl Fulton, stirring the beautiful red soup in the grey plate, was feeling just what she was feeling.

And the others? Face and Mug, Eddie and Harry, their spoons rising and falling – dabbing their lips with their napkins, crumbling bread, fiddling with the forks and glasses and talking.

'I met her at the Alpha show – the weirdest little person. She'd not only cut off her hair, but she seemed to have taken a dreadfully good snip off her legs and arms and her neck and her poor little nose as well.'

'Isn't she very *liée* with Michael Oat?'

'The man who wrote *Love in False Teeth*?'

'He wants to write a play for me. One act. One man. Decides to commit suicide. Gives all the reasons why he should and why he shouldn't. And just as he has made up his mind either to do it or not to do it – curtain. Not half a bad idea.'

'What's he going to call it – "Stomach Trouble"?'

'I *think* I've come across the *same* idea in a lit–tle French review, *quite* unknown in England.'

No, they didn't share it. They were dears – dears – and she loved having them there, at her table, and giving them delicious food and wine. In fact, she longed to tell them how delightful they were, and what a decorative group they made, how they seemed to set one another off and how they reminded her of a play by Chekhov!

Harry was enjoying his dinner. It was part of his – well, not his nature, exactly, and certainly not his pose – his – something or other – to talk about food and to glory in his 'shameless passion for the white flesh of the lobster' and 'the green of pistachio ices – green and cold like the eyelids of Egyptian dancers'.

When he looked up at her and said: 'Bertha, this is a very admirable *soufflée*!' she almost could have wept with childlike pleasure.

Oh, why did she feel so tender towards the whole world tonight? Everything was good – was right. All that happened seemed to fill again her brimming cup of bliss.

And still, in the back of her mind, there was the pear tree. It would be silver now, in the light of poor dear Eddie's moon, silver as Miss Fulton, who sat there turning a tangerine in her slender fingers that were so pale a light seemed to come from them.

What she simply couldn't make out – what was miraculous – was how she should have guessed Miss Fulton's mood so exactly and so instantly. For she never doubted for a moment that she was right, and yet what had she to go on? Less than nothing.

'I believe this does happen very, very rarely between women. Never between men,' thought Bertha. 'But while I am making the coffee in the drawing-room perhaps she will "give a sign".'

What she meant by that she did not know, and what would happen after that she could not imagine.

While she thought like this she saw herself talking and laughing. She had to talk because of her desire to laugh.

'I must laugh or die.'

But when she noticed Face's funny little habit of tucking some-thing down the front of her bodice – as if she kept a tiny, secret hoard of nuts there, too – Bertha had to dig her nails into her hands – so as not to laugh too much.

It was over at last. And: 'Come and see my new coffee machine,' said Bertha.

'We only have a new coffee machine once a fortnight,' said Harry. Face took her arm this time; Miss Fulton bent her head and followed after.

The fire had died down in the drawing-room to a red, flickering 'nest of baby phœnixes', said Face.

'Don't turn up the light for a moment. It is so lovely.' And down she crouched by the fire again. She was always cold . . . 'without her little red flannel jacket, of course,' thought Bertha.

At that moment Miss Fulton 'gave the sign'.

'Have you a garden?' said the cool, sleepy voice.

This was so exquisite on her part that all Bertha could do was to obey. She crossed the room, pulled the curtains apart, and opened those long windows.

'There!' she breathed.

And the two women stood side by side looking at the slender, flowering tree. Although it was so still it seemed, like the flame of a candle, to stretch up, to point, to quiver in the bright air, to grow taller and taller as they gazed – almost to touch the rim of the round, silver moon.

How long did they stand there? Both, as it were, caught in that circle of unearthly light, understanding each other perfectly, creat-ures of another world, and wondering what they were to do in this one with all this blissful treasure that burned in their bosoms and dropped, in silver flowers, from their hair and hands?

For ever? – for a moment? And did Miss Fulton murmur: 'Yes. Just *that*.' Or did Bertha dream it?

Then the light was snapped on and Face made the coffee and Harry said: 'My dear Mrs Knight, don't ask me about my baby. I never see her. I shan't feel the slightest interest in her until she has a lover,' and Mug took his eye out of the conservatory for a moment and then put it under glass again and Eddie Warren drank his coffee and set down the cup with a face of anguish as though he had drunk and seen the spider.

'What I want to do is to give the young men a show. I believe London is simply teeming with first-chop, unwritten plays. What I want to say to 'em is: "Here's the theatre. Fire ahead." '

'You know, my dear, I am going to decorate a room for the Jacob Nathans. Oh, I am so tempted to do a fried-fish scheme, with the backs of the chairs shaped like frying pans and lovely chip potatoes embroidered all over the curtains.'

'The trouble with our young writing men is that they are still too romantic. You can't put out to sea without being seasick and wanting a basin. Well, why won't they have the courage of those basins?'

'A *dreadful* poem about a *girl* who was *violated* by a beggar *without* a nose in a lit–tle wood . . . '

Miss Fulton sank into the lowest, deepest chair and Harry handed round the cigarettes.

From the way he stood in front of her shaking the silver box and saying abruptly: 'Egyptian? Turkish? Virginian? They're all mixed up,' Bertha realised that she not only bored him; he really disliked her. And she decided from the way Miss Fulton said: 'No, thank you, I won't smoke,' that she felt it, too, and was hurt.

'Oh, Harry, don't dislike her. You are quite wrong about her. She's wonderful, wonderful. And, besides, how can you feel so differently about someone who means so much to me. I shall try to tell you when we are in bed tonight what has been happening. What she and I have shared.'

At those last words something strange and almost terrifying darted into Bertha's mind. And this something blind and smiling whispered to her: 'Soon these people will go. The house will be quiet – quiet. The lights will be out. And you and he will be alone together in the dark room – the warm bed . . . '

She jumped up from her chair and ran over to the piano.

'What a pity someone does not play!' she cried. 'What a pity somebody does not play.'

For the first time in her life Bertha Young desired her husband.

Oh, she'd loved him – she'd been in love with him, of course, in every other way, but just not in that way. And, equally, of course, she'd understood that he was different. They'd discussed it so often. It had worried her dreadfully at first to find that she was so cold, but after a time it had not seemed to matter. They were so frank with each other – such good pals. That was the best of being modern.

But now ardently! Ardently! The word ached in her ardent body! Was this what that feeling of bliss had been leading up to? But then, then –

'My dear,' said Mrs Norman Knight, 'you know our shame. We are the victims of time and train. We live in Hampstead. It's been so nice.'

'I'll come with you into the hall,' said Bertha. 'I loved having you. But you must not miss the last train. That's so awful, isn't it?'

'Have a whisky, Knight, before you go?' called Harry.

'No, thanks, old chap.'

Bertha squeezed his hand for that as she shook it.

'Good night, goodbye,' she cried from the top step, feeling that this self of hers was taking leave of them for ever.

When she got back into the drawing-room the others were on the move.

' . . . Then you can come part of the way in my taxi.'

'I shall be *so* thankful *not* to have to face *another* drive *alone* after my *dreadful* experience.'

'You can get a taxi at the rank just at the end of the street. You won't have to walk more than a few yards.'

'That's a comfort. I'll go and put on my coat.'

Miss Fulton moved towards the hall and Bertha was following when Harry almost pushed past.

'Let me help you.'

Bertha knew that he was repenting his rudeness – she let him go. What a boy he was in some ways – so impulsive – so – simple.

And Eddie and she were left by the fire.

'I *wonder* if you have seen Bilks' *new* poem called *Table d'Hôte*,' said Eddie softly. 'It's *so* wonderful. In the last Anthology. Have you got a copy? I'd *so* like to *show* it to you. It begins with an *incredibly* beautiful line: "Why Must it Always be Tomato Soup?" '

'Yes,' said Bertha. And she moved noiselessly to a table opposite the drawing-room door and Eddie glided noiselessly after her. She picked up the little book and gave it to him; they had not made a sound.

While he looked it up she turned her head towards the hall. And she saw . . . Harry with Miss Fulton's coat in his arms and Miss Fulton with her back turned to him and her head bent. He tossed the coat away, put his hands on her shoulders and turned her violently to him. His lips said: 'I adore you,' and Miss Fulton laid her moonbeam fingers on his cheeks and smiled her sleepy smile. Harry's nostrils quivered; his lips curled back in a hideous grin while he whispered: 'Tomorrow,' and with her eyelids Miss Fulton said: 'Yes.'

'Here it is,' said Eddie. '"Why Must it Always be Tomato Soup?" It's so *deeply* true, don't you feel? Tomato soup is so *dreadfully* eternal.'

'If you prefer,' said Harry's voice, very loud, from the hall, 'I can phone you a cab to come to the door.'

'Oh, no. It's not necessary,' said Miss Fulton, and she came up to Bertha and gave her the slender fingers to hold.

'Goodbye. Thank you so much.'

'Goodbye,' said Bertha.

Miss Fulton held her hand a moment longer.

'Your lovely pear tree!' she murmured.

And then she was gone, with Eddie following, like the black cat following the grey cat.

'I'll shut up shop,' said Harry, extravagantly cool and collected.

'Your lovely pear tree – pear tree – pear tree!'

Bertha simply ran over to the long windows.

'Oh, what is going to happen now?' she cried.

But the pear tree was as lovely as ever and as full of flower and as still.

The Wind Blows

SUDDENLY – DREADFULLY – she wakes up. What has happened? Something dreadful has happened. No – nothing has happened. It is only the wind shaking the house, rattling the windows, banging a piece of iron on the roof and making her bed tremble. Leaves flutter past the window, up and away; down in the avenue a whole newspaper wags in the air like a lost kite and falls, spiked on a pine tree. It is cold. Summer is over – it is autumn – everything is ugly. The carts rattle by, swinging from side to side; two Chinamen lollop along under their wooden yokes with the straining vegetable baskets – their pigtails and blue blouses fly out in the wind. A white dog on three legs yelps past the gate. It is all over! What is? Oh, everything! And she begins to plait her hair with shaking fingers, not daring to look in the glass. Mother is talking to grandmother in the hall.

'A perfect idiot! Imagine leaving anything out on the line in weather like this . . . Now my best little Tenerife-work teacloth is simply in ribbons. *What* is that extraordinary smell? It's the porridge burning. Oh, heavens – this wind!'

She has a music lesson at ten o'clock. At the thought the minor movement of the Beethoven begins to play in her head, the trills long and terrible like little rolling drums . . . Marie Swainson runs into the garden next door to pick the 'chrysanths' before they are ruined. Her skirt flies up above her waist; she tries to beat it down, to tuck it between her legs while she stoops, but it is no use – up it flies. All the trees and bushes beat about her. She picks as quickly as she can, but she is quite distracted. She doesn't mind what she does – she pulls the plants up by the roots and bends and twists them, stamping her foot and swearing.

'For heaven's sake keep the front door shut! Go round to the back,' shouts someone. And then she hears Bogey: 'Mother, you're wanted on the telephone. Telephone, mother. It's the butcher.'

How hideous life is – revolting, simply revolting . . . And now her hat-elastic's snapped. Of course it would. She'll wear her old tam and slip out the back way. But mother has seen.

'Matilda. Matilda. Come back im–me–diately! What on earth have you got on your head? It looks like a tea-cosy. And why have you got that mane of hair on your forehead.'

'I can't come back, mother. I'll be late for my lesson.'

'Come back immediately!'

She won't. She won't. She hates mother. 'Go to hell,' she shouts, running down the road.

In waves, in clouds, in big round whirls the dust comes stinging, and with it little bits of straw and chaff and manure. There is a loud roaring sound from the trees in the gardens, and standing at the bottom of the road outside Mr Bullen's gate she can hear the sea sob: 'Ah! . . . Ah! . . . Ah–h!' But Mr Bullen's drawing-room is as quiet as a cave. The windows are closed, the blinds half pulled, and she is not late. The-girl-before-her has just started playing MacDowell's 'To an Iceberg'. Mr Bullen looks over at her and half smiles.

'Sit down,' he says. 'Sit over there in the sofa corner, little lady.'

How funny he is. He doesn't exactly laugh at you . . . but there is just something . . . Oh, how peaceful it is here. She likes this room. It smells of art serge and stale smoke and chrysanthemums . . . there is a big vase of them on the mantelpiece behind the pale photograph of Rubinstein . . . *à mon ami Robert Bullen* . . . Over the black glittering piano hangs 'Solitude' – a dark tragic woman draped in white, sitting on a rock, her knees crossed, her chin on her hands.

'No, no!' says Mr Bullen, and he leans over the other girl, puts his arms over her shoulders and plays the passage for her. The stupid – she's blushing! How ridiculous!

Now the-girl-before-her has gone; the front door slams. Mr Bullen comes back and walks up and down, very softly, waiting for her. What an extraordinary thing. Her fingers tremble so that she can't undo the knot in the music satchel. It's the wind . . . And her heart beats so hard she feels it must lift her blouse up and down. Mr Bullen does not say a word. The shabby red piano seat is long enough for two people to sit side by side. Mr Bullen sits down by her.

'Shall I begin with scales,' she asks, squeezing her hands together. 'I had some arpeggios, too.'

But he does not answer. She doesn't believe he even hears . . . and then suddenly his fresh hand with the ring on it reaches over and opens Beethoven.

'Let's have a little of the old master,' he says.

But why does he speak so kindly – so awfully kindly – and as though they had known each other for years and years and knew everything about each other.

He turns the page slowly. She watches his hand – it is a very nice hand and always looks as though it had just been washed.

'Here we are,' says Mr Bullen.

Oh, that kind voice – oh, that minor movement. Here come the little drums . . .

'Shall I take the repeat?'

'Yes, dear child.'

His voice is far, far too kind. The crotchets and quavers are dancing up and down the stave like little black boys on a fence. Why is he so . . . She will not cry – she has nothing to cry about . . .

'What is it, dear child?'

Mr Bullen takes her hands. His shoulder is there – just by her head. She leans on it ever so little, her cheek against the springy tweed.

'Life is so dreadful,' she murmurs, but she does not feel it's dreadful at all. He says something about 'waiting' and 'marking time' and 'that rare thing, a woman', but she does not hear. It is so comfortable . . . for ever . . .

Suddenly the door opens and in pops Marie Swainson, hours before her time.

'Take the allegretto a little faster,' says Mr Bullen, and gets up and begins to walk up and down again.

'Sit in the sofa corner, little lady,' he says to Marie.

The wind, the wind. It's frightening to be here in her room by herself. The bed, the mirror, the white jug and basin gleam like the sky outside. It's the bed that is frightening. There it lies, sound asleep . . . Does mother imagine for one moment that she is going to darn all those stockings knotted up on the quilt like a coil of snakes? She's not. No, mother. I do not see why I should . . . The wind – the wind! There's a funny smell of soot blowing down the chimney. Hasn't anyone written poems to the wind? . . . 'I bring fresh flowers to the leaves and showers' . . . What nonsense.

'Is that you, Bogey?'

'Come for a walk round the esplanade, Matilda. I can't stand this any longer.'

'Right-o. I'll put on my ulster. Isn't it an awful day!' Bogey's ulster is just like hers. Hooking the collar she looks at herself in the glass. Her face is white, they have the same excited eyes and hot lips. Ah, they know those two in the glass. Goodbye, dears; we shall be back soon.

'This is better, isn't it?'

'Hook on,' says Bogey.

They cannot walk fast enough. Their heads bent, their legs just touching, they stride like one eager person through the town, down the asphalt zigzag where the fennel grows wild and on to the esplanade. It is dusky – just getting dusky. The wind is so strong that they have to fight their way through it, rocking like two old drunkards. All the poor little pahutukawas on the esplanade are bent to the ground.

'Come on! Come on! Let's get near.'

Over by the breakwater the sea is very high. They pull off their hats and her hair blows across her mouth, tasting of salt. The sea is so high that the waves do not break at all; they thump against the rough stone wall and suck up the weedy, dripping steps. A fine spray skims from the water right across the esplanade. They are covered with drops; the inside of her mouth tastes wet and cold.

Bogey's voice is breaking. When he speaks he rushes up and down the scale. It's funny – it makes you laugh – and yet it just suits the day. The wind carries their voices – away fly the sentences like little narrow ribbons.

'Quicker! Quicker!'

It is getting very dark. In the harbour the coal hulks show two lights – one high on a mast, and one from the stern.

'Look, Bogey. Look over there.'

A big black steamer with a long loop of smoke streaming, with the portholes lighted, with lights everywhere, is putting out to sea. The wind does not stop her; she cuts through the waves, making for the open gate between the pointed rocks that leads to . . . It's the light that makes her look so awfully beautiful and mysterious . . . *They* are on board leaning over the rail arm in arm.

' . . . Who are they?'

' . . . Brother and sister.'

'Look, Bogey, there's the town. Doesn't it look small? There's the post-office clock chiming for the last time. There's the esplanade where we walked that windy day. Do you remember? I cried at my music lesson that day – how many years ago! Goodbye, little island, goodbye . . . '

Now the dark stretches a wing over the tumbling water. They can't see those two any more. Goodbye, goodbye. Don't forget . . . But the ship is gone, now.

The wind – the wind.

Psychology

WHEN SHE OPENED the door and saw him standing there she was more pleased than ever before, and he, too, as he followed her into the studio, seemed very very happy to have come.

'Not busy?'

'No. Just going to have tea.'

'And you are not expecting anybody?'

'Nobody at all.'

'Ah! That's good.'

He laid aside his coat and hat gently, lingeringly, as though he had time and to spare for everything, or as though he were taking leave of them for ever, and came over to the fire and held out his hands to the quick, leaping flame.

Just for a moment both of them stood silent in that leaping light. Still, as it were, they tasted on their smiling lips the sweet shock of their greeting.

Their secret selves whispered: 'Why should we speak? Isn't this enough?'

'More than enough. I never realised until this moment . . . '

'How good it is just to be with you . . . '

'Like this . . . '

'It's more than enough.'

But suddenly he turned and looked at her and she moved quickly away.

'Have a cigarette? I'll put the kettle on. Are you longing for tea?'

'No. Not longing.'

'Well, I am.'

'Oh, you.' He thumped the Armenian cushion and flung on to the *sommier*. 'You're a perfect little Chinee.'

'Yes, I am,' she laughed. 'I long for tea as strong men long for wine.'

She lighted the lamp under its broad orange shade, pulled the curtains and drew up the tea table. Two birds sang in the kettle; the fire fluttered. He sat up clasping his knees. It was delightful – this business of having tea – and she always had delicious things to eat – little sharp sandwiches, short sweet almond fingers, and a dark, rich cake tasting of rum – but it was an interruption. He wanted it over, the table pushed away, their two chairs drawn up to the light, and the moment come when he took out his pipe, filled it, and said, pressing the tobacco tight into the bowl: 'I have been thinking over what you said last time and it seems to me . . .'

Yes, that was what he waited for and so did she. Yes, while she shook the teapot hot and dry over the spirit flame she saw those other two, him, leaning back, taking his ease among the cushions, and her, curled up *en escargot* in the blue shell armchair. The picture was so clear and so minute it might have been painted on the blue teapot lid. And yet she couldn't hurry. She could almost have cried: 'Give me time.' She must have time in which to grow calm. She wanted time in which to free herself from all these familiar things with which she lived so vividly. For all these gay things round her were part of her – her offspring – and they knew it and made the largest, most vehement claims. But now they must go. They must be swept away, shooed away – like children, sent up the shadowy stairs, packed into bed and commanded to go to sleep – at once – without a murmur!

For the special thrilling quality of their friendship was in their complete surrender. Like two open cities in the midst of some vast plain their two minds lay open to each other. And it wasn't as if he rode into hers like a conqueror, armed to the eyebrows and seeing nothing but a gay silken flutter – nor did she enter his like a queen walking soft on petals. No, they were eager, serious travellers, absorbed in understanding what was to be seen and discovering what was hidden – making the most of this extraordinary absolute chance which made it possible for him to be utterly truthful to her and for her to be utterly sincere with him.

And the best of it was they were both of them old enough to enjoy their adventure to the full without any stupid emotional complication. Passion would have ruined everything; they quite saw that. Besides, all that sort of thing was over and done with for both of them – he was thirty-one, she was thirty – they had had their experiences, and very rich and varied they had been, but now was the time for harvest – harvest. Weren't his novels to be very big novels indeed? And her plays. Who else had her exquisite sense of real English Comedy? . . .

Carefully she cut the cake into thick little wads and he reached across for a piece.

'Do realise how good it is,' she implored. 'Eat it imaginatively. Roll your eyes if you can and taste it on the breath. It's not a sandwich from the hatter's bag – it's the kind of cake that might have been mentioned in the Book of Genesis . . . And God said: "Let there be cake. And there was cake. And God saw that it was good." '

'You needn't entreat me,' said he. 'Really you needn't. It's a queer thing but I always do notice what I eat here and never anywhere else. I suppose it comes of living alone so long and always reading while I feed . . . my habit of looking upon food as just food . . . something that's there, at certain times . . . to be devoured . . . to be . . . not there.' He laughed. 'That shocks you. Doesn't it?'

'To the bone,' said she.

'But – look here.' He pushed away his cup and began to speak very fast. 'I simply haven't got any external life at all. I don't know the names of things a bit – trees and so on – and I never notice places or furniture or what people look like. One room is just like another to me – a place to sit and read or talk in – except,' and here he paused, smiled in a strange naïve way, and said, 'except this studio.' He looked round him and then at her; he laughed in his astonishment and pleasure. He was like a man who wakes up in a train to find that he has arrived, already, at the journey's end.

'Here's another queer thing. If I shut my eyes I can see this place down to every detail – every detail . . . Now I come to think of it – I've never realised this consciously before. Often when I am away from here I revisit it in spirit – wander about among your red chairs, stare at the bowl of fruit on the black table – and just touch, very lightly, that marvel of a sleeping boy's head.'

He looked at it as he spoke. It stood on the corner of the mantel-piece; the head to one side down-drooping, the lips parted, as though in his sleep the little boy listened to some sweet sound . . .

'I love that little boy,' he murmured. And then they both were silent.

A new silence came between them. Nothing in the least like the satisfactory pause that had followed their greetings – the 'Well, here we are together again, and there's no reason why we shouldn't go on from just where we left off last time.' That silence could be contained in the circle of warm, delightful fire and lamplight. How many times hadn't they flung something into it just for the fun of watching the ripples break on the easy shores. But into this unfamiliar pool the head of the little boy sleeping his timeless sleep dropped – and the ripples flowed away, away – boundlessly far – into deep glittering darkness.

And then both of them broke it. She said: 'I must make up the fire,' and he said: 'I have been trying a new . . . ' Both of them escaped. She made up the fire and put the table back, the blue chair was wheeled forward, she curled up and he lay back among the cushions. Quickly! Quickly! They must stop it from happening again.

'Well, I read the book you left last time.'

'Oh, what do you think of it?'

They were off and all was as usual. But was it? Weren't they just a little too quick, too prompt with their replies, too ready to take each other up? Was this really anything more than a wonderfully good imitation of other occasions? His heart beat; her cheek burned and the stupid thing was she could not discover where exactly they were or what exactly was happening. She hadn't time to glance back. And just as she had got so far it happened again. They faltered, wavered, broke down, were silent. Again they were conscious of the boundless, questioning dark. Again, there they were – two hunters, bending over their fire, but hearing suddenly from the jungle beyond a shake of wind and a loud, questioning cry . . .

She lifted her head. 'It's raining,' she murmured. And her voice was like his when he had said: 'I love that little boy.'

Well. Why didn't they just give way to it – yield – and see what would happen then? But no. Vague and troubled though they were, they knew enough to realise their precious friendship was in danger. She was the one who would be destroyed – not they – and they'd be no party to that.

He got up, knocked out his pipe, ran his hand through his hair and said: 'I have been wondering very much lately whether the novel of the future will be a psychological novel or not. How sure are you that psychology qua psychology has got anything to do with literature at all?'

'Do you mean you feel there's quite a chance that the mysterious non-existent creatures – the young writers of today – are trying simply to jump the psychoanalyst's claim?'

'Yes, I do. And I think it's because this generation is just wise enough to know that it is sick and to realise that its only chance of recovery is by going into its symptoms – making an exhaustive study of them – tracking them down – trying to get at the root of the trouble.'

'But oh,' she wailed. 'What a dreadfully dismal outlook.'

'Not at all,' said he. 'Look here . . . ' On the talk went. And now it seemed they really had succeeded. She turned in her chair to look at him while she answered. Her smile said: 'We have won.' And he smiled back, confident: 'Absolutely.'

But the smile undid them. It lasted too long; it became a grin. They saw themselves as two little grinning puppets jigging away in nothingness.

'What have we been talking about?' thought he. He was so utterly bored he almost groaned.

'What a spectacle we have made of ourselves,' thought she. And she saw him laboriously – oh, laboriously – laying out the grounds and herself running after, putting here a tree and there a flowery shrub and here a handful of glittering fish in a pool. They were silent this time from sheer dismay.

The clock struck six merry little pings and the fire made a soft flutter. What fools they were – heavy, stodgy, elderly – with positively upholstered minds.

And now the silence put a spell upon them like solemn music. It was anguish – anguish for her to bear it and he would die – he'd die if it were broken . . . And yet he longed to break it. Not by speech. At any rate not by their ordinary maddening chatter. There was another way for them to speak to each other, and in the new way he wanted to murmur: 'Do you feel this too? Do you understand it at all?' . . .

Instead, to his horror, he heard himself say: 'I must be off; I'm meeting Brand at six.'

What devil made him say that instead of the other? She jumped – simply jumped out of her chair, and he heard her crying: 'You must rush, then. He's so punctual. Why didn't you say so before?'

'You've hurt me; you've hurt me! We've failed!' said her secret self while she handed him his hat and stick, smiling gaily. She wouldn't give him a moment for another word, but ran along the passage and opened the big outer door.

Could they leave each other like this? How could they? He stood on the step and she just inside holding the door. It was not raining now.

'You've hurt me – hurt me,' said her heart. 'Why don't you go? No, don't go. Stay. No – go!' And she looked out upon the night.

She saw the beautiful fall of the steps, the dark garden ringed with glittering ivy, on the other side of the road the huge bare willows and above them the sky big and bright with stars. But of course he would see nothing of all this. He was superior to it all. He – with his wonderful 'spiritual' vision!

She was right. He did see nothing at all. Misery! He'd missed it. It was too late to do anything now. Was it too late? Yes, it was. A cold snatch of hateful wind blew into the garden. Curse life! He heard her cry '*au revoir*' and the door slammed.

Running back into the studio she behaved so strangely. She ran up and down lifting her arms and crying: 'Oh! Oh! How stupid! How imbecile! How stupid!' And then she flung herself down on the *sommier* thinking of nothing – just lying there in her rage. All was over. What was over? Oh – something was. And she'd never see him again – never. After a long long time (or perhaps ten minutes) had passed in that black gulf her bell rang a sharp quick jingle. It was he, of course. And equally, of course, she oughtn't to have paid the slightest attention to it but just let it go on ringing and ringing. She flew to answer.

On the doorstep there stood an elderly virgin, a pathetic creature who simply idolised her (heaven knows why) and had this habit of turning up and ringing the bell and then saying, when she opened the door: 'My dear, send me away!' She never did. As a rule she asked her in and let her admire everything and accepted the bunch of slightly soiled-looking flowers – more than graciously. But today . . .

'Oh, I am so sorry,' she cried, 'but I've got someone with me. We are working on some woodcuts. I'm hopelessly busy all evening.'

'It doesn't matter. It doesn't matter at all, darling,' said the good friend. 'I was just passing and I thought I'd leave you some violets.' She fumbled down among the ribs of a large old umbrella. 'I put them down here. Such a good place to keep flowers out of the wind. Here they are,' she said, shaking out a little dead bunch.

For a moment she did not take the violets. But while she stood just inside, holding the door, a strange thing happened . . . Again she saw the beautiful fall of the steps, the dark garden ringed with glittering ivy, the willows, the big bright sky. Again she felt the silence that was like a question. But this time she did not hesitate. She moved forward. Very softly and gently, as though fearful of making a ripple in that boundless pool of quiet, she put her arms round her friend.

'My dear,' murmured her happy friend, quite overcome by this gratitude. 'They are really nothing. Just the simplest little thrippenny bunch.'

But as she spoke she was enfolded – more tenderly, more beautifully embraced, held by such a sweet pressure and for so long that the poor dear's mind positively reeled and she just had the strength to quaver: 'Then you really don't mind me too much?'

'Good-night, my friend,' whispered the other. 'Come again soon.'

'Oh, I will. I will.'

This time she walked back to the studio slowly, and standing in the middle of the room with half-shut eyes she felt so light, so rested, as if she had woken up out of a childish sleep. Even the act of breathing was a joy . . .

The *sommier* was very untidy. All the cushions 'like furious mountains' as she said; she put them in order before going over to the writing-table.

'I have been thinking over our talk about the psychological novel,' she dashed off, 'it really is intensely interesting' . . . And so on and so on.

At the end she wrote: 'Good-night, my friend. Come again soon.'

Pictures

EIGHT O'CLOCK in the morning. Miss Ada Moss lay in a black iron bedstead, staring up at the ceiling. Her room, a Bloomsbury top-floor back, smelled of soot and face powder and the paper of fried potatoes she brought in for supper the night before.

'Oh, dear,' thought Miss Moss, 'I am cold. I wonder why it is that I always wake up so cold in the mornings now. My knees and feet and my back – especially my back; it's like a sheet of ice. And I always was such a one for being warm in the old days. It's not as if I was skinny – I'm just the same full figure that I used to be. No, it's because I don't have a good hot dinner in the evenings.'

A pageant of Good Hot Dinners passed across the ceiling, each of them accompanied by a bottle of Nourishing Stout . . .

'Even if I were to get up now,' she thought, 'and have a sensible substantial breakfast . . . ' A pageant of Sensible Substantial Breakfasts followed the dinners across the ceiling, shepherded by an enormous, white, uncut ham. Miss Moss shuddered and disappeared under the bedclothes. Suddenly, in bounced the landlady.

'There's a letter for you, Miss Moss.'

'Oh,' said Miss Moss, far too friendly, 'thank you very much, Mrs Pine. It's very good of you, I'm sure, to take the trouble.'

'No trouble at all,' said the landlady. 'I thought perhaps it was the letter you'd been expecting.'

'Why,' said Miss Moss brightly, 'yes, perhaps it is.' She put her head on one side and smiled vaguely at the letter. 'I shouldn't be surprised.'

The landlady's eyes popped. 'Well, I should, Miss Moss,' said she, 'and that's how it is. And I'll trouble you to open it, if you please. Many is the lady in my place as would have done it for you and have been within her rights. For things can't go on like this, Miss Moss, no indeed they can't. What with week in week out and first you've got it and then you haven't, and then it's another letter lost in the post or another manager down at Brighton but will be back on

Tuesday for certain – I'm fair sick and tired and I won't stand it no more. Why should I, Miss Moss, I ask you, at a time like this, with prices flying up in the air and my poor dear lad in France? My sister Eliza was only saying to me yesterday – "Minnie," she says, "you're too soft-hearted. You could have let that room time and time again," says she, "and if people won't look after themselves in times like these, nobody else will," she says. "She may have had a College eddication and sung in West End concerts," says she, "but if your Lizzie says what's true," she says, "and she's washing her own wovens and drying them on the towel rail, it's easy to see where the finger's pointing. And it's high time you had done with it," says she.'

Miss Moss gave no sign of having heard this. She sat up in bed, tore open her letter and read:

DEAR MADAM
Yours to hand. Am not producing at present, but have filed photo for future ref.

Yours truly,
BACKWASH FILM CO.

This letter seemed to afford her peculiar satisfaction; she read it through twice before replying to the landlady.

'Well, Mrs Pine, I think you'll be sorry for what you said. This is from a manager, asking me to be there with evening dress at ten o'clock next Saturday morning.'

But the landlady was too quick for her. She pounced, secured the letter.

'Oh, is it! Is it indeed!' she cried.

'Give me back that letter. Give it back to me at once, you bad, wicked woman,' cried Miss Moss, who could not get out of bed because her nightdress was slit down the back. 'Give me back my private letter.' The landlady began slowly backing out of the room, holding the letter to her buttoned bodice.

'So it's come to this, has it?' said she. 'Well, Miss Moss, if I don't get my rent at eight o'clock tonight, we'll see who's a bad, wicked woman – that's all.' Here she nodded, mysteriously. 'And I'll keep this letter.' Here her voice rose. 'It will be a pretty little bit of evidence!' And here it fell, sepulchral, '*My lady*.'

The door banged and Miss Moss was alone. She flung off the bedclothes, and sitting on the side of the bed, furious and shivering, she stared at her fat white legs with their great knots of greeny-blue veins.

'Cockroach! That's what she is. She's a cockroach!' said Miss Moss. 'I could have her up for snatching my letter – I'm sure I could.' Still keeping on her nightdress she began to drag on her clothes.

'Oh, if I could only pay that woman, I'd give her a piece of my mind that she wouldn't forget. I'd tell her off proper.' She went over to the chest of drawers for a safety-pin, and seeing herself in the glass she gave a vague smile and shook her head. 'Well, old girl,' she murmured, 'you're up against it this time, and no mistake.' But the person in the glass made an ugly face at her.

'You silly thing,' scolded Miss Moss. 'Now what's the good of crying: you'll only make your nose red. No, you get dressed and go out and try your luck – that's what you've got to do.'

She unhooked her vanity bag from the bedpost, rooted in it, shook it, turned it inside out.

'I'll have a nice cup of tea at an ABC to settle me before I go anywhere,' she decided. 'I've got one and thrippence – yes, just one and three.'

Ten minutes later, a stout lady in blue serge, with a bunch of artificial 'parmas' at her bosom, a black hat covered with purple pansies, white gloves, boots with white uppers, and a vanity bag containing one and three, sang in a low contralto voice:

> Sweet–heart, remember when days are forlorn
> It al–ways is dar–kest before the dawn.

But the person in the glass made a face at her, and Miss Moss went out. There were grey crabs all the way down the street slopping water over grey stone steps. With his strange, hawking cry and the jangle of the cans the milk-boy went his rounds. Outside Brittweiler's Swiss House he made a splash, and an old brown cat without a tail appeared from nowhere, and began greedily and silently drinking up the spill. It gave Miss Moss a queer feeling to watch – a sinking – as you might say.

But when she came to the ABC she found the door propped open; a man went in and out carrying trays of rolls, and there was nobody inside except a waitress doing her hair and the cashier unlocking the cash-boxes. She stood in the middle of the floor but neither of them saw her.

'My boy came home last night,' sang the waitress.

'Oh, I say – how topping for you!' gurgled the cashier.

'Yes, wasn't it,' sang the waitress. 'He brought me a sweet little brooch. Look, it's got "Dieppe" written on it.'

The cashier ran across to look and put her arm round the waitress' neck.

'Oh, I say – how topping for you.'

'Yes, isn't it,' said the waitress. 'O–oh, he is brahn. "Hullo," I said, "hullo, old mahogany." '

'Oh, I say,' gurgled the cashier, running back into her cage and nearly bumping into Miss Moss on the way. 'You are a *treat*!' Then the man with the rolls came in again, swerving past her.

'Can I have a cup of tea, miss?' she asked

But the waitress went on doing her hair. 'Oh,' she sang, 'we're not *open* yet.' She turned round and waved her comb at the cashier.

'*Are* we, dear?'

'Oh, no,' said the cashier. Miss Moss went out.

'I'll go to Charing Cross. Yes, that's what I'll do,' she decided. 'But I won't have a cup of tea. No, I'll have a coffee. There's more of a tonic in coffee . . . Cheeky, those girls are! Her boy came home last night; he brought her a brooch with "Dieppe" written on it.' She began to cross the road . . .

'Look out, Fattie; don't go to sleep!' yelled a taxi driver. She pretended not to hear.

'No, I won't go to Charing Cross,' she decided. 'I'll go straight to Kig and Kadgit. They're open at nine. If I get there early Mr Kadgit may have something by the morning's post . . . I'm very glad you turned up so early, Miss Moss. I've just heard from a manager who wants a lady to play . . . I think you'll just suit him. I'll give you a card to go and see him. It's three pounds a week and all found. If I were you I'd hop round as fast as I could. Lucky you turned up so early . . . '

But there was nobody at Kig and Kadgit's except the charwoman wiping over the lino in the passage.

'Nobody here yet, miss,' said the char.

'Oh, isn't Mr Kadgit here?' said Miss Moss, trying to dodge the pail and brush. 'Well, I'll just wait a moment, if I may.'

'You can't wait in the waiting-room, miss. I 'aven't done it yet. Mr Kadgit's never 'ere before 'leven-thirty Saturdays. Sometimes 'e don't come at all.' And the char began crawling towards her.

'Dear me – how silly of me,' said Miss Moss. 'I forgot it was Saturday.'

'Mind your feet, *please*, miss,' said the char. And Miss Moss was outside again.

That was one thing about Beit and Bithems; it was lively. You walked into the waiting-room, into a great buzz of conversation, and there was everybody; you knew almost everybody. The early ones sat on chairs and the later ones sat on the early ones' laps, while the gentlemen leaned negligently against the walls or preened themselves in front of the admiring ladies.

'Hello,' said Miss Moss, very gay. 'Here we are again!'

And young Mr Clayton, playing the banjo on his walking-stick, sang: 'Waiting for the Robert E. Lee.'

'Mr Bithem here yet?' asked Miss Moss, taking out an old dead powder-puff and powdering her nose mauve.

'Oh, yes, dear,' cried the chorus. 'He's been here for ages. We've all been waiting here for more than an hour.'

'Dear me!' said Miss Moss. 'Anything doing, do you think?'

'Oh, a few jobs going for South Africa,' said young Mr Clayton. 'Hundred and fifty a week for two years, you know.'

'Oh!' cried the chorus. 'You *are* weird, Mr Clayton. Isn't he a *cure*? Isn't he a *scream*, dear? Oh, Mr Clayton, you do make me laugh. Isn't he a *comic*?'

A dark, mournful girl touched Miss Moss on the arm.

'I just missed a lovely job yesterday,' she said. 'Six weeks in the provinces and then the West End. The manager said I would have got it for certain if only I'd been robust enough. He said if my figure had been fuller, the part was made for me.' She stared at Miss Moss, and the dirty dark red rose under the brim of her hat looked, somehow, as though it shared the blow with her, and was crushed, too.

'Oh, dear, that was hard lines,' said Miss Moss trying to appear indifferent. 'What was it – if I may ask?'

But the dark, mournful girl saw through her and a gleam of spite came into her heavy eyes.

'Oh, no good to you, my dear,' said she. 'He wanted someone young, you know – a dark Spanish type – my style but more figure, that was all.'

The inner door opened and Mr Bithem appeared in his shirt-sleeves. He kept one hand on the door ready to whisk back again, and held up the other.

'Look here, ladies – ' and then he paused, grinned his famous grin before he said – '*and bhoys*'. The waiting-room laughed so loudly at this that he had to hold both hands up. 'It's no good waiting this morning. Come back Monday; I'm expecting several calls on Monday.'

Miss Moss made a desperate rush forward. 'Mr Bithem, I wonder if you've heard from . . . '

'Now let me see,' said Mr Bithem slowly, staring; he had only seen

Miss Moss four times a week for the past – how many weeks? 'Now, who are you?'

'Miss Ada Moss.'

'Oh, yes, yes; of course, my dear. Not yet, my dear. Now I had a call for twenty-eight ladies today, but they had to be young and able to hop it a bit – see? And I had another call for sixteen – but they had to know something about sand-dancing. Look here, my dear, I'm up to the eyebrows this morning. Come back on Monday week; it's no good coming before that.' He gave her a whole grin to herself and patted her fat back. 'Hearts of oak, dear lady,' said Mr Bithem, 'hearts of oak!'

At the North-East Film Company the crowd was all the way up the stairs. Miss Moss found herself next to a fair little baby thing about thirty in a white lace hat with cherries round it.

'What a crowd!' said she. 'Anything special on?'

'*Didn't* you know, dear?' said the baby, opening her immense pale eyes. 'There was a call at nine-thirty for *attractive* girls. We've all been waiting for *hours*. Have you played for this company before?' Miss Moss put her head on one side. 'No, I don't think I have.'

'They're a lovely company to play for,' said the baby. 'A friend of mine has a friend who gets thirty pounds a day . . . Have you *arcted* much for the *fil*-lums?'

'Well, I'm not an actress by profession,' confessed Miss Moss. 'I'm a contralto singer. But things have been so bad lately that I've been doing a little.'

'It's *like* that, isn't it, dear?' said the baby.

'I had a splendid education at the College of Music,' said Miss Moss, 'and I got my silver medal for singing. I've often sung at West End concerts. But I thought, for a change, I'd try my luck . . . '

'Yes, it's *like* that, isn't it, dear?' said the baby.

At that moment a beautiful typist appeared at the top of the stairs. 'Are you all waiting for the North-East call?'

'Yes!' cried the chorus.

'Well, it's off. I've just had a phone through.'

'But look here! What about our expenses?' shouted a voice.

The typist looked down at them, and she couldn't help laughing.

'Oh, you weren't to have been *paid*. The North-East never *pay* their crowds.'

There was only a little round window at the Bitter Orange Company. No waiting-room – nobody at all except a girl, who came to the window when Miss Moss knocked, and said: 'Well?'

'Can I see the producer, please?' said Miss Moss pleasantly. The girl leaned on the window-bar, half shut her eyes and seemed to go to sleep for a moment. Miss Moss smiled at her. The girl not only frowned; she seemed to smell something vaguely unpleasant; she sniffed. Suddenly she moved away, came back with a paper and thrust it at Miss Moss.

'Fill up the form!' said she. And banged the window down.

'Can you aviate – high-dive – drive a car – buckjump – shoot?' read Miss Moss. She walked along the street asking herself those questions. There was a high, cold wind blowing; it tugged at her, slapped her face, jeered; it knew she could not answer them. In the Square Gardens she found a little wire basket to drop the form into. And then she sat down on one of the benches to powder her nose. But the person in the pocket mirror made a hideous face at her, and that was too much for Miss Moss; she had a good cry. It cheered her wonderfully.

'Well, that's over,' she sighed. 'It's one comfort to be off my feet. And my nose will soon get cool in the air . . . It's very nice in here. Look at the sparrows. Cheep. Cheep. How close they come. I expect somebody feeds them. No, I've nothing for you, you cheeky little things . . . ' She looked away from them. What was the big building opposite – the Café de Madrid? My goodness, what a smack that little child came down! Poor little mite! Never mind – up again . . . By eight o'clock tonight . . . Café de Madrid. 'I could just go in and sit there and have a coffee, that's all,' thought Miss Moss. 'It's such a place for artists too. I might just have a stroke of luck . . . A dark handsome gentleman in a fur coat comes in with a friend, and sits at my table, perhaps. "No, old chap, I've searched London for a contralto and I can't find a soul. You see, the music is difficult; have a look at it." ' And Miss Moss heard herself saying: ' "Excuse me, I happen to be a contralto, and I have sung that part many times . . . " Extraordinary! "Come back to my studio and I'll try your voice now." . . . Ten pounds a week . . . Why should I feel nervous? It's not nervousness. Why shouldn't I go to the Café de Madrid? I'm a respectable woman – I'm a contralto singer. And I'm only trembling because I've had nothing to eat today . . . "A nice little piece of evidence, *my lady*." . . . Very well, Mrs Pine. Café de Madrid. They have concerts there in the evenings . . . "Why don't they begin?" The contralto has not arrived . . . "Excuse me, I happen to be a contralto; I have sung that music many times." '

It was almost dark in the café. Men, palms, red plush seats, white

marble tables, waiters in aprons, Miss Moss walked through them all.
Hardly had she sat down when a very stout gentleman wearing a very
small hat that floated on the top of his head like a little yacht flopped
into the chair opposite hers.

'Good evening!' said he.

Miss Moss said, in her cheerful way: 'Good evening!'

'Fine evening,' said the stout gentleman.

'Yes, very fine. Quite a treat, isn't it?' said she.

He crooked a sausage finger at the waiter – 'Bring me a large
whisky' – and turned to Miss Moss. 'What's yours?'

'Well, I think I'll take a brandy if it's all the same.'

Five minutes later the stout gentleman leaned across the table and
blew a puff of cigar smoke full in her face.

'That's a tempting bit o' ribbon!' said he.

Miss Moss blushed until a pulse at the top of her head that she
never had felt before pounded away.

'I always was one for pink,' said she.

The stout gentleman considered her, drumming with his fingers
on the table.

'I like 'em firm and well covered,' said he.

Miss Moss, to her surprise, gave a loud snigger.

Five minutes later the stout gentleman heaved himself up. 'Well,
am I goin' your way, or are you comin' mine?' he asked.

'I'll come with you, if it's all the same,' said Miss Moss. And she
sailed after the little yacht out of the café.

The Man Without a Temperament

HE STOOD at the hall door turning the ring, turning the heavy signet ring upon his little finger while his glance travelled coolly, deliberately, over the round tables and basket chairs scattered about the glassed-in veranda. He pursed his lips – he might have been going to whistle – but he did not whistle – only turned the ring – turned the ring on his pink, freshly washed hands.

Over in the corner sat The Two Topknots, drinking a decoction they always drank at this hour – something whitish, greyish, in glasses, with little husks floating on the top – and rooting in a tin full of paper shavings for pieces of speckled biscuit, which they broke, dropped into the glasses and fished for with spoons. Their two coils of knitting, like two snakes, slumbered beside the tray.

The American Woman sat where she always sat against the glass wall, in the shadow of a great creeping thing with wide open purple eyes that pressed – that flattened itself against the glass, hungrily watching her. And she knoo it was there – she knoo it was looking at her just that way. She played up to it; she gave herself little airs. Sometimes she even pointed at it, crying: 'Isn't that the most terrible thing you've ever seen! Isn't that ghoulish!' It was on the other side of the veranda, after all . . . and besides it couldn't touch her, could it, Klaymongso? She was an American Woman, wasn't she, Klaymongso, and she'd just go right away to her Consul. Klaymongso, curled in her lap, with her torn antique brocade bag, a grubby handkerchief, and a pile of letters from home on top of him, sneezed for reply.

The other tables were empty. A glance passed between the American and the Topknots. She gave a foreign little shrug; they waved an understanding biscuit. But he saw nothing. Now he was still, now from his eyes you saw he listened. 'Hoo-e–zip–zoo–oo!' sounded the lift. The iron cage clanged open. Light dragging steps sounded across the hall, coming towards him. A hand, like a leaf, fell on his shoulder. A soft voice said: 'Let's go and sit over there – where we can see the drive. The trees are so lovely.' And he moved forward with the hand still on his shoulder, and the light, dragging steps beside his. He pulled out a chair and she sank into it, slowly, leaning her head against the back, her arms falling along the sides.

'Won't you bring the other up closer? It's such miles away.' But he did not move.

'Where's your shawl?' he asked.

'Oh!' She gave a little groan of dismay. 'How silly I am, I've left it upstairs on the bed. Never mind. Please don't go for it. I shan't want it, I know I shan't.'

'You'd better have it.' And he turned and swiftly crossed the veranda into the dim hall with its scarlet plush-and-gilt furniture – conjuror's furniture – its Notice of Services at the English Church, its green baize board with the unclaimed letters climbing the black lattice, huge 'Presentation' clock that struck the hours and the half-hours, bundles of sticks and umbrellas and sunshades in the clasp of a brown wooden bear, past the two crippled palms, two ancient beggars at the foot of the staircase, up the marble stairs three at a time, past the life-size group on the landing of two stout peasant children with their marble pinnies full of marble grapes, and along the corridor, with its piled-up wreckage of old tin boxes, leather trunks, canvas holdalls, to their room.

The servant girl was in their room, singing loudly while she emptied soapy water into a pail. The windows were open wide, the shutters put back, and the light glared in. She had thrown the carpets and the big white pillows over the balcony rails; the nets were looped up from the beds; on the writing-table there stood a pan of fluff and match-ends. When she saw him her small impudent eyes snapped and her singing changed to humming. But he gave no sign. His eyes searched the glaring room. Where the devil was the shawl!

'*Vous désirez, monsieur?*' mocked the servant girl.

No answer. He had seen it. He strode across the room, grabbed the grey cobweb and went out, banging the door. The servant girl's voice at its loudest and shrillest followed him along the corridor.

'Oh, there you are. What happened? What kept you? The tea's here, you see. I've just sent Antonio off for the hot water. Isn't it extraordinary? I must have told him about it sixty times at least, and still he doesn't bring it. Thank you. That's very nice. One does just feel the air when one bends forward.'

'Thanks.' He took his tea and sat down in the other chair. 'No, nothing to eat.'

'Oh do! Just one, you had so little at lunch and it's hours before dinner.'

Her shawl dropped off as she bent forward to hand him the biscuits. He took one and put it in his saucer.

'Oh, those trees along the drive,' she cried, 'I could look at them for ever. They are like the most exquisite huge ferns. And you see that one with the grey-silver bark and the clusters of cream-coloured flowers, I pulled down a head of them yesterday to smell and the scent' – she shut her eyes at the memory and her voice thinned away, faint, airy – 'was like freshly ground nutmegs.' A little pause. She turned to him and smiled. 'You do know what nutmegs smell like – do you, Robert?'

And he smiled back at her. 'Now how am I going to prove to you that I do?'

Back came Antonio with not only the hot water – with letters on a salver and three rolls of paper.

'Oh, the post! Oh, how lovely! Oh, Robert, they mustn't be all for you! Have they just come, Antonio?' Her thin hands flew up and hovered over the letters that Antonio offered her, bending forward.

'Just this moment, signora,' grinned Antonio. 'I took-a them from the postman myself. I made-a the postman give them for me.'

'Noble Antonio!' laughed she. 'There – those are mine, Robert; the rest are yours.'

Antonio wheeled sharply, stiffened, the grin went out of his face. His striped linen jacket and his flat gleaming fringe made him look like a wooden doll.

Mr Salesby put the letters into his pocket; the papers lay on the table. He turned the ring, turned the signet ring on his little finger and stared in front of him, blinking, vacant.

But she – with her teacup in one hand, the sheets of thin paper in the other, her head tilted back, her lips open, a brush of bright colour on her cheek-bones, sipped, sipped, drank . . . drank . . .

'From Lottie,' came her soft murmur. 'Poor dear . . . such trouble . . . left foot. She thought . . . neuritis . . . Doctor Blyth . . . flat foot . . . massage. So many robins this year . . . maid most satisfactory . . . Indian colonel . . . every grain of rice separate . . . very heavy fall of snow.' And her wide lighted eyes looked up from the letter. 'Snow, Robert! Think of it!' And she touched the little dark violets pinned on her thin bosom and went back to the letter.

. . . Snow. Snow in London. Millie with the early morning cup of tea. 'There's been a terrible fall of snow in the night, sir.' 'Oh, has there, Millie?' The curtains ring apart, letting in the pale, reluctant light. He raises himself in the bed; he catches a glimpse of the solid houses opposite framed in white, of their window boxes full of great sprays of white coral . . . In the bathroom – overlooking the back garden. Snow – heavy snow over everything. The lawn is covered with a wavy pattern of cat's paws; there is a thick, thick icing on the garden table; the withered pods of the laburnum tree are white tassels; only here and there in the ivy is a dark leaf showing . . . Warming his back at the dining-room fire, the paper drying over a chair. Millie with the bacon. 'Oh, if you please, sir, there's two little boys come as will do the steps and front for a shilling, shall I let them?' . . . And then flying lightly, lightly down the stairs – Jinnie. 'Oh, Robert, isn't it wonderful! Oh, what a pity it has to melt. Where's the pussy-wee?' 'I'll get him from Millie' . . . 'Millie, you might just hand me up the kitten if you've got him down there.' 'Very good, sir.' He feels the little beating heart under his hand. 'Come on, old chap, your missus wants you.' 'Oh, Robert, do show him the snow – his first snow. Shall I open the window and give him a little piece on his paw to hold? . . .'

'Well, that's very satisfactory on the whole – very. Poor Lottie! Darling Anne! How I only wish I could send them something of this,' she cried, waving her letters at the brilliant, dazzling garden. 'More tea, Robert? Robert dear, more tea?'

'No, thanks, no. It was very good,' he drawled.

'Well mine wasn't. Mine was just like chopped hay. Oh, here comes the Honeymoon Couple.'

Half striding, half running, carrying a basket between them and rods and lines, they came up the drive, up the shallow steps.

'My! have you been out fishing?' cried the American Woman.

They were out of breath, they panted: 'Yes, yes, we have been out in a little boat all day. We have caught seven. Four are good to eat. But three we shall give away. To the children.'

Mrs Salesby turned her chair to look; the Topknots laid the snakes down. They were a very dark young couple – black hair, olive skin, brilliant eyes and teeth. He was dressed 'English fashion' in a flannel jacket, white trousers and shoes. Round his neck he wore a silk scarf; his head, with his hair brushed back, was bare. And he kept mopping his forehead, rubbing his hands with a brilliant handkerchief. Her white skirt had a patch of wet; her neck and throat were stained a deep pink. When she lifted her arms big half-hoops of perspiration showed under her armpits; her hair clung in wet curls to her cheeks. She looked as though her young husband had been dipping her in the sea, and fishing her out again to dry in the sun and then – in with her again – all day.

'Would Klaymongso like a fish?' they cried. Their laughing voices charged with excitement beat against the glassed-in veranda like birds, and a strange saltish smell came from the basket.

'You will sleep well tonight,' said a Topknot, picking her ear with a knitting needle while the other Topknot smiled and nodded.

The Honeymoon Couple looked at each other. A great wave seemed to go over them. They gasped, gulped, staggered a little and then came up laughing – laughing.

'We cannot go upstairs, we are too tired. We must have tea just as we are. Here – coffee. No – tea. No – coffee. Tea – coffee, Antonio!' Mrs Salesby turned.

'Robert! Robert!' Where was he? He wasn't there. Oh, there he was at the other end of the veranda, with his back turned, smoking a cigarette. 'Robert, shall we go for our little turn?'

'Right.' He stumped the cigarette into an ashtray and sauntered over, his eyes on the ground. 'Will you be warm enough?'

'Oh, quite.'

'Sure?'

'Well,' she put her hand on his arm, 'perhaps' – and gave his arm the faintest pressure – 'it's not upstairs, it's only in the hall – perhaps you'd get me my cape. Hanging up.'

He came back with it and she bent her small head while he dropped it on her shoulders. Then, very stiff, he offered her his arm. She bowed sweetly to the people on the veranda while he just covered a yawn, and they went down the steps together.

'*Vous avez voo ça!*' said the American Woman.

'He is not a man,' said the Two Topknots, 'he is an ox. I say to my sister in the morning and at night when we are in bed, I tell her – *No* man is he, but an ox!'

Wheeling, tumbling, swooping, the laughter of the Honeymoon Couple dashed against the glass of the veranda.

The sun was still high. Every leaf, every flower in the garden lay open, motionless, as if exhausted, and a sweet, rich, rank smell filled the quivering air. Out of the thick, fleshy leaves of a cactus there rose an aloe stem loaded with pale flowers that looked as though they had been cut out of butter; light flashed upon the lifted spears of the palms; over a bed of scarlet waxen flowers some big black insects 'zoom-zoomed'; a great, gaudy creeper, orange splashed with jet, sprawled against a wall.

'I don't need my cape after all,' said she. 'It's really too warm.' So he took it off and carried it over his arm. 'Let us go down this path here. I feel so well today – marvellously better. Good heavens – look at those children! And to think it's November!'

In a corner of the garden there were two brimming tubs of water. Three little girls, having thoughtfully taken off their drawers and hung them on a bush, their skirts clasped to their waists, were standing in the tubs and tramping up and down. They screamed, their hair fell over their faces, they splashed one another. But suddenly, the smallest, who had a tub to herself, glanced up and saw who was looking. For a moment she seemed overcome with terror, then clumsily she struggled and strained out of her tub, and still holding her clothes above her waist. 'The Englishman! The Englishman!' she shrieked and fled away to hide. Shrieking and screaming, the other two followed her. In a moment they were gone; in a moment there was nothing but the two brimming tubs and their little drawers on the bush.

'How – very – extraordinary!' said she. 'What made them so frightened? Surely they were much too young to . . . ' She looked up at him. She thought he looked pale – but wonderfully handsome with that great tropical tree behind him with its long, spiked thorns.

For a moment he did not answer. Then he met her glance, and smiling his slow smile, '*Très* rum!' said he.

Très rum! Oh, she felt quite faint. Oh, why should she love him so much just because he said a thing like that. *Très* rum! That was Robert all over. Nobody else but Robert could ever say such a thing. To be so wonderful, so brilliant, so learned, and then to say in that queer, boyish voice . . . She could have wept.

'You know you're very absurd, sometimes,' said she.

'I am,' he answered. And they walked on.

But she was tired. She had had enough. She did not want to walk any more.

'Leave me here and go for a little constitutional, won't you? I'll be in one of these long chairs. What a good thing you've got my cape; you won't have to go upstairs for a rug. Thank you, Robert, I shall look at that delicious heliotrope . . . You won't be gone long?'

'No – no. You don't mind being left?'

'Silly! I want you to go. I can't expect you to drag after your invalid wife every minute . . . How long will you be?'

He took out his watch. 'It's just after half-past four. I'll be back at a quarter-past five.'

'Back at a quarter-past five,' she repeated, and she lay still in the long chair and folded her hands.

He turned away. Suddenly he was back again. 'Look here, would you like my watch?' And he dangled it before her.

'Oh!' She caught her breath. 'Very, very much.' And she clasped the watch, the warm watch, the darling watch in her fingers. 'Now go quickly.'

The gates of the Pension Villa Excelsior were open wide, jammed open against some bold geraniums. Stooping a little, staring straight ahead, walking swiftly, he passed through them and began climbing the hill that wound behind the town like a great rope looping the villas together. The dust lay thick. A carriage came bowling along driving towards the Excelsior. In it sat the General and the Countess; they had been for his daily airing. Mr Salesby stepped to one side but the dust beat up, thick, white, stifling like wool. The Countess just had time to nudge the General.

'There he goes,' she said spitefully.

But the General gave a loud caw and refused to look.

'It is the Englishman,' said the driver, turning round and smiling. And the Countess threw up her hands and nodded so amiably that he spat with satisfaction and gave the stumbling horse a cut.

On – on – past the finest villas in the town, magnificent palaces, palaces worth coming any distance to see, past the public gardens with the carved grottoes and statues and stone animals drinking at the fountain, into a poorer quarter. Here the road ran narrow and foul between high lean houses, the ground floors of which were scooped and hollowed into stables and carpenters' shops. At a fountain ahead of him two old hags were beating linen. As he passed them they squatted back on their haunches, stared and then their 'A-hak-kak-kak!' with the slap, slap, of the stone on the linen sounded after him.

He reached the top of the hill; he turned a corner and the town was hidden. Down he looked into a deep valley with a dried-up river bed at the bottom. This side and that was covered with small dilapidated houses that had broken stone verandas where the fruit lay drying, tomato lanes in the garden, and from the gates to the doors a trellis of vines. The late sunlight, deep, golden, lay in the cup of the valley; there was a smell of charcoal in the air. In the gardens the men were cutting grapes. He watched a man standing in the greenish shade, raising up, holding a black cluster in one hand, taking the knife from his belt, cutting, laying the bunch in a flat boat-shaped basket. The man worked leisurely, silently, taking hundreds of years over the job. On the hedges on the other side of the road there were grapes small as berries, growing wild, growing among the stones. He leaned against a wall, filled his pipe, put a match to it . . .

Leaned across a gate, turned up the collar of his mackintosh. It was going to rain. It didn't matter, he was prepared for it. You didn't expect anything else in November. He looked over the bare field. From the corner by the gate there came the smell of swedes, a great stack of them, wet, rank coloured. Two men passed walking towards the straggling village. 'Good day!' 'Good day!' By Jove! he had to hurry if he was going to catch that train home. Over the gate, across a field, over the stile, into the lane, swinging along in the drifting rain and dusk . . . Just home in time for a bath and a change before supper . . . In the drawing-room; Jinnie is sitting pretty nearly in the fire. 'Oh, Robert, I didn't hear you come in. Did you have a good time? How nice you smell! A present?' 'Some bits of blackberry I picked for you. Pretty colour.' 'Oh, lovely, Robert! Dennis and Beaty are coming to supper.' Supper – cold beef, potatoes in their jackets, claret, household bread. They are gay – everybody's laughing. 'Oh, we all know Robert,' says Dennis, breathing on his eyeglasses and polishing them. 'By the way, Dennis, I picked up a very jolly little edition of . . . '

A clock struck. He wheeled sharply. What time was it. Five? A quarter past? Back, back the way he came. As he passed through the gates he saw her on the look-out. She got up, waved and slowly she came to meet him, dragging the heavy cape. In her hand she carried a spray of heliotrope.

'You're late,' she cried gaily. 'You're three minutes late. Here's your watch, it's been very good while you were away. Did you have a nice time? Was it lovely? Tell me. Where did you go?'

'I say – put this *on*,' he said, taking the cape from her.

'Yes, I will. Yes, it's getting chilly. Shall we go up to our room?'

When they reached the lift she was coughing. He frowned.

'It's nothing. I haven't been out too late. Don't be cross.' She sat down on one of the red-plush chairs while he rang and rang, and then, getting no answer, kept his finger on the bell.

'Oh, Robert, do you think you ought to?'

'Ought to what?'

The door of the *salon* opened. 'What is that? Who is making that noise?' sounded from within. Klaymongso began to yelp. 'Caw! Caw! Caw!' came from the General. A Topknot darted out with one hand to her ear, opened the staff door, 'Mr Queet! Mr Queet!' she bawled. That brought the manager up at a run.

'Is that you ringing the bell, Mr Salesby? Do you want the lift? Very good, sir. I'll take you up myself. Antonio wouldn't have been a minute, he was just taking off his apron – ' And having ushered them in, the oily manager went to the door of the *salon*. 'Very sorry you should have been troubled, ladies and gentlemen.' Salesby stood in the cage, sucking in his cheeks, staring at the ceiling and turning the ring, turning the signet ring on his little finger . . .

Arrived in their room he went swiftly over to the washstand, shook the bottle, poured her out a dose and brought it across.

'Sit down. Drink it. And don't talk.' And he stood over her while she obeyed. Then he took the glass, rinsed it and put it back in its case. 'Would you like a cushion?'

'No, I'm quite all right. Come over here. Sit down by me just a minute, will you, Robert? Ah, that's very nice.' She turned and thrust the piece of heliotrope in the lapel of his coat. 'That,' she said, 'is most becoming,' and then she leaned her head against his shoulder, and he put his arm round her.

'Robert – ' her voice like a sigh – like a breath.

'Yes – '

They sat there for a long while. The sky flamed, paled; the two white beds were like two ships . . . At last he heard the servant girl running along the corridor with the hot-water cans, and gently he released her and turned on the light.

'Oh, what time is it? Oh, what a heavenly evening. Oh, Robert, I was thinking while you were away this afternoon . . . '

They were the last couple to enter the dining-room. The Countess was there with her lorgnette and her fan, the General was there with his special chair and the air cushion and the small rug over his knees. The American Woman was there showing Klaymongso a copy of the *Saturday Evening Post* . . . 'We're having a feast of reason and a flow of soul.' The Two Topknots were there feeling over the peaches and the pears in their dish of fruit, and putting aside all they considered unripe or overripe to show to the manager, and the Honeymoon Couple leaned across the table, whispering, trying not to burst out laughing.

Mr Queet, in everyday clothes and white canvas shoes, served the soup, and Antonio, in full evening dress, handed it round.

'No,' said the American Woman, 'take it away, Antonio. We can't eat soup. We can't eat anything mushy, can we, Klaymongso?'

'Take them back and fill them to the rim!' said the Topknots, and they turned and watched while Antonio delivered the message.

'What is it? Rice? Is it cooked?' The Countess peered through her lorgnette. 'Mr Queet, the General can have some of this soup if it is cooked.'

'Very good, Countess.'

The Honeymoon Couple had their fish instead.

'Give me that one. That's the one I caught. No, it's not. Yes, it is. No, it's not. Well, it's looking at me with its eye so it must be. Tee! Hee! Hee!' Their feet were locked together under the table.

'Robert, you're not eating again. Is anything the matter?'

'No. Off food, that's all.'

'Oh, what a bother. There are eggs and spinach coming. You don't like spinach, do you. I must tell them in future . . . '

An egg and mashed potatoes for the General.

'Mr Queet! Mr Queet!'

'Yes, Countess.'

'The General's egg's too hard again.'

'Caw! Caw! Caw!'

'Very sorry, Countess. Shall I have you another cooked, General?'

. . . They are the first to leave the dining-room. She rises, gathering her shawl and he stands aside, waiting for her to pass, turning the ring, turning the signet ring on his little finger. In the hall Mr Queet hovers. 'I thought you might not want to wait for the lift. Antonio's just serving the finger-bowls. And I'm sorry the bell won't ring, it's out of order. I can't think what's happened.'

'Oh, I do hope . . . ' from her.

'Get in,' says he.

Mr Queet steps after them and slams the door . . .

' . . . Robert, do you mind if I go to bed very soon? Won't you go down to the *salon* or out into the garden? Or perhaps you might smoke a cigar on the balcony. It's lovely out there. And I like cigar smoke. I always did. But if you'd rather . . . '

'No, I'll sit here.'

He takes a chair and sits on the balcony. He hears her moving about in the room, lightly, lightly, moving and rustling. Then she comes over to him. 'Good-night, Robert.'

'Good-night.' He takes her hand and kisses the palm. 'Don't catch cold.'

The sky is the colour of jade. There are a great many stars; an enormous white moon hangs over the garden. Far away lightning flutters – flutters like a wing – flutters like a broken bird that tries to fly and sinks again and again struggles.

The lights from the *salon* shine across the garden path and there is the sound of a piano. And once the American Woman, opening the French window to let Klaymongso into the garden, cries: 'Have you seen this moon?' But nobody answers.

He gets very cold sitting there, staring at the balcony rail. Finally he comes inside. The moon – the room is painted white with moonlight. The light trembles in the mirrors; the two beds seem to float. She is asleep. He sees her through the nets, half sitting, banked up with pillows, her white hands crossed on the sheet. Her white cheeks, her fair hair pressed against the pillow, are silvered over. He undresses quickly, stealthily and gets into bed. Lying there, his hands clasped behind his head . . .

. . . In his study. Late summer. The virginia creeper just on the turn . . .

'Well, my dear chap, that's the whole story. That's the long and the short of it. If she can't cut away for the next two years and give a decent climate a chance she don't stand a dog's – h'm – show. Better be frank about these things.' 'Oh, certainly . . . ' 'And hang it all, old man, what's to prevent you going with her? It isn't as though you've got a regular job like us wage earners. You can do what you do wherever you are – ' 'Two years.' 'Yes, I should give it two years. You'll have no trouble about letting this house you know. As a matter of fact . . . '

. . . He is with her. 'Robert, the awful thing is – I suppose it's my illness – I simply feel I could not go alone. You see – you're everything. You're bread and wine, Robert, bread and wine. Oh, my darling – what am I saying? Of course I could, of course I won't take you away . . . '

He hears her stirring. Does she want something?

'Boogles?'

Good Lord! She is talking in her sleep. They haven't used that name for years.

'Boogles. Are you awake?'

'Yes, do you want anything?'

'Oh, I'm going to be a bother. I'm so sorry. Do you mind? There's a wretched mosquito inside my net – I can hear him singing. Would you catch him? I don't want to move because of my heart.'

'No, don't move. Stay where you are.' He switches on the light, lifts the net. 'Where is the little beggar? Have you spotted him?'

'Yes, there, over by the corner. Oh, I do feel such a fiend to have dragged you out of bed. Do you mind dreadfully?'

'No, of course not.' For a moment he hovers in his blue and white pyjamas. Then, 'Got him,' he said.

'Oh, good. Was he a juicy one?'

'Beastly.' He went over to the washstand and dipped his fingers in water. 'Are you all right now? Shall I switch off the light?'

'Yes, please. No. Boogles! Come back here a moment. Sit down by me. Give me your hand.' She turns his signet ring. 'Why weren't you asleep? Boogles, listen. Come closer. I sometimes wonder – do you mind awfully being out here with me?'

He bends down. He kisses her. He tucks her in, he smoothes the pillow.

'Rot!' he whispers.

Mr Reginald Peacock's Day

IF THERE WAS one thing that he hated more than another it was the way she had of waking him in the morning. She did it on purpose, of course. It was her way of establishing her grievance for the day, and he was not going to let her know how successful it was. But really, really, to wake a sensitive person like that was positively dangerous! It took him hours to get over it – simply hours. She came into the room buttoned up in an overall, with a handkerchief over her head – thereby proving that she had been up herself and slaving since dawn – and called in a low, warning voice: 'Reginald!'

'Eh! What! What's that? What's the matter?'

'It's time to get up; it's half-past eight.' And out she went, shutting the door quietly after her, to gloat over her triumph, he supposed.

He rolled over in the big bed, his heart still beating in quick, dull throbs, and with every throb he felt his energy escaping him, his – his inspiration for the day stifling under those thudding blows. It seemed that she took a malicious delight in making life more difficult for him than – Heaven knows – it was, by denying him his rights as an artist, by trying to drag him down to her level. What was the matter with her? What the hell did she want? Hadn't he three times as many pupils now as when they were first married, earned three times as much, paid for every stick and stone that they possessed, and now had begun to shell out for Adrian's kindergarten? . . . And had he ever reproached her for not having a penny to her name? Never a word – never a sign! The truth was that once you married a woman she became insatiable, and the truth was that nothing was more fatal for an artist than marriage, at any rate until he was well over forty . . . Why had he married her? He asked himself this question on an average about three times a day, but he never could answer it satisfactorily. She had caught him at a weak moment, when the first plunge into reality had bewildered and overwhelmed him for a time. Looking back, he saw a pathetic, youthful creature, half child, half wild untamed bird, totally incompetent to cope with bills and creditors and all the sordid details of existence. Well – she had done her best to clip his wings, if that was any satisfaction for her, and she could congratulate herself on the success of this early morning trick. One ought to wake exquisitely, reluctantly, he thought, slipping down in the warm bed. He began to imagine a series of enchanting scenes which ended with his latest, most charming pupil putting her bare, scented arms round his neck, and covering him with her long, perfumed hair. 'Awake, my love!' . . .

As was his daily habit, while the bathwater ran, Reginald Peacock tried his voice.

> When her mother tends her before the laughing mirror,
> Looping up her laces, tying up her hair,

he sang, softly at first, listening to the quality, nursing his voice until he came to the third line:

> Often she thinks, were this wild thing wedded . . .

and upon the word 'wedded' he burst into such a shout of triumph that the tooth-glass on the bathroom shelf trembled and even the bath tap seemed to gush stormy applause . . .

Well, there was nothing wrong with his voice, he thought, leaping into the bath and soaping his soft, pink body all over with a loofah shaped like a fish. He could fill Covent Garden with it! '*Wedded*,' he shouted again, seizing the towel with a magnificent operatic gesture, and went on singing while he rubbed as though he had been Lohengrin tipped out by an unwary Swan and drying himself in the greatest haste before that tiresome Elsa came along . . .

Back in his bedroom, he pulled the blind up with a jerk, and standing upon the pale square of sunlight that lay upon the carpet like a sheet of cream blotting-paper, he began to do his exercises – deep breathing, bending forward and back, squatting like a frog and shooting out his legs – for if there was one thing he had a horror of it was of getting fat, and men in his profession had a dreadful tendency that way. However, there was no sign of it at present. He was, he decided, just right, just in good proportion. In fact, he could not help a thrill of satisfaction when he saw himself in the glass, dressed in a morning coat, dark grey trousers, grey socks and a black tie with a silver thread in it. Not that he was vain – he couldn't stand vain men – no; the sight of himself gave him a thrill of purely artistic satisfaction. '*Voilà tout!*' said he, passing his hand over his sleek hair.

That little, easy French phrase blown so lightly from his lips, like a whiff of smoke, reminded him that someone had asked him again, the evening before, if he was English. People seemed to find it impossible to believe that he hadn't some southern blood. True, there was an emotional quality in his singing that had nothing of the John Bull in it . . . The door-handle rattled and turned round and round. Adrian's head popped through.

'Please, father, mother says breakfast is quite ready, please.'

'Very well,' said Reginald. Then, just as Adrian disappeared: 'Adrian!'

'Yes, father.'

'You haven't said "good morning".'

A few months ago Reginald had spent a weekend in a very aristo-cratic family, where the father received his little sons in the morning and shook hands with them. Reginald thought the practice charm-ing, and introduced it immediately, but Adrian felt dreadfully silly at having to shake hands with his own father every morning. And why did his father always sort of sing to him instead of talk? . . .

In excellent temper, Reginald walked into the dining-room and sat down before a pile of letters, a copy of *The Times*, and a little covered dish. He glanced at the letters and then at his breakfast. There were two thin slices of bacon and one egg.

'Don't you want any bacon?' he asked.

'No, I prefer a cold baked apple. I don't feel the need of bacon every morning.'

Now, did she mean that there was no need for him to have bacon every morning, either, and that she grudged having to cook it for him?

'If you don't want to cook the breakfast,' said he, 'why don't you keep a servant? You know we can afford one, and you know how I loathe to see my wife doing the work. Simply because all the women we have had in the past have been failures, and utterly upset my regime, and made it almost impossible for me to have any pupils here, you've given up trying to find a decent woman. It's not im-possible to train a servant – is it? I mean, it doesn't require genius?'

'But I prefer to do the work myself; it makes life so much more peaceful . . . Run along, Adrian darling, and get ready for school.'

'Oh no, that's not it!' Reginald pretended to smile. 'You do the work yourself, because, for some extraordinary reason, you love to humiliate me. Objectively, you may not know that, but, subjectively, it's the case.' This last remark so delighted him that he cut open an envelope as gracefully as if he had been on the stage . . .

DEAR MR PEACOCK,

I feel I cannot go to sleep until I have thanked you again for the wonderful joy your singing gave me this evening. Quite unforgettable. You make me wonder, as I have not wondered since I was a girl, if this is *all*. I mean, if this ordinary world is *all*. If there is not, perhaps, for those of us who understand, divine beauty and richness awaiting us if we only have the *courage* to see it. And to make it ours . . . The house is so quiet. I wish you were here now that I might thank you in person. You are doing a great thing. You are teaching the world to escape from life!

Yours, most sincerely,
ÆNONE FELL

P.S. – I am in every afternoon this week . . .

The letter was scrawled in violet ink on thick, handmade paper. Vanity, that bright bird, lifted its wings again, lifted them until he felt his breast would break.

'Oh well, don't let us quarrel,' said he, and actually flung out a hand to his wife.

But she was not great enough to respond.

'I must hurry and take Adrian to school,' said she. 'Your room is quite ready for you.'

Very well – very well – let there be open war between them! But he was hanged if he'd be the first to make it up again!

He walked up and down his room, and was not calm again until he heard the outer door close upon Adrian and his wife. Of course, if this went on, he would have to make some other arrangement. That was obvious. Tied and bound like this, how could he help the world to escape from life? He opened the piano and looked up his pupils for the morning. Miss Betty Brittle, the Countess Wilkowska and Miss Marian Morrow. They were charming, all three.

Punctually at half-past ten the door-bell rang. He went to the door. Miss Betty Brittle was there, dressed in white, with her music in a blue silk case.

'I'm afraid I'm early,' she said, blushing and shy, and she opened her big blue eyes very wide. 'Am I?'

'Not at all, dear lady. I am only too charmed,' said Reginald. 'Won't you come in?'

'It's such a heavenly morning,' said Miss Brittle. 'I walked across the park. The flowers were too marvellous.'

'Well, think about them while you sing your exercises,' said

Reginald, sitting down at the piano. 'It will give your voice colour and warmth.'

Oh, what an enchanting idea! What a *genius* Mr Peacock was. She parted her pretty lips, and began to sing like a pansy.

'Very good, very good, indeed,' said Reginald, playing chords that would waft a hardened criminal to heaven. 'Make the notes round. Don't be afraid. Linger over them, breathe them like a perfume.'

How pretty she looked, standing there in her white frock, her little blonde head tilted, showing her milky throat.

'Do you ever practise before a glass?' asked Reginald. 'You ought to, you know; it makes the lips more flexible. Come over here.'

They went over to the mirror and stood side by side.

'Now sing – moo–e–koo–e–oo–e–a'!

But she broke down, and blushed more brightly than ever.

'Oh,' she cried, 'I can't. It makes me feel so silly. It makes me want to laugh. I do look so absurd!'

'No, you don't. Don't be afraid,' said Reginald, but laughed, too, very kindly. 'Now, try again!'

The lesson simply flew, and Betty Brittle quite got over her shyness.

'When can I come again?' she asked, tying the music up again in the blue silk case. 'I want to take as many lessons as I can just now. Oh, Mr Peacock, I *do* enjoy them so much. May I come the day after tomorrow?'

'Dear lady, I shall be only too charmed,' said Reginald, bowing her out.

Glorious girl! And when they had stood in front of the mirror, her white sleeve had just touched his black one. He could feel – yes, he could actually feel a warm glowing spot, and he stroked it. She loved her lessons. His wife came in.

'Reginald, can you let me have some money? I must pay the dairy. And will you be in for dinner tonight?'

'Yes, you know I'm singing at Lord Timbuck's at half-past nine. Can you make me some clear soup, with an egg in it?'

'Yes. And the money, Reginald. It's eight and sixpence.'

'Surely that's very heavy – isn't it?'

'No, it's just what it ought to be. And Adrian must have milk.'

There she was – off again. Now she was standing up for Adrian against him.

'I have not the slightest desire to deny my child a proper amount of milk,' said he. 'Here is ten shillings.'

The door-bell rang. He went to the door.

'Oh,' said the Countess Wilkowska, 'the stairs. I have not a breath.' And she put her hand over her heart as she followed him into the music-room. She was all in black, with a little black hat with a floating veil – violets in her bosom.

'Do not make me sing exercises, today,' she cried, throwing out her hands in her delightful foreign way. 'No, today, I want only to sing songs . . . And may I take off my violets? They fade so soon.'

'They fade so soon – they fade so soon,' played Reginald on the piano.

'May I put them here?' asked the countess, dropping them in a little vase that stood in front of one of Reginald's photographs.

'Dear lady, I should be only too charmed!'

She began to sing, and all was well until she came to the phrase: 'You love me. Yes, I *know* you love me!' Down dropped his hands from the keyboard, he wheeled round, facing her.

'No, no; that's not good enough. You can do better than that,' cried Reginald ardently. 'You must sing as if you were in love. Listen; let me try and show you.' And he sang.

'Oh, yes, yes. I see what you mean,' stammered the little countess. 'May I try it again?'

'Certainly. Do not be afraid. Let yourself go. Confess yourself. Make proud surrender!' he called above the music. And she sang.

'Yes; better that time. But I still feel you are capable of more. Try it with me. There must be a kind of exultant defiance as well – don't you feel?' And they sang together.

Ah! now she was sure she understood. 'May I try once again?'

'You love me. Yes, I *know* you love me.'

The lesson was over before that phrase was quite perfect. The little foreign hands trembled as they put the music together.

'And you are forgetting your violets,' said Reginald softly.

'Yes, I think I will forget them,' said the countess, biting her underlip. What fascinating ways these foreign women have!

'And you will come to my house on Sunday and make music?' she asked.

'Dear lady, I shall be only too charmed!' said Reginald.

> Weep ye no more, sad fountains
> Why need ye flow so fast?

sang Miss Marian Morrow, but her eyes filled with tears and her chin trembled.

'Don't sing just now,' said Reginald. 'Let me play it for you.' He played so softly. 'Is there anything the matter?' asked Reginald. 'You're not quite happy this morning.'

No, she wasn't; she was awfully miserable.

'You don't care to tell me what it is?'

It really was nothing particular. She had those moods sometimes when life seemed almost unbearable.

'Ah, I know,' he said; 'if I could only help!'

'But you do; you do! Oh, if it were not for my lessons I don't feel I could go on.'

'Sit down in the armchair and smell the violets and let me sing to you. It will do you just as much good as a lesson.'

Why weren't all men like Mr Peacock?

'I wrote a poem after the concert last night – just about what I felt. Of course, it wasn't *personal*. May I send it to you?'

'Dear lady, I should be only too charmed!'

By the end of the afternoon he was quite tired and lay down on a sofa to rest his voice before dressing. The door of his room was open. He could hear Adrian and his wife talking in the dining-room.

'Do you know what that teapot reminds me of, Mummy? It reminds me of a little sitting-down kitten.'

'Does it, Mr Absurdity?'

Reginald dozed. The telephone bell woke him.

'Ænone Fell is speaking. Mr Peacock, I have just heard that you are singing at Lord Timbuck's tonight. Will you dine with me, and we can go on together afterwards?' And the words of his reply dropped like flowers down the telephone.

'Dear lady, I should be only too charmed.'

What a triumphant evening! The little dinner *tête-à-tête* with Ænone Fell, the drive to Lord Timbuck's in her white motor-car, when she thanked him again for the unforgettable joy. Triumph upon triumph! And Lord Timbuck's champagne simply flowed.

'Have some more champagne, Peacock,' said Lord Timbuck. Peacock, you notice – not Mr Peacock – but Peacock, as if he were one of them. And wasn't he? He was an artist. He could sway them all. And wasn't he teaching them all to escape from life? How he sang! And as he sang, as in a dream he saw their feathers and their flowers and their fans, offered to him, laid before him, like a huge bouquet.

'Have another glass of wine, Peacock.'

'I could have anyone I liked by lifting a finger,' thought Peacock, positively staggering home.

But as he let himself into the dark flat his marvellous sense of elation began to ebb away. He turned up the light in the bedroom. His wife lay asleep, squeezed over to her side of the bed. He remembered suddenly how she had said when he had told her he was going out to dinner: 'You might have let me know before!' And how he had answered: 'Can't you possibly speak to me without offending against even good manners?' It was incredible, he thought, that she cared so little for him – incredible that she wasn't interested in the slightest in his triumphs and his artistic career. When so many women in her place would have given their eyes . . . Yes, he knew it . . . Why not acknowledge it? . . . And there she lay, an enemy, even in her sleep . . . Must it ever be thus? he thought, the champagne still working. Ah, if we only were friends, how much I could tell her now! About this evening; even about Timbuck's manner to me, and all that they said to me and so on and so on. If only I felt that she was here to come back to – that I could confide in her – and so on and so on.

In his emotion he pulled off his evening-boot and simply hurled it in the corner. The noise woke his wife with a terrible start. She sat up, pushing back her hair. And he suddenly decided to have one more try to treat her as a friend, to tell her everything, to win her. Down he sat on the side of the bed, and seized one of her hands. But of all those splendid things he had to say, not one could he utter. For some fiendish reason, the only words he could get out were: 'Dear lady, I should be so charmed – so charmed!'

Sun and Moon

In the afternoon the chairs came, a whole big cart full of little gold ones with their legs in the air. And then the flowers came. When you stared down from the balcony at the people carrying them the flowerpots looked like funny awfully nice hats nodding up the path.

Moon thought they were hats. She said: 'Look. There's a man wearing a palm on his head.' But she never knew the difference between real things and not real ones.

There was nobody to look after Sun and Moon. Nurse was helping Annie alter mother's dress which was much-too-long-and-tight-under-the-arms and mother was running all over the house and telephoning father to be sure not to forget things. She only had time to say: 'Out of my way, children!'

They kept out of her way – at any rate Sun did. He did so hate being sent stumping back to the nursery. It didn't matter about Moon. If she got tangled in people's legs they only threw her up and shook her till she squeaked. But Sun was too heavy for that. He was so heavy that the fat man who came to dinner on Sundays used to say: 'Now, young man, let's try to lift you.' And then he'd put his thumbs under Sun's arms and groan and try and give it up at last saying: 'He's a perfect little ton of bricks!'

Nearly all the furniture was taken out of the dining-room. The big piano was put in a corner and then there came a row of flowerpots and then there came the goldy chairs. That was for the concert. When Sun looked in a white-faced man sat at the piano – not playing, but banging at it and then looking inside. He had a bag of tools on the piano and he had stuck his hat on a statue against the wall. Sometimes he just started to play and then he jumped up again and looked inside. Sun hoped he wasn't the concert.

But of course the place to be in was the kitchen. There was a man helping in a cap like a blancmange, and their real cook, Minnie, was all red in the face and laughing. Not cross at all. She gave them each an almond finger and lifted them up on to the flour bin so that they could watch the wonderful things she and the man were making for supper. Cook brought in the things and he put them on dishes and trimmed them. Whole fishes, with their heads and eyes and tails still on, he sprinkled with red and green and yellow bits; he made squiggles all over the jellies, he stuck a collar on a ham and put a very thin sort of a fork in it; he dotted almonds and tiny round biscuits on the creams. And more and more things kept coming.

'Ah, but you haven't seen the ice pudding,' said cook. 'Come along.' Why was she being so nice, thought Sun as she gave them each a hand. And they looked into the refrigerator.

Oh! Oh! Oh! It was a little house. It was a little pink house with white snow on the roof and green windows and a brown door and stuck in the door there was a nut for a handle.

When Sun saw the nut he felt quite tired and had to lean against cook.

'Let me touch it. Just let me put my finger on the roof,' said Moon, dancing. She always wanted to touch all the food. Sun didn't.

'Now, my girl, look sharp with the table,' said cook as the house-maid came in.

'It's a picture, Min,' said Nellie. 'Come along and have a look.' So they all went into the dining-room. Sun and Moon were almost frightened. They wouldn't go up to the table at first; they just stood at the door and made eyes at it.

It wasn't real night yet but the blinds were down in the dining-room and the lights turned on – and all the lights were red roses. Red ribbons and bunches of roses tied up the table at the corners. In the middle was a lake with rose petals floating on it.

'That's where the ice pudding is to be,' said cook.

Two silver lions with wings had fruit on their backs, and the salt cellars were tiny birds drinking out of basins.

And all the winking glasses and shining plates and sparkling knives and forks – and all the food. And the little red table napkins made into roses . . .

'Are people going to eat the food?' asked Sun.

'I should just think they were,' laughed cook, laughing with Nellie. Moon laughed, too; she always did the same as other people. But Sun didn't want to laugh. Round and round he walked with his hands behind his back. Perhaps he never would have stopped if nurse hadn't called suddenly: 'Now then, children. It's high time you were washed and dressed.' And they were marched off to the nursery.

While they were being unbuttoned mother looked in with a white thing over her shoulders; she was rubbing stuff on her face.

'I'll ring for them when I want them, nurse, and then they can just come down and be seen and go back again,' said she.

Sun was undressed first, nearly to his skin, and dressed again in a white shirt with red and white daisies speckled on it, breeches with strings at the sides and braces that came over, white socks and red shoes.

'Now you're in your Russian costume,' said nurse, flattening down his fringe.

'Am I?' said Sun.

'Yes. Sit quiet in that chair and watch your little sister.'

Moon took ages. When she had her socks put on she pretended to fall back on the bed and waved her legs at nurse as she always did, and every time nurse tried to make her curls with a finger and a wet brush she turned round and asked nurse to show her the photo in her brooch or something like that. But at last she was finished too. Her dress stuck out, with fur on it, all white; there was even fluffy stuff on the legs of her drawers. Her shoes were white with big blobs on them.

'There you are, my lamb,' said nurse. 'And you look like a sweet little cherub of a picture of a powder-puff!' Nurse rushed to the door. 'Ma'am, one moment.'

Mother came in again with half her hair down.

'Oh,' she cried. 'What a picture!'

'Isn't she,' said nurse.

And Moon held out her skirts by the tips and dragged one of her feet. Sun didn't mind people not noticing him – much . . .

After that they played clean tidy games up at the table while nurse stood at the door, and when the carriages began to come and the sound of laughter and voices and soft rustlings came from down below she whispered: 'Now then, children, stay where you are.' Moon kept jerking the tablecloth so that it all hung down her side and Sun hadn't any – and then she pretended she didn't do it on purpose.

At last the bell rang. Nurse pounced at them with the hair brush, flattened his fringe, made her bow stand on end and joined their hands together.

'Down you go!' she whispered.

And down they went. Sun did feel silly holding Moon's hand like that but Moon seemed to like it. She swung her arm and the bell on her coral bracelet jingled.

At the drawing-room door stood mother fanning herself with a black fan. The drawing-room was full of sweet-smelling, silky, rustling ladies and men in black with funny tails on their coats – like beetles. Father was among them, talking very loud, and rattling something in his pocket.

'What a picture!' cried the ladies. 'Oh, the ducks! Oh, the lambs! Oh, the sweets! Oh, the pets!'

All the people who couldn't get at Moon kissed Sun, and a skinny old lady with teeth that clicked said: 'Such a serious little poppet,' and rapped him on the head with something hard.

Sun looked to see if the same concert was there, but he was gone. Instead, a fat man with a pink head leaned over the piano talking to a girl who held a violin at her ear.

There was only one man that Sun really liked. He was a little grey man, with long grey whiskers, who walked about by himself. He came up to Sun and rolled his eyes in a very nice way and said: 'Hallo, my lad.' Then he went away. But soon he came back again and said: 'Fond of dogs?' Sun said: 'Yes.' But then he went away again, and though Sun looked for him everywhere he couldn't find him. He thought perhaps he'd gone outside to fetch in a puppy.

'Good-night, my precious babies,' said mother, folding them up in her bare arms. 'Fly up to your little nest.'

Then Moon went and made a silly of herself again. She put up her arms in front of everybody and said: 'My daddy must carry me.'

But they seemed to like it, and daddy swooped down and picked her up as he always did.

Nurse was in such a hurry to get them to bed that she even interrupted Sun over his prayers and said: 'Get on with them, child, *do*.' And the moment after they were in bed and in the dark except for the nightlight in its little saucer.

'Are you asleep?' asked Moon.

'No,' said Sun. 'Are you?'

'No,' said Moon.

A long while after Sun woke up again. There was a loud, loud noise of clapping from downstairs, like when it rains. He heard Moon turn over.

'Moon, are you awake?'

'Yes, are you.'

'Yes. Well, let's go and look over the stairs.'

They had just got settled on the top step when the drawing-room door opened and they heard the party cross over the hall into the dining-room. Then that door was shut; there was a noise of 'pops' and laughing. Then that stopped and Sun saw them all walking round and round the lovely table with their hands behind their backs like he had done . . . Round and round they walked, looking and staring. The man with the grey whiskers liked the little house best. When he saw the nut for a handle he rolled his eyes like he did before and said to Sun: 'Seen the nut?'

'Don't nod your head like that, Moon.'

'I'm not nodding. It's you.'

'It is not. I never nod my head.'

'O–oh, you do. You're nodding it now.'

'I'm not. I'm only showing you how not to do it.'

When they woke up again they could only hear father's voice very loud, and mother, laughing away. Father came out of the dining-room, bounded up the stairs, and nearly fell over them.

'Hallo!' he said. 'By Jove, Kitty, come and look at this.'

Mother came out. 'Oh, you naughty children,' said she from the hall.

'Let's have 'em down and give 'em a bone,' said father. Sun had never seen him so jolly.

'No, certainly not,' said mother.

'Oh, my daddy, do! Do have us down,' said Moon.

'I'm hanged if I won't,' cried father. 'I won't be bullied. Kitty – way there.' And he caught them up, one under each arm.

Sun thought mother would have been dreadfully cross. But she wasn't. She kept on laughing at father.

'Oh, you dreadful boy!' said she. But she didn't mean Sun.

'Come on, kiddies. Come and have some pickings,' said this jolly father. But Moon stopped a minute.

'Mother – your dress is right off one side.'

'Is it?' said mother. And father said 'Yes' and pretended to bite her white shoulder, but she pushed him away.

And so they went back to the beautiful dining-room.

But – oh! oh! what had happened. The ribbons and the roses were all pulled untied. The little red table napkins lay on the floor, all the shining plates were dirty and all the winking glasses. The lovely food that the man had trimmed was all thrown about, and there were bones and bits and fruit peel and shells everywhere. There was even a bottle lying down with stuff coming out of it on to the cloth and nobody stood it up again.

And the little pink house with the snow roof and the green

windows was broken – broken – half melted away in the centre of the table.

'Come on, Sun,' said father, pretending not to notice.

Moon lifted up her pyjama legs and shuffled up to the table and stood on a chair, squeaking away.

'Have a bit of this ice,' said father, smashing in some more of the roof.

Mother took a little plate and held it for him; she put her other arm round his neck.

'Daddy. Daddy,' shrieked Moon. 'The little handle's left. The little nut. Kin I eat it?' And she reached across and picked it out of the door and scrunched it up, biting hard and blinking.

'Here, my lad,' said father.

But Sun did not move from the door. Suddenly he put up his head and gave a loud wail.

'I think it's horrid – horrid – horrid!' he sobbed.

'There, you see!' said mother. 'You see!'

'Off with you,' said father, no longer jolly. 'This moment. Off you go!'

And wailing loudly, Sun stumped off to the nursery.

Feuille d'Album

HE REALLY WAS an impossible person. Too shy altogether. With absolutely nothing to say for himself. And such a weight. Once he was in your studio he never knew when to go, but would sit on and on until you nearly screamed, and burned to throw something enormous after him when he did finally blush his way out – something like the tortoise stove. The strange thing was that at first sight he looked most interesting. Everybody agreed about that. You would drift into the café one evening and there you would see, sitting in a corner, with a glass of coffee in front of him, a thin, dark boy, wearing a blue jersey with a little grey flannel jacket buttoned over it. And somehow that blue jersey and the grey jacket with the sleeves that were too short gave him the air of a boy that has made up his mind to run away to sea. Who has run away, in fact, and will get up in a moment and sling a knotted handkerchief containing his nightshirt and his mother's picture on the end of a stick, and walk out into the night and be drowned . . . Stumble over the wharf edge on his way to the ship, even . . . He had black close-cropped hair, grey eyes with long lashes, white cheeks and a mouth pouting as though he were determined not to cry . . . How could one resist him? Oh, one's heart was wrung at sight. And, as if that were not enough, there was his trick of blushing . . . Whenever the waiter came near him he turned crimson – he might have been just out of prison and the waiter in the know . . .

'Who is he, my dear? Do you know?'

'Yes. His name is Ian French. Painter. Awfully clever, they say. Someone started by giving him a mother's tender care. She asked him how often he heard from home, whether he had enough blankets on his bed, how much milk he drank a day. But when she went round to his studio to give an eye to his socks, she rang and rang, and though she could have sworn she heard someone breathing inside, the door was not answered . . . Hopeless!'

Someone else decided that he ought to fall in love. She summoned him to her side, called him 'boy', leaned over him so that he might smell the enchanting perfume of her hair, took his arm, told him how marvellous life could be if one only had the courage, and went round to his studio one evening and rang and rang . . . Hopeless.

'What the poor boy really wants is thoroughly rousing,' said a third. So off they went to cafés and cabarets, little dances, places where you drank something that tasted like tinned apricot juice, but cost twenty-seven shillings a bottle and was called champagne, other places, too thrilling for words, where you sat in the most awful gloom, and where someone had always been shot the night before. But he did not turn a hair. Only once he got very drunk, but instead of blossoming forth, there he sat, stony, with two spots of red on his cheeks, like, my dear, yes, the dead image of that ragtime thing they were playing, like a 'Broken Doll'. But when she took him back to his studio he had quite recovered, and said 'good-night' to her in the street below, as though they had walked home from church together . . . Hopeless.

After heaven knows how many more attempts – for the spirit of kindness dies very hard in women – they gave him up. Of course, they were still perfectly charming, and asked him to their shows, and spoke to him in the café, but that was all. When one is an artist one has no time simply for people who won't respond. Has one?

'And besides I really think there must be something rather fishy somewhere . . . don't you? It can't all be as innocent as it looks! Why come to Paris if you want to be a daisy in the field? No, I'm not suspicious. But – '

He lived at the top of a tall mournful building overlooking the river. One of those buildings that look so romantic on rainy nights and moonlight nights, when the shutters are shut, and the heavy door, and the sign advertising 'a little apartment to let immediately' gleams forlorn beyond words. One of those buildings that smell so unromantic all the year round, and where the concierge lives in a glass cage on the ground floor, wrapped up in a filthy shawl, stirring something in a saucepan and ladling out titbits to the swollen old dog lolling on a bead cushion . . . Perched up in the air the studio had a wonderful view. The two big windows faced the water; he could see the boats and the barges swinging up and down, and the fringe of an island planted with trees, like a round bouquet. The side window looked across to another house, shabbier still and smaller, and down below there was a flower market. You could see the tops of huge umbrellas, with frills of bright flowers escaping from them, booths covered with striped awning where they sold plants in boxes and clumps of wet gleaming palms in terracotta jars. Among the flowers the old women scuttled from side to side, like crabs. Really there was no need for him to go out. If he sat at the window until his white beard fell over the sill he still would have found something to draw . . .

How surprised those tender women would have been if they had managed to force the door. For he kept his studio as neat as a pin. Everything was arranged to form a pattern, a little 'still life' as it were – the saucepans with their lids on the wall behind the gas stove, the bowl of eggs, milk jug and teapot on the shelf, the books and the lamp with the crinkly paper shade on the table. An Indian curtain that had a fringe of red leopards marching round it covered his bed by day, and on the wall beside the bed on a level with your eyes when you were lying down there was a small neatly printed notice: Get up at once.

Every day was much the same. While the light was good he slaved at his painting, then cooked his meals and tidied up the place. And in the evenings he went off to the café, or sat at home reading or making out the most complicated list of expenses headed: 'What I ought to be able to do it on', and ending with a sworn statement . . . 'I swear not to exceed this amount for next month. Signed, Ian French.'

Nothing very fishy about this; but those far-seeing women were quite right. It wasn't all.

One evening he was sitting at the side window eating some prunes and throwing the stones on to the tops of the huge umbrellas in the deserted flower market. It had been raining – the first real spring rain of the year had fallen – a bright spangle hung on everything, and the air smelled of buds and moist earth. Many voices sounding languid and content rang out in the dusky air, and the people who had come to close their windows and fasten the shutters leaned out instead. Down below in the market the trees were peppered with new green. What kind of trees were they? he wondered. And now came the lamplighter. He stared at the house across the way, the small, shabby house, and suddenly, as if in answer to his gaze, two wings of windows opened and a girl came out on to the tiny balcony carrying a pot of daffodils. She was a strangely thin girl in a dark pinafore, with a pink handkerchief tied over her hair. Her sleeves were rolled up almost to her shoulders and her slender arms shone against the dark stuff.

'Yes, it is quite warm enough. It will do them good,' she said, putting down the pot and turning to someone in the room inside. As she turned she put her hands up to the handkerchief and tucked away some wisps of hair. She looked down at the deserted market and up at the sky, but where he sat there might have been a hollow in the air. She simply did not see the house opposite. And then she disappeared.

His heart fell out of the side window of his studio, and down to the balcony of the house opposite – buried itself in the pot of daffodils under the half-opened buds and spears of green . . . That room with the balcony was the sitting-room, and the one next door to it was the kitchen. He heard the clatter of the dishes as she washed up after supper, and then she came to the window; knocked a little mop against the ledge, and hung it on a nail to dry. She never sang or unbraided her hair, or held out her arms to the moon as young girls are supposed to do. And she always wore the same dark pinafore and the pink handkerchief over her hair . . . Whom did she live with? Nobody else came to those two windows, and yet she was always talking to someone in the room. Her mother, he decided, was an invalid. They took in sewing. The father was dead . . . He had been a journalist – very pale, with long moustaches, and a piece of black hair falling over his forehead.

By working all day they just made enough money to live on, but they never went out and they had no friends. Now when he sat down at his table he had to make an entirely new set of sworn statements . . . Not to go to the side window before a certain hour: signed, Ian French. Not to think about her until he had put away his painting things for the day: signed, Ian French.

It was quite simple. She was the only person he really wanted to know, because she was, he decided, the only other person alive who was just his age. He couldn't stand giggling girls, and he had no use for grown-up women . . . She was his age, she was – well, just like him. He sat in his dusky studio, tired, with one arm hanging over the back of his chair, staring in at her window and seeing himself in there with her. She had a violent temper; they quarrelled terribly at times, he and she. She had a way of stamping her foot and twisting her hands in her pinafore . . . furious. And she very rarely laughed. Only when she told him about an absurd little kitten she once had who used to roar and pretend to be a lion when it was given meat to eat. Things like that made her laugh . . . But as a rule they sat together very quietly; he, just as he was sitting now, and she with her hands folded in her lap and her feet tucked under, talking in low tones, or silent and tired after the day's work. Of course, she never asked him about his pictures, and of course he made the most wonderful drawings of her which she hated, because he made her so thin and so dark . . . But how could he get to know her? This might go on for years . . .

Then he discovered that once a week, in the evening, she went out shopping. On two successive Thursdays she came to the window wearing an old-fashioned cape over the pinafore, and carrying a basket. From where he sat he could not see the door of her house, but on the next Thursday evening at the same time he snatched up his cap and ran down the stairs. There was a lovely pink light over everything. He saw it glowing in the river, and the people walking towards him had pink faces and pink hands.

He leaned against the side of his house waiting for her and he had no idea of what he was going to do or say. 'Here she comes,' said a voice in his head. She walked very quickly, with small, light steps; with one hand she carried the basket, with the other she kept the cape together . . . What could he do? He could only follow . . . First she went into the grocer's and spent a long time in there, and then she went into the butcher's where she had to wait her turn. Then she was an age at the draper's matching something, and then she went to the fruit shop and bought a lemon. As he watched her he knew more surely than ever he must get to know her, now. Her composure, her seriousness and her loneliness, the very way she walked as though she was eager to be done with this world of grown-ups, all was so natural to him and so inevitable.

'Yes, she is always like that,' he thought proudly. 'We have nothing to do with these people.'

But now she was on her way home and he was as far off as ever . . . She suddenly turned into the dairy and he saw her through the window buying an egg. She picked it out of the basket with such care – a brown one, a beautifully shaped one, the one he would have chosen. And when she came out of the dairy he went in after her. In a moment he was out again, and following her past his house across the flower market, dodging among the huge umbrellas and treading on the fallen flowers and the round marks where the pots had stood . . . Through her door he crept, and up the stairs after, taking care to tread in time with her so that she should not notice. Finally, she stopped on the landing, and took the key out of her purse. As she put it into the door he ran up and faced her.

Blushing more crimson than ever, but looking at her severely, he said, almost angrily: 'Excuse me, mademoiselle, you dropped this.' And he handed her an egg.

A Dill Pickle

AND THEN, after six years, she saw him again. He was seated at one of those little bamboo tables decorated with a Japanese vase of paper daffodils. There was a tall plate of fruit in front of him, and very carefully, in a way she recognised immediately as his 'special' way, he was peeling an orange.

He must have felt that shock of recognition in her for he looked up and met her eyes. Incredible! He didn't know her! She smiled; he frowned. She came towards him. He closed his eyes an instant, but opening them his face lit up as though he had struck a match in a dark room. He laid down the orange and pushed back his chair, and she took her little warm hand out of her muff and gave it to him.

'Vera!' he exclaimed. 'How strange. Really, for a moment I didn't know you. Won't you sit down? You've had lunch? Won't you have some coffee?'

She hesitated, but of course she meant to.

'Yes, I'd like some coffee.' And she sat down opposite him.

'You've changed. You've changed very much,' he said, staring at her with that eager, lighted look. 'You look so well. I've never seen you look so well before.'

'Really?' She raised her veil and unbuttoned her high fur collar. 'I don't feel very well. I can't bear this weather, you know.'

'Ah, no. You hate the cold . . . '

'Loathe it.' She shuddered. 'And the worst of it is that the older one grows . . . '

He interrupted her. 'Excuse me,' and tapped on the table for the waitress. 'Please bring some coffee and cream.' To her: 'You are sure you won't eat anything? Some fruit, perhaps. The fruit here is very good.'

'No, thanks. Nothing.'

'Then that's settled.' And smiling just a hint too broadly he took up the orange again. 'You were saying – the older one grows – '

'The colder,' she laughed. But she was thinking how well she remembered that trick of his – the trick of interrupting her – and of how it used to exasperate her six years ago. She used to feel then as though he, quite suddenly, in the middle of what she was saying, put his hand over her lips, turned from her, attended to something different, and then took his hand away, and with just the same slightly too broad smile, gave her his attention again . . . Now we are ready. That is settled.

'The colder!' He echoed her words, laughing too. 'Ah, ah. You still say the same things. And there is another thing about you that is not changed at all – your beautiful voice – your beautiful way of speaking.' Now he was very grave; he leaned towards her, and she smelled the warm, stinging scent of the orange peel. 'You have only to say one word and I would know your voice among all other voices. I don't know what it is – I've often wondered – that makes your voice such a – haunting memory . . . Do you remember that first afternoon we spent together at Kew Gardens? You were so surprised because I did not know the names of any flowers. I am still just as ignorant for all your telling me. But whenever it is very fine and warm, and I see some bright colours – it's awfully strange – I hear your voice saying: "Geranium, marigold and verbena." And I feel those three words are all I recall of some forgotten, heavenly language . . . You remember that afternoon?'

'Oh, yes, very well.' She drew a long, soft breath, as though the paper daffodils between them were almost too sweet to bear. Yet, what had remained in her mind of that particular afternoon was an absurd scene over the tea table. A great many people taking tea in a Chinese pagoda, and he behaving like a maniac about the wasps – waving them away, flapping at them with his straw hat, serious and infuriated out of all proportion to the occasion. How delighted the sniggering tea drinkers had been. And how she had suffered.

But now, as he spoke, that memory faded. His was the truer. Yes, it had been a wonderful afternoon, full of geranium and marigold and verbena, and – warm sunshine. Her thoughts lingered over the last two words as though she sang them.

In the warmth, as it were, another memory unfolded. She saw herself sitting on a lawn. He lay beside her, and suddenly, after a long silence, he rolled over and put his head in her lap.

'I wish,' he said, in a low, troubled voice, 'I wish that I had taken poison and were about to die – here now!'

At that moment a little girl in a white dress, holding a long, dripping water lily, dodged from behind a bush, stared at them, and dodged back again. But he did not see. She leaned over him.

'Ah, why do you say that? I could not say that.'

But he gave a kind of soft moan, and taking her hand he held it to his cheek.

'Because I know I am going to love you too much – far too much. And I shall suffer so terribly, Vera, because you never, never will love me.'

He was certainly far better looking now than he had been then. He had lost all that dreamy vagueness and indecision. Now he had the air of a man who has found his place in life, and fills it with a confidence and an assurance which was, to say the least, impressive. He must have made money, too. His clothes were admirable, and at that moment he pulled a Russian cigarette case out of his pocket.

'Won't you smoke?'

'Yes, I will.' She hovered over them. 'They look very good.'

'I think they are. I get them made for me by a little man in St James's Street. I don't smoke very much. I'm not like you – but when I do, they must be delicious, very fresh cigarettes. Smoking isn't a habit with me; it's a luxury – like perfume. Are you still so fond of perfumes? Ah, when I was in Russia . . .'

She broke in: 'You've really been to Russia?'

'Oh, yes. I was there for over a year. Have you forgotten how we used to talk of going there?'

'No, I've not forgotten.'

He gave a strange half-laugh and leaned back in his chair. 'Isn't it curious. I have really carried out all those journeys that we planned. Yes, I have been to all those places that we talked of, and stayed in them long enough to – as you used to say, "air oneself" in them. In fact, I have spent the last three years of my life travelling all the time. Spain, Corsica, Siberia, Russia, Egypt. The only country left is China, and I mean to go there, too, when the war is over.'

As he spoke, so lightly, tapping the end of his cigarette against the ashtray, she felt the strange beast that had slumbered so long within her bosom stir, stretch itself, yawn, prick up its ears, and suddenly bound to its feet, and fix its longing, hungry stare upon those faraway places. But all she said was, smiling gently: 'How I envy you.'

He accepted that. 'It has been,' he said, 'very wonderful – especially Russia. Russia was all that we had imagined, and far, far more. I

even spent some days on a river boat on the Volga. Do you remember that boatman's song that you used to play?'

'Yes.' It began to play in her mind as she spoke.

'Do you ever play it now?'

'No, I've no piano.'

He was amazed at that. 'But what has become of your beautiful
piano?'

She made a little grimace. 'Sold. Ages ago.'

'But you were so fond of music,' he wondered.

'I've no time for it now,' said she.

He let it go at that. 'That river life,' he went on, 'is something quite
special. After a day or two you cannot realise that you have ever
known another. And it is not necessary to know the language – the
life of the boat creates a bond between you and the people that's
more than sufficient. You eat with them, pass the day with them, and
in the evening there is that endless singing.'

She shivered, hearing the boatman's song break out again loud and
tragic, and seeing the boat floating on the darkening river with
melancholy trees on either side . . . 'Yes, I should like that,' said she,
stroking her muff.

'You'd like almost everything about Russian life,' he said warmly.
'It's so informal, so impulsive, so free without question. And then the
peasants are so splendid. They are such human beings – yes, that is it.
Even the man who drives your carriage has – has some real part in
what is happening. I remember the evening a party of us, two friends
of mine and the wife of one of them, went for a picnic by the Black
Sea. We took supper and champagne and ate and drank on the grass.
And while we were eating the coachman came up. "Have a dill
pickle," he said. He wanted to share with us. That seemed to me so
right, so – you know what I mean?'

And she seemed at that moment to be sitting on the grass beside
the mysteriously Black Sea, black as velvet, and rippling against the
banks in silent, velvet waves. She saw the carriage drawn up to one
side of the road, and the little group on the grass, their faces and
hands white in the moonlight. She saw the pale dress of the woman
outspread and her folded parasol, lying on the grass like a huge pearl
crochet hook. Apart from them, with his supper in a cloth on his
knees, sat the coachman. 'Have a dill pickle,' said he, and although
she was not certain what a dill pickle was, she saw the greenish glass
jar with a red chilli like a parrot's beak glimmering through. She
sucked in her cheeks; the dill pickle was terribly sour . . .

'Yes, I know perfectly what you mean,' she said.

In the pause that followed they looked at each other. In the past when they had looked at each other like that they had felt such a boundless understanding between them that their souls had, as it were, put their arms round each other and dropped into the same sea, content to be drowned, like mournful lovers. But now, the surprising thing was that it was he who held back. He who said: 'What a marvellous listener you are. When you look at me with those wild eyes I feel that I could tell you things that I would never breathe to another human being.'

Was there just a hint of mockery in his voice or was it her fancy? She could not be sure.

'Before I met you,' he said, 'I had never spoken of myself to anybody. How well I remember one night, the night that I brought you the little Christmas tree, telling you all about my childhood. And of how I was so miserable that I ran away and lived under a cart in our yard for two days without being discovered. And you listened, and your eyes shone, and I felt that you had even made the little Christmas tree listen too, as in a fairy story.'

But of that evening she had remembered a little pot of caviare. It had cost seven and sixpence. He could not get over it. Think of it – a tiny jar like that costing seven and sixpence. While she ate it he watched her, delighted and shocked.

'No, really, that is eating money. You could not get seven shillings into a little pot that size. Only think of the profit they must make . . . ' And he had begun some immensely complicated calculations . . . But now goodbye to the caviare. The Christmas tree was on the table, and the little boy lay under the cart with his head pillowed on the yard dog.

'The dog was called Bosun,' she cried delightedly.

But he did not follow. 'Which dog? Had you a dog? I don't remember a dog at all.'

'No, no. I mean the yard dog when you were a little boy.' He laughed and snapped the cigarette case to.

'Was he? Do you know I had forgotten that. It seems such ages ago. I cannot believe that it is only six years. After I had recognised you today – I had to take such a leap – I had to take a leap over my whole life to get back to that time. I was such a kid then.' He drummed on the table. 'I've often thought how I must have bored you. And now I understand so perfectly why you wrote to me as you did – although at the time that letter nearly finished my life. I found it again the other day, and I couldn't help laughing as I read it. It was so clever – such a true picture of me.' He glanced up. 'You're not going?'

She had buttoned her collar again and drawn down her veil.

'Yes, I am afraid I must,' she said, and managed a smile. Now she knew that he had been mocking.

'Ah, no, please,' he pleaded. 'Don't go just for a moment,' and he caught up one of her gloves from the table and clutched at it as if that would hold her. 'I see so few people to talk to nowadays that I have turned into a sort of barbarian,' he said. 'Have I said something to hurt you?'

'Not a bit,' she lied. But as she watched him draw her glove through his fingers, gently, gently, her anger really did die down, and besides, at the moment he looked more like himself of six years ago . . .

'What I really wanted then,' he said softly, 'was to be a sort of carpet – to make myself into a sort of carpet for you to walk on so that you need not be hurt by the sharp stones and the mud that you hated so. It was nothing more positive than that – nothing more selfish. Only I did desire, eventually, to turn into a magic carpet and carry you away to all those lands you longed to see.'

As he spoke she lifted her head as though she drank something; the strange beast in her bosom began to purr . . .

'I felt that you were more lonely than anybody else in the world,' he went on, 'and yet, perhaps, that you were the only person in the world who was really truly alive. Born out of your time,' he murmured, stroking the glove, 'fated.'

Ah, God! What had she done! How had she dared to throw away her happiness like this. This was the only man who had ever understood her. Was it too late? Could it be too late? She was that glove that he held in his fingers . . .

'And then the fact that you had no friends and never had made friends with people. How I understood that, for neither had I. Is it just the same now?'

'Yes,' she breathed. 'Just the same. I am as alone as ever.'

'So am I,' he laughed gently, 'just the same.'

Suddenly with a quick gesture he handed her back the glove and scraped his chair on the floor. 'But what seemed to me so mysterious then is perfectly plain to me now. And to you, too, of course . . . It simply was that we were such egoists, so self-engrossed, so wrapped up in ourselves that we hadn't a corner in our hearts for anybody else. Do you know,' he cried, naïve and hearty, and dreadfully like another side of that old self again, 'I began studying a Mind System when I was in Russia, and I found that we were not peculiar at all. It's quite a well-known form of . . .'

She had gone. He sat there, thunderstruck, astounded beyond words . . . And then he asked the waitress for his bill.

'But the cream has not been touched,' he said. 'Please do not charge me for it.'

The Little Governess

OH, DEAR, how she wished that it wasn't night-time. She'd have much rather travelled by day, much much rather. But the lady at the Governess Bureau had said: 'You had better take an evening boat and then if you get into a compartment for "Ladies Only" in the train you will be far safer than sleeping in a foreign hotel. Don't go out of the carriage; don't walk about the corridors and *be sure* to lock the lavatory door if you go there. The train arrives at Munich at eight o'clock, and Frau Arnholdt says that the Hotel Grünewald is only one minute away. A porter can take you there. She will arrive at six the same evening, so you will have a nice quiet day to rest after the journey and rub up your German. And when you want anything to eat I would advise you to pop into the nearest baker's and get a bun and some coffee. You haven't been abroad before, have you?' 'No.' 'Well, I always tell my girls that it's better to mistrust people at first rather than trust them, and it's safer to suspect people of evil intentions rather than good ones . . . It sounds rather hard but we've got to be women of the world, haven't we?'

It had been nice in the Ladies' Cabin. The stewardess was so kind and changed her money for her and tucked up her feet. She lay on one of the hard pink-sprigged couches and watched the other passengers, friendly and natural, pinning their hats to the bolsters, taking off their boots and skirts, opening dressing-cases and arranging mysterious rustling little packages, tying their heads up in veils before lying down. *Thud, thud, thud*, went the steady screw of the steamer. The stewardess pulled a green shade over the light and sat down by the stove, her skirt turned back over her knees, a long piece of knitting on her lap. On a shelf above her head there was a water-bottle with a tight bunch of flowers stuck in it. 'I like travelling very much,' thought the little governess. She smiled and yielded to the warm rocking.

But when the boat stopped and she went up on deck, her dress-basket in one hand, her rug and umbrella in the other, a cold, strange wind flew under her hat. She looked up at the masts and spars of the ship black against a green glittering sky and down to the dark landing stage where strange muffled figures lounged, waiting; she moved forward with the sleepy flock, all knowing where to go to and what to do except her, and she felt afraid. Just a little – just enough to wish – oh, to wish that it was daytime and that one of those women who had smiled at her in the glass, when they both did their hair in the Ladies' Cabin, was somewhere near now. 'Tickets, please. Show your tickets. Have your tickets ready.' She went down the gangway balancing herself carefully on her heels. Then a man in a black leather cap came forward and touched her on the arm. 'Where for, miss?' He spoke English – he must be a guard or a stationmaster with a cap like that. She had scarcely answered when he pounced on her dress-basket. 'This way,' he shouted, in a rude, determined voice, and elbowing his way he strode past the people. 'But I don't want a porter.' What a horrible man! 'I don't want a porter. I want to carry it myself.' She had to run to keep up with him, and her anger, far stronger than she, ran before her and snatched the bag out of the wretch's hand. He paid no attention at all, but swung on down the long dark platform, and across a railway line. 'He is a robber.' She was sure he was a robber as she stepped between the silvery rails and felt the cinders crunch under her shoes. On the other side – oh, thank goodness! – there was a train with Munich written on it. The man stopped by the huge lighted carriages. 'Second class?' asked the insolent voice. 'Yes, a ladies' compartment.' She was quite out of breath. She opened her little purse to find something small enough to give this horrible man while he tossed her dress-basket into the rack of an empty carriage that had a ticket, *Dames Seules*, gummed on the window. She got into the train and handed him twenty centimes. 'What's this?' shouted the man, glaring at the money and then at her, holding it up to his nose, sniffing at it as though he had never in his life seen, much less held, such a sum. 'It's a franc. You know that, don't you? It's a franc. That's my fare!' A franc! Did he imagine that she was going to give him a franc for playing a trick like that just because she was a girl and travelling alone at night? Never, never! She squeezed her purse in her hand and simply did not see him – she looked at a view of St Malo on the wall opposite and simply did not hear him. 'Ah, no. Ah, no. Four sous. You make a mistake. Here, take it. It's a franc I want.' He leapt on to the step of the train and threw the money on to her lap. Trembling with terror she screwed herself tight, tight, and put out an icy hand and took the money – stowed it away in her hand. 'That's all you're going to get,' she said. For a minute or two she felt his sharp eyes pricking her all over, while he nodded slowly, pulling down his mouth: 'Ve—ry well. *Trrrès bien.*' He shrugged his shoulders and disappeared into the dark. Oh, the relief! How simply terrible that had been! As she stood up to feel if the dress-basket was firm she caught sight of herself in the mirror, quite white, with big round eyes. She untied her 'motor veil' and unbuttoned her green cape.

'But it's all over now,' she said to the mirror face, feeling in some way that it was more frightened than she.

People began to assemble on the platform. They stood together in little groups talking; a strange light from the station lamps painted their faces almost green. A little boy in red clattered up with a huge tea wagon and leaned against it, whistling and flicking his boots with a serviette. A woman in a black alpaca apron pushed a barrow with pillows for hire. Dreamy and vacant she looked – like a woman wheeling a perambulator – up and down, up and down – with a sleeping baby inside it. Wreaths of white smoke floated up from somewhere and hung below the roof like misty vines. 'How strange it all is,' thought the little governess, 'and the middle of the night, too.' She looked out from her safe corner, frightened no longer but proud that she had not given that franc. 'I can look after myself – of course I can. The great thing is not to – ' Suddenly from the corridor there came a stamping of feet and men's voices, high and broken with snatches of loud laughter. They were coming her way. The little governess shrank into her corner as four young men in bowler hats passed, staring through the door and window. One of them, bursting with the joke, pointed to the notice *Dames Seules* and the four bent down the better to see the one little girl in the corner. Oh dear, they were in the carriage next door. She heard them tramping about and then a sudden hush followed by a tall thin fellow with a tiny black moustache who flung her door open. 'If mademoiselle cares to come in with us,' he said, in French. She saw the others crowding behind him, peeping under his arm and over his shoulder, and she sat very straight and still. 'If mademoiselle will do us the honour,' mocked the tall man. One of them could be quiet no longer; his laughter went off in a loud crack. 'Mademoiselle is serious,' persisted the young man, bowing and grimacing. He took off his hat with a flourish, and she was alone again.

'*En voiture. En voi—ture!*' someone ran up and down beside the train. 'I wish it wasn't night-time. I wish there was another woman in the carriage. I'm frightened of the men next door.' The little governess looked out to see her porter coming back again – the same man making for her carriage with his arms full of luggage. But – but what *was* he doing? He put his thumb nail under the label *Dames Seules* and tore it right off and then stood aside squinting at her while an old man wrapped in a plaid cape climbed up the high step. 'But this is a ladies' compartment.' 'Oh, no, mademoiselle, you make a mistake. No, no, I assure you. Merci, monsieur.' '*En voi–turre!*' A shrill whistle. The porter stepped off triumphant and the train started. For a moment or two big tears brimmed her eyes and through them she saw the old man unwinding a scarf from his neck and untying the flaps of his Jaeger cap. He looked very old. Ninety at least. He had a white moustache and big gold-rimmed spectacles with little blue eyes behind them and pink wrinkled cheeks. A nice face – and charming the way he bent forward and said in halting French: 'Do I disturb you, mademoiselle? Would you rather I took all these things out of the rack and found another carriage?' What! that old man have to move all those heavy things just because she . . . 'No, it's quite all right. You don't disturb me at all.' 'Ah, a thousand thanks.' He sat down opposite her and unbuttoned the cape of his enormous coat and flung it off his shoulders.

The train seemed glad to have left the station. With a long leap it sprang into the dark. She rubbed a place in the window with her glove but she could see nothing – just a tree outspread like a black fan or a scatter of lights, or the line of a hill, solemn and huge. In the carriage next door the young men started singing '*Un, deux, trois*'. They sang the same song over and over at the tops of their voices.

'I never could have dared to go to sleep if I had been alone,' she decided. 'I *couldn't* have put my feet up or even taken off my hat.' The singing gave her a queer little tremble in her stomach and, hugging herself to stop it, with her arms crossed under her cape, she felt really glad to have the old man in the carriage with her. Careful to see that he was not looking she peeped at him through her long lashes. He sat extremely upright, the chest thrown out, the chin well in, knees pressed together, reading a German paper. That was why he spoke French so funnily. He was a German. Something in the army, she supposed – a colonel or a general – once, of course, not now; he was too old for that now. How spick and span he looked for an old man. He wore a pearl pin stuck in his black tie and a ring with a dark red stone in his little finger; the tip of a white silk handkerchief showed in the pocket of his double-breasted jacket. Somehow, altogether, he was really nice to look at. Most old men were so horrid. She couldn't bear them doddery – or they had a disgusting cough or something. But not having a beard – that made all the difference – and then his cheeks were so pink and his moustache so very white. Down went the German paper and the old man leaned forward with the same delightful courtesy: 'Do you speak German, mademoiselle?' '*Ja, ein wenig, mehr als Französisch,*' said the little governess, blushing a deep pink colour that spread slowly over her cheeks and made her blue eyes look almost black. 'Ach, so!' The old man bowed graciously. 'Then perhaps you would care to look at some illustrated papers.' He slipped a rubber band from a little roll of them and handed them across. 'Thank you very much.' She was very fond of looking at pictures, but first she would take off her hat and gloves. So she stood up, unpinned the brown straw and put it neatly in the rack beside the dress-basket, stripped off her brown kid gloves, paired them in a tight roll and put them in the crown of the hat for safety, and then sat down again, more comfortably this time, her feet crossed, the papers on her lap. How kindly the old man in the corner watched her bare little hand turning over the big white pages, watched her lips moving as she pronounced the long words to herself, rested upon her hair that fairly blazed under the light. Alas! how tragic for a little governess to possess hair that made one think of tangerines and marigolds, of apricots and tortoiseshell cats and champagne! Perhaps that was what the old man was thinking as he gazed and gazed, and that not even the dark ugly clothes could disguise her soft beauty. Perhaps the flush that licked his cheeks and lips was a flush of rage that anyone so young and tender should have to travel alone and unprotected through the night. Who knows he was not murmuring in his sentimental German fashion: '*Ja, es ist eine Tragödie!* Would to God I were the child's grandpapa!'

'Thank you very much. They were very interesting.' She smiled prettily handing back the papers. 'But you speak German extremely well,' said the old man. 'You have been in Germany before, of course?' 'Oh no, this is the first time' – a little pause, then – 'this is the first time that I have ever been abroad at all.' 'Really! I am surprised. You gave me the impression, if I may say so, that you were accustomed to travelling.' 'Oh, well – I have been about a good deal in England, and to Scotland, once.' 'So. I myself have been in England once, but I could not learn English.' He raised one hand and shook his head, laughing. 'No, it was too difficult for me . . . "Ow-do-you-do. Please vich is ze vay to Leicestaire Squaare." ' She laughed too. 'Foreigners always say . . . ' They had quite a little talk about it. 'But you will like Munich,' said the old man. 'Munich is a wonderful city. Museums, pictures, galleries, fine buildings and shops, concerts, theatres, restaurants – all are in Munich. I have travelled all over Europe many, many times in my life, but it is always to Munich that I return. You will enjoy yourself there.' 'I am not going to *stay* in Munich,' said the little governess, and she added shyly, 'I am going to a post as governess to a doctor's family in Augsburg.' 'Ah, that was it.' Augsburg he knew. Augsburg – well – was not beautiful. A solid manufacturing town. But if Germany was new to her he hoped she would find something interesting there too. 'I am sure I shall.' 'But what a pity not to see Munich before you go. You ought to take a little holiday on your way' – he smiled – 'and store up some pleasant memories.' 'I am afraid I could not do *that*,' said the little governess, shaking her head, suddenly important and serious. 'And also, if one is alone . . . ' He quite understood. He bowed, serious too. They were silent after that. The train shattered on, baring its dark, flaming breast to the hills and to the valleys. It was warm in the carriage. She seemed to lean against the dark rushing and to be carried away and away. Little sounds made themselves heard; steps in the corridor, doors opening and shutting – a murmur of voices – whistling . . . Then the window was pricked with long needles of rain . . . But it did not matter . . . it was outside . . . and she had her umbrella . . . she pouted, sighed, opened and shut her hands once and fell fast asleep.

'Pardon! Pardon!' The sliding back of the carriage door woke her with a start. What had happened? Someone had come in and gone out again. The old man sat in his corner, more upright than ever, his hands in the pockets of his coat, frowning heavily. 'Ha! ha! ha!' came from the carriage next door. Still half asleep, she put her hands to her hair to make sure it wasn't a dream. 'Disgraceful!' muttered the old man more to himself than to her. 'Common, vulgar fellows! I am afraid they disturbed you, gracious Fräulein, blundering in here like that.' No, not really. She was just going to wake up, and she took out her silver watch to look at the time. Half-past four. A cold blue light filled the window-panes. Now when she rubbed a place she could see bright patches of fields, a clump of white houses like mushrooms, a road 'like a picture' with poplar trees on either side, a thread of river. How pretty it was! How pretty and how different! Even those pink clouds in the sky looked foreign. It was cold, but she pretended that it was far colder and rubbed her hands together and shivered, pulling at the collar of her coat because she was so happy.

The train began to slow down. The engine gave a long shrill whistle. They were coming to a town. Taller houses, pink and yellow, glided by, fast asleep behind their green eyelids, and guarded by the poplar trees that quivered in the blue air as if on tiptoe, listening. In one house a woman opened the shutters, flung a red and white mattress across the window frame and stood staring at the train. A pale woman with black hair and a white woollen shawl over her shoulders. More women appeared at the doors and at the windows of the sleeping houses. There came a flock of sheep. The shepherd wore a blue blouse and pointed wooden shoes. Look! look what flowers – and by the railway station too! Standard roses like bridesmaids' bouquets, white geraniums, waxy pink ones that you would *never* see out of a greenhouse at home. Slower and slower. A man with a watering-can was spraying the platform. 'A–a–aah!' Somebody came running and waving his arms. A huge fat woman waddled through the glass doors of the station with a tray of strawberries. Oh, she was thirsty! She was very thirsty! 'Aa–a–ah!' The same somebody ran back again. The train stopped.

The old man pulled his coat round him and got up, smiling at her. He murmured something she didn't quite catch, but she smiled back at him as he left the carriage. While he was away the little governess looked at herself again in the glass, shook and patted herself with the precise practical care of a girl who is old enough to travel by herself and has nobody else to assure her that she is 'quite all right behind'. Thirsty and thirsty! The air tasted of water. She let down the window and the fat woman with the strawberries passed as if on purpose; holding up the tray to her. '*Nein, danke*,' said the little governess, looking at the big berries on their gleaming leaves. '*Wie viel?*' she asked as the fat woman moved away. 'Two marks fifty, Fräulein.' 'Good gracious!' She came in from the window and sat down in the corner, very sobered for a minute. Half a crown! 'H–o–o–o–o–o–e–e–e!' shrieked the train, gathering itself together to be off again. She hoped the old man wouldn't be left behind. Oh, it was daylight – everything was lovely if only she hadn't been so thirsty. Where *was* the old man – oh, here he was – she dimpled at him as though he were an old accepted friend as he closed the door and, turning, took from under his cape a basket of the strawberries. 'If Fräulein would honour me by accepting these . . . ' 'What, for me?' But she drew back and raised her hands as though he were about to put a wild little kitten on her lap.

'Certainly, for you,' said the old man. 'For myself it is twenty years since I was brave enough to eat strawberries.' 'Oh, thank you very much. *Danke bestens*,' she stammered, '*sie sind so sehr schön!*' 'Eat them and see,' said the old man, looking pleased and friendly. 'You won't have even one?' 'No, no, no.' Timidly and charmingly her hand hovered. They were so big and juicy she had to take two bites to them – the juice ran all down her fingers – and it was while she munched the berries that she first thought of the old man as a grandfather. What a perfect grandfather he would make! Just like one out of a book!

The sun came out, the pink clouds in the sky, the strawberry clouds, were eaten by the blue. 'Are they good?' asked the old man. 'As good as they look?'

When she had eaten them she felt she had known him for years. She told him about Frau Arnholdt and how she had got the place. Did he know the Hotel Grünewald? Frau Arnholdt would not arrive until the evening. He listened, listened until he knew as much about the affair as she did, until he said – not looking at her – but smoothing the palms of his brown suede gloves together: 'I wonder if you would let me show you a little of Munich today. Nothing much – but just perhaps a picture gallery and the Englischer Garten. It seems such a pity that you should have to spend the day at the hotel, and also a little uncomfortable . . . in a strange place. *Nicht wahr?* You would be back there by the early afternoon or whenever you wish, of course, and you would give an old man a great deal of pleasure.'

It was not until long after she had said 'Yes' – because the moment she had said it and he had thanked her he began telling her about his travels in Turkey and attar of roses – that she wondered whether she had done wrong. After all, she really did not know him. But he was so old and he had been so very kind – not to mention the strawberries . . . And she couldn't have explained the reason why she said 'No', and it was her *last* day in a way, her last day to really enjoy herself in. 'Was I wrong? Was I?' A drop of sunlight fell into her hands and lay there, warm and quivering. 'If I might accompany you as far as the hotel,' he suggested, 'and call for you again at about ten o'clock.' He took out his pocket-book and handed her a card. 'Herr Regierungs-rat . . . ' He had a title! Well, it was *bound* to be all right! So after that the little governess gave herself up to the excitement of being really abroad, to looking out and reading the foreign advertisement signs, to being told about the places they came to – having her attention and enjoyment looked after by the charming old grandfather – until they reached Munich and the Hauptbahnhof. 'Porter! Porter!' He found her a porter, disposed of his own luggage in a few words, guided her through the bewildering crowd out of the station, down the clean white steps into the white road to the hotel. He explained who she was to the manager as though all this had been bound to happen, and then for one moment her little hand lost itself in the big brown suede ones. 'I will call for you at ten o'clock.' He was gone.

'This way, Fräulein,' said a waiter, who had been dodging behind the manager's back, all eyes and ears for the strange couple. She followed him up two flights of stairs into a dark bedroom. He dashed down her dress-basket and pulled up a clattering, dusty blind. Ugh! what an ugly, cold room – what enormous furniture! Fancy spending the day in here! 'Is this the room Frau Arnholdt ordered?' asked the little governess. The waiter had a curious way of staring as if there was something *funny* about her. He pursed up his lips about to whistle, and then changed his mind. '*Gewiss*,' he said. Well, why didn't he go? Why did he stare so? '*Gehen Sie*,' said the little governess, with frigid English simplicity. His little eyes, like currants, nearly popped out of his doughy cheeks. '*Gehen Sie sofort*,' she repeated icily. At the door he turned. 'And the gentleman,' said he, 'shall I show the gentleman upstairs when he comes?'

Over the white streets big white clouds fringed with silver – and sunshine everywhere. Fat, fat coachmen driving fat cabs; funny women with little round hats cleaning the tramway lines; people laughing and pushing against one another; trees on both sides of the streets and everywhere you looked almost, immense fountains; a noise of laughing from the footpaths or the middle of the streets or the open windows. And beside her, more beautifully brushed than ever, with a rolled umbrella in one hand and yellow gloves instead of brown ones, her grandfather who had asked her to spend the day. She wanted to run, she wanted to hang on his arm, she wanted to cry every minute, 'Oh, I am so frightfully happy!' He guided her across the roads, stood still while she 'looked', and his kind eyes beamed on her and he said 'just whatever you wish'. She ate two white sausages and two little rolls of fresh bread at eleven o'clock in the morning and she drank some beer, which he told her wasn't intoxicating, wasn't at all like English beer, out of a glass like a flower vase. And then they took a cab and really she must have seen thousands and thousands of wonderful classical pictures in about a quarter of an hour! 'I shall have to think them over when I am alone.' . . . But when they came out of the picture gallery it was raining. The grandfather unfurled his umbrella and held it over the little governess. They started to walk to the restaurant for lunch, she very close beside him so that he should have some of the umbrella, too. 'It goes easier,' he remarked in a detached way, 'if you take my arm, Fräulein. And besides it is the custom in Germany.' So she took his arm and walked beside him while he pointed out the famous statues, so interested that he quite forgot to put down the umbrella even when the rain was long over.

After lunch they went to a café to hear a gypsy band, but she did not like that at all. Ugh! such horrible men were there with heads like eggs and cuts on their faces, so she turned her chair and cupped her burning cheeks in her hands and watched her old friend instead . . . Then they went to the Englischer Garten.

'I wonder what the time is,' asked the little governess. 'My watch has stopped. I forgot to wind it in the train last night. We've seen such a lot of things that I feel it must be quite late.' 'Late!' He stopped in front of her laughing and shaking his head in a way she had begun to know. 'Then you have not really enjoyed yourself. Late! Why, we have not had any ice-cream yet!' 'Oh, but I have enjoyed myself,' she cried, distressed, 'more than I can possibly say. It has been wonderful! Only Frau Arnholdt is to be at the hotel at six and I ought to be there by five.' 'So you shall. After the ice-cream I shall put you into a cab and you can go there comfortably.' She was happy again. The chocolate ice-cream melted – melted in little sips a long way down. The shadows of the trees danced on the tablecloths, and she sat with her back safely turned to the ornamental clock that pointed to twenty-five minutes to seven. 'Really and truly,' said the little governess earnestly, 'this has been the happiest day of my life. I've never even imagined such a day.' In spite of the ice-cream her grateful baby heart glowed with love for the fairy grandfather.

So they walked out of the garden down a long alley. The day was nearly over. 'You see those big buildings opposite,' said the old man. 'The third storey – that is where I live. I and the old housekeeper who looks after me.' She was very interested. 'Now just before I find a cab for you, will you come and see my little "home" and let me give you a bottle of the attar of roses I told you about in the train? For remembrance?' She would love to. 'I've never seen a bachelor's flat in my life,' laughed the little governess.

The passage was quite dark. 'Ah, I suppose my old woman has gone out to buy me a chicken. One moment.' He opened a door and stood aside for her to pass, a little shy but curious, into a strange room. She did not know quite what to say. It wasn't pretty. In a way it was very ugly – but neat, and, she supposed, comfortable for such an old man. 'Well, what do you think of it?' He knelt down and took from a cupboard a round tray with two pink glasses and a tall pink bottle. 'Two little bedrooms beyond,' he said gaily, 'and a kitchen. It's enough, eh?' 'Oh, quite enough.' 'And if ever you should be in Munich and care to spend a day or two – why there is always a little nest – a wing of a chicken, and a salad, and an old man delighted to be your host once more and many many times, dear little Fräulein!' He took the stopper out of the bottle and poured some wine into the two pink glasses. His hand shook and the wine spilled over the tray. It was very quiet in the room. She said: 'I think I ought to go now.' 'But you will have a tiny glass of wine with me – just one before you go?' said the old man. 'No, really no. I never drink wine. I – I have promised never to touch wine or anything like that.' And though he pleaded and though she felt dreadfully rude, especially when he seemed to take it to heart so, she was quite determined. 'No, *really*, please.' 'Well, will you just sit down on the sofa for five minutes and let me drink your health?' The little governess sat down on the edge of the red velvet couch and he sat down beside her and drank her health at a gulp. 'Have you really been happy today?' asked the old man, turning round, so close beside her that she felt his knee twitching against hers. Before she could answer he held her hands. 'And are you going to give me one little kiss before you go?' he asked, drawing her closer still.

It was a dream! It wasn't true! It wasn't the same old man at all. Ah, how horrible! The little governess stared at him in terror. 'No, no, no!' she stammered, struggling out of his hands. 'One little kiss. A kiss. What is it? Just a kiss, dear little Fräulein. A kiss.' He pushed his face forward, his lips smiling broadly; and how his little blue eyes gleamed behind the spectacles! 'Never – never. How can you!' She sprang up, but he was too quick and he held her against the wall, pressed against her his hard old body and his twitching knee and, though she shook her head from side to side, distracted, kissed her on the mouth. On the mouth! Where not a soul who wasn't a near relation had ever kissed her before . . .

She ran, ran down the street until she found a broad road with tram lines and a policeman standing in the middle like a clockwork doll. 'I want to get a tram to the Hauptbahnhof,' sobbed the little governess. 'Fräulein?' She wrung her hands at him. 'The Hauptbahnhof. There – there's one now,' and while he watched very much surprised, the little girl with her hat on one side, crying without a handkerchief, sprang on to the tram – not seeing the conductor's eyebrows, nor hearing the *hochwohlgebildete Dame* talking her over with a scandalised friend. She rocked herself and cried out loud and said, 'Ah, ah!' pressing her hands to her mouth. 'She has been to the dentist,' shrilled a fat old woman, too stupid to be uncharitable. '*Na, sagen Sie 'mal*, what toothache! The child hasn't one left in her mouth.' While the tram swung and jangled through a world full of old men with twitching knees.

When the little governess reached the hall of the Hotel Grünewald the same waiter who had come into her room in the morning was standing by a table, polishing a tray of glasses. The sight of the little governess seemed to fill him out with some inexplicable important content. He was ready for her question; his answer came pat and suave. 'Yes, Fräulein, the lady has been here. I told her that you had arrived and gone out again immediately with a gentleman. She asked me when you were coming back again – but of course I could not say. And then she went to the manager.' He took up a glass from the table, held it up to the light, looked at it with one eye closed, and started polishing it with a corner of his apron. '. . . ?' 'Pardon, Fräulein? Ach, no, Fräulein. The manager could tell her nothing – nothing.' He shook his head and smiled at the brilliant glass. 'Where is the lady now?' asked the little governess, shuddering so violently that she had to hold her handkerchief up to her mouth. 'How should I know?' cried the waiter, and as he swooped past her to pounce upon a new arrival his heart beat so hard against his ribs that he nearly chuckled aloud. 'That's it! that's it!' he thought. 'That will show her.' And as he swung the new arrival's box on to his shoulders – hoop! – as though he were a giant and the box a feather, he minced over again the little governess's words, '*Gehen Sie. Gehen Sie sofort.* Shall I! Shall I!' he shouted to himself.

Revelations

FROM EIGHT O'CLOCK in the morning until about half-past eleven Monica Tyrell suffered from her nerves, and suffered so terribly that these hours were – agonising, simply. It was not as though she could control them. 'Perhaps if I were ten years younger . . .' she would say. For now that she was thirty-three she had a queer little way of referring to her age on all occasions, of looking at her friends with grave, childish eyes and saying: 'Yes, I remember how twenty years ago . . .' or of drawing Ralph's attention to the girls – real girls – with lovely youthful arms and throats and swift hesitating movements who sat near them in restaurants. 'Perhaps if I were ten years younger . . .'

'Why don't you get Marie to sit outside your door and absolutely forbid anybody to come near your room until you ring your bell?'

'Oh, if it were as simple as that!' She threw her little gloves down and pressed her eyelids with her fingers in the way he knew so well. 'But in the first place I'd be so conscious of Marie sitting there, Marie shaking her finger at Rudd and Mrs Moon, Marie as a kind of cross between a wardress and a nurse for mental cases! And then, there's the post. One can't get over the fact that the post comes, and once it has come, who – who – could wait until eleven for the letters?'

His eyes grew bright; he quickly, lightly clasped her. '*My* letters, darling?'

'Perhaps,' she drawled, softly, and she drew her hand over his reddish hair, smiling too, but thinking: 'Heavens! What a stupid thing to say!'

But this morning she had been awakened by one great slam of the front door. Bang. The flat shook. What was it? She jerked up in bed, clutching the eiderdown; her heart beat. What could it be? Then she heard voices in the passage. Marie knocked, and, as the door opened, with a sharp tearing rip out flew the blind and the curtains, stiffening, flapping, jerking. The tassel of the blind knocked-knocked against the window. 'Eh–h, *voilà*!' cried Marie, setting down the tray and running. '*C'est le vent, madame. C'est un vent insupportable.*'

Up rolled the blind; the window went up with a jerk; a whitey-greyish light filled the room. Monica caught a glimpse of a huge pale sky and a cloud like a torn shirt dragging across before she hid her eyes with her sleeve.

'Marie! the curtains! Quick, the curtains!' Monica fell back into the bed and then, 'Ring-ting-a-ping-ping, ring-ting-a-ping-ping.' It was the telephone. The limit of her suffering was reached; she grew quite calm. 'Go and see, Marie.'

'It is monsieur. To know if madame will lunch at Princes' at one-thirty today.' Yes, it was monsieur himself. Yes, he had asked that the message be given to madame immediately. Instead of replying, Monica put her cup down and asked Marie in a small wondering voice what time it was. It was half-past nine. She lay still and half closed her eyes. 'Tell monsieur I cannot come,' she said gently. But as the door shut, anger – anger suddenly gripped her close, close, violent, half strangling her. How dared he? How dared Ralph do such a thing when he knew how agonising her nerves were in the morning! Hadn't she explained and described and even – though lightly, of course; she couldn't say such a thing directly – given him to understand that this was the one unforgivable thing.

And then to choose this frightful windy morning. Did he think it was just a fad of hers, a little feminine folly to be laughed at and tossed aside? Why, only last night she had said: 'Ah, but you must take me seriously, too.' And he had replied: 'My darling, you'll not believe me, but I know you infinitely better than you know yourself. Every delicate thought and feeling I bow to, I treasure. Yes, laugh! I love the way your lip lifts' – and he had leaned across the table – 'I don't care who sees that I adore all of you. I'd be with you on mountain-top and have all the searchlights of the world play upon us.'

'Heavens!' Monica almost clutched her head. Was it possible he had really said that? How incredible men were! And she had loved him – how could she have loved a man who talked like that. What had she been doing ever since that dinner party months ago, when he had seen her home and asked if he might come and 'see again that slow Arabian smile'? Oh, what nonsense – what utter nonsense – and yet she remembered at the time a strange deep thrill unlike anything she had ever felt before.

'Coal! Coal! Coal! Old iron! Old iron! Old iron!' sounded from below. It was all over. Understand her? He had understood nothing. That ringing her up on a windy morning was immensely significant. Would he understand that? She could almost have laughed. 'You rang me up when the person who understood me simply couldn't have.' It was the end. And when Marie said: 'Monsieur replied he would be in the vestibule in case madame changed her mind,' Monica said: 'No, not verbena, Marie. Carnations. Two handfuls.'

A wild white morning, a tearing, rocking wind. Monica sat down before the mirror. She was pale. The maid combed back her dark hair – combed it all back – and her face was like a mask, with pointed eyelids and dark red lips. As she stared at herself in the blueish shadowy glass she suddenly felt – oh, the strangest, most tremendous excitement filling her slowly, slowly, until she wanted to fling out her arms, to laugh, to scatter everything, to shock Marie, to cry: 'I'm free. I'm free. I'm free as the wind.' And now all this vibrating, trembling, exciting, flying world was hers. It was her kingdom. No, no, she belonged to nobody but Life.

'That will do, Marie,' she stammered. 'My hat, my coat, my bag. And now get me a taxi.' Where was she going? Oh, anywhere. She could not stand this silent flat, noiseless Marie, this ghostly, quiet, feminine interior. She must be out; she must be driving quickly – anywhere, anywhere.

'The taxi is here, madame.' As she pressed open the big outer doors of the flats the wild wind caught her and floated her across the pavement. Where to? She got in, and smiling radiantly at the cross, cold-looking driver, she told him to take her to her hairdresser's. What would she have done without her hairdresser? Whenever Monica had nowhere else to go to or nothing on earth to do she drove there. She might just have her hair waved, and by that time she'd have thought out a plan. The cross, cold driver drove at a tremendous pace, and she let herself be hurled from side to side. She wished he would go faster and faster. Oh, to be free of Princes' at one-thirty, of being the tiny kitten in the swansdown basket, of being the Arabian, and the grave, delighted child and the little wild creature . . . 'Never again,' she cried aloud, clenching her small fist. But the cab had stopped, and the driver was standing holding the door open for her.

The hairdresser's shop was warm and glittering. It smelled of soap and burnt paper and wallflower brilliantine. There was Madame behind the counter, round, fat, white, her head like a powder-puff rolling on a black satin pin-cushion. Monica always had the feeling

that they loved her in this shop and understood her – the real her –
far better than many of her friends did. She was her real self here,
and she and Madame had often talked – quite strangely – together.
Then there was George who did her hair, young, dark, slender
George. She was really fond of him.

But today – how curious! Madame hardly greeted her. Her face
was whiter than ever, but rims of bright red showed round her blue
bead eyes, and even the rings on her pudgy fingers did not flash.
They were cold, dead, like chips of glass. When she called through
the wall-telephone to George there was a note in her voice that had
never been there before. But Monica would not believe this. No, she
refused to. It was just her imagination. She sniffed greedily the
warm, scented air, and passed behind the velvet curtain into the
small cubicle.

Her hat and jacket were off and hanging from the peg, and still
George did not come. This was the first time he had ever not been
there to hold the chair for her, to take her hat and hang up her bag,
dangling it in his fingers as though it were something he'd never
seen before – something fairy. And how quiet the shop was! There
was not a sound even from Madame. Only the wind blew, shaking
the old house; the wind hooted, and the portraits of Ladies of
the Pompadour Period looked down and smiled, cunning and
sly. Monica wished she hadn't come. Oh, what a mistake to have
come! Fatal. Fatal. Where was George? If he didn't appear the next
moment she would go away. She took off the white kimono. She
didn't want to look at herself any more. When she opened a big
pot of cream on the glass shelf her fingers trembled. There was a
tugging feeling at her heart as though her happiness – her marvellous happiness – were trying to get free.

'I'll go. I'll not stay.' She took down her hat. But just at that
moment steps sounded, and, looking in the mirror, she saw George
bowing in the doorway. How queerly he smiled! It was the mirror of
course. She turned round quickly. His lips curled back in a sort of
grin, and – wasn't he unshaved? – he looked almost green in the face.

'Very sorry to have kept you waiting,' he mumbled, sliding, gliding
forward.

Oh, no, she wasn't going to stay. 'I'm afraid,' she began. But he
had lighted the gas and laid the tongs across, and was holding out
the kimono.

'It's a wind,' he said. Monica submitted. She smelled his fresh
young fingers pinning the jacket under her chin. 'Yes, there is a

wind,' said she, sinking back into the chair. And silence fell. George took out the pins in his expert way. Her hair tumbled back, but he didn't hold it as he usually did, as though to feel how fine and soft and heavy it was. He didn't say it 'was in a lovely condition'. He let it fall, and, taking a brush out of a drawer, he coughed faintly, cleared his throat and said dully: 'Yes, it's a pretty strong one, I should say it was.'

She had no reply to make. The brush fell on her hair. Oh, oh, how mournful, how mournful! It fell quick and light, it fell like leaves; and then it fell heavy, tugging like the tugging at her heart. 'That's enough,' she cried, shaking herself free.

'Did I do it too much?' asked George. He crouched over the tongs. 'I'm sorry.' There came the smell of burnt paper – the smell she loved – and he swung the hot tongs round in his hand, staring before him. 'I shouldn't be surprised if it rained.' He took up a piece of her hair, when – she couldn't bear it any longer – she stopped him. She looked at him; she saw herself looking at him in the white kimono like a nun. 'Is there something the matter here? Has something happened?' But George gave a half-shrug and a grimace. 'Oh, no, madame. Just a little occurrence.' And he took up the piece of hair again. But, oh, she wasn't deceived. That was it. Something awful had happened. The silence – really, the silence seemed to come drifting down like flakes of snow. She shivered. It was cold in the little cubicle, all cold and glittering. The nickel taps and jets and sprays looked somehow almost malignant. The wind rattled the window-frame; a piece of iron banged, and the young man went on changing the tongs, crouching over her. Oh, how terrifying Life was, thought Monica. How dreadful. It is the loneliness which is so appalling. We whirl along like leaves, and nobody knows – nobody cares where we fall, in what black river we float away. The tugging feeling seemed to rise into her throat. It ached, ached; she longed to cry. 'That will do,' she whispered. 'Give me the pins.' As he stood beside her, so submissive, so silent, she nearly dropped her arms and sobbed. She couldn't bear any more. Like a wooden man the gay young George still slid, glided, handed her her hat and veil, took the note, and brought back the change. She stuffed it into her bag. Where was she going now?

George took a brush. 'There is a little powder on your coat,' he murmured. He brushed it away. And then suddenly he raised himself and, looking at Monica, gave a strange wave with the brush and said: 'The truth is, madame, since you are an old customer – my little daughter died this morning. A first child' – and then his white face crumpled like paper, and he turned his back on her and began brushing the cotton kimono. 'Oh, oh,' Monica began to cry. She ran out of the shop into the taxi. The driver, looking furious, swung off the seat and slammed the door again. 'Where to?'

'Princes',' she sobbed. And all the way there she saw nothing but a tiny wax doll with a feather of gold hair, lying meek, its tiny hands and feet crossed. And then just before she came to Princes' she saw a flower shop full of white flowers. Oh, what a perfect thought. Lilies-of-the-valley, and white pansies, double white violets and white velvet ribbon . . . From an unknown friend . . . From one who understands . . . For a Little Girl . . . She tapped against the window, but the driver did not hear; and, anyway, they were at Princes' already.

The Escape

IT WAS HIS FAULT, wholly and solely his fault, that they had missed the train. What if the idiotic hotel people had refused to produce the bill? Wasn't that simply because he hadn't impressed upon the waiter at lunch that they must have it by two o'clock? Any other man would have sat there and refused to move until they handed it over. But no! His exquisite belief in human nature had allowed him to get up and expect one of those idiots to bring it to their room . . . And then, when the *voiture* did arrive, while they were still (oh, Heavens!) waiting for change, why hadn't he seen to the arrangement of the boxes so that they could, at least, have started the moment the money had come? Had he expected her to go outside, to stand under the awning in the heat and point with her parasol? Very amusing picture of English domestic life. Even when the driver had been told how fast he had to drive he had paid no attention whatsoever – just smiled. Oh, she groaned, if she'd been a driver she couldn't have stopped smiling herself at the absurd, ridiculous way he was urged to hurry. And she sat back and imitated his voice: '*Allez, vite, vite*' – and begged the driver's pardon for troubling him . . .

And then the station – unforgettable – with the sight of the jaunty little train shuffling away and those hideous children waving from the windows. 'Oh, why am I made to bear these things? Why am I exposed to them? . . . ' The glare, the flies, while they waited, and he and the stationmaster put their heads together over the timetable, trying to find this other train, which, of course, they wouldn't catch. The people who'd gathered round, and the woman who'd held up that baby with that awful, awful head . . . 'Oh, to care as I care – to feel as I feel, and never to be saved anything – never to know for one moment what it was to . . . to . . . '

Her voice had changed. It was shaking now – crying now. She fumbled with her bag, and produced from its little maw a scented handkerchief. She put up her veil and, as though she were doing it for somebody else, pitifully, as though she were saying to somebody else: 'I know, my darling,' she pressed the handkerchief to her eyes.

The little bag, with its shiny, silvery jaws open, lay on her lap. He could see her powder-puff, her rouge stick, a bundle of letters, a phial of tiny black pills like seeds, a broken cigarette, a mirror, white ivory tablets with lists on them that had been heavily scored through. He thought: 'In Egypt she would be buried with those things.'

They had left the last of the houses, those small straggling houses with bits of broken pot flung among the flowerbeds and half-naked hens scratching round the doorsteps. Now they were mounting a long steep road that wound round the hill and over into the next bay. The horses stumbled, pulling hard. Every five minutes, every two minutes the driver trailed the whip across them. His stout back was solid as wood; there were boils on his reddish neck, and he wore a new, a shining new straw hat . . .

There was a little wind, just enough wind to blow to satin the new leaves on the fruit trees, to stroke the fine grass, to turn to silver the smoky olives – just enough wind to start in front of the carriage a whirling, twirling snatch of dust that settled on their clothes like the finest ash. When she took out her powder-puff the powder came flying over them both.

'Oh, the dust,' she breathed, 'the disgusting, revolting dust.' And she put down her veil and lay back as if overcome.

'Why don't you put up your parasol?' he suggested. It was on the front seat, and he leaned forward to hand it to her. At that she suddenly sat upright and blazed again.

'Please leave my parasol alone! I don't want my parasol! And anyone who was not utterly insensitive would know that I'm far, far too exhausted to hold up a parasol. And with a wind like this tugging at it . . . Put it down at once,' she flashed, and then snatched the parasol from him, tossed it into the crumpled hood behind, and subsided, panting.

Another bend of the road, and down the hill there came a troop of little children, shrieking and giggling, little girls with sun-bleached hair, little boys in faded soldiers' caps. In their hands they carried flowers – any kind of flowers – grabbed by the head, and these they offered, running beside the carriage. Lilac, faded lilac, greeny-white snowballs, one arum lily, a handful of hyacinths. They thrust the flowers and their impish faces into the carriage; one even threw into her lap a bunch of marigolds. Poor little mice! He had his hand in his trouser pocket before her. 'For Heaven's sake don't give them anything. Oh, how typical of you! Horrid little monkeys! Now they'll follow us all the way. Don't encourage them; you *would* encourage beggars'; and she hurled the bunch out of the carriage with, 'Well, do it when I'm not there, please.'

He saw the queer shock on the children's faces. They stopped running, lagged behind, and then they began to shout something, and went on shouting until the carriage had rounded yet another bend.

'Oh, how many more are there before the top of the hill is reached? The horses haven't trotted once. Surely it isn't necessary for them to walk the whole way.'

'We shall be there in a minute now,' he said, and took out his cigarette-case. At that she turned round towards him. She clasped her hands and held them against her breast; her dark eyes looked immense, imploring, behind her veil; her nostrils quivered, she bit her lip, and her head shook with a little nervous spasm. But when she spoke, her voice was quite weak and very, very calm.

'I want to ask you something. I want to beg something of you,' she said. 'I've asked you hundreds and hundreds of times before, but you've forgotten. It's such a little thing, but if you knew what it meant to me . . . ' She pressed her hands together. 'But you can't know. No human creature could know and be so cruel.' And then, slowly, deliberately, gazing at him with those huge, sombre eyes: 'I beg and implore you for the last time that when we are driving together you won't smoke. If you could imagine,' she said, 'the anguish I suffer when that smoke comes floating across my face . . . '

'Very well,' he said. 'I won't. I forgot.' And he put the case back.

'Oh, no,' said she, and almost began to láugh, and put the back of her hand across her eyes. 'You couldn't have forgotten. Not that.'

The wind came, blowing stronger. They were at the top of the hill. 'Hoy-yip-yip-yip,' cried the driver. They swung down the road that fell into a small valley, skirted the sea coast at the bottom of it, and then coiled over a gentle ridge on the other side. Now there were houses again, blue-shuttered against the heat, with bright burning gardens, with geranium carpets flung over the pinkish walls. The coastline was dark; on the edge of the sea a white silky fringe just stirred. The carriage swung down the hill, bumped, shook. 'Yi–ip,' shouted the driver. She clutched the sides of the seat, she closed her eyes, and he knew she felt this was happening on purpose; this swinging and bumping, this was all done – and he was responsible for it, somehow – to spite her because she had asked if they couldn't go a little faster. But just as they reached the bottom of the valley there was one tremendous lurch. The carriage nearly overturned, and he saw her eyes blaze at him, and she positively hissed, 'I suppose you are enjoying this?'

They went on. They reached the bottom of the valley. Suddenly she stood up. '*Cocher! Cocher! Arrêtez-vous!*' She turned round and looked into the crumpled hood behind. 'I knew it,' she exclaimed. 'I knew it. I heard it fall, and so did you, at that last bump.'

'What? Where?'

'My parasol. It's gone. The parasol that belonged to my mother. The parasol that I prize more than – more than . . . ' She was simply beside herself. The driver turned round, his gay, broad face smiling.

'I, too, heard something,' said he, simply and gaily. 'But I thought as monsieur and madame said nothing . . . '

'There. You hear that. Then you must have heard it too. So that accounts for the extraordinary smile on your face . . . '

'Look here,' he said, 'it can't be gone. If it fell out it will be there still. Stay where you are. I'll fetch it.'

But she saw through that. Oh, how she saw through it! 'No, thank you.' And she bent her spiteful, smiling eyes upon him, regardless of the driver. 'I'll go myself. I'll walk back and find it, and trust you not to follow. For' – knowing the driver did not understand, she spoke softly, gently – 'if I don't escape from you for a minute I shall go mad.'

She stepped out of the carriage. 'My bag.' He handed it to her.

'Madame prefers . . . '

But the driver had already swung down from his seat, and was seated on the parapet reading a small newspaper. The horses stood with hanging heads. It was still. The man in the carriage stretched himself out, folded his arms. He felt the sun beat on his knees. His head was sunk on his breast. 'Hish, hish,' sounded from the sea. The wind sighed in the valley and was quiet. He felt himself, lying there, a hollow man, a parched, withered man, as it were, of ashes. And the sea sounded, 'Hish hish.'

It was then that he saw the tree, that he was conscious of its presence just inside a garden gate. It was an immense tree with a round, thick silver stem and a great arc of copper leaves that gave back the light and yet were sombre. There was something beyond the tree – a whiteness, a softness, an opaque mass, half-hidden – with delicate pillars. As he looked at the tree he felt his breathing die away and he became part of the silence. It seemed to grow, it seemed to expand in the quivering heat until the great carved leaves hid the sky, and yet it was motionless. Then from within its depths or from beyond there came the sound of a woman's voice. A woman was singing. The warm untroubled voice floated upon the air, and it was all part of the silence as he was part of it. Suddenly, as the voice rose, soft, dreaming, gentle, he knew that it would come floating to him from the hidden leaves and his peace was shattered. What was happening to him? Something stirred in his breast. Something dark, something unbearable and dreadful pushed in his bosom, and like a great weed it floated, rocked . . . it was warm, stifling. He tried to struggle, to tear at it, and at the same moment – all was over. Deep, deep, he sank into the silence, staring at the tree and waiting for the voice that came floating, falling, until he felt himself enfolded.

*   *   *

In the shaking corridor of the train. It was night. The train rushed and roared through the dark. He held on with both hands to the brass rail. The door of their carriage was open.

'Do not disturb yourself, monsieur. He will come in and sit down when he wants to. He likes – he likes – it is his habit . . . *Oui, madame, je suis un peu souffrante . . . Mes nerfs*. Oh, but my husband is never so happy as when he is travelling. He likes roughing it . . . My husband . . . My husband . . . '

The voices murmured, murmured. They were never still. But so great was his heavenly happiness as he stood there he wished he might live for ever.

THE GARDEN-PARTY
and other stories

To
JOHN MIDDLETON MURRY

First published 1922

At the Bay

VERY EARLY MORNING. The sun was not yet risen, and the whole of Crescent Bay was hidden under a white sea-mist. The big bush-covered hills at the back were smothered. You could not see where they ended and the paddocks and bungalows began. The sandy road was gone and the paddocks and bungalows the other side of it; there were no white dunes covered with reddish grass beyond them; there was nothing to mark which was beach and where was the sea. A heavy dew had fallen. The grass was blue. Big drops hung on the bushes and just did not fall; the silvery, fluffy toi-toi was limp on its long stalks, and all the marigolds and the pinks in the bungalow gardens were bowed to the earth with wetness. Drenched were the cold fuchsias, round pearls of dew lay on the flat nasturtium leaves. It looked as though the sea had beaten up softly in the darkness, as though one immense wave had come rippling, rippling – how far? Perhaps if you had waked up in the middle of the night you might have seen a big fish flicking in at the window and gone again . . .

Ah-Aah! sounded the sleepy sea. And from the bush there came the sound of little streams flowing, quickly, lightly, slipping between the smooth stones, gushing into ferny basins and out again; and there was the splashing of big drops on large leaves, and something else – what was it? – a faint stirring and shaking, the snapping of a twig and then such silence that it seemed someone was listening.

Round the corner of Crescent Bay, between the piled-up masses of broken rock, a flock of sheep came pattering. They were huddled together, a small, tossing, woolly mass, and their thin, stick-like legs trotted along quickly as if the cold and the quiet had frightened them. Behind them an old sheep-dog, his soaking paws covered with sand, ran along with his nose to the ground, but carelessly, as if thinking of something else. And then in the rocky gateway the shepherd himself appeared. He was a lean, upright old man, in a frieze coat that was covered with a web of tiny drops, velvet trousers tied under the knee, and a wideawake with a folded blue hand-kerchief round the brim. One hand was crammed into his belt, the other grasped a beautifully smooth yellow stick. And as he walked, taking his time, he kept up a very soft light whistling, an airy, far-away fluting that sounded mournful and tender. The old dog cut an ancient caper or two and then drew up sharp, ashamed of his levity, and walked a few dignified paces by his master's side. The sheep ran forward in little pattering rushes; they began to bleat, and ghostly flocks and herds answered them from under the sea. 'Baa! Baaa!' For a time they seemed to be always on the same piece of ground. There ahead was stretched the sandy road with shallow puddles; the same soaking bushes showed on either side and the same shadowy palings. Then something immense came into view; an enormous shock-haired giant with his arms stretched out. It was the big gum-tree outside Mrs Stubbs' shop, and as they passed by there was a strong whiff of eucalyptus. And now big spots of light gleamed in the mist. The shepherd stopped whistling; he rubbed his red nose and wet beard on his wet sleeve and, screwing up his eyes, glanced in the direction of the sea. The sun was rising. It was marvellous how quickly the mist thinned, sped away, dissolved from the shallow plain, rolled up from the bush and was gone as if in a hurry to escape; big twists and curls jostled and shouldered each other as the silvery beams broadened. The far-away sky – a bright, pure blue – was reflected in the puddles, and the drops, swimming along the tele-graph poles, flashed into points of light. Now the leaping, glittering sea was so bright it made one's eyes ache to look at it. The shepherd drew a pipe, the bowl as small as an acorn, out of his breast pocket, fumbled for a chunk of speckled tobacco, pared off a few shavings and stuffed the bowl. He was a grave, fine-looking old man. As he lit up and the blue smoke wreathed his head, the dog, watching, looked proud of him.

'Baa! Baaa!' The sheep spread out into a fan. They were just clear of the summer colony before the first sleeper turned over and lifted a drowsy head; their cry sounded in the dreams of little children . . . who lifted their arms to drag down, to cuddle the darling little woolly lambs of sleep. Then the first inhabitant appeared; it was the Burnells' cat Florrie, sitting on the gatepost, far too early as usual, looking for their milk-girl. When she saw the old sheep-dog she sprang up quickly, arched her back, drew in her tabby head, and seemed to give a little fastidious shiver. 'Ugh! What a coarse, revol-ting creature!' said Florrie. But the old sheep-dog, not looking up, waggled past, flinging out his legs from side to side. Only one of his ears twitched to prove that he saw, and thought her a silly young female.

The breeze of morning lifted in the bush and the smell of leaves and wet black earth mingled with the sharp smell of the sea. Myriads of birds were singing. A goldfinch flew over the shepherd's head and, perching on the tiptop of a spray, it turned to the sun, ruffling its small breast feathers. And now they had passed the fisherman's hut, passed the charred-looking little whare where Leila the milk-girl lived with her old Gran. The sheep strayed over a yellow swamp and Wag, the sheep-dog, padded after, rounded them up and headed them for the steeper, narrower rocky pass that led out of Crescent Bay and towards Daylight Cove. 'Baa! Baa!' Faint the cry came as they rocked along the fast-drying road. The shepherd put away his pipe, dropping it into his breast-pocket so that the little bowl hung over. And straightway the soft airy whistling began again. Wag ran out along a ledge of rock after something that smelled, and ran back again disgusted. Then pushing, nudging, hurrying, the sheep rounded the bend and the shepherd followed after out of sight.

2

A few moments later the back door of one of the bungalows opened, and a figure in a broad-striped bathing suit flung down the paddock, cleared the stile, rushed through the tussock grass into the hollow, staggered up the sandy hillock, and raced for dear life over the big porous stones, over the cold, wet pebbles, on to the hard sand that gleamed like oil. Splish-Splosh! Splish-Splosh! The water bubbled round his legs as Stanley Burnell waded out exulting. First man in as usual! He'd beaten them all again. And he swooped down to souse his head and neck.

'Hail, brother! All hail, Thou Mighty One!' A velvety bass voice came booming over the water.

Great Scott! Damnation take it! Stanley lifted up to see a dark head bobbing far out and an arm lifted. It was Jonathan Trout – there before him! 'Glorious morning!' sang the voice.

'Yes, very fine!' said Stanley briefly. Why the dickens didn't the fellow stick to his part of the sea? Why should he come barging over to this exact spot? Stanley gave a kick, a lunge and struck out, swimming overarm. But Jonathan was a match for him. Up he came, his black hair sleek on his forehead, his short beard sleek.

'I had an extraordinary dream last night!' he shouted.

What was the matter with the man? This mania for conversation irritated Stanley beyond words. And it was always the same – always some piffle about a dream he'd had, or some cranky idea he'd got hold of, or some rot he'd been reading. Stanley turned over on his back and kicked with his legs till he was a living waterspout. But even then . . . 'I dreamed I was hanging over a terrifically high cliff, shouting to someone below.' You would be! thought Stanley. He could stick no more of it. He stopped splashing. 'Look here, Trout,' he said, 'I'm in rather a hurry this morning.'

'You're *what*?' Jonathan was so surprised – or pretended to be – that he sank under the water, then reappeared again blowing.

'All I mean is,' said Stanley, 'I've no time to – to – to fool about. I want to get this over. I'm in a hurry. I've work to do this morning – see?'

Jonathan was gone before Stanley had finished. 'Pass, friend!' said the bass voice gently, and he slid away through the water with scarcely a ripple . . . But curse the fellow! He'd ruined Stanley's bathe. What an unpractical idiot the man was! Stanley struck out to sea again, and then as quickly swam in again, and away he rushed up the beach. He felt cheated.

Jonathan stayed a little longer in the water. He floated, gently moving his hands like fins, and letting the sea rock his long, skinny body. It was curious, but in spite of everything he was fond of Stanley Burnell. True, he had a fiendish desire to tease him sometimes, to poke fun at him, but at bottom he was sorry for the fellow. There was something pathetic in his determination to make a job of everything. You couldn't help feeling he'd be caught out one day, and then what an almighty cropper he'd come! At that moment an immense wave lifted Jonathan, rode past him, and broke along the beach with a joyful sound. What a beauty! And now there came another. That was the way to live – carelessly, recklessly, spending oneself. He got on to his feet and began to wade towards the shore, pressing his toes into the firm, wrinkled sand. To take things easy, not to fight against the ebb and flow of life, but to give way to it – that was what was needed. It was this tension that was all wrong. To live – to live! And the perfect morning, so fresh and fair, basking in the light, as though laughing at its own beauty, seemed to whisper, 'Why not?'

But now he was out of the water Jonathan turned blue with cold. He ached all over; it was as though someone was wringing the blood out of him. And stalking up the beach, shivering, all his muscles tight, he too felt his bathe was spoilt. He'd stayed in too long.

3

Beryl was alone in the living-room when Stanley appeared, wearing a blue serge suit, a stiff collar and a spotted tie. He looked almost uncannily clean and brushed; he was going to town for the day. Dropping into his chair, he pulled out his watch and put it beside his plate.

'I've just got twenty-five minutes,' he said. 'You might go and see if the porridge is ready, Beryl?'

'Mother's just gone for it,' said Beryl. She sat down at the table and poured out his tea.

'Thanks!' Stanley took a sip. 'Hallo!' he said in an astonished voice, 'you've forgotten the sugar.'

'Oh, sorry!' But even then Beryl didn't help him; she pushed the basin across. What did this mean? As Stanley helped himself his blue eyes widened; they seemed to quiver. He shot a quick glance at his sister-in-law and leaned back.

'Nothing wrong, is there?' he asked carelessly, fingering his collar.

Beryl's head was bent; she turned her plate in her fingers.

'Nothing,' said her light voice. Then she too looked up, and smiled at Stanley. 'Why should there be?'

'O-oh! No reason at all as far as I know. I thought you seemed rather – '

At that moment the door opened and the three little girls appeared, each carrying a porridge plate. They were dressed alike in blue jerseys and knickers; their brown legs were bare, and each had her hair plaited and pinned up in what was called a horse's tail. Behind them came Mrs Fairfield with the tray.

'Carefully, children,' she warned. But they were taking the very greatest care. They loved being allowed to carry things. 'Have you said good morning to your father?'

'Yes, grandma.' They settled themselves on the bench opposite Stanley and Beryl.

'Good morning, Stanley!' Old Mrs Fairfield gave him his plate.

'Morning, mother! How's the boy?'

'Splendid! He only woke up once last night. What a perfect morning!' The old woman paused, her hand on the loaf of bread, to gaze out of the open door into the garden. The sea sounded. Through the wide-open window streamed the sun on to the yellow varnished walls and bare floor. Everything on the table flashed and glittered. In the middle there was an old salad bowl filled with yellow and red nasturtiums. She smiled, and a look of deep content shone in her eyes.

'You might cut me a slice of that bread, mother,' said Stanley. 'I've only twelve and a half minutes before the coach passes. Has anyone given my shoes to the servant girl?'

'Yes, they're ready for you.' Mrs Fairfield was quite unruffled.

'Oh, Kezia! Why are you such a messy child!' cried Beryl despairingly.

'Me, Aunt Beryl?' Kezia stared at her. What had she done now? She had only dug a river down the middle of her porridge, filled it, and was eating the banks away. But she did that every single morning, and no one had said a word up till now.

'Why can't you eat your food properly like Isabel and Lottie?' How unfair grown-ups are!

'But Lottie always makes a floating island, don't you, Lottie?'

'I don't,' said Isabel smartly. 'I just sprinkle mine with sugar and put on the milk and finish it. Only babies play with their food.'

Stanley pushed back his chair and got up.

'Would you get me those shoes, mother? And, Beryl, if you've finished, I wish you'd cut down to the gate and stop the coach. Run in to your mother, Isabel, and ask her where my bowler hat's been put. Wait a minute – have you children been playing with my stick?'

'No, father!'

'But I put it here.' Stanley began to bluster. 'I remember distinctly putting it in this corner. Now, who's had it? There's no time to lose. Look sharp! The stick's got to be found.'

Even Alice, the servant-girl, was drawn into the chase. 'You haven't been using it to poke the kitchen fire with by any chance?'

Stanley dashed into the bedroom where Linda was lying. 'Most extraordinary thing. I can't keep a single possession to myself. They've made away with my stick, now!'

'Stick, dear? What stick?' Linda's vagueness on these occasions could not be real, Stanley decided. Would nobody sympathise with him?

'Coach! Coach, Stanley!' Beryl's voice cried from the gate.

Stanley waved his arm to Linda. 'No time to say goodbye!' he cried. And he meant that as a punishment to her.

He snatched his bowler hat, dashed out of the house, and swung down the garden path. Yes, the coach was there waiting, and Beryl, leaning over the open gate, was laughing up at somebody or other just as if nothing had happened. The heartlessness of women! The way they took it for granted it was your job to slave away for them while they didn't even take the trouble to see that your walking-stick wasn't lost. Kelly trailed his whip across the horses.

'Goodbye, Stanley,' called Beryl, sweetly and gaily. It was easy enough to say goodbye! And there she stood, idle, shading her eyes with her hand. The worst of it was Stanley had to shout goodbye too, for the sake of appearances. Then he saw her turn, give a little skip and run back to the house. She was glad to be rid of him!

Yes, she was thankful. Into the living-room she ran and called 'He's gone!' Linda cried from her room: 'Beryl! Has Stanley gone?' Old Mrs Fairfield appeared, carrying the boy in his little flannel coatee.

'Gone?'

'Gone!'

Oh, the relief, the difference it made to have the man out of the house. Their very voices were changed as they called to one another; they sounded warm and loving and as if they shared a secret. Beryl went over to the table. 'Have another cup of tea, mother. It's still hot.' She wanted, somehow, to celebrate the fact that they could do what they liked now. There was no man to disturb them; the whole perfect day was theirs.

'No, thank you, child,' said old Mrs Fairfield, but the way at that moment she tossed the boy up and said 'a-goos-a-goos-a-ga!' to him meant that she felt the same. The little girls ran into the paddock like chickens let out of a coop.

Even Alice, the servant-girl, washing up the dishes in the kitchen, caught the infection and used the precious tank water in a perfectly reckless fashion.

'Oh, these men!' said she, and she plunged the teapot into the bowl and held it under the water even after it had stopped bubbling, as if it too was a man and drowning was too good for them.

4

'Wait for me, Isa-bel! Kezia, wait for me!'

There was poor little Lottie, left behind again, because she found it so fearfully hard to get over the stile by herself. When she stood on the first step her knees began to wobble; she grasped the post. Then you had to put one leg over. But which leg? She never could decide. And when she did finally put one leg over with a sort of stamp of despair – then the feeling was awful. She was half in the paddock still and half in the tussock grass. She clutched the post desperately and lifted up her voice. 'Wait for me!'

'No, don't you wait for her, Kezia!' said Isabel. 'She's such a little silly. She's always making a fuss. Come on!' And she tugged Kezia's jersey. 'You can use my bucket if you come with me,' she said kindly. 'It's bigger than yours.' But Kezia couldn't leave Lottie all by herself. She ran back to her. By this time Lottie was very red in the face and breathing heavily.

'Here, put your other foot over,' said Kezia.

'Where?'

Lottie looked down at Kezia as if from a mountain height.

'Here where my hand is.' Kezia patted the place.

'Oh, there do you mean!' Lottie gave a deep sigh and put the second foot over.

'Now – sort of turn round and sit down and slide,' said Kezia.

'But there's nothing to sit down on, Kezia,' said Lottie.

She managed it at last, and once it was over she shook herself and began to beam.

'I'm getting better at climbing over stiles, aren't I, Kezia?'

Lottie's was a very hopeful nature.

The pink and the blue sunbonnet followed Isabel's bright red sunbonnet up that sliding, slipping hill. At the top they paused to decide where to go and to have a good stare at who was there already. Seen from behind, standing against the skyline, gesticulating largely with their spades, they looked like minute puzzled explorers.

The whole family of Samuel Josephs was there already with their lady-help, who sat on a camp-stool and kept order with a whistle that she wore tied round her neck, and a small cane with which she directed operations. The Samuel Josephs never played by themselves or managed their own game. If they did, it ended in the boys pouring water down the girls' necks or the girls trying to put little black crabs into the boys' pockets. So Mrs S. J. and the poor lady-help drew up what she called a 'brogramme' every morning to keep them 'abused and out of bischief'. It was all competitions or races or round games. Everything began with a piercing blast of the lady-help's whistle and ended with another. There were even prizes – large, rather dirty paper parcels which the lady-help with a sour little smile drew out of a bulging string kit. The Samuel Josephs fought fearfully for the prizes and cheated and pinched one another's arms – they were all expert pinchers. The only time the Burnell children ever played with them Kezia had got a prize, and when she undid three bits of paper she found a very small rusty button-hook. She couldn't understand why they made such a fuss . . .

But they never played with the Samuel Josephs now or even went to their parties. The Samuel Josephs were always giving children's parties at the Bay and there was always the same food. A big wash-handbasin of very brown fruit-salad, buns cut into four and a wash-hand jug full of something the lady-help called 'Limonadear'. And you went away in the evening with half the frill torn off your frock or something spilled all down the front of your open-work pinafore, leaving the Samuel Josephs leaping like savages on their lawn. No! They were too awful.

On the other side of the beach, close down to the water, two little boys, their knickers rolled up, twinkled like spiders. One was digging, the other pattered in and out of the water, filling a small bucket. They were the Trout boys, Pip and Rags. But Pip was so busy digging and Rags was so busy helping that they didn't see their little cousins until they were quite close.

'Look!' said Pip. 'Look what I've discovered.' And he showed them an old wet, squashed-looking boot. The three little girls stared.

'Whatever are you going to do with it?' asked Kezia.

'Keep it, of course!' Pip was very scornful. 'It's a find – see?'

Yes, Kezia saw that. All the same . . .

'There's lots of things buried in the sand,' explained Pip. 'They get chucked up from wrecks. Treasure. Why – you might find – '

'But why does Rags have to keep on pouring water in?' asked Lottie.

'Oh, that's to moisten it,' said Pip, 'to make the work a bit easier. Keep it up, Rags.'

And good little Rags ran up and down, pouring in the water that turned brown like cocoa.

'Here, shall I show you what I found yesterday?' said Pip mysteriously, and he stuck his spade into the sand. 'Promise not to tell.'

They promised.

'Say, cross my heart straight dinkum.'

The little girls said it.

Pip took something out of his pocket, rubbed it a long time on the front of his jersey, then breathed on it and rubbed it again.

'Now turn round!' he ordered.

They turned round.

'All look the same way! Keep still! Now!'

And his hand opened; he held up to the light something that flashed, that winked, that was a most lovely green.

'It's a nemeral,' said Pip solemnly.

'Is it really, Pip?' Even Isabel was impressed.

The lovely green thing seemed to dance in Pip's fingers. Aunt Beryl had a nemeral in a ring, but it was a very small one. This one was as big as a star and far more beautiful.

5

As the morning lengthened whole parties appeared over the sand-hills and came down on the beach to bathe. It was understood that at eleven o'clock the women and children of the summer colony had the sea to themselves. First the women undressed, pulled on their bathing dresses and covered their heads in hideous caps like sponge bags; then the children were unbuttoned. The beach was strewn with little heaps of clothes and shoes; the big summer hats, with stones on them to keep them from blowing away, looked like immense shells. It was strange that even the sea seemed to sound differently when all those leaping, laughing figures ran into the waves. Old Mrs Fairfield, in a lilac cotton dress and a black hat tied under the chin, gathered her little brood and got them ready. The little Trout boys whipped their shirts over their heads, and away the five sped, while their grandma sat with one hand in her knitting-bag ready to draw out the ball of wool when she was satisfied they were safely in.

The firm compact little girls were not half so brave as the tender, delicate-looking little boys. Pip and Rags, shivering, crouching down, slapping the water, never hesitated. But Isabel, who could swim twelve strokes, and Kezia, who could nearly swim eight, only followed on the strict understanding they were not to be splashed. As for Lottie, she didn't follow at all. She liked to be left to go in her own way, please. And that way was to sit down at the edge of the water, her legs straight, her knees pressed together, and to make vague motions with her arms as if she expected to be wafted out to sea. But when a bigger wave than usual, an old whiskery one, came lolloping along in her direction, she scrambled to her feet with a face of horror and flew up the beach again.

'Here, mother, keep those for me, will you?'

Two rings and a thin gold chain were dropped into Mrs Fairfield's lap.

'Yes, dear. But aren't you going to bathe here?'

'No-o,' Beryl drawled. She sounded vague. 'I'm undressing farther along. I'm going to bathe with Mrs Harry Kember.'

'Very well.' But Mrs Fairfield's lips set. She disapproved of Mrs Harry Kember. Beryl knew it.

Poor old mother, she smiled, as she skimmed over the stones. Poor old mother! Old! Oh, what joy, what bliss it was to be young . . .

'You look very pleased,' said Mrs Harry Kember. She sat hunched up on the stones, her arms round her knees, smoking.

'It's such a lovely day,' said Beryl, smiling down at her.

'Oh my dear!' Mrs Harry Kember's voice sounded as though she knew better than that. But then her voice always sounded as though she knew something better about you than you did yourself. She was a long, strange-looking woman with narrow hands and feet. Her face, too, was long and narrow and exhausted-looking; even her fair curled fringe looked burnt out and withered. She was the only woman at the Bay who smoked, and she smoked incessantly, keeping the cigarette between her lips while she talked, and only taking it out when the ash was so long you could not understand why it did not fall. When she was not playing bridge – she played bridge every day of her life – she spent her time lying in the full glare of the sun. She could stand any amount of it; she never had enough. All the same, it did not seem to warm her. Parched, withered, cold, she lay stretched on the stones like a piece of tossed-up driftwood. The women at the Bay thought she was very, very fast. Her lack of vanity, her slang, the way she treated men as though she was one of them, and the fact that she didn't care twopence about her house and called the servant Gladys 'Glad-eyes', was disgraceful. Standing on the veranda steps Mrs Kember would call in her indifferent, tired voice, 'I say, Glad-eyes, you might heave me a handkerchief if I've got one, will you?' And Glad-eyes, a red bow in her hair instead of a cap, and white shoes, came running with an impudent smile. It was an absolute scandal! True, she had no children, and her husband . . . Here the voices were always raised; they became fervent. How can he have married her? How can he, how can he? It must have been money, of course, but even then!

Mrs Kember's husband was at least ten years younger than she was, and so incredibly handsome that he looked like a mask or a most perfect illustration in an American novel rather than a man. Black hair, dark blue eyes, red lips, a slow sleepy smile, a fine tennis player, a perfect dancer, and with it all a mystery. Harry Kember was like a man walking in his sleep. Men couldn't stand him, they couldn't get a word out of the chap; he ignored his wife just as she ignored him. How did he live? Of course there were stories, but such stories! They simply couldn't be told. The women he'd been seen with, the places he'd been seen in . . . but nothing was ever certain, nothing definite.

Some of the women at the Bay privately thought he'd commit a murder one day. Yes, even while they talked to Mrs Kember and took in the awful concoction she was wearing, they saw her, stretched as she lay on the beach; but cold, bloody, and still with a cigarette stuck in the corner of her mouth.

Mrs Kember rose, yawned, unsnapped her belt buckle, and tugged at the tape of her blouse. And Beryl stepped out of her skirt and shed her jersey, and stood up in her short white petticoat, and her camisole with ribbon bows on the shoulders.

'Mercy on us,' said Mrs Harry Kember, 'what a little beauty you are!'

'Don't!' said Beryl softly; but, drawing off one stocking and then the other, she felt a little beauty.

'My dear – why not?' said Mrs Harry Kember, stamping on her own petticoat. Really – her underclothes! A pair of blue cotton knickers and a linen bodice that reminded one somehow of a pillow-case . . . 'And you don't wear stays, do you?' She touched Beryl's waist, and Beryl sprang away with a small affected cry. Then 'Never!' she said firmly.

'Lucky little creature,' sighed Mrs Kember, unfastening her own.

Beryl turned her back and began the complicated movements of someone who is trying to take off her clothes and to pull on her bathing-dress all at one and the same time.

'Oh, my dear – don't mind me,' said Mrs Harry Kember. 'Why be shy? I shan't eat you. I shan't be shocked like those other ninnies.' And she gave her strange neighing laugh and grimaced at the other women.

But Beryl was shy. She never undressed in front of anybody. Was that silly? Mrs Harry Kember made her feel it was silly, even something to be ashamed of. Why be shy indeed! She glanced quickly at her friend standing so boldly in her torn chemise and lighting a fresh cigarette; and a quick, bold, evil feeling started up in her breast. Laughing recklessly, she drew on the limp, sandy-feeling bathing-dress that was not quite dry and fastened the twisted buttons.

'That's better,' said Mrs Harry Kember. They began to go down the beach together. 'Really, it's a sin for you to wear clothes, my dear. Somebody's got to tell you some day.'

The water was quite warm. It was that marvellous transparent blue, flecked with silver, but the sand at the bottom looked gold; when you kicked with your toes there rose a little puff of gold-dust. Now the waves just reached her breast. Beryl stood, her arms outstretched, gazing out, and as each wave came she gave the slightest little jump, so that it seemed it was the wave which lifted her so gently.

'I believe in pretty girls having a good time,' said Mrs Harry Kember. 'Why not? Don't you make a mistake, my dear. Enjoy yourself.' And suddenly she turned turtle, disappeared, and swam away quickly, quickly, like a rat. Then she flicked round and began swimming back. She was going to say something else. Beryl felt that she was being poisoned by this cold woman, but she longed to hear. But oh, how strange, how horrible! As Mrs Harry Kember came up close she looked, in her black waterproof bathing-cap, with her sleepy face lifted above the water, just her chin touching, like a horrible caricature of her husband.

6

In a steamer chair, under a manuka tree that grew in the middle of the front grass patch, Linda Burnell dreamed the morning away. She did nothing. She looked up at the dark, close, dry leaves of the manuka, at the chinks of blue between, and now and again a tiny yellowish flower dropped on her. Pretty – yes, if you held one of those flowers on the palm of your hand and looked at it closely, it was an exquisite small thing. Each pale yellow petal shone as if each was the careful work of a loving hand. The tiny tongue in the centre gave it the shape of a bell. And when you turned it over the outside was a deep bronze colour. But as soon as they flowered, they fell and were scattered. You brushed them off your frock as you talked; the horrid little things got caught in one's hair. Why, then, flower at all? Who takes the trouble – or the joy – to make all these things that are wasted, wasted . . . It was uncanny.

On the grass beside her, lying between two pillows, was the boy. Sound asleep he lay, his head turned away from his mother. His fine dark hair looked more like a shadow than like real hair, but his ear was a bright, deep coral. Linda clasped her hands above her head and crossed her feet. It was very pleasant to know that all these bungalows were empty, that everybody was down on the beach, out of sight, out of hearing. She had the garden to herself; she was alone.

Dazzling white the picotees shone; the golden-eyed marigold glittered; the nasturtiums wreathed the veranda poles in green and gold flame. If only one had time to look at these flowers long enough, time to get over the sense of novelty and strangeness, time to know them! But as soon as one paused to part the petals, to

discover the under-side of the leaf, along came Life and one was
swept away. And, lying in her cane chair, Linda felt so light; she felt
like a leaf. Along came Life like a wind and she was seized and
shaken; she had to go. Oh dear, would it always be so? Was there
no escape?

. . . Now she sat on the veranda of their Tasmanian home, leaning
against her father's knee. And he promised, 'As soon as you and I are
old enough, Linny, we'll cut off somewhere, we'll escape. Two boys
together. I have a fancy I'd like to sail up a river in China.' Linda saw
that river, very wide, covered with little rafts and boats. She saw the
yellow hats of the boatmen and she heard their high, thin voices as
they called . . .

'Yes, papa.'

But just then a very broad young man with bright ginger hair
walked slowly past their house, and slowly, solemnly even, uncovered. Linda's father pulled her ear teasingly, in the way he had.

'Linny's beau,' he whispered.

'Oh, papa, fancy being married to Stanley Burnell!'

Well, she was married to him. And what was more she loved him.
Not the Stanley whom every one saw, not the everyday one; but a
timid, sensitive, innocent Stanley who knelt down every night to say
his prayers, and who longed to be good. Stanley was simple. If he
believed in people – as he believed in her, for instance – it was with
his whole heart. He could not be disloyal; he could not tell a lie. And
how terribly he suffered if he thought anyone – she – was not being
dead straight, dead sincere with him! 'This is too subtle for me!' He
flung out the words, but his open, quivering, distraught look was like
the look of a trapped beast.

But the trouble was – here Linda felt almost inclined to laugh,
though Heaven knows it was no laughing matter – she saw her
Stanley so seldom. There were glimpses, moments, breathing spaces
of calm, but all the rest of the time it was like living in a house that
couldn't be cured of the habit of catching on fire, on a ship that got
wrecked every day. And it was always Stanley who was in the thick of
the danger. Her whole time was spent in rescuing him, and restoring
him, and calming him down, and listening to his story. And what was
left of her time was spent in the dread of having children.

Linda frowned; she sat up quickly in her steamer chair and clasped
her ankles. Yes, that was her real grudge against life; that was what
she could not understand. That was the question she asked and
asked, and listened in vain for the answer. It was all very well to say it

was the common lot of women to bear children. It wasn't true. She, for one, could prove that wrong. She was broken, made weak, her courage was gone, through child-bearing. And what made it doubly hard to bear was, she did not love her children. It was useless pretending. Even if she had had the strength she never would have nursed and played with the little girls. No, it was as though a cold breath had chilled her through and through on each of those awful journeys; she had no warmth left to give them. As to the boy – well, thank Heaven, mother had taken him; he was mother's, or Beryl's, or anybody's who wanted him. She had hardly held him in her arms. She was so indifferent about him that as he lay there . . . Linda glanced down.

The boy had turned over. He lay facing her, and he was no longer asleep. His dark-blue, baby eyes were open; he looked as though he was peeping at his mother. And suddenly his face dimpled; it broke into a wide, toothless smile, a perfect beam, no less.

'I'm here!' that happy smile seemed to say. 'Why don't you like me?'

There was something so quaint, so unexpected about that smile that Linda smiled herself. But she checked herself and said to the boy coldly, 'I don't like babies.'

'Don't like babies?' The boy couldn't believe her. 'Don't like me? ' He waved his arms foolishly at his mother.

Linda dropped off her chair on to the grass.

'Why do you keep on smiling?' she said severely. 'If you knew what I was thinking about, you wouldn't.'

But he only squeezed up his eyes, slyly, and rolled his head on the pillow. He didn't believe a word she said.

'We know all about that!' smiled the boy.

Linda was so astonished at the confidence of this little creature . . . Ah no, be sincere. That was not what she felt; it was something far different, it was something so new, so . . . The tears danced in her eyes; she breathed in a small whisper to the boy, 'Hallo, my funny!'

But by now the boy had forgotten his mother. He was serious again. Something pink, something soft waved in front of him. He made a grab at it and it immediately disappeared. But when he lay back, another, like the first, appeared. This time he determined to catch it. He made a tremendous effort and rolled right over.

7

The tide was out; the beach was deserted; lazily flopped the warm sea. The sun beat down, beat down hot and fiery on the fine sand, baking the grey and blue and black and white-veined pebbles. It sucked up the little drop of water that lay in the hollow of the curved shells; it bleached the pink convolvulus that threaded through and through the sand-hills. Nothing seemed to move but the small sand-hoppers. Pit-pit-pit! They were never still.

Over there on the weed-hung rocks that looked at low tide like shaggy beasts come down to the water to drink, the sunlight seemed to spin like a silver coin dropped into each of the small rock pools. They danced, they quivered, and minute ripples laved the porous shores. Looking down, bending over, each pool was like a lake with pink and blue houses clustered on the shores; and oh! the vast mountainous country behind those houses – the ravines, the passes, the dangerous creeks and fearful tracks that led to the water's edge. Underneath waved the sea-forest – pink thread-like trees, velvet anemones, and orange berry-spotted weeds. Now a stone on the bottom moved, rocked, and there was a glimpse of a black feeler; now a thread-like creature wavered by and was lost. Something was happening to the pink, waving trees; they were changing to a cold moonlight blue. And now there sounded the faintest 'plop'. Who made that sound? What was going on down there? And how strong, how damp the seaweed smelt in the hot sun . . .

The green blinds were drawn in the bungalows of the summer colony. Over the verandas, prone on the paddock, flung over the fences, there were exhausted-looking bathing-dresses and rough striped towels. Each back window seemed to have a pair of sand-shoes on the sill and some lumps of rock or a bucket or a collection of pawa shells. The bush quivered in a haze of heat; the sandy road was empty except for the Trouts' dog Snooker, who lay stretched in the very middle of it. His blue eye was turned up, his legs stuck out stiffly, and he gave an occasional desperate-sounding puff, as much as to say he had decided to make an end of it and was only waiting for some kind cart to come along.

'What are you looking at, my grandma? Why do you keep stopping and sort of staring at the wall?'

Kezia and her grandmother were taking their siesta together. The little girl, wearing only her short drawers and her under-bodice, her arms and legs bare, lay on one of the puffed-up pillows of her grandma's bed, and the old woman, in a white ruffled dressing-gown, sat in a rocker at the window, with a long piece of pink knitting in her lap. This room that they shared, like the other rooms of the bungalow, was of light varnished wood and the floor was bare. The furniture was of the shabbiest, the simplest. The dressing-table, for instance, was a packing-case in a sprigged muslin petticoat, and the mirror above was very strange; it was as though a little piece of forked lightning was imprisoned in it. On the table there stood a jar of sea-pinks, pressed so tightly together they looked more like a velvet pincushion, and a special shell which Kezia had given her grandma for a pin-tray, and another even more special which she had thought would make a very nice place for a watch to curl up in.

'Tell me, grandma,' said Kezia.

The old woman sighed, whipped the wool twice round her thumb, and drew the bone needle through. She was casting on.

'I was thinking of your Uncle William, darling,' she said quietly.

'My Australian Uncle William?' said Kezia. She had another.

'Yes, of course.'

'The one I never saw?'

'That was the one.'

'Well, what happened to him?' Kezia knew perfectly well, but she wanted to be told again.

'He went to the mines, and he got a sunstroke there and died,' said old Mrs Fairfield.

Kezia blinked and considered the picture again . . . a little man fallen over like a tin soldier by the side of a big black hole.

'Does it make you sad to think about him, grandma?' She hated her grandma to be sad.

It was the old woman's turn to consider. Did it make her sad? To look back, back. To stare down the years, as Kezia had seen her doing. To look after them as a woman does, long after they were out of sight. Did it make her sad? No, life was like that.

'No, Kezia.'

'But why?' asked Kezia. She lifted one bare arm and began to draw things in the air. 'Why did Uncle William have to die? He wasn't old.'

Mrs Fairfield began counting the stitches in threes. 'It just happened,' she said in an absorbed voice.

'Does everybody have to die?' asked Kezia.

'Everybody!'

'Me?' Kezia sounded fearfully incredulous.

'Some day, my darling.'

'But, grandma.' Kezia waved her left leg and waggled the toes. They felt sandy. 'What if I just won't?'

The old woman sighed again and drew a long thread from the ball.

'We're not asked, Kezia,' she said sadly. 'It happens to all of us sooner or later.'

Kezia lay still thinking this over. She didn't want to die. It meant she would have to leave here, leave everywhere, for ever, leave – leave her grandma. She rolled over quickly.

'Grandma,' she said in a startled voice.

'What, my pet!'

'You're not to die.' Kezia was very decided.

'Ah, Kezia' – her grandma looked up and smiled and shook her head – 'don't let's talk about it.'

'But you're not to. You couldn't leave me. You couldn't not be there.' This was awful. 'Promise me you won't ever do it, grandma,' pleaded Kezia.

The old woman went on knitting.

'Promise me! Say never!'

But still her grandma was silent.

Kezia rolled off her bed; she couldn't bear it any longer, and lightly she leapt on to her grandma's knees, clasped her hands round the old woman's throat and began kissing her, under the chin, behind the ear, and blowing down her neck.

'Say never . . . say never . . . say never – ' She gasped between the kisses. And then she began, very softly and lightly, to tickle her grandma.

'Kezia!' The old woman dropped her knitting. She swung back in the rocker. She began to tickle Kezia. 'Say never, say never, say never,' gurgled Kezia, while they lay there laughing in each other's arms. 'Come, that's enough, my squirrel! That's enough, my wild pony!' said old Mrs Fairfield, setting her cap straight. 'Pick up my knitting.'

Both of them had forgotten what the 'never' was about.

8

The sun was still full on the garden when the back door of the Burnells' shut with a bang, and a very gay figure walked down the path to the gate. It was Alice, the servant-girl, dressed for her afternoon out. She wore a white cotton dress with such large red spots on it and so many that they made you shudder, white shoes and a leghorn turned up under the brim with poppies. Of course she wore gloves, white ones, stained at the fastenings with iron-mould, and in one hand she carried a very dashed-looking sunshade which she referred to as her 'perishall'.

Beryl, sitting in the window, fanning her freshly-washed hair, thought she had never seen such a guy. If Alice had only blacked her face with a piece of cork before she started out, the picture would have been complete. And where did a girl like that go to in a place like this? The heart-shaped Fijian fan beat scornfully at that lovely bright mane. She supposed Alice had picked up some horrible common larrikin and they'd go off into the bush together. Pity to have made herself so conspicuous; they'd have hard work to hide with Alice in that rig-out.

But no, Beryl was unfair. Alice was going to tea with Mrs Stubbs, who'd sent her an 'invite' by the little boy who called for orders. She had taken ever such a liking to Mrs Stubbs ever since the first time she went to the shop to get something for her mosquitoes.

'Dear heart!' Mrs Stubbs had clapped her hand to her side. 'I never seen anyone so eaten. You might have been attacked by canningbals.'

Alice did wish there'd been a bit of life on the road though. Made her feel so queer, having nobody behind her. Made her feel all weak in the spine. She couldn't believe that someone wasn't watching her. And yet it was silly to turn round; it gave you away. She pulled up her gloves, hummed to herself and said to the distant gum-tree, 'Shan't be long now.' But that was hardly company.

Mrs Stubbs's shop was perched on a little hillock just off the road. It had two big windows for eyes, a broad veranda for a hat, and the sign on the roof, scrawled MRS. STUBBS'S, was like a little card stuck rakishly in the hat crown.

On the veranda there hung a long string of bathing-dresses, clinging together as though they'd just been rescued from the sea rather than waiting to go in, and beside them there hung a cluster of sandshoes so extraordinarily mixed that to get at one pair you had to tear apart and forcibly separate at least fifty. Even then it was the rarest thing to find the left that belonged to the right. So many people had lost patience and gone off with one shoe that fitted and one that was a little too big . . . Mrs Stubbs prided herself on keeping something of everything. The two windows, arranged in the form of precarious pyramids, were crammed so tight, piled so high, that it seemed only a conjurer could prevent them from toppling over. In the left-hand corner of one window, glued to the pane by four gelatine lozenges, there was – and there had been from time immemorial – a notice.

LOST! HANSOME GOLE BROOCH
SOLID GOLD
ON OR NEAR BEACH
REWARD OFFERED

Alice pressed open the door. The bell jangled, the red serge curtains parted, and Mrs Stubbs appeared. With her broad smile and the long bacon knife in her hand, she looked like a friendly brigand. Alice was welcomed so warmly that she found it quite difficult to keep up her 'manners'. They consisted of persistent little coughs and hems, pulls at her gloves, tweaks at her skirt, and a curious difficulty in seeing what was set before her or understanding what was said.

Tea was laid on the parlour table – ham, sardines, a whole pound of butter, and such a large johnny cake that it looked like an advertisement for somebody's baking-powder. But the Primus stove roared so loudly that it was useless to try to talk above it. Alice sat down on the edge of a basket-chair while Mrs Stubbs pumped the stove still higher. Suddenly Mrs Stubbs whipped the cushion off a chair and disclosed a large brown-paper parcel.

'I've just had some new photers taken, my dear,' she shouted cheerfully to Alice. 'Tell me what you think of them.'

In a very dainty, refined way Alice wet her finger and put the tissue back from the first one. Life! How many there were! There were three dozzing at least. And she held it up to the light.

Mrs Stubbs sat in an armchair, leaning very much to one side. There was a look of mild astonishment on her large face, and well there might be. For though the armchair stood on a carpet, to the left of it, miraculously skirting the carpet-border, there was a dashing water-fall. On her right stood a Grecian pillar with a giant fern-tree on either side of it, and in the background towered a gaunt mountain, pale with snow.

'It is a nice style, isn't it?' shouted Mrs Stubbs; and Alice had just screamed 'Sweetly' when the roaring of the Primus stove died down, fizzled out, ceased, and she said 'Pretty' in a silence that was frightening.

'Draw up your chair, my dear,' said Mrs Stubbs, beginning to pour out. 'Yes,' she said thoughtfully, as she handed the tea, 'but I don't care about the size. I'm having an enlargemint. All very well for Christmas cards, but I never was the one for small photers myself.

You get no comfort out of them. To say the truth, I find them dis'eartening.'

Alice quite saw what she meant.

'Size,' said Mrs Stubbs. 'Give me size. That was what my poor dear husband was always saying. He couldn't stand anything small. Gave him the creeps. And, strange as it may seem, my dear' – here Mrs Stubbs creaked and seemed to expand herself at the memory – 'it was dropsy that carried him off at the larst. Many's the time they drawn one and a half pints from 'im at the 'ospital . . . It seemed like a judgmint.'

Alice burned to know exactly what it was that was drawn from him. She ventured, 'I suppose it was water.'

But Mrs Stubbs fixed Alice with her eyes and replied meaningly, 'It was liquid, my dear.'

Liquid! Alice jumped away from the word like a cat and came back to it, nosing and wary.

'That's 'im!' said Mrs Stubbs, and she pointed dramatically to the life-size head and shoulders of a burly man with a dead white rose in the buttonhole of his coat that made you think of a curl of cold mutting fat. Just below, in silver letters on a red cardboard ground, were the words, 'Be not afraid, it is I.'

'It's ever such a fine face,' said Alice faintly.

The pale-blue bow on the top of Mrs Stubbs's fair frizzy hair quivered. She arched her plump neck. What a neck she had! It was bright pink where it began and then it changed to warm apricot, and that faded to the colour of a brown egg and then to a deep creamy.

'All the same, my dear,' she said surprisingly, 'freedom's best!' Her soft, fat chuckle sounded like a purr. 'Freedom's best,' said Mrs Stubbs again.

Freedom! Alice gave a loud, silly little titter. She felt awkward. Her mind flew back to her own kitching. Ever so queer! She wanted to be back in it again.

9

A strange company assembled in the Burnells' washhouse after tea. Round the table there sat a bull, a rooster, a donkey that kept forgetting it was a donkey, a sheep and a bee. The washhouse was the perfect place for such a meeting because they could make as much noise as they liked, and nobody ever interrupted. It was a small tin shed standing apart from the bungalow. Against the wall there was a deep trough and in the corner a copper with a basket of clothes-pegs on top of it. The little window, spun over with cobwebs, had a piece of candle and a mouse-trap on the dusty sill. There were clotheslines criss-crossed overhead and, hanging from a peg on the wall, a very big, a huge, rusty horseshoe. The table was in the middle with a form at either side.

'You can't be a bee, Kezia. A bee's not an animal. It's a ninseck.'

'Oh, but I do want to be a bee frightfully,' wailed Kezia . . . A tiny bee, all yellow-furry, with striped legs. She drew her legs up under her and leaned over the table. She felt she was a bee.

'A ninseck must be an animal,' she said stoutly. 'It makes a noise. It's not like a fish.'

'I'm a bull, I'm a bull!' cried Pip. And he gave such a tremendous bellow- -how did he make that noise? – that Lottie looked quite alarmed.

'I'll be a sheep,' said little Rags. 'A whole lot of sheep went past this morning.'

'How do you know?'

'Dad heard them. Baa!' He sounded like the little lamb that trots behind and seems to wait to be carried.

'Cock-a-doodle-do!' shrilled Isabel. With her red cheeks and bright eyes she looked like a rooster.

'What'll I be?' Lottie asked everybody, and she sat there smiling, waiting for them to decide for her. It had to be an easy one.

'Be a donkey, Lottie.' It was Kezia's suggestion. 'Hee-haw! You can't forget that.'

'Hee-haw!' said Lottie solemnly. 'When do I have to say it?'

'I'll explain, I'll explain,' said the bull. It was he who had the cards. He waved them round his head. 'All be quiet! All listen!' And he waited for them. 'Look here, Lottie.' He turned up a card. 'It's got two spots on it – see? Now, if you put that card in the middle and somebody else has one with two spots as well, you say "Hee-haw", and the card's yours.'

'Mine?' Lottie was round-eyed. 'To keep?'

'No, silly. Just for the game, see? Just while we're playing.' The bull was very cross with her.

'Oh, Lottie, you are a little silly,' said the proud rooster.

Lottie looked at both of them. Then she hung her head; her lip quivered. 'I don't want to play,' she whispered. The others glanced at one another like conspirators. All of them knew what that meant. She would go away and be discovered somewhere standing with her pinny thrown over her head, in a corner, or against a wall, or even behind a chair.

'Yes, you do, Lottie. It's quite easy,' said Kezia.

And Isabel, repentant, said exactly like a grown-up, 'Watch me, Lottie, and you'll soon learn.'

'Cheer up, Lot,' said Pip. 'There, I know what I'll do. I'll give you the first one. It's mine, really, but I'll give it to you. Here you are.' And he slammed the card down in front of Lottie.

Lottie revived at that. But now she was in another difficulty. 'I haven't got a hanky,' she said; 'I want one badly, too.'

'Here, Lottie, you can use mine.' Rags dipped into his sailor blouse and brought up a very wet-looking one, knotted together. 'Be very careful,' he warned her. 'Only use that corner. Don't undo it. I've got a little starfish inside I'm going to try and tame.'

'Oh, come on, you girls,' said the bull. 'And mind – you're not to look at your cards. You've got to keep your hands under the table till I say "Go".'

Smack went the cards round the table. They tried with all their might to see, but Pip was too quick for them. It was very exciting, sitting there in the washhouse; it was all they could do not to burst into a little chorus of animals before Pip had finished dealing.

'Now, Lottie, you begin.'

Timidly Lottie stretched out a hand, took the top card off her pack, had a good look at it – it was plain she was counting the spots – and put it down.

'No, Lottie, you can't do that. You mustn't look first. You must turn it the other way over.'

'But then everybody will see it the same time as me,' said Lottie.

The game proceeded. Mooe-ooo-er! The bull was terrible. He charged over the table and seemed to eat the cards up.

Bss-ss! said the bee.

Cock-a-doodle-do! Isabel stood up in her excitement and moved her elbows like wings.

Baa! Little Rags put down the King of Diamonds and Lottie put down the one they called the King of Spain. She had hardly any cards left.

'Why don't you call out, Lottie?'

'I've forgotten what I am,' said the donkey woefully.

'Well, change! Be a dog instead! Bow-wow!'

'Oh yes. That's much easier.' Lottie smiled again. But when she and Kezia both had a one Kezia waited on purpose. The others made signs to Lottie and pointed. Lottie turned very red; she looked bewildered, and at last she said, 'Hee-haw! Ke-zia.'

'Ss! Wait a minute!' They were in the very thick of it when the bull stopped them, holding up his hand. 'What's that? What's that noise?'

'What noise? What do you mean?' asked the rooster.

'Ss! Shut up! Listen!' They were mouse-still. 'I thought I heard a – a sort of knocking,' said the bull.

'What was it like?' asked the sheep faintly.

No answer.

The bee gave a shudder. 'Whatever did we shut the door for?' she said softly. Oh, why, why had they shut the door?

While they were playing, the day had faded; the gorgeous sunset had blazed and died. And now the quick dark came racing over the sea, over the sand-hills, up the paddock. You were frightened to look in the corners of the washhouse, and yet you had to look with all your might. And somewhere, far away, grandma was lighting a lamp. The blinds were being pulled down; the kitchen fire leapt in the tins on the mantelpiece.

'It would be awful now,' said the bull, 'if a spider was to fall from the ceiling on to the table, wouldn't it?'

'Spiders don't fall from ceilings.'

'Yes, they do. Our Min told us she'd seen a spider as big as a saucer, with long hairs on it like a gooseberry.'

Quickly all the little heads were jerked up; all the little bodies drew together, pressed together.

'Why doesn't somebody come and call us?' cried the rooster.

Oh, those grown-ups, laughing and snug, sitting in the lamp-light, drinking out of cups! They'd forgotten about them. No, not really forgotten. That was what their smile meant. They had decided to leave them there all by themselves.

Suddenly Lottie gave such a piercing scream that all of them jumped off the forms, all of them screamed too. 'A face – a face looking!' shrieked Lottie.

It was true, it was real. Pressed against the window was a pale face, black eyes, a black beard.

'Grandma! Mother! Somebody!'

But they had not got to the door, tumbling over one another, before it opened for Uncle Jonathan. He had come to take the little boys home.

10

He had meant to be there before, but in the front garden he had come upon Linda walking up and down the grass, stopping to pick off a dead pink or give a top-heavy carnation something to lean against, or to take a deep breath of something, and then walking on again, with her little air of remoteness. Over her white frock she wore a yellow, pink-fringed shawl from the Chinaman's shop.

'Hallo, Jonathan!' called Linda. And Jonathan whipped off his shabby panama, pressed it against his breast, dropped on one knee, and kissed Linda's hand.

'Greeting, my Fair One! Greeting, my Celestial Peach Blossom!' boomed the bass voice gently. 'Where are the other noble dames?'

'Beryl's out playing bridge and mother's giving the boy his bath . . . Have you come to borrow something?'

The Trouts were for ever running out of things and sending across to the Burnells' at the last moment.

But Jonathan only answered, 'A little love, a little kindness'; and he walked by his sister-in-law's side.

Linda dropped into Beryl's hammock under the manuka-tree, and Jonathan stretched himself on the grass beside her, pulled a long stalk and began chewing it. They knew each other well. The voices of children cried from the other gardens. A fisherman's light cart shook along the sandy road, and from far away they heard a dog barking; it was muffled as though the dog had its head in a sack. If you listened you could just hear the soft swish of the sea at full tide sweeping the pebbles. The sun was sinking.

'And so you go back to the office on Monday, do you, Jonathan?' asked Linda.

'On Monday the cage door opens and clangs to upon the victim for another eleven months and a week,' answered Jonathan.

Linda swung a little. 'It must be awful,' she said slowly.

'Would ye have me laugh, my fair sister? Would ye have me weep?'

Linda was so accustomed to Jonathan's way of talking that she paid no attention to it.

'I suppose,' she said vaguely, 'one gets used to it. One gets used to anything.'

'Does one? Hum!' The 'Hum' was so deep it seemed to boom from underneath the ground. 'I wonder how it's done,' brooded Jonathan; 'I've never managed it.'

Looking at him as he lay there, Linda thought again how attractive he was. It was strange to think that he was only an ordinary clerk, that Stanley earned twice as much money as he. What was the matter with Jonathan? He had no ambition; she supposed that was it. And yet one felt he was gifted, exceptional. He was passionately fond of music; every spare penny he had went on books. He was always full of new ideas, schemes, plans. But nothing came of it all. The new fire blazed in Jonathan; you almost heard it roaring softly as he explained, described and dilated on the new thing; but a moment later it had fallen in and there was nothing but ashes, and Jonathan went about with a look like hunger in his black eyes. At these times he exaggerated his absurd manner of speaking, and he sang in church – he was the leader of the choir – with such fearful dramatic intensity that the meanest hymn put on an unholy splendour.

'It seems to me just as imbecile, just as infernal, to have to go to the office on Monday,' said Jonathan, 'as it always has done and always will do. To spend all the best years of one's life sitting on a stool from nine to five, scratching in somebody's ledger! It's a queer use to make of one's . . . one and only life, isn't it? Or do I fondly dream?' He rolled over on the grass and looked up at Linda. 'Tell me, what is the difference between my life and that of an ordinary prisoner. The only difference I can see is that I put myself in jail and nobody's ever going to let me out. That's a more intolerable situation than the other. For if I'd been – pushed in, against my will – kicking, even – once the door was locked, or at any rate in five years or so, I might have accepted the fact and begun to take an interest in the flight of flies or counting the warder's steps along the passage with particular attention to variations of tread and so on. But as it is, I'm like an insect that's flown into a room of its own accord. I dash against the walls, dash against the windows, flop against the ceiling, do everything on God's earth, in fact, except fly out again. And all the while I'm thinking, like that moth, or that butterfly, or whatever it is, "The shortness of life! The shortness of life!" I've only one night or one day, and there's this vast dangerous garden, waiting out there, undiscovered, unexplored.'

'But, if you feel like that, why – ' began Linda quickly.

'Ah!' cried Jonathan. And that 'ah!' was somehow almost exultant. 'There you have me. Why? Why indeed? There's the maddening, mysterious question. Why don't I fly out again? There's the window or the door or whatever it was I came in by. It's not hopelessly shut –

is it? Why don't I find it and be off? Answer me that, little sister.' But
he gave her no time to answer.

'I'm exactly like that insect again. For some reason' – Jonathan
paused between the words – 'it's not allowed, it's forbidden, it's
against the insect law, to stop banging and flopping and crawling
up the pane even for an instant. Why don't I leave the office? Why
don't I seriously consider, this moment, for instance, what it is that
prevents me leaving? It's not as though I'm tremendously tied. I've
two boys to provide for, but, after all, they're boys. I could cut off to
sea, or get a job up-country, or – ' Suddenly he smiled at Linda and
said in a changed voice, as if he were confiding a secret, 'Weak . . .
weak. No stamina. No anchor. No guiding principle, let us call it.'
But then the dark velvety voice rolled out:

> Would ye hear the story
> How it unfolds itself . . .

and they were silent.

The sun had set. In the western sky there were great masses
of crushed-up rose-coloured clouds. Broad beams of light shone
through the clouds and beyond them as if they would cover the
whole sky. Overhead the blue faded; it turned a pale gold, and the
bush outlined against it gleamed dark and brilliant like metal. Sometimes when those beams of light show in the sky they are very awful.
They remind you that up there sits Jehovah, the jealous God, the
Almighty, Whose eye is upon you, ever watchful, never weary. You
remember that at His coming the whole earth will shake into one
ruined graveyard; the cold, bright angels will drive you this way and
that, and there will be no time to explain what could be explained so
simply . . . But tonight it seemed to Linda there was something
infinitely joyful and loving in those silver beams. And now no sound
came from the sea. It breathed softly as if it would draw that tender,
joyful beauty into its own bosom.

'It's all wrong, it's all wrong,' came the shadowy voice of Jonathan.
'It's not the scene, it's not the setting for . . . three stools, three desks,
three inkpots and a wire blind.'

Linda knew that he would never change, but she said, 'Is it too late,
even now?'

'I'm old – I'm old,' intoned Jonathan. He bent towards her, he
passed his hand over his head. 'Look!' His black hair was speckled all
over with silver, like the breast plumage of a black fowl.

Linda was surprised. She had no idea that he was grey. And yet, as he stood up beside her and sighed and stretched, she saw him, for the first time, not resolute, not gallant, not careless, but touched already with age. He looked very tall on the darkening grass, and the thought crossed her mind, 'He is like a weed.'

Jonathan stooped again and kissed her fingers.

'Heaven reward thy sweet patience, lady mine,' he murmured. 'I must go seek those heirs to my fame and fortune . . . ' He was gone.

11

Light shone in the windows of the bungalow. Two square patches of gold fell upon the pinks and the peaked marigolds. Florrie, the cat, came out on to the veranda, and sat on the top step, her white paws close together, her tail curled round. She looked content, as though she had been waiting for this moment all day.

'Thank goodness, it's getting late,' said Florrie. 'Thank goodness, the long day is over.' Her greengage eyes opened.

Presently there sounded the rumble of the coach, the crack of Kelly's whip. It came near enough for one to hear the voices of the men from town, talking loudly together. It stopped at the Burnells' gate.

Stanley was half-way up the path before he saw Linda. 'Is that you, darling?'

'Yes, Stanley.'

He leapt across the flower-bed and seized her in his arms. She was enfolded in that familiar, eager, strong embrace.

'Forgive me, darling, forgive me,' stammered Stanley, and he put his hand under her chin and lifted her face to him.

'Forgive you?' smiled Linda. 'But whatever for?'

'Good God! You can't have forgotten,' cried Stanley Burnell. 'I've thought of nothing else all day. I've had the hell of a day. I made up my mind to dash out and telegraph, and then I thought the wire mightn't reach you before I did. I've been in tortures, Linda.'

'But, Stanley,' said Linda, 'what must I forgive you for?'

'Linda!' – Stanley was very hurt – 'didn't you realise – you must have realised – I went away without saying goodbye to you this morning? I can't imagine how I can have done such a thing. My confounded temper, of course. But – well' – and he sighed and took her in his arms again – 'I've suffered for it enough today.'

'What's that you've got in your hand?' asked Linda. 'New gloves? Let me see.'

'Oh, just a cheap pair of wash-leather ones,' said Stanley humbly.

'I noticed Bell was wearing some in the coach this morning, so, as I was passing the shop, I dashed in and got myself a pair. What are you smiling at? You don't think it was wrong of me, do you?'

'On the con-trary, darling,' said Linda, 'I think it was most sensible.'

She pulled one of the large, pale gloves on her own fingers and looked at her hand, turning it this way and that. She was still smiling.

Stanley wanted to say, 'I was thinking of you the whole time I bought them.' It was true, but for some reason he couldn't say it. 'Let's go in,' said he.

12

Why does one feel so different at night? Why is it so exciting to be awake when everybody else is asleep? Late – it is very late! And yet every moment you feel more and more wakeful, as though you were slowly, almost with every breath, waking up into a new, wonderful, far more thrilling and exciting world than the daylight one. And what is this queer sensation that you're a conspirator? Lightly, stealthily you move about your room. You take something off the dressing-table and put it down again without a sound. And everything, even the bedpost, knows you, responds, shares your secret . . .

You're not very fond of your room by day. You never think about it. You're in and out, the door opens and slams, the cupboard creaks. You sit down on the side of your bed, change your shoes and dash out again. A dive down to the glass, two pins in your hair, powder your nose and off again. But now – it's suddenly dear to you. It's a darling little funny room. It's yours. Oh, what a joy it is to own things! Mine – my own!

'My very own for ever?'

'Yes.' Their lips met.

No, of course, that had nothing to do with it. That was all nonsense and rubbish. But, in spite of herself, Beryl saw so plainly two people standing in the middle of her room. Her arms were round his neck; he held her. And now he whispered, 'My beauty, my little beauty!' She jumped off her bed, ran over to the window and kneeled on the window-seat, with her elbows on the sill. But the beautiful night, the garden, every bush, every leaf, even the white palings, even the stars, were conspirators too. So bright was the moon that the flowers were bright as by day; the shadow of the nasturtiums, exquisite lily-like leaves and wide-open flowers, lay across the silvery veranda. The manuka-tree, bent by the southerly winds, was like a bird on one leg stretching out a wing.

But when Beryl looked at the bush, it seemed to her the bush was sad.

'We are dumb trees, reaching up in the night, imploring we know not what,' said the sorrowful bush.

It is true when you are by yourself and you think about life, it is always sad. All that excitement and so on has a way of suddenly leaving you, and it's as though, in the silence, somebody called your name, and you heard your name for the first time. 'Beryl!'

'Yes, I'm here. I'm Beryl. Who wants me?'

'Beryl!'

'Let me come.'

It is lonely living by oneself. Of course, there are relations, friends, heaps of them; but that's not what she means. She wants someone who will find the Beryl they none of them know, who will expect her to be that Beryl always. She wants a lover.

'Take me away from all these other people, my love. Let us go far away. Let us live our life, all new, all ours, from the very beginning. Let us make our fire. Let us sit down to eat together. Let us have long talks at night.'

And the thought was almost, 'Save me, my love. Save me!'

. . . 'Oh, go on! Don't be a prude, my dear. You enjoy yourself while you're young. That's my advice.' And a high rush of silly laughter joined Mrs Harry Kember's loud, indifferent neigh.

You see, it's so frightfully difficult when you've nobody. You're so at the mercy of things. You can't just be rude. And you've always this horror of seeming inexperienced and stuffy like the other ninnies at the Bay. And – and it's fascinating to know you've power over people. Yes, that is fascinating . . .

Oh why, oh why doesn't 'he' come soon?

If I go on living here, thought Beryl, anything may happen to me.

'But how do you know he is coming at all?' mocked a small voice within her.

But Beryl dismissed it. She couldn't be left. Other people, perhaps, but not she. It wasn't possible to think that Beryl Fairfield never married, that lovely fascinating girl.

'Do you remember Beryl Fairfield?'

'Remember her! As if I could forget her! It was one summer at the Bay that I saw her. She was standing on the beach in a blue' – no, pink – 'muslin frock, holding on a big cream' – no, black – 'straw hat. But it's years ago now.'

'She's as lovely as ever, more so if anything.'

Beryl smiled, bit her lip, and gazed over the garden. As she gazed, she saw somebody, a man, leave the road, step along the paddock beside their palings as if he was coming straight towards her. Her heart beat. Who was it? Who could it be? It couldn't be a burglar, certainly not a burglar, for he was smoking and he strolled lightly. Beryl's heart leapt; it seemed to turn right over, and then to stop. She recognized him.

'Good evening, Miss Beryl,' said the voice softly.

'Good evening.'

'Won't you come for a little walk?' it drawled.

Come for a walk – at that time of night! 'I couldn't. Everybody's in bed. Everybody's asleep.'

'Oh,' said the voice lightly, and a whiff of sweet smoke reached her. 'What does everybody matter? Do come! It's such a fine night. There's not a soul about.'

Beryl shook her head. But already something stirred in her, something reared its head.

The voice said, 'Frightened?' It mocked, 'Poor little girl!'

'Not in the least,' said she. As she spoke that weak thing within her seemed to uncoil, to grow suddenly tremendously strong; she longed to go!

And just as if this was quite understood by the other, the voice said, gently and softly, but finally, 'Come along!'

Beryl stepped over her low window, crossed the veranda, ran down the grass to the gate. He was there before her.

'That's right,' breathed the voice, and it teased, 'You're not frightened, are you? You're not frightened?'

She was; now she was here she was terrified, and it seemed to her everything was different. The moonlight stared and glittered; the shadows were like bars of iron. Her hand was taken.

'Not in the least,' she said lightly. 'Why should I be?'

Her hand was pulled gently, tugged. She held back.

'No, I'm not coming any farther,' said Beryl.

'Oh, rot!' Harry Kember didn't believe her. 'Come along! We'll just go as far as that fuchsia bush. Come along!'

The fuchsia bush was tall. It fell over the fence in a shower. There was a little pit of darkness beneath.

'No, really, I don't want to,' said Beryl.

For a moment Harry Kember didn't answer. Then he came close to her, turned to her, smiled and said quickly, 'Don't be silly! Don't be silly!'

His smile was something she'd never seen before. Was he drunk? That bright, blind, terrifying smile froze her with horror. What was she doing? How had she got here? the stern garden asked her as the gate pushed open, and quick as a cat Harry Kember came through and snatched her to him.

'Cold little devil! Cold little devil!' said the hateful voice.

But Beryl was strong. She slipped, ducked, wrenched free.

'You are vile, vile,' said she.

'Then why in God's name did you come?' stammered Harry Kember.

Nobody answered him.

A cloud, small, serene, floated across the moon. In that moment of darkness the sea sounded deep, troubled. Then the cloud sailed away, and the sound of the sea was a vague murmur, as though it waked out of a dark dream. All was still.

The Garden-Party

AND AFTER ALL the weather was ideal. They could not have had a more perfect day for a garden-party if they had ordered it. Windless, warm, the sky without a cloud. Only the blue was veiled with a haze of light gold, as it is sometimes in early summer. The gardener had been up since dawn, mowing the lawns and sweeping them, until the grass and the dark flat rosettes where the daisy plants had been seemed to shine. As for the roses, you could not help feeling they understood that roses are the only flowers that impress people at garden-parties; the only flowers that everybody is certain of knowing. Hundreds, yes, literally hundreds, had come out in a single night; the green bushes bowed down as though they had been visited by archangels.

Breakfast was not yet over before the men came to put up the marquee.

'Where do you want the marquee put, mother?'

'My dear child, it's no use asking me. I'm determined to leave everything to you children this year. Forget I am your mother. Treat me as an honoured guest.'

But Meg could not possibly go and supervise the men. She had washed her hair before breakfast, and she sat drinking her coffee in a green turban, with a dark wet curl stamped on each cheek. Jose, the butterfly, always came down in a silk petticoat and a kimono jacket.

'You'll have to go, Laura; you're the artistic one.'

Away Laura flew, still holding her piece of bread-and-butter. It's so delicious to have an excuse for eating out of doors, and besides, she loved having to arrange things; she always felt she could do it so much better than anybody else.

Four men in their shirt-sleeves stood grouped together on the garden path. They carried staves covered with rolls of canvas, and they had big tool-bags slung on their backs. They looked impressive. Laura wished now that she had not got the bread-and-butter, but there was nowhere to put it, and she couldn't possibly throw it away.

She blushed and tried to look severe and even a little bit short-sighted as she came up to them.

'Good morning,' she said, copying her mother's voice. But that sounded so fearfully affected that she was ashamed, and stammered like a little girl, 'Oh – er – have you come – is it about the marquee?'

'That's right, miss,' said the tallest of the men, a lanky, freckled fellow, and he shifted his tool-bag, knocked back his straw hat and smiled down at her. 'That's about it.'

His smile was so easy, so friendly that Laura recovered. What nice eyes he had, small, but such a dark blue! And now she looked at the others, they were smiling too. 'Cheer up, we won't bite,' their smile seemed to say. How very nice workmen were! And what a beautiful morning! She mustn't mention the morning; she must be business-like. The marquee.

'Well, what about the lily-lawn? Would that do?'

And she pointed to the lily-lawn with the hand that didn't hold the bread-and-butter. They turned, they stared in the direction. A little fat chap thrust out his under-lip, and the tall fellow frowned.

'I don't fancy it,' said he. 'Not conspicuous enough. You see, with a thing like a marquee,' and he turned to Laura in his easy way, 'you want to put it somewhere where it'll give you a bang slap in the eye, if you follow me.'

Laura's upbringing made her wonder for a moment whether it was quite respectful of a workman to talk to her of bangs slap in the eye. But she did quite follow him.

'A corner of the tennis-court,' she suggested. 'But the band's going to be in one corner.'

'H'm, going to have a band, are you?' said another of the work-men. He was pale. He had a haggard look as his dark eyes scanned the tennis-court. What was he thinking?

'Only a very small band,' said Laura gently. Perhaps he wouldn't mind so much if the band was quite small. But the tall fellow inter-rupted.

'Look here, miss, that's the place. Against those trees. Over there. That'll do fine.'

Against the karakas. Then the karaka-trees would be hidden. And they were so lovely, with their broad, gleaming leaves, and their clusters of yellow fruit. They were like trees you imagined growing on a desert island, proud, solitary, lifting their leaves and fruits to the sun in a kind of silent splendour. Must they be hidden by a marquee?

They must. Already the men had shouldered their staves and were making for the place. Only the tall fellow was left. He bent down, pinched a sprig of lavender, put his thumb and forefinger to his nose and snuffed up the smell. When Laura saw that gesture she forgot all about the karakas in her wonder at him caring for things like that – caring for the smell of lavender. How many men that she knew would have done such a thing? Oh, how extraordinarily nice work-men were, she thought. Why couldn't she have workmen for her friends rather than the silly boys she danced with and who came to Sunday night supper? She would get on much better with men like these.

It's all the fault, she decided, as the tall fellow drew something on the back of an envelope, something that was to be looped up or left to hang, of these absurd class distinctions. Well, for her part, she didn't feel them. Not a bit, not an atom . . . And now there came the chock-chock of wooden hammers. Someone whistled, someone sang out, 'Are you right there, matey?' 'Matey!' The friendliness of it, the – the – Just to prove how happy she was, just to show the tall fellow how at home she felt, and how she despised stupid conventions, Laura took a big bite of her bread-and-butter as she stared at the little drawing. She felt just like a work-girl.

'Laura, Laura, where are you? Telephone, Laura!' a voice cried from the house.

'Coming!' Away she skimmed, over the lawn, up the path, up the steps, across the veranda, and into the porch. In the hall her father and Laurie were brushing their hats ready to go to the office.

'I say, Laura,' said Laurie very fast, 'you might just give a squiz at my coat before this afternoon. See if it wants pressing.'

'I will,' said she. Suddenly she couldn't stop herself. She ran at Laurie and gave him a small, quick squeeze. 'Oh, I do love parties, don't you?' gasped Laura.

'Ra-ther,' said Laurie's warm, boyish voice, and he squeezed his sister too, and gave her a gentle push. 'Dash off to the telephone, old girl.'

The telephone. 'Yes, yes; oh yes. Kitty? Good morning, dear. Come to lunch? Do, dear. Delighted of course. It will only be a very scratch meal – just the sandwich crusts and broken meringue-shells and what's left over. Yes, isn't it a perfect morning? Your white? Oh, I certainly should. One moment – hold the line. Mother's calling.' And Laura sat back. 'What, mother? Can't hear.'

Mrs Sheridan's voice floated down the stairs. 'Tell her to wear that sweet hat she had on last Sunday.'

'Mother says you're to wear that sweet hat you had on last Sunday. Good. One o'clock. Bye-bye.'

Laura put back the receiver, flung her arms over her head, took a deep breath, stretched and let them fall. 'Huh,' she sighed, and the moment after the sigh she sat up quickly. She was still, listening. All the doors in the house seemed to be open. The house was alive with soft, quick steps and running voices. The green baize door that led to the kitchen regions swung open and shut with a muffled thud. And now there came a long, chuckling absurd sound. It was the heavy piano being moved on its stiff castors. But the air! If you stopped to notice, was the air always like this? Little faint winds were playing chase, in at the tops of the windows, out at the doors. And there were two tiny spots of sun, one on the inkpot, one on a silver photograph frame, playing too. Darling little spots. Especially the one on the inkpot lid. It was quite warm. A warm little silver star. She could have kissed it.

The front door bell pealed, and there sounded the rustle of Sadie's print skirt on the stairs. A man's voice murmured; Sadie answered, careless, 'I'm sure I don't know. Wait. I'll ask Mrs Sheridan.'

'What is it, Sadie?' Laura came into the hall.

'It's the florist, Miss Laura.'

It was, indeed. There, just inside the door, stood a wide, shallow tray full of pots of pink lilies. No other kind. Nothing but lilies – canna lilies, big pink flowers, wide open, radiant, almost frighteningly alive on bright crimson stems.

'O-oh, Sadie!' said Laura, and the sound was like a little moan. She crouched down as if to warm herself at that blaze of lilies; she felt they were in her fingers, on her lips, growing in her breast.

'It's some mistake,' she said faintly. 'Nobody ever ordered so many. Sadie, go and find mother.'

But at that moment Mrs Sheridan joined them.

'It's quite right,' she said calmly. 'Yes, I ordered them. Aren't they lovely?' She pressed Laura's arm. 'I was passing the shop yesterday, and I saw them in the window. And I suddenly thought for once in my life I shall have enough canna lilies. The garden-party will be a good excuse.'

'But I thought you said you didn't mean to interfere,' said Laura. Sadie had gone. The florist's man was still outside at his van. She put her arm round her mother's neck and gently, very gently, she bit her mother's ear.

'My darling child, you wouldn't like a logical mother, would you? Don't do that. Here's the man.'

He carried more lilies still, another whole tray.

'Bank them up, just inside the door, on both sides of the porch, please,' said Mrs Sheridan. 'Don't you agree, Laura?'

'Oh, I *do*, mother.'

In the drawing-room Meg, Jose and good little Hans had at last succeeded in moving the piano.

'Now, if we put this chesterfield against the wall and move everything out of the room except the chairs, don't you think?'

'Quite.'

'Hans, move these tables into the smoking-room, and bring a sweeper to take these marks off the carpet and – one moment, Hans – ' Jose loved giving orders to the servants, and they loved obeying her. She always made them feel they were taking part in some drama. 'Tell mother and Miss Laura to come here at once.'

'Very good, Miss Jose.'

She turned to Meg. 'I want to hear what the piano sounds like, just in case I'm asked to sing this afternoon. Let's try over "This life is Weary".'

Pom! Ta-ta-ta *Tee*-ta! The piano burst out so passionately that Jose's face changed. She clasped her hands. She looked mournfully and enigmatically at her mother and Laura as they came in.

> This Life is *Wee*-ary,
> A Tear – a Sigh.
> A Love that *Chan*-ges,
> This Life is *Wee*-ary,
> A Tear – a Sigh.
> A Love that *Chan*-ges,
> And then . . . Goodbye!

But at the word 'Goodbye,' and although the piano sounded more desperate than ever, her face broke into a brilliant, dreadfully unsympathetic smile.

'Aren't I in good voice, mummy?' she beamed.

> This Life is *Wee*-ary,
> Hope comes to Die.
> A Dream – a *Wa*-kening.

But now Sadie interrupted them. 'What is it, Sadie?'

'If you please, m'm, cook says have you got the flags for the sandwiches?'

'The flags for the sandwiches, Sadie?' echoed Mrs Sheridan dreamily. And the children knew by her face that she hadn't got them. 'Let me see.' And she said to Sadie firmly, 'Tell cook I'll let her have them in ten minutes.'

Sadie went.

'Now, Laura,' said her mother quickly, 'come with me into the smoking-room. I've got the names somewhere on the back of an envelope. You'll have to write them out for me. Meg, go upstairs this minute and take that wet thing off your head. Jose, run and finish dressing this instant. Do you hear me, children, or shall I have to tell your father when he comes home tonight? And – and, Jose, pacify cook if you do go into the kitchen, will you? I'm terrified of her this morning.'

The envelope was found at last behind the dining-room clock, though how it had got there Mrs Sheridan could not imagine.

'One of you children must have stolen it out of my bag, because I remember vividly – cream cheese and lemon-curd. Have you done that?'

'Yes.'

'Egg and – ' Mrs Sheridan held the envelope away from her. 'It looks like mice. It can't be mice, can it?'

'Olive, pet,' said Laura, looking over her shoulder.

'Yes, of course, olive. What a horrible combination it sounds. Egg and olive.'

They were finished at last, and Laura took them off to the kitchen. She found Jose there pacifying the cook, who did not look at all terrifying.

'I have never seen such exquisite sandwiches,' said Jose's rapturous voice. 'How many kinds did you say there were, cook? Fifteen?'

'Fifteen, Miss Jose.'

'Well, cook, I congratulate you.'

Cook swept up crusts with the long sandwich knife, and smiled broadly.

'Godber's has come,' announced Sadie, issuing out of the pantry. She had seen the man pass the window.

That meant the cream puffs had come. Godber's were famous for their cream puffs. Nobody ever thought of making them at home.

'Bring them in and put them on the table, my girl,' ordered cook.

Sadie brought them in and went back to the door. Of course Laura and Jose were far too grown-up to really care about such things. All the same, they couldn't help agreeing that the puffs looked very attractive. Very. Cook began arranging them, shaking off the extra icing sugar.

'Don't they carry one back to all one's parties?' said Laura.

'I suppose they do,' said practical Jose, who never liked to be carried back. 'They look beautifully light and feathery, I must say.'

'Have one each, my dears,' said cook in her comfortable voice. 'Yer ma won't know.'

Oh, impossible. Fancy cream puffs so soon after breakfast. The very idea made one shudder. All the same, two minutes later Jose and Laura were licking their fingers with that absorbed inward look that only comes from whipped cream.

'Let's go into the garden, out by the back way,' suggested Laura. 'I want to see how the men are getting on with the marquee. They're such awfully nice men.'

But the back door was blocked by cook, Sadie, Godber's man and Hans.

Something had happened.

'Tuk-tuk-tuk,' clucked cook like an agitated hen. Sadie had her hand clapped to her cheek as though she had toothache. Hans's face was screwed up in the effort to understand. Only Godber's man seemed to be enjoying himself; it was his story.

'What's the matter? What's happened?'

'There's been a horrible accident,' said cook. 'A man killed.'

'A man killed! Where? How? When?'

But Godber's man wasn't going to have his story snatched from under his very nose.

'Know those little cottages just below here, miss?' Know them? Of course, she knew them. 'Well, there's a young chap living there, name of Scott, a carter. His horse shied at a traction-engine, corner of Hawke Street this morning, and he was thrown out on the back of his head. Killed.'

'Dead!' Laura stared at Godber's man.

'Dead when they picked him up,' said Godber's man with relish. 'They were taking the body home as I come up here.' And he said to the cook, 'He's left a wife and five little ones.'

'Jose, come here.' Laura caught hold of her sister's sleeve and dragged her through the kitchen to the other side of the green baize door. There she paused and leaned against it. 'Jose!' she said, horrified, 'however are we going to stop everything?'

'Stop everything, Laura!' cried Jose in astonishment. 'What do you mean?'

'Stop the garden-party, of course.' Why did Jose pretend?

But Jose was still more amazed. 'Stop the garden-party? My dear Laura, don't be so absurd. Of course we can't do anything of the kind. Nobody expects us to. Don't be so extravagant.'

'But we can't possibly have a garden-party with a man dead just outside the front gate.'

That really was extravagant, for the little cottages were in a lane to themselves at the very bottom of a steep rise that led up to the house. A broad road ran between. True, they were far too near. They were the greatest possible eyesore, and they had no right to be in that neighbourhood at all. They were little mean dwellings painted a chocolate brown. In the garden patches there was nothing but cabbage stalks, sick hens and tomato cans. The very smoke coming out of their chimneys was poverty-stricken. Little rags and shreds of smoke, so unlike the great silvery plumes that uncurled from the Sheridans' chimneys. Washerwomen lived in the lane and sweeps and a cobbler, and a man whose house-front was studded all over with minute bird-cages. Children swarmed. When the Sheridans were little they were forbidden to set foot there because of the revolting language and of what they might catch. But since they were grown up, Laura and Laurie on their prowls sometimes walked through. It was disgusting and sordid. They came out with a shudder. But still one must go everywhere; one must see everything. So through they went.

'And just think of what the band would sound like to that poor woman,' said Laura.

'Oh, Laura!' Jose began to be seriously annoyed. 'If you're going to stop a band playing every time someone has an accident, you'll lead a very strenuous life. I'm every bit as sorry about it as you. I feel just as sympathetic.' Her eyes hardened. She looked at her sister just as she used to when they were little and fighting together. 'You won't bring a drunken workman back to life by being sentimental,' she said softly.

'Drunk! Who said he was drunk?' Laura turned furiously on Jose. She said, just as they had used to say on those occasions, 'I'm going straight up to tell mother.'

'Do, dear,' cooed Jose.

'Mother, can I come into your room?' Laura turned the big glass door-knob.

'Of course, child. Why, what's the matter? What's given you such a colour?' And Mrs Sheridan turned round from her dressing-table. She was trying on a new hat.

'Mother, a man's been killed,' began Laura.

'Not in the garden?' interrupted her mother.

'No, no!'

'Oh, what a fright you gave me!' Mrs Sheridan sighed with relief, and took off the big hat and held it on her knees.

'But listen, mother,' said Laura. Breathless, half-choking, she told the dreadful story. 'Of course, we can't have our party, can we?' she pleaded. 'The band and everybody arriving. They'd hear us, mother; they're nearly neighbours!'

To Laura's astonishment her mother behaved just like Jose; it was harder to bear because she seemed amused. She refused to take Laura seriously.

'But, my dear child, use your common sense. It's only by accident we've heard of it. If someone had died there normally – and I can't understand how they keep alive in those poky little holes – we should still be having our party, shouldn't we?'

Laura had to say 'yes' to that, but she felt it was all wrong. She sat down on her mother's sofa and pinched the cushion frill.

'Mother, isn't it terribly heartless of us?' she asked.

'Darling!' Mrs Sheridan got up and came over to her, carrying the hat. Before Laura could stop her she had popped it on. 'My child!' said her mother, 'the hat is yours. It's made for you. It's much too young for me. I have never seen you look such a picture. Look at yourself!' And she held up her hand-mirror.

'But, mother,' Laura began again. She couldn't look at herself; she turned aside.

This time Mrs Sheridan lost patience just as Jose had done.

'You are being very absurd, Laura,' she said coldly. 'People like that don't expect sacrifices from us. And it's not very sympathetic to spoil everybody's enjoyment as you're doing now.'

'I don't understand,' said Laura, and she walked quickly out of the room into her own bedroom. There, quite by chance, the first thing she saw was this charming girl in the mirror, in her black hat trimmed with gold daisies, and a long black velvet ribbon. Never had she imagined she could look like that. Is mother right? she thought. And now she hoped her mother was right. Am I being extravagant? Perhaps it was extravagant. Just for a moment she had another glimpse of that poor woman and those little children, and the body being carried into the house. But it all seemed blurred, unreal, like a picture in the newspaper. I'll remember it again after the party's over, she decided. And somehow that seemed quite the best plan . . .

Lunch was over by half-past one. By half-past two they were all ready for the fray. The green-coated band had arrived and was established in a corner of the tennis-court.

'My dear!' trilled Kitty Maitland, 'aren't they too like frogs for words? You ought to have arranged them round the pond with the conductor in the middle on a leaf.'

Laurie arrived and hailed them on his way to dress. At the sight of him Laura remembered the accident again. She wanted to tell him. If Laurie agreed with the others, then it was bound to be all right. And she followed him into the hall.

'Laurie!'

'Hallo!' He was half-way upstairs, but when he turned round and saw Laura he suddenly puffed out his cheeks and goggled his eyes at her. 'My word, Laura! You do look stunning,' said Laurie. 'What an absolutely topping hat!'

Laura said faintly 'Is it?' and smiled up at Laurie, and didn't tell him after all.

Soon after that people began coming in streams. The band struck up; the hired waiters ran from the house to the marquee. Wherever you looked there were couples strolling, bending to the flowers, greeting, moving on over the lawn. They were like bright birds that had alighted in the Sheridans' garden for this one afternoon, on their way to – where? Ah, what happiness it is to be with people who all are happy, to press hands, press cheeks, smile into eyes.

'Darling Laura, how well you look!'

'What a becoming hat, child!'

'Laura, you look quite Spanish. I've never seen you look so striking.'

And Laura, glowing, answered softly, 'Have you had tea? Won't you have an ice? The passion-fruit ices really are rather special.' She ran to her father and begged him. 'Daddy darling, can't the band have something to drink?'

And the perfect afternoon slowly ripened, slowly faded, slowly its petals closed.

'Never a more delightful garden-party . . . ' 'The greatest success . . . ' 'Quite the most . . . '

Laura helped her mother with the goodbyes. They stood side by side in the porch till it was all over.

'All over, all over, thank heaven,' said Mrs Sheridan. 'Round up the others, Laura. Let's go and have some fresh coffee. I'm exhausted. Yes, it's been very successful. But oh, these parties, these parties! Why will you children insist on giving parties!' And they all of them sat down in the deserted marquee.

'Have a sandwich, daddy dear. I wrote the flag.'

'Thanks.' Mr Sheridan took a bite and the sandwich was gone. He took another. 'I suppose you didn't hear of a beastly accident that happened today?' he said.

'My dear,' said Mrs Sheridan, holding up her hand, 'we did. It nearly ruined the party. Laura insisted we should put it off.'

'Oh, mother!' Laura didn't want to be teased about it.

'It was a horrible affair all the same,' said Mr Sheridan. 'The chap was married too. Lived just below in the lane, and leaves a wife and half a dozen kiddies, so they say.'

An awkward little silence fell. Mrs Sheridan fidgeted with her cup. Really, it was very tactless of father . . .

Suddenly she looked up. There on the table were all those sandwiches, cakes, puffs, all uneaten, all going to be wasted. She had one of her brilliant ideas.

'I know,' she said. 'Let's make up a basket. Let's send that poor creature some of this perfectly good food. At any rate, it will be the greatest treat for the children. Don't you agree? And she's sure to have neighbours calling in and so on. What a point to have it all ready prepared. Laura!' She jumped up. 'Get me the big basket out of the stairs cupboard.'

'But, mother, do you really think it's a good idea?' said Laura.

Again, how curious, she seemed to be different from them all. To take scraps from their party. Would the poor woman really like that?

'Of course! What's the matter with you today? An hour or two ago you were insisting on us being sympathetic, and now – '

Oh well! Laura ran for the basket. It was filled, it was heaped by her mother.

'Take it yourself, darling,' said she. 'Run down just as you are. No, wait, take the arum lilies too. People of that class are so impressed by arum lilies.'

'The stems will ruin her lace frock,' said practical Jose.

So they would. Just in time. 'Only the basket, then. And, Laura!' –

her mother followed her out of the marquee – 'don't on any account – '

'What mother?'

No, better not put such ideas into the child's head! 'Nothing! Run along.'

It was just growing dusky as Laura shut their garden gates. A big dog ran by like a shadow. The road gleamed white, and down below in the hollow the little cottages were in deep shade. How quiet it seemed after the afternoon. Here she was going down the hill to somewhere where a man lay dead, and she couldn't realise it. Why couldn't she? She stopped a minute. And it seemed to her that kisses, voices, tinkling spoons, laughter, the smell of crushed grass were somehow inside her. She had no room for anything else. How strange! She looked up at the pale sky, and all she thought was, 'Yes, it was the most successful party.'

Now the broad road was crossed. The lane began, smoky and dark. Women in shawls and men's tweed caps hurried by. Men hung over the palings; the children played in the doorways. A low hum came from the mean little cottages. In some of them there was a flicker of light, and a shadow, crab-like, moved across the window. Laura bent her head and hurried on. She wished now she had put on a coat. How her frock shone! And the big hat with the velvet streamer – if only it was another hat! Were the people looking at her? They must be. It was a mistake to have come; she knew all along it was a mistake. Should she go back even now?

No, too late. This was the house. It must be. A dark knot of people stood outside. Beside the gate an old, old woman with a crutch sat in a chair, watching. She had her feet on a newspaper. The voices stopped as Laura drew near. The group parted. It was as though she was expected, as though they had known she was coming here.

Laura was terribly nervous. Tossing the velvet ribbon over her shoulder, she said to a woman standing by, 'Is this Mrs Scott's house?' and the woman, smiling queerly, said, 'It is, my lass.'

Oh, to be away from this! She actually said, 'Help me, God,' as she walked up the tiny path and knocked. To be away from those staring eyes, or to be covered up in anything, one of those women's shawls even. I'll just leave the basket and go, she decided. I shan't even wait for it to be emptied.

Then the door opened. A little woman in black showed in the gloom.

Laura said, 'Are you Mrs Scott?' But to her horror the woman answered, 'Walk in please, miss,' and she was shut in the passage.

'No,' said Laura, 'I don't want to come in. I only want to leave this basket. Mother sent – '

The little woman in the gloomy passage seemed not to have heard her. 'Step this way, please, miss,' she said in an oily voice, and Laura followed her.

She found herself in a wretched little low kitchen, lighted by a smoky lamp. There was a woman sitting before the fire.

'Em,' said the little creature who had let her in. 'Em! It's a young lady.' She turned to Laura. She said meaningly, 'I'm 'er sister, miss. You'll excuse 'er, won't you?'

'Oh, but of course!' said Laura. 'Please, please don't disturb her. I – I only want to leave – '

But at that moment the woman at the fire turned round. Her face, puffed up, red, with swollen eyes and swollen lips, looked terrible. She seemed as though she couldn't understand why Laura was there. What did it mean? Why was this stranger standing in the kitchen with a basket? What was it all about? And the poor face puckered up again.

'All right, my dear,' said the other. 'I'll thenk the young lady.'

And again she began, 'You'll excuse her, miss, I'm sure,' and her face, swollen too, tried an oily smile.

Laura only wanted to get out, to get away. She was back in the passage. The door opened. She walked straight through into the bedroom, where the dead man was lying.

'You'd like a look at 'im, wouldn't you?' said Em's sister, and she brushed past Laura over to the bed. 'Don't be afraid, my lass,' – and now her voice sounded fond and sly, and fondly she drew down the sheet – ''e looks a picture. There's nothing to show. Come along, my dear.'

Laura came.

There lay a young man, fast asleep – sleeping so soundly, so deeply, that he was far, far away from them both. Oh, so remote, so peaceful. He was dreaming. Never wake him up again. His head was sunk in the pillow, his eyes were closed; they were blind under the closed eyelids. He was given up to his dream. What did garden-parties and baskets and lace frocks matter to him? He was far from all those things. He was wonderful, beautiful. While they were laughing and while the band was playing, this marvel had come to the lane. Happy . . . happy . . .

All is well, said that sleeping face. This is just as it should be. I am content.

But all the same you had to cry, and she couldn't go out of the room without saying something to him. Laura gave a loud childish sob.

'Forgive my hat,' she said.

And this time she didn't wait for Em's sister. She found her way out of the door, down the path, past all those dark people. At the corner of the lane she met Laurie.

He stepped out of the shadow. 'Is that you, Laura?'

'Yes.'

'Mother was getting anxious. Was it all right?'

'Yes, quite. Oh, Laurie!' She took his arm, she pressed up against him.

'I say, you're not crying, are you?' asked her brother.

Laura shook her head. She was.

Laurie put his arm round her shoulder. 'Don't cry,' he said in his warm, loving voice. 'Was it awful?'

'No,' sobbed Laura. 'It was simply marvellous. But Laurie – ' She stopped, she looked at her brother. 'Isn't life,' she stammered, 'isn't life – ' But what life was she couldn't explain. No matter. He quite understood.

'*Isn't* it, darling?' said Laurie.

The Daughters of the Late Colonel

I

THE WEEK AFTER was one of the busiest weeks of their lives. Even when they went to bed it was only their bodies that lay down and rested; their minds went on, thinking things out, talking things over, wondering, deciding, trying to remember where . . .

Constantia lay like a statue, her hands by her sides, her feet just overlapping each other, the sheet up to her chin. She stared at the ceiling.

'Do you think father would mind if we gave his top-hat to the porter?'

'The porter?' snapped Josephine. 'Why ever the porter? What a very extraordinary idea!'

'Because,' said Constantia slowly, 'he must often have to go to funerals. And I noticed at – at the cemetery that he only had a bowler.' She paused. 'I thought then how very much he'd appreciate a top-hat. We ought to give him a present, too. He was always very nice to father.'

'But,' cried Josephine, flouncing on her pillow and staring across the dark at Constantia, 'father's head!' And suddenly, for one awful moment, she nearly giggled. Not, of course, that she felt in the least like giggling. It must have been habit. Years ago, when they had stayed awake at night talking, their beds had simply heaved. And now the porter's head, disappearing, popped out, like a candle, under father's hat . . . The giggle mounted, mounted; she clenched her hands; she fought it down; she frowned fiercely at the dark and said 'Remember' terribly sternly.

'We can decide tomorrow,' she said.

Constantia had noticed nothing; she sighed.

'Do you think we ought to have our dressing-gowns dyed as well?'

'Black?' almost shrieked Josephine.

'Well, what else?' said Constantia. 'I was thinking – it doesn't seem quite sincere, in a way, to wear black out of doors and when we're fully dressed, and then when we're at home – '

'But nobody sees us,' said Josephine. She gave the bedclothes such a twitch that both her feet became uncovered, and she had to creep up the pillows to get them well under again.

'Kate does,' said Constantia. 'And the postman very well might.'

Josephine thought of her dark-red slippers, which matched her dressing-gown, and of Constantia's favourite indefinite green ones which went with hers. Black! Two black dressing-gowns and two pairs of black woolly slippers, creeping off to the bathroom like black cats.

'I don't think it's absolutely necessary,' said she.

Silence. Then Constantia said, 'We shall have to post the papers with the notice in them tomorrow to catch the Ceylon mail . . . How many letters have we had up till now?'

'Twenty-three.'

Josephine had replied to them all, and twenty-three times when she came to 'We miss our dear father so much' she had broken down and had to use her handkerchief, and on some of them even to soak up a very light-blue tear with an edge of blotting-paper. Strange! She couldn't have put it on – but twenty-three times. Even now, though, when she said over to herself sadly 'We miss our dear father so much', she could have cried if she'd wanted to.

'Have you got enough stamps?' came from Constantia.

'Oh, how can I tell?' said Josephine crossly. 'What's the good of asking me that now?'

'I was just wondering,' said Constantia mildly.

Silence again. There came a little rustle, a scurry, a hop.

'A mouse,' said Constantia.

'It can't be a mouse because there aren't any crumbs,' said Josephine.

'But it doesn't know there aren't,' said Constantia.

A spasm of pity squeezed her heart. Poor little thing! She wished she'd left a tiny piece of biscuit on the dressing-table. It was awful to think of it not finding anything. What would it do?

'I can't think how they manage to live at all,' she said slowly.

'Who?' demanded Josephine.

And Constantia said more loudly than she meant to, 'Mice.'

Josephine was furious. 'Oh, what nonsense, Con!' she said. 'What have mice got to do with it? You're asleep.'

'I don't think I am,' said Constantia. She shut her eyes to make sure. She was.

Josephine arched her spine, pulled up her knees, folded her arms so that her fists came under her ears, and pressed her cheek hard against the pillow.

2

Another thing which complicated matters was they had Nurse Andrews staying on with them that week. It was their own fault; they had asked her. It was Josephine's idea. On the morning – well, on the last morning, when the doctor had gone, Josephine had said to Constantia, 'Don't you think it would be rather nice if we asked Nurse Andrews to stay on for a week as our guest?'

'Very nice,' said Constantia.

'I thought,' went on Josephine quickly, 'I should just say this afternoon, after I've paid her, "My sister and I would be very pleased, after all you've done for us, Nurse Andrews, if you would stay on for a week as our guest." I'd have to put that in about being our guest in case – '

'Oh, but she could hardly expect to be paid!' cried Constantia.

'One never knows,' said Josephine sagely.

Nurse Andrews had, of course, jumped at the idea. But it was a bother. It meant they had to have regular sit-down meals at the proper times, whereas if they'd been alone they could just have asked Kate if she wouldn't have minded bringing them a tray wherever they were. And meal-times now that the strain was over were rather a trial.

Nurse Andrews was simply fearful about butter. Really they couldn't help feeling that about butter, at least, she took advantage of their kindness. And she had that maddening habit of asking for just an inch more of bread to finish what she had on her plate, and then, at the last mouthful, absent-mindedly – of course it wasn't absent-mindedly – taking another helping. Josephine got very red when this happened, and she fastened her small, bead-like eyes on the tablecloth as if she saw a minute strange insect creeping through the web of it. But Constantia's long, pale face lengthened and set, and she gazed away – away – far over the desert, to where that line of camels unwound like a thread of wool . . .

'When I was with Lady Tukes,' said Nurse Andrews, 'she had such a dainty little contrayvance for the buttah. It was a silvah Cupid balanced on the – on the bordah of a glass dish, holding a tayny fork. And when you wanted some buttah you simply pressed his foot and he bent down and speared you a piece. It was quite a gayme.'

Josephine could hardly bear that. But 'I think those things are very extravagant' was all she said.

'But whey?' asked Nurse Andrews, beaming through her eyeglasses. 'No one, surely, would take more buttah than one wanted – would one?'

'Ring, Con,' cried Josephine. She couldn't trust herself to reply.

And proud young Kate, the enchanted princess, came in to see what the old tabbies wanted now. She snatched away their plates of mock something or other and slapped down a white, terrified blancmange.

'Jam, please, Kate,' said Josephine kindly.

Kate knelt and burst open the sideboard, lifted the lid of the jam-pot, saw it was empty, put it on the table, and stalked off.

'I'm afraid,' said Nurse Andrews a moment later, 'there isn't any.'

'Oh, what a bother!' said Josephine. She bit her lip. 'What had we better do?'

Constantia looked dubious. 'We can't disturb Kate again,' she said softly.

Nurse Andrews waited, smiling at them both. Her eyes wandered, spying at everything behind her eyeglasses. Constantia in despair went back to her camels. Josephine frowned heavily – concentrated. If it hadn't been for this idiotic woman she and Con would, of course, have eaten their blancmange without. Suddenly the idea came.

'I know,' she said. 'Marmalade. There's some marmalade in the sideboard. Get it, Con.'

'I hope,' laughed Nurse Andrews – and her laugh was like a spoon tinkling against a medicine-glass – 'I hope it's not very bittah marmalayde.'

3

But, after all, it was not long now, and then she'd be gone for good. And there was no getting over the fact that she had been very kind to father. She had nursed him day and night at the end. Indeed, both Constantia and Josephine felt privately she had rather overdone the not leaving him at the very last. For when they had gone in to say goodbye Nurse Andrews had sat beside his bed the whole time, holding his wrist and pretending to look at her watch. It couldn't have been necessary. It was so tactless, too. Supposing father had wanted to say something – something private to them. Not that he had. Oh, far from it! He lay there, purple, a dark, angry purple in the face, and never even looked at them when they came in. Then, as they were standing there, wondering what to do, he had suddenly opened one eye. Oh, what a difference it would have made, what a difference to their memory of him, how much easier to tell people about it, if he had only opened both! But no – one eye only. It glared at them a moment and then . . . went out.

4

It had made it very awkward for them when Mr Farolles, of St John's, called the same afternoon.

'The end was quite peaceful, I trust?' were the first words he said as he glided towards them through the dark drawing-room.

'Quite,' said Josephine faintly. They both hung their heads. Both of them felt certain that eye wasn't at all a peaceful eye.

'Won't you sit down?' said Josephine.

'Thank you, Miss Pinner,' said Mr Farolles gratefully. He folded his coat-tails and began to lower himself into father's armchair, but just as he touched it he almost sprang up and slid into the next chair instead.

He coughed. Josephine clasped her hands; Constantia looked vague.

'I want you to feel, Miss Pinner,' said Mr Farolles, 'and you, Miss Constantia, that I'm trying to be helpful. I want to be helpful to you both, if you will let me. These are the times,' said Mr Farolles, very simply and earnestly, 'when God means us to be helpful to one another.'

'Thank you very much, Mr Farolles,' said Josephine and Constantia.

'Not at all,' said Mr Farolles gently. He drew his kid gloves through his fingers and leaned forward. 'And if either of you would like a little Communion, either or both of you, here and now, you have only to tell me. A little Communion is often very help – a great comfort,' he added tenderly.'

But the idea of a little Communion terrified them. What! In the drawing-room by themselves – with no – no altar or anything! The piano would be much too high, thought Constantia, and Mr Farolles could not possibly lean over it with the chalice. And Kate would be sure to come bursting in and interrupt them, thought Josephine. And supposing the bell rang in the middle? It might be somebody important – about their mourning. Would they get up reverently and go out, or would they have to wait . . . in torture?

'Perhaps you will send round a note by your good Kate if you would care for it later,' said Mr Farolles.

'Oh yes, thank you very much!' they both said.

Mr Farolles got up and took his black straw hat from the round table.

'And about the funeral,' he said softly. 'I may arrange that – as your dear father's old friend and yours, Miss Pinner – and Miss Constantia?'

Josephine and Constantia got up too.

'I should like it to be quite simple,' said Josephine firmly, 'and not too expensive. At the same time, I should like – '

'A good one that will last,' thought dreamy Constantia, as if Josephine were buying a nightgown. But, of course, Josephine didn't say that. 'One suitable to our father's position.' She was very nervous.

'I'll run round to our good friend Mr Knight,' said Mr Farolles soothingly. 'I will ask him to come and see you. I am sure you will find him very helpful indeed.'

5

Well, at any rate, all that part of it was over, though neither of them could possibly believe that father was never coming back. Josephine had had a moment of absolute terror at the cemetery, while the coffin was lowered, to think that she and Constantia had done this thing without asking his permission. What would father say when he found out? For he was bound to find out sooner or later. He always did. 'Buried. You two girls had me buried!' She heard his stick thumping. Oh, what would they say? What possible excuse could they make? It sounded such an appallingly heartless thing to do. Such a wicked advantage to take of a person because he happened to be helpless at the moment. The other people seemed to treat it all as a matter of course. They were strangers; they couldn't be expected to understand that father was the very last person for such a thing to happen to. No, the entire blame for it all would fall on her and Constantia. And the expense, she thought, stepping into the tight-buttoned cab. When she had to show him the bills. What would he say then?

She heard him absolutely roaring. 'And do you expect me to pay for this gimcrack excursion of yours?'

'Oh,' groaned poor Josephine aloud, 'we shouldn't have done it, Con!'

And Constantia, pale as a lemon in all that blackness, said in a frightened whisper, 'Done what, Jug?'

'Let them bu-bury father like that,' said Josephine, breaking down and crying into her new, queer-smelling mourning handkerchief.

'But what else could we have done?' asked Constantia wonderingly. 'We couldn't have kept him, Jug – we couldn't have kept him unburied. At any rate, not in a flat that size.'

Josephine blew her nose; the cab was dreadfully stuffy.

'I don't know,' she said forlornly. 'It is all so dreadful. I feel we ought to have tried to, just for a time at least. To make perfectly sure. One thing's certain' – and her tears sprang out again – 'father will never forgive us for this – never!'

6

Father would never forgive them. That was what they felt more than ever when, two mornings later, they went into his room to go through his things. They had discussed it quite calmly. It was even down on Josephine's list of things to be done. 'Go through father's things and settle about them.' But that was a very different matter from saying after breakfast: 'Well, are you ready, Con?'

'Yes, Jug – when you are.'

'Then I think we'd better get it over.'

It was dark in the hall. It had been a rule for years never to disturb father in the morning, whatever happened. And now they were going to open the door without knocking even . . . Constantia's eyes were enormous at the idea; Josephine felt weak in the knees.

'You – you go first,' she gasped, pushing Constantia.

But Constantia said, as she always had said on those occasions, 'No, Jug, that's not fair. You're the eldest.'

Josephine was just going to say – what at other times she wouldn't have owned to for the world – what she kept for her very last weapon, 'But you're the tallest,' when they noticed that the kitchen door was open, and there stood Kate . . .

'Very stiff,' said Josephine, grasping the door handle and doing her best to turn it. As if anything ever deceived Kate!

It couldn't be helped. That girl was . . . Then the door was shut behind them, but – but they weren't in father's room at all. They might have suddenly walked through the wall by mistake into a different flat altogether. Was the door just behind them? They were too frightened to look. Josephine knew that if it was it was holding itself tight shut; Constantia felt that, like the doors in dreams, it hadn't any handle at all. It was the coldness which made it so awful. Or the whiteness – which? Everything was covered. The blinds were down, a cloth hung over the mirror, a sheet hid the bed; a huge fan of white paper filled the fireplace. Constantia timidly put out her hand; she almost expected a snowflake to fall. Josephine felt a queer tingling in her nose, as if her nose was freezing. Then a cab klop-klopped over the cobbles below, and the quiet seemed to shake into little pieces.

'I had better pull up a blind,' said Josephine bravely.

'Yes, it might be a good idea,' whispered Constantia.

They only gave the blind a touch, but it flew up and the cord flew after, rolling round the blind-stick, and the little tassel tapped as if trying to get free. That was too much for Constantia.

'Don't you think – don't you think we might put it off for another day?' she whispered.

'Why?' snapped Josephine, feeling, as usual, much better now that she knew for certain that Constantia was terrified. 'It's got to be done. But I do wish you wouldn't whisper, Con.'

'I didn't know I was whispering,' whispered Constantia.

'And why do you keep staring at the bed?' said Josephine, raising her voice almost defiantly. 'There's nothing on the bed.'

'Oh, Jug, don't say so!' said poor Connie. 'At any rate, not so loudly.'

Josephine felt herself that she had gone too far. She took a wide swerve over to the chest of drawers, put out her hand, but quickly drew it back again.

'Connie!' she gasped, and she wheeled round and leaned with her back against the chest of drawers.

'Oh, Jug – what?'

Josephine could only glare. She had the most extraordinary feeling that she had just escaped something simply awful. But how could she explain to Constantia that father was in the chest of drawers? He was in the top drawer with his handkerchiefs and neckties, or in the next with his shirts and pyjamas, or in the lowest of all with his suits. He was watching there, hidden away – just behind the door-handle – ready to spring.

She pulled a funny old-fashioned face at Constantia, just as she used to in the old days when she was going to cry.

'I can't open,' she nearly wailed.

'No, don't, Jug,' whispered Constantia earnestly. 'It's much better not to. Don't let's open anything. At any rate, not for a long time.'

'But – but it seems so weak,' said Josephine, breaking down.

'But why not be weak for once, Jug?' argued Constantia, whispering quite fiercely. 'If it is weak.' And her pale stare flew from the locked writing-table – so safe – to the huge glittering wardrobe, and she began to breathe in a queer, panting away. 'Why shouldn't we be weak for once in our lives, Jug? It's quite excusable. Let's be weak – be weak, Jug. It's much nicer to be weak than to be strong.'

And then she did one of those amazingly bold things that she'd done about twice before in their lives: she marched over to the wardrobe, turned the key, and took it out of the lock. Took it out of the lock and held it up to Josephine, showing Josephine by her extraordinary smile that she knew what she'd done – she'd risked deliberately father being in there among his overcoats.

If the huge wardrobe had lurched forward, had crashed down on Constantia, Josephine wouldn't have been surprised. On the contrary, she would have thought it the only suitable thing to happen. But nothing happened. Only the room seemed quieter than ever, and the bigger flakes of cold air fell on Josephine's shoulders and knees. She began to shiver.

'Come, Jug,' said Constantia, still with that awful callous smile, and Josephine followed just as she had that last time, when Constantia had pushed Benny into the round pond.

7

But the strain told on them when they were back in the dining-room. They sat down, very shaky, and looked at each other.

'I don't feel I can settle to anything,' said Josephine, 'until I've had something. Do you think we could ask Kate for two cups of hot water?'

'I really don't see why we shouldn't,' said Constantia carefully. She was quite normal again. 'I won't ring. I'll go to the kitchen door and ask her.'

'Yes, do,' said Josephine, sinking down into a chair. 'Tell her, just two cups, Con, nothing else – on a tray.'

'She needn't even put the jug on, need she?' said Constantia, as though Kate might very well complain if the jug had been there.

'Oh no, certainly not! The jug's not at all necessary. She can pour it direct out of the kettle,' cried Josephine, feeling that would be a labour-saving indeed.

Their cold lips quivered at the greenish brims. Josephine curved her small red hands round the cup; Constantia sat up and blew on the wavy steam, making it flutter from one side to the other.

'Speaking of Benny,' said Josephine.

And though Benny hadn't been mentioned Constantia immediately looked as though he had.

'He'll expect us to send him something of father's, of course. But it's so difficult to know what to send to Ceylon.'

'You mean things get unstuck so on the voyage,' murmured Constantia.

'No, lost,' said Josephine sharply. 'You know there's no post. Only runners.'

Both paused to watch a black man in white linen drawers running through the pale fields for dear life, with a large brown-paper parcel in his hands. Josephine's black man was tiny; he scurried along glistening like an ant. But there was something blind and tireless about Constantia's tall, thin fellow, which made him, she decided, a very unpleasant person indeed . . . On the veranda, dressed all in white and wearing a cork helmet, stood Benny. His right hand shook up and down, as father's did when he was impatient. And behind him, not in the least interested, sat Hilda, the unknown sister-in-law. She swung in a cane rocker and flicked over the leaves of the 'Tatler'.

'I think his watch would be the most suitable present,' said Josephine.

Constantia looked up; she seemed surprised.

'Oh, would you trust a gold watch to a native?'

'But of course, I'd disguise it,' said Josephine. 'No one would know it was a watch.' She liked the idea of having to make a parcel such a curious shape that no one could possibly guess what it was. She even thought for a moment of hiding the watch in a narrow cardboard corset-box that she'd kept by her for a long time, waiting for it to come in for something. It was such beautiful, firm cardboard. But, no, it wouldn't be appropriate for this occasion. It had lettering on it: *Medium Women's* 28. *Extra Firm Busks*. It would be almost too much of a surprise for Benny to open that and find father's watch inside.

'And of course it isn't as though it would be going – ticking, I mean,' said Constantia, who was still thinking of the native love of jewellery. 'At least,' she added, 'it would be very strange if after all that time it was.'

8

Josephine made no reply. She had flown off on one of her tangents. She had suddenly thought of Cyril. Wasn't it more usual for the only grandson to have the watch? And then dear Cyril was so appreciative, and a gold watch meant so much to a young man. Benny, in all probability, had quite got out of the habit of watches; men so seldom wore waistcoats in those hot climates. Whereas Cyril in London wore them from year's end to year's end. And it would be so nice for her and Constantia, when he came to tea, to know it was there. 'I see you've got on grandfather's watch, Cyril.' It would be somehow so satisfactory.

Dear boy! What a blow his sweet, sympathetic little note had been! Of course they quite understood; but it was most unfortunate.

'It would have been such a point, having him,' said Josephine.

'And he would have enjoyed it so,' said Constantia, not thinking what she was saying.

However, as soon as he got back he was coming to tea with his aunties. Cyril to tea was one of their rare treats.

'Now, Cyril, you mustn't be frightened of our cakes. Your Auntie Con and I bought them at Buszard's this morning. We know what a man's appetite is. So don't be ashamed of making a good tea.'

Josephine cut recklessly into the rich dark cake that stood for her winter gloves or the soling and heeling of Constantia's only respectable shoes. But Cyril was most unmanlike in appetite.

'I say, Aunt Josephine, I simply can't. I've only just had lunch, you know.'

'Oh, Cyril, that can't be true! It's after four,' cried Josephine. Constantia sat with her knife poised over the chocolate-roll.

'It is, all the same,' said Cyril. 'I had to meet a man at Victoria, and he kept me hanging about till . . . there was only time to get lunch and to come on here. And he gave me – phew' – Cyril put his hand to his forehead – 'a terrific blow-out,' he said.

It was disappointing – today of all days. But still he couldn't be expected to know.

'But you'll have a meringue, won't you, Cyril?' said Aunt Josephine. 'These meringues were bought specially for you. Your dear father was so fond of them. We were sure you are, too.'

'I am, Aunt Josephine,' cried Cyril ardently. 'Do you mind if I take half to begin with?'

'Not at all, dear boy; but we mustn't let you off with that.'

'Is your dear father still so fond of meringues?' asked Auntie Con gently. She winced faintly as she broke through the shell of hers.

'Well, I don't quite know, Auntie Con,' said Cyril breezily.

At that they both looked up.

'Don't know?' almost snapped Josephine. 'Don't know a thing like that about your own father, Cyril?'

'Surely,' said Auntie Con softly.

Cyril tried to laugh it off. 'Oh, well,' he said, 'it's such a long time since – ' He faltered. He stopped. Their faces were too much for him.

'Even so,' said Josephine.

And Auntie Con looked.

Cyril put down his teacup. 'Wait a bit,' he cried. 'Wait a bit, Aunt Josephine. What am I thinking of?'

He looked up. They were beginning to brighten. Cyril slapped his knee.

'Of course,' he said, 'it was meringues. How could I have forgotten? Yes, Aunt Josephine, you're perfectly right. Father's most frightfully keen on meringues.'

They didn't only beam. Aunt Josephine went scarlet with pleasure; Auntie Con gave a deep, deep sigh.

'And now, Cyril, you must come and see father,' said Josephine. 'He knows you were coming today.'

'Right,' said Cyril, very firmly and heartily. He got up from his chair; suddenly he glanced at the clock.

'I say, Auntie Con, isn't your clock a bit slow? I've got to meet a man at – at Paddington just after five. I'm afraid I shan't be able to stay very long with grandfather.'

'Oh, he won't expect you to stay very long!' said Aunt Josephine.

Constantia was still gazing at the clock. She couldn't make up her mind if it was fast or slow. It was one or the other, she felt almost certain of that. At any rate, it had been.

Cyril still lingered. 'Aren't you coming along, Auntie Con?'

'Of course,' said Josephine, 'we shall all go. Come on, Con.'

9

They knocked at the door, and Cyril followed his aunts into grandfather's hot, sweetish room.

'Come on,' said Grandfather Pinner. 'Don't hang about. What is it? What've you been up to?'

He was sitting in front of a roaring fire, clasping his stick. He had a thick rug over his knees. On his lap there lay a beautiful pale yellow silk handkerchief.

'It's Cyril, father,' said Josephine shyly. And she took Cyril's hand and led him forward.

'Good afternoon, grandfather,' said Cyril, trying to take his hand out of Aunt Josephine's. Grandfather Pinner shot his eyes at Cyril in the way he was famous for. Where was Auntie Con? She stood on the other side of Aunt Josephine; her long arms hung down in front of her; her hands were clasped. She never took her eyes off grandfather.

'Well,' said Grandfather Pinner, beginning to thump, 'what have you got to tell me?'

What had he, what had he got to tell him? Cyril felt himself smiling like a perfect imbecile. The room was stifling, too.

But Aunt Josephine came to his rescue. She cried brightly, 'Cyril says his father is still very fond of meringues, father dear.'

'Eh?' said Grandfather Pinner, curving his hand like a purple meringue-shell over one ear.

Josephine repeated, 'Cyril says his father is still very fond of meringues.'

'Can't hear,' said old Colonel Pinner. And he waved Josephine away with his stick, then pointed with his stick to Cyril. 'Tell me what she's trying to say,' he said.

(My God!) 'Must I?' said Cyril, blushing and staring at Aunt Josephine.

'Do, dear,' she smiled. 'It will please him so much.'

'Come on, out with it!' cried Colonel Pinner testily, beginning to thump again.

And Cyril leaned forward and yelled, 'Father's still very fond of meringues.'

At that Grandfather Pinner jumped as though he had been shot.

'Don't shout!' he cried. 'What's the matter with the boy? Meringues! What about 'em?'

'Oh, Aunt Josephine, must we go on?' groaned Cyril desperately.

'It's quite all right, dear boy,' said Aunt Josephine, as though he and she were at the dentist's together. 'He'll understand in a minute.' And she whispered to Cyril, 'He's getting a bit deaf, you know.' Then she leaned forward and really bawled at Grandfather Pinner, 'Cyril only wanted to tell you, father dear, that his father is still very fond of meringues.'

Colonel Pinner heard that time, heard and brooded, looking Cyril up and down.

'What an esstrordinary thing!' said old Grandfather Pinner. 'What an esstrordinary thing to come all this way here to tell me!'

And Cyril felt it was.

'Yes, I shall send Cyril the watch,' said Josephine.

'That would be very nice,' said Constantia. 'I seem to remember last time he came there was some little trouble about the time.'

10

They were interrupted by Kate bursting through the door in her usual fashion, as though she had discovered some secret panel in the wall.

'Fried or boiled?' asked the bold voice.

Fried or boiled? Josephine and Constantia were quite bewildered for the moment. They could hardly take it in.

'Fried or boiled what, Kate?' asked Josephine, trying to begin to concentrate.

Kate gave a loud sniff. 'Fish.'

'Well, why didn't you say so immediately?' Josephine reproached her gently. 'How could you expect us to understand, Kate? There are a great many things in this world you know, which are fried or boiled.' And after such a display of courage she said quite brightly to Constantia, 'Which do you prefer, Con?'

'I think it might be nice to have it fried,' said Constantia. 'On the other hand, of course, boiled fish is very nice. I think I prefer both equally well . . . Unless you . . . In that case – '

'I shall fry it,' said Kate, and she bounced back, leaving their door open and slamming the door of her kitchen.

Josephine gazed at Constantia; she raised her pale eyebrows until they rippled away into her pale hair. She got up. She said in a very lofty, imposing way, 'Do you mind following me into the drawing-room, Constantia? I've got something of great importance to discuss with you.'

For it was always to the drawing-room they retired when they wanted to talk over Kate.

Josephine closed the door meaningly. 'Sit down, Constantia,' she said, still very grand. She might have been receiving Constantia for the first time. And Con looked round vaguely for a chair, as though she felt indeed quite a stranger.

'Now the question is,' said Josephine, bending forward, 'whether we shall keep her or not.'

'That is the question,' agreed Constantia.

'And this time,' said Josephine firmly, 'we must come to a definite decision.'

Constantia looked for a moment as though she might begin going over all the other times, but she pulled herself together and said, 'Yes, Jug.'

'You see, Con,' explained Josephine, 'everything is so changed now.' Constantia looked up quickly. 'I mean,' went on Josephine, 'we're not dependent on Kate as we were.' And she blushed faintly. 'There's not father to cook for.'

'That is perfectly true,' agreed Constantia. 'Father certainly doesn't want any cooking now, whatever else – '

Josephine broke in sharply, 'You're not sleepy, are you, Con?'

'Sleepy, Jug?' Constantia was wide-eyed.

'Well, concentrate more,' said Josephine sharply, and she returned to the subject. 'What it comes to is, if we did' – and this she barely breathed, glancing at the door – 'give Kate notice' – she raised her voice again – 'we could manage our own food.'

'Why not?' cried Constantia. She couldn't help smiling. The idea was so exciting. She clasped her hands. 'What should we live on, Jug?'

'Oh, eggs in various forms!' said Jug, lofty again. 'And, besides, there are all the cooked foods.'

'But I've always heard,' said Constantia, 'they are considered so very expensive.'

'Not if one buys them in moderation,' said Josephine. But she tore herself away from this fascinating bypath and dragged Constantia after her.

'What we've got to decide now, however, is whether we really do trust Kate or not.'

Constantia leaned back. Her flat little laugh flew from her lips.

'Isn't it curious, Jug,' said she, 'that just on this one subject I've never been able to quite make up my mind?'

11

She never had. The whole difficulty was to prove anything. How did one prove things, how could one? Suppose Kate had stood in front of her and deliberately made a face. Mightn't she very well have been in pain? Wasn't it impossible, at any rate, to ask Kate if she was making a face at her? If Kate answered 'No' – and, of course, she would say 'No' – what a position! How undignified! Then again Constantia suspected, she was almost certain that Kate went to her chest of drawers when she and Josephine were out, not to take things but to spy. Many times she had come back to find her amethyst cross in the most unlikely places, under her lace ties or on top of her evening Bertha. More than once she had laid a trap for Kate. She had arranged things in a special order and then called Josephine to witness.

'You see, Jug?'

'Quite, Con.'

'Now we shall be able to tell.'

But, oh dear, when she did go to look, she was as far off from a proof as ever! If anything was displaced, it might so very well have happened as she closed the drawer; a jolt might have done it so easily.

'You come, Jug, and decide. I really can't. It's too difficult.'

But after a pause and a long glare Josephine would sigh, 'Now you've put the doubt into my mind, Con, I'm sure I can't tell myself.'

'Well, we can't postpone it again,' said Josephine. 'If we postpone it this time – '

12

But at that moment in the street below a barrel-organ struck up. Josephine and Constantia sprang to their feet together.

'Run, Con,' said Josephine. 'Run quickly. There's sixpence on the – '

Then they remembered. It didn't matter. They would never have to stop the organ-grinder again. Never again would she and Constantia be told to make that monkey take his noise somewhere else. Never would sound that loud, strange bellow when father thought they were not hurrying enough. The organ-grinder might play there all day and the stick would not thump.

> It never will thump again,
> It never will thump again,

played the barrel-organ.

What was Constantia thinking? She had such a strange smile; she looked different. She couldn't be going to cry.

'Jug, Jug,' said Constantia softly, pressing her hands together. 'Do you know what day it is? It's Saturday. It's a week today, a whole week.'

A week since father died,
A week since father died,

cried the barrel-organ. And Josephine, too, forgot to be practical and sensible; she smiled faintly, strangely. On the Indian carpet there fell a square of sunlight, pale red; it came and went and came – and stayed, deepened – until it shone almost golden.

'The sun's out,' said Josephine, as though it really mattered.

A perfect fountain of bubbling notes shook from the barrel-organ, round, bright notes, carelessly scattered.

Constantia lifted her big, cold hands as if to catch them, and then her hands fell again. She walked over to the mantelpiece to her favourite Buddha. And the stone and gilt image, whose smile always gave her such a queer feeling, almost a pain and yet a pleasant pain, seemed today to be more than smiling. He knew something; he had a secret. 'I know something that you don't know,' said her Buddha. Oh, what was it, what could it be? And yet she had always felt there was . . . something.

The sunlight pressed through the windows, thieved its way in, flashed its light over the furniture and the photographs. Josephine watched it. When it came to mother's photograph, the enlargement over the piano, it lingered as though puzzled to find so little remained of mother, except the earrings shaped like tiny pagodas and a black feather boa. Why did the photographs of dead people always fade so? wondered Josephine. As soon as a person was dead their photograph died too. But, of course, this one of mother was very old. It was thirty-five years old. Josephine remembered standing on a chair and pointing out that feather boa to Constantia and telling her that it was a snake that had killed their mother in Ceylon . . . Would everything have been different if mother hadn't died? She didn't see why. Aunt Florence had lived with them until they had left school, and they had moved three times and had their yearly holiday and . . . and there'd been changes of servants, of course.

Some little sparrows, young sparrows they sounded, chirped on the window-ledge. 'Yeep – eyeep – yeep.' But Josephine felt they were not sparrows, not on the window-ledge. It was inside her, that queer little crying noise. 'Yeep – eyeep – yeep.' Ah, what was it crying, so weak and forlorn?

If mother had lived, might they have married? But there had been nobody for them to marry. There had been father's Anglo-Indian friends before he quarrelled with them. But after that she and

Constantia never met a single man except clergymen. How did one meet men? Or even if they'd met them, how could they have got to know men well enough to be more than strangers? One read of people having adventures, being followed, and so on. But nobody had ever followed Constantia and her. Oh yes, there had been one year at Eastbourne a mysterious man at their boarding-house who had put a note on the jug of hot water outside their bedroom door! But by the time Connie had found it the steam had made the writing too faint to read; they couldn't even make out to which of them it was addressed. And he had left next day. And that was all. The rest had been looking after father, and at the same time keeping out of father's way. But now? But now? The thieving sun touched Josephine gently. She lifted her face. She was drawn over to the window by gentle beams . . .

Until the barrel-organ stopped playing Constantia stayed before the Buddha, wondering, but not as usual, not vaguely. This time her wonder was like longing. She remembered the times she had come in here, crept out of bed in her nightgown when the moon was full, and lain on the floor with her arms outstretched, as though she was crucified. Why? The big, pale moon had made her do it. The horrible dancing figures on the carved screen had leered at her and she hadn't minded. She remembered too how, whenever they were at the seaside, she had gone off by herself and got as close to the sea as she could, and sung something, something she had made up, while she gazed all over that restless water. There had been this other life, running out, bringing things home in bags, getting things on approval, discussing them with Jug, and taking them back to get more things on approval, and arranging father's trays and trying not to annoy father. But it all seemed to have happened in a kind of tunnel. It wasn't real. It was only when she came out of the tunnel into the moonlight or by the sea or into a thunderstorm that she really felt herself. What did it mean? What was it she was always wanting? What did it all lead to? Now? Now?

She turned away from the Buddha with one of her vague gestures. She went over to where Josephine was standing. She wanted to say something to Josephine, something frightfully important, about – about the future and what . . .

'Don't you think perhaps – ' she began.

But Josephine interrupted her. 'I was wondering if now – ' she murmured. They stopped; they waited for each other.

'Go on, Con,' said Josephine.

'No, no, Jug; after you,' said Constantia.

'No, say what you were going to say. You began,' said Josephine.

'I . . . I'd rather hear what you were going to say first,' said Constantia.

'Don't be absurd, Con.'

'Really, Jug.'

'Connie!'

'Oh, Jug!'

A pause. Then Constantia said faintly, 'I can't say what I was going to say, Jug, because I've forgotten what it was . . . that I was going to say.'

Josephine was silent for a moment. She stared at a big cloud where the sun had been. Then she replied shortly, 'I've forgotten too.'

Mr and Mrs Dove

OF COURSE HE KNEW – no man better – that he hadn't a ghost of a chance, he hadn't an earthly. The very idea of such a thing was preposterous. So preposterous that he'd perfectly understand it if her father – well, whatever her father chose to do he'd perfectly understand. In fact, nothing short of desperation, nothing short of the fact that this was positively his last day in England for God knows how long, would have screwed him up to it. And even now . . . He chose a tie out of the chest of drawers, a blue and cream check tie, and sat on the side of his bed. Supposing she replied, 'What impertinence!' would he be surprised? Not in the least, he decided, turning up his soft collar and turning it down over the tie. He expected her to say something like that. He didn't see, if he looked at the affair dead soberly, what else she could say.

Here he was! And nervously he tied a bow in front of the mirror, jammed his hair down with both hands, pulled out the flaps of his jacket pockets. Making between 500 and 600 pounds a year on a fruit farm in – of all places – Rhodesia. No capital. Not a penny coming to him. No chance of his income increasing for at least four years. As for looks and all that sort of thing, he was completely out of the running. He couldn't even boast of top-hole health, for the East Africa business had knocked him out so thoroughly that he'd had to take six months' leave. He was still fearfully pale – worse even than usual this afternoon, he thought, bending forward and peering into the mirror. Good heavens! What had happened? His hair looked almost bright green. Dash it all, he hadn't green hair at all events. That was a bit too steep. And then the green light trembled in the glass; it was the shadow from the tree outside. Reggie turned away, took out his cigarette case, but remembering how the mater hated him to smoke in his bedroom, put it back again and drifted over to the chest of drawers. No, he was dashed if he could think of one blessed thing in his favour, while she . . . Ah! . . . He stopped dead, folded his arms, and leaned hard against the chest of drawers.

And in spite of her position, her father's wealth, the fact that she was an only child and far and away the most popular girl in the neighbourhood; in spite of her beauty and her cleverness – cleverness! – it was a great deal more than that, there was really nothing she couldn't do; he fully believed, had it been necessary, she would have been a genius at anything – in spite of the fact that her parents adored her, and she them, and they'd as soon let her go all that way as . . . In spite of every single thing you could think of, so terrific was his love that he couldn't help hoping. Well, was it hope? Or was this queer, timid longing to have the chance of looking after her, of making it his job to see that she had everything she wanted, and that nothing came near her that wasn't perfect – just love? How he loved her! He squeezed hard against the chest of drawers and murmured to it, 'I love her, I love her!' And just for the moment he was with her on the way to Umtali. It was night. She sat in a corner asleep. Her soft chin was tucked into her soft collar, her gold-brown lashes lay on her cheeks. He doted on her delicate little nose, her perfect lips, her ear like a baby's, and the gold-brown curl that half covered it. They were passing through the jungle. It was warm and dark and far away. Then she woke up and said, 'Have I been asleep?' and he answered, 'Yes. Are you all right? Here, let me – ' And he leaned forward to . . . He bent over her. This was such bliss that he could dream no further. But it gave him the courage to bound downstairs, to snatch his straw hat from the hall, and to say as he closed the front door, 'Well, I can only try my luck, that's all.'

But his luck gave him a nasty jar, to say the least, almost immediately. Promenading up and down the garden path with Chinny and Biddy, the ancient Pekes, was the mater. Of course Reginald was fond of the mater and all that. She – she meant well, she had no end of grit, and so on. But there was no denying it, she was rather a grim parent. And there had been moments, many of them, in Reggie's life, before Uncle Alick died and left him the fruit farm, when he was convinced that to be a widow's only son was about the worst punishment a chap could have. And what made it rougher than ever was that she was positively all that he had. She wasn't only a combined parent, as it were, but she had quarrelled with all her own and the governor's relations before Reggie had won his first trouser pockets. So that whenever Reggie was homesick out there, sitting on his dark veranda by starlight, while the gramophone cried, 'Dear, what is Life but Love?' his only vision was of the mater, tall and stout, rustling down the garden path, with Chinny and Biddy at her heels . . .

The mater, with her scissors outspread to snap the head of a dead something or other, stopped at the sight of Reggie.

'You are not going out, Reginald?' she asked, seeing that he was.

'I'll be back for tea, mater,' said Reggie weakly, plunging his hands into his jacket pockets.

Snip. Off came a head. Reggie almost jumped.

'I should have thought you could have spared your mother your last afternoon,' said she.

Silence. The Pekes stared. They understood every word of the mater's. Biddy lay down with her tongue poked out; she was so fat and glossy she looked like a lump of half-melted toffee. But Chinny's porcelain eyes gloomed at Reginald, and he sniffed faintly, as though the whole world were one unpleasant smell. Snip, went the scissors again. Poor little beggars; they were getting it!

'And where are you going, if your mother may ask?' asked the mater.

It was over at last, but Reggie did not slow down until he was out of sight of the house and half-way to Colonel Proctor's. Then only he noticed what a top-hole afternoon it was. It had been raining all the morning, late summer rain, warm, heavy, quick, and now the sky was clear, except for a long tail of little clouds, like ducklings, sailing over the forest. There was just enough wind to shake the last drops off the trees; one warm star splashed on his hand. Ping! – another drummed on his hat. The empty road gleamed, the hedges smelled of briar, and how big and bright the hollyhocks glowed in the cottage gardens. And here was Colonel Proctor's – here it was already. His hand was on the gate, his elbow jogged the syringa bushes, and petals and pollen scattered over his coat sleeve. But wait a bit. This was too quick altogether. He'd meant to think the whole thing out again. Here, steady. But he was walking up the path, with the huge rose bushes on either side. It can't be done like this. But his hand had grasped the bell, given it a pull, and started it pealing wildly, as if he'd come to say the house was on fire. The housemaid must have been in the hall, too, for the front door flashed open, and Reggie was shut in the empty drawing-room before that confounded bell had stopped ringing. Strangely enough, when it did, the big room, shadowy, with someone's parasol lying on top of the grand piano, bucked him up – or rather, excited him. It was so quiet, and yet in one moment the door would open, and his fate be decided. The feeling was not unlike that of being at the dentist's; he was almost reckless. But at the same time, to his immense surprise, Reggie heard himself saying, 'Lord,

Thou knowest, Thou hast not done much for me . . . ' That pulled him up; that made him realise again how dead serious it was. Too late. The door handle turned. Anne came in, crossed the shadowy space between them, gave him her hand, and said, in her small, soft voice, 'I'm so sorry, father is out. And mother is having a day in town, hat-hunting. There's only me to entertain you, Reggie.'

Reggie gasped, pressed his own hat to his jacket buttons, and stammered out, 'As a matter of fact, I've only come . . . to say goodbye.'

'Oh!' cried Anne softly – she stepped back from him and her grey eyes danced – 'what a very short visit!'

Then, watching him, her chin tilted, she laughed outright, a long, soft peal, and walked away from him over to the piano, and leaned against it, playing with the tassel of the parasol.

'I'm so sorry,' she said, 'to be laughing like this. I don't know why I do. It's just a bad ha – habit.' And suddenly she stamped her grey shoe, and took a pocket-handkerchief out of her white woolly jacket. 'I really must conquer it, it's too absurd,' said she.

'Good heavens, Anne,' cried Reggie, 'I love to hear you laughing! I can't imagine anything more – '

But the truth was, and they both knew it, she wasn't always laughing; it wasn't really a habit. Only ever since the day they'd met, ever since that very first moment, for some strange reason that Reggie wished to God he understood, Anne had laughed at him. Why? It didn't matter where they were or what they were talking about. They might begin by being as serious as possible, dead serious – at any rate, as far as he was concerned – but then suddenly, in the middle of a sentence, Anne would glance at him, and a little quick quiver passed over her face. Her lips parted, her eyes danced, and she began laughing.

Another queer thing about it was, Reggie had an idea she didn't herself know why she laughed. He had seen her turn away, frown, suck in her cheeks, press her hands together. But it was no use. The long, soft peal sounded, even while she cried, 'I don't know why I'm laughing.' It was a mystery . . .

Now she tucked the handkerchief away.

'Do sit down,' said she. 'And smoke, won't you? There are cigarettes in that little box beside you. I'll have one too.' He lighted a match for her, and as she bent forward he saw the tiny flame glow in the pearl ring she wore. 'It is tomorrow that you're going, isn't it?' said Anne.

'Yes, tomorrow as ever was,' said Reggie, and he blew a little fan of smoke. Why on earth was he so nervous? Nervous wasn't the word for it.

'It's – it's frightfully hard to believe,' he added.

'Yes – isn't it?' said Anne softly, and she leaned forward and rolled the point of her cigarette round the green ash-tray. How beautiful she looked like that! – simply beautiful – and she was so small in that immense chair. Reginald's heart swelled with tenderness, but it was her voice, her soft voice, that made him tremble. 'I feel you've been here for years,' she said.

Reginald took a deep breath of his cigarette. 'It's ghastly, this idea of going back,' be said.

'Coo-roo-coo-coo-coo,' sounded from the quiet.

'But you're fond of being out there, aren't you?' said Anne. She hooked her finger through her pearl necklace. 'Father was saying only the other night how lucky he thought you were to have a life of your own.' And she looked up at him. Reginald's smile was rather wan. 'I don't feel fearfully lucky,' he said lightly.

'Roo-coo-coo-coo,' came again. And Anne murmured, 'You mean it's lonely.'

'Oh, it isn't the loneliness I care about,' said Reginald, and he stumped his cigarette savagely on the green ash-tray. 'I could stand any amount of it, used to like it even. It's the idea of – ' Suddenly, to his horror, he felt himself blushing.

'Roo-coo-coo-coo! Roo-coo-coo-coo!'

Anne jumped up. 'Come and say goodbye to my doves,' she said. 'They've been moved to the side veranda. You do like doves, don't you, Reggie?'

'Awfully,' said Reggie, so fervently that as he opened the French window for her and stood to one side, Anne ran forward and laughed at the doves instead.

To and fro, to and fro over the fine red sand on the floor of the dove house, walked the two doves. One was always in front of the other. One ran forward, uttering a little cry, and the other followed, solemnly bowing and bowing. 'You see,' explained Anne, 'the one in front, she's Mrs Dove. She looks at Mr Dove and gives that little laugh and runs forward, and he follows her, bowing and bowing. And that makes her laugh again. Away she runs, and after her,' cried Anne, and she sat back on her heels, 'comes poor Mr Dove, bowing and bowing . . . and that's their whole life. They never do anything else, you know.' She got up and took some yellow grains out of a bag on the roof of the dove house. 'When you think of them, out in Rhodesia, Reggie, you can be sure that is what they will be doing . . . '

Reggie gave no sign of having seen the doves or of having heard a word. For the moment he was conscious only of the immense effort it took to tear his secret out of himself and offer it to Anne. 'Anne, do you think you could ever care for me?' It was done. It was over. And in the little pause that followed Reginald saw the garden open to the light, the blue quivering sky, the flutter of leaves on the veranda poles, and Anne turning over the grains of maize on her palm with one finger. Then slowly she shut her hand, and the new world faded as she murmured slowly, 'No, never in that way.' But he had scarcely time to feel anything before she walked quickly away, and he followed her down the steps, along the garden path, under the pink rose arches, across the lawn. There, with the gay herbaceous border behind her, Anne faced Reginald. 'It isn't that I'm not awfully fond of you,' she said. 'I am. But' – her eyes widened – 'not in the way' – a quiver passed over her face – 'one ought to be fond of – ' Her lips parted, and she couldn't stop herself. She began laughing. 'There, you see, you see,' she cried, 'it's your check t-tie. Even at this moment, when one would think one really would be solemn, your tie reminds me fearfully of the bow-tie that cats wear in pictures! Oh, please forgive me for being so horrid, please!'

Reggie caught hold of her little warm hand. 'There's no question of forgiving you,' he said quickly. 'How could there be? And I do believe I know why I make you laugh. It's because you're so far above me in every way that I am somehow ridiculous. I see that, Anne. But if I were to – '

'No, no.' Anne squeezed his hand hard. 'It's not that. That's all wrong. I'm not far above you at all. You're much better than I am. You're marvellously unselfish and . . . and kind and simple. I'm none of those things. You don't know me. I'm the most awful character,' said Anne. 'Please don't interrupt. And besides, that's not the point. The point is' – she shook her head – 'I couldn't possibly marry a man I laughed at. Surely you see that. The man I marry – ' breathed Anne softly. She broke off. She drew her hand away, and looking at Reggie she smiled strangely, dreamily. 'The man I marry – '

And it seemed to Reggie that a tall, handsome, brilliant stranger stepped in front of him and took his place – the kind of man that Anne and he had seen often at the theatre, walking on to the stage from nowhere, without a word catching the heroine in his arms, and after one long, tremendous look, carrying her off to anywhere . . .

Reggie bowed to his vision. 'Yes, I see,' he said huskily.

'Do you?' said Anne. 'Oh, I do hope you do. Because I feel so horrid about it. It's so hard to explain. You know I've never – ' She stopped. Reggie looked at her. She was smiling. 'Isn't it funny?' she said. 'I can say anything to you. I always have been able to from the very beginning.'

He tried to smile, to say 'I'm glad.' She went on. 'I've never known anyone I like as much as I like you. I've never felt so happy with anyone. But I'm sure it's not what people and what books mean when they talk about love. Do you understand? Oh, if you only knew how horrid I feel. But we'd be like . . . like Mr and Mrs Dove.'

That did it. That seemed to Reginald final, and so terribly true that he could hardly bear it. 'Don't drive it home,' he said, and he turned away from Anne and looked across the lawn. There was the gardener's cottage, with the dark ilex-tree beside it. A wet, blue thumb of transparent smoke hung above the chimney. It didn't look real. How his throat ached! Could he speak? He had a shot. 'I must be getting along home,' he croaked, and he began walking across the lawn. But Anne ran after him. 'No, don't. You can't go yet,' she said imploringly. 'You can't possibly go away feeling like that.' And she stared up at him frowning, biting her lip.

'Oh, that's all right,' said Reggie, giving himself a shake. 'I'll . . . I'll – ' And he waved his hand as much to say 'get over it.'

'But this is awful,' said Anne. She clasped her hands and stood in front of him. 'Surely you do see how fatal it would be for us to marry, don't you?'

'Oh, quite, quite,' said Reggie, looking at her with haggard eyes.

'How wrong, how wicked, feeling as I do. I mean, it's all very well for Mr and Mrs Dove. But imagine that in real life – imagine it!'

'Oh, absolutely,' said Reggie, and he started to walk on. But again Anne stopped him. She tugged at his sleeve, and to his astonishment, this time, instead of laughing, she looked like a little girl who was going to cry.

'Then why, if you understand, are you so un-unhappy?' she wailed. 'Why do you mind so fearfully? Why do you look so aw-awful?'

Reggie gulped, and again he waved something away. 'I can't help it,' he said, 'I've had a blow. If I cut off now, I'll be able to – '

'How can you talk of cutting off now?' said Anne scornfully. She stamped her foot at Reggie; she was crimson. 'How can you be so cruel? I can't let you go until I know for certain that you are just as happy as you were before you asked me to marry you. Surely you must see that, it's so simple.'

But it did not seem at all simple to Reginald. It seemed impossibly difficult.

'Even if I can't marry you, how can I know that you're all that way away, with only that awful mother to write to, and that you're miserable, and that it's all my fault?'

'It's not your fault. Don't think that. It's just fate.' Reggie took her hand off his sleeve and kissed it. 'Don't pity me, dear little Anne,' he said gently. And this time he nearly ran, under the pink arches, along the garden path.

'Roo-coo-coo-coo! Roo-coo-coo-coo!' sounded from the veranda. 'Reggie, Reggie,' from the garden.

He stopped, he turned. But when she saw his timid, puzzled look, she gave a little laugh.

'Come back, Mr Dove,' said Anne. And Reginald came slowly across the lawn.

The Young Girl

IN HER BLUE DRESS, with her cheeks lightly flushed, her blue, blue eyes, and her gold curls pinned up as though for the first time – pinned up to be out of the way for her flight – Mrs Raddick's daughter might have just dropped from this radiant heaven. Mrs Raddick's timid, faintly astonished, but deeply admiring glance looked as if she believed it, too; but the daughter didn't appear any too pleased – why should she? – to have alighted on the steps of the Casino. Indeed, she was bored – bored as though Heaven had been full of casinos with snuffy old saints for croupiers and crowns to play with.

'You don't mind taking Hennie?' said Mrs Raddick. 'Sure you don't? There's the car, and you'll have tea and we'll be back here on this step – right here – in an hour. You see, I want her to go in. She's not been before, and it's worth seeing. I feel it wouldn't be fair to her.'

'Oh, shut up, mother,' said she wearily. 'Come along. Don't talk so much. And your bag's open; you'll be losing all your money again.'

'I'm sorry, darling,' said Mrs Raddick.

'Oh, do come in! I want to make money,' said the impatient voice. 'It's all jolly well for you – but I'm broke!'

'Here – take fifty francs, darling, take a hundred!' I saw Mrs Raddick pressing notes into her hand as they passed through the swing doors.

Hennie and I stood on the steps a minute, watching the people. He had a very broad, delighted smile.

'I say,' he cried, 'there's an English bulldog. Are they allowed to take dogs in there?'

'No, they're not.'

'He's a ripping chap, isn't he? I wish I had one. They're such fun. They frighten people so, and they're never fierce with their – the people they belong to.' Suddenly he squeezed my arm. 'I say, do look at that old woman. Who is she? Why does she look like that? Is she a gambler?'

The ancient, withered creature, wearing a green satin dress, a black velvet cloak and a white hat with purple feathers, jerked slowly, slowly up the steps as though she were being drawn up on wires. She stared in front of her, she was laughing and nodding and cackling to herself; her claws clutched round what looked like a dirty boot-bag.

But just at that moment there was Mrs Raddick again with – her – and another lady hovering in the background. Mrs Raddick rushed at me. She was brightly flushed, gay, a different creature. She was like a woman who is saying 'goodbye' to her friends on the station platform, with not a minute to spare before the train starts.

'Oh, you're here, still. Isn't that lucky! You've not gone. Isn't that fine! I've had the most dreadful time with – her,' and she waved to her daughter, who stood absolutely still, disdainful, looking down, twiddling her foot on the step, miles away. 'They won't let her in. I swore she was twenty-one. But they won't believe me. I showed the man my purse; I didn't dare to do more. But it was no use. He simply scoffed . . . And now I've just met Mrs MacEwen from New York, and she just won thirteen thousand in the Salle Privée – and she wants me to go back with her while the luck lasts. Of course I can't leave – her. But if you'd – '

At that 'she' looked up; she simply withered her mother. 'Why can't you leave me?' she said furiously. 'What utter rot! How dare you make a scene like this? This is the last time I'll come out with you. You really are too awful for words.' She looked her mother up and down. 'Calm yourself,' she said superbly.

Mrs Raddick was desperate, just desperate. She was 'wild' to go back with Mrs MacEwen, but at the same time . . .

I seized my courage. 'Would you – do you care to come to tea with – us?'

'Yes, yes, she'll be delighted. That's just what I wanted, isn't it, darling? Mrs MacEwen . . . I'll be back here in an hour . . . or less . . . I'll – '

Mrs R. dashed up the steps. I saw her bag was open again.

So we three were left. But really it wasn't my fault. Hennie looked crushed to the earth, too. When the car was there she wrapped her dark coat round her – to escape contamination. Even her little feet looked as though they scorned to carry her down the steps to us.

'I am so awfully sorry,' I murmured as the car started.

'Oh, I don't mind,' said she. 'I don't want to look twenty-one. Who would – if they were seventeen! It's' – and she gave a faint shudder – 'the stupidity I loathe, and being stared at by old fat men. Beasts!'

Hennie gave her a quick look and then peered out of the window.

We drew up before an immense palace of pink-and-white marble with orange-trees outside the doors in gold-and-black tubs.

'Would you care to go in?' I suggested.

She hesitated, glanced, bit her lip, and resigned herself. 'Oh well, there seems nowhere else,' said she. 'Get out, Hennie.'

I went first – to find the table, of course – she followed. But the worst of it was having her little brother, who was only twelve, with us. That was the last, final straw – having that child, trailing at her heels.

There was one table. It had pink carnations and pink plates with little blue tea-napkins for sails.

'Shall we sit here?'

She put her hand wearily on the back of a white wicker chair.

'We may as well. Why not?' said she.

Hennie squeezed past her and wriggled on to a stool at the end. He felt awfully out of it. She didn't even take her gloves off. She lowered her eyes and drummed on the table. When a faint violin sounded she winced and bit her lip again. Silence.

The waitress appeared. I hardly dared to ask her. 'Tea – coffee? China tea – or iced tea with lemon?'

Really she didn't mind. It was all the same to her. She didn't really want anything. Hennie whispered, 'Chocolate!'

But just as the waitress turned away she cried out carelessly, 'Oh, you may as well bring me a chocolate, too.'

While we waited she took out a little, gold powder-box with a mirror in the lid, shook the poor little puff as though she loathed it, and dabbed her lovely nose.

'Hennie,' she said, 'take those flowers away.' She pointed with her puff to the carnations, and I heard her murmur, 'I can't bear flowers on a table.' They had evidently been giving her intense pain, for she positively closed her eyes as I moved them away.

The waitress came back with the chocolate and the tea. She put the big, frothing cups before them and pushed across my clear glass. Hennie buried his nose, emerged, with, for one dreadful moment, a little trembling blob of cream on the tip. But he hastily wiped it off like a little gentleman. I wondered if I should dare draw her attention to her cup. She didn't notice it – didn't see it – until suddenly, quite by chance, she took a sip. I watched anxiously; she faintly shuddered.

'Dreadfully sweet!' said she.

A tiny boy with a head like a raisin and a chocolate body came round with a tray of pastries – row upon row of little freaks, little inspirations, little melting dreams. He offered them to her. 'Oh, I'm not at all hungry. Take them away.'

He offered them to Hennie. Hennie gave me a swift look – it must have been satisfactory – for he took a chocolate cream, a coffee éclair, a meringue stuffed with chestnut and a tiny horn filled with fresh strawberries. She could hardly bear to watch him. But just as the boy swerved away she held up her plate.

'Oh well, give me one,' said she.

The silver tongs dropped one, two, three – and a cherry tartlet. 'I don't know why you're giving me all these,' she said, and nearly smiled. 'I shan't eat them; I couldn't!'

I felt much more comfortable. I sipped my tea, leaned back, and even asked if I might smoke. At that she paused, the fork in her hand, opened her eyes, and really did smile. 'Of course,' said she. 'I always expect people to.'

But at that moment a tragedy happened to Hennie. He speared his pastry horn too hard, and it flew in two, and one half spilled on the table. Ghastly affair! He turned crimson. Even his ears flared, and one ashamed hand crept across the table to take what was left of the body away.

'You utter little beast!' said she.

Good heavens! I had to fly to the rescue. I cried hastily, 'Will you be abroad long?'

But she had already forgotten Hennie. I was forgotten, too. She was trying to remember something . . . She was miles away.

'I – don't – know,' she said slowly, from that far place.

'I suppose you prefer it to London. It's more – more – '

When I didn't go on she came back and looked at me, very puzzled. 'More – ?'

'Enfin – gayer,' I cried, waving my cigarette.

But that took a whole cake to consider. Even then, 'Oh well, that depends!' was all she could safely say.

Hennie had finished. He was still very warm.

I seized the butterfly list off the table. 'I say – what about an ice, Hennie? What about tangerine and ginger? No, something cooler. What about a fresh pineapple cream?'

Hennie strongly approved. The waitress had her eye on us. The order was taken when she looked up from her crumbs.

'Did you say tangerine and ginger? I like ginger. You can bring me one.' And then quickly, 'I wish that orchestra wouldn't play things from the year One. We were dancing to that all last Christmas. It's too sickening!'

But it was a charming air. Now that I noticed it, it warmed me.

'I think this is rather a nice place, don't you, Hennie?' I said.

Hennie said: 'Ripping!' He meant to say it very low, but it came out very high in a kind of squeak.

Nice? This place? Nice? For the first time she stared about her, trying to see what there was . . . She blinked; her lovely eyes wondered. A very good-looking elderly man stared back at her through a monocle on a black ribbon. But him she simply couldn't see. There was a hole in the air where he was. She looked through and through him.

Finally the little flat spoons lay still on the glass plates. Hennie looked rather exhausted, but she pulled on her white gloves again. She had some trouble with her diamond wrist-watch; it got in her way. She tugged at it – tried to break the stupid little thing – it wouldn't break. Finally, she had to drag her glove over. I saw, after that, she couldn't stand this place a moment longer, and, indeed, she jumped up and turned away while I went through the vulgar act of paying for the tea.

And then we were outside again. It had grown dusky. The sky was sprinkled with small stars; the big lamps glowed. While we waited for the car to come up she stood on the step, just as before, twiddling her foot, looking down.

Hennie bounded forward to open the door and she got in and sank back with – oh – such a sigh!

'Tell him,' she gasped, 'to drive as fast as he can.'

Hennie grinned at his friend the chauffeur. 'Allie veet!' said he. Then he composed himself and sat on the small seat facing us.

The gold powder-box came out again. Again the poor little puff was shaken; again there was that swift, deadly-secret glance between her and the mirror.

We tore through the black-and-gold town like a pair of scissors tearing through brocade. Hennie had great difficulty not to look as though he were hanging on to something.

And when we reached the Casino, of course Mrs Raddick wasn't there. There wasn't a sign of her on the steps – not a sign.

'Will you stay in the car while I go and look?'

But no – she wouldn't do that. Good heavens, no! Hennie

could stay. She couldn't bear sitting in a car. She'd wait on the steps.

'But I scarcely like to leave you,' I murmured. 'I'd very much rather not leave you here.'

At that she threw back her coat; she turned and faced me; her lips parted. 'Good heavens – why! I – I don't mind it a bit. I – I like waiting.' And suddenly her cheeks crimsoned, her eyes grew dark – for a moment I thought she was going to cry. 'L – let me, please,' she stammered, in a warm, eager voice. 'I like it. I love waiting! Really – really I do! I'm always waiting – in all kinds of places . . .'

Her dark coat fell open, and her white throat – all her soft young body in the blue dress – was like a flower that is just emerging from its dark bud.

Life of Ma Parker

WHEN THE LITERARY GENTLEMAN, whose flat old Ma Parker cleaned every Tuesday, opened the door to her that morning, he asked after her grandson. Ma Parker stood on the doormat inside the dark little hall, and she stretched out her hand to help her gentleman shut the door before she replied. 'We buried 'im yesterday, sir,' she said quietly.

'Oh, dear me! I'm sorry to hear that,' said the literary gentleman in a shocked tone. He was in the middle of his breakfast. He wore a very shabby dressing-gown and carried a crumpled newspaper in one hand. But he felt awkward. He could hardly go back to the warm sitting-room without saying something – something more. Then because these people set such store by funerals he said kindly, 'I hope the funeral went off all right.'

'Beg parding, sir?' said old Ma Parker huskily.

Poor old bird! She did look dashed. 'I hope the funeral was a – a – success,' said he. Ma Parker gave no answer. She bent her head and hobbled off to the kitchen, clasping the old fish bag that held her cleaning things and an apron and a pair of felt shoes. The literary gentleman raised his eyebrows and went back to his breakfast.

'Overcome, I suppose,' he said aloud, helping himself to the marmalade.

Ma Parker drew the two jetty spears out of her toque and hung it behind the door. She unhooked her worn jacket and hung that up too. Then she tied her apron and sat down to take off her boots. To take off her boots or to put them on was an agony to her, but it had been an agony for years. In fact, she was so accustomed to the pain that her face was drawn and screwed up ready for the twinge before she'd so much as untied the laces. That over, she sat back with a sigh and softly rubbed her knees . . .

'Gran! Gran!' Her little grandson stood on her lap in his button boots. He'd just come in from playing in the street.

'Look what a state you've made your gran's skirt into – you wicked boy!'

But he put his arms round her neck and rubbed his cheek against hers.

'Gran, gi' us a penny!' he coaxed.

'Be off with you; Gran ain't got no pennies.'

'Yes, you 'ave.'

'No, I ain't.'

'Yes, you 'ave. Gi' us one!'

Already she was feeling for the old, squashed, black leather purse.

'Well, what'll you give your gran?'

He gave a shy little laugh and pressed closer. She felt his eyelid quivering against her cheek. 'I ain't got nothing,' he murmured . . .

The old woman sprang up, seized the iron kettle off the gas stove and took it over to the sink. The noise of the water drumming in the kettle deadened her pain, it seemed. She filled the pail, too, and the washing-up bowl.

It would take a whole book to describe the state of that kitchen. During the week the literary gentleman 'did' for himself. That is to say, he emptied the tea leaves now and again into a jam jar set aside for that purpose, and if he ran out of clean forks he wiped over one or two on the roller towel. Otherwise, as he explained to his friends, his 'system' was quite simple, and he couldn't understand why people made all this fuss about house-keeping.

'You simply dirty everything you've got, get a hag in once a week to clean up, and the thing's done.'

The result looked like a gigantic dustbin. Even the floor was littered with toast crusts, envelopes, cigarette ends. But Ma Parker bore him no grudge. She pitied the poor young gentleman for having no one to look after him. Out of the smudgy little window you could see an immense expanse of sad-looking sky, and whenever there were clouds they looked very worn, old clouds, frayed at the edges, with holes in them, or dark stains like tea.

While the water was heating, Ma Parker began sweeping the floor. 'Yes,' she thought, as the broom knocked, 'what with one thing and another I've had my share. I've had a hard life.'

Even the neighbours said that of her. Many a time, hobbling home with her fish bag, she heard them, waiting at the corner, or leaning over the area railings, say among themselves, 'She's had a hard life, has Ma Parker.' And it was so true she wasn't in the least proud of it.

It was just as if you were to say she lived in the basement-back at Number 27. A hard life! . . .

At sixteen she'd left Stratford and come up to London as kitching-maid. Yes, she was born in Stratford-on-Avon. Shakespeare, sir? No, people were always arsking her about him. But she'd never heard his name until she saw it on the theatres.

Nothing remained of Stratford except that 'sitting in the fireplace of a evening you could see the stars through the chimley,' and 'Mother always 'ad 'er side of bacon, 'anging from the ceiling.' And there was something – a bush, there was – at the front door, that smelt ever so nice. But the bush was very vague. She'd only remembered it once or twice in the hospital, when she'd been taken bad.

That was a dreadful place – her first place. She was never allowed out. She never went upstairs except for prayers morning and evening. It was a fair cellar. And the cook was a cruel woman. She used to snatch away her letters from home before she'd read them, and throw them in the range because they made her dreamy . . . And the beedles! Would you believe it? – until she came to London she'd never seen a black beedle. Here Ma always gave a little laugh, as though – not to have seen a black beedle! Well! It was as if to say you'd never seen your own feet.

When that family was sold up she went as 'help' to a doctor's house, and after two years there, on the run from morning till night, she married her husband. He was a baker.

'A baker, Mrs Parker!' the literary gentleman would say. For occasionally he laid aside his tomes and lent an ear, at least, to this product called Life. 'It must be rather nice to be married to a baker!'

Mrs Parker didn't look so sure.

'Such a clean trade,' said the gentleman.

Mrs Parker didn't look convinced.

'And didn't you like handing the new loaves to the customers?'

'Well, sir,' said Mrs Parker, 'I wasn't in the shop above a great deal. We had thirteen little ones and buried seven of them. If it wasn't the 'ospital it was the infirmary, you might say!'

'You might, indeed, Mrs Parker!' said the gentleman, shuddering, and taking up his pen again.

Yes, seven had gone, and while the six were still small her husband was taken ill with consumption. It was flour on the lungs, the doctor told her at the time . . . Her husband sat up in bed with his shirt pulled over his head, and the doctor's finger drew a circle on his back.

'Now, if we were to cut him open here, Mrs Parker,' said the doctor, 'you'd find his lungs chock-a-block with white powder. Breathe, my good fellow!' And Mrs Parker never knew for certain whether she saw or whether she fancied she saw a great fan of white dust come out of her poor dead husband's lips . . .

But the struggle she'd had to bring up those six little children and keep herself to herself. Terrible it had been! Then, just when they were old enough to go to school her husband's sister came to stop with them to help things along, and she hadn't been there more than two months when she fell down a flight of steps and hurt her spine. And for five years Ma Parker had another baby – and such a one for crying! – to look after. Then young Maudie went wrong and took her sister Alice with her; the two boys emigrimated, and young Jim went to India with the army, and Ethel, the youngest, married a good-for-nothing little waiter who died of ulcers the year little Lennie was born. And now little Lennie – my grandson . . .

The piles of dirty cups, dirty dishes, were washed and dried. The ink-black knives were cleaned with a piece of potato and finished off with a piece of cork. The table was scrubbed, and the dresser and the sink that had sardine tails swimming in it . . .

He'd never been a strong child – never from the first. He'd been one of those fair babies that everybody took for a girl. Silvery fair curls he had, blue eyes, and a little freckle like a diamond on one side of his nose. The trouble she and Ethel had had to rear that child! The things out of the newspapers they tried him with! Every Sunday morning Ethel would read aloud while Ma Parker did her washing.

DEAR SIR
Just a line to let you know my little Myrtil was laid out for dead . . . After four bottils . . . gained 8 lbs. in 9 weeks, and is still putting it on.

And then the egg-cup of ink would come off the dresser and the letter would be written, and Ma would buy a postal order on her way to work next morning. But it was no use. Nothing made little Lennie put it on. Taking him to the cemetery, even, never gave him a colour; a nice shake-up in the bus never improved his appetite.

But he was gran's boy from the first . . .

'Whose boy are you?' said old Ma Parker, straightening up from the stove and going over to the smudgy window. And a little voice, so warm, so close, it half stifled her – it seemed to be in her breast under her heart – laughed out, and said, 'I'm gran's boy!'

At that moment there was a sound of steps, and the literary gentleman appeared, dressed for walking.

'Oh, Mrs Parker, I'm going out.'

'Very good, sir.'

'And you'll find your half-crown in the tray of the inkstand.'

'Thank you, sir.'

'Oh, by the way, Mrs Parker,' said the literary gentleman quickly, 'you didn't throw away any cocoa last time you were here – did you?'

'No, sir.' 'Very strange. I could have sworn I left a teaspoonful of cocoa in the tin.' He broke off. He said softly and firmly, 'You'll always tell me when you throw things away – won't you, Mrs Parker?' And he walked off very well pleased with himself, convinced, in fact, he'd shown Mrs Parker that under his apparent carelessness he was as vigilant as a woman.

The door banged. She took her brushes and cloths into the bedroom. But when she began to make the bed, smoothing, tucking, patting, the thought of little Lennie was unbearable. Why did he have to suffer so? That's what she couldn't understand. Why should a little angel child have to arsk for his breath and fight for it? There was no sense in making a child suffer like that.

. . . From Lennie's little box of a chest there came a sound as though something was boiling. There was a great lump of something bubbling in his chest that he couldn't get rid of. When he coughed the sweat sprang out on his head; his eyes bulged, his hands waved, and the great lump bubbled as a potato knocks in a saucepan. But what was more awful than all was when he didn't cough he sat against the pillow and never spoke or answered, or even made as if he heard. Only he looked offended.

'It's not your poor old gran's doing it, my lovey,' said old Ma Parker, patting back the damp hair from his little scarlet ears. But Lennie moved his head and edged away. Dreadfully offended with her he looked – and solemn. He bent his head and looked at her sideways as though he couldn't have believed it of his gran.

But at the last . . . Ma Parker threw the counterpane over the bed. No, she simply couldn't think about it. It was too much – she'd had too much in her life to bear. She'd borne it up till now, she'd kept herself to herself, and never once had she been seen to cry. Never by a living soul. Not even her own children had seen Ma break down. She'd kept a proud face always. But now! Lennie gone – what had she? She had nothing. He was all she'd got from life, and now he was took too. Why must it all have happened to me? she wondered.

'What have I done?' said old Ma Parker. 'What have I done?'

As she said those words she suddenly let fall her brush. She found herself in the kitchen. Her misery was so terrible that she pinned on her hat, put on her jacket and walked out of the flat like a person in a dream. She did not know what she was doing. She was like a person so dazed by the horror of what has happened that he walks away – anywhere, as though by walking away he could escape . . .

It was cold in the street. There was a wind like ice. People went flitting by, very fast; the men walked like scissors; the women trod like cats. And nobody knew – nobody cared. Even if she broke down, if at last, after all these years, she were to cry, she'd find herself in the lock-up as like as not.

But at the thought of crying it was as though little Lennie leapt in his gran's arms. Ah, that's what she wants to do, my dove. Gran wants to cry. If she could only cry now, cry for a long time, over everything, beginning with her first place and the cruel cook, going on to the doctor's, and then the seven little ones, death of her husband, the children's leaving her, and all the years of misery that led up to Lennie. But to have a proper cry over all these things would take a long time. All the same, the time for it had come. She must do it. She couldn't put it off any longer; she couldn't wait any more . . . Where could she go?

'She's had a hard life, has Ma Parker.' Yes, a hard life, indeed! Her chin began to tremble; there was no time to lose. But where? Where?

She couldn't go home; Ethel was there. It would frighten Ethel out of her life. She couldn't sit on a bench anywhere; people would come arsking her questions. She couldn't possibly go back to the gentleman's flat; she had no right to cry in strangers' houses. If she sat on some steps a policeman would speak to her.

Oh, wasn't there anywhere where she could hide and keep herself to herself and stay as long as she liked, not disturbing anybody, and nobody worrying her? Wasn't there anywhere in the world where she could have her cry out – at last?

Ma Parker stood, looking up and down. The icy wind blew out her apron into a balloon. And now it began to rain. There was nowhere.

Marriage à la Mode

ON HIS WAY to the station William remembered with a fresh pang of disappointment that he was taking nothing down to the kiddies. Poor little chaps! It was hard lines on them. Their first words always were as they ran to greet him, 'What have you got for me, daddy?' and he had nothing. He would have to buy them some sweets at the station. But that was what he had done for the past four Saturdays; their faces had fallen last time when they saw the same old boxes produced again.

And Paddy had said, 'I had red ribbing on mine bee-fore!'

And Johnny had said, 'It's always pink on mine. I hate pink.'

But what was William to do? The affair wasn't so easily settled. In the old days, of course, he would have taken a taxi off to a decent toyshop and chosen them something in five minutes. But nowadays they had Russian toys, French toys, Serbian toys – toys from God knows where. It was over a year since Isabel had scrapped the old donkeys and engines and so on because they were so 'dreadfully sentimental' and 'so appallingly bad for the babies' sense of form'.

'It's so important,' the new Isabel had explained, 'that they should like the right things from the very beginning. It saves so much time later on. Really, if the poor pets have to spend their infant years staring at these horrors, one can imagine them growing up and asking to be taken to the Royal Academy.'

And she spoke as though a visit to the Royal Academy was certain immediate death to anyone . . .

'Well, I don't know,' said William slowly. 'When I was their age I used to go to bed hugging an old towel with a knot in it.'

The new Isabel looked at him, her eyes narrowed, her lips apart.

'Dear William! I'm sure you did!' She laughed in the new way.

Sweets it would have to be, however, thought William gloomily, fishing in his pocket for change for the taxi-man. And he saw the kiddies handing the boxes round – they were awfully generous little chaps – while Isabel's precious friends didn't hesitate to help themselves . . .

What about fruit? William hovered before a stall just inside the station. What about a melon each? Would they have to share that, too? Or a pineapple, for Pad, and a melon for Johnny? Isabel's friends could hardly go sneaking up to the nursery at the children's meal-times. All the same, as he bought the melon William had a horrible vision of one of Isabel's young poets lapping up a slice, for some reason, behind the nursery door.

With his two very awkward parcels he strode off to his train. The platform was crowded, the train was in. Doors banged open and shut. There came such a loud hissing from the engine that people looked dazed as they scurried to and fro. William made straight for a first-class smoker, stowed away his suitcase and parcels, and taking a huge wad of papers out of his inner pocket, he flung down in the corner and began to read.

'Our client moreover is positive . . . We are inclined to reconsider . . . in the event of – ' Ah, that was better. William pressed back his flattened hair and stretched his legs across the carriage floor. The familiar dull gnawing in his breast quietened down. 'With regard to our decision – ' He took out a blue pencil and scored a paragraph slowly.

Two men came in, stepped across him, and made for the farther corner. A young fellow swung his golf clubs into the rack and sat down opposite. The train gave a gentle lurch, they were off. William glanced up and saw the hot, bright station slipping away. A red-faced girl raced along by the carriages, there was something strained and almost desperate in the way she waved and called. 'Hysterical!' thought William dully. Then a greasy, black-faced workman at the end of the platform grinned at the passing train. And William thought, 'A filthy life!' and went back to his papers.

When he looked up again there were fields, and beasts standing for shelter under the dark trees. A wide river, with naked children splashing in the shallows, glided into sight and was gone again. The sky shone pale, and one bird drifted high like a dark fleck in a jewel.

'We have examined our client's correspondence files . . . ' The last sentence he had read echoed in his mind. 'We have examined . . . ' William hung on to that sentence, but it was no good; it snapped in the middle, and the fields, the sky, the sailing bird, the water, all said, 'Isabel.' The same thing happened every Saturday afternoon. When he was on his way to meet Isabel there began those countless imaginary meetings. She was at the station, standing just a little apart from everybody else; she was sitting in the open taxi outside; she was at the garden gate; walking across the parched grass; at the door, or just inside the hall.

And her clear, light voice said, 'It's William,' or 'Hillo, William!' or 'So William has come!' He touched her cool hand, her cool cheek.

The exquisite freshness of Isabel! When he had been a little boy, it was his delight to run into the garden after a shower of rain and shake the rose bush over him. Isabel was that rose bush, petal-soft, sparkling and cool. And he was still that little boy. But there was no running into the garden now, no laughing and shaking. The dull, persistent gnawing in his breast started again. He drew up his legs, tossed the papers aside, and shut his eyes.

'What is it, Isabel? What is it?' he said tenderly. They were in their bedroom in the new house. Isabel sat on a painted stool before the dressing-table that was strewn with little black and green boxes.

'What is what, William?' And she bent forward, and her fine light hair fell over her cheeks.

'Ah, you know!' He stood in the middle of the room and he felt a stranger. At that Isabel wheeled round quickly and faced him.

'Oh, William!' she cried imploringly, and she held up the hair-brush: 'Please! Please don't be so dreadfully stuffy and – tragic. You're always saying or looking or hinting that I've changed. Just because I've got to know really congenial people, and go about more, and am frightfully keen on – on everything, you behave as though I'd – ' Isabel tossed back her hair and laughed – 'killed our love or something. It's so awfully absurd' – she bit her lip – 'and it's so maddening, William. Even this new house and the servants you grudge me.'

'Isabel!'

'Yes, yes, it's true in a way,' said Isabel quickly. 'You think they are another bad sign. Oh, I know you do. I feel it,' she said softly, 'every time you come up the stairs. But we couldn't have gone on living in that other poky little hole, William. Be practical, at least! Why, there wasn't enough room for the babies even.'

No, it was true. Every morning when he came back from chambers it was to find the babies with Isabel in the back drawing-room. They were having rides on the leopard skin thrown over the sofa back, or they were playing shops with Isabel's desk for a counter, or Pad was sitting on the hearthrug rowing away for dear life with a little brass fire shovel, while Johnny shot at pirates with the tongs. Every evening they each had a pick-a-back up the narrow stairs to their fat old Nanny.

Yes, he supposed it was a poky little house. A little white house with blue curtains and a window-box of petunias. William met their friends at the door with 'Seen our petunias? Pretty terrific for London, don't you think?'

But the imbecile thing, the absolutely extraordinary thing was that he hadn't the slightest idea that Isabel wasn't as happy as he. God, what blindness! He hadn't the remotest notion in those days that she really hated that inconvenient little house, that she thought the fat Nanny was ruining the babies, that she was desperately lonely, pining for new people and new music and pictures and so on. If they hadn't gone to that studio party at Moira Morrison's – if Moira Morrison hadn't said as they were leaving, 'I'm going to rescue your wife, selfish man. She's like an exquisite little Titania' – if Isabel hadn't gone with Moira to Paris – if – if . . .

The train stopped at another station. Bettingford. Good heavens! They'd be there in ten minutes. William stuffed the papers back into his pockets; the young man opposite had long since disappeared. Now the other two got out. The late afternoon sun shone on women in cotton frocks and little sunburnt, barefoot children. It blazed on a silky yellow flower with coarse leaves which sprawled over a bank of rock. The air ruffling through the window smelled of the sea. Had Isabel the same crowd with her this weekend, wondered William?

And he remembered the holidays they used to have, the four of them, with a little farm girl, Rose, to look after the babies. Isabel wore a jersey and her hair in a plait; she looked about fourteen. Lord! how his nose used to peel! And the amount they ate, and the amount they slept in that immense feather bed with their feet locked together . . . William couldn't help a grim smile as he thought of Isabel's horror if she knew the full extent of his sentimentality.

*   *   *

'Hillo, William!' She was at the station after all, standing just as he had imagined, apart from the others, and – William's heart leapt – she was alone.

'Hallo, Isabel!' William stared. He thought she looked so beautiful that he had to say something, 'You look very cool.'

'Do I?' said Isabel. 'I don't feel very cool. Come along, your horrid old train is late. The taxi's outside.' She put her hand lightly on his arm as they passed the ticket collector. 'We've all come to meet you,' she said. 'But we've left Bobby Kane at the sweet shop, to be called for.'

'Oh!' said William. It was all he could say for the moment.

There in the glare waited the taxi, with Bill Hunt and Dennis Green sprawling on one side, their hats tilted over their faces, while on the other, Moira Morrison, in a bonnet like a huge strawberry, jumped up and down.

'No ice! No ice! No ice!' she shouted gaily.

And Dennis chimed in from under his hat. 'Only to be had from the fishmonger's.'

And Bill Hunt, emerging, added, 'With whole fish in it.'

'Oh, what a bore!' wailed Isabel. And she explained to William how they had been chasing round the town for ice while she waited for him. 'Simply everything is running down the steep cliffs into the sea, beginning with the butter.'

'We shall have to anoint ourselves with butter,' said Dennis. 'May thy head, William, lack not ointment.'

'Look here,' said William, 'how are we going to sit? I'd better get up by the driver.'

'No, Bobby Kane's by the driver,' said Isabel. 'You're to sit between Moira and me.' The taxi started. 'What have you got in those mysterious parcels?'

'De-cap-it-ated heads!' said Bill Hunt, shuddering beneath his hat.

'Oh, fruit!' Isabel sounded very pleased. 'Wise William! A melon and a pineapple. How too nice!'

'No, wait a bit,' said William, smiling. But he really was anxious. 'I brought them down for the kiddies.'

'Oh, my dear!' Isabel laughed, and slipped her hand through his arm. 'They'd be rolling in agonies if they were to eat them. No' – she patted his hand – 'you must bring them something next time. I refuse to part with my pineapple.'

'Cruel Isabel! Do let me smell it!' said Moira. She flung her arms across William appealingly. 'Oh!' The strawberry bonnet fell forward: she sounded quite faint.

'A Lady in Love with a Pineapple,' said Dennis, as the taxi drew up before a little shop with a striped blind. Out came Bobby Kane, his arms full of little packets.

'I do hope they'll be good. I've chosen them because of the colours. There are some round things which really look too divine. And just look at this nougat,' he cried ecstatically, 'just look at it! It's a perfect little ballet.'

But at that moment the shopman appeared. 'Oh, I forgot. They're none of them paid for,' said Bobby, looking frightened. Isabel gave the shopman a note, and Bobby was radiant again. 'Hallo, William! I'm sitting by the driver.' And bareheaded, all in white, with his sleeves rolled up to the shoulders, he leapt into his place. 'Avanti!' he cried . . .

After tea the others went off to bathe, while William stayed and made his peace with the kiddies. But Johnny and Paddy were asleep, the rose-red glow had paled, bats were flying, and still the bathers had not returned. As William wandered downstairs, the maid crossed the hall carrying a lamp. He followed her into the sitting-room. It was a long room, coloured yellow. On the wall opposite William someone had painted a young man, over life-size, with very wobbly legs, offering a wide-eyed daisy to a young woman who had one very short arm and one very long, thin one. Over the chairs and sofa there hung strips of black material, covered with big splashes like broken eggs, and everywhere one looked there seemed to be an ash-tray full of cigarette ends. William sat down in one of the arm- chairs. Nowadays, when one felt with one hand down the sides, it wasn't to come upon a sheep with three legs or a cow that had lost one horn, or a very fat dove out of the Noah's Ark. One fished up yet another little paper-covered book of smudged-looking poems . . . He thought of the wad of papers in his pocket, but he was too hungry and tired to read. The door was open; sounds came from the kitchen. The servants were talking as if they were alone in the house. Suddenly there came a loud screech of laughter and an equally loud 'Sh!' They had remembered him. William got up and went through the French windows into the garden, and as he stood there in the shadow he heard the bathers coming up the sandy road; their voices rang through the quiet.

'I think it's up to Moira to use her little arts and wiles.'

A tragic moan from Moira.

'We ought to have a gramophone for the weekends that played "The Maid of the Mountains".'

'Oh no! Oh no!' cried Isabel's voice. 'That's not fair to William. Be nice to him, my children! He's only staying until tomorrow evening.'

'Leave him to me,' cried Bobby Kane. 'I'm awfully good at looking after people.'

The gate swung open and shut. William moved on the terrace; they had seen him. 'Hallo, William!' And Bobby Kane, flapping his towel, began to leap and pirouette on the parched lawn. 'Pity you didn't come, William. The water was divine. And we all went to a little pub afterwards and had sloe gin.'

The others had reached the house. 'I say, Isabel,' called Bobby, 'would you like me to wear my Nijinsky dress tonight?'

'No,' said Isabel, 'nobody's going to dress. We're all starving. William's starving, too. Come along, *mes amis*, let's begin with sardines.'

'I've found the sardines,' said Moira, and she ran into the hall, holding a box high in the air.

'A Lady with a Box of Sardines,' said Dennis gravely.

'Well, William, and how's London?' asked Bill Hunt, drawing the cork out of a bottle of whisky.

'Oh, London's not much changed,' answered William.

'Good old London,' said Bobby, very hearty, spearing a sardine.

But a moment later William was forgotten. Moira Morrison began wondering what colour one's legs really were under water.

'Mine are the palest, palest mushroom colour.'

Bill and Dennis ate enormously. And Isabel filled glasses, and changed plates, and found matches, smiling blissfully. At one moment, she said, 'I do wish, Bill, you'd paint it.'

'Paint what?' said Bill loudly, stuffing his mouth with bread.

'Us,' said Isabel, 'round the table. It would be so fascinating in twenty years' time.'

Bill screwed up his eyes and chewed. 'Light's wrong,' he said rudely, 'far too much yellow'; and went on eating. And that seemed to charm Isabel, too.

But after supper they were all so tired they could do nothing but yawn until it was late enough to go to bed . . .

It was not until William was waiting for his taxi the next afternoon that he found himself alone with Isabel. When he brought his suitcase down into the hall, Isabel left the others and went over to him. She stooped down and picked up the suitcase. 'What a weight!' she said, and she gave a little awkward laugh. 'Let me carry it! To the gate.'

'No, why should you?' said William. 'Of course not. Give it to me.'

'Oh, please, do let me,' said Isabel. 'I want to, really.' They walked together silently. William felt there was nothing to say now.

'There,' said Isabel triumphantly, setting the suitcase down, and she looked anxiously along the sandy road. 'I hardly seem to have seen you this time,' she said breathlessly. 'It's so short, isn't it? I feel you've only just come. Next time –' The taxi came into sight. 'I hope they look after you properly in London. I'm so sorry the babies have been out all day, but Miss Neil had arranged it. They'll hate missing you. Poor William, going back to London.' The taxi turned. 'Goodbye!' She gave him a little hurried kiss; she was gone.

Fields, trees, hedges streamed by. They shook through the empty, blind-looking little town, ground up the steep pull to the station.

The train was in. William made straight for a first-class smoker, flung back into the corner, but this time he let the papers alone. He folded his arms against the dull, persistent gnawing, and began in his mind to write a letter to Isabel.

*   *   *

The post was late as usual. They sat outside the house in long chairs under coloured parasols. Only Bobby Kane lay on the turf at Isabel's feet. It was dull, stifling; the day drooped like a flag.

'Do you think there will be Mondays in Heaven?' asked Bobby childishly.

And Dennis murmured, 'Heaven will be one long Monday.'

But Isabel couldn't help wondering what had happened to the salmon they had for supper last night. She had meant to have fish mayonnaise for lunch and now . . .

Moira was asleep. Sleeping was her latest discovery. 'It's so wonderful. One simply shuts one's eyes, that's all. It's so delicious.'

When the old ruddy postman came beating along the sandy road on his tricycle one felt the handle-bars ought to have been oars.

Bill Hunt put down his book. 'Letters,' he said complacently, and they all waited. But, heartless postman – O malignant world! There was only one, a fat one for Isabel. Not even a paper.

'And mine's only from William,' said Isabel mournfully.

'From William – already?'

'He's sending you back your marriage lines as a gentle reminder.'

'Does everybody have marriage lines? I thought they were only for servants.'

'Pages and pages! Look at her! A Lady reading a Letter,' said Dennis.

'My darling, precious Isabel.' Pages and pages there were. As Isabel read on her feeling of astonishment changed to a stifled feeling. What on earth had induced William . . . ? How extraordinary it was . . . What could have made him . . . ? She felt confused, more and more excited, even frightened. It was just like William. Was it? It was absurd, of course, it must be absurd, ridiculous. 'Ha, ha, ha!

Oh dear!' What was she to do? Isabel flung back in her chair and laughed till she couldn't stop laughing.

'Do, do tell us,' said the others. 'You must tell us.'

'I'm longing to,' gurgled Isabel. She sat up, gathered the letter, and waved it at them. 'Gather round,' she said. 'Listen, it's too marvellous. A love-letter!'

'A love-letter! But how divine!' 'Darling, precious Isabel.' But she had hardly begun before their laughter interrupted her.

'Go on, Isabel, it's perfect.'

'It's the most marvellous find.'

'Oh, do go on, Isabel!'

'God forbid, my darling, that I should be a drag on your happiness.'

'Oh! oh! oh!'

'Sh! sh! sh!'

And Isabel went on. When she reached the end they were hysterical: Bobby rolled on the turf and almost sobbed.

'You must let me have it just as it is, entire, for my new book,' said Dennis firmly. 'I shall give it a whole chapter.'

'Oh, Isabel,' moaned Moira, 'that wonderful bit about holding you in his arms!'

'I always thought those letters in divorce cases were made up. But they pale before this.'

'Let me hold it. Let me read it, mine own self,' said Bobby Kane.

But, to their surprise, Isabel crushed the letter in her hand. She was laughing no longer. She glanced quickly at them all; she looked exhausted. 'No, not just now. Not just now,' she stammered.

And before they could recover she had run into the house, through the hall, up the stairs into her bedroom. Down she sat on the side of the bed. 'How vile, odious, abominable, vulgar,' muttered Isabel. She pressed her eyes with her knuckles and rocked to and fro. And again she saw them, but not four, more like forty, laughing, sneering, jeering, stretching out their hands while she read them William's letter. Oh, what a loathsome thing to have done. How could she have done it! 'God forbid, my darling, that I should be a drag on your happiness.' William! Isabel pressed her face into the pillow. But she felt that even the grave bedroom knew her for what she was, shallow, tinkling, vain . . .

Presently from the garden below there came voices.

'Isabel, we're all going for a bathe. Do come!'

'Come, thou wife of William!'

'Call her once before you go, call once yet!'

Isabel sat up. Now was the moment, now she must decide. Would she go with them, or stay here and write to William. Which, which should it be? 'I must make up my mind.' Oh, but how could there be any question? Of course she would stay here and write.

'Titania!' piped Moira.

'Isa-bel?'

No, it was too difficult. 'I'll – I'll go with them, and write to William later. Some other time. Later. Not now. But I shall certainly write,' thought Isabel hurriedly.

And, laughing, in the new way, she ran down the stairs.

The Voyage

THE PICTON BOAT was due to leave at half-past eleven. It was a beautiful night, mild, starry, only when they got out of the cab and started to walk down the Old Wharf that jutted out into the harbour, a faint wind blowing off the water ruffled under Fenella's hat, and she put up her hand to keep it on. It was dark on the Old Wharf, very dark; the wool sheds, the cattle trucks, the cranes standing up so high, the little squat railway engine, all seemed carved out of solid darkness. Here and there on a rounded wood-pile, that was like the stalk of a huge black mushroom, there hung a lantern, but it seemed afraid to unfurl its timid, quivering light in all that blackness; it burned softly, as if for itself.

Fenella's father pushed on with quick, nervous strides. Beside him her grandma bustled along in her crackling black ulster; they went so fast that she had now and again to give an undignified little skip to keep up with them. As well as her luggage strapped into a neat sausage, Fenella carried clasped to her her grandma's umbrella, and the handle, which was a swan's head, kept giving her shoulder a sharp little peck as if it too wanted her to hurry . . . Men, their caps pulled down, their collars turned up, swung by; a few women all muffled scurried along; and one tiny boy, only his little black arms and legs showing out of a white woolly shawl, was jerked along angrily between his father and mother; he looked like a baby fly that had fallen into the cream.

Then suddenly, so suddenly that Fenella and her grandma both leapt, there sounded from behind the largest wool shed, that had a trail of smoke hanging over it, 'Mia-oo-oo-O-O!'

'First whistle,' said her father briefly, and at that moment they came in sight of the Picton boat. Lying beside the dark wharf, all strung, all beaded with round golden lights, the Picton boat looked as if she was more ready to sail among stars than out into the cold sea. People pressed along the gangway. First went her grandma, then her father, then Fenella. There was a high step down on to the deck, and an old sailor in a jersey standing by gave her his dry, hard hand. They were there; they stepped out of the way of the hurrying people, and standing under a little iron stairway that led to the upper deck they began to say goodbye.

'There, mother, there's your luggage!' said Fenella's father, giving grandma another strapped-up sausage.

'Thank you, Frank.'

'And you've got your cabin tickets safe?'

'Yes, dear.'

'And your other tickets?'

Grandma felt for them inside her glove and showed him the tips. 'That's right.'

He sounded stern, but Fenella, eagerly watching him, saw that he looked tired and sad. 'Mia-oo-oo-O-O!' The second whistle blared just above their heads, and a voice like a cry shouted, 'Any more for the gangway?'

'You'll give my love to father,' Fenella saw her father's lips say. And her grandma, very agitated, answered, 'Of course I will, dear. Go now. You'll be left. Go now, Frank. Go now.'

'It's all right, mother. I've got another three minutes.' To her surprise Fenella saw her father take off his hat. He clasped grandma in his arms and pressed her to him. 'God bless you, mother!' she heard him say.

And grandma put her hand, with the black thread glove that was worn through on her ring finger, against his cheek, and she sobbed, 'God bless you, my own brave son!'

This was so awful that Fenella quickly turned her back on them, swallowed once, twice, and frowned terribly at a little green star on a mast head. But she had to turn round again; her father was going.

'Goodbye, Fenella. Be a good girl.' His cold, wet moustache brushed her cheek. But Fenella caught hold of the lapels of his coat.

'How long am I going to stay?' she whispered anxiously. He wouldn't look at her. He shook her off gently, and gently said, 'We'll see about that. Here! Where's your hand?' He pressed something into her palm. 'Here's a shilling in case you should need it.'

A shilling! She must be going away for ever! 'Father!' cried Fenella. But he was gone. He was the last off the ship. The sailors put their shoulders to the gangway. A huge coil of dark rope went flying through the air and fell 'thump' on the wharf. A bell rang; a whistle shrilled. Silently the dark wharf began to slip, to slide, to edge away from them. Now there was a rush of water between. Fenella strained to see with all her might. 'Was that father turning round?' – or waving? – or standing alone? – or walking off by himself? The strip of water grew broader, darker. Now the Picton boat began to swing round steady, pointing out to sea. It was no good looking any longer. There was nothing to be seen but a few lights, the face of the town clock hanging in the air, and more lights, little patches of them, on the dark hills.

The freshening wind tugged at Fenella's skirts; she went back to her grandma. To her relief grandma seemed no longer sad. She had put the two sausages of luggage one on top of the other, and she was sitting on them, her hands folded, her head a little on one side. There was an intent, bright look on her face. Then Fenella saw that her lips were moving and guessed that she was praying. But the old woman gave her a bright nod as if to say the prayer was nearly over. She unclasped her hands, sighed, clasped them again, bent forward, and at last gave herself a soft shake.

'And now, child,' she said, fingering the bow of her bonnet-strings, 'I think we ought to see about our cabins. Keep close to me, and mind you don't slip.'

'Yes, grandma!'

'And be careful the umbrellas aren't caught in the stair rail. I saw a beautiful umbrella broken in half like that on my way over.'

'Yes, grandma.'

Dark figures of men lounged against the rails. In the glow of their pipes a nose shone out, or the peak of a cap, or a pair of surprised-looking eyebrows. Fenella glanced up. High in the air, a little figure, his hands thrust in his short jacket pockets, stood staring out to sea. The ship rocked ever so little, and she thought the stars rocked too. And now a pale steward in a linen coat, holding a tray high in the palm of his hand, stepped out of a lighted doorway and skimmed past them. They went through that doorway. Carefully over the high brass-bound step on to the rubber mat and then down such a terribly steep flight of stairs that grandma had to put both feet on each step, and Fenella clutched the clammy brass rail and forgot all about the swan-necked umbrella.

At the bottom grandma stopped; Fenella was rather afraid she was going to pray again. But no, it was only to get out the cabin tickets. They were in the saloon. It was glaring bright and stifling; the air smelled of paint and burnt chop-bones and india-rubber. Fenella wished her grandma would go on, but the old woman was not to be hurried. An immense basket of ham sandwiches caught her eye. She went up to them and touched the top one delicately with her finger.

'How much are the sandwiches?' she asked.

'Tuppence!' bawled a rude steward, slamming down a knife and fork.

Grandma could hardly believe it.

'Twopence each?' she asked.

'That's right,' said the steward, and he winked at his companion.

Grandma made a small, astonished face. Then she whispered primly to Fenella. 'What wickedness!' And they sailed out at the further door and along a passage that had cabins on either side. Such a very nice stewardess came to meet them. She was dressed all in blue, and her collar and cuffs were fastened with large brass buttons. She seemed to know grandma well.

'Well, Mrs Crane,' said she, unlocking their washstand. 'We've got you back again. It's not often you give yourself a cabin.'

'No,' said grandma. 'But this time my dear son's thoughtfulness – '

'I hope – ' began the stewardess. Then she turned round and took a long, mournful look at grandma's blackness and at Fenella's black coat and skirt, black blouse, and hat with a crape rose.

Grandma nodded. 'It was God's will,' said she.

The stewardess shut her lips and, taking a deep breath, she seemed to expand.

'What I always say is,' she said, as though it was her own discovery, 'sooner or later each of us has to go, and that's a certingty.' She paused. 'Now, can I bring you anything, Mrs Crane? A cup of tea? I know it's no good offering you a little something to keep the cold out.'

Grandma shook her head. 'Nothing, thank you. We've got a few wine biscuits, and Fenella has a very nice banana.'

'Then I'll give you a look later on,' said the stewardess, and she went out, shutting the door.

What a very small cabin it was! It was like being shut up in a box with grandma. The dark round eye above the washstand gleamed at them dully. Fenella felt shy. She stood against the door, still clasping her luggage and the umbrella. Were they going to get undressed in here? Already her grandma had taken off her bonnet, and, rolling up the strings, she fixed each with a pin to the lining before she hung the bonnet up. Her white hair shone like silk; the little bun at the back was covered with a black net. Fenella hardly ever saw her grandma with her head uncovered; she looked strange.

'I shall put on the woollen fascinator your dear mother crocheted for me,' said grandma, and, unstrapping the sausage, she took it out and wound it round her head; the fringe of grey bobbles danced at her eyebrows as she smiled tenderly and mournfully at Fenella. Then she undid her bodice, and something under that, and something else underneath that. Then there seemed a short, sharp tussle, and grandma flushed faintly. Snip! Snap! She had undone her stays. She breathed a sigh of relief, and sitting on the plush couch, she slowly and carefully pulled off her elastic-sided boots and stood them side by side.

By the time Fenella had taken off her coat and skirt and put on her flannel dressing-gown grandma was quite ready.

'Must I take off my boots, grandma? They're lace.'

Grandma gave them a moment's deep consideration. 'You'd feel a great deal more comfortable if you did, child,' said she. She kissed Fenella. 'Don't forget to say your prayers. Our dear Lord is with us when we are at sea even more than when we are on dry land. And because I am an experienced traveller,' said grandma briskly, 'I shall take the upper berth.'

'But, grandma, however will you get up there?'

Three little spider-like steps were all Fenella saw. The old woman gave a small silent laugh before she mounted them nimbly, and she peered over the high bunk at the astonished Fenella.

'You didn't think your grandma could do that, did you?' said she. And as she sank back Fenella heard her light laugh again.

The hard square of brown soap would not lather, and the water in the bottle was like a kind of blue jelly. How hard it was, too, to turn down those stiff sheets; you simply had to tear your way in. If everything had been different, Fenella might have got the giggles . . . At last she was inside, and while she lay there panting, there sounded from above a long, soft whispering, as though someone was gently, gently rustling among tissue paper to find something. It was grandma saying her prayers . . .

A long time passed. Then the stewardess came in; she trod softly and leaned her hand on grandma's bunk.

'We're just entering the Straits,' she said.

'Oh!'

'It's a fine night, but we're rather empty. We may pitch a little.'

And indeed at that moment the Picton Boat rose and rose and hung in the air just long enough to give a shiver before she swung down again, and there was the sound of heavy water slapping against her sides. Fenella remembered she had left the swan-necked umbrella standing up on the little couch. If it fell over, would it break? But grandma remembered too, at the same time.

'I wonder if you'd mind, stewardess, laying down my umbrella,' she whispered.

'Not at all, Mrs Crane.' And the stewardess, coming back to grand-ma, breathed, 'Your little granddaughter's in such a beautiful sleep.'

'God be praised for that!' said grandma.

'Poor little motherless mite!' said the stewardess. And grandma was still telling the stewardess all about what happened when Fenella fell asleep.

But she hadn't been asleep long enough to dream before she woke up again to see something waving in the air above her head. What was it? What could it be? It was a small grey foot. Now another joined it. They seemed to be feeling about for something; there came a sigh.

'I'm awake, grandma,' said Fenella.

'Oh, dear, am I near the ladder?' asked grandma. 'I thought it was this end.'

'No, grandma, it's the other. I'll put your foot on it. Are we there?' asked Fenella.

'In the harbour,' said grandma. 'We must get up, child. You'd better have a biscuit to steady yourself before you move.'

But Fenella had hopped out of her bunk. The lamp was still burning, but night was over, and it was cold. Peering through that round eye she could see far off some rocks. Now they were scattered over with foam; now a gull flipped by; and now there came a long piece of real land.

'It's land, grandma,' said Fenella, wonderingly, as though they had been at sea for weeks together. She hugged herself; she stood on one leg and rubbed it with the toes of the other foot; she was trembling. Oh, it had all been so sad lately. Was it going to change? But all her grandma said was, 'Make haste, child. I should leave your nice banana for the stewardess as you haven't eaten it.' And Fenella put on her black clothes again and a button sprang off one of her gloves and rolled to where she couldn't reach it. They went up on deck.

But if it had been cold in the cabin, on deck it was like ice. The sun was not up yet, but the stars were dim, and the cold pale sky was the same colour as the cold pale sea. On the land a white mist rose and fell. Now they could see quite plainly dark bush. Even the shapes of the umbrella ferns showed, and those strange silvery withered trees that are like skeletons . . . Now they could see the landing-stage and some little houses, pale too, clustered together, like shells on the lid of a box. The other passengers tramped up and down, but more slowly than they had the night before, and they looked gloomy.

And now the landing-stage came out to meet them. Slowly it swam towards the Picton boat, and a man holding a coil of rope, and a cart with a small drooping horse and another man sitting on the step, came too.

'It's Mr Penreddy, Fenella, come for us,' said grandma. She sounded pleased. Her white waxen cheeks were blue with cold, her chin trembled, and she had to keep wiping her eyes and her little pink nose.

'You've got my –'

'Yes, grandma.' Fenella showed it to her.

The rope came flying through the air, and 'smack' it fell on to the deck. The gangway was lowered. Again Fenella followed her grandma on to the wharf over to the little cart, and a moment later they were bowling away. The hooves of the little horse drummed over the wooden piles, then sank softly into the sandy road. Not a soul was to be seen; there was not even a feather of smoke. The mist rose and fell and the sea still sounded asleep as slowly it turned on the beach.

'I seen Mr Crane yestiddy,' said Mr Penreddy. 'He looked himself then. Missus knocked him up a batch of scones last week.'

And now the little horse pulled up before one of the shell-like houses. They got down. Fenella put her hand on the gate, and the big, trembling dew-drops soaked through her glove-tips. Up a little path of round white pebbles they went, with drenched sleeping flowers on either side. Grandma's delicate white picotees were so heavy with dew that they were fallen, but their sweet smell was part of the cold morning. The blinds were down in the little house; they mounted the steps on to the veranda. A pair of old bluchers was on one side of the door, and a large red watering-can on the other.

'Tut! tut! Your grandpa,' said grandma. She turned the handle. Not a sound. She called, 'Walter!' And immediately a deep voice that sounded half-stifled called back, 'Is that you, Mary?'

'Wait, dear,' said grandma. 'Go in there.' She pushed Fenella gently into a small dusky sitting-room.

On the table a white cat, that had been folded up like a camel, rose, stretched itself, yawned, and then sprang on to the tips of its toes. Fenella buried one cold little hand in the white, warm fur, and smiled timidly while she stroked and listened to grandma's gentle voice and the rolling tones of grandpa.

A door creaked. 'Come in, dear.' The old woman beckoned, Fenella followed. There, lying to one side on an immense bed, lay grandpa. Just his head with a white tuft and his rosy face and long silver beard showed over the quilt. He was like a very old wide-awake bird.

'Well, my girl!' said grandpa. 'Give us a kiss!' Fenella kissed him. 'Ugh!' said grandpa. 'Her little nose is as cold as a button. What's that she's holding? Her grandma's umbrella?'

Fenella smiled again, and crooked the swan neck over the bed-rail. Above the bed there was a big text in a deep black frame:

> Lost! One Golden Hour
> Set with Sixty Diamond Minutes.
> No Reward Is Offered
> For It Is Gone For Ever!

'Yer grandma painted that,' said grandpa. And he ruffled his white tuft and looked at Fenella so merrily she almost thought he winked at her.

Miss Brill

ALTHOUGH IT WAS so brilliantly fine – the blue sky powdered with gold and great spots of light like white wine splashed over the *Jardins Publiques* – Miss Brill was glad that she had decided on her fur. The air was motionless, but when you opened your mouth there was just a faint chill, like a chill from a glass of iced water before you sip, and now and again a leaf came drifting – from nowhere, from the sky. Miss Brill put up her hand and touched her fur. Dear little thing! It was nice to feel it again. She had taken it out of its box that afternoon, shaken out the moth-powder, given it a good brush, and rubbed the life back into the dim little eyes. 'What has been happening to me?' said the sad little eyes. Oh, how sweet it was to see them snap at her again from the red eiderdown! . . . But the nose, which was of some black composition, wasn't at all firm. It must have had a knock, somehow. Never mind – a little dab of black sealing-wax when the time came – when it was absolutely necessary . . . Little rogue! Yes, she really felt like that about it. Little rogue biting its tail just by her left ear. She could have taken it off and laid it on her lap and stroked it. She felt a tingling in her hands and arms, but that came from walking, she supposed. And when she breathed, something light and sad – no, not sad, exactly – something gentle seemed to move in her bosom.

There were a number of people out this afternoon, far more than last Sunday. And the band sounded louder and gayer. That was because the Season had begun. For although the band played all the year round on Sundays, out of season it was never the same. It was like someone playing with only the family to listen; it didn't care how it played if there weren't any strangers present. Wasn't the conductor wearing a new coat, too? She was sure it was new. He scraped with his foot and flapped his arms like a rooster about to crow, and the bandsmen sitting in the green rotunda blew out their cheeks and glared at the music. Now there came a little 'flutey' bit – very pretty! – a little chain of bright drops. She was sure it would be repeated. It was; she lifted her head and smiled.

Only two people shared her 'special' seat: a fine old man in a velvet coat, his hands clasped over a huge carved walking-stick, and a big old woman, sitting upright, with a roll of knitting on her embroidered apron. They did not speak. This was disappointing, for Miss Brill always looked forward to the conversation. She had become really quite expert, she thought, at listening as though she didn't listen, at sitting in other people's lives just for a minute while they talked round her.

She glanced, sideways, at the old couple. Perhaps they would go soon. Last Sunday, too, hadn't been as interesting as usual. An Englishman and his wife, he wearing a dreadful Panama hat and she button boots. And she'd gone on the whole time about how she ought to wear spectacles; she knew she needed them; but that it was no good getting any; they'd be sure to break and they'd never keep on. And he'd been so patient. He'd suggested everything – gold rims, the kind that curved round your ears, little pads inside the bridge. No, nothing would please her. 'They'll always be sliding down my nose!' Miss Brill had wanted to shake her.

The old people sat on the bench, still as statues. Never mind, there was always the crowd to watch. To and fro, in front of the flower-beds and the band rotunda, the couples and groups paraded, stopped to talk, to greet, to buy a handful of flowers from the old beggar who had his tray fixed to the railings. Little children ran among them, swooping and laughing; little boys with big white silk bows under their chins, little girls, little French dolls, dressed up in velvet and lace. And sometimes a tiny staggerer came suddenly rocking into the open from under the trees, stopped, stared, as suddenly sat down 'flop', until its small high-stepping mother, like a young hen, rushed scolding to its rescue. Other people sat on the benches and green chairs, but they were nearly always the same, Sunday after Sunday, and – Miss Brill had often noticed – there was something funny about nearly all of them. They were odd, silent, nearly all old, and from the way they stared they looked as though they'd just come from dark little rooms or even – even cupboards!

Behind the rotunda the slender trees with yellow leaves down drooping, and through them just a line of sea, and beyond the blue sky with gold-veined clouds.

Tum-tum-tum tiddle-um! tiddle-um! tum tiddley-um tum ta! blew the band.

Two young girls in red came by and two young soldiers in blue met them, and they laughed and paired and went off arm-in-arm.

Two peasant women with funny straw hats passed, gravely, leading beautiful smoke-coloured donkeys. A cold, pale nun hurried by. A beautiful woman came along and dropped her bunch of violets, and a little boy ran after to hand them to her, and she took them and threw them away as if they'd been poisoned. Dear me! Miss Brill didn't know whether to admire that or not! And now an ermine toque and a gentleman in grey met just in front of her. He was tall, stiff, dignified, and she was wearing the ermine toque she'd bought when her hair was yellow. Now everything, her hair, her face, even her eyes, was the same colour as the shabby ermine, and her hand, in its cleaned glove, lifted to dab her lips, was a tiny yellowish paw. Oh, she was so pleased to see him – delighted! She rather thought they were going to meet that afternoon. She described where she'd been – everywhere, here, there, along by the sea. The day was so charming – didn't he agree? And wouldn't he, perhaps? . . . But he shook his head, lighted a cigarette, slowly breathed a great deep puff into her face, and even while she was still talking and laughing, flicked the match away and walked on. The ermine toque was alone; she smiled more brightly than ever. But even the band seemed to know what she was feeling and played more softly, played tenderly, and the drum beat, 'The Brute! The Brute!' over and over. What would she do? What was going to happen now? But as Miss Brill wondered, the ermine toque turned, raised her hand as though she'd seen someone else, much nicer, just over there, and pattered away. And the band changed again and played more quickly, more gaily than ever, and the old couple on Miss Brill's seat got up and marched away, and such a funny old man with long whiskers hobbled along in time to the music and was nearly knocked over by four girls walking abreast.

Oh, how fascinating it was! How she enjoyed it! How she loved sitting here, watching it all! It was like a play. It was exactly like a play. Who could believe the sky at the back wasn't painted? But it wasn't till a little brown dog trotted on solemn and then slowly trotted off, like a little 'theatre' dog, a little dog that had been drugged, that Miss Brill discovered what it was that made it so exciting. They were all on the stage. They weren't only the audience, not only looking on; they were acting. Even she had a part and came every Sunday. No doubt somebody would have noticed if she hadn't been there; she was part of the performance after all. How strange she'd never thought of it like that before! And yet it explained why she made such a point of starting from home at just

the same time each week – so as not to be late for the performance – and it also explained why she had quite a queer, shy feeling
at telling her English pupils how she spent her Sunday afternoons.
No wonder! Miss Brill nearly laughed out loud. She was on
the stage. She thought of the old invalid gentleman to whom she
read the newspaper four afternoons a week while he slept in the
garden. She had got quite used to the frail head on the cotton
pillow, the hollowed eyes, the open mouth and the high pinched
nose. If he'd been dead she mightn't have noticed for weeks; she
wouldn't have minded. But suddenly he knew he was having the
paper read to him by an actress! 'An actress!' The old head lifted;
two points of light quivered in the old eyes. 'An actress – are ye?'
And Miss Brill smoothed the newspaper as though it were the
manuscript of her part and said gently: 'Yes, I have been an actress
for a long time.'

The band had been having a rest. Now they started again. And
what they played was warm, sunny, yet there was just a faint chill –
a something, what was it? – not sadness – no, not sadness – a
something that made you want to sing. The tune lifted, lifted, the
light shone; and it seemed to Miss Brill that in another moment all
of them, all the whole company, would begin singing. The young
ones, the laughing ones who were moving together, they would
begin, and the men's voices, very resolute and brave, would join
them. And then she too, she too, and the others on the benches –
they would come in with a kind of accompaniment – something
low, that scarcely rose or fell, something so beautiful – moving . . .
And Miss Brill's eyes filled with tears and she looked smiling at
all the other members of the company. Yes, we understand, we
understand, she thought – though what they understood she
didn't know.

Just at that moment a boy and girl came and sat down where the
old couple had been. They were beautifully dressed; they were in
love. The hero and heroine, of course, just arrived from his father's
yacht. And still soundlessly singing, still with that trembling smile,
Miss Brill prepared to listen.

'No, not now,' said the girl. 'Not here, I can't.'

'But why? Because of that stupid old thing at the end there?' asked
the boy. 'Why does she come here at all – who wants her? Why
doesn't she keep her silly old mug at home?'

'It's her fu-ur which is so funny,' giggled the girl. 'It's exactly like a
fried whiting.'

'Ah, be off with you!' said the boy in an angry whisper. Then: 'Tell me, *ma petite chère* – '

'No, not here,' said the girl. 'Not yet.'

*   *   *

On her way home she usually bought a slice of honey-cake at the baker's. It was her Sunday treat. Sometimes there was an almond in her slice, sometimes not. It made a great difference. If there was an almond it was like carrying home a tiny present – a surprise – something that might very well not have been there. She hurried on the almond Sundays and struck the match for the kettle in quite a dashing way.

But today she passed the baker's by, climbed the stairs, went into the little dark room – her room like a cupboard – and sat down on the red eiderdown. She sat there for a long time. The box that the fur came out of was on the bed. She unclasped the necklet quickly; quickly, without looking, laid it inside. But when she put the lid on she thought she heard something crying.

Her First Ball

EXACTLY WHEN the ball began Leila would have found it hard to say. Perhaps her first real partner was the cab. It did not matter that she shared the cab with the Sheridan girls and their brother. She sat back in her own little corner of it, and the bolster on which her hand rested felt like the sleeve of an unknown young man's dress suit; and away they bowled, past waltzing lamp-posts and houses and fences and trees.

'Have you really never been to a ball before, Leila? But, my child, how too weird – ' cried the Sheridan girls.

'Our nearest neighbour was fifteen miles,' said Leila softly, gently opening and shutting her fan.

Oh dear, how hard it was to be indifferent like the others! She tried not to smile too much; she tried not to care. But every single thing was so new and exciting . . . Meg's tuberoses, Jose's long loop of amber, Laura's little dark head, pushing above her white fur like a flower through snow. She would remember for ever. It even gave her a pang to see her cousin Laurie throw away the wisps of tissue paper he pulled from the fastenings of his new gloves. She would like to have kept those wisps as a keepsake, as a remembrance. Laurie leaned forward and put his hand on Laura's knee.

'Look here, darling,' he said. 'The third and the ninth as usual. Twig?'

Oh, how marvellous to have a brother! In her excitement Leila felt that if there had been time, if it hadn't been impossible, she couldn't have helped crying because she was an only child, and no brother had ever said 'Twig?' to her; no sister would ever say, as Meg said to Jose that moment, 'I've never known your hair go up more successfully than it has tonight!'

But, of course, there was no time. They were at the drill hall already; there were cabs in front of them and cabs behind. The road was bright on either side with moving fan-like lights, and on the pavement gay couples seemed to float through the air; little satin shoes chased each other like birds.

'Hold on to me, Leila; you'll get lost,' said Laura.

'Come on, girls, let's make a dash for it,' said Laurie.

Leila put two fingers on Laura's pink velvet cloak, and they were somehow lifted past the big golden lantern, carried along the passage, and pushed into the little room marked 'Ladies'. Here the crowd was so great there was hardly space to take off their things; the noise was deafening. Two benches on either side were stacked high with wraps. Two old women in white aprons ran up and down tossing fresh armfuls. And everybody was pressing forward trying to get at the little dressing-table and mirror at the far end.

A great quivering jet of gas lighted the ladies' room. It couldn't wait; it was dancing already. When the door opened again and there came a burst of tuning from the drill hall, it leaped almost to the ceiling.

Dark girls, fair girls were patting their hair, tying ribbons again, tucking handkerchiefs down the fronts of their bodices, smoothing marble-white gloves. And because they were all laughing it seemed to Leila that they were all lovely.

'Aren't there any invisible hair-pins?' cried a voice. 'How most extraordinary! I can't see a single invisible hair-pin.'

'Powder my back, there's a darling,' cried someone else.

'But I must have a needle and cotton. I've torn simply miles and miles of the frill,' wailed a third.

Then, 'Pass them along, pass them along!' The straw basket of programmes was tossed from arm to arm. Darling little pink-and-silver programmes, with pink pencils and fluffy tassels. Leila's fingers shook as she took one out of the basket. She wanted to ask someone, 'Am I meant to have one too?' but she had just time to read: 'Waltz 3. *Two, Two in a Canoe*. Polka 4. *Making the Feathers Fly*', when Meg cried, 'Ready, Leila?' and they pressed their way through the crush in the passage towards the big double doors of the drill hall.

Dancing had not begun yet, but the band had stopped tuning, and the noise was so great it seemed that when it did begin to play it would never be heard. Leila, pressing close to Meg, looking over Meg's shoulder, felt that even the little quivering coloured flags strung across the ceiling were talking. She quite forgot to be shy; she forgot how in the middle of dressing she had sat down on the bed with one shoe off and one shoe on and begged her mother to ring up her cousins and say she couldn't go after all. And the rush of longing she had had to be sitting on the veranda of their forsaken up-country home, listening to the baby owls crying 'More pork' in the moonlight, was changed to a rush of joy so sweet that it was hard to bear alone. She clutched her fan, and, gazing at the gleaming, golden floor, the azaleas, the lanterns, the stage at one end with its red carpet and gilt chairs and the band in a corner, she thought breathlessly, 'How heavenly; how simply heavenly!'

All the girls stood grouped together at one side of the doors, the men at the other, and the chaperones in dark dresses, smiling rather foolishly, walked with little careful steps over the polished floor towards the stage.

'This is my little country cousin Leila. Be nice to her. Find her partners; she's under my wing,' said Meg, going up to one girl after another.

Strange faces smiled at Leila – sweetly, vaguely. Strange voices answered, 'Of course, my dear.' But Leila felt the girls didn't really see her. They were looking towards the men. Why didn't the men begin? What were they waiting for? There they stood, smoothing their gloves, patting their glossy hair and smiling among themselves. Then, quite suddenly, as if they had only just made up their minds that that was what they had to do, the men came gliding over the parquet. There was a joyful flutter among the girls. A tall, fair man flew up to Meg, seized her programme, scribbled something; Meg passed him on to Leila. 'May I have the pleasure?' He ducked and smiled. There came a dark man wearing an eyeglass, then cousin Laurie with a friend, and Laura with a little freckled fellow whose tie was crooked. Then quite an old man – fat, with a big bald patch on his head – took her programme and murmured, 'Let me see, let me see!' And he was a long time comparing his programme, which looked black with names, with hers. It seemed to give him so much trouble that Leila was ashamed. 'Oh, please don't bother,' she said eagerly. But instead of replying the fat man wrote something, glanced at her again. 'Do I remember this bright little face?' he said softly. 'Is it known to me of yore?' At that moment the band began playing; the fat man disappeared. He was tossed away on a great wave of music that came flying over the gleaming floor, breaking the groups up into couples, scattering them, sending them spinning . . .

Leila had learned to dance at boarding school. Every Saturday afternoon the boarders were hurried off to a little corrugated iron mission hall where Miss Eccles (of London) held her 'select' classes.

But the difference between that dusty-smelling hall – with calico texts on the walls, the poor terrified little woman in a brown velvet toque with rabbit's ears thumping the cold piano, Miss Eccles poking the girls' feet with her long white wand – and this was so tremendous that Leila was sure if her partner didn't come and she had to listen to that marvellous music and to watch the others sliding, gliding over the golden floor, she would die at least, or faint, or lift her arms and fly out of one of those dark windows that showed the stars.

'Ours, I think – ' Someone bowed, smiled, and offered her his arm; she hadn't to die after all. Someone's hand pressed her waist, and she floated away like a flower that is tossed into a pool.

'Quite a good floor, isn't it?' drawled a faint voice close to her ear.

'I think it's most beautifully slippery,' said Leila.

'Pardon!' The faint voice sounded surprised. Leila said it again. And there was a tiny pause before the voice echoed, 'Oh, quite!' and she was swung round again.

He steered so beautifully. That was the great difference between dancing with girls and men, Leila decided. Girls banged into each other, and stamped on each other's feet; the girl who was gentleman always clutched you so.

The azaleas were separate flowers no longer; they were pink and white flags streaming by.

'Were you at the Bells' last week?' the voice came again. It sounded tired. Leila wondered whether she ought to ask him if he would like to stop.

'No, this is my first dance,' said she.

Her partner gave a little gasping laugh. 'Oh, I say,' he protested.

'Yes, it is really the first dance I've ever been to.' Leila was most fervent. It was such a relief to be able to tell somebody. 'You see, I've lived in the country all my life up till now . . . '

At that moment the music stopped, and they went to sit on two chairs against the wall. Leila tucked her pink satin feet under and fanned herself, while she blissfully watched the other couples passing and disappearing through the swing doors.

'Enjoying yourself, Leila?' asked Jose, nodding her golden head.

Laura passed and gave her the faintest little wink; it made Leila wonder for a moment whether she was quite grown up after all. Certainly her partner did not say very much. He coughed, tucked his handkerchief away, pulled down his waistcoat, took a minute thread off his sleeve. But it didn't matter. Almost immediately the band started and her second partner seemed to spring from the ceiling.

'Floor's not bad,' said the new voice. Did one always begin with the floor? And then, 'Were you at the Neaves' on Tuesday?' And again Leila explained. Perhaps it was a little strange that her partners were not more interested. For it was thrilling. Her first ball! She was only at the beginning of everything. It seemed to her that she had never known what the night was like before. Up till now it had been dark, silent, beautiful very often – oh yes – but mournful somehow. Solemn. And now it would never be like that again – it had opened dazzling bright.

'Care for an ice?' said her partner. And they went through the swing doors, down the passage, to the supper room. Her cheeks burned, she was fearfully thirsty. How sweet the ices looked on little glass plates and how cold the frosted spoon was, iced too! And when they came back to the hall there was the fat man waiting for her by the door. It gave her quite a shock again to see how old he was; he ought to have been on the stage with the fathers and mothers. And when Leila compared him with her other partners he looked shabby. His waistcoat was creased, there was a button off his glove, his coat looked as if it was dusty with French chalk.

'Come along, little lady,' said the fat man. He scarcely troubled to clasp her, and they moved away so gently, it was more like walking than dancing. But he said not a word about the floor. 'Your first dance, isn't it?' he murmured.

'How did you know?'

'Ah,' said the fat man, 'that's what it is to be old!' He wheezed faintly as he steered her past an awkward couple. 'You see, I've been doing this kind of thing for the last thirty years.'

'Thirty years?' cried Leila. Twelve years before she was born!

'It hardly bears thinking about, does it?' said the fat man gloomily. Leila looked at his bald head, and she felt quite sorry for him.

'I think it's marvellous to be still going on,' she said kindly.

'Kind little lady,' said the fat man, and he pressed her a little closer, and hummed a bar of the waltz. 'Of course,' he said, 'you can't hope to last anything like as long as that. No-o,' said the fat man, 'long before that you'll be sitting up there on the stage, looking on, in your nice black velvet. And these pretty arms will have turned into little short fat ones, and you'll beat time with such a different kind of fan – a black bony one.' The fat man seemed to shudder. 'And you'll smile away like the poor old dears up there, and point to your daughter, and tell the elderly lady next to you how some dreadful man tried to kiss her at the club ball. And your heart will ache, ache' – the fat man squeezed her closer still, as if he really was sorry for that poor heart – 'because no one wants to kiss you now. And you'll say how unpleasant these polished floors are to walk on, how dangerous they are. Eh, Mademoiselle Twinkletoes?' said the fat man softly.

Leila gave a light little laugh, but she did not feel like laughing. Was it – could it all be true? It sounded terribly true. Was this first ball only the beginning of her last ball, after all? At that the music seemed to change; it sounded sad, sad; it rose upon a great sigh. Oh, how quickly things changed! Why didn't happiness last for ever? For ever wasn't a bit too long.

'I want to stop,' she said in a breathless voice. The fat man led her to the door.

'No,' she said, 'I won't go outside. I won't sit down. I'll just stand here, thank you.' She leaned against the wall, tapping with her foot, pulling up her gloves and trying to smile. But deep inside her a little girl threw her pinafore over her head and sobbed. Why had he spoiled it all?

'I say, you know,' said the fat man, 'you mustn't take me seriously, little lady.'

'As if I should!' said Leila, tossing her small dark head and sucking her underlip . . .

Again the couples paraded. The swing doors opened and shut. Now new music was given out by the bandmaster. But Leila didn't want to dance any more. She wanted to be home, or sitting on the veranda listening to those baby owls. When she looked through the dark windows at the stars, they had long beams like wings . . .

But presently a soft, melting, ravishing tune began, and a young man with curly hair bowed before her. She would have to dance, out of politeness, until she could find Meg. Very stiffly she walked into the middle; very haughtily she put her hand on his sleeve. But in one minute, in one turn, her feet glided, glided. The lights, the azaleas, the dresses, the pink faces, the velvet chairs, all became one beautiful flying wheel. And when her next partner bumped her into the fat man and he said, 'Pardon,' she smiled at him more radiantly than ever. She didn't even recognise him again.

The Singing Lesson

WITH DESPAIR – cold, sharp despair – buried deep in her heart like a wicked knife, Miss Meadows, in cap and gown and carrying a little baton, trod the cold corridors that led to the music hall. Girls of all ages, rosy from the air, and bubbling over with that gleeful excitement that comes from running to school on a fine autumn morning, hurried, skipped, fluttered by; from the hollow classrooms came a quick drumming of voices; a bell rang; a voice like a bird cried, 'Muriel.' And then there came from the staircase a tremendous knock-knock-knocking. Someone had dropped her dumb-bells.

The Science Mistress stopped Miss Meadows.

'Good mor-ning,' she cried, in her sweet, affected drawl. 'Isn't it cold? It might be win-ter.'

Miss Meadows, hugging the knife, stared in hatred at the Science Mistress. Everything about her was sweet, pale, like honey. You would not have been surprised to see a bee caught in the tangles of that yellow hair.

'It is rather sharp,' said Miss Meadows, grimly.

The other smiled her sugary smile.

'You look fro-zen,' said she. Her blue eyes opened wide; there came a mocking light in them. (Had she noticed anything?)

'Oh, not quite as bad as that,' said Miss Meadows, and she gave the Science Mistress, in exchange for her smile, a quick grimace and passed on . . .

Forms Four, Five, and Six were assembled in the music hall. The noise was deafening. On the platform, by the piano, stood Mary Beazley, Miss Meadows' favourite, who played accompaniments. She was turning the music stool. When she saw Miss Meadows she gave a loud, warning 'Sh-sh! girls!' and Miss Meadows, her hands thrust in her sleeves, the baton under her arm, strode down the centre aisle, mounted the steps, turned sharply, seized the brass music stand, planted it in front of her, and gave two sharp taps with her baton for silence.

'Silence, please! Immediately!' and, looking at nobody, her glance swept over that sea of coloured flannel blouses, with bobbing pink faces and hands, quivering butterfly hair-bows, and music-books outspread. She knew perfectly well what they were thinking. 'Meady is in a wax.' Well, let them think it! Her eyelids quivered; she tossed her head, defying them. What could the thoughts of those creatures matter to someone who stood there bleeding to death, pierced to the heart, to the heart, by such a letter –

. . . 'I feel more and more strongly that our marriage would be a mistake. Not that I do not love you. I love you as much as it is possible for me to love any woman, but, truth to tell, I have come to the conclusion that I am not a marrying man, and the idea of settling down fills me with nothing but – ' and the word 'disgust' was scratched out lightly and 'regret' written over the top.

Basil! Miss Meadows stalked over to the piano. And Mary Beazley, who was waiting for this moment, bent forward; her curls fell over her cheeks while she breathed, 'Good morning, Miss Meadows,' and she motioned towards rather than handed to her mistress a beautiful yellow chrysanthemum. This little ritual of the flower had been gone through for ages and ages, quite a term and a half. It was as much part of the lesson as opening the piano. But this morning, instead of taking it up, instead of tucking it into her belt while she leant over Mary and said, 'Thank you, Mary. How very nice! Turn to page thirty-two,' what was Mary's horror when Miss Meadows totally ignored the chrysanthemum, made no reply to her greeting, but said in a voice of ice, 'Page fourteen, please, and mark the accents well.'

Staggering moment! Mary blushed until the tears stood in her eyes, but Miss Meadows was gone back to the music stand; her voice rang through the music hall.

'Page fourteen. We will begin with page fourteen. "A Lament". Now, girls, you ought to know it by this time. We shall take it all together; not in parts, all together. And without expression. Sing it, though, quite simply, beating time with the left hand.'

She raised the baton; she tapped the music stand twice. Down came Mary on the opening chord; down came all those left hands, beating the air, and in chimed those young, mournful voices:

Fast! Ah, too Fast Fade the Ro-o-ses of Pleasure;
    Soon Autumn yields unto Wi-i-nter Drear.
Fleetly! Ah, Fleetly Mu-u-sic's Gay Measure
    Passes away from the Listening Ear.

Good Heavens, what could be more tragic than that lament! Every note was a sigh, a sob, a groan of awful mournfulness. Miss Meadows lifted her arms in the wide gown and began conducting with both hands. ' . . . I feel more and more strongly that our marriage would be a mistake . . . ' she beat. And the voices cried: *Fleetly! Ah, Fleetly*. What could have possessed him to write such a letter! What could have led up to it! It came out of nothing. His last letter had been all about a fumed-oak bookcase he had bought for 'our' books, and a 'natty little hall-stand' he had seen, 'a very neat affair with a carved owl on a bracket, holding three hat-brushes in its claws'. How she had smiled at that! So like a man to think one needed three hat-brushes! *From the Listening Ear*, sang the voices.

'Once again,' said Miss Meadows. 'But this time in parts. Still without expression.' *Fast! Ah, too Fast*. With the gloom of the contraltos added, one could scarcely help shuddering. *Fade the Roses of Pleasure*. Last time he had come to see her, Basil had worn a rose in his buttonhole. How handsome he had looked in that bright blue suit, with that dark red rose! And he knew it, too. He couldn't help knowing it. First he stroked his hair, then his moustache; his teeth gleamed when he smiled.

'The headmaster's wife keeps on asking me to dinner. It's a perfect nuisance. I never get an evening to myself in that place.'

'But can't you refuse?'

'Oh, well, it doesn't do for a man in my position to be unpopular.'

Music's Gay Measure, wailed the voices. The willow trees, outside the high, narrow windows, waved in the wind. They had lost half their leaves. The tiny ones that clung wriggled like fishes caught on a line. ' . . . I am not a marrying man . . . ' The voices were silent; the piano waited.

'Quite good,' said Miss Meadows, but still in such a strange, stony tone that the younger girls began to feel positively frightened. 'But now that we know it, we shall take it with expression. As much expression as you can put into it. Think of the words, girls. Use your imaginations. *Fast! Ah, too Fast*,' cried Miss Meadows. 'That ought to break out – a loud, strong *forte* – a lament. And then in the second line, *Winter Drear*, make that *Drear* sound as if a cold wind were blowing through it. *Dre-ear*! ' said she so awfully that Mary Beazley, on the music stool, wriggled her spine. 'The third line should be one crescendo. *Fleetly! Ah, Fleetly Music's Gay Measure*. Breaking on the first word of the last line, *Passes*.' And then on the word, *Away*, you must begin to die . . . to fade . . . until *the*

Listening Ear is nothing more than a faint whisper . . . You can slow down as much as you like almost on the last line. Now, please.'

Again the two light taps; she lifted her arms again. *Fast! Ah, too Fast.* ' . . . and the idea of settling down fills me with nothing but disgust – ' Disgust was what he had written. That was as good as to say their engagement was definitely broken off. Broken off! Their engagement! People had been surprised enough that she had got engaged. The Science Mistress would not believe it at first. But nobody had been as surprised as she. She was thirty. Basil was twenty-five. It had been a miracle, simply a miracle, to hear him say, as they walked home from church that very dark night, 'You know, somehow or other, I've got fond of you.' And he had taken hold of the end of her ostrich feather boa. *Passes away from the Listening Ear*.

'Repeat! Repeat!' said Miss Meadows. 'More expression, girls! Once more!'

Fast! Ah, too Fast. The older girls were crimson; some of the younger ones began to cry. Big spots of rain blew against the windows, and one could hear the willows whispering, ' . . . not that I do not love you . . . '

'But, my darling, if you love me,' thought Miss Meadows, 'I don't mind how much it is. Love me as little as you like.' But she knew he didn't love her. Not to have cared enough to scratch out that word 'disgust', so that she couldn't read it! *Soon Autumn yields unto Winter Drear.* She would have to leave the school, too. She could never face the Science Mistress or the girls after it got known. She would have to disappear somewhere. *Passes away.* The voices began to die, to fade, to whisper . . . to vanish . . .

Suddenly the door opened. A little girl in blue walked fussily up the aisle, hanging her head, biting her lips, and twisting the silver bangle on her red little wrist. She came up the steps and stood before Miss Meadows.

'Well, Monica, what is it?'

'Oh, if you please, Miss Meadows,' said the little girl, gasping, 'Miss Wyatt wants to see you in the mistress's room.'

'Very well,' said Miss Meadows. And she called to the girls, 'I shall put you on your honour to talk quietly while I am away.' But they were too subdued to do anything else. Most of them were blowing their noses.

The corridors were silent and cold; they echoed to Miss Meadows' steps. The head mistress sat at her desk. For a moment she did not look up. She was as usual disentangling her eyeglasses, which had got caught in her lace tie. 'Sit down, Miss Meadows,' she said very kindly. And then she picked up a pink envelope from the blotting-pad. 'I sent for you just now because this telegram has come for you.'

'A telegram for me, Miss Wyatt?'

Basil! He had committed suicide, decided Miss Meadows. Her hand flew out, but Miss Wyatt held the telegram back a moment. 'I hope it's not bad news,' she said, no more than kindly. And Miss Meadows tore it open.

'Pay no attention to letter, must have been mad, bought hat-stand today – Basil,' she read. She couldn't take her eyes off the telegram.

'I do hope it's nothing very serious,' said Miss Wyatt, leaning forward.

'Oh, no, thank you, Miss Wyatt,' blushed Miss Meadows. 'It's nothing bad at all. It's' – and she gave an apologetic little laugh – 'it's from my fiancé saying that . . . saying that – ' There was a pause. 'I *see*,' said Miss Wyatt. And another pause. Then – 'You've fifteen minutes more of your class, Miss Meadows, haven't you?'

'Yes, Miss Wyatt.' She got up. She half ran towards the door.

'Oh, just one minute, Miss Meadows,' said Miss Wyatt. 'I must say I don't approve of my teachers having telegrams sent to them in school hours, unless in case of very bad news, such as death,' explained Miss Wyatt, 'or a very serious accident, or something to that effect. Good news, Miss Meadows, will always keep, you know.'

On the wings of hope, of love, of joy, Miss Meadows sped back to the music hall, up the aisle, up the steps, over to the piano.

'Page thirty-two, Mary,' she said, 'page thirty-two,' and, picking up the yellow chrysanthemum, she held it to her lips to hide her smile. Then she turned to the girls, rapped with her baton: 'Page thirty-two, girls. Page thirty-two.'

> We come here Today with Flowers o'erladen,
> With Baskets of Fruit and Ribbons to boot,
> To-oo Congratulate . . .

'Stop! Stop!' cried Miss Meadows. 'This is awful. This is dreadful.' And she beamed at her girls. 'What's the matter with you all? Think, girls, think of what you're singing. Use your imaginations. *With Flowers o'erladen. Baskets of Fruit and Ribbons to boot*. And *Congratulate*.' Miss Meadows broke off. 'Don't look so doleful, girls. It ought to sound warm, joyful, eager. *Congratulate*. Once more. Quickly. All together. Now then!'

And this time Miss Meadows' voice sounded over all the other voices – full, deep, glowing with expression.

The Stranger

IT SEEMED to the little crowd on the wharf that she was never going to move again. There she lay, immense, motionless on the grey crinkled water, a loop of smoke above her, an immense flock of gulls screaming and diving after the galley droppings at the stern. You could just see little couples parading – little flies walking up and down the dish on the grey crinkled tablecloth. Other flies clustered and swarmed at the edge. Now there was a gleam of white on the lower deck – the cook's apron or the stewardess perhaps. Now a tiny black spider raced up the ladder on to the bridge.

In the front of the crowd a strong-looking, middle-aged man, dressed very well, very snugly in a grey overcoat, grey silk scarf, thick gloves and dark felt hat, marched up and down, twirling his folded umbrella. He seemed to be the leader of the little crowd on the wharf and at the same time to keep them together. He was something between the sheep-dog and the shepherd.

But what a fool – what a fool he had been not to bring any glasses! There wasn't a pair of glasses between the whole lot of them.

'Curious thing, Mr Scott, that none of us thought of glasses. We might have been able to stir 'em up a bit. We might have managed a little signalling. "Don't hesitate to land. Natives harmless." Or: "A welcome awaits you. All is forgiven." What? Eh?'

Mr Hammond's quick, eager glance, so nervous and yet so friendly and confiding, took in everybody on the wharf, roped in even those old chaps lounging against the gangways. They knew, every man-jack of them, that Mrs Hammond was on that boat, and that he was so tremendously excited it never entered his head not to believe that this marvellous fact meant something to them too. It warmed his heart towards them. They were, he decided, as decent a crowd of people – Those old chaps over by the gangways, too – fine, solid old chaps. What chests – by Jove! And he squared his own, plunged his thick-gloved hands into his pockets, rocked from heel to toe.

'Yes, my wife's been in Europe for the last ten months. On a visit to our eldest girl, who was married last year. I brought her up here, as far as Salisbury, myself. So I thought I'd better come and fetch her back. Yes, yes, yes.' The shrewd grey eyes narrowed again and searched anxiously, quickly, the motionless liner. Again his overcoat was unbuttoned. Out came the thin, butter-yellow watch again, and for the twentieth – fiftieth – hundredth time he made the calculation.

'Let me see now. It was two fifteen when the doctor's launch went off. Two fifteen. It is now exactly twenty-eight minutes past four. That is to say, the doctor's been gone two hours and thirteen minutes. Two hours and thirteen minutes! Whee-ooh!' He gave a queer little half-whistle and snapped his watch to again. 'But I think we should have been told if there was anything up – don't you, Mr Gaven?'

'Oh, yes, Mr Hammond! I don't think there's anything to – anything to worry about,' said Mr Gaven, knocking out his pipe against the heel of his shoe. 'At the same time – '

'Quite so! Quite so!' cried Mr Hammond. 'Dashed annoying!' He paced quickly up and down and came back again to his stand between Mr and Mrs Scott and Mr Gaven. 'It's getting quite dark, too,' and he waved his folded umbrella as though the dusk at least might have had the decency to keep off for a bit. But the dusk came slowly, spreading like a slow stain over the water. Little Jean Scott dragged at her mother's hand.

'I wan' my tea, mammy!' she wailed.

'I expect you do,' said Mr Hammond. 'I expect all these ladies want their tea.' And his kind, flushed, almost pitiful glance roped them all in again. He wondered whether Janey was having a final cup of tea in the saloon out there. He hoped so; he thought not. It would be just like her not to leave the deck. In that case perhaps the deck steward would bring her up a cup. If he'd been there he'd have got it for her – somehow. And for a moment he was on deck, standing over her, watching her little hand fold round the cup in the way she had, while she drank the only cup of tea to be got on board . . . But now he was back here, and the Lord only knew when that cursed Captain would stop hanging about in the stream. He took another turn, up and down, up and down. He walked as far as the cab-stand to make sure his driver hadn't disappeared; back he swerved again to the little flock huddled in the shelter of the banana crates. Little Jean Scott was still wanting her tea. Poor little beggar! He wished he had a bit of chocolate on him.

'Here, Jean!' he said. 'Like a lift up?' And easily, gently, he swung the little girl on to a higher barrel. The movement of holding her, steadying her, relieved him wonderfully, lightened his heart.

'Hold on,' he said, keeping an arm round her.

'Oh, don't worry about Jean, Mr Hammond!' said Mrs Scott.

'That's all right, Mrs Scott. No trouble. It's a pleasure. Jean's a little pal of mine, aren't you, Jean?'

'Yes, Mr Hammond,' said Jean, and she ran her finger down the dent of his felt hat.

But suddenly she caught him by the ear and gave a loud scream. 'Lo-ok, Mr Hammond! She's moving! Look, she's coming in!'

By Jove! So she was. At last! She was slowly, slowly turning round. A bell sounded far over the water and a great spout of steam gushed into the air. The gulls rose; they fluttered away like bits of white paper. And whether that deep throbbing was her engines or his heart Mr Hammond couldn't say. He had to nerve himself to bear it, whatever it was. At that moment old Captain Johnson, the harbour-master, came striding down the wharf, a leather portfolio under his arm.

'Jean'll be all right,' said Mr Scott. 'I'll hold her.' He was just in time. Mr Hammond had forgotten about Jean. He sprang away to greet old Captain Johnson.

'Well, Captain,' the eager, nervous voice rang out again, 'you've taken pity on us at last.'

'It's no good blaming me, Mr Hammond,' wheezed old Captain Johnson, staring at the liner. 'You got Mrs Hammond on board, ain't yer?'

'Yes, yes!' said Hammond, and he kept by the harbour-master's side. 'Mrs Hammond's there. Hul-lo! We shan't be long now!'

With her telephone ring-ringing, the thrum of her screw filling the air, the big liner bore down on them, cutting sharp through the dark water so that big white shavings curled to either side. Hammond and the harbour-master kept in front of the rest. Hammond took off his hat; he raked the decks – they were crammed with passengers; he waved his hat and bawled a loud, strange 'Hul-lo!' across the water; and then turned round and burst out laughing and said something – nothing – to old Captain Johnson.

'Seen her?' asked the harbour-master.

'No, not yet. Steady – wait a bit!' And suddenly, between two great clumsy idiots – 'Get out of the way there!' he signed with his umbrella – he saw a hand raised – a white glove shaking a handkerchief.

Another moment, and – thank God, thank God! – there she was.
There was Janey. There was Mrs Hammond, yes, yes, yes – standing
by the rail and smiling and nodding and waving her handkerchief.

'Well that's first class – first class! Well, well, well!' He positively
stamped. Like lightning he drew out his cigar-case and offered it to
old Captain Johnson. 'Have a cigar, Captain! They're pretty good.
Have a couple! Here' – and he pressed all the cigars in the case on the
harbour-master – 'I've a couple of boxes up at the hotel.'

'Thanks, Mr Hammond!' wheezed old Captain Johnson.

Hammond stuffed the cigar-case back. His hands were shaking,
but he'd got hold of himself again. He was able to face Janey. There
she was, leaning on the rail, talking to some woman and at the same
time watching him, ready for him. It struck him, as the gulf of water
closed, how small she looked on that huge ship. His heart was wrung
with such a spasm that he could have cried out. How little she looked
to have come all that long way and back by herself! Just like her,
though. Just like Janey. She had the courage of a – And now the crew
had come forward and parted the passengers; they had lowered the
rails for the gangways.

The voices on shore and the voices on board flew to greet each
other.

'All well?'

'All well.'

'How's mother?'

'Much better.'

'Hullo, Jean!'

'Hillo, Aun' Emily!'

'Had a good voyage?'

'Splendid!'

'Shan't be long now!'

'Not long now.'

The engines stopped. Slowly she edged to the wharf-side.

'Make way there – make way – make way!' And the wharf hands
brought the heavy gangways along at a sweeping run. Hammond
signed to Janey to stay where she was. The old harbour-master
stepped forward; he followed. As to 'ladies first', or any rot like that,
it never entered his head.

'After you, Captain!' he cried genially. And, treading on the old
man's heels, he strode up the gangway on to the deck in a bee-line to
Janey, and Janey was clasped in his arms.

'Well, well, well! Yes, yes! Here we are at last!' he stammered. It

was all he could say. And Janey emerged, and her cool little voice –
the only voice in the world for him – said, 'Well, darling! Have you
been waiting long?'

No; not long. Or, at any rate, it didn't matter. It was over now. But
the point was, he had a cab waiting at the end of the wharf. Was she
ready to go off. Was her luggage ready? In that case they could cut
off sharp with her cabin luggage and let the rest go hang until
tomorrow. He bent over her and she looked up with her familiar
half-smile. She was just the same. Not a day changed. Just as he'd
always known her. She laid her small hand on his sleeve.

'How are the children, John?' she asked.

(Hang the children!) 'Perfectly well. Never better in their lives.'

'Haven't they sent me letters?'

'Yes, yes – of course! I've left them at the hotel for you to digest
later on.'

'We can't go quite so fast,' said she. 'I've got people to say goodbye to – and then there's the Captain.' As his face fell she gave his
arm a small understanding squeeze. 'If the Captain comes off the
bridge I want you to thank him for having looked after your wife so
beautifully.' Well, he'd got her. If she wanted another ten minutes –
As he gave way she was surrounded. The whole first-class seemed to
want to say goodbye to Janey.

'Goodbye, dear Mrs Hammond! And next time you're in Sydney
I'll expect you.'

'Darling Mrs Hammond! You won't forget to write to me, will
you?'

'Well, Mrs Hammond, what this boat would have been without
you!'

It was as plain as a pikestaff that she was by far the most popular
woman on board. And she took it all – just as usual. Absolutely
composed. Just her little self – just Janey all over; standing there with
her veil thrown back. Hammond never noticed what his wife had on.
It was all the same to him whatever she wore. But today he did notice
that she wore a black 'costume' – didn't they call it? – with white
frills, trimmings he supposed they were, at the neck and sleeves. All
this while Janey handed him round.

'John, dear!' And then: 'I want to introduce you to – '

Finally they did escape, and she led the way to her stateroom. To
follow Janey down the passage that she knew so well – that was
so strange to him; to part the green curtains after her and to step
into the cabin that had been hers gave him exquisite happiness.

But – confound it! – the stewardess was there on the floor, strapping up the rugs.

'That's the last, Mrs Hammond,' said the stewardess, rising and pulling down her cuffs.

He was introduced again, and then Janey and the stewardess disappeared into the passage. He heard whisperings. She was getting the tipping business over, he supposed. He sat down on the striped sofa and took his hat off. There were the rugs she had taken with her; they looked good as new. All her luggage looked fresh, perfect. The labels were written in her beautiful little clear hand – 'Mrs John Hammond'.

'Mrs John Hammond!' He gave a long sigh of content and leaned back, crossing his arms. The strain was over. He felt he could have sat there for ever sighing his relief – the relief at being rid of that horrible tug, pull, grip on his heart. The danger was over. That was the feeling. They were on dry land again.

But at that moment Janey's head came round the corner.

'Darling – do you mind? I just want to go and say goodbye to the doctor.'

Hammond started up. 'I'll come with you.'

'No, no!' she said. 'Don't bother. I'd rather not. I'll not be a minute.'

And before he could answer she was gone. He had half a mind to run after her; but instead he sat down again.

Would she really not be long? What was the time now? Out came the watch; he stared at nothing. That was rather queer of Janey, wasn't it? Why couldn't she have told the stewardess to say goodbye for her? Why did she have to go chasing after the ship's doctor? She could have sent a note from the hotel even if the affair had been urgent. Urgent? Did it – could it mean that she had been ill on the voyage – she was keeping something from him? That was it! He seized his hat. He was going off to find that fellow and to wring the truth out of him at all costs. He thought he'd noticed just something. She was just a touch too calm – too steady. From the very first moment –

The curtains rang. Janey was back. He jumped to his feet.

'Janey, have you been ill on this voyage? You have!'

'Ill?' Her airy little voice mocked him. She stepped over the rugs, and came up close, touched his breast, and looked up at him.

'Darling,' she said, 'don't frighten me. Of course I haven't! Whatever makes you think I have? Do I look ill?'

But Hammond didn't see her. He only felt that she was looking at him and that there was no need to worry about anything. She was here to look after things. It was all right. Everything was.

The gentle pressure of her hand was so calming that he put his over hers to hold it there. And she said: 'Stand still. I want to look at you. I haven't seen you yet. You've had your beard beautifully trimmed, and you look – younger, I think, and decidedly thinner! Bachelor life agrees with you.'

'Agrees with me!' He groaned for love and caught her close again. And again, as always, he had the feeling that he was holding something that never was quite his – his. Something too delicate, too precious, that would fly away once he let go.

'For God's sake let's get off to the hotel so that we can be by ourselves!' And he rang the bell hard for someone to look sharp with the luggage.

*   *   *

Walking down the wharf together she took his arm. He had her on his arm again. And the difference it made to get into the cab after Janey – to throw the red-and-yellow striped blanket round them both – to tell the driver to hurry because neither of them had had any tea. No more going without his tea or pouring out his own. She was back. He turned to her, squeezed her hand, and said gently, teasingly, in the 'special' voice he had for her: 'Glad to be home again, dearie?' She smiled; she didn't even bother to answer, but gently she drew his hand away as they came to the brighter streets.

'We've got the best room in the hotel,' he said. 'I wouldn't be put off with another. And I asked the chambermaid to put in a bit of a fire in case you felt chilly. She's a nice, attentive girl. And I thought now we were here we wouldn't bother to go home tomorrow, but spend the day looking round and leave the morning after. Does that suit you? There's no hurry, is there? The children will have you soon enough . . . I thought a day's sight-seeing might make a nice break in your journey – eh, Janey?'

'Have you taken the tickets for the day after?' she asked.

'I should think I have!' He unbuttoned his overcoat and took out his bulging pocket-book. 'Here we are! I reserved a first-class carriage to Cooktown. There it is – "Mr and Mrs John Hammond". I thought we might as well do ourselves comfortably, and we don't want other people butting in, do we? But if you'd like to stop here a bit longer – ?'

'Oh, no!' said Janey quickly. 'Not for the world! The day after tomorrow, then. And the children – '

But they had reached the hotel. The manager was standing in the broad, brilliantly-lighted porch. He came down to greet them. A porter ran from the hall for their boxes.

'Well, Mr Arnold, here's Mrs Hammond at last!'

The manager led them through the hall himself and pressed the elevator-bell. Hammond knew there were business pals of his sitting at the little hall tables having a drink before dinner. But he wasn't going to risk interruption; he looked neither to the right nor the left. They could think what they pleased. If they didn't understand, the more fools they – and he stepped out of the lift, unlocked the door of their room, and shepherded Janey in. The door shut. Now, at last, they were alone together. He turned up the light. The curtains were drawn; the fire blazed. He flung his hat on to the huge bed and went towards her.

But – would you believe it! – again they were interrupted. This time it was the porter with the luggage. He made two journeys of it, leaving the door open in between, taking his time, whistling through his teeth in the corridor. Hammond paced up and down the room, tearing off his gloves, tearing off his scarf. Finally he flung his overcoat on to the bedside.

At last the fool was gone. The door clicked. Now they were alone. Said Hammond: 'I feel I'll never have you to myself again. These cursed people! Janey' – and he bent his flushed, eager gaze upon her – 'let's have dinner up here. If we go down to the restaurant we'll be interrupted, and then there's the confounded music' (the music he'd praised so highly, applauded so loudly last night!). 'We shan't be able to hear each other speak. Let's have something up here in front of the fire. It's too late for tea. I'll order a little supper, shall I? How does that idea strike you?'

'Do, darling!' said Janey. 'And while you're away – the children's letters – '

'Oh, later on will do!' said Hammond.

'But then we'd get it over,' said Janey. 'And I'd first have time to – '

'Oh, I needn't go down!' explained Hammond. 'I'll just ring and give the order . . . you don't want to send me away, do you?'

Janey shook her head and smiled.

'But you're thinking of something else. You're worrying about something,' said Hammond. 'What is it? Come and sit here – come and sit on my knee before the fire.'

'I'll just unpin my hat,' said Janey, and she went over to the dressing-table. 'A-ah!' She gave a little cry.

'What is it?'

'Nothing, darling. I've just found the children's letters. That's all right! They will keep. No hurry now!' She turned to him, clasping them. She tucked them into her frilled blouse. She cried quickly, gaily: 'Oh, how typical this dressing-table is of you!'

'Why? What's the matter with it?' said Hammond.

'If it were floating in eternity I should say "John!" ' laughed Janey, staring at the big bottle of hair tonic, the wicker bottle of eau-de-Cologne, the two hair-brushes, and a dozen new collars tied with pink tape. 'Is this all your luggage?'

'Hang my luggage!' said Hammond; but all the same he liked being laughed at by Janey. 'Let's talk. Let's get down to things. Tell me' – and as Janey perched on his knees he leaned back and drew her into the deep, ugly chair – 'tell me you're really glad to be back, Janey.'

'Yes, darling, I am glad,' she said.

But just as when he embraced her he felt she would fly away, so Hammond never knew – never knew for dead certain that she was as glad as he was. How could he know? Would he ever know? Would he always have this craving – this pang like hunger, somehow, to make Janey so much part of him that there wasn't any of her to escape? He wanted to blot out everybody, everything. He wished now he'd turned off the light. That might have brought her nearer. And now those letters from the children rustled in her blouse. He could have chucked them into the fire.

'Janey,' he whispered.

'Yes, dear?' She lay on his breast, but so lightly, so remotely. Their breathing rose and fell together.

'Janey!'

'What is it?'

'Turn to me,' he whispered. A slow, deep flush flowed into his forehead. 'Kiss me, Janey! You kiss me!'

It seemed to him there was a tiny pause – but long enough for him to suffer torture – before her lips touched his, firmly, lightly – kissing them as she always kissed him, as though the kiss – how could he describe it? – confirmed what they were saying, signed the contract. But that wasn't what he wanted; that wasn't at all what he thirsted for. He felt suddenly, horribly tired.

'If you knew,' he said, opening his eyes, 'what it's been like –

waiting today. I thought the boat never would come in. There we were, hanging about. What kept you so long?'

She made no answer. She was looking away from him at the fire. The flames hurried – hurried over the coals, flickered, fell.

'Not asleep, are you?' said Hammond, and he jumped her up and down.

'No,' she said. And then: 'Don't do that, dear. No, I was thinking. As a matter of fact,' she said, 'one of the passengers died last night – a man. That's what held us up. We brought him in – I mean, he wasn't buried at sea. So, of course, the ship's doctor and the shore doctor – '

'What was it?' asked Hammond uneasily. He hated to hear of death. He hated this to have happened. It was, in some queer way, as though he and Janey had met a funeral on their way to the hotel.

'Oh, it wasn't anything in the least infectious!' said Janey. She was speaking scarcely above her breath. 'It was heart.' A pause. 'Poor fellow!' she said. 'Quite young.' And she watched the fire flicker and fall. 'He died in my arms,' said Janey.

The blow was so sudden that Hammond thought he would faint. He couldn't move; he couldn't breathe. He felt all his strength flowing – flowing into the big dark chair, and the big dark chair held him fast, gripped him, forced him to bear it.

'What?' he said dully. 'What's that you say?'

'The end was quite peaceful,' said the small voice. 'He just' – and Hammond saw her lift her gentle hand – 'breathed his life away at the end.' And her hand fell.

'Who – else was there?' Hammond managed to ask.

'Nobody. I was alone with him.'

Ah, my God, what was she saying! What was she doing to him! This would kill him! And all the while she spoke: 'I saw the change coming and I sent the steward for the doctor, but the doctor was too late. He couldn't have done anything, anyway.'

'But – why you, why you?' moaned Hammond.

At that Janey turned quickly, quickly searched his face.

'You don't mind, John, do you?' she asked. 'You don't – It's nothing to do with you and me.'

Somehow or other he managed to shake some sort of smile at her. Somehow or other he stammered: 'No – go – on, go on! I want you to tell me.'

'But, John darling – '

'Tell me, Janey!'

'There's nothing to tell,' she said, wondering. 'He was one of the first-class passengers. I saw he was very ill when he came on board . . . But he seemed to be so much better until yesterday. He had a severe attack in the afternoon – excitement – nervousness, I think, about arriving. And after that he never recovered.'

'But why didn't the stewardess – '

'Oh, my dear – the stewardess!' said Janey. 'What would he have felt? And besides . . . he might have wanted to leave a message . . . to – '

'Didn't he?' muttered Hammond. 'Didn't he say anything?'

'No, darling, not a word!' She shook her head softly. 'All the time I was with him he was too weak . . . he was too weak even to move a finger . . . '

Janey was silent. But her words, so light, so soft, so chill, seemed to hover in the air, to rain into his breast like snow.

The fire had gone red. Now it fell in with a sharp sound and the room was colder. Cold crept up his arms. The room was huge, immense, glittering. It filled his whole world. There was the great blind bed, with his coat flung across it like some headless man saying his prayers. There was the luggage, ready to be carried away again, anywhere, tossed into trains, carted on to boats.

. . . 'He was too weak. He was too weak to move a finger.' And yet he died in Janey's arms. She – who'd never – never once in all these years – never on one single solitary occasion –

No; he mustn't think of it. Madness lay in thinking of it. No, he wouldn't face it. He couldn't stand it. It was too much to bear!

And now Janey touched his tie with her fingers. She pinched the edges of the tie together.

'You're not – sorry I told you, John darling? It hasn't made you sad? It hasn't spoilt our evening – our being alone together?'

But at that he had to hide his face. He put his face into her bosom and his arms enfolded her.

Spoilt their evening! Spoilt their being alone together! They would never be alone together again.

Bank Holiday

A STOUT MAN with a pink face wears dingy white flannel trousers, a blue coat with a pink handkerchief showing, and a straw hat much too small for him, perched at the back of his head. He plays the guitar. A little chap in white canvas shoes, his face hidden under a felt hat like a broken wing, breathes into a flute; and a tall thin fellow, with bursting over-ripe button boots, draws ribbons – long, twisted, streaming ribbons – of tune out of a fiddle. They stand, unsmiling, but not serious, in the broad sunlight opposite the fruit-shop; the pink spider of a hand beats the guitar, the little squat hand, with a brass-and-turquoise ring, forces the reluctant flute, and the fiddler's arm tries to saw the fiddle in two.

A crowd collects, eating oranges and bananas, tearing off the skins, dividing, sharing. One young girl has even a basket of strawberries, but she does not eat them. 'Aren't they dear!' She stares at the tiny pointed fruits as if she were afraid of them. The Australian soldier laughs. 'Here, go on, there's not more than a mouthful.' But he doesn't want her to eat them, either. He likes to watch her little frightened face, and her puzzled eyes lifted to his: 'Aren't they a price!' He pushes out his chest and grins. Old fat women in velvet bodices – old dusty pin-cushions – lean old hags like worn umbrellas with a quivering bonnet on top; young women, in muslins, with hats that might have grown on hedges, and high pointed shoes; men in khaki, sailors, shabby clerks, young Jews in fine cloth suits with padded shoulders and wide trousers, 'hospital boys' in blue – the sun discovers them – the loud, bold music holds them together in one big knot for a moment. The young ones are larking, pushing each other on and off the pavement, dodging, nudging; the old ones are talking: 'So I said to 'im, if you wants the doctor to yourself, fetch 'im, says I.'

'An' by the time they was cooked there wasn't so much as you could put in the palm of me 'and!'

The only ones who are quiet are the ragged children. They stand, as close up to the musicians as they can get, their hands behind their

backs, their eyes big. Occasionally a leg hops, an arm wags. A tiny
staggerer, overcome, turns round twice, sits down solemn, and then
gets up again.

'Ain't it lovely?' whispers a small girl behind her hand.

And the music breaks into bright pieces, and joins together again,
and again breaks, and is dissolved, and the crowd scatters, moving
slowly up the hill.

At the corner of the road the stalls begin.

'Ticklers! Tuppence a tickler! 'Ool 'ave a tickler? Tickle 'em up,
boys.' Little soft brooms on wire handles. They are eagerly bought
by the soldiers.

'Buy a golliwog! Tuppence a golliwog!'

'Buy a jumping donkey! All alive-oh!'

'Su-perior chewing gum. Buy something to do, boys.'

'Buy a rose. Give 'er a rose, boy. Roses, lady?'

'Fevvers! Fevvers!' They are hard to resist. Lovely, streaming
feathers, emerald green, scarlet, bright blue, canary yellow. Even the
babies wear feathers threaded through their bonnets.

And an old woman in a three-cornered paper hat cries as if it
were her final parting advice, the only way of saving yourself or of
bringing him to his senses: 'Buy a three-cornered 'at, my dear, an'
put it on!'

It is a flying day, half sun, half wind. When the sun goes in a
shadow flies over; when it comes out again it is fiery. The men and
women feel it burning their backs, their breasts and their arms; they
feel their bodies expanding, coming alive . . . so that they make large
embracing gestures, lift up their arms, for nothing, swoop down on a
girl, blurt into laughter.

Lemonade! A whole tank of it stands on a table covered with a
cloth; and lemons like blunted fishes blob in the yellow water. It
looks solid, like a jelly, in the thick glasses. Why can't they drink it
without spilling it? Everybody spills it, and before the glass is handed
back the last drops are thrown in a ring.

Round the ice-cream cart, with its striped awning and bright
brass cover, the children cluster. Little tongues lick, lick round
the cream trumpets, round the squares. The cover is lifted, the
wooden spoon plunges in; one shuts one's eyes to feel it, silently
scrunching.

'Let these little birds tell you your future!' She stands beside the
cage, a shrivelled ageless Italian, clasping and unclasping her dark
claws. Her face, a treasure of delicate carving, is tied in a green-and-

gold scarf. And inside their prison the love-birds flutter towards the papers in the seed-tray.

'You have great strength of character. You will marry a red-haired man and have three children. Beware of a blonde woman.' Look out! Look out! A motor-car driven by a fat chauffeur comes rushing down the hill. Inside there a blonde woman, pouting, leaning forward – rushing through your life – beware! Beware!

'Ladies and gentlemen, I am an auctioneer by profession, and if what I tell you is not the truth I am liable to have my licence taken away from me and a heavy imprisonment.' He holds the licence across his chest; the sweat pours down his face into his paper collar; his eyes look glazed. When he takes off his hat there is a deep pucker of angry flesh on his forehead. Nobody buys a watch.

Look out again! A huge barouche comes swinging down the hill with two old, old babies inside. She holds up a lace parasol; he sucks the knob of his cane, and the fat old bodies roll together as the cradle rocks, and the steaming horse leaves a trail of manure as it ambles down the hill.

Under a tree, Professor Leonard, in cap and gown, stands beside his banner. He is here 'for one day', from the London, Paris and Brussels Exhibition, to tell your fortune from your face. And he stands, smiling encouragement, like a clumsy dentist. When the big men, romping and swearing a moment before, hand across their sixpence, and stand before him, they are suddenly serious, dumb, timid, almost blushing as the Professor's quick hand notches the printed card. They are like little children caught playing in a forbidden garden by the owner, stepping from behind a tree.

The top of the hill is reached. How hot it is! How fine it is! The public-house is open, and the crowd presses in. The mother sits on the pavement edge with her baby, and the father brings her out a glass of dark, brownish stuff, and then savagely elbows his way in again. A reek of beer floats from the public-house, and a loud clatter and rattle of voices.

The wind has dropped, and the sun burns more fiercely than ever. Outside the two swing-doors there is a thick mass of children like flies at the mouth of a sweet-jar.

And up, up the hill come the people, with ticklers and golliwogs, and roses and feathers. Up, up they thrust into the light and heat, shouting, laughing, squealing, as though they were being pushed by something, far below, and by the sun, far ahead of them – drawn up into the full, bright, dazzling radiance to . . . what?

An Ideal Family

THAT EVENING for the first time in his life, as he pressed through the swing door and descended the three broad steps to the pavement, old Mr Neave felt he was too old for the spring. Spring – warm, eager, restless – was there, waiting for him in the golden light, ready in front of everybody to run up, to blow in his white beard, to drag sweetly on his arm. And he couldn't meet her, no; he couldn't square up once more and stride off, jaunty as a young man. He was tired and, although the late sun was still shining, curiously cold, with a numbed feeling all over. Quite suddenly he hadn't the energy, he hadn't the heart to stand this gaiety and bright movement any longer; it confused him. He wanted to stand still, to wave it away with his stick, to say, 'Be off with you!' Suddenly it was a terrible effort to greet as usual – tipping his wideawake with his stick – all the people whom he knew, the friends, acquaintances, shopkeepers, postmen, drivers. But the gay glance that went with the gesture, the kindly twinkle that seemed to say, 'I'm a match and more for any of you' – that old Mr Neave could not manage at all. He stumped along, lifting his knees high as if he were walking through air that had somehow grown heavy and solid like water. And the homeward-looking crowd hurried by, the trams clanked, the light carts clattered, the big swinging cabs bowled along with that reckless, defiant indifference that one knows only in dreams . . .

It had been a day like other days at the office. Nothing special had happened. Harold hadn't come back from lunch until close on four. Where had he been? What had he been up to? He wasn't going to let his father know. Old Mr Neave had happened to be in the vestibule, saying goodbye to a caller, when Harold sauntered in, perfectly turned out as usual, cool, suave, smiling that peculiar little half-smile that women found so fascinating.

Ah, Harold was too handsome, too handsome by far; that had been the trouble all along. No man had a right to such eyes, such lashes, and such lips; it was uncanny. As for his mother, his sisters, and the servants, it was not too much to say they made a young god of him; they worshipped Harold, they forgave him everything; and he had needed some forgiving ever since the time when he was thirteen and he had stolen his mother's purse, taken the money, and hidden the purse in the cook's bedroom. Old Mr Neave struck sharply with his stick upon the pavement edge. But it wasn't only his family who spoiled Harold, he reflected, it was everybody; he had only to look and to smile, and down they went before him. So perhaps it wasn't to be wondered at that he expected the office to carry on the tradition. H'm, h'm! But it couldn't be done. No business – not even a success-ful, established, big paying concern – could be played with. A man had either to put his whole heart and soul into it, or it went all to pieces before his eyes . . .

And then Charlotte and the girls were always at him to make the whole thing over to Harold, to retire, and to spend his time enjoying himself. Enjoying himself! Old Mr Neave stopped dead under a group of ancient cabbage palms outside the Government buildings! Enjoying himself! The wind of evening shook the dark leaves to a thin airy cackle. Sitting at home, twiddling his thumbs, conscious all the while that his life's work was slipping away, dissolving, disapp-earing through Harold's fine fingers, while Harold smiled . . .

'Why will you be so unreasonable, father? There's absolutely no need for you to go to the office. It only makes it very awkward for us when people persist in saying how tired you're looking. Here's this huge house and garden. Surely you could be happy in – in – appreciating it for a change. Or you could take up some hobby.'

And Lola the baby had chimed in loftily, 'All men ought to have hobbies. It makes life impossible if they haven't.'

Well, well! He couldn't help a grim smile as painfully he began to climb the hill that led into Harcourt Avenue. Where would Lola and her sisters and Charlotte be if he'd gone in for hobbies, he'd like to know? Hobbies couldn't pay for the town house and the seaside bungalow, and their horses, and their golf, and the sixty-guinea gramophone in the music-room for them to dance to. Not that he grudged them these things. No, they were smart, good-looking girls, and Charlotte was a remarkable woman; it was natural for them to be in the swim. As a matter of fact, no other house in the town was as popular as theirs; no other family entertained so much. And how many times old Mr Neave, pushing the cigar box across the smoking-room table, had listened to praises of his wife, his girls, of himself even.

'You're an ideal family, sir, an ideal family. It's like something one reads about or sees on the stage.'

'That's all right, my boy,' old Mr Neave would reply. 'Try one of those; I think you'll like them. And if you care to smoke in the garden, you'll find the girls on the lawn, I dare say.'

That was why the girls had never married, so people said. They could have married anybody. But they had too good a time at home. They were too happy together, the girls and Charlotte. H'm, h'm! Well, well. Perhaps so . . .

By this time he had walked the length of fashionable Harcourt Avenue; he had reached the corner house, their house. The carriage gates were pushed back; there were fresh marks of wheels on the drive. And then he faced the big white-painted house, with its wide-open windows, its tulle curtains floating outwards, its blue jars of hyacinths on the broad sills. On either side of the carriage porch their hydrangeas – famous in the town – were coming into flower; the pinkish, bluish masses of flower lay like light among the spreading leaves. And somehow, it seemed to old Mr Neave that the house and the flowers, and even the fresh marks on the drive, were saying, 'There is young life here. There are girls – '

The hall, as always, was dusky with wraps, parasols, gloves, piled on the oak chests. From the music-room sounded the piano, quick, loud and impatient. Through the drawing-room door that was ajar voices floated.

'And were there ices?' came from Charlotte. Then the creak, creak of her rocker.

'Ices!' cried Ethel. 'My dear mother, you never saw such ices. Only two kinds. And one a common little strawberry shop ice, in a sopping wet frill.'

'The food altogether was too appalling,' came from Marion.

'Still, it's rather early for ices,' said Charlotte easily.

'But why, if one has them at all . . . ' began Ethel.

'Oh, quite so, darling,' crooned Charlotte.

Suddenly the music-room door opened and Lola dashed out. She started, she nearly screamed, at the sight of old Mr Neave.

'Gracious, father! What a fright you gave me! Have you just come home? Why isn't Charles here to help you off with your coat?'

Her cheeks were crimson from playing, her eyes glittered, the hair fell over her forehead. And she breathed as though she had come running through the dark and was frightened. Old Mr Neave stared at his youngest daughter; he felt he had never seen her before. So that was Lola, was it? But she seemed to have forgotten her father; it was not for him that she was waiting there. Now she put the tip of her crumpled handkerchief between her teeth and tugged at it angrily. The telephone rang. A-ah! Lola gave a cry like a sob and dashed past him. The door of the telephone-room slammed, and at the same moment Charlotte called, 'Is that you, father?'

'You're tired again,' said Charlotte reproachfully, and she stopped the rocker and offered her warm plum-like cheek. Bright-haired Ethel pecked his beard, Marion's lips brushed his ear.

'Did you walk back, father?' asked Charlotte.

'Yes, I walked home,' said old Mr Neave, and he sank into one of the immense drawing-room chairs.

'But why didn't you take a cab?' said Ethel. 'There are hundred of cabs about at that time.'

'My dear Ethel,' cried Marion, 'if father prefers to tire himself out, I really don't see what business of ours it is to interfere.'

'Children, children!' coaxed Charlotte.

But Marion wouldn't be stopped. 'No, mother, you spoil father, and it's not right. You ought to be stricter with him. He's very naughty.' She laughed her hard, bright laugh and patted her hair in a mirror. Strange! When she was a little girl she had such a soft, hesitating voice; she had even stuttered, and now, whatever she said – even if it was only 'Jam, please, father' – it rang out as though she were on the stage.

'Did Harold leave the office before you, dear?' asked Charlotte, beginning to rock again.

'I'm not sure,' said Old Mr Neave. 'I'm not sure. I didn't see him after four o'clock.'

'He said – ' began Charlotte.

But at that moment Ethel, who was twitching over the leaves of some paper or other, ran to her mother and sank down beside her chair.

'There, you see,' she cried. 'That's what I mean, mummy. Yellow, with touches of silver. Don't you agree?'

'Give it to me, love,' said Charlotte. She fumbled for her tortoise-shell spectacles and put them on, gave the page a little dab with her plump small fingers, and pursed up her lips. 'Very sweet!' she crooned vaguely; she looked at Ethel over her spectacles. 'But I shouldn't have the train.'

'Not the train!' wailed Ethel tragically. 'But the train's the whole point.'

'Here, mother, let me decide.' Marion snatched the paper playfully from Charlotte. 'I agree with mother,' she cried triumphantly. 'The train overweights it.'

Old Mr Neave, forgotten, sank into the broad lap of his chair, and, dozing, heard them as though he dreamed. There was no doubt about it, he was tired out; he had lost his hold. Even Charlotte and the girls were too much for him tonight. They were too . . . too . . . But all his drowsing brain could think of was – too rich for him. And somewhere at the back of everything he was watching a little withered ancient man climbing up endless flights of stairs. Who was he?

'I shan't dress tonight,' he muttered.

'What do you say, father?'

'Eh, what, what?' Old Mr Neave woke with a start and stared across at them. 'I shan't dress tonight,' he repeated.

'But, father, we've got Lucile coming, and Henry Davenport, and Mrs Teddie Walker.'

'It will look so very out of the picture.'

'Don't you feel well, dear?'

'You needn't make any effort. What is Charles for?'

'But if you're really not up to it,' Charlotte wavered.

'Very well! Very well!' Old Mr Neave got up and went to join that little old climbing fellow just as far as his dressing-room . . .

There young Charles was waiting for him. Carefully, as though everything depended on it, he was tucking a towel round the hot-water can. Young Charles had been a favourite of his ever since as a little red-faced boy he had come into the house to look after the fires. Old Mr Neave lowered himself into the cane lounge by the window, stretched out his legs, and made his little evening joke, 'Dress him up, Charles!' And Charles, breathing intensely and frowning, bent forward to take the pin out of his tie.

H'm, h'm! Well, well! It was pleasant by the open window, very pleasant – a fine mild evening. They were cutting the grass on the tennis court below; he heard the soft churr of the mower. Soon the girls would begin their tennis parties again. And at the thought he seemed to hear Marion's voice ring out, 'Good for you, partner . . . Oh, played, partner . . . Oh, very nice indeed.' Then Charlotte calling from the veranda, 'Where is Harold?' And Ethel, 'He's certainly not here, mother.' And Charlotte's vague, 'He said – '

Old Mr Neave sighed, got up, and putting one hand under his beard, he took the comb from young Charles, and carefully combed the white beard over. Charles gave him a folded handkerchief, his watch and seals, and spectacle case.

'That will do, my lad.' The door shut, he sank back, he was alone . . .

And now that little ancient fellow was climbing down endless flights that led to a glittering, gay dining-room. What legs he had! They were like a spider's – thin, withered.

'You're an ideal family, sir, an ideal family.'

But if that were true, why didn't Charlotte or the girls stop him? Why was he all alone, climbing up and down? Where was Harold? Ah, it was no good expecting anything from Harold. Down, down went the little old spider, and then, to his horror, old Mr Neave saw him slip past the dining-room and make for the porch, the dark drive, the carriage gates, the office. Stop him, stop him, somebody!

Old Mr Neave started up. It was dark in his dressing-room; the window shone pale. How long had he been asleep? He listened, and through the big, airy, darkened house there floated far-away voices, far-away sounds. Perhaps, he thought vaguely, he had been asleep for a long time. He'd been forgotten. What had all this to do with him – this house and Charlotte, the girls and Harold – what did he know about them? They were strangers to him. Life had passed him by. Charlotte was not his wife. His wife!

. . . A dark porch, half hidden by a passion-vine, that drooped sorrowful, mournful, as though it understood. Small, warm arms were round his neck. A face, little and pale, lifted to his, and a voice breathed, 'Goodbye, my treasure.'

My treasure! 'Goodbye, my treasure!' Which of them had spoken? Why had they said goodbye? There had been some terrible mistake. She was his wife, that little pale girl, and all the rest of his life had been a dream.

Then the door opened, and young Charles, standing in the light, put his hands by his side and shouted like a young soldier, 'Dinner is on the table, sir!'

'I'm coming, I'm coming,' said old Mr Neave.

The Lady's Maid

Eleven o'clock. A knock at the door.

. . . I hope I haven't disturbed you, madam. You weren't asleep –
were you? But I've just given my lady her tea, and there was such a
nice cup over, I thought, perhaps . . .

. . . Not at all, madam. I always make a cup of tea last thing. She
drinks it in bed after her prayers to warm her up. I put the kettle on
when she kneels down and I say to it, 'Now you needn't be in too
much of a hurry to say your prayers.' But it's always boiling before
my lady is half through. You see, madam, we know such a lot of
people, and they've all got to be prayed for – every one. My lady
keeps a list of the names in a little red book. Oh dear! whenever
someone new has been to see us and my lady says afterwards, 'Ellen,
give me my little red book,' I feel quite wild, I do. 'There's another,'
I think, 'keeping her out of her bed in all weathers.' And she won't
have a cushion, you know, madam; she kneels on the hard carpet. It
fidgets me something dreadful to see her, knowing her as I do. I've
tried to cheat her; I've spread out the eiderdown. But the first time I
did it – oh, she gave me such a look – holy it was, madam. 'Did our
Lord have an eiderdown, Ellen?' she said. But – I was younger at the
time – I felt inclined to say, 'No, but our Lord wasn't your age, and
he didn't know what it was to have your lumbago.' Wicked – wasn't
it? But she's too good, you know, madam. When I tucked her up just
now and seen – saw her lying back, her hands outside and her head
on the pillow – so pretty – I couldn't help thinking, 'Now you look
just like your dear mother when I laid her out!'

. . . Yes, madam, it was all left to me. Oh, she did look sweet. I did
her hair, soft-like, round her forehead, all in dainty curls, and just to
one side of her neck I put a bunch of most beautiful purple pansies.
Those pansies made a picture of her, madam! I shall never forget
them. I thought tonight, when I looked at my lady, 'Now, if only the
pansies was there no one could tell the difference.'

. . . Only the last year, madam. Only after she'd got a little – well –

feeble as you might say. Of course, she was never dangerous; she was the sweetest old lady. But how it took her was – she thought she'd lost something. She couldn't keep still, she couldn't settle. All day long she'd be up and down, up and down; you'd meet her everywhere – on the stairs, in the porch, making for the kitchen. And she'd look up at you, and she'd say – just like a child, 'I've lost it, I've lost it.' 'Come along,' I'd say, 'come along, and I'll lay out your patience for you.' But she'd catch me by the hand – I was a favourite of hers – and whisper, 'Find it for me, Ellen. Find it for me.' Sad, wasn't it?

. . . No, she never recovered, madam. She had a stroke at the end. Last words she ever said was – very slow, 'Look in – the – Look – in – ' And then she was gone.

. . . No, madam, I can't say I noticed it. Perhaps some girls. But you see, it's like this, I've got nobody but my lady. My mother died of consumption when I was four, and I lived with my grandfather, who kept a hairdresser's shop. I used to spend all my time in the shop under a table dressing my doll's hair – copying the assistants, I suppose. They were ever so kind to me. Used to make me little wigs, all colours, the latest fashions and all. And there I'd sit all day, quiet as quiet – the customers never knew. Only now and again I'd take my peep from under the tablecloth.

. . . But one day I managed to get a pair of scissors and – would you believe it, madam? I cut off all my hair; snipped it off all in bits, like the little monkey I was. Grandfather was furious! He caught hold of the tongs – I shall never forget it – grabbed me by the hand and shut my fingers in them. 'That'll teach you!' he said. It was a fearful burn. I've got the mark of it today.

. . . Well, you see, madam, he'd taken such pride in my hair. He used to sit me up on the counter, before the customers came, and do it something beautiful – big, soft curls and waved over the top. I remember the assistants standing round, and me ever so solemn with the penny grandfather gave me to hold while it was being done . . . But he always took the penny back afterwards. Poor grandfather! Wild, he was, at the fright I'd made of myself. But he frightened me that time. Do you know what I did, madam? I ran away. Yes, I did, round the corners, in and out, I don't know how far I didn't run. Oh, dear, I must have looked a sight, with my hand rolled up in my pinny and my hair sticking out. People must have laughed when they saw me . . .

. . . No, madam, grandfather never got over it. He couldn't bear the sight of me after. Couldn't eat his dinner, even, if I was there. So my aunt took me. She was a cripple, an upholstress. Tiny! She had to stand on the sofas when she wanted to cut out the backs. And it was helping her I met my lady . . .

. . . Not so very, madam. I was thirteen, turned. And I don't remember ever feeling – well – a child, as you might say. You see there was my uniform, and one thing and another. My lady put me into collars and cuffs from the first. Oh yes – once I did! That was – funny! It was like this. My lady had her two little nieces staying with her – we were at Sheldon at the time- -and there was a fair on the common.

'Now, Ellen,' she said, 'I want you to take the two young ladies for a ride on the donkeys.' Off we went; solemn little loves they were; each had a hand. But when we came to the donkeys they were too shy to go on. So we stood and watched instead. Beautiful those donkeys were! They were the first I'd seen out of a cart – for pleasure as you might say. They were a lovely silver-grey, with little red saddles and blue bridles and bells jing-a-jingling on their ears. And quite big girls – older than me, even – were riding them, ever so gay. Not at all common, I don't mean, madam, just enjoying themselves. And I don't know what it was, but the way the little feet went, and the eyes – so gentle – and the soft ears – made me want to go on a donkey more than anything in the world!

. . . Of course, I couldn't. I had my young ladies. And what would I have looked like perched up there in my uniform? But all the rest of the day it was donkeys – donkeys on the brain with me. I felt I should have burst if I didn't tell someone; and who was there to tell? But when I went to bed – I was sleeping in Mrs James's bedroom, our cook that was, at the time – as soon as the lights was out, there they were, my donkeys, jingling along, with their neat little feet and sad eyes . . . Well, madam, would you believe it, I waited for a long time and pretended to be asleep, and then suddenly I sat up and called out as loud as I could, 'I do want to go on a donkey. I do want a donkey-ride!' You see, I had to say it, and I thought they wouldn't laugh at me if they knew I was only dreaming. Artful – wasn't it? Just what a silly child would think . . .

. . . No, madam, never now. Of course, I did think of it at one time. But it wasn't to be. He had a little flower-shop just down the road and across from where we was living. Funny – wasn't it? And me such a one for flowers. We were having a lot of company at the time, and I was in and out of the shop more often than not, as the saying is.

And Harry and I (his name was Harry) got to quarrelling about how things ought to be arranged – and that began it. Flowers! you wouldn't believe it, madam, the flowers he used to bring me. He'd stop at nothing. It was lilies-of-the-valley more than once, and I'm not exaggerating! Well, of course, we were going to be married and live over the shop, and it was all going to be just so, and I was to have the window to arrange . . . Oh, how I've done that window of a Saturday! Not really, of course, madam, just dreaming, as you might say. I've done it for Christmas – motto in holly, and all – and I've had my Easter lilies with a gorgeous star all daffodils in the middle. I've hung – well, that's enough of that. The day came he was to call for me to choose the furniture. Shall I ever forget it? It was a Tuesday. My lady wasn't quite herself that afternoon. Not that she'd said anything, of course; she never does or will. But I knew by the way that she kept wrapping herself up and asking me if it was cold – and her little nose looked . . . pinched. I didn't like leaving her; I knew I'd be worrying all the time. At last I asked her if she'd rather I put it off. 'Oh no, Ellen,' she said, 'you mustn't mind about me. You mustn't disappoint your young man.' And so cheerful, you know, madam, never thinking about herself. It made me feel worse than ever. I began to wonder . . . then she dropped her handkerchief and began to stoop down to pick it up herself – a thing she never did. 'Whatever are you doing!' I cried, running to stop her. 'Well,' she said, smiling, you know, madam, 'I shall have to begin to practise.' Oh, it was all I could do not to burst out crying. I went over to the dressing-table and made believe to rub up the silver, and I couldn't keep myself in, and I asked her if she'd rather I . . . didn't get married. 'No, Ellen,' she said – that was her voice, madam, like I'm giving you – 'No, Ellen, not for the wide world!' But while she said it, madam – I was looking in her glass; of course, she didn't know I could see her – she put her little hand on her heart just like her dear mother used to, and lifted her eyes . . . Oh, madam!

When Harry came I had his letters all ready, and the ring and a ducky little brooch he'd given me – a silver bird it was, with a chain in its beak, and on the end of the chain a heart with a dagger. Quite the thing! I opened the door to him. I never gave him time for a word. 'There you are,' I said. 'Take them all back,' I said, 'it's all over. I'm not going to marry you,' I said, 'I can't leave my lady.' White! he turned as white as a woman. I had to slam the door, and there I stood, all of a tremble, till I knew he had gone. When I opened the door – believe me or not, madam – that man was gone! I ran out into the road just as I was, in my apron and my house-shoes, and there I stayed in the middle of the road ... staring. People must have laughed if they saw me ...

... Goodness gracious! – What's that? It's the clock striking! And here I've been keeping you awake. Oh, madam, you ought to have stopped me ... Can I tuck in your feet? I always tuck in my lady's feet, every night, just the same. And she says, 'Good night, Ellen. Sleep sound and wake early!' I don't know what I should do if she didn't say that, now.

... Oh dear, I sometimes think ... whatever should I do if anything were to ... But, there, thinking's no good to anyone – is it, madam? Thinking won't help. Not that I do it often. And if ever I do I pull myself up sharp, 'Now, then, Ellen. At it again – you silly girl! If you can't find anything better to do than to start thinking! ...'

THE DOVES' NEST
and other stories

To
WALTER DE LA MARE

First published 1923

INTRODUCTORY NOTE

Katherine Mansfield died at Fontainebleau on January 9, 1923, at the age of thirty-four.

The Doves' Nest contains all the complete stories, and several fragments of stories, which she wrote at the same time as, or after, those published in *The Garden-Party and Other Stories*. Her earlier work, belonging to the period between her first book, *In a German Pension*, and her second, *Bliss and Other Stories*, is collected in the next section of the present volume (p. 521 *seq*). Thus the continuity of her writing will be preserved, and an opportunity given to those who care for such things to follow the development of a talent now generally recognised as among the rarest of her generation.

The title *The Doves' Nest and Other Stories* is the title which Katherine Mansfield intended to give to this collection. Whether the stories which compose it are those she would finally have included in it, I cannot say. Her standard of self-criticism was continually changing, and changing always in the direction of a greater rigour. In writings which I thought perfect she, with her keener insight, discerned unworthy elements. Now that I am forced to depend upon my own sole judgement, it has seemed to me that there is not a scrap of her writing – not even the tiniest fragment – during this final period which does not bear the visible impress of her exquisite individuality and her creative power.

On October 27, 1921, soon after she had finished and sent to her publisher the stories which compose *The Garden-Party*, she wrote the following plan of her new book in her journal. (The letters L. and N.Z. mean that the stories were to have London or New Zealand for their setting.)

STORIES FOR MY NEW BOOK

N.Z. 'Honesty': The Doctor, Arnold Cullen and his wife Lydia, and Archie the friend.

L.   'Second Violin': Alexander and his friend in the train. Spring . . . wet lilac . . . spouting rain.

N.Z.   'Six Years After': A wife and husband on board a steamer. They see someone who reminds them. The cold buttons.

L.   'Lives Like Logs of Driftwood': This wants to be a long, very well written story. The men are important, especially the lesser man. It wants a great deal of working . . . newspaper office.

N.Z.   'A Weak Heart': Roddie on his bike in the evening, with his hands in his pockets, *doing marvels* by that dark tree at the corner of May Street.

L.   'Widowed': Geraldine and Jimmie, a house overlooking Sloane Street and Square. Wearing those buds at her breast. 'Married or not married' . . . From autumn to spring.

N.Z.   'Our Maude': Husband and wife play duets: *And* a *one* a *two* a *three* a *one* a *two three one!* His white waist-coats. Wifeling and Mahub! What a girl you are!

N.Z.   'At Karori': The little lamp. I seen it. And then they were silent.

N.Z.   'Aunt Anne': Her life with the Tannhäuser overture.

Of these stories, only the one called 'At Karori' and subsequently entitled 'The Doll's House' was finished, three days later, on October 30. Of some of the remaining stories there are considerable fragments, of three of them I have so far discovered no trace at all. All the fragments I have found which indubitably belong to any of these stories I have included in this volume. I have also included other fragments which seemed to possess a separate existence, but I have reserved most of the shorter pieces for publication with her Journal.

Between October 1921, when the original plan of this volume was sketched, and the end of January 1922, she finished other stories which she had not foreseen. These were 'A Cup of Tea', 'Honeymoon', 'Taking the Veil', and the long, unfinished, yet somehow complete piece, 'A Married Man's Story'. In January she also began 'The Doves' Nest', a story which was particularly important to her, and with the writing of which – at least at the beginning – she was satisfied. She wrote in her journal on New Year's Day, 1922:

Wrote 'The Doves' Nest' this afternoon. I was in no mood to write; it seemed impossible. Yet, when I had finished three pages, they 'were all right'! This is a proof (never to be too often proved) that when one has thought out a story nothing remains but the *labour*.

She worked on and off at 'The Doves' Nest' during the following summer also. Unfortunately I can find no trace of her own manuscript. There is a fair, clean copy, typewritten by herself, of the portion printed in this book, but nothing more.

In February 1922 began three months of an exacting medical treatment in Paris, during which work became more and more a physical impossibility. Nevertheless, at the beginning of this time, on February 20, she wrote 'The Fly'. On her return to Switzerland in June she tried to resume work on 'The Doves' Nest' and she wrote the scenario of a play; but again physical weakness made work in the mountains impossible. To ease the strain on her heart she descended into the valley in June. At Sierre she wrote more of 'The Doves' Nest', much more, alas, than remains; she also began the unfinished piece called 'Father and the Girls' and finished the short story called 'The Canary'. These were the last of the stories written by her which can be exactly dated. There is reason, however, to believe that the passage of the story called 'Six Years After' which ends with the words: 'Can one do nothing for the dead? And for a long time the answer had been – Nothing!' was actually the last piece written by her. It seems to belong to the autumn of 1922, when she had, for a time, practically abandoned writing.

It was not, however, because of her physical weakness that she stopped writing in the late summer of 1922. The power of her spirit to triumph over the frailty of her body had been proved over and over again. She stopped writing deliberately, not under compulsion. She felt that her whole attitude to life needed to be renewed, and she determined that she would write no more until it had been renewed.

Perhaps an idea of the way of her mind – or rather her whole being – was moving, may be gleaned from some extracts from her journal. At first, her dissatisfaction with her work took shape in a feeling that she was not exerting the whole of her powers or expressing the whole of her knowledge in her writings. As early as July 1921, when she was still engaged on the last of the stories for *The Garden-Party*, she wrote:

July 1921. I finished 'Mr and Mrs Dove' yesterday. I am not altogether pleased with it. It's a little bit made up. It's not inevitable. I meant to imply that those two may not be happy together – that that is the kind of reason for which a young girl marries. But have I done so? I don't think so. Besides it's not *strong* enough. I want to be nearer – far nearer than that. I want to use all my force, even when I am taking a fine line. And I have a sneaking notion that I have, at the end, used the doves *unwarrantably*. *Tu sais ce que je veux dire*. I used them to round off something – didn't I? Is that quite my game? No, it's not. It's not quite the kind of truth I'm after. Now for *Susannah*. All must be *deeply felt*.

And a few days later she wrote:

July 23. Finished 'An Ideal Family' yesterday. It seems to me better than the 'Doves', but still it's not good enough. I worked at it hard enough, God knows, and yet I didn't get the deepest truth out of the idea, even once. What is this feeling? I feel again that this kind of knowledge is too easy for me; it's even a kind of trickery. I know so much more. It looks and smells like a story, but I wouldn't buy it. I don't want to possess it – to live with it. *No*. Once I have written two more, I shall tackle something different – a long story – 'At the Bay', with more *difficult* relationships. That's the whole problem.

Yet a little later her vision of the cause of her own dissatisfaction deepened, and she began to define it in terms – of the insufficient clarity of her own spirit, and of the incompleteness of her inward life – which were to become more and more familiar.

Well, I must confess I have had an idle day – God knows why. All was to be written, but I just didn't write it. I thought I would, but I felt tired after tea, and rested instead. Is it good or bad in me to behave so? I have a sense of guilt, but at the same time I know that to rest is the very best thing I can do. And for some reason there is a kind of booming in my head – which is horrid. But marks of earthly degradation still pursue me. I am not crystal clear. Above all else, I do still lack application. It's not right. There is so much to do, and I do so little. Look at the stories that wait and wait, just at the threshold. Why don't I let them in? And their place would be taken by others who are lurking beyond just out there – waiting for the chance.

Next day. Yet take this morning, for instance. I don't want to write anything. It's grey; it's heavy and dull. And short stories seem unreal, and not worth doing. I don't want to write? I want to *live*. What does one mean by that? It's not too easy to say. But there you are!

Aug. 21. All this that I write, all that I am, is on the border of the sea. It's a kind of playing. I want to put all my force behind it, but somehow I *cannot*.

And again in the autumn of the year her incessant effort towards an inward purity – who but she would have dreamed that she lacked it? – as a condition of soul essential to writing as she purposed to write, becomes still more manifest.

Oct. 16. Another radiant day. J. is typing my last story, 'The Garden-Party', which I finished on my birthday. It took me nearly a month to 'recover' from 'At the Bay'. I made at least four false starts. But I could not get away from the sound of the sea and Beryl fanning her hair at the window. These things would not *die down*. But now I am not at all sure about that story. It seems to me it is a little 'wispy' – not what it might have been. The 'G.-P.' is better. But that is not *good enough*, either . . . The last few days, what one notices more than anything is the blue. Blue sky, blue mountains – all is a heavenly blueness! And clouds of all kinds – wings, soft white clouds, almost hard little golden islands, great mock-mountains. The gold deepens on the slopes. In fact, in sober fact, it is perfection. But the late evening is the time of times. Then, with that unearthly beauty before one, it is not hard to realise how far one has to go. To write something that will be worthy of that rising moon, that pale light. To be 'simple' enough as one would be simple before God.

Nov. 21. Since then I have only written 'The Doll's House'. A bad spell has been on me. I have begun two stories, but then told them and they felt betrayed. It is absolutely fatal to give way to this temptation . . . Today I begin to write, seriously, 'The Weak Heart' – a story which fascinates me *deeply*. What I feel it needs so peculiarly is a very subtle variation of tense from the present to the past and back again – and softness, lightness, and the feeling that all is in bud, with a play of humour over the character of Roddie. And the feeling of the Thorndon Baths, the wet, moist, oozy . . . no, I know how it must be done.

May I be found worthy to do it! Lord, make me crystal clear for thy light to shine through.

The two stories which she told and then was forced to abandon 'because they felt betrayed' were 'Honesty' and 'All Serene'. Of 'Weak Heart', as she subsequently called it, only fragments remain.

There is the opening copied in careful writing, a few hurriedly written sentences from the middle – themes, as it were, hastily noted – and then, obviously written at top speed and decipherable only with great difficulty, the end.

The two following passages from her journal belong to the same months, October and November 1921. But they were written in another book, and one of them should be placed in point of time between the two previous entries. Katherine Mansfield's attempts at keeping a regular journal were intermittent. Nearly all the passages quoted here as from her 'journal' were written on random pages of the little copybooks in which she composed her stories. In order to appreciate the first of the following passages fully it should be remembered that it was written immediately after she had finished 'At the Bay'.

Oct. 1921. I wonder why it should be so difficult to be humble. I do not think that I am a good writer; I realise my faults better than anyone else could realise them. I know exactly when I fail. And yet, when I have finished a story and before I have begun another, I catch myself *preening* my feathers. It is disheartening. There seems to be some bad old pride in my heart; a root of it that puts out a thick shoot on the slightest provocation . . . This interferes very much with work. One can't be calm, clear, good as one must be, while it goes on. I look at the mountains, I try to pray – and I think of something *clever*. It's a kind of excitement within one which shouldn't be there. Calm yourself. Clear yourself. And anything that I write in this mood will be no good; it will be full of *sediment*. If I were well, I would go off by myself somewhere and sit under a tree. One must learn, one must practise to *forget* oneself. I can't tell the truth about Aunt Anne unless I am free to enter into her life without self-consciousness. Oh, God! I am divided still, I am bad, I fail in my personal life. I lapse into impatience, temper, vanity, and so I fail as thy priest. Perhaps poetry will help.

I have just thoroughly cleaned and attended to my fountain pen. If after this it leaks, then it is *no* gentleman!

Nov. 13, 1921. It is time I started a new journal. Come, my unseen, my unknown, let us talk together. Yes, for the last two weeks I have written scarcely anything. I have been idle; I have *failed*. Why? Many reasons. There has been a kind of confusion in my consciousness. It has seemed as though there was no time to work. The mornings, if they are sunny, are taken up with sun-treatment;

the post eats away the afternoon. And at night I am tired. But it goes deeper. Yes, you are right. I haven't felt able to yield to the kind of contemplation that is necessary. I haven't felt pure in heart, not humble, not good. There's been a stirring up of sediment. I look at the mountains and I see nothing but mountains. Be frank! I read rubbish . . . Out of hand? Yes, that describes it. Dissipated, vague, not *positive*, and above all, above everything, not working as I should be working – wasting time.

Wasting time! The old cry – the first and last cry. Why do ye tarry? Ah, why indeed? My deepest desire is to be a writer, to have 'a body of work' done – and there the work is, there the stories wait for me, *grow tired*, wilt, fade, because I will not come. When first they knock, how eager and fresh they are! And I hear and I *acknowledge* them, and still I go on sitting at the window, playing with the ball of wool. What is to be done?

I must make another effort at once. I must begin all over again. I must try and write simply, fully, freely, from my heart. *Quietly*, caring nothing for success or failure, but just going on . . .

But now to resolve! And especially to keep in touch with life. With the sky, this moon, these stars, these cold candid peaks.

During the following summer at Sierre in Switzerland one could have believed that Katherine Mansfield had finally accomplished the task of inward purification she had set herself, and to me it seems that there is a halcyon clarity and calm diffused through the unfinished stories written there. But she was still secretly dissatisfied with herself and her work, and in the autumn, after a brief return to London, she deliberately decided to risk everything, to abandon the writing that was dearer than all else to her, in order to achieve that newness of heart without which her work and her life seemed to her unprofitable. At the end of October she retired, by herself, to a settlement at Fontainebleau, where she found what she sought. A few days after she had taken this final step, she wrote in a letter:

No treatment on earth is any good to me really. It's all pretence. M. did make me heavier and a trifle stronger. But that was all, if I really face the facts. The miracle never came near happening. It couldn't. And as for my spirit – well, as a result of that life at the Victoria-Palace I stopped being a writer. I have only written long or short scraps since 'The Fly'. If I had gone on with my old life, I never would have written again, for I was dying of poverty of life.

I wish, when one writes about things, one didn't dramatise them so. I feel awfully happy about all this – And it's all as simple as can be . . .

But in any case I shan't write any stories for three months, and I'll not have a book ready before the spring. It doesn't matter . . .

And again, in reply to a friend who pleaded with her not to abandon writing, she wrote, on October 26:

As for writing stories and being true to one's gift – I could not write them if I were not here, even. I am at an end of my source for a time. Life has brought me no *flow*. I want to write, but differently – far more steadily.

She believed that she could not express the change that had taken place in her even in letters, though indeed her letters were radiant with happiness:

And yet I realise as I write, all this is no use. An old personality is trying to get back to the outside and observe, and it's not true to the facts at all. What I write seems so petty. In fact I cannot express myself in writing just now. The old mechanism isn't mine any longer and I can't control the new. I just have to talk this baby talk.

'I am not in a mood for books at present,' she wrote finally, shortly before Christmas, 'though I know that in future I shall want to write them more than anything else. But different books.'

What those 'different books' would have been we shall never know. She was seized by a sudden and fatal hæmorrhage on the evening of January 9. She is buried in the communal cemetery of Avon, near Fontainebleau. On her gravestone are inscribed the words of Shakespeare she chose for the titlepage of *Bliss*, words which had long been cherished by her and were to prove prophetic:

But I tell you, my lord fool, out of this nettle, danger, we pluck this flower, safety.

J. M. M.

The Doll's House

WHEN DEAR OLD MRS HAY went back to town after staying with the Burnells she sent the children a doll's house. It was so big that the carter and Pat carried it into the courtyard, and there it stayed, propped up on two wooden boxes beside the feed-room door. No harm could come to it; it was summer. And perhaps the smell of paint would have gone off by the time it had to be taken in. For, really, the smell of paint coming from that doll's house ('Sweet of old Mrs Hay, of course; most sweet and generous!') – but the smell of paint was quite enough to make anyone seriously ill, in Aunt Beryl's opinion. Even before the sacking was taken off. And when it was . . .

There stood the doll's house, a dark, oily, spinach green, picked out with bright yellow. Its two solid little chimneys, glued on to the roof, were painted red and white, and the door, gleaming with yellow varnish, was like a little slab of toffee. Four windows, real windows, were divided into panes by a broad streak of green. There was actually a tiny porch, too, painted yellow, with big lumps of congealed paint hanging along the edge.

But perfect, perfect little house! Who could possibly mind the smell. It was part of the joy, part of the newness.

'Open it quickly, someone!'

The hook at the side was stuck fast. Pat prised it open with his penknife, and the whole house front swung back, and – there you were, gazing at one and the same moment into the drawing-room and dining-room, the kitchen and two bedrooms. That is the way for a house to open! Why don't all houses open like that? How much more exciting than peering through the slit of a door into a mean little hall with a hat-stand and two umbrellas! That is – isn't it? – what you long to know about a house when you put your hand on the knocker. Perhaps it is the way God opens houses at the dead of night when He is taking a quiet turn with an angel . . .

'Oh-oh!' The Burnell children sounded as though they were in despair. It was too marvellous; it was too much for them. They had never seen anything like it in their lives. All the rooms were papered. There were pictures on the walls, painted on the paper, with gold frames complete. Red carpet covered all the floors except the kitchen; red plush chairs in the drawing-room, green in the dining-room; tables, beds with real bedclothes, a cradle, a stove, a dresser with tiny plates and one big jug. But what Kezia liked more than anything, what she liked frightfully, was the lamp. It stood in the middle of the dining-room table, an exquisite little amber lamp with a white globe. It was even filled all ready for lighting, though, of course, you couldn't light it. But there was something inside that looked like oil and moved when you shook it.

The father and mother dolls, who sprawled very stiff as though they had fainted in the drawing-room, and their two little children asleep upstairs, were really too big for the doll's house. They didn't look as though they belonged. But the lamp was perfect. It seemed to smile at Kezia, to say, 'I live here.' The lamp was real.

The Burnell children could hardly walk to school fast enough the next morning. They burned to tell everybody, to describe, to – well – to boast about their doll's house before the school-bell rang.

'I'm to tell,' said Isabel, 'because I'm the eldest. And you two can join in after. But I'm to tell first.'

There was nothing to answer. Isabel was bossy, but she was always right, and Lottie and Kezia knew too well the powers that went with being eldest. They brushed through the thick buttercups at the road edge and said nothing.

'And I'm to choose who's to come and see it first. Mother said I might.'

For it had been arranged that while the doll's house stood in the courtyard they might ask the girls at school, two at a time, to come and look. Not to stay to tea, of course, or to come traipsing through the house. But just to stand quietly in the courtyard while Isabel pointed out the beauties, and Lottie and Kezia looked pleased . . .

But hurry as they might, by the time they had reached the tarred palings of the boys' playground the bell had begun to jangle. They only just had time to whip off their hats and fall into line before the roll was called. Never mind. Isabel tried to make up for it by looking very important and mysterious and by whispering behind her hand to the girls near her, 'Got something to tell you at playtime.'

Playtime came and Isabel was surrounded. The girls of her class nearly fought to put their arms round her, to walk away with her, to beam flatteringly, to be her special friend. She held quite a court under the huge pine trees at the side of the playground. Nudging, giggling together, the little girls pressed up close. And the only two who stayed outside the ring were the two who were always outside, the little Kelveys. They knew better than to come anywhere near the Burnells.

For the fact was, the school the Burnell children went to was not at all the kind of place their parents would have chosen if there had been any choice. But there was none. It was the only school for miles. And the consequence was all the children of the neighbourhood, the Judge's little girls, the doctor's daughters, the store-keeper's children, the milkman's, were forced to mix together. Not to speak of there being an equal number of rude, rough little boys as well. But the line had to be drawn somewhere. It was drawn at the Kelveys. Many of the children, including the Burnells, were not allowed even to speak to them. They walked past the Kelveys with their heads in the air, and as they set the fashion in all matters of behaviour, the Kelveys were shunned by everybody. Even the teacher had a special voice for them, and a special smile for the other children when Lil Kelvey came up to her desk with a bunch of dreadfully common-looking flowers.

They were the daughters of a spry, hard-working little washer-woman, who went about from house to house by the day. This was awful enough. But where was Mr Kelvey? Nobody knew for certain. But everybody said he was in prison. So they were the daughters of a washerwoman and a gaolbird. Very nice company for other people's children! And they looked it. Why Mrs Kelvey made them so conspicuous was hard to understand. The truth was they were dressed in 'bits' given to her by the people for whom she worked. Lil, for instance, who was a stout, plain child, with big freckles, came to school in a dress made from a green art-serge tablecloth of the Burnells', with red plush sleeves from the Logans' curtains. Her hat, perched on top of her high forehead, was a grown-up woman's hat, once the property of Miss Lecky, the post-mistress. It was turned up at the back and trimmed with a large scarlet quill. What a little guy she looked! It was impossible not to laugh. And her little sister, our Else, wore a long white dress, rather like a nightgown, and a pair of little boy's boots. But whatever our Else wore she would have looked strange. She was a tiny wishbone of a child, with cropped hair and enormous solemn eyes – a little white owl. Nobody had ever seen her smile; she scarcely ever spoke. She went through life holding on to Lil, with a piece of Lil's skirt screwed up in her hand. Where Lil went, our Else followed. In the playground, on the road going to and from school, there was Lil marching in front and our Else holding on behind. Only when she wanted anything, or when she was out of breath, our Else gave Lil a tug, a twitch, and Lil stopped and turned round. The Kelveys never failed to understand each other.

Now they hovered at the edge; you couldn't stop them listening. When the little girls turned round and sneered, Lil, as usual, gave her silly, shamefaced smile, but our Else only looked.

And Isabel's voice, so very proud, went on telling. The carpet made a great sensation, but so did the beds with real bedclothes, and the stove with an oven door.

When she finished Kezia broke in. 'You've forgotten the lamp, Isabel.'

'Oh yes,' said Isabel, 'and there's a teeny little lamp, all made of yellow glass, with a white globe that stands on the dining-room table. You couldn't tell it from a real one.'

'The lamp's best of all,' cried Kezia. She thought Isabel wasn't making half enough of the little lamp. But nobody paid any attention. Isabel was choosing the two who were to come back with them that afternoon and see it. She chose Emmie Cole and Lena Logan. But when the others knew they were all to have a chance, they couldn't be nice enough to Isabel. One by one they put their arms round Isabel's waist and walked her off. They had something to whisper to her, a secret. 'Isabel's *my* friend.'

Only the little Kelveys moved away forgotten; there was nothing more for them to hear.

Days passed, and as more children saw the doll's house, the fame of it spread. It became the one subject, the rage. The one question was, 'Have you seen Burnells' doll's house? Oh, ain't it lovely!' 'Haven't you seen it? Oh, I say!'

Even the dinner hour was given up to talking about it. The little girls sat under the pines eating their thick mutton sandwiches and big slabs of johnny cake spread with butter. While always, as near as they could get, sat the Kelveys, our Else holding on to Lil, listening too, while they chewed their jam sandwiches out of a newspaper soaked with large red blobs.

'Mother,' said Kezia, 'can't I ask the Kelveys just once?'

'Certainly not, Kezia.'

'But why not?'

'Run away, Kezia; you know quite well why not.'

At last everybody had seen it except them. On that day the subject rather flagged. It was the dinner hour. The children stood together under the pine trees, and suddenly, as they looked at the Kelveys eating out of their paper, always by themselves, always listening, they wanted to be horrid to them. Emmie Cole started the whisper.

'Lil Kelvey's going to be a servant when she grows up.'

'O-oh, how awful!' said Isabel Burnell, and she made eyes at Emmie.

Emmie swallowed in a very meaning way and nodded to Isabel as she'd seen her mother do on those occasions.

'It's true – it's true – it's true,' she said.

Then Lena Logan's little eyes snapped. 'Shall I ask her?' she whispered.

'Bet you don't,' said Jessie May.

'Pooh, I'm not frightened,' said Lena. Suddenly she gave a little squeal and danced in front of the other girls. 'Watch! Watch me! Watch me now!' said Lena. And sliding, gliding, dragging one foot, giggling behind her hand, Lena went over to the Kelveys.

Lil looked up from her dinner. She wrapped the rest quickly away. Our Else stopped chewing. What was coming now?

'Is it true you're going to be a servant when you grow up, Lil Kelvey?' shrilled Lena.

Dead silence. But instead of answering, Lil only gave her silly, shamefaced smile. She didn't seem to mind the question at all. What a sell for Lena! The girls began to titter.

Lena couldn't stand that. She put her hands on her hips; she shot forward. 'Yah, yer father's in prison!' she hissed spitefully.

This was such a marvellous thing to have said that the little girls rushed away in a body, deeply, deeply excited, wild with joy. Someone found a long rope, and they began skipping. And never did they skip so high, run in and out so fast, or do such daring things as on that morning.

In the afternoon Pat called for the Burnell children with the buggy and they drove home. There were visitors. Isabel and Lottie, who liked visitors, went upstairs to change their pinafores. But Kezia thieved out at the back. Nobody was about; she began to swing on the big white gates of the courtyard. Presently, looking along the road, she saw two little dots. They grew bigger, they were coming towards her. Now she could see that one was in front and one close behind. Now she could see that they were the Kelveys. Kezia stopped swinging. She slipped off the gate as if she was going to run away. Then she hesitated. The Kelveys came nearer, and beside them walked their shadows, very long, stretching right across the road with their heads in the buttercups. Kezia clambered back on the gate; she had made up her mind; she swung out.

'Hullo,' she said to the passing Kelveys.

They were so astounded that they stopped. Lil gave her silly smile. Our Else stared.

'You can come and see our doll's house if you want to,' said Kezia, and she dragged one toe on the ground. But at that Lil turned red and shook her head quickly.

'Why not?' asked Kezia.

Lil gasped, then she said, 'Your ma told our ma you wasn't to speak to us.'

'Oh, well,' said Kezia. She didn't know what to reply. 'It doesn't matter. You can come and see our doll's house all the same. Come on. Nobody's looking.'

But Lil shook her head still harder.

'Don't you want to?' asked Kezia.

Suddenly there was a twitch, a tug at Lil's skirt. She turned round. Our Else was looking at her with big, imploring eyes; she was frowning; she wanted to go. For a moment Lil looked at our Else very doubtfully. But then our Else twitched her skirt again. She started forward. Kezia led the way. Like two little stray cats they followed across the courtyard to where the doll's house stood.

'There it is,' said Kezia.

There was a pause. Lil breathed loudly, almost snorted; our Else was still as stone.

'I'll open it for you,' said Kezia kindly. She undid the hook and they looked inside.

'There's the drawing-room and the dining-room, and that's the – '

'Kezia!'

Oh, what a start they gave!

'Kezia!'

It was Aunt Beryl's voice. They turned round. At the back door stood Aunt Beryl, staring as if she couldn't believe what she saw.

'How dare you ask the little Kelveys into the courtyard!' said her cold, furious voice. 'You know as well as I do, you're not allowed to talk to them. Run away, children, run away at once. And don't come back again,' said Aunt Beryl. And she stepped into the yard and shooed them out as if they were chickens.

'Off you go immediately!' she called, cold and proud.

They did not need telling twice. Burning with shame, shrinking together, Lil huddling along like her mother, our Else dazed, somehow they crossed the big courtyard and squeezed through the white gate.

'Wicked, disobedient little girl!' said Aunt Beryl bitterly to Kezia, and she slammed the doll's house to.

The afternoon had been awful. A letter had come from Willie Brent, a terrifying, threatening letter, saying if she did not meet him that evening in Pulman's Bush, he'd come to the front door and ask the reason why! But now that she had frightened those little rats of Kelveys and given Kezia a good scolding, her heart felt lighter. That ghastly pressure was gone. She went back to the house humming.

When the Kelveys were well out of sight of Burnells', they sat down to rest on a big red drainpipe by the side of the road. Lil's cheeks were still burning; she took off the hat with the quill and held it on her knee. Dreamily they looked over the hay paddocks, past the creek, to the group of wattles where Logan's cows stood waiting to be milked. What were their thoughts?

Presently our Else nudged up close to her sister. But now she had forgotten the cross lady. She put out a finger and stroked her sister's quill; she smiled her rare smile.

'I seen the little lamp,' she said softly.

Then both were silent once more.

Honeymoon

AND WHEN THEY CAME out of the lace shop there was their own driver and the cab they called their own cab waiting for them under a plane tree. What luck! Wasn't it luck? Fanny pressed her husband's arm. These things seemed always to be happening to them ever since they – came abroad. Didn't he think so too? But George stood on the pavement edge, lifted his stick, and gave a loud 'Hi!' Fanny sometimes felt a little uncomfortable about the way George summoned cabs, but the drivers didn't seem to mind, so it must have been all right. Fat, good-natured, and smiling, they stuffed away the little newspaper they were reading, whipped the cotton cover off the horse, and were ready to obey.

'I say,' George said as he helped Fanny in, 'suppose we go and have tea at the place where the lobsters grow. Would you like to?'

'Most awfully,' said Fanny fervently, as she leaned back wondering why the way George put things made them sound so very nice.

'R-right, *bien*.' He was beside her. '*Allay*,' he cried gaily, and off they went.

Off they went, spanking along lightly, under the green and gold shade of the plane trees, through the small streets that smelled of lemons and fresh coffee, past the fountain square where women, with water-pots lifted, stopped talking to gaze after them, round the corner past the café, with its pink and white umbrellas, green tables, and blue siphons, and so to the sea front. There a wind, light, warm, came flowing over the boundless sea. It touched George, and Fanny it seemed to linger over while they gazed at the dazzling water. And George said, 'Jolly, isn't it?' And Fanny, looking dreamy, said, as she said at least twenty times a day since they – came abroad: 'Isn't it extraordinary to think that here we are quite alone, away from everybody, with nobody to tell us to go home, or to – to order us about except ourselves?'

George had long since given up answering 'Extraordinary!' As a rule he merely kissed her. But now he caught hold of her hand, stuffed it into his pocket, pressed her fingers, and said, 'I used to keep a white mouse in my pocket when I was a kid.'

'Did you?' said Fanny, who was intensely interested in everything George had ever done. 'Were you very fond of white mice?'

'Fairly,' said George, without conviction. He was looking at something, bobbing out there beyond the bathing steps. Suddenly he almost jumped in his seat. 'Fanny!' he cried. 'There's a chap out there bathing. Do you see? I'd no idea people had begun. I've been missing it all these days.' George glared at the reddened face, the reddened arm, as though he could not look away. 'At any rate,' he muttered, 'wild horses won't keep me from going in tomorrow morning.'

Fanny's heart sank. She had heard for years of the frightful dangers of the Mediterranean. It was an absolute death-trap. Beautiful, treacherous Mediterranean. There it lay curled before them, its white, silky paws touching the stones and gone again . . . But she'd made up her mind long before she was married that never would she be the kind of woman who interfered with her husband's pleasures, so all she said was, airily, 'I suppose one has to be very up in the currents, doesn't one?'

'Oh, I don't know,' said George. 'People talk an awful lot of rot about the danger.'

But now they were passing a high wall on the land side, covered with flowering heliotrope, and Fanny's little nose lifted. 'Oh, George,' she breathed. 'The smell! The most divine . . .'

'Topping villa,' said George. 'Look, you can see it through the palms.'

'Isn't it rather large?' said Fanny, who somehow could not look at any villa except as a possible habitation for herself and George.

'Well, you'd need a crowd of people if you stayed there long,' replied George. 'Deadly, otherwise. I say, it is ripping. I wonder who it belongs to.' And he prodded the driver in the back.

The lazy, smiling driver, who had no idea, replied, as he always did on these occasions, that it was the property of a wealthy Spanish family.

'Masses of Spaniards on this coast,' commented George, leaning back again, and they were silent until, as they rounded a bend, the big, bone-white hotel-restaurant came into view. Before it there was a small terrace built up against the sea, planted with umbrella palms, set out with tables, and at their approach, from the terrace, from the hotel, waiters came running to receive, to welcome Fanny and George, to cut them off from any possible kind of escape.

'Outside?'

Oh, but of course they would sit outside. The sleek manager, who was marvellously like a fish in a frock-coat, skimmed forward.

'Dis way, sir. Dis way, sir. I have a very nice little table,' he gasped. 'Just the little table for you, sir, over in de corner. Dis way.'

So George, looking most dreadfully bored, and Fanny, trying to look as though she'd spent years of life threading her way through strangers, followed after.

'Here you are, sir. Here you will be very nice,' coaxed the manager, taking the vase off the table, and putting it down again as if it were a fresh little bouquet out of the air. But George refused to sit down immediately. He saw through these fellows; he wasn't going to be done. These chaps were always out to rush you. So he put his hands in his pockets, and said to Fanny, very calmly, 'This all right for you? Anywhere else you'd prefer? How about over there?' And he nodded to a table right over the other side.

What it was to be a man of the world! Fanny admired him deeply, but all she wanted to do was to sit down and look like everybody else.

'I – I like this,' said she.

'Right,' said George hastily, and he sat down almost before Fanny, and said quickly, 'Tea for two and chocolate éclairs.'

'Very good, sir,' said the manager, and his mouth opened and shut as though he was ready for another dive under the water. 'You will not 'ave toasts to start with? We 'ave very nice toasts, sir.'

'No,' said George shortly. 'You don't want toast, do you, Fanny?'

'Oh no, thank you, George,' said Fanny, praying the manager would go.

'Or perhaps de lady might like to look at de live lobsters in de tank while de tea is coming?' And he grimaced and smirked and flicked his serviette like a fin.

George's face grew stony. He said 'No' again, and Fanny bent over the table, unbuttoning her gloves. When she looked up the man was gone. George took off his hat, tossed it on to a chair, and pressed back his hair.

'Thank God,' said he, 'that chap's gone. These foreign fellows bore me stiff. The only way to get rid of them is simply to shut up as you saw I did. Thank heaven!' sighed George again, with so much emotion that if it hadn't been ridiculous Fanny might have imagined that he had been as frightened of the manager as she. As it was she felt a rush of love for George. His hands were on the table, brown, large hands that she knew so well. She longed to take one of them and squeeze it hard. But, to her astonishment, George did just that thing. Leaning across the table, he put his hand over hers, and said, without looking at her, 'Fanny, darling Fanny!'

'Oh, George!' It was in that heavenly moment that Fanny heard a *twing-twing-tootle-tootle*, and a light strumming. There's going to be music, she thought, but the music didn't matter just then. Nothing mattered except love. Faintly smiling she gazed into that faintly smiling face, and the feeling was so blissful that she felt inclined to say to George, 'Let us stay here – where we are – at this little table. It's perfect, and the sea is perfect. Let us stay.' But instead her eyes grew serious.

'Darling,' said Fanny. 'I want to ask you something fearfully important. Promise me you'll answer. Promise.'

'I promise,' said George, too solemn to be quite as serious as she.

'It's this.' Fanny paused a moment, looked down, looked up again. 'Do you feel,' she said softly, 'that you really know me now? But really, really know *me*?'

It was too much for George. Know his Fanny? He gave a broad, childish grin. 'I should jolly well think I do,' he said emphatically. 'Why, what's up?'

Fanny felt he hadn't quite understood. She went on quickly: 'What I mean is this. So often people, even when they love each other, don't seem to – to – it's so hard to say – know each other perfectly. They don't seem to want to. And I think that's awful. They misunderstand each other about the most important things of all.' Fanny looked horrified. 'George, we couldn't do that, could we? We never could.'

'Couldn't be done,' laughed George, and he was just going to tell her how much he liked her little nose, when the waiter arrived with the tea and the band struck up. It was a flute, a guitar, and a violin, and it played so gaily that Fanny felt if she wasn't careful even the cups and saucers might grow little wings and fly away. George absorbed three chocolate éclairs, Fanny two. The funny-tasting tea – 'Lobster in the kettle,' shouted George above the music – was nice all the same, and when the tray was pushed aside and George was smoking, Fanny felt bold enough to look at the other people. But it was the band grouped under one of the dark trees that fascinated her most. The fat man stroking the guitar was like a picture. The dark man playing the flute kept raising his eyebrows as though he was astonished at the sounds that came from it. The fiddler was in shadow.

The music stopped as suddenly as it had begun. It was then she noticed a tall old man with white hair standing beside the musicians. Strange she hadn't noticed him before. He wore a very high, glazed collar, a coat green at the seams, and shamefully shabby button boots. Was he another manager? He did not look like a manager, and yet he stood there gazing over the tables as though thinking of something different and far away from all this. Who could he be?

Presently, as Fanny watched him, he touched the points of his collar with his fingers, coughed slightly, and half turned to the band. It began to play again. Something boisterous, reckless, full of fire, full of passion, was tossed into the air, was tossed to that quiet figure, which clasped its hands, and still with that far-away look, began to sing.

'Good Lord!' said George. It seemed that everybody was equally astonished. Even the little children eating ices stared, with their spoons in the air . . . Nothing was heard except a thin, faint voice, the memory of a voice singing something in Spanish. It wavered, beat on, touched the high notes, fell again, seemed to implore, to entreat, to beg for something, and then the tune changed, and it was resigned, it bowed down, it knew it was denied.

Almost before the end a little child gave a squeak of laughter, but everybody was smiling – except Fanny and George. Is life like this too? thought Fanny. There are people like this. There is suffering. And she looked at that gorgeous sea, lapping the land as though it loved it, and the sky, bright with the brightness before evening. Had she and George the right to be so happy? Wasn't it cruel? There must be something else in life which made all these things possible. What was it? She turned to George.

But George had been feeling differently from Fanny. The poor old boy's voice was funny in a way, but, God, how it made you realise what a terrific thing it was to be at the beginning of everything, as they were, he and Fanny! George, too, gazed at the bright, breathing water, and his lips opened as if he could drink it. How fine it was! There was nothing like the sea for making a chap feel fit. And there sat Fanny, his Fanny, leaning forward, breathing so gently.

'Fanny!' George called to her.

As she turned to him something in her soft, wondering look made George feel that for two pins he would jump over the table and carry her off.

'I say,' said George rapidly, 'let's go, shall we? Let's go back to the hotel. Come. Do, Fanny darling. Let's go now.'

The band began to play. 'Oh, God!' almost groaned George. 'Let's go before the old codger begins squawking again.'

And a moment later they were gone.

A Cup of Tea

ROSEMARY FELL was not exactly beautiful. No, you couldn't have called her beautiful. Pretty? Well, if you took her to pieces . . . But why be so cruel as to take anyone to pieces? She was young, brilliant, extremely modern, exquisitely well dressed, amazingly well read in the newest of the new books, and her parties were the most delicious mixture of the really important people and . . . artists – quaint creatures, discoveries of hers, some of them too terrifying for words, but others quite presentable and amusing.

Rosemary had been married two years. She had a duck of a boy. No, not Peter – Michael. And her husband absolutely adored her. They were rich, really rich, not just comfortably well off, which is odious and stuffy and sounds like one's grandparents. But if Rosemary wanted to shop she would go to Paris as you and I would go to Bond Street. If she wanted to buy flowers, the car pulled up at that perfect shop in Regent Street, and Rosemary inside the shop just gazed in her dazzled, rather exotic way, and said: 'I want those and those and those. Give me four bunches of those. And that jar of roses. Yes, I'll have all the roses in the jar. No, no lilac. I hate lilac. It's got no shape.' The attendant bowed and put the lilac out of sight, as though this was only too true; lilac was dreadfully shapeless. 'Give me those stumpy little tulips. Those red and white ones.' And she was followed to the car by a thin shop-girl staggering under an immense white paper armful that looked like a baby in long clothes . . .

One winter afternoon she had been buying something in a little antique shop in Curzon Street. It was a shop she liked. For one thing, one usually had it to oneself. And then the man who kept it was ridiculously fond of serving her. He beamed whenever she came in. He clasped his hands; he was so gratified he could scarcely speak. Flattery, of course. All the same, there was something . . .

'You see, madam,' he would explain in his low respectful tones, 'I love my things. I would rather not part with them than sell them to someone who does not appreciate them, who has not that fine feeling which is so rare . . . ' And, breathing deeply, he unrolled a tiny square of blue velvet and pressed it on the glass counter with his pale finger-tips.

Today it was a little box. He had been keeping it for her. He had shown it to nobody as yet. An exquisite little enamel box with a glaze so fine it looked as though it had been baked in cream. On the lid a minute creature stood under a flowery tree, and a more minute creature still had her arms round his neck. Her hat, really no bigger than a geranium petal, hung from a branch; it had green ribbons. And there was a pink cloud like a watchful cherub floating above their heads. Rosemary took her hands out of her long gloves. She always took off her gloves to examine such things. Yes, she liked it very much. She loved it; it was a great duck. She must have it. And, turning the creamy box, opening and shutting it, she couldn't help noticing how charming her hands were against the blue velvet. The shopman, in some dim cavern of his mind, may have dared to think so too. For he took a pencil, leant over the counter, and his pale bloodless fingers crept timidly towards those rosy, flashing ones, as he murmured gently: 'If I may venture to point out to madam, the flowers on the little lady's bodice.'

'Charming!' Rosemary admired the flowers. But what was the price? For a moment the shopman did not seem to hear. Then a murmur reached her. 'Twenty-eight guineas, madam.'

'Twenty-eight guineas.' Rosemary gave no sign. She laid the little box down; she buttoned her gloves again. Twenty-eight guineas. Even if one is rich . . . She looked vague. She stared at a plump tea-kettle like a plump hen above the shopman's head, and her voice was dreamy as she answered: 'Well, keep it for me – will you? I'll . . . '

But the shopman had already bowed as though keeping it for her was all any human being could ask. He would be willing, of course, to keep it for her for ever.

The discreet door shut with a click. She was outside on the step, gazing at the winter afternoon. Rain was falling, and with the rain it seemed the dark came too, spinning down like ashes. There was a cold bitter taste in the air, and the new-lighted lamps looked sad. Sad were the lights in the houses opposite. Dimly they burned as if regretting something. And people hurried by, hidden under their hateful umbrellas. Rosemary felt a strange pang. She pressed her muff against her breast; she wished she had the little box, too, to cling to. Of course, the car was there. She'd only to cross the pavement. But still she waited. There are moments, horrible moments in life, when one emerges from shelter and looks out, and it's awful. One oughtn't to give way to them. One ought to go home and have an extra-special tea. But at the very instant of thinking that, a young girl, thin, dark, shadowy – where had she come from? – was standing at Rosemary's elbow and a voice like a sigh, almost like a sob, breathed: 'Madam, may I speak to you a moment?'

'Speak to me?' Rosemary turned. She saw a little battered creature with enormous eyes, someone quite young, no older than herself, who clutched at her coat-collar with reddened hands, and shivered as though she had just come out of the water.

'M-madam,' stammered the voice. 'Would you let me have the price of a cup of tea?'

'A cup of tea?' There was something simple, sincere in that voice; it wasn't in the least the voice of a beggar. 'Then have you no money at all?' asked Rosemary.

'None, madam,' came the answer.

'How extraordinary!' Rosemary peered through the dusk, and the girl gazed back at her. How more than extraordinary! And suddenly it seemed to Rosemary such an adventure. It was like something out of a novel by Dostoevsky, this meeting in the dusk. Supposing she took the girl home? Supposing she did do one of those things she was always reading about or seeing on the stage, what would happen? It would be thrilling. And she heard herself saying afterwards to the amazement of her friends: 'I simply took her home with me,' as she stepped forward and said to that dim person beside her: 'Come home to tea with me.'

The girl drew back startled. She even stopped shivering for a moment. Rosemary put out a hand and touched her arm. 'I mean it,' she said, smiling. And she felt how simple and kind her smile was. 'Why won't you? Do. Come home with me now in my car and have tea.'

'You – you don't mean it, madam,' said the girl, and there was pain in her voice.

'But I do,' cried Rosemary. 'I want you to. To please me. Come along.'

The girl put her fingers to her lips and her eyes devoured Rosemary. 'You're – you're not taking me to the police station?' she stammered.

'The police station!' Rosemary laughed out. 'Why should I be so cruel? No, I only want to make you warm and to hear – anything you care to tell me.'

Hungry people are easily led. The footman held the door of the car open, and a moment later they were skimming through the dusk.

'There!' said Rosemary. She had a feeling of triumph as she slipped her hand through the velvet strap. She could have said, 'Now I've got you,' as she gazed at the little captive she had netted. But of course she meant it kindly. Oh, more than kindly. She was going to prove to this girl that – wonderful things did happen in life, that – fairy godmothers were real, that – rich people had hearts, and that women *were* sisters. She turned impulsively, saying: 'Don't be frightened. After all, why shouldn't you come back with me? We're both women. If I'm the more fortunate, you ought to expect . . . '

But happily at that moment, for she didn't know how the sentence was going to end, the car stopped. The bell was rung, the door opened, and with a charming, protecting, almost embracing movement, Rosemary drew the other into the hall. Warmth, softness, light, a sweet scent, all those things so familiar to her she never even thought about them, she watched that other receive. It was fascinating. She was like the rich little girl in her nursery with all the cupboards to open, all the boxes to unpack.

'Come, come upstairs,' said Rosemary, longing to begin to be generous. 'Come up to my room.' And, besides, she wanted to spare this poor little thing from being stared at by the servants; she decided as they mounted the stairs she would not even ring for Jeanne, but take off her things by herself. The great thing was to be natural!

And 'There!' cried Rosemary again, as they reached her beautiful big bedroom with the curtains drawn, the fire leaping on her wonderful lacquer furniture, her gold cushions and the primrose and blue rugs.

The girl stood just inside the door; she seemed dazed. But Rosemary didn't mind that.

'Come and sit down,' she cried, dragging her big chair up to the fire, 'in this comfy chair. Come and get warm. You look so dreadfully cold.'

'I daren't, madam,' said the girl, and she edged backwards.

'Oh, please,' – Rosemary ran forward – 'you mustn't be frightened, you mustn't, really. Sit down, and when I've taken off my things we shall go into the next room and have tea and be cosy. Why are you afraid?' And gently she half pushed the thin figure into its deep cradle.

But there was no answer. The girl stayed just as she had been put, with her hands by her sides and her mouth slightly open. To be quite sincere, she looked rather stupid. But Rosemary wouldn't acknowledge it. She leant over her, saying: 'Won't you take off your hat? Your pretty hair is all wet. And one is so much more comfortable without a hat, isn't one?'

There was a whisper that sounded like 'Very good, madam,' and the crushed hat was taken off.

'And let me help you off with your coat, too,' said Rosemary.

The girl stood up. But she held on to the chair with one hand and let Rosemary pull. It was quite an effort. The other scarcely helped her at all. She seemed to stagger like a child, and the thought came and went through Rosemary's mind, that if people wanted helping they must respond a little, just a little, otherwise it became very difficult indeed. And what was she to do with the coat now? She left it on the floor, and the hat too. She was just going to take a cigarette off the mantelpiece when the girl said quickly, but so lightly and strangely: 'I'm very sorry, madam, but I'm going to faint. I shall go off, madam, if I don't have something.'

'Good heavens, how thoughtless I am!' Rosemary rushed to the bell.

'Tea! Tea at once! And some brandy immediately!'

The maid was gone again, but the girl almost cried out: 'No, I don't want no brandy. I never drink brandy. It's a cup of tea I want, madam.' And she burst into tears.

It was a terrible and fascinating moment. Rosemary knelt beside her chair.

'Don't cry, poor little thing,' she said. 'Don't cry.' And she gave the other her lace handkerchief. She really was touched beyond words. She put her arm round those thin, bird-like shoulders.

Now at last the other forgot to be shy, forgot everything except that they were both women, and gasped out: 'I can't go on no longer like this. I can't bear it. I can't bear it. I shall do away with myself. I can't bear no more.'

'You shan't have to. I'll look after you. Don't cry any more. Don't you see what a good thing it was that you met me? We'll have tea and you'll tell me everything. And I shall arrange something. I promise. *Do* stop crying. It's so exhausting. Please!'

The other did stop just in time for Rosemary to get up before the tea came. She had the table placed between them. She plied the poor little creature with everything, all the sandwiches, all the bread and butter, and every time her cup was empty she filled it with tea, cream and sugar. People always said sugar was so nourishing. As for herself she didn't eat; she smoked and looked away tactfully so that the other should not be shy.

And really the effect of that slight meal was marvellous. When the tea-table was carried away a new being, a light, frail creature with tangled hair, dark lips, deep, lighted eyes, lay back in the big chair in a kind of sweet languor, looking at the blaze. Rosemary lit a fresh cigarette; it was time to begin.

'And when did you have your last meal?' she asked softly.

But at that moment the door-handle turned.

'Rosemary, may I come in?' It was Philip.

'Of course.'

He came in. 'Oh, I'm so sorry,' he said, and stopped and stared.

'It's quite all right,' said Rosemary, smiling. 'This is my friend, Miss – '

'Smith, madam,' said the languid figure, who was strangely still and unafraid.

'Smith,' said Rosemary. 'We are going to have a little talk.'

'Oh yes,' said Philip. 'Quite,' and his eye caught sight of the coat and hat on the floor. He came over to the fire and turned his back to it. 'It's a beastly afternoon,' he said curiously, still looking at that listless figure, looking at its hands and boots, and then at Rosemary again.

'Yes, isn't it?' said Rosemary enthusiastically. 'Vile.'

Philip smiled his charming smile. 'As a matter of fact,' said he, 'I wanted you to come into the library for a moment. Would you? Will Miss Smith excuse us?'

The big eyes were raised to him, but Rosemary answered for her: 'Of course she will.' And they went out of the room together.

'I say,' said Philip, when they were alone. 'Explain. Who is she? What does it all mean?'

Rosemary, laughing, leaned against the door and said: 'I picked her up in Curzon Street. Really. She's a real pick-up. She asked me for the price of a cup of tea, and I brought her home with me.'

'But what on earth are you going to do with her?' cried Philip.

'Be nice to her,' said Rosemary quickly. 'Be frightfully nice to her. Look after her. I don't know how. We haven't talked yet. But show her – treat her – make her feel – '

'My darling girl,' said Philip, 'you're quite mad, you know. It simply can't be done.'

'I knew you'd say that,' retorted Rosemary. 'Why not? I want to. Isn't that a reason? And besides, one's always reading about these things. I decided – '

'But,' said Philip slowly, and he cut the end of a cigar, 'she's so astonishingly pretty.'

'Pretty?' Rosemary was so surprised that she blushed. 'Do you think so? I – I hadn't thought about it.'

'Good Lord!' Philip struck a match. 'She's absolutely lovely. Look again, my child. I was bowled over when I came into your room just now. However . . . I think you're making a ghastly mistake. Sorry, darling, if I'm crude and all that. But let me know if Miss Smith is going to dine with us in time for me to look up *The Milliner's Gazette*.'

'You absurd creature!' said Rosemary, and she went out of the library, but not back to her bedroom. She went to her writing-room and sat down at her desk. Pretty! Absolutely lovely! Bowled over! Her heart beat like a heavy bell. Pretty! Lovely! She drew her cheque-book towards her. But no, cheques would be no use, of course. She opened a drawer and took out five pound notes, looked at them, put two back, and holding the three squeezed in her hand, she went back to her bedroom.

Half an hour later Philip was still in the library, when Rosemary came in.

'I only wanted to tell you,' said she, and she leaned against the door again and looked at him with her dazzled exotic gaze, 'Miss Smith won't dine with us tonight.'

Philip put down the paper. 'Oh, what's happened? Previous engagement?'

Rosemary came over and sat down on his knee. 'She insisted on going,' said she, 'so I gave the poor little thing a present of money. I couldn't keep her against her will, could I?' she added softly.

Rosemary had just done her hair, darkened her eyes a little, and put on her pearls. She put up her hands and touched Philip's cheeks.

'Do you like me?' said she, and her tone, sweet, husky, troubled him.

'I like you awfully,' he said, and he held her tighter. 'Kiss me.'

There was a pause.

Then Rosemary said dreamily: 'I saw a fascinating little box today. It cost twenty-eight guineas. May I have it?'

Philip jumped her on his knee. 'You may, little wasteful one,' said he.

But that was not really what Rosemary wanted to say.

'Philip,' she whispered, and she pressed his head against her bosom, 'am I *pretty*?'

Taking the Veil

IT SEEMED IMPOSSIBLE that anyone should be unhappy on such a beautiful morning. Nobody was, decided Edna, except herself. The windows were flung wide in the houses. From within there came the sound of pianos, little hands chased after each other and ran away from each other, practising scales. The trees fluttered in the sunny gardens, all bright with spring flowers. Street boys whistled, a little dog barked; people passed by, walking so lightly, so swiftly, they looked as though they wanted to break into a run. Now she actually saw in the distance a parasol, peach-coloured, the first parasol of the year.

Perhaps even Edna did not look quite as unhappy as she felt. It is not easy to look tragic at eighteen, when you are extremely pretty, with the cheeks and lips and shining eyes of perfect health. Above all, when you are wearing a French blue frock and your new spring hat trimmed with cornflowers. True, she carried under her arm a book bound in horrid black leather. Perhaps the book provided a gloomy note, but only by accident; it was the ordinary Library binding. For Edna had made going to the Library an excuse for getting out of the house to think, to realise what had happened, to decide somehow what was to be done now.

An awful thing had happened. Quite suddenly, at the theatre last night, when she and Jimmy were seated side by side in the dress-circle, without a moment's warning – in fact, she had just finished a chocolate almond and passed the box to him again – she had fallen in love with an actor. But – fallen – in – love . . .

The feeling was unlike anything she had ever imagined before. It wasn't in the least pleasant. It was hardly thrilling. Unless you can call the most dreadful sensation of hopeless misery, despair, agony and wretchedness, thrilling. Combined with the certainty that if that actor met her on the pavement after, while Jimmy was fetching their cab, she would follow him to the ends of the earth, at a nod, at a sign, without giving another thought to Jimmy or her father and mother or her happy home and countless friends again . . .

The play had begun fairly cheerfully. That was at the chocolate almond stage. Then the hero had gone blind. Terrible moment! Edna had cried so much she had to borrow Jimmy's folded, smooth-feeling handkerchief as well. Not that crying mattered. Whole rows were in tears. Even the men blew their noses with a loud trumpeting noise and tried to peer at the programme instead of looking at the stage. Jimmy, most mercifully dry-eyed – for what would she have done without his handkerchief? – squeezed her free hand, and whispered 'Cheer up, darling girl!' And it was then she had taken a last chocolate almond to please him and passed the box again. Then there had been that ghastly scene with the hero alone on the stage in a deserted room at twilight, with a band playing outside and the sound of cheering coming from the street. He had tried – ah! how painfully, how pitifully! – to grope his way to the window. He had succeeded at last. There he stood holding the curtain while one beam of light, just one beam, shone full on his raised sightless face, and the band faded away into the distance . . .

It was – really, it was absolutely – oh, the most – it was simply – in fact, from that moment Edna knew that life could never be the same. She drew her hand away from Jimmy's, leaned back, and shut the chocolate box for ever. This at last was love!

Edna and Jimmy were engaged. She had had her hair up for a year and a half; they had been publicly engaged for a year. But they had known they were going to marry each other ever since they walked in the Botanical Gardens with their nurses, and sat on the grass with a wine biscuit and a piece of barley-sugar each for their tea. It was so much an accepted thing that Edna had worn a wonderfully good imitation of an engagement ring out of a cracker all the time she was at school. And up till now they had been devoted to each other.

But now it was over. It was so completely over that Edna found it difficult to believe that Jimmy did not realise it too. She smiled wisely, sadly, as she turned into the gardens of the Convent of the Sacred Heart and mounted the path that led through them to Hill Street. How much better to know it now than to wait until after they were married! Now it was possible that Jimmy would get over it. No, it was no use deceiving herself; he would never get over it! His life was wrecked, was ruined; that was inevitable. But he was young . . . Time, people always said, Time might make a little, just a little difference. In forty years when he was an old man, he might be able to think of her calmly – perhaps. But she – what did the future hold for her?

Edna had reached the top of the path. There under a new-leafed tree, hung with little bunches of white flowers, she sat down on a green bench and looked over the Convent flower-beds. In the one nearest to her there grew tender stocks, with a border of blue, shell-like pansies, with at one corner a clump of creamy freesias, their light spears of green criss-crossed over the flowers. The Convent pigeons were tumbling high in the air, and she could hear the voice of Sister Agnes who was giving a singing lesson. *Ah-me*, sounded the deep tones of the nun, and *Ah-me*, they were echoed . . .

If she did not marry Jimmy, of course she would marry nobody. The man she was in love with, the famous actor – Edna had far too much common-sense not to realise that would never be. It was very odd. She didn't even want it to be. Her love was too intense for that. It had to be endured, silently; it had to torment her. It was, she supposed, simply that kind of love.

'But, Edna!' cried Jimmy. 'Can you never change? Can I never hope again?'

Oh, what sorrow to have to say it, but it must be said. 'No, Jimmy, I will never change.'

Edna bowed her head; and a little flower fell on her lap, and the voice of Sister Agnes cried suddenly *Ah-no*, and the echo came, *Ah-no* . . .

At that moment the future was revealed. Edna saw it all. She was astonished; it took her breath away at first. But, after all, what could be more natural? She would go into a convent . . . Her father and mother do everything to dissuade her, in vain. As for Jimmy, his state of mind hardly bears thinking about. Why can't they understand? How can they add to her suffering like this? The world is cruel, terribly cruel! After a last scene when she gives away her jewellery and so on to her best friends – she so calm, they so broken-hearted – into a convent she goes. No, one moment. The very evening of her going is the actor's last evening at Port Willin. He receives by a strange messenger a box. It is full of white flowers. But there is no name, no card. Nothing? Yes, under the roses, wrapped in a white handkerchief, Edna's last photograph with, written underneath,

The world forgetting, by the world forgot.

Edna sat very still under the trees; she clasped the black book in her fingers as though it were her missal. She takes the name of Sister Angela. Snip! Snip! All her lovely hair is cut off. Will she be allowed to send one curl to Jimmy? It is contrived somehow. And in a blue gown with a white head-band Sister Angela goes from the convent to the chapel, from the chapel to the convent with something unearthly in her look, in her sorrowful eyes, and in the gentle smile with which they greet the little children who run to her. A saint! She hears it whispered as she paces the chill, wax-smelling corridors. A saint! And visitors to the chapel are told of the nun whose voice is heard above the other voices, of her youth, her beauty, of her tragic, tragic love. 'There is a man in this town whose life is ruined . . . '

A big bee, a golden furry fellow, crept into a freesia, and the delicate flower leaned over, swung, shook; and when the bee flew away it fluttered still as though it were laughing. Happy, careless flower!

Sister Angela looked at it and said, 'Now it is winter.' One night, lying in her icy cell, she hears a cry. Some stray animal is out there in the garden, a kitten or a lamb or – well, whatever little animal might be there. Up rises the sleepless nun. All in white, shivering but fearless, she goes and brings it in. But next morning, when the bell rings for matins, she is found tossing in high fever . . . in delirium . . . and she never recovers. In three days all is over. The service has been said in the chapel, and she is buried in the corner of the cemetery reserved for the nuns, where there are plain little crosses of wood. Rest in Peace, Sister Angela . . .

Now it is evening. Two old people leaning on each other come slowly to the grave and kneel down sobbing, 'Our daughter! Our only daughter!' Now there comes another. He is all in black; he comes slowly. But when he is there and lifts his black hat, Edna sees to her horror his hair is snow-white. Jimmy! Too late, too late! The tears are running down his face; he is crying *now*. Too late, too late! The wind shakes the leafless trees in the churchyard. He gives one awful bitter cry.

Edna's black book fell with a thud to the garden path. She jumped up, her heart beating. My darling! No, it's not too late. It's all been a mistake, a terrible dream. Oh, that white hair! How could she have done it? She has not done it. Oh, heavens! Oh, what happiness! She is free, young, and nobody knows her secret. Everything is still possible for her and Jimmy. The house they have planned may still be built, the little solemn boy with his hands behind his back watching them plant the standard roses may still be born. His baby sister . . . But when Edna got as far as his baby sister, she stretched out her arms as though the little love came flying through the air to her, and gazing at the garden, at the white sprays on the tree, at those darling pigeons blue against the blue, and the Convent with its narrow windows, she realised that now at last for the first time in her life – she had never imagined any feeling like it before – she knew what it was to be in love, but – in – love!

The Fly

'Y'ARE VERY SNUG IN HERE,' piped old Mr Woodifield, and he peered out of the great, green-leather armchair by his friend the boss's desk as a baby peers out of its pram. His talk was over; it was time for him to be off. But he did not want to go. Since he had retired, since his . . . stroke, the wife and the girls kept him boxed up in the house every day of the week except Tuesday. On Tuesday he was dressed and brushed and allowed to cut back to the City for the day. Though what he did there the wife and girls couldn't imagine. Made a nuisance of himself to his friends, they supposed . . . Well, perhaps so. All the same, we cling to our last pleasures as the tree clings to its last leaves. So there sat old Woodifield, smoking a cigar and staring almost greedily at the boss, who rolled in his office chair, stout, rosy, five years older than he, and still going strong, still at the helm. It did one good to see him.

Wistfully, admiringly, the old voice added, 'It's snug in here, upon my word!'

'Yes, it's comfortable enough,' agreed the boss, and he flipped the *Financial Times* with a paper-knife. As a matter of fact he was proud of his room; he liked to have it admired, especially by old Woodifield. It gave him a feeling of deep, solid satisfaction to be planted there in the midst of it in full view of that frail old figure in the muffler.

'I've had it done up lately,' he explained, as he had explained for the past – how many? – weeks. 'New carpet,' and he pointed to the bright red carpet with a pattern of large white rings. 'New furniture,' and he nodded towards the massive bookcase and the table with legs like twisted treacle. 'Electric heating!' He waved almost exultantly towards the five transparent, pearly sausages glowing so softly in the tilted copper pan.

But he did not draw old Woodifield's attention to the photograph over the table of a grave-looking boy in uniform standing in one of those spectral photographers' parks with photographers' storm-clouds behind him. It was not new. It had been there for over six years.

'There was something I wanted to tell you,' said old Woodifield, and his eyes grew dim remembering. 'Now what was it? I had it in my mind when I started out this morning.' His hands began to tremble, and patches of red showed above his beard.

Poor old chap, he's on his last pins, thought the boss. And, feeling kindly, he winked at the old man, and said jokingly, 'I tell you what. I've got a little drop of something here that'll do you good before you go out into the cold again. It's beautiful stuff. It wouldn't hurt a child.' He took a key off his watch-chain, unlocked a cupboard below his desk, and drew forth a dark, squat bottle. 'That's the medicine,' said he. 'And the man from whom I got it told me on the strict Q.T. it came from the cellars at Windsor Castle.'

Old Woodifield's mouth fell open at the sight. He couldn't have looked more surprised if the boss had produced a rabbit.

'It's whisky, ain't it?' he piped feebly.

The boss turned the bottle and lovingly showed him the label. Whisky it was.

'D'you know,' said he, peering up at the boss wonderingly, 'they won't let me touch it at home.' And he looked as though he was going to cry.

'Ah, that's where we know a bit more than the ladies,' cried the boss, swooping across for two tumblers that stood on the table with the water-bottle, and pouring a generous finger into each. 'Drink it down. It'll do you good. And don't put any water with it. It's sacrilege to tamper with stuff like this. Ah!' He tossed off his, pulled out his handkerchief, hastily wiped his moustaches, and cocked an eye at old Woodifield, who was rolling his in his chaps.

The old man swallowed, was silent a moment, and then said faintly, 'It's nutty!'

But it warmed him; it crept into his chill old brain – he remembered.

'That was it,' he said, heaving himself out of his chair. 'I thought you'd like to know. The girls were in Belgium last week having a look at poor Reggie's grave, and they happened to come across your boy's. They're quite near each other, it seems.'

Old Woodifield paused, but the boss made no reply. Only a quiver in his eyelids showed that he heard.

'The girls were delighted with the way the place is kept,' piped the old voice. 'Beautifully looked after. Couldn't be better if they were at home. You've not been across, have yer?'

'No, no!' For various reasons the boss had not been across.

'There's miles of it,' quavered old Woodifield, 'and it's all as neat as a garden. Flowers growing on all the graves. Nice broad paths.' It was plain from his voice how much he liked a nice broad path.

The pause came again. Then the old man brightened wonderfully.

'D'you know what the hotel made the girls pay for a pot of jam?' he piped. 'Ten francs! Robbery, I call it. It was a little pot, so Gertrude says, no bigger than a half-crown. And she hadn't taken more than a spoonful when they charged her ten francs. Gertrude brought the pot away with her to teach 'em a lesson. Quite right, too; it's trading on our feelings. They think because we're over there having a look round we're ready to pay anything. That's what it is.' And he turned towards the door.

'Quite right, quite right!' cried the boss, though what was quite right he hadn't the least idea. He came round by his desk, followed the shuffling footsteps to the door, and saw the old fellow out. Woodifield was gone.

For a long moment the boss stayed, staring at nothing, while the grey-haired office messenger, watching him, dodged in and out of his cubby-hole like a dog that expects to be taken for a run. Then: 'I'll see nobody for half an hour, Macey,' said the boss. 'Understand? Nobody at all.'

'Very good, sir.'

The door shut, the firm heavy steps recrossed the bright carpet, the fat body plumped down in the spring chair, and leaning forward, the boss covered his face with his hands. He wanted, he intended, he had arranged to weep . . .

It had been a terrible shock to him when old Woodifield sprang that remark upon him about the boy's grave. It was exactly as though the earth had opened and he had seen the boy lying there with Woodifield's girls staring down at him. For it was strange. Although over six years had passed away, the boss never thought of the boy except as lying unchanged, unblemished in his uniform, asleep for ever. 'My son!' groaned the boss. But no tears came yet. In the past, in the first months and even years after the boy's death, he had only to say those words to be overcome by such grief that nothing short of a violent fit of weeping could relieve him. Time, he had declared then, he had told everybody, could make no difference. Other men perhaps might recover, might live their loss down, but not he. How was it possible? His boy was an only son. Ever since his birth the boss had worked at building up this business for him; it had no other meaning if it was not for the boy. Life itself had come to have no other meaning. How on earth could he have slaved, denied himself, kept going all those years without the promise for ever before him of the boy's stepping into his shoes and carrying on where he left off?

And that promise had been so near being fulfilled. The boy had been in the office learning the ropes for a year before the war. Every morning they had started off together; they had come back by the same train. And what congratulations he had received as the boy's father! No wonder; he had taken to it marvellously. As to his popularity with the staff, every man jack of them down to old Macey couldn't make enough of the boy. And he wasn't in the least spoilt. No, he was just his bright natural self, with the right word for everybody, with that boyish look and his habit of saying, 'Simply splendid!'

But all that was over and done with as though it never had been. The day had come when Macey had handed him the telegram that brought the whole place crashing about his head. 'Deeply regret to inform you . . .' And he had left the office a broken man, with his life in ruins.

Six years ago, six years . . . How quickly time passed! It might have happened yesterday. The boss took his hands from his face; he was puzzled. Something seemed to be wrong with him. He wasn't feeling as he wanted to feel. He decided to get up and have a look at the boy's photograph. But it wasn't a favourite photograph of his; the expression was unnatural. It was cold, even stern-looking. The boy had never looked like that.

At that moment the boss noticed that a fly had fallen into his broad inkpot, and was trying feebly but desperately to clamber out again. Help! help! said those struggling legs. But the sides of the inkpot were wet and slippery; it fell back again and began to swim. The boss took up a pen, picked the fly out of the ink, and shook it on to a piece of blotting-paper. For a fraction of a second it lay still on the dark patch that oozed round it. Then the front legs waved, took hold, and, pulling its small, sodden body up, it began the immense task of cleaning the ink from its wings. Over and under, over and under, went a leg along a wing as the stone goes over and under the scythe. Then there was a pause, while the fly, seeming to stand on the tips of its toes, tried to expand first one wing and then the other. It succeeded at last, and, sitting down, it began, like a minute cat, to clean its face. Now one could imagine that the little front legs rubbed against each other lightly, joyfully. The horrible danger was over; it had escaped; it was ready for life again.

But just then the boss had an idea. He plunged his pen back into the ink, leaned his thick wrist on the blotting-paper, and as the fly tried its wings down came a great heavy blot. What would it make of that? What indeed! The little beggar seemed absolutely cowed, stunned, and afraid to move because of what would happen next. But then, as if painfully, it dragged itself forward. The front legs waved, caught hold, and, more slowly this time, the task began from the beginning.

He's a plucky little devil, thought the boss, and he felt a real admiration for the fly's courage. That was the way to tackle things; that was the right spirit. Never say die; it was only a question of . . . But the fly had again finished its laborious task, and the boss had just time to refill his pen, to shake fair and square on the new-cleaned body yet another dark drop. What about it this time? A painful moment of suspense followed. But behold, the front legs were again waving; the boss felt a rush of relief. He leaned over the fly and said to it tenderly, 'You artful little b—' And he actually had the brilliant notion of breathing on it to help the drying process. All the same, there was something timid and weak about its efforts now, and the boss decided that this time should be the last, as he dipped the pen deep into the inkpot.

It was. The last blot fell on the soaked blotting-paper, and the draggled fly lay in it and did not stir. The back legs were stuck to the body; the front legs were not to be seen.

'Come on,' said the boss. 'Look sharp!' And he stirred it with his pen – in vain. Nothing happened or was likely to happen. The fly was dead.

The boss lifted the corpse on the end of the paper-knife and flung it into the waste-paper basket. But such a grinding feeling of wretchedness seized him that he felt positively frightened. He started forward and pressed the bell for Macey.

'Bring me some fresh blotting-paper,' he said sternly, 'and look sharp about it.' And while the old dog padded away he fell to wondering what it was he had been thinking about before. What was it? It was . . . He took out his handkerchief and passed it inside his collar. For the life of him he could not remember.

The Canary

... YOU SEE THAT BIG NAIL to the right of the front door? I can scarcely
look at it even now and yet I could not bear to take it out. I should
like to think it was there always even after my time. I sometimes hear
the next people saying, 'There must have been a cage hanging from
there.' And it comforts me; I feel he is not quite forgotten.

... You cannot imagine how wonderfully he sang. It was not like
the singing of other canaries. And that isn't just my fancy. Often,
from the window, I used to see people stop at the gate to listen, or
they would lean over the fence by the mock-orange for quite a long
time – carried away. I suppose it sounds absurd to you – it wouldn't if
you had heard him – but it really seemed to me that he sang whole
songs with a beginning and an end to them.

For instance, when I'd finished the house in the afternoon, and
changed my blouse and brought my sewing on to the veranda here,
he used to hop, hop, hop from one perch to another, tap against the
bars as if to attract my attention, sip a little water just as a professional singer might, and then break into a song so exquisite that I
had to put my needle down to listen to him. I can't describe it; I wish
I could. But it was always the same, every afternoon, and I felt that I
understood every note of it.

... I loved him. How I loved him! Perhaps it does not matter so
very much what it is one loves in this world. But love something one
must. Of course there was always my little house and the garden, but
for some reason they were never enough. Flowers respond wonderfully, but they don't sympathise. Then I loved the evening star. Does
that sound foolish? I used to go into the backyard, after sunset, and
wait for it until it shone above the dark gum tree. I used to whisper,
'There you are, my darling.' And just in that first moment it seemed
to be shining for me alone. It seemed to understand this . . . something which is like longing, and yet it is not longing. Or regret –
it is more like regret. And yet regret for what? I have much to be
thankful for.

. . . But after he came into my life I forgot the evening star; I did not need it any more. But it was strange. When the Chinaman who came to the door with birds to sell held him up in his tiny cage, and instead of fluttering, fluttering, like the poor little goldfinches, he gave a faint, small chirp, I found myself saying, just as I had said to the star over the gum tree, 'There you are, my darling.' From that moment he was mine.

. . . It surprises me even now to remember how he and I shared each other's lives. The moment I came down in the morning and took the cloth off his cage he greeted me with a drowsy little note. I knew it meant 'Missus! Missus!' Then I hung him on the nail outside while I got my three young men their breakfasts, and I never brought him in until we had the house to ourselves again. Then, when the washing-up was done, it was quite a little entertainment. I spread a newspaper over a corner of the table, and when I put the cage on it he used to beat with his wings despairingly, as if he didn't know what was coming. 'You're a regular little actor,' I used to scold him. I scraped the tray, dusted it with fresh sand, filled his seed and water tins, tucked a piece of chickweed and half a chilli between the bars. And I am perfectly certain he understood and appreciated every item of this little performance. You see by nature he was exquisitely neat. There was never a speck on his perch. And you'd only to see him enjoy his bath to realise he had a real small passion for cleanliness. His bath was put in last. And the moment it was in he positively leapt into it. First he fluttered one wing, then the other, then he ducked his head and dabbled his breast feathers. Drops of water were scattered all over the kitchen, but still he would not get out. I used to say to him, 'Now that's quite enough. You're only showing off.' And at last out he hopped and, standing on one leg, he began to peck himself dry. Finally he gave a shake, a flick, a twitter and he lifted his throat – Oh, I can hardly bear to recall it. I was always cleaning the knives at the time. And it almost seemed to me the knives sang too, as I rubbed them bright on the board.

. . . Company, you see – that was what he was. Perfect company. If you have lived alone you will realise how precious that is. Of course there were my three young men who came in to supper every evening, and sometimes they stayed in the dining-room afterwards reading the paper. But I could not expect them to be interested in the little things that made my day. Why should they be? I was nothing to them. In fact, I overheard them one evening talking about me on the stairs as 'the Scarecrow'. No matter. It doesn't matter. Not in the least. I quite understand. They are young. Why should I mind? But I remember feeling so especially thankful that I was not quite alone that evening. I told him, after they had gone out. I said, 'Do you know what they call Missus?' And he put his head on one side and looked at me with his little bright eye until I could not help laughing. It seemed to amuse him.

. . . Have you kept birds? If you haven't all this must sound, perhaps, exaggerated. People have the idea that birds are heartless, cold little creatures, not like dogs or cats. My washer-woman used to say on Mondays when she wondered why I didn't keep 'a nice fox-terrier,' 'There's no comfort, Miss, in a canary.' Untrue. Dreadfully untrue. I remember one night. I had had a very awful dream – dreams can be dreadfully cruel – even after I had woken up I could not get over it. So I put on my dressing-gown and went down to the kitchen for a glass of water. It was a winter night and raining hard. I suppose I was still half asleep, but through the kitchen window, that hadn't a blind, it seemed to me the dark was staring in, spying. And suddenly I felt it was unbearable that I had no one to whom I could say 'I've had such a dreadful dream,' or – or 'Hide me from the dark.' I even covered my face for a minute. And then there came a little 'Sweet! Sweet!' His cage was on the table, and the cloth had slipped so that a chink of light shone through. 'Sweet, Sweet!' said the darling little fellow again, softly, as much as to say, 'I'm here, Missus! I'm here!' That was so beautifully comforting that I nearly cried.

. . . And now he's gone. I shall never have another bird, another pet of any kind. How could I? When I found him, lying on his back, with his eye dim and his claws wrung, when I realised that never again should I hear my darling sing, something seemed to die in me. My heart felt hollow, as if it was his cage. I shall get over it. Of course. I must. One can get over anything in time. And people always say I have a cheerful disposition. They are quite right. I thank my God I have.

. . . All the same, without being morbid, and giving way to – to memories and so on, I must confess that there does seem to me something sad in life. It is hard to say what it is. I don't mean the sorrow that we all know, like illness and poverty and death. No, it is something different. It is there, deep down, deep down, part of one, like one's breathing. However hard I work and tire myself I have only to stop to know it is there, waiting. I often wonder if everybody feels the same. One can never know. But isn't it extraordinary that under his sweet, joyful little singing it was just this – sadness? – Ah, what is it? – that I heard.

A Married Man's Story

I

IT IS EVENING. Supper is over. We have left the small, cold dining-room, we have come back to the sitting-room where there is a fire. All is as usual. I am sitting at my writing-table which is placed across a corner so that I am behind it, as it were, and facing the room. The lamp with the green shade is alight; I have before me two large books of reference, both open, a pile of papers ... All the paraphernalia, in fact, of an extremely occupied man. My wife, with her little boy on her lap, is in a low chair before the fire. She is about to put him to bed before she clears away the dishes and piles them up in the kitchen for the servant girl tomorrow morning. But the warmth, the quiet, and the sleepy baby, have made her dreamy. One of his red woollen boots is off, one is on. She sits, bent forward, clasping the little bare foot, staring into the glow, and as the fire quickens, falls, flares again, her shadow – an immense *Mother and Child* – is here and gone again upon the wall ...

Outside it is raining. I like to think of that cold drenched window behind the blind, and beyond, the dark bushes in the garden, their broad leaves bright with rain, and beyond the fence, the gleaming road with the two hoarse little gutters singing against each other, and the wavering reflections of the lamps, like fishes' tails. While I am here, I am there, lifting my face to the dim sky, and it seems to me it must be raining all over the world – that the whole earth is drenched, is sounding with a soft, quick patter or hard, steady drumming, or gurgling and something that is like sobbing and laughing mingled together, and that light, playful splashing that is of water falling into still lakes and flowing rivers. And all at one and the same moment I am arriving in a strange city, slipping under the hood of the cab while the driver whips the cover off the breathing horse, running from shelter to shelter, dodging someone, swerving by someone else. I am conscious of tall houses, their doors and shutters sealed against the night, of dripping balconies and sodden flowerpots. I am brushing through deserted gardens and falling into moist smelling summer-houses (you know how soft and almost crumbling the wood of a summer-house is in the rain); I am standing on the dark quayside giving my ticket into the wet, red hand of the old sailor in an oilskin. How strong the sea smells! How loudly the tied-up boats knock against one another! I am crossing the wet stackyard, hooded in an old sack, carrying a lantern, while the house-dog, like a soaking doormat, springs, shakes himself over me. And now I am walking along a deserted road – it is impossible to miss the puddles, and the trees are stirring – stirring.

But one could go on with such a catalogue for ever – on and on – until one lifted the single arum lily leaf and discovered the tiny snails clinging, until one counted . . . and what then? Aren't those just the signs, the traces of my feeling? The bright green streaks made by someone who walks over the dewy grass? Not the feeling itself. And as I think that a mournful, glorious voice begins to sing in my bosom. Yes, perhaps that is nearer what I mean. What a voice! What power! What velvety softness! Marvellous!

Suddenly my wife turns round quickly. She knows – how long has she known? – that I am not 'working'. It is strange that with her full, open gaze she should smile so timidly – and that she should say in such a hesitating voice, 'What are you thinking?'

I smile and draw two fingers across my forehead in the way I have. 'Nothing,' I answer softly.

At that she stirs and, still trying not to make it sound important, she says, 'Oh, but you must have been thinking of something!'

Then I really meet her gaze, meet it fully, and I fancy her face quivers. Will she never grow accustomed to these simple – one might say – everyday little lies? Will she never learn not to expose herself – or to build up defences?

'Truly, I was thinking of nothing.'

There! I seem to see it dart at her. She turns away, pulls the other red sock off the baby, sits him up, and begins to unbutton him behind. I wonder if that little soft rolling bundle sees anything, feels anything? Now she turns him over on her knee, and in this light, his soft arms and legs waving, he is extraordinarily like a young crab. A queer thing is I can't connect him with my wife and myself – I've never accepted him as ours. Each time when I come into the hall and see the perambulator I catch myself thinking: 'H'm, someone has brought a baby!' Or, when his crying wakes me at night, I feel inclined to blame my wife for having brought the baby in from outside. The truth is, that though one might suspect her of strong maternal feelings, my wife doesn't seem to me the type of woman who bears children in her own body. There's an immense difference! Where is that . . . animal ease and playfulness, that quick kissing and cuddling one has been taught to expect of young mothers? She hasn't a sign of it. I believe that when she ties its bonnet she feels like an aunt and not a mother. But of course I may be wrong; she may be passionately devoted . . . I don't think so. At any rate, isn't it a trifle indecent to feel like this about one's own wife? Indecent or not, one has these feelings. And one other thing. How can I reasonably expect my wife, *a broken-hearted woman*, to spend her time tossing the baby? But that is beside the mark. She never even began to toss when her heart was whole.

And now she has carried the baby to bed. I hear her soft, deliberate steps moving between the dining-room and the kitchen, there and back again, to the tune of the clattering dishes. And now all is quiet. What is happening now? Oh, I know just as surely as if I'd gone to see – she is standing in the middle of the kitchen facing the rainy window. Her head is bent, with one finger she is tracing something – nothing – on the table. It is cold in the kitchen; the gas jumps; the tap drips; it's a forlorn picture. And nobody is going to come behind her, to take her in his arms, to kiss her soft hair, to lead her to the fire and to rub her hands warm again. Nobody is going to call her or to wonder what she is doing out there. And she knows it. And yet, being a woman, deep down, deep down, she really does expect the miracle to happen; she really could embrace that dark, dark deceit, rather than live – like this.

2

To live like this . . . I write those words very carefully, very beautifully. For some reason I feel inclined to sign them, or to write underneath – Trying a New Pen. But, seriously, isn't it staggering to think what may be contained in one innocent-looking little phrase? It tempts me – it tempts me terribly. Scene: The supper-table. My wife has just handed me my tea. I stir it, lift the spoon, idly chase and then carefully capture a speck of tea-leaf, and having brought it ashore, I murmur, quite gently, 'How long shall we continue to live – like – this?' And immediately there is that famous 'blinding flash and deafening roar. Huge pieces of débris (I must say I like débris) are flung into the air . . . and when the dark clouds of smoke have drifted away . . . ' But this will never happen; I shall never know it.

It will be found upon me 'intact', as they say. 'Open my heart and you will see . . . '

Why? Ah, there you have me! There is the most difficult question of all to answer. Why do people stay together? Putting aside 'for the sake of the children', and 'the habit of years' and 'economic reasons' as lawyers' nonsense – it's not much more – if one really does try to find out why it is that people don't leave each other, one discovers a mystery. It is because they can't; they are bound. And nobody on earth knows what are the bonds that bind them except those two. Am I being obscure? Well, the thing itself isn't so frightfully crystal clear, is it? Let me put it like this. Supposing you are taken, absolutely, first into his confidence and then into hers. Supposing you know all there is to know about the situation. And having given it not only your deepest sympathy but your most honest impartial criticism, you declare, very calmly (but not without the slightest suggestion of relish – for there is – I swear there is – in the very best of us – something that leaps up and cries 'A-ahh!' for joy at the thought of destroying), 'Well, my opinion is that you two people ought to part. You'll do no earthly good together. Indeed, it seems to me, it's the duty of either to set the other free.' What happens then? He – and she – agree. It is their conviction too. You are only saying what they have been thinking all last night. And away they go to act on your advice, immediately . . . And the next time you hear of them they are still together. You see – you've reckoned without the unknown quantity – which is their secret relation to each other – and that they can't disclose even if they want to. Thus far you may tell and no further. Oh, don't misunderstand me! It need not necessarily have anything to do with their sleeping together . . . But this brings me to a thought I've often half entertained. Which is that human beings, as we know them, don't choose each other at all. It is the owner, the second self inhabiting them, who makes the choice for his own particular purposes, and – this may sound absurdly far-fetched – it's the second self in the other which responds. Dimly – dimly – or so it has seemed to me – we realise this, at any rate to the extent that we realise the hopelessness of trying to escape. So that, what it all amounts to is – if the impermanent selves of my wife and me are happy – *tant mieux pour nous* – if miserable – *tant pis* . . . But I don't know, I don't know. And it may be that it's something entirely individual in me – this sensation (yes, it is even a sensation) of how extraordinarily *shell-like* we are as we are – little creatures, peering out of the sentry-box at the gate, ogling through our glass case at the entry, wan little servants, who never can say for certain, even, if the master is out or in . . .

The door opens . . . My wife. She says, 'I am going to bed.'

And I look up vaguely, and vaguely say, 'You are going to bed.'

'Yes.' A tiny pause. 'Don't forget – will you? – to turn out the gas in the hall.'

And again I repeat, 'The gas in the hall.'

There was a time – the time before – when this habit of mine – it really has become a habit now – it wasn't one then – was one of our sweetest jokes together. It began, of course, when on several occasions I really was deeply engaged and I didn't hear. I emerged only to see her shaking her head and laughing at me, 'You haven't heard a word!'

'No. What did you say?'

Why should she think that so funny and charming? She did – it delighted her. 'Oh, my darling, it's so like you! It's so – so – ' And I knew she loved me for it. I knew she positively looked forward to coming in and disturbing me, and so – as one does – I played up. I was guaranteed to be wrapped away every evening at 10.30 p.m. But now? For some reason I feel it would be crude to stop my performance. It's simplest to play on. But what is she waiting for tonight? Why doesn't she go? Why prolong this? She is going. No, her hand on the door-knob, she turns round again, and she says in the most curious, small, breathless voice, 'You're not cold?'

Oh, it's not fair to be as pathetic as that! That was simply damnable. I shuddered all over before I managed to bring out a slow 'No-o!' while my left hand ruffles the reference pages.

She is gone; she will not come back again tonight. It is not only I who recognise that – the room changes too. It relaxes, like an old actor. Slowly the mask is rubbed off; the look of strained attention changes to an air of heavy, sullen brooding. Every line, every fold breathes fatigue. The mirror is quenched; the ash whitens; only my sly lamp burns on . . . But what a cynical indifference to me it all shows! Or should I perhaps be flattered? No, we understand each other. You know those stories of little children who are suckled by wolves and accepted by the tribe, and how for ever after they move freely among their fleet, grey brothers? Something like that has happened to me. But wait! That about the wolves won't do. Curious! Before I wrote it down, while it was still in my head, I was delighted with it. It seemed to express, and more, to suggest, just what I wanted to say. But written, I can smell the falseness immediately and the . . .

source of the smell is in that word fleet. Don't you agree? Fleet, grey
brothers! 'Fleet.' A word I never use. When I wrote 'wolves' it
skimmed across my mind like a shadow and I couldn't resist it. Tell
me! Tell me! Why is it so difficult to write simply – and not simply
only but *sotto voce*, if you know what I mean? That is how I long to
write. No fine effects – no bravura. But just the plain truth, as only a
liar can tell it.

3

I light a cigarette, lean back, inhale deeply – and find myself wondering if my wife is asleep. Or is she lying in her cold bed, staring into
the dark, with those trustful, bewildered eyes? Her eyes are like the
eyes of a cow that is being driven along a road. 'Why am I being driven
– what harm have I done?' But I really am not responsible for that
look; it's her natural expression. One day, when she was turning out a
cupboard, she found a little old photograph of herself, taken when she
was a girl at school. In her confirmation dress, she explained. And
there were the eyes, even then. I remember saying to her, 'Did you
always look so sad?' Leaning over my shoulder, she laughed lightly,
'Do I look sad? I think it's just . . . me.' And she waited for me to say
something about it. But I was marvelling at her courage at having
shown it to me at all. It was a hideous photograph! And I wondered
again if she realised how plain she was, and comforted herself with the
idea that people who loved each other didn't criticise but accepted
everything, or if she really rather liked her appearance and expected
me to say something complimentary.

Oh, that was base of me! How could I have forgotten all the num-
berless times when I have known her turn away to avoid the light,
press her face into my shoulders. And, above all, how could I have
forgotten the afternoon of our wedding-day when we sat on the green
bench in the Botanical Gardens and listened to the band; how, in an
interval between two pieces, she suddenly turned to me and said in the
voice in which one says, 'Do you think the grass is damp?' or 'Do you
think it's time for tea?' . . . 'Tell me, do you think physical beauty is so
very important?' I don't like to think how often she had rehearsed that
question. And do you know what I answered? At that moment, as if at
my command, there came a great gush of hard, bright sound from the
band, and I managed to shout above it cheerfully, 'I didn't hear what
you said.' Devilish! Wasn't it? Perhaps not wholly. She looked like the
poor patient who hears the surgeon say, 'It will certainly be necessary
to perform the operation – but not now!'

4

But all this conveys the impression that my wife and I were never really happy together. Not true! Not true! We were marvellously, radiantly happy. We were a model couple. If you had seen us together, any time, any place, if you had followed us, tracked us down, spied, taken us off our guard, you still would have been forced to confess, 'I have never seen a more ideally suited pair.' Until last autumn.

But really to explain what happened then I should have to go back and back – I should have to dwindle until my two hands clutched the banisters, the stair-rail was higher than my head, and I peered through to watch my father padding softly up and down. There were coloured windows on the landings. As he came up, first his bald head was scarlet, then it was yellow. How frightened I was! And when they put me to bed, it was to dream that we were living inside one of my father's big coloured bottles. For he was a chemist. I was born nine years after my parents were married. I was an only child, and the effort to produce even me – small, withered bud I must have been – sapped all my mother's strength. She never left her room again. Bed, sofa, window, she moved between the three. Well I can see her, on the window days, sitting, her cheek in her hand, staring out. Her room looked over the street. Opposite there was a wall plastered with advertisements for travelling shows and circuses and so on. I stand beside her, and we gaze at the slim lady in a red dress hitting a dark gentlemen over the head with her parasol, or at the tiger peering through the jungle while the clown, close by, balances a bottle on his nose, or at a little golden-haired girl sitting on the knee of an old black man in a broad cotton hat . . . She says nothing. On sofa days there is a flannel dressing-gown that I loathe and a cushion that keeps on slipping off the hard sofa. I pick it up. It has flowers and writing sewn on. I ask what the writing says, and she whispers, 'Sweet Repose!' In bed her fingers plait, in tight little plaits, the fringe of the quilt and her lips are thin. And that is all there is of my mother, except the last queer 'episode' that comes later.

My father . . . Curled up in the corner on the lid of a round box that held sponges, I stared at my father so long, it's as though his image, cut off at the waist by the counter, has remained solid in my memory. Perfectly bald, polished head, shaped like a thin egg, creased, creamy cheeks, little bags under the eyes, large pale ears like handles. His manner was discreet, sly, faintly amused and tinged with impudence.

Long before I could appreciate it I knew the mixture . . . I even used to copy him in my corner, bending forward, with a small reproduction of his faint sneer. In the evening his customers were, chiefly, young women; some of them came in every day for his famous fivepenny pick-me-up. Their gaudy looks, their voices, their free ways fascinated me. I longed to be my father, handing them across the counter the little glass of bluish stuff they tossed off so greedily. God knows what it was made of. Years after I drank some, just to see what it tasted like, and I felt as though someone had given me a terrific blow on the head; I felt stunned.

One of those evenings I remember vividly. It was cold; it must have been autumn, for the flaring gas was lighted after my tea. I sat in my corner and my father was mixing something; the shop was empty. Suddenly the bell jangled and a young woman rushed in, crying so loud, sobbing so hard, that it didn't sound real. She wore a green cape trimmed with fur and a hat with cherries dangling. My father came from behind the screen. But she couldn't stop herself at first. She stood in the middle of the shop and wrung her hands and moaned; I've never heard such crying since. Presently she managed to gasp out, 'Give me a pick-me-up!' Then she drew a long breath, trembled away from him and quavered, 'I've had *bad news!*' And in the flaring gaslight I saw the whole side of her face was puffed up and purple; her lip was cut and her eyelid looked as though it was gummed fast over the wet eye. My father pushed the glass across the counter, and she took the purse out of her stocking and paid him. But she couldn't drink; clutching the glass, she stared in front of her as if she could not believe what she saw. Each time she put her head back the tears spurted out again. Finally she put the glass down. It was no use. Holding the cape with one hand, she ran in the same way out of the shop again. My father gave no sign. But long after she had gone I crouched in my corner, and when I think back it's as though I felt my whole body vibrating – 'So that's what it is outside,' I thought. 'That's what it's like out there.'

5

Do you remember your childhood? I am always coming across these marvellous accounts by writers who declare that they remember 'everything'. I certainly don't. The dark stretches, the blanks, are much bigger than the bright glimpses. I seem to have spent most of my time like a plant in a cupboard. Now and again, when the sun shone, a careless hand thrust me out on to the window-sill, and a careless hand whipped me in again – and that was all. But what happened in the darkness – I wonder? Did one grow? Pale stem . . . timid leaves . . . white reluctant bud. No wonder I was hated at school. Even the masters shrank from me. I somehow knew that my soft, hesitating voice disgusted them. I knew, too, how they turned away from my shocked, staring eyes. I was small and thin and I smelled of the shop; my nickname was Gregory Powder. School was a tin building, stuck on the raw hillside. There were dark red streaks like blood in the oozing clay banks of the playground. I hide in the dark passage, where the coats hang, and am discovered there by one of the masters. 'What are you doing there in the dark?' His terrible voice kills me; I die before his eyes. I am standing in a ring of thrust-out heads; some are grinning, some look greedy, some are spitting. And it is always cold. Big crushed-up clouds press across the sky; the rusty water in the school tank is frozen; the bell sounds numb. One day they put a dead bird in my overcoat pocket. I found it just when I reached home. Oh, what a strange flutter there was at my heart when I drew out that terribly soft, cold little body, with the legs thin as pins and the claws wrung. I sat on the back door step in the yard and put the bird in my cap. The feathers round the neck looked wet and there was a tiny tuft just above the closed eyes that stood up too. How tightly the beak was shut! I could not see the mark where it was divided. I stretched out one wing and touched the soft, secret down underneath; I tried to make the claws curl round my little finger. But I didn't feel sorry for it – no! I wondered. The smoke from our kitchen chimney poured downwards, and flakes of soot floated – soft, light in the air. Through a big crack in the cement yard a poor-looking plant with dull, reddish flowers had pushed its way. I looked at the dead bird again . . . And that is the first time that I remember singing – rather . . . listening to a silent voice inside a little cage that was me.

6

But what has all this to do with my married happiness? How can all this affect my wife and me? Why – to tell what happened last autumn – do I run all this way back into the Past? The Past – what is the Past? I might say the star-shaped flake of soot on a leaf of the poor-looking plant, and the bird lying on the quilted lining of my cap, and my father's pestle and my mother's cushion belong to it. But that is not to say they are any less mine than they were when I looked upon them with my very eyes and touched them with these fingers.

No, they are more – they are a living part of me. Who am I, in fact, as I sit here at this table, but my own past? If I deny that, I am nothing. And if I were to try to divide my life into childhood, youth, early manhood and so one, it would be a kind of affectation; I should know I was doing it just because of the pleasantly important sensation it gives one to rule lines and to use green ink for childhood, red for the next stage, and purple for the period of adolescence. For, one thing I have learnt, one thing I do believe is, Nothing Happens Suddenly. Yes, that is my religion, I suppose.

My mother's death, for instance. Is it more distant from me today than it was then? It is just as close, as strange, as puzzling, and, in spite of all the countless times I have recalled the circumstances, I know no more now than I did then, whether I dreamed them, or whether they really occurred. It happened when I was thirteen and I slept in a little strip of a room on what was called the half-landing. One night I woke up with a start to see my mother, in her night-gown, without even the hated flannel dressing-gown, sitting on my bed. But the strange thing which frightened me was, she wasn't looking at me. Her head was bent; the short, thin trail of hair lay between her shoulders; her hands were pressed between her knees and my bed shook; she was shivering. It was the first time I had ever seen her out of her own room. I said, or I think I said, 'Is that you, Mother?' And as she turned round, I saw in the moonlight how queer she looked. Her face looked small – quite different. She looked like one of the boys at the school baths, who sits on a step, shivering just like that, and wants to go in and yet is frightened.

'Are you awake?' she said. Her eyes opened; I think she smiled. She leaned towards me. 'I've been poisoned,' she whispered. 'Your father's poisoned me.' And she nodded. Then, before I could say a word, she was gone; I thought I heard the door shut. I sat quite still, I couldn't move, I think I expected something else to happen. For a long time I listened for something; there wasn't a sound. The candle was by my bed, but I was too frightened to stretch out my hand for the matches. But even while I wondered what I ought to do, even while my heart thumped – everything became confused. I lay down and pulled the blankets round me. I fell asleep, and the next morning my mother was found dead of failure of the heart.

Did that visit happen? Was it a dream? Why did she come to tell me? Or why, if she came, did she go away so quickly? And her expression – so joyous under the frightened look – was that real? I believed it fully the afternoon of the funeral, when I saw my father dressed up for his part, hat and all. That tall hat so gleaming black and round was like a cork covered with black sealing-wax, and the rest of my father was awfully like a bottle, with his face for the label – *Deadly Poison*. It flashed into my mind as I stood opposite him in the hall. And Deadly Poison, or old D. P., was my private name for him from that day.

7

Late, it grows late. I love the night. I love to feel the tide of darkness rising slowly and slowly washing, turning over and over, lifting, floating, all that lies strewn upon the dark beach, all that lies hid in rocky hollows. I love, I love this strange feeling of drifting – whither? After my mother's death I hated to go to bed. I used to sit on the window-sill, folded up, and watch the sky. It seemed to me the moon moved much faster than the sun. And one big, bright green star I chose for my own. My star! But I never thought of it beckoning to me or twinkling merrily for my sake. Cruel, indifferent, splendid – it burned in the airy night. No matter – it was mine! But, growing close up against the window, there was a creeper with small, bunched-up pink and purple flowers. These did know me. These, when I touched them at night, welcomed my fingers; the little tendrils, so weak, so delicate, knew I would not hurt them. When the wind moved the leaves I felt I understood their shaking. When I came to the window, it seemed to me the flowers said among themselves, 'The boy is here.'

As the months passed there was often a light in my father's room below. And I heard voices and laughter. 'He's got some woman with him,' I thought. But it meant nothing to me. Then the gay voice, the sound of the laughter, gave me the idea it was one of the girls who used to come to the shop in the evenings – and gradually I began to imagine which girl it was. It was the dark one in the red coat and skirt who once had given me a penny. A merry face stooped over me – warm breath tickled my neck – there were little beads of black on her long lashes, and when she opened her arms to kiss me there came a marvellous wave of scent! Yes, that was the one.

Time passed, and I forgot the moon and my green star and my shy creeper – I came to the window to wait for the light in my father's window, to listen for the laughing voice, until one night I dozed and I dreamed she came again – again she drew me to her, something soft, scented, warm and merry hung over me like a cloud. But when I tried to see, her eyes only mocked me, her red lips opened and she hissed, 'Little sneak! Little sneak!' But not as if she were angry, – as if she understood, and her smile somehow was like a rat – hateful!

The night after, I lighted the candle and sat down at the table instead. By and by, as the flame steadied, there was a small lake of liquid wax, surrounded by a white, smooth wall. I took a pin and made little holes in this wall and then sealed them up faster than the wax could escape. After a time I fancied the candle flame joined in the game; it leapt up, quivered, wagged; it even seemed to laugh. But while I played with the candle and smiled and broke off the tiny white peaks of wax that rose above the wall and floated them on my lake, a feeling of awful dreariness fastened on me – yes, that's the word. It crept up from my knees to my thighs, into my arms; I ached all over with misery. And I felt so strangely that I couldn't move. Something bound me there by the table – I couldn't even let the pin drop that I held between my finger and thumb. For a moment I came to a stop, as it were.

Then the shrivelled case of the bud split and fell, the plant in the cupboard came into flower. 'Who am I?' I thought. 'What is all this?' And I looked at my room, at the broken bust of the man called Hahnemann on top of the cupboard, at my little bed with the pillow like an envelope. I saw it all, but not as I had seen before . . . Everything lived, everything. But that was not all. I was equally alive and – it's the only way I can express it – the barriers were down between us – I had come into my own world!

8

The barriers were down. I had been all my life a little outcast; but until that moment no one had 'accepted' me; I had lain in the cupboard – or the cave forlorn. But now I was taken, I was accepted, claimed. I did not consciously turn away from the world of human beings; I had never known it; but I from that night did beyond words consciously turn towards my silent brothers . . .

The Doves' Nest

I

AFTER LUNCH MILLY and her mother were sitting as usual on the balcony beyond the salon admiring for the five-hundredth time the stocks, the roses, the small, bright grass beneath the palms, and the oranges against a wavy line of blue, when a card was brought them by Marie. Visitors at the Villa Martin were very rare. True, the English clergyman, Mr Sandiman, had called, and he had come a second time with his wife to tea. But an awful thing had happened on that second occasion. Mother had made a mistake. She had said 'More tea, Mr Sandybags?' Oh, what a frightful thing to have happened! How could she have done it? Milly still flamed at the thought. And he had evidently not forgiven them; he'd never come again. So this card put them both into quite a flutter.

Mr Walter Prodger, they read. And then an American address, so very much abbreviated that neither of them understood it. Walter Prodger? But they'd never heard of him. Mother looked from the card to Milly.

'Prodger, dear?' she asked mildly, as though helping Milly to a slice of never-before-tasted pudding.

And Milly seemed to be holding her plate back in the way she answered 'I – don't – know, Mother.'

'These are the occasions,' said Mother, becoming a little flustered, 'when one does so feel the need of our dear English servants. Now if I could just say, "What is he like, Annie?" I should know whether to see him or not. But he may be some common man, selling something – one of those American inventions for peeling things, you know, dear. Or he may even be some kind of foreign sharper.' Mother winced at the hard, bright little word as though she had given herself a dig with her embroidery scissors.

But here Marie smiled at Milly and murmured, '*C'est un très beau Monsieur.*'

'What does she say, dear?'

'She says he looks very nice, Mother.'

'Well, we'd better – ' began Mother. 'Where is he now, I wonder.'
Marie answered 'In the vestibule, Madame.'

In the hall! Mother jumped up, seriously alarmed. In the hall, with all those valuable little foreign things that didn't belong to them scattered over the tables.

'Show him in, Marie. Come, Milly, come, dear. We will see him in the salon. Oh, why isn't Miss Anderson here?' almost wailed Mother.

But Miss Anderson, Mother's new companion, never was on the spot when she was wanted. She had been engaged to be a comfort, a support to them both. Fond of travelling, a cheerful disposition, a good packer and so on. And then, when they had come all this way and taken the Villa Martin and moved in, she had turned out to be a Roman Catholic. Half her time, more than half, was spent wearing out the knees of her skirts in cold churches. It was really too . . .

The door opened. A middle-aged, clean-shaven, very well-dressed stranger stood bowing before them. His bow was stately. Milly saw it pleased Mother very much; she bowed her Queen Alexandra bow back. As for Milly, she never could bow. She smiled, feeling shy, but deeply interested.

'Have I the pleasure,' said the stranger very courteously, with a strong American accent, 'of speaking with Mrs Wyndham Fawcett?'

'I am Mrs Fawcett,' said Mother graciously, 'and this is my daughter, Mildred.'

'Pleased to meet you, Miss Fawcett.' And the stranger shot a fresh, chill hand at Milly, who grasped it just in time before it was gone again.

'Won't you sit down?' said Mother, and she waved faintly at all the gilt chairs.

'Thank you, I will,' said the stranger.

Down he sat, still solemn, crossing his legs and, most surprisingly, his arms as well. His face looked at them over his dark arms as over a gate.

'Milly, sit down, dear.'

So Milly sat down, too, on the Madame Récamier couch and traced a filet lace flower with her finger. There was a little pause. She saw the stranger swallow; Mother's fan opened and shut.

Then he said, 'I took the liberty of calling, Mrs Fawcett, because I had the pleasure of your husband's acquaintance in the States when he was lecturing there some years ago. I should like very much to renoo our – well – I venture to hope we might call it friendship. Is he with you at present? Are you expecting him out? I noticed his name was not mentioned in the local paper. But I put that down to a foreign custom, perhaps – giving precedence to the lady.'

And here the stranger looked as though he might be going to smile.

But as a matter of fact it was extremely awkward. Mother's mouth shook. Milly squeezed her hands between her knees, but she watched hard from under her eyebrows. Good, noble little Mummy! How Milly admired her as she heard her say, gently and quite simply, 'I am sorry to say my husband died two years ago.'

Mr Prodger gave a great start. 'Did he?' He thrust out his under lip, frowned, pondered. 'I am truly sorry to hear that, Mrs Fawcett. I hope you'll believe me when I say I had no idea your husband had . . . passed over.'

'Of course.' Mother softly stroked her skirt.

'I do trust,' said Mr Prodger, more seriously still, 'that my inquiry didn't give you too much pain.'

'No, no. It's quite all right,' said the gentle voice.

But Mr Prodger insisted. 'You're sure? You're positive?'

At that Mother raised her head and gave him one of her still, bright, exalted glances that Milly knew so well. 'I'm not in the least hurt,' she said, as one might say it from the midst of the fiery furnace.

Mr Prodger looked relieved. He changed his attitude and continued. 'I hope this regrettable circumstance will not deprive me of your – '

'Oh, certainly not. We shall be delighted. We are always so pleased to know anyone who – ' Mother gave a little bound, a little flutter. She flew from her shadowy branch on to a sunny one. 'Is this your first visit to the Riviera?'

'It is,' said Mr Prodger. 'The fact is I was in Florence until recently. But I took a heavy cold there – '

'Florence so damp,' cooed Mother.

'And the doctor recommended I should come here for the sunshine before I started for home.'

'The sun is so very lovely here,' agreed Mother enthusiastically.

'Well, I don't think we get too much of it,' said Mr Prodger dubiously, and two lines showed at his lips. 'I seem to have been sitting around in my hotel more days than I care to count.'

'Ah, hotels are so very trying,' said Mother, and she drooped sympathetically at the thought of a lonely man in an hotel . . . 'You are alone here?' she asked gently, just in case . . . one never knew . . . it was better to be on the safe, the tactful side.

But her fears were groundless.

'Oh yes, I'm alone,' cried Mr Prodger, more heartily than he had spoken yet, and he took a speck of thread off his immaculate trouser leg. Something in his voice puzzled Milly. What was it?

'Still, the scenery is so very beautiful,' said Mother, 'that one really does not feel the need of friends. I was only saying to my daughter yesterday, I could live here for years without going outside the garden gate. It is all so beautiful.'

'Is that so?' said Mr Prodger soberly. He added, 'You have a very charming villa.' And he glanced round the salon. 'Is all this antique furniture genuine, may I ask?'

'I believe so,' said Mother. 'I was certainly given to understand it was. Yes, we love our villa. But, of course, it is very large for two, that is to say three, ladies. My companion, Miss Anderson, is with us. But unfortunately she is a Roman Catholic and so she is out most of the time.'

Mr Prodger bowed as one who agreed that Roman Catholics were very seldom in.

'But I am so fond of space,' continued Mother, 'and so is my daughter. We both love large rooms and plenty of them – don't we, Milly?'

This time Mr Prodger looked at Milly quite cordially and remarked, 'Yes, young people like plenty of room to run about.'

He got up, put one hand behind his back, slapped the other upon it and went over to the balcony.

'You've a view of the sea from here,' he observed.

The ladies might well have noticed it; the whole Mediterranean swung before the windows.

'We are so fond of the sea,' said Mother, getting up too.

Mr Prodger looked towards Milly. 'Do you see those yachts, Miss Fawcett?'

Milly saw them.

'Do you happen to know what they're doing?' asked Mr Prodger.

What they were doing? What a funny question! Milly stared and bit her lip.

'They're racing!' said Mr Prodger, and this time he did actually smile at her.

'Oh yes, of course,' stammered Milly. 'Of course they are.' She knew that.

'Well, they're not always at it,' said Mr Prodger good-humouredly. And he turned to Mother and began to take a ceremonious farewell.

THE DOVES' NEST AND OTHER STORIES

'I wonder,' hesitated Mother, folding her little hands and eyeing him, 'if you would care to lunch with us? – if you would not be too dull with two ladies. We should be so very pleased.'

Mr Prodger became intensely serious again. He seemed to brace himself to meet the luncheon invitation. 'Thank you very much, Mrs Fawcett. I should be delighted.'

'That will be very nice,' said Mother warmly. 'Let me see. Today is Monday – isn't it, Milly? Would Wednesday suit you?'

Mr Prodger replied, 'It would suit me excellently to lunch with you on Wednesday, Mrs Fawcett. At *mee-dee*, I presume, as they call it here.'

'Oh no! We keep our English times. At one o'clock,' said Mother.

And that being arranged, Mr Prodger became more and more ceremonious and bowed himself out of the room.

Mother rang for Marie to look after him, and a moment later the big glass hall-door shut.

'Well!' said Mother. She was all smiles. Little smiles, like butterflies, alighting on her lips and gone again. 'That was an adventure, Milly, wasn't it, dear? And I thought he was such a very charming man, didn't you?'

Milly made a little face at Mother and rubbed her eyes.

'Of course you did. You must have, dear. And his appearance was so satisfactory – wasn't it?' Mother was obviously enraptured. 'I mean he looked so very well kept. Did you notice his hands? Every nail shone like a diamond. I must say I do like to see . . . '

She broke off. She came over to Milly and patted her big collar straight.

'You do think it was right of me to ask him to lunch – don't you, dear?' said Mother pathetically.

Mother made her feel so big, so tall. But she was tall. She could pick Mother up in her arms. Sometimes, rare moods came when she did. Swooped on Mother who squeaked like a mouse and even kicked. But not lately. Very seldom now . . .

'It was so strange,' said Mother. There was the still, bright, exalted glance again. 'I suddenly seemed to hear Father say to me "Ask him to lunch." And then there was some – warning . . . I think it was about the wine. But that I didn't catch – very unfortunately,' she added mournfully. She put her hand on her breast; she bowed her head. 'Father is still so near,' she whispered.

Milly looked out of the window. She hated Mother going on like this. But, of course, she couldn't say anything. Out of the window there was the sea and the sunlight silver on the palms, like water dripping from silver oars. Milly felt a yearning – what was it? – it was like a yearning to fly.

But Mother's voice brought her back to the salon, to the gilt chairs, the gilt couches, sconces, cabinets, the tables with the heavy-sweet flowers, the faded brocade, the pink-spotted Chinese dragons on the mantelpiece and the two Turks' heads in the fireplace that supported the broad logs.

'I think a leg of lamb would be nice, don't you, dear?' said Mother. 'The lamb is so very small and delicate just now. And men like nothing so much as plain roast meat. Yvonne prepares it so nicely, too, with that little frill of paper lace round the top of the leg. It always reminds me of something – I can't think what. But it certainly makes it look very attractive indeed.'

2

Wednesday came. And the flutter that Mother and Milly had felt over the visiting-card extended to the whole villa. Yes, it was not too much to say that the whole villa thrilled and fluttered at the idea of having a man to lunch. Old, flat-footed Yvonne came waddling back from market with a piece of gorgonzola in so perfect a condition that when she found Marie in the kitchen she flung down her great basket, snatched the morsel up and held it, rustling in its paper, to her quivering bosom.

'*J'ai trouvé un morceau de gorgonzola*,' she panted, rolling up her eyes as though she invited the heavens themselves to look down upon it. '*J'ai un morceau de gorgonzola ici pour un prr-ince, ma fille.*' And hissing the word '*prr-ince*' like lightning, she thrust the morsel under Marie's nose. Marie, who was a delicate creature, almost swooned at the shock.

'Do you think,' cried Yvonne scornfully, 'that I would ever buy such cheese *pour ces dames?* Never. Never. *Jamais de ma vie.*' Her sausage finger wagged before her nose, and she minced in a dreadful imitation of Mother's French, 'We have none of us large appetites, Yvonne. We are very fond of boiled eggs and mashed potatoes and a nice, plain salad. Ah-Bah!' With a snort of contempt she flung away her shawl, rolled up her sleeves, and began unpacking the basket. At the bottom there was a flat bottle which, sighing, she laid aside.

'*De quoi pour mes cors*,' said she.

And Marie, seizing a bottle of Sauterne and bearing it off to the dining-room, murmured as she shut the kitchen door behind her, '*Et voilà pour les cors de Monsieur!*'

The dining-room was a large room panelled in dark wood. It had a massive mantelpiece and carved chairs covered in crimson damask. On the heavy, polished table stood an oval glass dish decorated with little gilt swags. This dish, which it was Marie's duty to keep filled with fresh flowers, fascinated her. The sight of it gave her a *frisson*. It reminded her always, as it lay solitary on the dark expanse, of a little tomb. And one day, passing through the long windows on to the stone terrace and down the steps into the garden, she had the happy thought of so arranging the flowers that they would be appropriate to one of the ladies on a future tragic occasion. Her first creation had been terrible. *Tomb of Mademoiselle Anderson* in black pansies, lily-of-the-valley and a frill of heliotrope. It gave her a most intense, curious pleasure to hand Miss Anderson the potatoes at lunch and at the same time to gaze beyond her at her triumph. It was like (*O ciel!*) – it was like handing potatoes to a corpse.

The *Tomb of Madame* was, on the contrary, almost gay. Foolish little flowers, half yellow, half blue, hung over the edge, wisps of green trailed across and in the middle there was a large scarlet rose. *Cœur saignant*, Marie had called it. But it did not look in the least like a *cœur saignant*. It looked flushed and cheerful, like Mother emerging from the luxury of a warm bath.

Milly's of course, was all white. White stocks, little white rose-buds, with a sprig or two of dark box edging. It was Mother's favourite.

Poor innocent! Marie, at the sideboard, had to turn her back when she heard Mother exclaim, 'Isn't it pretty, Milly? Isn't it sweetly pretty? Most artistic. So original.' And she had said to Marie, '*C'est très joli, Marie. Très original.*'

Marie's smile was so remarkable that Milly, peeling a tangerine, remarked to Mother, 'I don't think she likes you to admire them. It makes her uncomfortable.'

But today – the glory of her opportunity made Marie feel quite faint as she seized her flower scissors. *Tombeau d'un beau Monsieur.* She was forbidden to cut the orchids that grew round the fountain basin. But what were orchids for if not for such an occasion? Her fingers trembled as the scissors snipped away. They were enough; Marie added two small sprays of palm. And back in the dining-room she had the happy idea of binding the palm together with a twist of gold thread deftly torn off the fringe of the dining-room curtains.

The effect was superb. Marie almost seemed to see her *beau Monsieur*, very small, very small, at the bottom of the bowl, in full evening dress with a ribbon across his chest and his ears white as wax.

What surprised Milly, however, was that Miss Anderson should pay any attention to Mr Prodger's coming. She rustled to breakfast in her best black silk blouse, her Sunday blouse, with the large, painful-looking crucifix dangling over the front. Milly was alone when Miss Anderson entered the dining-room. This was unfortunate, for she always tried to avoid being left alone with Miss Anderson. She could not say exactly why; it was a feeling. She had the feeling that Miss Anderson might say something about God, or something fearfully intimate. Oh, she would sink through the floor if such a thing happened; she would expire. Supposing she were to say 'Milly, do you believe in our Lord?' Heavens! It simply didn't bear thinking about.

'Good morning, my dear,' said Miss Anderson, and her fingers, cold, pale, like church candles, touched Milly's cheeks.

'Good morning, Miss Anderson. May I give you some coffee?' said Milly, trying to be natural.

'Thank you, dear child,' said Miss Anderson, and laughing her light, nervous laugh, she hooked on her eyeglasses and stared at the basket of rolls. 'And is it today that you expect your guest?' she asked.

Now why did she ask that? Why pretend when she knew perfectly well? That was all part of her strangeness. Or was it because she wanted to be friendly? Miss Anderson was more than friendly; she was genial. But there was always this something. Was she spying? People said at school that Roman Catholics spied . . . Miss Anderson rustled, rustled about the house like a dead leaf. Now she was on the stairs, now in the upstairs passage. Sometimes, at night, when Milly was feverish she woke up and heard that rustle outside her door. Was Miss Anderson looking through the keyhole? And one night she actually had the idea that Miss Anderson had bored two holes in the wall above her head and was watching her from there. The feeling was so strong that next time she went into Miss Anderson's room her eyes flew to the spot. To her horror a large picture hung there. Had it been there before? . . .

'Guest?' The crisp breakfast roll broke in half at the word.

'Yes, I think it is,' said Milly vaguely, and her blue, flower-like eyes were raised to Miss Anderson in a vague stare.

'It will make quite a little change in our little party,' said the much-too-pleasant voice. 'I confess I miss very much the society of men. I have had such a great deal of it in my life. I think that ladies by themselves are apt to get a little – h'm – h'm . . . ' And helping herself to cherry jam, she spilt it on the cloth.

Milly took a large, childish bite out of her roll. There was nothing to reply to this. But how young Miss Anderson made her feel! She made her want to be naughty, to pour milk over her head or make a noise with a spoon.

'Ladies by themselves,' went on Miss Anderson, who realised none of this, 'are very apt to find their interests limited.'

'Why?' said Milly, goaded to reply. People always said that; it sounded most unfair.

'I think,' said Miss Anderson, taking off her eyeglasses and looking a little dim, 'it is the absence of political discussion.'

'Oh, politics!' cried Milly airily. 'I hate politics. Father always said – ' But here she pulled up short. She crimsoned. She didn't want to talk about Father to Miss Anderson.

'Oh! Look! Look! A butterfly!' cried Miss Anderson, softly and hastily. 'Look, what a darling!' Her own cheeks flushed a slow red at the sight of the darling butterfly fluttering so softly over the glittering table.

That was very nice of Miss Anderson – fearfully nice of her. She must have realised that Milly didn't want to talk about Father and so she had mentioned the butterfly on purpose. Milly smiled at Miss Anderson as she never had smiled at her before. And she said in her warm, youthful voice, 'He is a duck, isn't he? I love butterflies. I think they are great lambs.'

3

The morning whisked away as foreign mornings do. Mother had half decided to wear her hat at lunch.

'What do you think, Milly? Do you think as head of the house it might be appropriate? On the other hand, one does not want to do anything at all extreme.'

'Which do you mean, Mother? Your mushroom or the jampot?'

'Oh, not the jampot, dear.' Mother was quite used to Milly's name for it. 'I somehow don't feel myself in a hat without a brim. And to tell you the truth, I am still not quite certain whether I was wise in buying a jampot. I cannot help the feeling that if I were to meet Father in it he would be a little too surprised. More than once lately,' went on Mother quickly, 'I have thought of taking off the trimming, turning it upside down and making it into a nice little work-bag. What do you think, dear? But we must not go into it now, Milly. This is not the moment for such schemes. Come on to the balcony. I have told Marie we shall have coffee there. What about bringing out that big chair with the nice, substantial legs for Mr Prodger? Men are so fond of nice, substantial . . . No, not by yourself, love! Let me help you.'

When the chair was carried out Milly thought it looked exactly like Mr Prodger. It *was* Mr Prodger admiring the view.

'No, don't sit down on it. You mustn't,' she cried hastily, as Mother began to subside. She put her arm through Mother's and drew her back into the salon.

Happily, at that moment there was a rustle and Miss Anderson was upon them. In excellent time, for once. She carried a copy of the *Morning Post*.

'I have been trying to find out from this,' said she, lightly tapping the newspaper with her eyeglasses, 'whether Congress is sitting at present. But unfortunately, after reading my copy right through, I happened to glance at the heading and discovered it was five weeks old.'

Congress! Would Mr Prodger expect them to talk about Congress? The idea terrified Mother. Congress! The American parliament, of course, composed of senators – grey-bearded old men in frock-coats and turn-down collars, rather like missionaries. But she did not feel at all competent to discuss them.

'I think we had better not be too intellectual,' she suggested timidly, fearful of disappointing Miss Anderson, but more fearful still of the alternative.

'Still, one likes to be prepared,' said Miss Anderson. And after a pause she added softly, 'One never knows.'

Ah, how true that was! One never does. Miss Anderson and Mother seemed both to ponder this truth. They sat silent, with head bent, as though listening to the whisper of the words.

'One never knows,' said the pink-spotted dragons on the mantelpiece and the Turks' heads pondered. Nothing is known – nothing. Everybody just waits for things to happen as they were waiting there for the stranger who came walking towards them through the sun and shadow under the budding plane trees, or driving, perhaps, in one of the small, cotton-covered cabs . . . An angel passed over the Villa Martin. In that moment of hovering silence something timid, something beseeching seemed to lift, seemed to offer itself, as the flowers in the salon, uplifted, gave themselves to the light.

Then Mother said, 'I hope Mr Prodger will not find the scent of the mimosa too powerful. Men are not fond of flowers in a room as a rule. I have heard it causes actual hay-fever in some cases. What do you think, Milly? Ought we perhaps – ' But there was no time to do anything. A long, firm trill sounded from the hall door. It was a trill so calm and composed and unlike the tentative little push they gave the bell that it brought them back to the seriousness of the moment. They heard a man's voice; the door clicked shut again. He was inside. A stick rattled on the table. There was a pause, and then the door handle of the salon turned and Marie, in frilled muslin cuffs and an apron shaped like a heart, ushered in Mr Prodger.

Only Mr Prodger, after all? But whom had Milly expected to see? The feeling was there and gone again that she would not have been surprised to see somebody quite different, before she realised this wasn't quite the same Mr Prodger as before. He was smarter than ever: all brushed, combed, shining. The ears that Marie had seen white as wax flashed as if they had been pink enamelled. Mother fluttered up in her pretty little way, so hoping he had not found the heat of the day too trying to be out in . . . but happily it was a little early in the year for dust. Then Miss Anderson was introduced. Milly was ready this time for that fresh hand, but she almost gasped; it was so very chill. It was like a hand stretched out to you from the water. Then together they all sat down.

'Is this your first visit to the Riviera?' asked Miss Anderson graciously, dropping her handkerchief.

'It is,' answered Mr Prodger composedly, and he folded his arms as before. 'I was in Florence until recently, but I caught a heavy cold – '

'Florence so – ' began Mother, when the beautiful brass gong, that burned like a fallen sun in the shadows of the hall, began to throb. First it was a low muttering, then it swelled, it quickened, it burst into a clash of triumph under Marie's sympathetic fingers. Never had they been treated to such a performance before. Mr Prodger was all attention.

'That's a very fine gong,' he remarked approvingly.

'We think it is so very oriental,' said Mother. 'It gives our little meals quite an Eastern flavour. Shall we . . . '

Their guest was at the door bowing.

'So many gentlemen and only one lady,' fluttered Mother. 'What I mean is the boot is on the other shoe. That is to say – come, Milly, come, dear.' And she led the way to the dining-room.

Well, there they were. The cold, fresh napkins were shaken out of their charming shapes and Marie handed the omelette. Mr Prodger sat on Mother's right, facing Milly, and Miss Anderson had her back to the long windows. But after all – why should the fact of their having a man with them make such a difference? It did; it made all the difference. Why should they feel so stirred at the sight of that large hand outspread, moving among the wine glasses? Why should the sound of that loud, confident 'Ah-hm!' change the very look of the dining-room? It was not a favourite room of theirs as a rule – it was overpowering. They bobbed uncertainly at the pale table with a curious feeling of exposure. They were like those meek guests who arrive unexpectedly at the fashionable hotel and are served with whatever may be ready, while the real luncheon, the real guests lurk important and contemptuous in the background. And although it was impossible for Marie to be other than deft, nimble and silent, what heart could she have in ministering to that most uninspiring of spectacles – three ladies dining alone?

Now all was changed. Marie filled their glasses to the brim as if to reward them for some marvellous feat of courage. These timid English ladies had captured a live lion, a real one, smelling faintly of eau-de-Cologne, and with a tip of handkerchief showing, white as a flake of snow.

'He is worthy of it,' decided Marie, eyeing her orchids and palms.

Mr Prodger touched his hot plate with appreciative fingers.

'You'll hardly believe it, Mrs Fawcett,' he remarked, turning to Mother, 'but this is the first hot plate I've happened on since I left the States. I had begun to believe there were two things that just weren't to be had in Europe. One was a hot plate and the other was a glass of cold water. Well, the cold water one can do without; but a hot plate is more difficult. I'd got so discouraged with the cold wet ones I encountered everywhere that when I was arranging with Cook's Agency about my room here I explained to them: "I don't mind where I go to. I don't care what the expense may be. But for mercy's sake find me an hotel where I can get a hot plate by ringing for it." '

Mother, though outwardly all sympathy, found this a little bewildering. She had a momentary vision of Mr Prodger ringing for hot plates to be brought to him at all hours. Such strange things to want in any numbers.

'I have always heard the American hotels are so very well equipped,' said Miss Anderson. 'Telephones in all the rooms and even tape machines.'

Milly could see Miss Anderson reading that tape machine.

'I should like to go to America awfully,' she cried, as Marie brought in the lamb and set it before Mother.

'There's certainly nothing wrong with America,' said Mr Prodger soberly. 'America's a great country. What are they? Peas? Well, I just take a few. I don't eat peas as a rule. No, no salad, thank you. Not with the hot meat.'

'But what makes you want to go to America?' Miss Anderson ducked forward, smiling at Milly, and her eyeglasses fell into her plate, just escaping the gravy.

Because one wants to go everywhere, was the real answer. But Milly's flower-blue gaze rested thoughtfully on Miss Anderson as she said, 'The ice-cream. I adore ice-cream.'

'Do you?' said Mr Prodger, and he put down his fork; he seemed moved. 'So you're fond of ice-cream, are you, Miss Fawcett?'

Milly transferred her dazzling gaze to him. It said she was.

'Well,' said Mr Prodger quite playfully, and he began eating again, 'I'd like to see you get it. I'm sorry we can't manage to ship some across. I like to see young people have just what they want. It seems right, somehow.'

Kind man! Would he have any more lamb?

Lunch passed so pleasantly, so quickly, that the famous piece of gorgonzola was on the table in all its fatness and richness before there had been an awkward moment. The truth was that Mr Prodger proved most easy to entertain, most ready to chat. As a rule men were not fond of chat as Mother understood it. They did not seem to understand that it does not matter very much what one says; the important thing is not to let the conversation drop. Strange! Even the best of men ignored that simple rule. They refused to realise that conversation is like a dear little baby that is brought in to be handed round. You must rock it, nurse it, keep it on the move if you want it to keep on smiling. What could be simpler? But even Father . . . Mother winced away from memories that were not as sweet as memories ought to be.

All the same, she could not help hoping that Father saw what a successful little lunch party it was. He did so love to see Milly happy, and the child looked more animated than she had done for weeks. She had lost that dreamy expression, which, though very sweet, did not seem natural at her age. Perhaps what she wanted was not so much Easton's Syrup as taking out of herself.

'I have been very selfish,' thought Mother, blaming herself as usual. She put her hand on Milly's arm; she pressed it gently as they rose from the table. And Marie held the door open for the white and the grey figure; for Miss Anderson, who peered shortsightedly, as though looking for something; for Mr Prodger, who brought up the rear, walking stately, with the benign air of a Monsieur who had eaten well.

4

Beyond the balcony, the gardens, the palms and the sea lay bathed in quivering brightness. Not a leaf moved; the oranges were little worlds of burning light. There was the sound of grasshoppers ringing their tiny tambourines, and the hum of bees as they hovered, as though to taste their joy in advance, before burrowing close into the warm wide-open stocks and roses. The sound of the sea was like a breath, was like a sigh.

Did the little group on the balcony hear it? Mother's fingers moved among the black and gold coffee-cups; Miss Anderson brought the most uncomfortable chair out of the salon and sat down. Mr Prodger put his large hand on to the yellow stone ledge of the balcony and remarked gravely, 'This balcony rail is just as hot as it can be.'

'They say,' said Mother, 'that the greatest heat of the day is at about half-past two. We have certainly noticed it is very hot then.'

'Yes, it's lovely then,' murmured Milly, and she stretched out her hand to the sun. 'It's simply baking!'

'Then you're not afraid of the sunshine?' said Mr Prodger, taking his coffee from Mother. 'No, thank you. I won't take any cream. Just one lump of sugar.' And he sat down balancing the little, chattering cup on his broad knee.

'No, I adore it,' answered Milly, and she began to nibble the lump of sugar . . .

Six Years After

IT WAS NOT THE AFTERNOON to be on deck – on the contrary, it was exactly the afternoon when there is no snugger place than a warm cabin, a warm bunk. Tucked up with a rug, a hot-water bottle and a piping hot cup of tea she would not have minded the weather in the least. But he – hated cabins, hated to be inside anywhere more than was absolutely necessary. He had a passion for keeping, as he called it, above board, especially when he was travelling. And it wasn't surprising, considering the enormous amount of time he spent cooped up in the office. So, when he rushed away from her as soon as they got on board and came back five minutes later to say he had secured two deck-chairs on the lee side and the steward was undoing the rugs, her voice through the high sealskin collar murmured 'Good'; and because he was looking at her, she smiled with bright eyes and blinked quickly, as if to say, 'Yes, perfectly all right – absolutely.' And she meant it.

'Then we'd better – ' said he, and he tucked her hand inside his arm and began to rush her off to where their chairs stood. But she just had time to breathe, 'Not so fast, Daddy, please,' when he remembered too and slowed down.

Strange! They had been married twenty-eight years, and it was still an effort to him, each time, to adapt his pace to hers.

'Not cold, are you?' he asked, glancing sideways at her. Her little nose, geranium pink above the dark fur, was answer enough. But she thrust her free hand into the velvet pocket of her jacket and murmured gaily, 'I shall be glad of my rug.'

He pressed her tighter to his side – a quick, nervous pressure. He knew, of course, that she ought to be down in the cabin; he knew that it was no afternoon for her to be sitting on deck, in this cold and raw mist, lee side or no lee side, rugs or no rugs, and he realised how she must be hating it. But he had come to believe that it really was easier for her to make these sacrifices than it was for him. Take their present case, for instance. If he had gone down to the cabin with her, he would have been miserable the whole time, and he couldn't have helped showing it. At any rate, she would have found him out. Whereas, having made up her mind to fall in with his ideas, he would have betted anybody she would even go so far as to enjoy the experience. Not because she was without personality of her own. Good Lord! She was absolutely brimming with it. But because . . . but here his thoughts always stopped. Here they always felt the need of a cigar, as it were. And, looking at the cigar-tip, his fine blue eyes narrowed. It was a law of marriage, he supposed . . . All the same, he always felt guilty when he asked these sacrifices of her. That was what the quick pressure meant. His being said to her being: 'You do understand, don't you?' and there was an answering tremor of her fingers, 'I *understand*.'

Certainly the steward – good little chap – had done all in his power to make them comfortable. He had put up their chairs in whatever warmth there was and out of the smell. She did hope he would be tipped adequately. It was on occasions like these (and her life seemed to be full of such occasions) that she wished it was the woman who controlled the purse.

'Thank you, steward. That will do beautifully.'

'Why are stewards so often delicate-looking?' she wondered, as her feet were tucked under. 'This poor little chap looks as though he'd got a chest, and yet one would have thought . . . the sea air . . . '

The button of the pigskin purse was undone. The tray was tilted. She saw sixpences, shillings, half-crowns.

'I should give him five shillings,' she decided, 'and tell him to buy himself a good nourishing – '

He was given a shilling, and he touched his cap and seemed genuinely grateful.

Well, it might have been worse. It might have been sixpence. It might, indeed. For at that moment Father turned towards her and said, half apologetically, stuffing the purse back, 'I gave him a shilling. I think it was worth it, don't you?'

'Oh, quite! Every bit!' said she.

It is extraordinary how peaceful it feels on a little steamer once the bustle of leaving port is over. In a quarter of an hour one might have been at sea for days. There is something almost touching, childish, in the way people submit themselves to the new conditions. They go to bed in the early afternoon, they shut their eyes and 'it's night' like little children who turn the table upside down and cover themselves with the table-cloth. And those who remain on deck – they seem to be always the same, those few hardened men travellers – pause, light their pipes, stamp softly, gaze out to sea, and their voices are subdued as they walk up and down. The long-legged little girl chases after the red-cheeked boy, but soon both are captured; and the old sailor, swinging an unlighted lantern, passes and disappears . . .

He lay back, the rug up to his chin, and she saw he was breathing deeply. Sea air! If anyone believed in sea air it was he. He had the strongest faith in its tonic qualities. But the great thing was, according to him, to fill the lungs with it the moment you came on board. Otherwise, the sheer strength of it was enough to give you a chill . . .

She gave a small chuckle, and he turned to her quickly. 'What is it?'

'It's your cap,' she said. 'I never can get used to you in a cap. You look such a thorough burglar.'

'Well, what the deuce am I to wear?' He shot up one grey eyebrow and wrinkled his nose. 'It's a very good cap, too. Very fine specimen of its kind. It's got a very rich white satin lining.' He paused. He declaimed, as he had hundreds of times before at this stage, 'Rich and rare were the gems she wore.'

But she was thinking he really was childishly proud of the white satin lining. He would like to have taken off his cap and made her feel it. 'Feel the quality!' How often had she rubbed between finger and thumb his coat, his shirt cuff, tie, sock, linen handkerchief, while he said that.

She slipped down more deeply into her chair.

And the little steamer pressed on, pitching gently, over the grey, unbroken, gently moving water, that was veiled with slanting rain.

Far out, as though idly, listlessly, gulls were flying. Now they settled on the waves, now they beat up into the rainy air and shone against the pale sky like the lights within a pearl. They looked cold and lonely. How lonely it will be when we have passed by, she thought. There will be nothing but the waves and those birds and rain falling.

She gazed through the rust-spotted railing along which big drops trembled, until suddenly she shut her lids. It was as if a warning voice inside her had said, 'Don't look!'

'No, I won't,' she decided. 'It's too depressing, much too depressing.'

But, immediately, she opened her eyes and looked again. Lonely birds, water lifting, white pale sky – how were they changed?

And it seemed to her there was a presence far out there, between the sky and the water; someone very desolate and longing watched them pass and cried as if to stop them – but cried to her alone.

'Mother!'

'Don't leave me,' sounded in the cry. 'Don't forget me! You are forgetting me, you know you are!' And it was as though from her own breast there came the sound of childish weeping.

'My son – my precious child – it isn't true!'

Sh! How was it possible that she was sitting there on that quiet steamer beside Father and at the same time she was hushing and holding a little slender boy – so pale – who had just waked out of a dreadful dream?

'I dreamed I was in a wood – somewhere far away from everybody – and I was lying down and a great blackberry vine grew over me. And I called and called to you – and you wouldn't come – you wouldn't come – so I had to lie there for ever.'

What a terrible dream! He had always had terrible dreams. How often, years ago, when he was small, she had made some excuse and escaped from their friends in the dining-room or the drawing-room to come to the foot of the stairs and listen. 'Mother!' And when he was asleep, his dream had journeyed with her back into the circle of lamplight; it had taken its place there like a ghost. And now –

Far more often – at all times – in all places – like now, for instance – she never settled down, she was never off her guard for a moment but she heard him. He wanted her. 'I am coming as fast as I can! As fast as I can!' But the dark stairs have no ending, and the worst dream of all – the one that is always the same – goes for ever and ever uncomforted.

This is anguish! How is it to be borne? Still, it is not the idea of her suffering which is unbearable – it is his. Can one do nothing for the dead? And for a long time the answer had been – Nothing!

. . . But softly without a sound the dark curtain has rolled down. There is no more to come. That is the end of the play. But it can't end like that – so suddenly. There must be more. No, it's cold, it's still. There is nothing to be gained by waiting.

But – did he go back again? Or, when the war was over, did he come home for good? Surely, he will marry – later on – not for several years. Surely, one day I shall remember his wedding and my first grandchild – a beautiful dark-haired boy born in the early morning – a lovely morning – spring!

'Oh, Mother, it's not fair to me to put these ideas into my head! Stop, Mother, stop! When I think of all I have missed, I can't bear it.'

'I can't bear it!' She sits up breathing the words and tosses the dark rug away. It is colder than ever, and now the dusk is falling, falling like ash upon the pallid water.

And the little steamer, growing determined, throbbed on, pressed on, as if at the end of the journey there waited . . .

Daphne

I HAD BEEN in Port Willin six months when I decided to give a one-man show. Not that I was particularly keen, but little Field, the picture-shop man, had just started a gallery and he wanted me – begged me, rather – to kick off for him. He was a decent little chap; I hadn't the heart to refuse. And besides, as it happened, I had a good deal of stuff that I felt it would be rather fun to palm off on anyone who was fool enough to buy it. So with these high aims I had the cards printed, the pictures framed in plain white frames, and God knows how many cups and saucers ordered for the Private View.

What was I doing in Port Willin? Oh well – why not? I'll own it does sound an unlikely spot, but when you are an impermanent movable, as I am, it's just those unlikely spots that have a trick of holding you. I arrived, intending to stay a week and go on to Fiji. But I had letters to one or two people, and the morning of my arrival, hanging over the side of the ship while we were waiting in the stream, with nothing on earth to do but stare, I took an extraordinary fancy to the shape – to the look of the place.

It's a small town, you know, planted at the edge of a fine deep harbour like a lake. Behind it, on either side, there are hills. The houses are built of light painted wood. They have iron roofs coloured red. And there are big dark plumy trees massed together, breaking up those light shapes, giving a depth – warmth – making a composition of it well worth looking at . . . Well, we needn't go into that – But it had me that fine morning. And the first days after my arrival, walking, or driving out in one of the big swinging, rocking cabs, I took an equal fancy to the people.

Not to quite all of them. The men left me cold. Yes, I must say, colonial men are not the brightest specimens. But I never struck a place where the average of female attractiveness was so high. You can't help noticing it, for a peculiarity of Port Willin is the number of its teashops and the vast quantity of tea absorbed by its inhabitants. Not tea only – sandwiches, cream cakes, ices, fruit salad with fresh pine-apples. From eleven o'clock in the morning you meet with couples and groups of girls and young married women hurrying off to their first tea: It was a real eleven o'clock function. Even the business men knocked off and went to a café. And the same thing happened in the afternoon. From four until half-past six the streets were gay as a garden. Which reminds me, it was early spring when I arrived and the town smelled of moist earth and the first flowers. In fact, wherever one went one got a strong whiff, like the whiff of violets in a wood, which was enough in itself to make one feel like lingering . . .

There was a theatre too, a big bare building plastered over with red and blue bills which gave it an oriental look in that blue air, and a touring company was playing *San Toy*. I went my first evening. I found it, for some reason, fearfully exciting. The inside smelled of gas, of glue and burnt paper. Whistling draughts cut along the corridors – a strong wind among the orchestra kept the palms trembling, and now and again the curtain blew out and there was a glimpse of a pair of large feet walking rapidly away. But what women! What girls in muslin dresses with velvet sashes and little caps edged with swansdown! In the intervals long ripples of laughter sounded from the stalls, from the dress-circle. And I leaned against a pillar that looked as though it was made of wedding-cake icing – and fell in love with whole rows at a time . . .

Then I presented my letters, I was asked out to dine, and I met these charmers in their own homes. That decided it. They were something I had never known before – so gay, so friendly, so impressed with the idea of one's being an artist! It was rather like finding oneself in the playground of an extremely attractive girls' school.

I painted the Premier's daughter, a dark beauty, against a tree hung with long, bell-like flowers as white as wax. I painted a girl with a pigtail curled up on a white sofa playing with a pale-red fan . . . and a little blonde in a black jacket with pearl grey gloves . . . I painted like fury.

I'm fond of women. As a matter of fact I'm a great deal more at my ease with women than I am with men. Because I've cultivated them, I suppose. You see, it's like this with me. I've always had enough money to live on, and the consequence is I have never had to mix with people more than I wished. And I've equally always had – well, I suppose you might call it – a passion for painting. Painting is far and away the most important thing in life – as I see it. But – my work's my own affair. It's the separate compartment which is me. No strangers allowed in. I haven't the smallest desire to explain what it is I'm after – or to hear other men. If people like my work I'm pleased. If they don't – well, if I was a shrugging person, I'd shrug. This sounds arrogant. It isn't; I know my limitations. But the truth about oneself always sounds arrogant, as no doubt you've observed.

But women – well, I can only speak for myself – I find the presence of women, the consciousness of women, an absolute necessity. I know they are considered a distraction, that the very Big Pots seal themselves in their hives to keep away. All I can say is work without women would be to me like dancing without music or food without wine or a sailing boat without a breeze. They just give me that . . . what is it? Stimulus is not enough; inspiration is far too much. That – well, if I knew what it is, I should have solved a bigger problem than my own! And problems aren't in my line.

I expected a mob at my Private View, and I got it, too . . . What I hadn't reckoned on was that there would be no men. It was one thing to ask a painter fellow to knock you up something to the tune of fifty guineas or so, but it was quite another to make an ass of yourself staring. The Port Willin men would as soon have gazed into shops. True, when you came to Europe, you visited the galleries, but then you shop-gazed too. It didn't matter what you did in Europe. You could walk about for a week without being recognised.

So there were little Field and I absolutely alone among all that loveliness; it frightened him out of his life, but I didn't mind, I thought it rather fun, especially as the sightseers didn't hesitate to find my pictures amusing. I'm by no means an out-and-out modern, as they say; people like violins and landscapes of telegraph poles leave me cold. But Port Willin is still trying to swallow Rossetti, and 'Hope' by Watts is looked upon as very advanced. It was natural my pictures should surprise them. The fat old Lady Mayoress became quite hysterical. She drew me over to one drawing; she patted my arm with her fan.

'I don't wonder you drew her slipping out,' she gurgled. 'And how depressed she looks! The poor dear never could have sat down in it. It's much too small. There ought to be a little cake of Pears' Soap on the floor.' And overcome by her own joke, she flopped on the little double bench that ran down the middle of the room, and even her fan seemed to laugh.

At that moment two girls passed in front of us. One I knew, a big fair girl called May Pollock, pulled her companion by the sleeve.

'Daphne!' she said. 'Daphne!' And the other turned towards her, then towards us, smiled and was born, christened part of my world from that moment.

'Daphne!' Her quick, beautiful smile answered . . .

Saturday morning was gloriously fine. When I woke up and saw the sun streaming over the polished floor I felt like a little boy who has been promised a picnic. It was all I could do not to telephone Daphne. Was she feeling the same? It seemed somehow such a terrific lark that we should be going off together like this, just with a couple of rucksacks and our bathing suits. I thought of other weekends, the preparation, the emotional tension, the amount of managing they'd needed. But I couldn't really think of them; I couldn't be bothered, they belonged to another life . . .

It seemed to me suddenly so preposterous that two people should be as happy as we were and not be happier. Here we were, alone, miles away from everybody, free as air, and in love with each other. I looked again at Daphne, at her slender shoulders, her throat, her bosom, and, passionately in love, I decided, with fervour: Wouldn't it be rather absurd, then, to behave like a couple of children? Wouldn't she even, in spite of all she had said, be disappointed if we did? . . .

And I went off at a tremendous pace, not because I thought she'd run after me, but I did think she might call, or I might look round . . .

It was one of those still, hushed days when the sea and the sky seem to melt into one another, and it is long before the moisture dries on the leaves and grasses. One of those days when the sea smells strong and there are gulls standing in a row on the sand. The smoke from our wood fire hung in the air and the smoke of my pipe mingled with it. I caught myself staring at nothing. I felt dull and angry. I couldn't get over the ridiculous affair. You see, my *amour propre* was wounded.

Monday morning was grey, cloudy, one of those mornings peculiar to the seaside when everything, the sea most of all, seems exhausted and sullen. There had been a very high tide, the road was wet – on the beach there stood a long line of sickly-looking gulls . . .

When we got on board she sat down on one of the green benches and, muttering something about a pipe, I walked quickly away. It was intolerable that we should still be together after what had happened.

It was indecent. I only asked – I only longed for one thing – to be free of this still, unsmiling and pitiful – that was the worst of it – creature who had been my playful Daphne.

For answer I telephoned her at once and asked if I might come and see her that evening. Her voice sounded grave, unlike the voice I remembered, and she seemed to deliberate. There was a long pause before she said, 'Yes – perhaps that would be best.'

'Then I shall come at half-past six.'

'Very well.'

And we went into a room full of flowers and very large art photographs of the 'Harbour by Night', 'A Misty Day', 'Moonrise over the Water', and I know I wondered if she admired them.

'Why did you send me that letter?'

'Oh, but I had to,' said Daphne. 'I meant every word of it. I only let you come tonight to . . . No, I know I shall disappoint you. I'm wiser than you are for all your experience. I shan't be able to live up to it. I'm not the person for you. Really I'm not!' . . .

Father and the Girls

I

AT MIDDAY, ERNESTINE, who had come down from the mountains with her mother to work in the vineyards belonging to the hotel, heard the faint, far-away *chuff-chuff* of the train from Italy. Trains were a novelty to Ernestine; they were fascinating, unknown, terrible. What were they like as they came tearing their way through the valley, plunging between the mountains as if not even the mountains could stop them? When she saw the dark, flat breast of the engine, so bare, so powerful, hurled as it were towards her, she felt a weakness – she could have sunk to the earth. And yet she must look. So she straightened up, stopped pulling at the blue-green leaves, tugging at the long, bright-green, curly suckers, and, with eyes like a bird, stared. The vines were very tall. There was nothing to be seen of Ernestine but her beautiful, youthful bosom buttoned into a blue cotton jacket and her small, dark head covered with a faded cherry-coloured handkerchief.

Chiff-chuff-chaff. Chiff-chuff-chaff, sounded the train. Now a wisp of white smoke shone and melted. Now there was another, and the monster itself came into sight and snorting horribly drew up at a little, toy-like station five minutes away. The railway ran at the bottom of the hotel garden which was perched high and surrounded by a stone wall. Steps cut in the stone led to the terraces where the vines were planted. Ernestine, looking out from the leaves like a bright bird, saw the terrible engine and looked beyond it at doors swinging open, at strangers stepping down. She would never know who they were or where they had come from. A moment ago they were not here; perhaps by tomorrow they would be gone again. And looking like a bird herself, she remembered how, at home, in the late autumn, she had sometimes seen strange birds in the fir-tree that were there one day and gone the next. Where from? Where to? She felt an ache in her bosom. Wings were tight-folded there. Why could she not stretch them out and fly away and away? . . .

2

From the first-class carriage tall, thin Emily alighted and gave her hand to Father whose brittle legs seemed to wave in the air as they felt for the iron step. Taller, thinner Edith followed, carrying Father's light overcoat, his field-glasses on a strap and his new Baedeker. The blond hotel porter came forward. Wasn't that nice? He could speak as good English as you or me. So Edith had no trouble at all in explaining how, as they were going on by the morning train tomorrow, they would only need their suitcases and what was left in the compartment. Was there a carriage outside? Yes, a carriage was there. But if they cared to walk there was a private entrance through the hotel gardens . . . No, they wouldn't walk.

'You wouldn't care to walk, would you, Father dear?'

'No, Edith, I won't walk. Do you girls wanna walk?'

'Why no, Father, not without you, dear.'

And the blond hotel porter leading, they passed through the little knot of sturdy peasants at the station gate to where the carriage waited under a group of limes.

'Did you ever see anything as big as that horse, Edith!' cried Emily. She was always the first to exclaim about things.

'It is a very big horse,' sang Edith, more sober. 'It's a farm horse, from the look of it, and it's been working. See how hot it is.' Edith had so much observation. The big, brown horse, his sides streaked with dark sweat, tossed his head and the bells on his collar set up a loud jangling.

'Hu-yup!' called the young peasant driver warningly, from his seat on the high box.

Father, who was just about to get in, drew back, a little scared.

'You don't think that horse will run away with us, do you, Edith?' he quavered.

'Why no, Father dear,' coaxed Edith. 'That horse is just as tame as you or me.' So in they got, the three of them. And as the horse bounded forward his ears seemed to twitch in surprise at his friend the driver. Call that a load? Father and the girls weighed nothing. They might have been three bones, three broomsticks, three umbrellas bouncing up and down on the hard seats of the carriage. It was a mercy the hotel was so close. Father could never have stood that for more than a minute, especially at the end of a journey. Even as it was his face was quite green when Emily helped him out, straightened him, and gave him a little pull.

'It's shaken you, dear, hasn't it?' she said tenderly.

But he refused her arm into the hotel. That would create a wrong impression.

'No, no, Emily. I'm all right. All right,' said Father, as staggering a little he followed them through big glass doors into a hall as dim as a church and as chill and as deserted.

My! Wasn't that hall cold! The cold seemed to come leaping at them from the floor. It clasped the peaked knees of Edith and Emily; it leapt high as the fluttering heart of Father. For a moment they hesitated, drew together, almost gasped. But then out from the Bureau a cheerful young person, her smiling face spotted with mosquito bites, ran to meet them, and welcomed them with such real enthusiasm (in English too) that the chill first moment was forgotten.

'Aw-yes. Aw-yes. I can let you ave very naice rooms on de firs floor wid a lif. Two rooms and bart and dressing-room for de chentleman. Beautiful rooms wid sun but nort too hot. Very naice. Till tomorrow. I taike you. If you please. It is dis way. You are tired wid the churney? Launch is at half-pas tvelf. Hort worter? Aw-yes. It is wid de bart. If you please.'

Father and the girls were drawn by her cheerful smiles and becks and nods along a cloister-like corridor, into the lift and up, until she flung open a heavy, dark door and stood aside for them to enter.

'It is a suite,' she explained. 'Wid a hall and tree doors.' Quickly she opened them. 'Now I gaw to see when your luggage is gum.'

And she went.

'Well!' cried Emily.

Edith stared.

Father craned his thin, old neck, looking, too.

'Did you – ever see the like, Edith?' cried Emily, in a little rush.

And Edith softly clasped her hands. Softly she sang 'No, I never did, Emily. I've never seen anything just like this before.'

'Sims to me a nice room,' quavered Father, still hovering. 'Do you girls wanna change it?'

Change it! 'Why, Father dear, it's just the loveliest thing we've ever set eyes on, isn't it, Emily? Sit down, Father dear, sit down in the armchair.'

Father's pale claws gripped the velvet arms. He lowered himself; he sank with an old man's quick sigh.

Edith still stood, as if bewitched, at the door. But Emily ran over to the window and leaned out, quite girlish . . .

For a long time now – for how long? – for countless ages – Father and the girls had been on the wing. Nice, Montreux, Biarritz, Naples, Mentone, Lake Maggiore, they had seen them all and many, many more. And still they beat on, beat on, flying as if unwearied, never stopping anywhere for long. But the truth was – Oh, better not inquire what the truth was. Better not ask what it was that kept them going. Or why the only word that daunted Father was the word – home . . .

Home! To sit around, doing nothing, listening to the clock, counting up the years, thinking back . . . thinking! To stay fixed in one place as if waiting for something or somebody. No! no! Better far to be blown over the earth like the husk, like the withered pod that the wind carries and drops and bears aloft again.

'Are you ready, girls?'

'Yes, Father dear.'

'Then we'd better be off if we're to make that train.'

But oh, it was a weariness, it was an unspeakable weariness. Father made no secret of his age; he was eighty-four. As for Edith and Emily – well, he looked now like their elder brother. An old, old brother and two ancient sisters, so the lovely room might have summed them up. But its shaded brightness, its beauty, the flutter of leaves at the creamy stone windows seemed only to whisper 'Rest! Stay!'

Edith looked at the pale, green-panelled walls, at the doors that had lozenges and squares of green picked out in gold. She made the amazing discovery that the floor had the same pattern in wood that was traced on the high, painted ceiling. But the colour of the shining floor was marvellous; it was like tortoiseshell. In one corner there was a huge, tilted stove, milky white and blue. The low wooden bed, with its cover of quilted yellow satin, had sheaves of corn carved on the bedposts. It looked to fanciful, tired Edith – yes – that bed looked as if it were breathing, softly, gently breathing. Outside the narrow, deep-set windows, beyond their wreaths of green, she could see a whole, tiny landscape bright as a jewel in the summer heat.

'Rest! Stay!' Was it the sound of the leaves outside? No, it was in the air; it was the room itself that whispered joyfully, shyly. Edith felt so strange that she could keep quiet no longer.

'This is a very old room, Emily,' she warbled softly. 'I know what it is. This hotel has not always been a hotel. It's been an old château. I feel as sure of that as that I'm standing here.' Perhaps she wanted to convince herself that she was standing there. 'Do you see that stove?'

She walked over to the stove. 'It's got figures on it. Emily,' she warbled faintly, 'it's 1623.'

'Isn't that too wonderful!' cried Emily.

Even Father was deeply moved.

'1623? Nearly three hundred years old.' And suddenly, in spite of his tiredness, he gave a thin, airy, old man's chuckle. 'Makes yer feel quite a chicken, don't it?' said Father.

Emily's breathless little laugh answered him; it, too, was gay.

'I'm going to see what's behind that door,' she cried. And half running to the door in the middle wall she lifted the slender steel catch. It led into a larger room, into Edith's and her bedroom. But the walls were the same and the floor, and there were the same deep-set windows. Only two beds instead of one stood side by side with blue silk quilts instead of yellow. And what a beautiful old chest there was under the windows!

'Oh,' cried Emily, in rapture. 'Isn't it all too perfectly historical for words, Edith! It makes me feel – ' She stopped, she looked at Edith who had followed her and whose thin shadow lay on the sunny floor. 'Queer!' said Emily, trying to put all she felt into that one word. 'I don't know what it is.'

Perhaps if Edith, the discoverer, had had time she might have satisfied Emily. But a knock sounded at the outer door; it was the luggage boy. And while he brought in their suitcases there came from downstairs the ringing of the luncheon bell. Father mustn't be kept waiting. Once a bell had gone he liked to follow it up right then. So without even a glance at the mirror – they had reached the age when it is as natural to avoid mirrors as it is to peer into them when one is young – Edith and Emily were ready.

'Are you ready, girls?'

'Yes, Father dear.'

And off they went again, to the left, to the right, down a stone staircase with a broad, worn balustrade, to the left again, finding their way as if by instinct – Edith first, then Father, and Emily close behind.

But when they reached the *salle à manger*, which was as big as a ballroom, it was still empty. All gay, all glittering, the long French windows open on to the green and gold garden, the *salle à manger* stretched before them. And the fifty little tables with the fifty posts of dahlias looked as if they might begin dancing with . . .

All Serene!

AT BREAKFAST THAT MORNING they were in wonderfully good spirits. Who was responsible – he or she? It was true she made a point of looking her best in the morning; she thought it part of her duty to him – to their love, even, to wear charming little caps, funny little coats, coloured mules at breakfast time, and to see that the table was perfect as he and she – fastidious pair! – understood the word. But he, too, so fresh, well-groomed and content, contributed his share . . . She had been down first, sitting at her place when he came in. He leaned over the back of her chair, his hands on her shoulders; he bent down and lightly rubbed his cheek against hers, murmuring gently but with just enough pride of proprietorship to make her flush with delight, 'Give me my tea, love.' And she lifted the silver teapot that had a silver pear modelled on the lid and gave him his tea.

'Thanks . . . You know you look awfully well this morning!'

'Do I?'

'Yes. Do that again. Look at me again. It's your eyes. They're like a child's. I've never known anyone have such shining eyes as you.'

'Oh, dear!' She sighed for joy. 'I do love having sweet things said to me!'

'Yes, you do – spoilt child! Shall I give you some of this?'

'No, thank you . . . Darling!' Her hand flew across the table and clasped his hand.

'Yes?'

But she said nothing, only 'Darling!' again. There was the look on his face she loved – a kind of sweet jesting. He was pretending he didn't know what she meant, and yet of course he did know. He was pretending to be feeling 'Here she is – trust a woman – all ready for a passionate love scene over the breakfast table at nine o'clock in the morning.' But she wasn't deceived. She knew he felt just the same as she did. That amused tolerance, that mock despair was part of the ways of men – no more.

'May I be allowed to *use* this knife please, or to put it down?'

Really! Mona had never yet got accustomed to her husband's smile. They had been married for three years. She was in love with him for countless reasons, but apart from them all, a special reason all to itself, was because of his smile. If it hadn't sounded nonsense she would have said she fell in love at first sight over and over again when he smiled. Other people felt the charm of it, too. Other women, she was certain. Sometimes she thought that even the servants watched for it . . .

'Don't forget we're going to the theatre tonight.'

'Oh, good egg! I had forgotten. It's ages since we went to a show.'

'Yes, isn't it? I feel quite thrilled.'

'Don't you think we might have a tiny small celebration at dinner?' ('Tiny small' was one of her expressions. But why did it sound so sweet when he used it?)

'Yes, let's. You mean champagne?' And she looked into the distance, and said in a far-away voice: 'Then I must revise the sweet.'

At that moment the maid came in with the letters. There were four for him, three for her. No, one of hers belonged to him, too, rather a grimy little envelope with a dab of sealing-wax on the back.

'Why do you get all the letters?' she wailed, handing it across. 'It's awfully unfair. I love letters and I never get any.'

'Well, I do like that!' said he. 'How can you sit there and tell such awful bangers? It's the rarest thing on earth for me to get a letter in the morning. It's always you who get those mysterious epistles from girls you were at college with or faded aunts. Here, have half my pear – it's a beauty.' She held out her plate.

The Rutherfords never shared their letters. It was her idea that they should not. He had been violently opposed to it at first. She couldn't help laughing; he had so absolutely misunderstood her reason.

'Good God! my dear. You're perfectly welcome to open any letters of mine that come to the house – or to read any letters of mine that may be lying about. I think I can promise you . . . '

'Oh no, no, darling, that's not what I mean. I don't suspect you.' And she put her hands on his cheeks and kissed him quickly. He looked like an offended boy. 'But so many of Mother's old friends write to me – confide in me – don't you know? – tell me things they wouldn't for the world tell a man. I feel it wouldn't be fair to them. Don't you see?'

He gave way at last. But 'I'm old-fashioned,' he said, and his smile was a little rueful. 'I like to feel my wife reads my letters.'

'My precious dear! I've made you unhappy.' She felt so repentant; she didn't know quite about what. 'Of course I'd love to read . . .'

'No, no! That's all right. It's understood. We'll keep the bond.' And they had kept it.

He slit open the grimy envelope. He began to read.

'Damn!' he said and thrust out his underlip.

'Why, what is it? Something horrid?'

'No – annoying. I shall be late this evening. A man wants to meet me at the office at six o'clock.'

'Was that a business letter?' She sounded surprised.

'Yes, why?'

'It looked so awfully unbusinesslike. The sealing-wax and the funny writing – much more like a woman's than a man's.'

He laughed. He folded the letter, put it in his pocket and picked up the envelope. 'Yes,' he said, 'it is queer, isn't it. I shouldn't have noticed. How quick you are! But it does look exactly like a woman's hand. That capital R, for instance' – he flipped the envelope across to her.

'Yes, and that squiggle underneath. I should have said a rather uneducated female . . .'

'As a matter of fact,' said Hugh, 'he's a mining engineer.' And he got up, began to stretch and then stopped. 'I say, what a glorious morning! Why do I have to go to the office instead of staying at home and playing with you?' And he came over to her and locked his arms round her neck. 'Tell me that, little lovely one.'

'Oh,' she leaned against him, 'I wish you could. Life's arranged badly for people like you and me. And now you're going to be late this evening.'

'Never mind,' said he. 'All the rest of the time's ours. Every single bit of it. We shan't come back from the theatre to find – '

'Our porch black with mining engineers.' She laughed. Did other people – could other people – was it possible that anyone before had ever loved as they loved? She squeezed her head against him – she heard his watch ticking – precious watch!

'What are those purple floppy flowers in my bedroom?' he murmured.

'Petunias.'

'You smell exactly like a petunia.'

And he raised her up. She drew towards him. 'Kiss me,' said he.

2

It was her habit to sit on the bottom stair and watch his final preparations. Strange it should be so fascinating to see someone brush his hat, choose a pair of gloves and give a last quick look in the round mirror. But it was the same when he was shaving. Then she loved to curl up on the hard little couch in his dressing-room; she was as absorbed, as intent as he. How fantastic he looked, like a pierrot, like a mask, with those dark eyebrows, liquid eyes and the brush of fresh colour on his cheek-bones above the lather! But that was not her chief feeling. No, it was what she felt on the stairs, too. It was, 'So this is my husband, so this is the man I've married, this is the stranger who walked across the lawn that afternoon swinging his tennis racket and bowed, rolling up his shirtsleeves. This is not only my lover and my husband but my brother, my dearest friend, my playmate, even at times a kind of very perfect father too. And here is where we live. Here is his room – and here is our hall.' She seemed to be showing their house and him to her other self, the self she had been before she had met him. Deeply admiring, almost awed by so much happiness, that other self looked on . . .

'Will I do?' He stood there smiling, stroking on his gloves. But although he wouldn't like her to say the things she often longed to say about his appearance, she did think she detected that morning just the very faintest boyish showing-off. Children who know they are admired look like that at their mother.

'Yes, you'll do . . . ' Perhaps at that moment she was proud of him as a mother is proud; she could have blessed him before he went his way. Instead she stood in the porch thinking, 'There he goes. The man I've married. The stranger who came across the lawn.' The fact was never less wonderful . . .

It was never less wonderful, never. It was even more wonderful if anything, and the reason was – Mona ran back into the house, into the drawing-room and sat down to the piano. Oh, why bother about reasons – She began to sing,

> See, love, I bring thee flowers
> To charm thy pain!

But joy – joy breathless and exulting thrilled in her voice, on the word 'pain' her lips parted in such a happy – dreadfully unsympathetic smile that she felt quite ashamed. She stopped playing, she turned round on the piano stool facing the room. How different it looked in the morning, how severe and remote. The grey chairs with the fuchsia-coloured cushions, the black and gold carpet, the bright green silk curtains might have belonged to anybody. It was like a stage setting with the curtain still down. She had no right to be there, and as she thought that a queer little chill caught her; it seemed so extraordinary that anything, even a chair, should turn away from, should not respond to her happiness.

'I don't like this room in the morning, I don't like it at all,' she decided, and she ran upstairs to finish dressing. Ran into their big, shadowy bedroom . . . and leaned over the starry petunias . . .

A Bad Idea

SOMETHING'S HAPPENED to me – something bad. And I don't know what to do about it. I don't see any way out for the life of me. The worst of it is, I can't get this thing into focus – if you know what I mean. I just feel in a muddle – in the hell of a muddle. It ought to be plain to anyone that I'm not the kind of man to get mixed up in a thing like this. I'm not one of your actor Johnnies, or a chap in a book. I'm – well, I knew what I was all right until yesterday. But now – I feel helpless, yes, that's the word, helpless. Here I sit, chucking stones at the sea like a child that's missed its mother. And everybody else has cut along home hours ago and tea's over and it's getting on for time to light the lamp. I shall have to go home too, sooner or later. I see that, of course. In fact, would you believe it? at this very moment I wish I was there in spite of everything. What's she doing? My wife, I mean. Has she cleared away? Or has she stayed there staring at the table with the plates pushed back? My God! when I think that I could howl like a dog – if you know what I mean . . .

I should have realised it was all U.P. this morning when she didn't get up for breakfast. I did, in a way. But I couldn't face it. I had the feeling that if I said nothing special and just treated it as one of her bad headache days and went off to the office, by the time I got back this evening the whole affair would have blown over somehow. No, that wasn't it. I felt a bit like I do now, 'helpless'. What was I to do? Just go on. That was all I could think of. So I took her up a cup of tea and a couple of slices of thin bread and butter as per usual on her headache days. The blind was still down. She was lying on her back. I think she had a wet handkerchief on her forehead. I'm not sure, for I couldn't look at her. It was a beastly feeling. And she said in a weak kind of voice, 'Put the jug on the table, will you?' I put it down. I said, 'Can I do anything?' And she said, 'No. I'll be all right in half an hour.' But her voice, you know! It did for me. I barged out as quick as I could, snatched my hat and stick from the hall-stand and dashed off for the tram.

Here's a queer thing – you needn't believe me if you don't want to – the moment I got out of the house I forgot that about my wife. It was a splendid morning, soft, with the sun making silver ducks on the sea. The kind of morning when you know it's going to keep hot and fine all day. Even the tram bell sounded different, and the little school kids crammed between people's knees had bunches of flowers. I don't know – I can't understand why – I just felt happy, but happy in a way I'd never been before, happy to beat the band! That wind that had been so strong the night before was still blowing a bit. It felt like her – the other – touching me. Yes, it did. Brought it back, every bit of it. If I told you how it took me, you'd say I was mad. I felt reckless – didn't care if I was late for the office or not and I wanted to do every one a kindness. I helped the little kids out of the tram. One little chap dropped his cap, and when I picked it up for him and said, 'Here, sonny!' . . . well, it was all I could do not to make a fool of myself.

At the office it was just the same. It seemed to me I'd never known the fellows at the office before. When old Fisher came over to my desk and put down a couple of giant sweet peas as per usual with his 'Beat 'em, old man, beat 'em!' – I didn't feel annoyed. I didn't care that he was riddled with conceit about his garden. I just looked at them and I said quietly, 'Yes, you've done it this time.' He didn't know what to make of it. Came back in about five minutes and asked me if I had a headache.

And so it went on all day. In the evening I dashed home with the home-going crowd, pushed open the gate, saw the hall-door open as it always is and sat down on the little chair just inside to take off my boots. My slippers were there, of course. This seemed to me a good sign. I put my boots into the rack in the cupboard under the stairs, changed my office coat and made for the kitchen. I knew my wife was there. Wait a bit. The only thing I couldn't manage was my whistling as per usual, 'I often lie awake and think, What a dreadful thing is work . . . ' I had a try, but nothing came of it. Well, I opened the kitchen door and said, 'Hullo! How's everybody?' But as soon as I'd said that – even before – I knew the worst had happened. She was standing at the table beating the salad dressing. And when she looked up and gave a kind of smile and said 'Hullo!' you could have knocked me down! My wife looked dreadful – there's no other word for it. She must have been crying all day. She'd put some white flour stuff on her face to take away the marks – but it only made her look worse. She must have seen I spotted something, for she caught up the cup of cream and poured some into the salad bowl – like she always does, you know, so quick, so neat, in her own way – and began beating again. I said, 'Is your head better?' But she didn't seem to hear. She said, 'Are you going to water the garden before or after supper?' What could I say? I said, 'After,' and went off to the dining-room, opened the evening paper and sat by the open window – well, hiding behind that paper, I suppose.

I shall never forget sitting there. People passing by, going down the road, sounded so peaceful. And a man passed with some cows. I – I envied him. My wife came in and out. Then she called me to supper and we sat down. I suppose we ate some cold meat and salad. I don't remember. We must have. But neither of us spoke. It's like a dream now. Then she got up, changed the plates, and went to the larder for the pudding. Do you know what the pudding was? Well, of course, it wouldn't mean anything to you. It was my favourite – the kind she only made me on special occasions – honeycomb cream . . .

A Man and his Dog

TO LOOK AT MR POTTS one would have thought that there at least went someone who had nothing to boast about. He was a little, insignificant fellow with a crooked tie, a hat too small for him and a coat too large. The brown canvas portfolio that he carried to and from the Post Office every day was not like a businessman's portfolio. It was like a child's school satchel; it did up even with a round-eyed button. One imagined there were crumbs and an apple core inside. And then there was something funny about his boots, wasn't there? Through the laces his coloured socks peeped out. What the dickens had the chap done with the tongues? 'Fried 'em,' suggested the wit of the Chesney bus. Poor old Potts! 'More likely buried 'em in his garden.' Under his arm he clasped an umbrella. And in wet weather when he put it up he disappeared completely. He was not. He was a walking umbrella – no more – the umbrella became his shell.

Mr Potts lived in a little bungalow on Chesney Flat. The bulge of the water tank to one side gave it a mournful air, like a little bungalow with the toothache. There was no garden. A path had been cut in the paddock turf from the gate to the front door, and two beds, one round, one oblong, had been cut in what was going to be the front lawn. Down that path went Potts every morning at half-past eight and was picked up by the Chesney bus; up that path walked Potts every evening while the great kettle of a bus droned on. In the late evening, when he crept as far as the gate, eager to smoke a pipe – he wasn't allowed to smoke any nearer to the house than that – so humble, so modest was his air, that the big, merrily shining stars seemed to wink at each other, to laugh, to say, 'Look at him! Let's throw something!'

When Potts got out of the tram at the Fire Station to change into the Chesney bus he saw that something was up. The car was there all right, but the driver was off his perch; he was flat on his face half under the engine, and the conductor, his cap off, sat on a step rolling a cigarette and looking dreamy. A little group of business-men and a woman clerk or two stood staring at the empty car; there was something mournful, pitiful about the way it leaned to one side and shivered faintly when the driver shook something. It was like someone who'd had an accident and tries to say: 'Don't touch me! Don't come near me! Don't hurt me!'

But all this was so familiar – the cars had only been running to Chesney the last few months – that nobody said anything, nobody asked anything. They just waited on the off chance. In fact, two or three decided to walk it as Potts came up. But Potts didn't want to walk unless he had to. He was tired. He'd been up half the night rubbing his wife's chest – she had one of her mysterious pains – and helping the sleepy servant girl heat compresses and hot-water bottles and make tea. The window was blue and the roosters had started crowing before he lay down finally with feet like ice. And all this was familiar, too.

Standing at the edge of the pavement and now and again changing his brown canvas portfolio from one hand to the other Potts began to live over the night before. But it was vague, shadowy. He saw himself moving like a crab, down the passage to the cold kitchen and back again. The two candles quivered on the dark chest of drawers, and as he bent over his wife her big eyes suddenly flashed and she cried: 'I get no sympathy – no sympathy. You only do it because you have to. Don't contradict me. I can see you grudge doing it.'

Trying to soothe her only made matters worse. There had been an awful scene ending with her sitting up and saying solemnly with her hand raised: 'Never mind, it will not be for long now.' But the sound of these words frightened her so terribly that she flung back on the pillow and sobbed, 'Robert! Robert!' Robert was the name of the young man to whom she had been engaged years ago, before she met Potts. And Potts was very glad to hear him invoked. He had come to know that meant the crisis was over and she'd begin to quieten down . . .

By this time Potts had wheeled round; he had walked across the pavement to the paling fence that ran beside. A piece of light grass pushed through the fence and some slender silky daisies. Suddenly he saw a bee alight on one of the daisies and the flower leaned over, swayed, shook, while the little bee clung and rocked. And as it flew away the petals fluttered as if joyfully . . . Just for an instant Potts dropped into the world where this happened. He brought from it the timid smile with which he walked back to the car. But now everybody had disappeared except one young girl who stood beside the empty car reading.

At the tail of the procession came Potts in a cassock so much too large for him that it looked like a night-shirt and you felt that he ought to be carrying not a hymn and a prayer book but a candle. His voice was a very light plaintive tenor. It surprised everybody. It seemed to surprise him, too. But it was so plaintive that when he cried 'for the wings, for the wings of a dove,' the ladies in the congregation wanted to club together and buy him a pair.

Lino's nose quivered so pitifully, there was such a wistful, timid look in his eyes, that Potts' heart was wrung. But, of course, he would not show it. 'Well,' he said sternly, 'I suppose you'd better come home.' And he got up off the bench. Lino got up, too, but stood still, holding up a paw.

'But there's one thing,' said Potts, turning and facing him squarely, 'that we'd better be clear about before you do come. And it's this.' He pointed his finger at Lino, who started as though he expected to be shot. But he kept his bewildered wistful eyes upon his master. 'Stop this pretence of being a fighting dog,' said Potts more sternly than ever. 'You're not a fighting dog. You're a watch dog. That's what you are. Very well. Stick to it. But it's this infernal boasting I can't stand. It's that that gets me.'

In the moment's pause that followed while Lino and his master looked at each other it was curious how strong a resemblance was between them. Then Potts turned again and made for home.

And timidly, as though falling over his own paws, Lino followed after the humble little figure of his master . . .

Such a Sweet Old Lady

WHY DID OLD Mrs Travers wake so early nowadays? She would like
to have slept for another three hours at least. But no, every morning
at almost precisely the same time, at half-past four, she was wide
awake. For – nowadays, again – she woke always in the same way,
with a slight start, a small shock, lifting her head from the pillow with
a quick glance as if she fancied someone had called her, or as if she
were trying to remember for certain whether this was the same
wallpaper, the same window she had seen last night before Warner
switched off the light . . . Then the small, silvery head pressed the
white pillow again, and just for a moment, before the agony of lying
awake began, old Mrs Travers was happy. Her heart quietened down,
she breathed deeply, she even smiled. Yet once more the tide of
darkness had risen, had floated her, had carried her away; and once
more it had ebbed, it had withdrawn, casting her up where it had
found her, shut in by the same wallpaper, stared at by the same
window – still safe – still *there!*

Now the church clock sounded from outside, slow, languid, faint,
as if it chimed the half-hour in its sleep. She felt under the pillow for
her watch; yes, it said the same: half-past four. Three and a half hours
before Warner came in with her tea. Oh dear, would she be able to
stand it? She moved her legs restlessly. And, staring at the prim,
severe face of the watch, it seemed to her that the hands – the minute
hand especially – knew that she was watching them and held back –
just a very little – on purpose . . . Very strange, she had never got over
the feeling that watch hated her. It had been Henry's. Twenty years
ago, when standing by poor Henry's bed she had taken it into her
hands for the first time and wound it, it had felt cold and heavy. And
two days later, when she undid a hook of her crape bodice and thrust
it inside, it had lain in her bosom like a stone . . . It had never felt at
home there. It's place was – ticking, keeping perfect time, against
Henry's firm ribs. It had never trusted her, just as he had never
trusted her in those ways. And on the rare occasions when she had

forgotten to wind it, she had felt a pang of almost terror, and she had murmured as she fitted the little key: 'Forgive me, Henry!'

Old Mrs Travers sighed and pushed the watch under the pillow again. It seemed to her that lately this feeling that it hated her had become more definite . . . Perhaps that was because she looked at it so often, especially now that she was away from home. Foreign clocks never go. They are always stopped at twenty minutes to two. Twenty minutes to two! Such an unpleasant time, neither one thing nor the other. If one arrived anywhere lunch was over and it was too early to expect a cup of tea . . . But she mustn't begin thinking about tea. Old Mrs Travers pulled herself up in the bed and, like a tired baby, she lifted her arms and let them fall on the eider-down.

The room was gay with morning light. The big french window on to the balcony was open and the palm outside flung its quivering spider-like shadow over the bedroom walls. Although their hotel did not face the front, at this early hour you could smell the sea, you could hear it breathing, and flying high on golden wings sea-gulls skimmed past. How peaceful the sky looked, as though it was tenderly smiling! Far away – far away from this satin-stripe wallpaper, the glass-covered table, the yellow brocade sofa and chairs, and the mirrors that showed you your side view, your back view, your three-quarters view as well.

Ernestine had been enthusiastic about this room.

'It's just the very room for you, Mother! So bright and attractive and non-depressing! With a balcony, too, so that on wet days you can still have your chair outside and look at those lovely palms. And Gladys can have the little room adjoining, which makes it so beautifully easy for Warner to keep her eye on you both . . . You couldn't have a nicer room, could you, Mother? I can't get over that sweet balcony! So nice for Gladys! Cecil and I haven't got one at all . . .'

But all the same, in spite of Ernestine, she never sat on that balcony. For some strange reason that she couldn't explain she hated looking at palms. Nasty foreign things, she called them in her mind. When they were still they drooped, they looked draggled like immense untidy birds, and when they moved they reminded her always of spiders. Why did they never look just natural and peaceful and shady like English trees? Why were they for ever writhing and twisting or standing sullen? It tried her even to think of them, or in fact of anything foreign . . .

Honesty

I

THERE WAS AN EXPRESSION Rupert Henderson was very fond of
using: 'If you want my *honest* opinion . . . ' He had an honest opinion
on every subject under the sun, and nothing short of a passion for
delivering it. But Archie Cullen's pet phrase was 'I cannot *honestly*
say . . . ' Which meant that he had not really made up his mind. He
had not really made up his mind on any subject whatsoever. Why?
Because he could not. He was unlike other men. He was minus
something – or was it plus? No matter. He was not in the least
proud of the fact. It depressed him – one might go so far as to say –
terribly at times.

Rupert and Archie lived together. That is to say, Archie lived in
Rupert's rooms. Oh, he paid his share, his half in everything; the
arrangement was a purely, strictly business arrangement. But perhaps
it was because Rupert had invited Archie that Archie remained always
– his guest. They each had a bedroom – there was a common sitting-
room and a largish bathroom which Rupert used as a dressing-room
as well. The first morning after his arrival Archie had left his sponge
in the bathroom, and a moment after there was a knock at his door
and Rupert said, kindly but firmly, 'Your sponge, I fancy.' The first
evening Archie had brought his tobacco jar into the sitting-room
and placed it on a corner of the mantel-piece. Rupert was reading
the newspaper. It was a round china jar, the surface painted and
roughened to represent a sea-urchin. On the lid was a spray of china
seaweed with two berries for a knob. Archie was excessively fond of it.
But after dinner, when Rupert took out his pipe and pouch, he
suddenly fixed his eyes on this object, blew through his moustaches,
gasped, and said in a wondering, astonished voice, 'I say! Is that yours
or Mrs Head's?' Mrs Head was their landlady.

'It's mine,' said Archie, and he blushed and smiled just a trifle
timidly.

'I *say!*' said Rupert again – this time very meaningly.

'Would you rather I . . . ' said Archie, and he moved in his chair to get up.

'No, no! Certainly not! On no account!' answered Rupert, and he actually raised his hand. 'But perhaps' – and here he smiled at Archie and gazed about him – 'perhaps we might find some spot for it that was a trifle less conspicuous.'

The spot was not decided on, however, and Archie nipped his sole personal possession into his bedroom as soon as Rupert was out of the way.

But it was chiefly at meals that the attitude of host and guest was most marked. For instance, on each separate occasion, even before they sat down, Rupert said, 'Would you mind cutting the bread, Archie?' Had he not made such a point of it, it is possible that Archie in a moment of abstractedness might have grasped the bread knife . . . An unpleasant thought! Again, Archie was never allowed to serve. Even at breakfast, the hot dishes and the tea, both were dispensed by Rupert. True, he had half apologised about the tea; he seemed to feel the necessity of some slight explanation, there.

'I'm rather a fad about my tea,' said he. 'Some people, females especially, pour in the milk first. Fatal habit, for more reasons than one. In my opinion, the cup should be filled just *so* and the tea then coloured. Sugar, Archie?'

'Oh, please,' said Archie, almost bowing over the table. Rupert was so very impressive.

'But I suppose,' said his friend, 'you don't notice any of these little things?'

And Archie answered vaguely, stirring: 'No, I don't suppose I do.'

Rupert sat down and unfolded his napkin.

'It would be very inconsistent with your character and disposition,' said he genially, 'if you did! Kidneys and bacon? Scrambled eggs? Either? Both? Which?'

Poor Archie hated scrambled eggs, but, alas! he was practically certain that scrambled eggs were expected of him too. This 'psychological awareness', as Rupert called it, which existed between them, might after a time make things a trifle difficult. He felt a little abject as he murmured, 'Eggs, please.' And he saw by Rupert's expression that he had chosen right. Rupert helped him to eggs largely.

2

Psychological awareness . . . perhaps it was that which explained their intimacy. One might have been tempted to say it was a case of mutual fascination. But whereas Archie's reply to the suggestion would have been a slow 'Poss-ibly!', Rupert would have flouted it at once.

'Fascination! The word's preposterous in this connection. What on earth would there be in Cullen to fascinate me even if I was in the habit of being fascinated by my fellow creatures; which I certainly am not. No, I'll own I am deeply interested. I confess my belief is, I understand him better than anybody else. And if you want my honest opinion, I am certain that my – my – h'm – influence over – sympathy for – him – call it what you like, is all to the good. There is a psychological awareness . . . Moreover, as a companion, instinctively I find him extremely agreeable. He stimulates some part of my mind which is less active without him. But fascination – wide of the mark, my dear – wide!'

But supposing one remained unconvinced? Supposing one still played with the idea. Wasn't it possible to see Rupert and Archie as the python and the rabbit keeping house together? Rupert that handsome, well-fed python with his moustaches, his glare, his habit of uncoiling before the fire and swaying against the mantelpiece, pipe and pouch in hand. And Archie, soft, hunched, timid, sitting in the lesser armchair, there and not there, flicking back into the darkness at a word but emerging again at a look – with sudden wholly unexpected starts of playfulness (instantly suppressed by the python). Of course, there was no question of anything so crude and dreadful as the rabbit being eaten by his housemate. Neverthe-less, it was a strange fact, after a typical evening the one looked immensely swelled, benign and refreshed, and the other, pale, small and exhausted . . . And more often than not Rupert's final comment was – ominous this – as he doused his whisky with soda: 'This has been very absorbing, Archie.' And Archie gasped out, 'Oh, *very!*'

3

Archie Cullen was a journalist and the son of a journalist. He had no private money, no influential connections, scarcely any friends. His father had been one of those weak, disappointed, unsuccessful men who see in their sons a weapon for themselves. He would get his own back on life through Archie. Archie would show them the stuff he – his father was made of. Just you wait till my son comes along! This, though highly consoling to Mr Cullen *père*, was terribly poor fun for Archie. At two and a half his infant nose was put to the grindstone and even on Sundays it was not taken off. Then his father took him out walking and improved the occasion by making him spell the shop signs, count the yachts racing in the harbour, divide them by four and multiply the result by three.

But the experiment was an amazing success. Archie turned away from the distractions of life, shut his ears, folded his feet, sat over the table with his book, and when the holidays came he didn't like them; they made him uneasy; so he went on reading for himself. He was a model boy. On prize-giving days his father accompanied him to school, carried the great wad of stiff books home for him and, flinging them on the dining-room table, he surveyed them with an exultant smile. My prizes! The little sacrifice stared at them, too, through his spectacles as other little boys stared at puddings. He ought, of course, at this juncture to have been rescued by a doting mother who, though cowed herself, rose on the . . .

Susannah

OF COURSE THERE WOULD HAVE BEEN NO QUESTION of their going to the exhibition if Father had not had the tickets given to him. Little girls cannot expect to be given treats that cost extra money when only to feed them, buy them clothes, pay for their lessons and the house they live in takes their kind generous Father all day and every day working hard from morning till night – 'except Saturday afternoons and Sundays,' said Susannah.

'Susannah!' Mother was very shocked. 'But do you know what would happen to your poor Father if he didn't have a holiday on Saturday afternoons and Sundays?'

'No,' said Susannah. She looked interested. 'What?'

'He would die,' said their Mother impressively.

'Would he?' said Susannah, opening her eyes. She seemed astounded, and Sylvia and Phyllis, who were four and five years older than she, chimed in with 'Of course' in a very superior tone. What a little silly-billy she was not to know that! They sounded so convinced and cheerful that their Mother felt a little shaken and hastened to change the subject . . .

'So that is why,' she said a little vaguely, 'you must each thank Father separately before you go.'

'And then will he give us the money?' asked Phyllis.

'And then I shall ask him for whatever is necessary,' said their Mother firmly. She sighed suddenly and got up. 'Run along, children, and ask Miss Wade to dress you and get ready herself and then to come down to the dining-room. And now, Susannah, you are not to let go Miss Wade's hand from the moment you are through the gates until you are out again.'

'Well – what if I go on a horse?' inquired Susannah.

'Go on a horse – nonsense, child! You're much too young for horses! Only big girls and boys can ride.'

'There're roosters for small children,' said Susannah, undaunted.

'I know, because Irene Heywood went on one and when she got off she fell over.'

'All the more reason why you shouldn't go on,' said her Mother.

But Susannah looked as though falling over had no terrors for her. On the contrary.

About the exhibition, however, Sylvia and Phyllis knew as little as Susannah. It was the first that had ever come to their town. One morning, as Miss Wade, their lady help, rushed them along to the Heywoods', whose governess they shared, they had seen carts piled with great long planks of wood, sacks, what looked like whole doors, and white flagstaffs, passing through the wide gate of the Recreation Ground. And by the time they were bowled home to their dinners there were the beginnings of a high, thin fence, dotted with flag-staffs, built all round the railings. From inside came a tremendous noise of hammering, shouting, clanging; a little engine, hidden away, went *Chuff-chuff-chuff. Chuff!* And round, woolly balls of smoke were tossed over the palings.

First it was the day after the day after tomorrow, then plain day after tomorrow, then tomorrow, and at last, the day itself. When Susannah woke up in the morning there was a little gold spot of sunlight watching her from the wall; it looked as though it had been there for a long time, waiting to remind her: 'It's today – you're going today – this afternoon. Here she is!'

[second version]

That afternoon they were allowed to cut jugs and basins out of a draper's catalogue, and at tea-time they had real tea in the doll's tea-set on the table. This was a very nice treat, indeed, except that the doll's teapot wouldn't pour out even after you'd poked a pin down the spout and blown into it.

But the next afternoon, which was Saturday, Father came home in high feather. The front door banged so hard that the whole house shook, and he shouted to Mother from the hall.

'Oh, how more than good of you, darling!' cried Mother, 'but how unnecessary too. Of course, they'll simply love it. But to have spent all that money! You shouldn't have done it, Daddy dear! They've totally forgotten all about it. And what is this! Half a crown?' cried Mother. 'No! Two shillings, I see,' she corrected quickly, 'to spend as well. Children! Children! Come down, downstairs!'

Down they came, Phyllis and Sylvia leading, Susannah holding on. 'Do you know what Father's done?' And Mother held up her hand.

What was she holding? Three cherry tickets and a green one. 'He's bought you tickets. You're to go to the circus, this very afternoon, all of you, with Miss Wade. What do you say to that?'

'Oh, Mummy! Lovely! Lovely!' cried Phyllis and Sylvia.

'Isn't it?' said Mother. 'Run upstairs. Run and ask Miss Wade to get you ready. Don't dawdle. Up you go! All of you.'

Away flew Phyllis and Sylvia, but still Susannah stayed where she was at the bottom of the stairs, hanging her head.

'Go along,' said Mother. And Father said sharply, 'What the devil's the matter with the child?'

Susannah's face quivered. 'I don't want to go,' she whispered.

'What! Don't want to go to the Exhibition! After Father's – You naughty, ungrateful child! Either you go to the Exhibition, Susannah, or you will be packed off to bed at once.'

Susannah's head bent low, lower still. All her little body bent forward. She looked as though she was going to bow down, to bow down to the ground, before her kind generous Father and beg for his forgiveness . . .

Second Violin

A FEBRUARY MORNING, windy, cold, with chill-looking clouds hurrying over a pale sky and chill snowdrops for sale in the grey streets. People look small and shrunken as they flit by; they look scared as if they were trying to hide inside their coats from something big and brutal. The shop doors are closed, the awnings are furled, and the policemen at the crossings are lead policemen. Huge empty vans shake past with a hollow sound; and there is a smell of soot and wet stone staircases, a raw, grimy smell . . .

Flinging her small scarf over her shoulder again, clasping her violin, Miss Bray darts along to orchestra practice. She is conscious of her cold hands, her cold nose and her colder feet. She can't feel her toes at all. Her feet are just little slabs of cold, all of a piece, like the feet of china dolls. Winter is a terrible time for thin people – terrible! Why should it hound them down, fasten on them, worry them so? Why not, for a change, take a nip, take a snap at the fat ones who wouldn't notice? But no! It is sleek, warm, cat-like summer that makes the fat one's life a misery. Winter is all for bones . . .

Threading her way, like a needle, in and out and along, went Miss Bray, and she thought of nothing but the cold. She had just come out of her kitchen, which was pleasantly snug in the morning, with her gas-fire going for her breakfast and the window closed. She had just drunk three large cups of really boiling tea. Surely, they ought to have warmed her. One always read in books of people going on their way warmed and invigorated by even one cup. And she had three! How she loved her tea! She was getting fonder and fonder of it. Stirring the cup, Miss Bray looked down. A little fond smile parted her lips, and she breathed tenderly, 'I love my tea.'

But all the same, in spite of the books, it didn't keep her warm. Cold! Cold! And now as she turned the corner she took such a gulp of damp, cold air that her eyes filled. *Yi-yi-yi*, a little dog yelped; he looked as though he'd been hurt. She hadn't time to look round, but that high, sharp yelping soothed her, was a comfort even. She could have made just that sound herself.

And here was the Academy. Miss Bray pressed with all her might against the stiff, sulky door, squeezed through into the vestibule hung with pallid notices and concert programmes, and stumbled up the dusty stairs and along the passage to the dressing-room. Through the open door there came such shrill loud laughter, such high, indifferent voices that it sounded like a play going on in there. It was hard to believe people were not laughing and talking like that . . . on purpose. 'Excuse me – pardon – sorry,' said Miss Bray, nudging her way in and looking quickly round the dingy little room. Her two friends had not yet come.

The First Violins were there; a dreamy, broad-faced girl leaned against her 'cello; two Violas sat on a bench, bent over a music book, and the Harp, a small grey little person, who only came occasionally, leaned against a bench and looked for her pocket in her underskirt . . .

'I've a run of three twice, ducky,' said Ma, 'a pair of queens make eight, and one for his nob makes nine.'

With an awful hollow groan Alexander, curling his little finger high, pegged nine for Ma. And 'Wait now, wait now,' said she, and her quick short little hands snatched at the other cards. 'My crib, young man!' She spread them out, leaned back, twitched her shawl, put her head on one side. 'H'm, not so bad! A flush of four and a pair!'

'Betrayed! Betrayed!' moaned Alexander, bowing his dark head over the cribbage board, 'and by a woo-man.' He sighed deeply, shuffled the cards and said to Ma, 'Cut for me, my love!'

Although, of course, he was only having his joke like all professional young gentlemen, something in the tone in which he said 'my love!' gave Ma quite a turn. Her lips trembled as she cut the cards, she felt a sudden pang as she watched those long slim fingers dealing.

Ma and Alexander were playing cribbage in the basement kitchen of number 9 Bolton Street. It was late, it was on eleven, and Sunday night, too – shocking! They sat at the kitchen table that was covered with a worn art serge cloth spotted with candle grease. On one corner of it stood three glasses, three spoons, a saucer of sugar lumps and a bottle of gin. The stove was still alight and the lid of the kettle had just begun to lift, cautiously, stealthily, as though there was someone inside who wanted to have a peep and pop back again. On the horse-hair sofa against the wall by the door the owner of the third glass lay asleep, gently snoring. Perhaps because he had his back to them, perhaps because his feet poked out from the short overcoat covering him, he looked forlorn, pathetic and the long, fair hair covering his collar looked forlorn and pathetic, too.

'Well, well,' said Ma, sighing as she put out two cards and arranged the others in a fan, 'such is life. I little thought when I saw the last of you this morning that we'd be playing a game together tonight.'

'The caprice of destiny,' murmured Alexander. But, as a matter of fact, it was no joking matter. By some infernal mischance that morning he and Rinaldo had missed the train that all the company travelled by. That was bad enough. But being Sunday, there was no other train until midnight, and as they had a full rehearsal at 10 o'clock on Monday it meant going by that, or getting what the company called the beetroot. But God! what a day it had been. They had left the luggage at the station and come back to Ma's, back to Alexander's frowsy bedroom with the bed unmade and water standing about. Rinaldo had spent the whole day sitting on the side of the bed swinging his leg, dropping ash on the floor and saying, 'I wonder what made us lose that train. Strange we should have lost it. I bet the others are wondering what made us lose it, too.' And Alexander had stayed by the window gazing into the small garden that was so black with grime even the old lean cat who came and scraped seemed revolted by it, too. It was only after Ma had seen the last of her Sunday visitors . . .

Mr and Mrs Williams

THAT WINTER Mr and Mrs Williams of The Rowans, Wickenham, Surrey, astonished their friends by announcing that they were going for a three weeks' holiday to Switzerland. Switzerland! How very enterprising and exciting! There was quite a flutter in Wickenham households at the news. Husbands coming home from the city in the evening were greeted immediately with: 'My dear, have you heard the news about the Williams?'

'No! What's up now?'

'They're off to Switzerland.'

'Switzerland! What the dickens are they going there for?'

That, of course, was only the extravagance of the moment. One knew perfectly well why people went. But nobody in Wickenham ever plunged so far away from home at that time of year. It was not considered 'necessary' – as golf, bridge, a summer holiday at the sea, an account at Harrods and a small car as soon as one could afford it, were considered necessary . . .

'Won't you find the initial expenditure very heavy?' asked stout old Mrs Prean, meeting Mrs Williams quite by chance at their nice obliging grocer's. And she brushed the crumbs of a sample cheese biscuit off her broad bosom.

'Oh, we shall get our kit over there,' said Mrs Williams.

'Kit' was a word in high favour among the Wickenham ladies. It was left over from the war, of course, with 'cheery', 'wash-out', 'Hun', 'Boche', and 'Bolshy'. As a matter of fact, Bolshy was post-war. But it belonged to the same mood. ('My dear, my housemaid is an absolute little Hun, and I'm afraid the cook is turning Bolshy . . . ') There was a fascination in those words. To use them was like opening one's Red Cross cupboard again and gazing at the remains of the bandages, body-belts, tins of anti-insecticide and so on. One was stirred, one got a far-away thrill, like the thrill of hearing a distant band. It reminded you of those exciting, busy, of course anxious, but tremendous days when the whole of Wickenham was one united family. And, although one's husband was away, one had for a substitute three large photographs of him in uniform. One in a silver frame on the table by the bed, one in the regimental colours on the piano, and one in leather to match the dining-room chairs.

'Cook strongly advised us to buy nothing here,' went on Mrs Williams.

'Cook!' cried Mrs Prean, greatly astounded. 'What can – '

'Oh – *Thomas* Cook, of course, I mean,' said Mrs Williams, smiling brightly. Mrs Prean subsided.

'But you will surely not depend upon the resources of a little Swiss village for clothes?' she persisted, deeply interested, as usual, in other people's affairs.

'Oh no, certainly not.' Mrs Williams was quite shocked. 'We shall get all we need in the way of clothes from Harrods.'

That was what Mrs Prean had wished to hear. That was as it should be.

'The great secret, my dear' (she always knew the great secret), 'the great secret' – and she put her hand on Mrs Williams' arm and spoke very distinctly – 'is plenty of long-sleeved woven combies!'

'Thank you, m'm.'

Both ladies started. There at their side was Mr Wick, the nice grocer, holding Mrs Prean's parcel by a loop of pink string. Dear me – how very awkward! He must have . . . he couldn't possibly not have . . . In the emotion of the moment Mrs Prean, thinking to gloss it over tactfully, nodded significantly at Mrs Williams and said, accepting the parcel, 'And that is what I always tell my dear son!' But this was too swift for Mrs Williams to follow.

Her embarrassment continued and, ordering the sardines, she just stopped herself from saying 'Three large pairs, Mr Wick, please,' instead of 'Three large tins.'

2

As a matter of fact it was Mrs Williams' Aunt Aggie's happy release which had made their scheme possible. Happy release it was! After fifteen years in a wheel-chair passing in and out of the little house at Ealing she had, to use the nurse's expression, 'just glided away at the last'. Glided away . . . it sounded as though Aunt Aggie had taken the wheel-chair with her. One saw her, in her absurd purple velvet, steering carefully among the stars and whimpering faintly, as was her terrestrial wont, when the wheel jolted over a particularly large one.

Aunt Aggie had left her dear niece Gwendolen two hundred and fifty pounds. Not a vast sum by any means but quite a nice little windfall. Gwendolen, in that dashing mood that only women know, decided immediately to spend it – part of it on the house and the rest on a treat for Gerald. And the lawyer's letter happening to come at tea-time together with a copy of the *Sphere* full of the most fascinating, thrilling photographs of holiday-makers at Mürren and St Moritz and Montana, the question of the treat was settled.

'You would like to go to Switzerland, wouldn't you, Gerald?'

'Very much.'

'You're – awfully good at skating and all that kind of thing – aren't you?'

'Fairly.'

'You do feel it's a thing to be done – don't you?'

'How do you mean?'

But Gwendolen only laughed. That was so like Gerald. She knew, in his heart of hearts, he was every bit as keen as she was. But he had this horror of showing his feelings – like all men. Gwendolen understood it perfectly and wouldn't have had him different for the world . . .

'I'll write to Cook's at once and tell them we don't want to go to a very fashionable place and we don't want one of those big jazzy hotels! I'd much prefer a really small out-of-the-way place where we could really go in for the sports seriously.' This was quite untrue, but, like so many of Gwendolen's statements, it was made to please Gerald. 'Don't you agree?'

Gerald lit his pipe for reply.

As you have gathered, the Christian names of Mr and Mrs Williams were Gwendolen and Gerald. How well they went together! They sounded married. Gwendolen-Gerald. Gwendolen wrote them, bracketed, on bits of blotting-paper, on the backs of old envelopes, on the Stores' catalogue. They looked married. Gerald, when they were on their honeymoon, had made an awfully good joke about them. He had said one morning, 'I say, has it ever struck you that both our names begin with *G*? Gwendolen-Gerald. You're a *G*,' and he had pointed his razor at her – he was shaving – 'and I'm a *G*. Two *Gs*. Gee-Gee. See?'

Oh, Gwendolen saw immediately. It was really most witty. Quite brilliant! And so – sweet and unexpected of him to have thought of it. Gee-Gee. Oh, *very* good! She wished she could have told it to people. She had an idea that some people thought Gerald had not a very strong sense of humour. But it was a little too intimate. All the more precious for that reason, however.

'My dear, did you think of it at this moment? I mean – did you just make it up on the spot?'

Gerald, rubbing the lather with a finger, nodded. 'Flashed into my mind while I was soaping my face,' said he seriously. 'It's a queer thing' – and he dipped the razor into the pot of hot water – 'I've noticed it before. Shaving gives me ideas.' It did, indeed, thought Gwendolen . . .

Weak Heart

ALTHOUGH IT SOUNDED all the year round, although it rang out sometimes as early as half-past six in the morning, sometimes as late as half-past ten at night, it was in the spring, when Bengel's violet patch just inside the gate was blue with flowers, that that piano . . . made the passers-by not only stop talking, but slow down, pause, look suddenly – if they were men – grave, even stern, and if they were women – dreamy, even sorrowful.

Tarana Street was beautiful in the spring; there was not a single house without its garden and trees and a plot of grass big enough to be called 'the lawn'. Over the low painted fences, you could see, as you ran by, whose daffys were out, whose wild snowdrop border was over and who had the biggest hyacinths, so pink and white, the colour of cocoanut ice. But nobody had violets that grew, that smelled in the spring sun like Bengel's. Did they really smell like that? Or did you shut your eyes and lean over the fence because of Edie Bengel's piano?

A little wind ruffles among the leaves like a joyful hand looking for the finest flowers; and the piano sounds gay, tender, laughing. Now a cloud, like a swan, flies across the sun, the violets shine cold, like water, and a sudden questioning cry rings from Edie Bengel's piano.

. . . Ah, if life must pass so quickly, why is the breath of these flowers so sweet? What is the meaning of this feeling of longing, of sweet trouble – of flying joy? Goodbye! Farewell! The young bees lie half awake on the slender dandelions, silver are the pink-tipped arrowy petals of the daisies; the new grass shakes in the light. Everything is beginning again, marvellous as ever, heavenly fair. 'Let me stay! Let me stay!' pleads Edie Bengel's piano.

It is the afternoon, sunny and still. The blinds are down in the front to save the carpets, but upstairs the slats are open and in the golden light little Mrs Bengel is feeling under her bed for the square bonnet box. She is flushed. She feels timid, excited, like a girl. And now the tissue paper is parted, her best bonnet, the one trimmed with a jet butterfly, which reposes on top, is lifted out and solemnly blown upon.

Dipping down to the glass she tries it with fingers that tremble. She twitches her dolman round her slender shoulders, clasps her purse and before leaving the bedroom kneels down a moment to ask God's blessing on her 'goings out'. And as she kneels there quivering, she is rather like a butterfly herself, fanning her wings before her Lord. When the door is open the sound of the piano coming up through the silent house is almost frightening, so bold, so defiant, so reckless it rolls under Edie's fingers. And just for a moment the thought comes to Mrs Bengel and is gone again, that there is a stranger with Edie in the drawing-room, but a fantastic person, out of a book, a – a – villain. It's very absurd. She flits across the hall, turns the door handle and confronts her flushed daughter. Edie's hands drop from the keys. She squeezes them between her knees, her head is bent, her curls are fallen forward. She gazes at her mother with brilliant eyes. There is something painful in that glance, something very strange. It is dusky in the drawing-room, the top of the piano is open. Edie has been playing from memory; it's as though the air still tingles.

'I'm going, dear,' said Mrs Bengel softly, so softly it is like a sigh.

'Yes, Mother,' came from Edie.

'I don't expect I shall be long.'

Mrs Bengel lingers. She would very much like just a word of sympathy, of understanding, even from Edie, to cheer her on her way.

But Edie murmurs, 'I'll put the kettle on in half an hour.'

'Do, dear!' Mrs Bengel grasped at that even. A nervous little smile touched her lips. 'I expect I shall want my tea.'

But to that Edie makes no reply; she frowns, she stretches out a hand, quickly unscrews one of the piano candlesticks, lifts off a pink china ring and screws all tight again. The ring has been rattling. As the front door bangs softly after her mother Edie and the piano seem to plunge together into deep dark water, into waves that flow over both, relentless. She plays on desperately until her nose is white and her heart beats. It is her way of getting over her nervousness and her way too of praying. Would they accept her? Would she be allowed to go? Was it possible that in a week's time she would be one of Miss Farmer's girls, wearing a red and blue hat-band, running up the broad steps leading to the big grey painted house that buzzed, that hummed as you went by? Their pew in Church faced Miss Farmer's boarders. Would she at last know the names of the girls she had looked at so often? The pretty pale one with red hair, the dark one with a fringe, the fair one who held Miss Farmer's hand during the sermon? . . . But after all . . .

It was Edie's fourteenth birthday. Her father gave her a silver brooch with a bar of music, two crotchets, two quavers and a minim headed by a very twisted treble clef. Her mother gave her blue satin gloves and two boxes for gloves and handkerchiefs, hand-painted the glove box with a sprig of gold roses tying up the capital G and the handkerchief box with a marvellously lifelike butterfly quivering on the capital H. From the aunts in . . .

There was a tree at the corner of Tarana Street and May Street. It grew so close to the pavement that the heavy boughs stretched over, and on that part of the pavement there was always a fine sifting of minute twigs.

But in the dusk, lovers parading came into its shade as into a tent. There, however long they had been together, they greeted each other again with long kisses, with embraces that were sweet torture, agony to bear, agony to end.

Edie never knew that Roddie 'loved' it, Roddie never knew that it meant anything to Edie.

Roddie, spruce, sleek with water, bumped his new bike down the wooden steps, through the gate. He was off for a spin, and looking at that tree, dark in the glow of evening, he felt the tree was watching him. He wanted to do marvels, to astonish, to shock, to amaze it.

Roddie had a complete new outfit for the occasion. A black serge suit, a black tie, a straw hat so white it was almost silver, a dazzling white straw hat with a broad black band. Attached to the hat there was a thick guard that somehow reminded one of a fishing line and the little clasp on the brim was like a fly . . . He stood at the graveside, his legs apart, his hands loosely clasped, and watched Edie being lowered into the grave – as a half-grown boy watches anything, a man at work, or a bicycle accident, or a chap cleaning a spring-carriage wheel – but suddenly as the men drew back he gave a violent start, turned, muttered something to his father and dashed away, so fast that people looked positively frightened, through the cemetery, down the avenue of dripping clay banks into Tarana Road, and started pelting for home. His suit was very tight and hot. It was like a dream. He kept his head down and his fists clenched, he couldn't look up, nothing could have made him look higher than the tops of the fences – What was he thinking of as he pressed along? On, on until the gate was reached, up the steps, in at the front door, through the hall, up to the drawing-room.

'Edie!' called Roddie. 'Edie, old girl!'

And he gave a low strange squawk and cried 'Edie!' and stared across at Edie's piano.

But cold, solemn, as if frozen, heavily the piano stared back at Roddie. Then it answered, but on its own behalf, on behalf of the house and the violet patch, the garden, the velvet tree at the corner of May Street, and all that was delightful: 'There is nobody here of that name, young man!'

Widowed

THEY CAME DOWN TO BREAKFAST next morning absolutely their own selves. Rosy, fresh, and just chilled enough by the cold air blowing through the bedroom windows to be very ready for hot coffee.

'Nippy.' That was Geraldine's word as she buttoned on her orange coat with pink-washed fingers. 'Don't you find it decidedly nippy?' And her voice, so matter-of-fact, so natural, sounded as though they had been married for years.

Parting his hair with two brushes (marvellous feat for a woman to watch) in the little round mirror, he had replied, lightly clapping the brushes together, 'My dear, have you got enough *on*?' and he, too, sounded as though well he knew from the experience of years her habit of clothing herself underneath in wisps of chiffon and two satin bows . . . Then they ran down to breakfast, laughing together and terribly startling the shy parlour-maid who, after talking it over with Cook, had decided to be invisible until she was rung for.

'Good morning, Nellie, I think we shall want more toast than *that*,' said the smiling Geraldine as she hung over the breakfast table. She deliberated – 'Ask Cook to make us four more pieces, please.'

Marvellous, the parlour-maid thought it was. And as she closed the door she heard the voice say, 'I do so hate to be short of toast, don't you?'

He was standing in the sunny window. Geraldine went up to him. She put her hand on his arm and gave it a gentle squeeze. How pleasant it was to feel that rough man's-tweed again. Ah, how pleasant! She rubbed her hand against it, touched it with her cheek, sniffed the smell.

The window looked out on to flower beds, a tangle of Michaelmas daisies, late dahlias, hanging heavy, and shaggy little asters. Then there came a lawn strewn with yellow leaves with a broad path

beyond and a row of gold-fluttering trees. An old gardener, in woollen
mitts, was sweeping the path, brushing the leaves into a neat little
heap. Now, the broom tucked in his arm, he fumbled in his coat
pocket, brought out some matches, and scooping a hole in the leaves
he set fire to them.

Such lovely blue smoke came breathing into the air through those
dry leaves; there was something so calm and orderly in the way
the pile burned that it was a pleasure to watch. The old gardener
stumped away and came back with a handful of withered twigs. He
flung them on and stood by, and little light flames began to flicker.

'I do think,' said Geraldine, 'I do think there is nothing nicer than
a real satisfactory fire.'

'Jolly, isn't it,' he murmured back, and they went to their first
breakfast.

Just over a year ago, thirteen months, to be exact, she had
been standing before the dining-room window of the little house in
Sloane Street. It looked over the railed gardens. Breakfast was over,
cleared away and done with . . . she had a fat bunch of letters in her
hand that she meant to answer, snugly, over the fire. But before
settling down, the autumn sun, the freshness had drawn her to the
window. Such a perfect morning for the Row. Jimmie had gone
riding.

'Goodbye, dear thing.'

'Goodbye, Gerry mine.' And then the morning kiss, quick and
firm. He looked so handsome in his riding kit. She imagined him as
she stood there . . . riding. Geraldine was not very good at imagining
things. But there was mist, a thud of hooves and Jimmie's moustache
was damp. From the garden there sounded the creak of a gardener's
barrow. An old man came into sight with a load of leaves and a
broom lying across. He stopped; he began to sweep. 'What enormous
tufts of irises grew in London gardens,' mused Geraldine. 'Why?'
And now the smoke of a real fire ascended.

'There is nothing nicer,' she thought, 'than a really satisfactory fire.'

Just at that moment the telephone bell rang. Geraldine sat down at
Jimmie's desk to answer it. It was Major Hunter.

'Good morning, Major. You're a very early bird!'

'Good morning, Mrs Howard. Yes. I am.' (Geraldine made a little
surprised face at herself. How odd he sounded!) 'Mrs Howard, I'm
coming round to see you . . . now . . . I'm taking a taxi. . . . Please
don't go out. And – and – ' the voice stammered, 'p-please don't let
the servants go out.'

'*Par*-don?' This last was so very peculiar, though the whole thing had been peculiar enough, that Geraldine couldn't believe what she heard. But he was gone. He had rung off. What on earth – and putting down the receiver, she took up a pencil and drew what she always drew when she sat down before a piece of blotting-paper – the behind of a little cat with whiskers and tail complete. Geraldine must have drawn that little cat hundreds of times, all over the world, in hotels, in clubs, at steamer desks, waiting at the bank. The little cat was her sign, her mark. She had copied it from a little girl at school when she thought it most wonderful. And she never tried anything else. She was . . . not very good at drawing. This particular cat was drawn with an extra firm pen and even its whiskers looked surprised.

'Not to let the servants go out!' But she had never heard anything so peculiar in her life. She must have made a mistake. Geraldine couldn't help a little giggle of amusement. And why should he tell her he was taking a taxi? And why – above all – should he be coming to see her at that hour of the morning?

Then – it came over her – like a flash she remembered Major Hunter's mania for old furniture. They had been discussing it at the Carlton the last time they lunched together. And he had said something to Jimmie about some – Jacobean or Queen Anne – Geraldine knew nothing about these things – something or other. Could he possibly be bringing it round? But of course. He must be. And that explained the remark about the servants. He wanted them to help getting it into the house. What a bore! Geraldine did hope it would tone in. And really, she must say she thought Major Hunter was taking a good deal for granted to produce a thing that size at that hour of the day without a word of warning. They hardly knew him well enough for that. Why make such a mystery of it too? Geraldine hated mysteries. But she had heard his head was rather troublesome at times ever since the Somme affair. Perhaps this was one of his bad days. In that case, a pity Jimmie was not back. She rang. Mullins answered.

'Oh, Mullins, I'm expecting Major Hunter in a few moments. He's bringing something rather heavy. He may want you to help with it. And Cook had better be ready too.'

Geraldine's manner was slightly lofty with her servants. She enjoyed carrying things off with a high hand. All the same, Mullins did look surprised. She seemed to hover for a moment before she went out. It annoyed Geraldine greatly. What was there to be surprised at? What could have been simpler? she thought, sitting down to her batch of letters, and the fire, and the clock and her pen began to whisper together.

There was the taxi – making an enormous noise at the door. She thought she heard the driver's voice too, arguing. It took her a long moment to clasp her writing-case and to get up out of the low chair. The bell rang. She went straight to the dining-room door –

And there was Major Hunter in his riding kit, coming quickly towards her, and behind him, through the open door at the bottom of the steps, she saw something big, something grey. It was an ambulance.

'There's been an accident,' cried Geraldine sharply.

'Mrs Howard.' Major Hunter ran forward. He put out his icy cold hand and wrung hers. 'You'll be brave, won't you?' he said, he pleaded.

But of course she would be brave.

'Is it serious?'

Major Hunter nodded gravely. He said the one word 'Yes.'

'Very serious?'

Now he raised his head. He looked her full in the eyes. She'd never realised until that moment that he was extraordinarily handsome though in a melodrama kind of way. 'It's as bad as it can be, Mrs Howard,' said Major Hunter simply. 'But – go in there,' he said hastily, and he almost pushed her into her own dining-room. 'We must bring him in – where can we – '

'Can he be taken upstairs?' asked Geraldine.

'Yes, yes, of course.' Major Hunter looked at her so strangely – so painfully.

'There's his dressing-room,' said Geraldine. 'It's on the first floor. I'll lead the way,' and she put her hand on the Major's arm. 'It's quite all right, Major,' she said, 'I'm not going to break down – ' and she actually smiled, a confident brilliant smile.

To her amazement, as Major Hunter turned away he burst out with, 'Ah, my God! I'm so sorry.'

Poor man. He was quite overcome. 'Brandy afterwards,' thought Geraldine. 'Not now, of course.'

It was a painful moment when she heard those measured deliberate steps in the hall. But Geraldine, realising this was not the moment, and there was nothing to be gained by it, refrained from looking.

'This way, Major.' She skimmed on in front, up the stairs, along the passage; she flung open the door of Jimmie's gay, living, breathing dressing-room and stood to one side – for Major Hunter, for the two stretcher-bearers. Only then she realised that it must be a scalp wound – some injury to the head. For there was nothing to be seen of Jimmie; the sheet was pulled right over . . .

SOMETHING CHILDISH
and other stories

To
H. M. TOMLINSON

First published 1924

INTRODUCTORY NOTE

Most of the stories and sketches in this collection were written in the years between the publication of Katherine Mansfield's first book, *In a German Pension*, in 1911, and the publication of her second, *Bliss and other stories*, in 1920. There are a few exceptions. The first story, 'The Tiredness of Rosabel', was written in 1908 when Katherine Mansfield was nineteen years old, and the three stories following also were written before *In a German Pension* was published: while 'Sixpence' and 'Poison' were written after 'Bliss' had appeared. 'Sixpence' was excluded from *The Garden-Party and other stories* by Katherine Mansfield because she thought it 'sentimental'; 'Poison' was excluded because I thought it was not wholly successful. I have since changed my mind: it now seems to me a little masterpiece.

I have no doubt that Katherine Mansfield, were she still alive, would not have suffered some of these stories to appear. When she was urged to allow *In a German Pension* to be republished, she would always reply: 'Not now; not yet – not until I have a body of work done and it can be seen in perspective. It is not true of me now: I am not like that any more. When the time for a collected edition comes – ' she would end, laughing. The time has come.

The stories are arranged in chronological order.

J. M. M.

The Tiredness of Rosabel

AT THE CORNER of Oxford Circus Rosabel bought a bunch of violets, and that was practically the reason why she had so little tea – for a scone and a boiled egg and a cup of cocoa at Lyons are not ample sufficiency after a hard day's work in a millinery establishment. As she swung on to the step of the Atlas bus, grabbed her skirt with one hand and clung to the railing with the other, Rosabel thought she would have sacrificed her soul for a good dinner – roast duck and green peas, chestnut stuffing, pudding with brandy sauce – something hot and strong and filling. She sat down next to a girl very much her own age who was reading *Anna Lombard* in a cheap, paper-covered edition, and the rain had tear-spattered the pages. Rosabel looked out of the windows; the street was blurred and misty, but light striking on the panes turned their dullness to opal and silver, and the jewellers' shops seen through this, were fairy palaces. Her feet were horribly wet, and she knew the bottom of her skirt and petticoat would be coated with black, greasy mud. There was a sickening smell of warm humanity – it seemed to be oozing out of everybody in the bus – and everybody had the same expression, sitting so still, staring in front of them. How many times had she read these advertisements – 'Sapolio Saves Time, Saves Labour' – 'Heinz's Tomato Sauce' – and the inane, annoying dialogue between doctor and judge concerning the superlative merits of 'Lamplough's Pyretic Saline'. She glanced at the book which the girl read so earnestly, mouthing the words in a way that Rosabel detested, licking her first finger and thumb each time that she turned the page. She could not see very clearly; it was something about a hot, voluptuous night, a band playing, and a girl with lovely, white shoulders. Oh, heavens! Rosabel stirred suddenly and unfastened the two top buttons of her coat . . . she felt almost stifled. Through her half-closed eyes the whole row of people on the opposite seat seemed to resolve into one fatuous, staring face . . .

And this was her corner. She stumbled a little on her way out and lurched against the girl next her. 'I beg your pardon,' said Rosabel, but the girl did not even look up. Rosabel saw that she was smiling as she read.

Westbourne Grove looked as she had always imagined Venice to look at night, mysterious, dark, even the hansoms were like gondolas dodging up and down, and the lights trailing luridly – tongues of flame licking the wet street – magic fish swimming in the Grand Canal. She was more than glad to reach Richmond Road, but from the corner of the street until she came to No. 26 she thought of those four flights of stairs. Oh, why four flights! It was really criminal to expect people to live so high up. Every house ought to have a lift, something simple and inexpensive, or else an electric staircase like the one at Earl's Court – but four flights! When she stood in the hall and saw the first flight ahead of her and the stuffed albatross head on the landing, glimmering ghost-like in the light of the little gas jet, she almost cried. Well, they had to be faced; it was very like bicycling up a steep hill, but there was not the satisfaction of flying down the other side . . .

Her own room at last! She closed the door, lit the gas, took off her hat and coat, skirt, blouse, unhooked her old flannel dressing-gown from behind the door, pulled it on, then unlaced her boots – on consideration her stockings were not wet enough to change. She went over to the wash-stand. The jug had not been filled again today. There was just enough water to soak the sponge, and the enamel was coming off the basin – that was the second time she had scratched her chin.

It was just seven o'clock. If she pulled the blind up and put out the gas it was much more restful – Rosabel did not want to read. So she knelt down on the floor, pillowing her arms on the window-sill . . . just one little sheet of glass between her and the great wet world outside!

She began to think of all that had happened during the day. Would she ever forget that awful woman in the grey mackintosh who had wanted a trimmed motor-cap – 'something purple with something rosy each side' – or the girl who had tried on every hat in the shop and then said she would 'call in tomorrow and decide definitely'. Rosabel could not help smiling; the excuse was worn so thin . . .

But there had been one other – a girl with beautiful red hair and a white skin and eyes the colour of that green ribbon shot with gold they had got from Paris last week. Rosabel had seen her electric brougham at the door; a man had come in with her, quite a young man, and so well dressed.

'What is it exactly that I want, Harry?' she had said, as Rosabel took the pins out of her hat, untied her veil, and gave her a hand-mirror.

'You must have a black hat,' he had answered, 'a black hat with a feather that goes right round it and then round your neck and ties in a bow under your chin, and the ends tuck into your belt – a decent-sized feather.'

The girl glanced at Rosabel laughingly. 'Have you any hats like that?'

They had been very hard to please; Harry would demand the impossible, and Rosabel was almost in despair. Then she remembered the big, untouched box upstairs.

'Oh, one moment, Madam,' she had said. 'I think perhaps I can show you something that will please you better.' She had run up, breathlessly, cut the cords, scattered the tissue paper, and yes, there was the very hat – rather large, soft, with a great, curled feather, and a black velvet rose, nothing else. They had been charmed. The girl had put it on and then handed it to Rosabel.

'Let me see how it looks on you,' she said, frowning a little, very serious indeed.

Rosabel turned to the mirror and placed it on her brown hair, then faced them.

'Oh, Harry, isn't it adorable,' the girl cried, 'I must have that!' She smiled again at Rosabel. 'It suits you beautifully.'

A sudden, ridiculous feeling of anger had seized Rosabel. She longed to throw the lovely, perishable thing in the girl's face, and bent over the hat, flushing.

'It's exquisitely finished off inside, Madam,' she said. The girl swept out to her brougham, and left Harry to pay and bring the box with him.

'I shall go straight home and put it on before I come out to lunch with you,' Rosabel heard her say.

The man leant over her as she made out the bill, then, as he counted the money into her hand – 'Ever been painted?' he said.

'No,' said Rosabel shortly, realising the swift change in his voice, the slight tinge of insolence, of familiarity.

'Oh, well you ought to be,' said Harry. 'You've got such a damned pretty little figure.'

Rosabel did not pay the slightest attention. How handsome he had been! She had thought of no one else all day; his face fascinated her; she could see clearly his fine, straight eyebrows, and his hair grew back from his forehead with just the slightest suspicion of crisp curl, his laughing, disdainful mouth. She saw again his slim hands counting the money into hers . . . Rosabel suddenly pushed the hair back from her face, her forehead was hot . . . if those slim hands could rest one moment . . . the luck of that girl!

Suppose they changed places. Rosabel would drive home with him, of course they were in love with each other, but not engaged, very nearly, and she would say – 'I won't be one moment.' He would wait in the brougham while her maid took the hat-box up the stairs, following Rosabel. Then the great, white and pink bedroom with roses everywhere in dull silver vases. She would sit down before the mirror and the little French maid would fasten her hat and find her a thin, fine veil and another pair of white suede gloves – a button had come off the gloves she had worn that morning. She had scented her furs and gloves and handkerchief, taken a big muff and run downstairs. The butler opened the door, Harry was waiting, they drove away together . . . *That* was life, thought Rosabel! On the way to the Carlton they stopped at Gerard's, Harry bought her great sprays of Parma violets, filled her hands with them.

'Oh, they are sweet!' she said, holding them against her face.

'It is as you always should be,' said Harry, 'with your hands full of violets.'

(Rosabel realised that her knees were getting stiff; she sat down on the floor and leant her head against the wall.) Oh, that lunch! The table covered with flowers, a band hidden behind a grove of palms playing music that fired her blood like wine – the soup, and oysters, and pigeons, and creamed potatoes, and champagne, of course, and afterwards coffee and cigarettes. She would lean over the table fingering her glass with one hand, talking with that charming gaiety which Harry so appreciated. Afterwards a matinée, something that gripped them both, and then tea at the 'Cottage'.

'Sugar? Milk? Cream?' The little homely questions seemed to suggest a joyous intimacy. And then home again in the dusk, and the scent of the Parma violets seemed to drench the air with their sweetness.

'I'll call for you at nine,' he said as he left her.

The fire had been lighted in her boudoir, the curtains drawn, there were a great pile of letters waiting her – invitations for the Opera, dinners, balls, a weekend on the river, a motor tour – she glanced through them listlessly as she went upstairs to dress. A fire in her bedroom, too, and her beautiful, shining dress spread on the bed –

white tulle over silver, silver shoes, silver scarf, a little silver fan. Rosabel knew that she was the most famous woman at the ball that night; men paid her homage, a foreign Prince desired to be presented to this English wonder. Yes, it was a voluptuous night, a band playing, and *her* lovely white shoulders . . .

But she became very tired. Harry took her home, and came in with her for just one moment. The fire was out in the drawing-room, but the sleepy maid waited for her in her boudoir. She took off her cloak, dismissed the servant, and went over to the fireplace, and stood peeling off her gloves; the firelight shone on her hair, Harry came across the room and caught her in his arms – 'Rosabel, Rosabel, Rosabel . . . ' Oh, the haven of those arms, and she was very tired.

(The real Rosabel, the girl crouched on the floor in the dark, laughed aloud, and put her hand up to her hot mouth.)

Of course they rode in the park next morning, the engagement had been announced in the *Court Circular*, all the world knew, all the world was shaking hands with her . . .

They were married shortly afterwards at St George's, Hanover Square, and motored down to Harry's old ancestral home for the honeymoon; the peasants in the village curtseyed to them as they passed; under the folds of the rug he pressed her hands convulsively. And that night she wore again her white and silver frock. She was tired after the journey and went upstairs to bed . . . quite early . . .

The real Rosabel got up from the floor and undressed slowly, folding her clothes over the back of a chair. She slipped over her head her coarse, calico nightdress, and took the pins out of her hair – the soft, brown flood of it fell round her, warmly. Then she blew out the candle and groped her way into bed, pulling the blankets and grimy 'honeycomb' quilt closely round her neck, cuddling down in the darkness . . .

So she slept and dreamed, and smiled in her sleep, and once threw out her arm to feel for something which was not there, dreaming still.

And the night passed. Presently the cold fingers of dawn closed over her uncovered hand; grey light flooded the dull room. Rosabel shivered, drew a little gasping breath, sat up. And because her heritage was that tragic optimism, which is all too often the only inheritance of youth, still half asleep, she smiled, with a little nervous tremor round her mouth.

(1908)

How Pearl Button was Kidnapped

PEARL BUTTON swung on the little gate in front of the House of Boxes. It was the early afternoon of a sunshiny day with little winds playing hide-and-seek in it. They blew Pearl Button's pinafore frill into her mouth, and they blew the street dust all over the House of Boxes. Pearl watched it – like a cloud – like when mother peppered her fish and the top of the pepper-pot came off. She swung on the little gate, all alone, and she sang a small song. Two big women came walking down the street. One was dressed in red and the other was dressed in yellow and green. They had pink handkerchiefs over their heads, and both of them carried a big flax basket of ferns. They had no shoes and stockings on, and they came walking along, slowly, because they were so fat, and talking to each other and always smiling. Pearl stopped swinging, and when they saw her they stopped walking. They looked and looked at her and then they talked to each other, waving their arms and clapping their hands together. Pearl began to laugh.

The two women came up to her, keeping close to the hedge and looking in a frightened way towards the House of Boxes.

'Hallo, little girl!' said one.

Pearl said, 'Hallo!'

'You all alone by yourself?'

Pearl nodded.

'Where's your mother?'

'In the kitching, ironing-because-its-Tuesday.'

The women smiled at her and Pearl smiled back. 'Oh,' she said, 'haven't you got very white teeth indeed! Do it again.'

The dark women laughed, and again they talked to each other with funny words and wavings of the hands. 'What's your name?' they asked her.

'Pearl Button.'

'You coming with us, Pearl Button? We got beautiful things to show you,' whispered one of the women. So Pearl got down from the gate and she slipped out into the road. And she walked between the two dark women down the windy road, taking little running steps to keep up, and wondering what they had in their House of Boxes.

They walked a long way. 'You tired?' asked one of the women, bending down to Pearl. Pearl shook her head. They walked much further. 'You not tired?' asked the other woman. And Pearl shook her head again, but tears shook from her eyes at the same time and her lips trembled. One of the women gave over her flax basket of ferns and caught Pearl Button up in her arms, and walked with Pearl Button's head against her shoulder and her dusty little legs dangling. She was softer than a bed and she had a nice smell – a smell that made you bury your head and breathe and breathe it . . .

They set Pearl Button down in a log room full of other people the same colour as they were – and all these people came close to her and looked at her, nodding and laughing and throwing up their eyes. The woman who had carried Pearl took off her hair ribbon and shook her curls loose. There was a cry from the other women, and they crowded close and some of them ran a finger through Pearl's yellow curls, very gently, and one of them, a young one, lifted all Pearl's hair and kissed the back of her little white neck. Pearl felt shy but happy at the same time. There were some men on the floor, smoking, with rugs and feather mats round their shoulders. One of them made a funny face at her and he pulled a great big peach out of his pocket and set it on the floor, and flicked it with his finger as though it were a marble. It rolled right over to her. Pearl picked it up. 'Please can I eat it?' she asked. At that they all laughed and clapped their hands, and the man with the funny face made another at her and pulled a pear out of his pocket and sent it bobbling over the floor. Pearl laughed. The women sat on the floor and Pearl sat down too. The floor was very dusty. She carefully pulled up her pinafore and dress and sat on her petticoat as she had been taught to sit in dusty places, and she ate the fruit, the juice running all down her front.

'Oh!' she said in a very frightened voice to one of the women, 'I've spilt all the juice!'

'That doesn't matter at all,' said the woman, patting her cheek. A man came into the room with a long whip in his hand. He shouted something. They all got up, shouting, laughing, wrapping themselves up in rugs and blankets and feather mats. Pearl was carried again, this time into a great cart, and she sat on the lap of one of her women with the driver beside her. It was a green cart with a red pony and a black pony. It went very fast out of the town. The driver stood up and waved the whip round his head. Pearl peered over the shoulder of her woman. Other carts were behind like a procession. She waved at them. Then the country came. First fields of short grass with sheep on them and little bushes of white flowers and pink briar rose baskets – then big trees on both sides of the road – and nothing to be seen except big trees. Pearl tried to look through them but it was quite dark. Birds were singing. She nestled closer in the big lap. The woman was warm as a cat, and she moved up and down when she breathed, just like purring. Pearl played with a green ornament round her neck, and the woman took the little hand and kissed each of her fingers and then turned it over and kissed the dimples. Pearl had never been happy like this before. On the top of a big hill they stopped. The driving man turned to Pearl and said, 'Look, look!' and pointed with his whip.

And down at the bottom of the hill was something perfectly different – a great big piece of blue water was creeping over the land. She screamed and clutched at the big woman. 'What is it, what is it?'

'Why,' said the woman, 'it's the sea.'

'Will it hurt us – is it coming?'

'Ai-e, no, it doesn't come to us. It's very beautiful. You look again.'

Pearl looked. 'You're sure it can't come,' she said.

'Ai-e, no. It stays in its place,' said the big woman. Waves with white tops came leaping over the blue. Pearl watched them break on a long piece of land covered with garden-path shells. They drove round a corner.

There were some little houses down close to the sea, with wood fences round them and gardens inside. They comforted her. Pink and red and blue washing hung over the fences, and as they came near more people came out, and five yellow dogs with long thin tails. All the people were fat and laughing, with little naked babies holding on to them or rolling about in the gardens like puppies. Pearl was lifted down and taken into a tiny house with only one room and a veranda. There was a girl there with two pieces of black hair down to her feet. She was setting the dinner on the floor. 'It *is* a funny place,' said Pearl, watching the pretty girl while the woman unbuttoned her little drawers for her. She was very hungry. She ate meat and vegetables and fruit and the woman gave her milk out of a green cup. And it was quite silent except for the sea outside and the laughs of the two women watching her. 'Haven't you got any Houses of Boxes?' she said. 'Don't you all live in a row? Don't the men go to offices? Aren't there any nasty things?'

They took off her shoes and stockings, her pinafore and dress. She walked about in her petticoat and then she walked outside with the grass pushing between her toes. The two women came out with different sorts of baskets. They took her hands. Over a little paddock, through a fence, and then on warm sand with brown grass in it they went down to the sea. Pearl held back when the sand grew wet, but the women coaxed, 'Nothing to hurt, very beautiful. You come.' They dug in the sand and found some shells which they threw into the baskets. The sand was wet as mud pies. Pearl forgot her fright and began digging too. She got hot and wet, and suddenly over her feet broke a little line of foam. 'Oo, oo!' she shrieked, dabbling with her feet. 'Lovely, lovely!' She paddled in the shallow water. It was warm. She made a cup of her hands and caught some of it. But it stopped being blue in her hands. She was so excited that she rushed over to her woman and flung her little thin arms round the woman's neck, hugging her, kissing . . .

Suddenly the girl gave a frightful scream. The woman raised herself and Pearl slipped down on the sand and looked towards the land. Little men in blue coats – little blue men came running, running towards her with shouts and whistlings – a crowd of little blue men to carry her back to the House of Boxes.

(1910)

The Journey to Bruges

'YOU GOT THREE-QUARTERS of an hour,' said the porter. 'You got an hour mostly. Put it in the cloak-room, lady.'

A German family, their luggage neatly buttoned into what appeared to be odd canvas trouser legs, filled the entire space before the counter, and a homeopathic young clergyman, his black dicky flapping over his shirt, stood at my elbow. We waited and waited, for the cloak-room porter could not get rid of the German family, who appeared by their enthusiasm and gestures to be explaining to him the virtue of so many buttons. At last the wife of the party seized her particular packet and started to undo it. Shrugging his shoulders, the porter turned to me. 'Where for?' he asked.

'Ostend.'

'Wot are you putting it in here for?'

I said, 'Because I've a long time to wait.'

He shouted, 'Train's in 2.20. No good bringing it here. Hi, you there, lump it off!'

My porter lumped it. The young clergyman, who had listened and remarked, smiled at me radiantly. 'The train is in,' he said, 'really in. You've only a few moments, you know.' My sensitiveness glimpsed a symbol in his eye. I ran to the bookstall. When I returned I had lost my porter. In the teasing heat I ran up and down the platform. The whole travelling world seemed to possess a porter and glory in him except me. Savage and wretched I saw them watch me with that delighted relish of the hot in the very much hotter. 'One could have a fit running in weather like this,' said a stout lady, eating a farewell present of grapes. Then I was informed that the train was not yet in. I had been running up and down the Folkestone express. On a higher platform I found my porter sitting on the suitcase.

'I knew you'd be doin' that,' he said airily. 'I nearly come and stop you. I seen you from 'ere.'

I dropped into a smoking compartment with four young men, two of whom were saying goodbye to a pale youth with a cane. 'Well, goodbye, old chap. It's frightfully good of you to have come down. I knew you. I knew the same old slouch. Now, look here, when we come back we'll have a night of it. What? Ripping of you to have come, old man.' This from an enthusiast, who lit a cigar as the train swung out, turned to his companion and said, 'Frightfully nice chap, but – lord – what a bore!' His companion, who was dressed entirely in mole, even unto his socks and hair, smiled gently. I think his brain must have been the same colour: he proved so gentle and sympathetic a listener. In the opposite corner to me sat a beautiful young Frenchman with curly hair and a watch-chain from which dangled a silver fish, a ring, a silver shoe, and a medal. He stared out of the window the whole time, faintly twitching his nose. Of the remaining member there was nothing to be seen from behind his luggage but a pair of tan shoes and a copy of *The Snark's Summer Annual*.

'Look here, old man,' said the Enthusiast, 'I want to change all our places. You know those arrangements you've made – I want to cut them out altogether. Do you mind?'

'No,' said the Mole faintly. 'But why?'

'Well, I was thinking it over in bed last night, and I'm hanged if I can see the good of us paying fifteen bob if we don't want to. You see what I mean?' The Mole took off his pince-nez and breathed on them. 'Now I don't want to unsettle you,' went on the Enthusiast, 'because, after all, it's your party – you asked me. I wouldn't upset it for anything, but – there you are – you see – what?'

Suggested the Mole: 'I'm afraid people will be down on me for taking you abroad.'

Straightway the other told him how sought after he had been. From far and near, people who were full up for the entire month of August had written and begged for him. He wrung the Mole's heart by enumerating those longing homes and vacant chairs dotted all over England, until the Mole deliberated between crying and going to sleep. He chose the latter.

They all went to sleep except the young Frenchman, who took a little pocket edition out of his coat and nursed it on his knee while he gazed at the warm, dusty country. At Shorncliffe the train stopped. Dead silence. There was nothing to be seen but a large white cemetery. Fantastic it looked in the late afternoon sun, its full-length marble angels appearing to preside over a cheerless picnic of the Shorncliffe departed on the brown field. One white butterfly flew over the railway lines. As we crept out of the station I saw a poster advertising the *Athenaeum*. The Enthusiast grunted and yawned, shook himself into existence by rattling the money in his trouser pockets. He jabbed the Mole in the ribs. 'I say, we're nearly there! Can you get down those beastly golf-clubs of mine from the rack?' My heart yearned over the Mole's immediate future, but he was cheerful and offered to find me a porter at Dover, and strapped my parasol in with my rugs. We saw the sea. 'It's going to be beastly rough,' said the Enthusiast. 'Gives you a head, doesn't it? Look here, I know a tip for sea-sickness, and it's this: You lie on your back – flat – you know, cover your face, and eat nothing but biscuits.'

'Dover!' shouted a guard.

In the act of crossing the gangway we renounced England. The most blatant British female produced her mite of French: we 'S'il vous plaît?'d one another on the deck, 'Merci'd one another on the stairs, and 'Pardon'd to our heart's content in the saloon. The stewardess stood at the foot of the stairs, a stout, forbidding female, pock-marked, her hands hidden under a businesslike-looking apron. She replied to our salutations with studied indifference, mentally ticking off her prey. I descended to the cabin to remove my hat. One old lady was already established there.

She lay on a rose and white couch, a black shawl tucked round her, fanning herself with a black feather fan. Her grey hair was half covered with a lace cap and her face gleamed from the black drapings and rose pillows with charming old-world dignity. There was about her a faint rustling and the scents of camphor and lavender. As I watched her, thinking of Rembrandt and, for some reason, Anatole France, the stewardess bustled up, placed a canvas stool at her elbow, spread a newspaper upon it, and banged down a receptacle rather like a baking tin . . .

I went up on deck. The sea was bright green, with rolling waves. All the beauty and artificial flower of France had removed their hats and bound their heads in veils. A number of young German men, displaying their national bulk in light-coloured suits cut in the pattern of pyjamas, promenaded. French family parties – the female element in chairs, the male in graceful attitudes against the ship's side – talked already with that brilliance which denotes friction! I found a chair in a corner against a white partition, but unfortunately this partition had a window set in it for the purpose of providing endless amusement for the curious, who peered through it, watching those bold and brave spirits who walked 'for'ard' and were drenched and beaten by the waves. In the first half-hour the excitement of getting wet and being pleaded with, and rushing into dangerous places to return and be rubbed down, was all-absorbing. Then it palled – the parties drifted into silence. You would catch them staring intently at the ocean – and yawning. They grew cold and snappy. Suddenly a young lady in a white woollen hood with cherry bows got up from her chair and swayed over to the railings. We watched her, vaguely sympathetic. The young man with whom she had been sitting called to her.

'Are you better?' Negative expressed.

He sat up in his chair. 'Would you like me to hold your head?'

'No,' said her shoulders.

'Would you care for a coat round you? . . . Is it over? . . . Are you going to remain there?' . . . He looked at her with infinite tenderness. I decided never again to call men unsympathetic, and to believe in the all-conquering power of love until I died – but never put it to the test. I went down to sleep.

I lay down opposite the old lady, and watched the shadows spinning over the ceilings and the wave-drops shining on the portholes.

In the shortest sea voyage there is no sense of time. You have been down in the cabin for hours or days or years. Nobody knows or cares. You know all the people to the point of indifference. You do not believe in dry land any more – you are caught in the pendulum itself, and left there, idly swinging. The light faded.

I fell asleep, to wake to find the stewardess shaking me. 'We are there in two minutes,' said she. Forlorn ladies, freed from the embrace of Neptune, knelt upon the floor and searched for their shoes and hairpins – only the old and dignified one lay passive, fanning herself. She looked at me and smiled.

'*Grâce de Dieu, c'est fini*,' she quavered in a voice so fine it seemed to quaver on a thread of lace.

I lifted up my eyes. '*Oui, c'est fini!*'

'*Vous allez à Strasbourg, Madame?*'

'No,' I said. 'Bruges.'

'That is a great pity,' said she, closing her fan and the conversation. I could not think why, but I had visions of myself perhaps travelling in the same railway carriage with her, wrapping her in the black shawl, of her falling in love with me and leaving me unlimited quantities of money and old lace . . . These sleepy thoughts pursued me until I arrived on deck.

The sky was indigo blue, and a great many stars were shining: our little ship stood black and sharp in the clear air. 'Have you the tickets? . . . Yes, they want the tickets . . . Produce your tickets!' . . .

We were squeezed over the gangway, shepherded into the custom-house, where porters heaved our luggage on to long wooden slabs, and an old man wearing horn spectacles checked it without a word. 'Follow me!' shouted the villainous-looking creature whom I had endowed with my worldly goods. He leapt on to a railway line, and I leapt after him. He raced along a platform, dodging the passengers and fruit wagons, with the security of a cinematograph figure. I reserved a seat and went to buy fruit at a little stall displaying grapes and greengages. The old lady was there, leaning on the arm of a large blond man, in white, with a flowing tie. We nodded.

'Buy me,' she said in her delicate voice, 'three ham sandwiches, *mon cher*!'

'And some cakes,' said he.

'Yes, and perhaps a bottle of lemonade.'

'Romance is an imp!' thought I, climbing up into the carriage. The train swung out of the station; the air, blowing through the open windows, smelled of fresh leaves. There were sudden pools of light in the darkness; when I arrived at Bruges the bells were ringing, and white and mysterious shone the moon over the Grand' Place.

(1910)

A Truthful Adventure

'THE LITTLE TOWN lies spread before the gaze of the eager traveller like a faded tapestry threaded with the silver of its canals, made musical by the great chiming belfry. Life is long since asleep in Bruges; fantastic dreams alone breathe over tower and mediaeval house front, enchanting the eye, inspiring the soul and filling the mind with the great beauty of contemplation.'

I read this sentence from a guide-book while waiting for Madame in the hotel sitting-room. It sounded extremely comforting, and my tired heart, tucked away under a thousand and one grey city wrappings, woke and exulted within me . . . I wondered if I had enough clothes with me to last for at least a month. 'I shall dream away whole days,' I thought, 'take a boat and float up and down the canals, or tether it to a green bush tangling the water side, and absorb mediaeval house fronts. At evensong I shall lie in the long grass of the Béguinage meadow and look up at the elm trees – their leaves touched with gold light and quivering in the blue air – listening the while to the voices of nuns at prayer in the little chapel, and growing full enough of grace to last me the whole winter.'

While I soared magnificently upon these very new feathers Madame came in and told me that there was no room at all for me in the hotel – not a bed, not a corner. She was extremely friendly and seemed to find a fund of secret amusement in the fact; she looked at me as though expecting me to break into delighted laughter. 'To-morrow,' she said, 'there may be. I am expecting a young gentleman who is suddenly taken ill to move from number eleven. He is at present at the chemist's – perhaps you would care to see the room?'

'Not at all,' said I. 'Neither shall I wish tomorrow to sleep in the bedroom of an indisposed young gentleman.'

'But he will be gone,' cried Madame, opening her blue eyes wide and laughing with that French cordiality so enchanting to English hearing. I was too tired and hungry to feel either appreciative or argumentative. 'Perhaps you can recommend me another hotel?'

'Impossible!' She shook her head and turned up her eyes, mentally counting over the blue bows painted on the ceiling. 'You see, it is the season in Bruges, and people do not care to let their rooms for a very short time' – not a glance at my little suitcase lying between us, but I looked at it gloomily, and it seemed to dwindle before my desperate gaze – become small enough to hold nothing but a collapsible folding tooth-brush.

'My large box is at the station,' I said coldly, buttoning my gloves. Madame started. 'You have more luggage . . . Then you intend to make a long stay in Bruges, perhaps?'

'At least a fortnight – perhaps a month.' I shrugged my shoulders.

'One moment,' said Madame. 'I shall see what I can do.' She disappeared, I am sure not further than the other side of the door, for she reappeared immediately and told me I might have a room at her private house – 'just round the corner and kept by an old servant who, although she has a wall eye, has been in our family for fifteen years. The porter will take you there, and you can have supper before you go.'

I was the only guest in the dining-room. A tired waiter provided me with an omelette and a pot of coffee, then leaned against a sideboard and watched me while I ate, the limp table napkin over his arm seeming to symbolise the very man. The room was hung with mirrors reflecting unlimited empty tables and watchful waiters and solitary ladies finding sad comfort in omelettes, and sipping coffee to the rhythm of Mendelssohn's 'Spring Song' played over three times by the great chiming belfry.

'Are you ready, Madame?' asked the waiter. 'It is I who carry your luggage.'

'Quite ready.'

He heaved the suitcase on to his shoulder and strode before me – past the little pavement cafés where men and women, scenting our approach, laid down their beer and their postcards to stare after us, down a narrow street of shuttered houses, through the Place van Eyck, to a red-brick house. The door was opened by the wall-eyed family treasure, who held a candle like a miniature frying-pan in her hand. She refused to admit us until we had both told the whole story.

'C'est ça, c'est ça,' said she. 'Jean, number five!'

She shuffled up the stairs, unlocked a door and lit another miniature frying-pan upon the bed-table. The room was papered in pink, having a pink bed, a pink door and a pink chair. On pink mats on the mantelpiece obese young cherubs burst out of pink eggshells with trumpets in their mouths. I was brought a can of hot water; I shut and locked the door. 'Bruges at last,' I thought as I climbed into a bed so slippery with fine linen that one felt like a fish endeavouring to swim over an ice pond, and this quiet house with the old 'typical' servant – the Place van Eyck, with the white statue surrounded by those dark and heavy trees – there was almost a touch of Verlaine in that . . .

Bang! went the door. I started up in terror and felt for the frying-pan, but it was the room next to mine suddenly invaded. 'Ah! home at last,' cried a female voice. '*Mon Dieu*, my feet! Would you go down to Marie, *mon cher*, and ask her for the tin bath and some hot water?'

'No, that is too much,' boomed the answer. 'You have washed them three times today already.'

'But you do not know the pain I suffer; they are quite inflamed. Look only!'

'I have looked three times already; I am tired. I beg of you come to bed.'

'It would be useless; I could not sleep. *Mon Dieu, mon Dieu*, how a woman suffers!' A masculine snort accompanied by the sounds of undressing.

'Then, if I wait until the morning will you promise not to drag me to a picture gallery?'

'Yes, yes, I promise.'

'But truly?'

'I have said so.'

'Now can I believe you?'

A long groan.

'It is absurd to make that noise, for you know yourself the same thing happened last evening and this morning.'

. . . There was only one thing to be done. I coughed and cleared my throat in that unpleasant and obtrusive way of strange people in next-door bedrooms. It acted like a charm, their conversation sifted into a whisper for female voice only! I fell asleep.

'Barquettes for hire. Visit the Venice of the North by boat. Explore the little known and fascinating by-ways.' With the memory of the guide-book clinging about me I went into the shop and demanded a boat. 'Have you a small canoe?'

'No, Mademoiselle, but a little boat – very suitable.'

'I wish to go alone and return when I like.'

'Then you have been here before?'

'No.'

450 SOMETHING CHILDISH AND OTHER STORIES

The boatman looked puzzled. 'It is not safe for Mademoiselle to go without a guide for the first time.'

'Then I will take one on the condition that he is silent and points out no beauties to me.'

'But the names of the bridges?' cried the boatman – 'the famous house fronts?'

I ran down to the landing stage. 'Pierre, Pierre!' called the water-man. A burly young Belgian, his arms full of carpet strips and red velvet pillows, appeared and tossed his spoil into an immense craft. On the bridge above the landing stage a crowd collected, watching the proceedings, and just as I took my seat a fat couple who had been hanging over the parapet rushed down the steps and declared they must come too. 'Certainly, certainly,' said Pierre, handing in the lady with charming grace. 'Mademoiselle will not mind at all.' They sat in the stern, the gentleman held the lady's hand, and we twisted among these 'silver ribbons' while Pierre threw out his chest and chanted the beauties of Bruges with the exultant abandon of a Latin lover. 'Turn your head this way – to the left – to the right – now, wait one moment – look up at the bridge – observe this house front. Mademoiselle, do you wish to see the Lac d'Amour?'

I looked vague; the fat couple answered for me.

'Then we shall disembark.'

We rowed close into a little parapet. We caught hold of a bush and I jumped out. 'Now, Monsieur,' who successfully followed, and, kneeling on the bank, gave Madame the crook of his walking-stick for support. She stood up, smiling and vigorous, clutched the walking-stick, strained against the boat side and the next moment had fallen flat into the water. 'Ah! what has happened – what has happened!' screamed Monsieur, clutching her arm, for the water was not deep, reaching only to her waist mark. Somehow or other we fished her up on to the bank, where she sat and gasped, wringing her black alpaca skirt.

'It is all over – a little accident!' said she, amazingly cheerful.

But Pierre was furious. 'It is the fault of Mademoiselle for wishing to see the Lac d'Amour,' said he. 'Madame had better walk though the meadow and drink something hot at the little café opposite.'

'No, no,' said she, but Monsieur seconded Pierre.

'You will await our return,' said Pierre, loathing me. I nodded and turned my back, for the sight of Madame flopping about on the meadow grass like a large, ungainly duck was too much. One cannot expect to travel in upholstered boats with people who are enlightened enough to understand laughter that has its wellspring in sympathy. When they were out of sight I ran as fast as I could over the meadow, crawled through a fence and never went near the Lac d'Amour again. 'They may think me as drowned as they please,' thought I, 'I have had quite enough of canals to last me a lifetime.'

In the Béguinage meadow at evensong little groups of painters are dotted about in the grass with spindle-legged easels which seem to possess a separate individuality and stand rudely defying their efforts and returning their long, long gaze with an unfinished stare. English girls wearing flower-wreathed hats and the promise of young American manhood give expression to their souls with a gaiety and 'camaraderie', sort of 'the world is our shining play-ground' spirit – theoretically delightful. They call to one another and throw cigarettes and fruit and chocolates with youthful naïveté, while parties of tourists who have escaped the clutches of an old woman lying in wait for them in the shadow of the chapel door pause thoughtfully in front of the easels to 'see and remark, and say whose?'

I was lying under a tree with the guilty consciousness of no sketchbook – watching the swifts wheel and dip in the bright air, and wondering if all the brown dogs resting in the grass belonged to the young painters, when two people passed me, a man and a girl, their heads bent over a book. There was something vaguely familiar in their walk. Suddenly they looked down at me – we stared – opened our mouths. She swooped down upon me, and he took off his immaculate straw hat and placed it under his left arm.

'Katherine! How extraordinary! How incredible after all these years!' cried she. Turning to the man: 'Guy, can you believe it? – It's Katherine, in Bruges of all places in the world!'

'Why not?' said I, looking very bright and trying to remember her name.

'But, my dear, the last time we met was in New Zealand – only think of the miles!'

Of course, she was Betty Sinclair; I'd been to school with her.

'Where are you staying – have you been here long? Oh, you haven't changed a day – not a day. I'd have known you anywhere.'

She beckoned to the young man, and said, blushing as though she were ashamed of the fact, but it had to be faced, 'This is my husband.' We shook hands. He sat down and chewed a grass twig. Silence fell while Betty recovered breath and squeezed my hand.

'I didn't know you were married,' I said stupidly.

'Oh, my dear – got a baby!' said Betty. 'We live in England now. We're frightfully keen on the Suffrage, you know.'

Guy removed the straw. 'Are you with us?' he asked, intensely.

I shook my head. He put the straw back again and narrowed his eyes.

'Then here's the opportunity,' said Betty. 'My dear, how long are you going to stay? We must go about together and have long talks. Guy and I aren't a honeymoon couple, you know. We love to have other people with us sometimes.'

The belfry clashed into 'See the Conquering Hero Comes!'

'Unfortunately I have to go home quite soon. I've had an urgent letter.'

'How disappointing! You know Bruges is simply packed with treasures and churches and pictures. There's an outdoor concert tonight in the Grand' Place, and a competition of bell-ringers tomorrow to go on for a whole week.'

'Go I must,' I said, so firmly that my soul felt imperative marching orders, stimulated by the belfry.

'But the quaint streets and the Continental smells, and the lace-makers – if we could just wander about – we three – and absorb it all.' I sighed and bit my underlip.

'What's your objection to the vote?' asked Guy, watching the nuns wending their way in sweet procession among the trees.

'I always had the idea you were so frightfully keen on the future of women,' said Betty. 'Come to dinner with us tonight. Let's thrash the whole subject out. You know, after the strenuous life in London, one does seem to see things in such a different light in this old world city.'

'Oh, a very different light indeed,' I answered, shaking my head at the familiar guide-book emerging from Guy's pocket.

(1910)

New Dresses

MRS CARSFIELD and her mother sat at the dining-room table putting the finishing touches to some green cashmere dresses. They were to be worn by the two Misses Carsfield at church on the following day, with apple-green sashes, and straw hats with ribbon tails. Mrs Carsfield had set her heart on it, and this being a late night for Henry, who was attending a meeting of the Political League, she and the old mother had the dining-room to themselves and could make 'a peaceful litter' as she expressed it. The red cloth was taken off the table – where stood the wedding-present sewing-machine, a brown work-basket, the 'material', and some torn fashion journals. Mrs Carsfield worked the machine, slowly, for she feared the green thread would give out, and had a sort of tired hope that it might last longer if she was careful to use a little at a time; the old woman sat in a rocking-chair, her skirt turned back, and her felt-slippered feet on a hassock, tying the machine threads and stitching some narrow lace on the necks and cuffs. The gas jet flickered. Now and again the old woman glanced up at the jet and said, 'There's water in the pipe, Anne, that's what's the matter,' then was silent, to say again a moment later, 'There must be water in that pipe, Anne,' and again, with quite a burst of energy, '*Now* there is – I'm *certain* of it.'

Anne frowned at the sewing-machine. 'The way mother *harps* on things – it gets frightfully on my nerves,' she thought. 'And always when there's no earthly opportunity to better a thing . . . I suppose it's old age – but most aggravating.' Aloud she said: 'Mother, I'm having a really substantial hem in this dress of Rose's – the child has got so leggy lately. And don't put any lace on Helen's cuffs; it will make a distinction, and besides she's so careless about rubbing her hands on anything grubby.'

'Oh, there's plenty,' said the old woman. 'I'll put it a little higher up.' And she wondered why Anne had such a down on Helen – Henry was just the same. They seemed to want to hurt Helen's feelings – the distinction was merely an excuse.

'Well,' said Mrs Carsfield, 'you didn't see Helen's clothes when I took them off tonight. Black from head to foot after a week. And when I compared them before her eyes with Rose's she merely shrugged, you know that habit she's got, and began stuttering. I really shall have to see Dr Malcolm about her stuttering, if only to give her a good fright. I believe it's merely an affectation she's picked up at school – that she can help it.'

'Anne, you know she's always stuttered. You did just the same when you were her age, she's highly strung.' The old woman took off her spectacles, breathed on them, and rubbed them with a corner of her sewing apron.

'Well, the last thing in the world to do her any good is to let her imagine *that*,' answered Anne, shaking out one of the green frocks and pricking at the pleats with her needle. 'She is treated exactly like Rose, and the Boy hasn't a nerve. Did you see him when I put him on the rocking-horse today, for the first time? He simply gurgled with joy. He's more the image of his father every day.'

'Yes, he certainly is a thorough Carsfield,' assented the old woman, nodding her head.

'Now that's another thing about Helen,' said Anne. 'The peculiar way she treats Boy, staring at him and frightening him as she does. You remember when he was a baby how she used to take away his bottle to see what he would do? Rose is perfect with the child – but Helen . . .'

The old woman put down her work on the table. A little silence fell, and through the silence the loud ticking of the dining-room clock. She wanted to speak her mind to Anne once and for all about the way she and Henry were treating Helen, ruining the child, but the ticking noise distracted her. She could not think of the words and sat there stupidly, her brain going *tick*, *tick* to the dining-room clock.

'How loudly that clock ticks,' was all she said.

'Oh, there's mother – off the subject again – giving me no help or encouragement,' thought Anne. She glanced at the clock.

'Mother, if you've finished that frock, would you go into the kitchen and heat up some coffee and perhaps cut a plate of ham. Henry will be in directly. I'm practically through with this second frock by myself.' She held it up for inspection. 'Aren't they charming? They ought to last the children a good two years, and then I expect they'll do for school – lengthened, and perhaps dyed.'

'I'm glad we decided on the more expensive material,' said the old woman.

Left alone in the dining-room Anne's frown deepened and her mouth drooped – a sharp line showed from nose to chin. She breathed deeply and pushed back her hair. There seemed to be no air in the room, she felt stuffed up, and it seemed so useless to be tiring herself out with fine sewing for Helen. One never got through with children and never had any gratitude from them – except Rose – who was exceptional. Another sign of old age in mother was her absurd point of view about Helen and her 'touchiness' on the subject. There was one thing, Mrs Carsfield said to herself. She was determined to keep Helen apart from Boy. He had all his father's sensitiveness to unsympathetic influences. A blessing that the girls were at school all day!

At last the dresses were finished and folded over the back of the chair. She carried the sewing-machine over to the book-shelves, spread the tablecloth, and went over to the window. The blind was up, she could see the garden quite plainly: there must be a moon about. And then she caught sight of something shining on the garden seat. A book, yes, it must be a book, left there to get soaked through by the dew. She went out into the hall, put on her goloshes, gathered up her skirt, and ran into the garden. Yes, it was a book. She picked it up carefully. Damp already – and the cover bulging. She shrugged her shoulders in the way that her little daughter had caught from her. In the shadowy garden that smelled of grass and rose leaves Anne's heart hardened. Then the gate clicked and she saw Henry striding up the front path.

'Henry!' she called.

'Hullo,' he cried, 'what on earth are you doing down there. . . . Moon-gazing, Anne?' She ran forward and kissed him.

'Oh, look at this book,' she said. 'Helen's been leaving it about again. My dear, how you smell of cigars!'

Said Henry: 'You've got to smoke a decent cigar when you're with these other chaps. Looks so bad if you don't. But come inside, Anne; you haven't got anything on. Let the book go hang! You're cold, my dear, you're shivering.' He put his arm round her shoulder. 'See the moon over there, by the chimney? Fine night. By Jove! I had the fellows roaring tonight – I made a colossal joke. One of them said: "Life is a game of cards", and I, without thinking, just straight out . . . ' Henry paused by the door and held up a finger. 'I said . . . well, I've forgotten the exact words, but they shouted, my dear, simply shouted. No, I'll remember what I said in bed tonight; you know I always do.'

'I'll take this book into the kitchen to dry on the stove-rack,' said Anne, and she thought, as she banged the pages, 'Henry has been drinking beer again, that means indigestion tomorrow. No use mentioning Helen tonight.'

When Henry had finished the supper he lay back in the chair, picking his teeth, and patted his knee for Anne to come and sit there.

'Hullo,' he said, jumping her up and down, 'what's the green fandangles on the chair back? What have you and mother been up to, eh?'

Said Anne airily, casting a most careless glance at the green dresses, 'Only some frocks for the children. Remnants for Sunday.'

The old woman put the plate and cup and saucer together, then lighted a candle.

'I think I'll go to bed,' she said cheerfully.

'Oh, dear me, how unwise of mother,' thought Anne. 'She makes Henry suspect by going away like that, as she always does if there's any unpleasantness brewing.'

'No, don't go to bed yet, mother,' cried Henry jovially. 'Let's have a look at the things.' She passed him over the dresses, faintly smiling. Henry rubbed them through his fingers.

'So these are the remnants, are they, Anne? Don't feel much like the Sunday trousers my mother used to make me out of an ironing blanket. How much did you pay for this a yard, Anne?'

Anne took the dresses from him and played with a button of his waistcoat.

'Forget the exact price, darling. Mother and I rather skimped them, even though they were so cheap. What can great big men bother about clothes . . . ? Was Lumley there tonight?'

'Yes, he says their kid was a bit bandy-legged at just the same age as Boy. He told me of a new kind of chair for children that the draper has just got in – makes them sit with their legs straight. By the way, have you got this month's draper's bill?'

She had been waiting for that – had known it was coming. She slipped off his knee and yawned.

'Oh, dear me,' she said, 'I think I'll follow mother. Bed's the place for me.' She stared at Henry vacantly. 'Bill – bill did you say, dear? Oh, I'll look it out in the morning.'

'No, Anne, hold on.' Henry got up and went over to the cupboard where the bill file was kept. 'Tomorrow's no good – because it's Sunday. I want to get that account off my chest before I turn in. Sit down there – in the rocking-chair – you needn't stand!'

She dropped into the chair and began humming, all the while her thoughts coldly busy and her eyes fixed on her husband's broad back as he bent over the cupboard door. He dawdled over finding the file.

'He's keeping me in suspense on purpose,' she thought. 'We can afford it – otherwise why should I do it? I know our income and our expenditure. I'm not a fool. They're a hell upon earth every month, these bills.' And she thought of her bed upstairs, yearned for it, imagining she had never felt so tired in her life.

'Here we are!' said Henry. He slammed the file on to the table. 'Draw up your chair . . .'

'Clayton: Seven yards green cashmere at five shillings a yard – thirty-five shillings.' He read the item twice – then folded the sheet over and bent towards Anne. He was flushed and his breath smelt of beer. She knew exactly how he took things in that mood, and she raised her eyebrows and nodded.

'Do you mean to tell me,' stormed Henry, 'that lot over there cost thirty-five shillings – that stuff you've been mucking up for the children. Good God! Anybody would think you'd married a million-aire. You could buy your mother a trousseau with that money. You're making yourself a laughing-stock for the whole town. How do you think I can buy Boy a chair or anything else – if you chuck away my earnings like that? Time and again you impress upon me the impossibility of keeping Helen decent; and then you go decking her out the next moment in thirty-five shillings' worth of green cashmere . . .'

On and on stormed the voice.

'He'll have calmed down in the morning, when the beer's worked off,' thought Anne, and later, as she toiled up to bed, 'When he sees how they'll last, he'll understand . . .'

A brilliant Sunday morning. Henry and Anne, quite reconciled, sitting in the dining-room waiting for church time to the tune of Carsfield junior, who steadily thumped the shelf of his high chair with a gravy spoon given him from the breakfast table by his father.

'That beggar's got muscle,' said Henry proudly. 'I've timed him by my watch. He's kept that up for five minutes without stopping.'

'Extraordinary,' said Anne, buttoning her gloves. 'I think he's had that spoon almost long enough now, dear, don't you? I'm so afraid of him putting it into his mouth.'

'Oh, I've got an eye on him.' Henry stood over his small son. 'Go it, old man. Tell mother boys like to kick up a row.'

458 SOMETHING CHILDISH AND OTHER STORIES

Anne kept silence. At any rate, it would keep his eye off the children when they came down in those cashmeres. She was still wondering if she had drummed into their minds often enough the supreme importance of being careful and of taking them off immediately after church before dinner, and why Helen was fidgety when she was pulled about at all, when the door opened and the old woman ushered them in, complete to the straw hats with ribbon tails.

She could not help thrilling, they looked so very superior – Rose carrying her prayer-book in a white case embroidered with a pink woollen cross. But she feigned indifference immediately and the lateness of the hour. Not a word more on the subject from Henry, even with the thirty-five shillings' worth walking hand in hand before him all the way to church. Anne decided that was really generous and noble of him. She looked up at him, walking with the shoulders thrown back. How fine he looked in that long black coat with the white silk tie just showing! And the children looked worthy of him. She squeezed his hand in church, conveying by that silent pressure 'It was for your sake I made the dresses; of course, you can't understand that, but *really*, Henry.' And she fully believed it.

On their way home the Carsfield family met Doctor Malcolm out walking with a black dog carrying his stick in its mouth. Doctor Malcolm stopped and asked after Boy so intelligently that Henry invited him to dinner.

'Come and pick a bone with us and see Boy for yourself,' he said. And Doctor Malcolm accepted. He walked beside Henry and shouted over his shoulder, 'Helen, keep an eye on *my* boy baby, will you, and see he doesn't swallow that walking-stick. Because, if he does, a tree will grow right out of his mouth or it will go to his tail and make it so stiff that a wag will knock you into kingdom come!'

'Oh, Doctor Malcolm!' laughed Helen, stooping over the dog. 'Come along, doggie, give it up, there's a good boy!'

'Helen, your dress!' warned Anne.

'Yes, indeed,' said Doctor Malcolm. 'They are looking top-notchers today – the two young ladies.'

'Well, it really *is* Rose's colour,' said Anne. 'Her complexion is so much more vivid than Helen's.'

Rose blushed. Doctor Malcolm's eyes twinkled, and he kept a tight rein on himself from saying she looked like a tomato in a lettuce salad.

'That child wants taken down a peg,' he decided. 'Give me Helen every time. She'll come to her own yet and lead them just the dance they need.'

Boy was having his midday sleep when they arrived home, and Doctor Malcolm begged that Helen might show him round the garden. Henry, repenting already of his generosity, gladly assented, and Anne went into the kitchen to interview the servant girl.

'Mumma, let me come too and taste the gravy,' begged Rose.

'Huh!' muttered Doctor Malcolm. 'Good riddance.'

He established himself on the garden bench – put up his feet and took off his hat to give the sun 'a chance of growing a second crop', he told Helen.

She asked soberly: 'Doctor Malcolm, do you really like my dress.'

'Of course I do, my lady. Don't you?'

'Oh yes, I'd like to be born and die in it. But it was such a fuss – tryings on, you know, and pullings, and "don'ts". I believe mother would kill me if it got hurt. I even knelt on my petticoat all through church because of dust on the hassock.'

'Bad as that!' asked Doctor Malcolm, rolling his eyes at Helen.

'Oh, *far* worse,' said the child, then burst into laughter and shouted 'Hellish!' dancing over the lawn.

'Take care, they'll hear you, Helen.'

'Oh, booh! It's just dirty old cashmere – serve them right. They can't see me if they're not here to see and so it doesn't matter. It's only with them I feel funny.'

'Haven't you got to remove your finery before dinner?'

'No, because you're here.'

'Oh my prophetic soul!' groaned Doctor Malcolm.

Coffee was served in the garden. The servant girl brought out some cane chairs and a rug for Boy. The children were told to go away and play.

'Leave off worrying Doctor Malcolm, Helen,' said Henry. 'You mustn't be a plague to people who are not members of your own family.' Helen pouted and dragged over to the swing for comfort. She swung high, and thought Doctor Malcolm was a most beautiful man – and wondered if his dog had finished the plate of bones in the back yard. Decided to go and see. Slower she swung, then took a flying leap; her tight skirt caught on a nail – there was a sharp, tearing sound – quickly she glanced at the others – they had not noticed – and then at the frock – at a hole big enough to stick her hand through. She felt neither frightened nor sorry. 'I'll go and change it,' she thought.

'Helen, where are you going to?' called Anne.

'Into the house for a book.'

The old woman noticed that the child held her skirt in a peculiar way. Her petticoat string must have come untied. But she made no remark. Once in the bedroom Helen unbuttoned the frock, slipped out of it, and wondered what to do next. Hide it somewhere – she glanced all round the room – there was nowhere safe from them. Except the top of the cupboard – but even standing on a chair she could not throw so high – it fell back on top of her every time – the horrid, hateful thing. Then her eyes lighted on her school satchel hanging on the end of the bedpost. Wrap it in her school pinafore – put it in the bottom of the bag with the pencil case on top. They'd never look there. She returned to the garden in the everyday dress – but forgot about the book.

'A-ah,' said Anne, smiling ironically. 'What a new leaf for Doctor Malcolm's benefit! Look, mother, Helen has changed without being told to.'

'Come here, dear, and be done up properly.' She whispered to Helen: 'Where did you leave your dress?'

'Left it on the side of the bed. *Where* I took it off,' sang Helen.

Doctor Malcolm was talking to Henry of the advantages derived from public school education for the sons of commercial men, but he had his eye on the scene and, watching Helen, he smelt a rat – smelt a Hamelin tribe of them.

Confusion and consternation reigned. One of the green cashmeres had disappeared – spirited off the face of the earth – during the time that Helen took it off and the children's tea.

'Show me the exact spot,' scolded Mrs Carsfield for the twentieth time. 'Helen, tell the truth.'

'Mumma, I *swear* I left it on the floor.'

'Well, it's no good swearing if it's not there. It can't have been stolen!'

'I did see a very funny-looking man in a white cap walking up and down the road and staring in the windows as I came up to change.' Sharply Anne eyed her daughter.

'Now,' she said, 'I *know* you are telling lies.'

She turned to the old woman, in her voice something of pride and joyous satisfaction. 'You hear, mother – this cock-and-bull story?'

When they were near the end of the bed Helen blushed and turned away from them. And now and again she wanted to shout 'I tore it, I tore it,' and she fancied she had said it and seen their faces, just as sometimes in bed she dreamed she had got up and dressed. But as the evening wore on she grew quite careless – glad only of one thing – people had to go to sleep at night. Viciously she stared at the sun shining through the window space and making a pattern of the curtain on the bare nursery floor. And then she looked at Rose, painting a text at the nursery table with a whole egg-cup full of water to herself . . .

Henry visited their bedroom the last thing. She heard him come creaking into their room and hid under the bedclothes. But Rose betrayed her.

'Helen's not asleep,' piped Rose.

Henry sat by the bedside pulling his moustache.

'If it were not Sunday, Helen, I would whip you. As it is, and I must be at the office early tomorrow, I shall give you a sound smacking after tea in the evening . . . Do you hear me?'

She grunted.

'You love your father and mother, don't you?'

No answer.

Rose gave Helen a dig with her foot.

'Well,' said Henry, sighing deeply, 'I suppose you love Jesus?'

'Rose has scratched my leg with her toe-nail,' answered Helen.

Henry strode out of the room and flung himself on to his own bed with his outdoor boots on the starched bolster, Anne noticed, but he was too overcome for her to venture a protest. The old woman was in the bedroom, too, idly combing the hairs from Anne's brush. Henry told them the story, and was gratified to observe Anne's tears.

'It *is* Rose's turn for her toe-nails after the bath next Saturday,' commented the old woman.

In the middle of the night Henry dug his elbow into Mrs Carsfield.

'I've got an idea,' he said. 'Malcolm's at the bottom of this.'

'No . . . how . . . why . . . where . . . bottom of what?'

'Those damned green dresses.'

'Wouldn't be surprised,' she managed to articulate, thinking 'imagine his rage if I woke *him* up to tell him an idiotic thing like that!'

'Is Mrs Carsfield at home?' asked Doctor Malcolm.

'No, sir, she's out visiting,' answered the servant girl.

'Is Mr Carsfield anywhere about?'

'Oh no, sir, he's never home midday.'

'Show me into the drawing-room.'

The servant girl opened the drawing-room door, cocked her eye at the doctor's bag. She wished he would leave it in the hall – even if she could only *feel* the outside without opening it . . . But the doctor kept it in his hand.

The old woman sat in the drawing-room, a roll of knitting on her lap. Her head had fallen back – her mouth was open – she was asleep and quietly snoring. She started up at the sound of the doctor's footsteps and straightened her cap.

'Oh, Doctor – you *did* take me by surprise. I was dreaming that Henry had bought Anne five little canaries. Please sit down!'

'No, thanks. I just popped in on the chance of catching you alone . . . You see this bag?'

The old woman nodded.

'Now, are you any good at opening bags?'

'Well, my husband was a great traveller and once I spent a whole night in a railway train.'

'Well, have a go at opening this one.'

The old woman knelt on the floor – her fingers trembled.

'There's nothing startling inside?' she asked.

'Well, it won't bite exactly,' said Doctor Malcolm.

The catch sprang open – the bag yawned like a toothless mouth, and she saw, folded in its depths – green cashmere – with narrow lace on the neck and sleeves.

'Fancy that!' said the old woman mildly. 'May I take it out, Doctor?' She professed neither astonishment nor pleasure – and Malcolm felt disappointed.

'Helen's dress,' he said, and bending towards her, raised his voice. 'That young spark's Sunday rig-out.'

'I'm not deaf, Doctor,' answered the old woman. 'Yes, I thought it looked like it. I told Anne only this morning it was bound to turn up somewhere.' She shook the crumpled frock and looked it over. 'Things always do if you give them time; I've noticed that so often – it's such a blessing.'

'You know Lindsay – the postman? Gastric ulcers – called there this morning . . . Saw this brought in by Lena, who'd got it from Helen on her way to school. Said the kid fished it out of her satchel rolled in a pinafore, and said her mother had told her to give it away because it did not fit her. When I saw the tear I understood yesterday's "new leaf", as Mrs Carsfield put it. Was up to the dodge in a jiffy. Got the dress – bought some stuff at Clayton's and made my sister Bertha sew it while I had dinner. I knew what would be happening this end of the line – and I knew you'd see Helen through for the sake of getting one in at Henry.'

'How thoughtful of you, Doctor!' said the old woman. 'I'll tell Anne I found it under my dolman.'

'Yes, that's your ticket,' said Doctor Malcolm.

'But, of course, Helen would have forgotten the whipping by tomorrow morning and I'd promised her a new doll . . . ' The old woman spoke regretfully.

Doctor Malcolm snapped his bag together. 'It's no good talking to the old bird,' he thought, 'she doesn't take in half I say. Don't seem to have got any forrader than doing Helen out of a doll.'

(1910)

The Woman at the Store

ALL THAT DAY the heat was terrible. The wind blew close to the ground; it rooted among the tussock grass, slithered along the road, so that the white pumice dust swirled in our faces, settled and sifted over us and was like a dry-skin itching for growth on our bodies. The horses stumbled along, coughing and chuffing. The pack-horse was sick – with a big open sore rubbed under the belly. Now and again she stopped short, threw back her head, looked at us as though she were going to cry, and whinnied. Hundreds of larks shrilled; the sky was slate colour, and the sound of the larks reminded me of slate pencils scraping over its surface. There was nothing to be seen but wave after wave of tussock grass, patched with purple orchids and manuka bushes covered with thick spider webs.

Jo rode ahead. He wore a blue galatea shirt, corduroy trousers and riding boots. A white handkerchief, spotted with red – it looked as though his nose had been bleeding on it – was knotted round his throat. Wisps of white hair straggled from under his wideawake – his moustache and eyebrows were called white – he slouched in the saddle, grunting. Not once that day had he sung

> I don't care, for don't you see,
> My wife's mother was in front of me!

It was the first day we had been without it for a month, and now there seemed something uncanny in his silence. Jim rode beside me, white as a clown; his black eyes glittered and he kept shooting out his tongue and moistening his lips. He was dressed in a Jaeger vest and a pair of blue duck trousers, fastened round the waist with a plaited leather belt. We had hardly spoken since dawn. At noon we had lunched off fly biscuits and apricots by the side of a swampy creek.

'My stomach feels like the crop of a hen,' said Jo. 'Now then, Jim, you're the bright boy of the party – where's this 'ere store you kep' on talking about. "Oh yes," you says, "I know a fine store, with a paddock for the horses and a creek runnin' through, owned by a friend of mine who'll give yer a bottle of whisky before 'e shakes hands with yer." I'd like ter see that place – merely as a matter of curiosity – not that I'd ever doubt yer word – as yer know very well – *but . . .*'

Jim laughed. 'Don't forget there's a woman too, Jo, with blue eyes and yellow hair, who'll promise you something else before she shakes hands with you. Put that in your pipe and smoke it.'

'The heat's making you balmy,' said Jo. But he dug his knees into the horse. We shambled on. I half fell asleep and had a sort of uneasy dream that the horses were not moving forward at all – then that I was on a rocking-horse, and my old mother was scolding me for raising such a fearful dust from the drawing-room carpet. 'You've entirely worn off the pattern of the carpet,' I heard her saying, and she gave the reins a tug. I snivelled and woke to find Jim leaning over me, maliciously smiling.

'That was a case of all but,' said he. 'I just caught you. What's up? Been bye-bye?'

'No!' I raised my head. 'Thank the Lord we're arriving somewhere.'

We were on the brow of the hill, and below us there was a whare roofed with corrugated iron. It stood in a garden, rather far back from the road – a big paddock opposite, and a creek and a clump of young willow trees. A thin line of blue smoke stood up straight from the chimney of the whare; and as I looked a woman came out, followed by a child and a sheep dog – the woman carrying what appeared to me a black stick. She made gestures at us. The horses put on a final spurt, Jo took off his wideawake, shouted, threw out his chest, and began singing 'I don't care, for don't you see . . .' The sun pushed through the pale clouds and shed a vivid light over the scene. It gleamed on the woman's yellow hair, over her flapping pinafore and the rifle she was carrying. The child hid behind her, and the yellow dog, a mangy beast, scuttled back into the whare, his tail between his legs. We drew rein and dismounted.

'Hallo,' screamed the woman. 'I thought you was three 'awks. My kid comes runnin' in ter me. "Mumma," says she, "there's three brown things comin' over the 'ill," says she. An' I comes out smart, I can tell yer. "They'll be 'awks," I says to her. Oh, the 'awks about 'ere, yer wouldn't believe.'

The 'kid' gave us the benefit of one eye from behind the woman's pinafore – then retired again.

'Where's your old man?' asked Jim.

The woman blinked rapidly, screwing up her face.

'Away shearin'. Bin away a month. I suppose ye're not goin' to stop, are yer? There's a storm comin' up.'

'You bet we are,' said Jo. 'So you're on your lonely, missus?'

She stood, pleating the frills of her pinafore, and glancing from one to the other of us, like a hungry bird. I smiled at the thought of how Jim had pulled Jo's leg about her. Certainly her eyes were blue, and what hair she had was yellow, but ugly. She was a figure of fun. Looking at her, you felt there was nothing but sticks and wires under that pinafore – her front teeth were knocked out, she had red, pulpy hands and she wore on her feet a pair of dirty Bluchers.

'I'll go and turn out the horses,' said Jim. 'Got any embrocation? Poi's rubbed herself to hell!'

''Arf a mo!' The woman stood silent a moment, her nostrils expanding as she breathed. Then she shouted violently, 'I'd rather you didn't stop . . . You *can't*, and there's the end of it. I don't let out that paddock any more. You'll have to go on; I ain't got nothing!'

'Well, I'm blest!' said Jo heavily. He pulled me aside. 'Gone a bit off 'er dot,' he whispered. 'Too much alone, *you know*,' very significantly. 'Turn the sympathetic tap on 'er, she'll come round all right.'

But there was no need – she had come round by herself.

'Stop if yer like!' she muttered, shrugging her shoulders. To me – 'I'll give yer the embrocation if yer come along.'

'Right-o, I'll take it down to them.' We walked together up the garden path. It was planted on both sides with cabbages. They smelled like stale dish-water. Of flowers there were double poppies and sweet-williams. One little patch was divided off by pawa shells – presumably it belonged to the child – for she ran from her mother and began to grub in it with a broken clothes-peg. The yellow dog lay across the doorstep, biting fleas; the woman kicked him away.

'Gar-r, get away, you beast . . . the place ain't tidy. I 'aven't 'ad time ter fix things today – been ironing. Come right in.'

It was a large room, the walls plastered with old pages of English periodicals. Queen Victoria's Jubilee appeared to be the most recent number. A table with an ironing board and wash-tub on it, some wooden forms, a black horsehair sofa and some broken cane chairs pushed against the walls. The mantelpiece above the stove was draped in pink paper, further ornamented with dried grasses and ferns and a coloured print of Richard Seddon. There were four doors – one, judging from the smell, led into the 'Store', one on to the 'backyard', through a third I saw the bedroom. Flies buzzed in circles round the ceiling, and treacle papers and bundles of dried clover were pinned to the window curtains.

I was alone in the room; she had gone into the store for the embrocation. I heard her stamping about and muttering to herself: 'I got some, now where did I put that bottle? . . . It's behind the pickles . . . no, it ain't.' I cleared a place on the table and sat there, swinging my legs. Down in the paddock I could hear Jo singing and the sound of hammer strokes as Jim drove in the tent pegs. It was sunset. There is no twilight in our New Zealand days, but a curious half-hour when everything appears grotesque – it frightens – as though the savage spirit of the country walked abroad and sneered at what it saw. Sitting alone in the hideous room I grew afraid. The woman next door was a long time finding that stuff. What was she doing in there? Once I thought I heard her bang her hands down on the counter, and once she half moaned, turning it into a cough and clearing her throat. I wanted to shout 'Buck up!' but I kept silent.

'Good Lord, what a life!' I thought. 'Imagine being here day in, day out, with that rat of a child and a mangy dog. Imagine bothering about ironing. *Mad*, of course she's mad! Wonder how long she's been here – wonder if I could get her to talk.'

At that moment she poked her head round the door.

'Wot was it yer wanted?' she asked.

'Embrocation.'

'Oh, I forgot. I got it, it was in front of the pickle jars.'

She handed me the bottle.

'My, you do look tired, you do! Shall I knock yer up a few scones for supper! There's some tongue in the store, too, and I'll cook yer a cabbage if you fancy it.'

'Right-o.' I smiled at her. 'Come down to the paddock and bring the kid for tea.'

She shook her head, pursing up her mouth.

'Oh no. I don't fancy it. I'll send the kid down with the things and a billy of milk. Shall I knock up a few extry scones to take with yer ter-morrow?'

'Thanks.'

She came and stood by the door.

'How old is the kid?'

'Six – come next Christmas. I 'ad a bit of trouble with 'er one way an' another. I 'adn't any milk till a month after she was born and she sickened like a cow.'

'She's not like you – takes after her father?' Just as the woman had shouted her refusal at us before, she shouted at me then.

'No, she don't! She's the dead spit of me. Any fool could see that. Come on in now, Else, you stop messing in the dirt.'

I met Jo climbing over the paddock fence.

'What's the old bitch got in the store?' he asked.

'Don't know – didn't look.'

'Well, of all the fools. Jim's slanging you. What have you been doing all the time?'

'She couldn't find this stuff. Oh, my shakes, you are smart!'

Jo had washed, combed his wet hair in a line across his forehead, and buttoned a coat over his shirt. He grinned.

Jim snatched the embrocation from me. I went to the end of the paddock where the willows grew and bathed in the creek. The water was clear and soft as oil. Along the edges held by the grass and rushes white foam tumbled and bubbled. I lay in the water and looked up at the trees that were still a moment, then quivered lightly and again were still. The air smelt of rain. I forgot about the woman and the kid until I came back to the tent. Jim lay by the fire watching the billy boil.

I asked where Jo was, and if the kid had brought our supper.

'Pooh,' said Jim, rolling over and looking up at the sky. 'Didn't you see how Jo had been titivating? He said to me before he went up to the whare, "Dang it! she'll look better by night light – at any rate, my buck, she's female flesh!" '

'You had Jo about her looks – you had me too.'

'No – look here. I can't make it out. It's four years since I came past this way and I stopped here two days. The husband was a pal of mine once, down the West Coast – a fine, big chap, with a voice on him like a trombone. She's been barmaid down the Coast – as pretty as a wax doll. The coach used to come this way then once a fortnight, that was before they opened the railway up Napier way, and she had no end of a time! Told me once in a confidential moment that she knew one hundred and twenty-five different ways of kissing!'

'Oh, go on, Jim! She isn't the same woman!'

'Course she is . . . I can't make it out. What I think is the old man's cleared out and left her: that's all my eye about shearing. Sweet life! The only people who come through now are Maoris and sun-downers!'

Through the dark we saw the gleam of the kid's pinafore. She trailed over to us with a basket in her hand, the milk billy in the other. I unpacked the basket, the child standing by.

'Come over here,' said Jim, snapping his fingers at her.

She went, the lamp from the inside of the tent cast a bright light over her. A mean, undersized brat, with whitish hair and weak eyes. She stood, legs wide apart and her stomach protruding.

'What do you do all day?' asked Jim.

She scraped out one ear with her little finger, looked at the result and said, 'Draw.'

'Huh! What do you draw? Leave your ears alone!'

'Pictures.'

'What on?'

'Bits of butter paper an' a pencil of my Mumma's.'

'Boh! What a lot of words at one time!' Jim rolled his eyes at her. 'Baa-lambs and moo-cows?'

'No, everything. I'll draw all of you when you're gone, and your horses and the tent, and that one' – she pointed to me – 'with no clothes on in the creek. I looked at her where she couldn't see me from.'

'Thanks very much. How ripping of you,' said Jim. 'Where's Dad?'

The kid pouted. 'I won't tell you because I don't like yer face!' She started operations on the other ear.

'Here,' I said. 'Take the basket, get along home and tell the other man supper's ready.'

'I don't want to.'

'I'll give you a box on the ear if you don't,' said Jim savagely.

'Hie! I'll tell Mumma. I'll tell Mumma.' The kid fled.

We ate until we were full, and had arrived at the smoke stage before Jo came back, very flushed and jaunty, a whisky bottle in his hand.

''Ave a drink – you two!' he shouted, carrying off matters with a high hand. ''Ere, shove along the cups.'

'One hundred and twenty-five different ways,' I murmured to Jim.

'What's that? Oh! stow it!' said Jo. 'Why 'ave you always got your knife into me. You gas like a kid at a Sunday School beano. She wants us to go there tonight and have a comfortable chat. I' – he waved his hand airily – 'I got 'er round.'

'Trust you for that,' laughed Jim. 'But did she tell you where the old man's got to?'

Jo looked up. 'Shearing! You 'eard 'er, you fool!'

The woman had fixed up the room, even to a light bouquet of sweet-williams on the table. She and I sat one side of the table, Jo and Jim the other. An oil lamp was set between us, the whisky bottle and glasses, and a jug of water. The kid knelt against one of the forms, drawing on butter paper; I wondered, grimly, if she was attempting the creek episode. But Jo had been right about night time. The woman's hair was tumbled – two red spots burned in her cheeks – her eyes shone – and we knew that they were kissing feet under the table. She had changed the blue pinafore for a white calico dressing-jacket and a black skirt – the kid was decorated to the extent of a blue sateen hair ribbon. In the stifling room, with the flies buzzing against the ceiling and dropping on to the table, we got slowly drunk.

'Now listen to me,' shouted the woman, banging her fist on the table. 'It's six years since I was married, and four miscarriages. I says to 'im, I says, what do you think I'm doin' up 'ere? If you was back at the Coast I'd 'ave you lynched for child murder. Over and over I tells 'im – you've broken my spirit and spoiled my looks, and wot for – that's wot I'm driving at.' She clutched her head with her hands and stared round at us. Speaking rapidly, 'Oh, some days – an' months of them – I 'ear them two words knockin' inside me all the time – "Wot for!" but sometimes I'll be cooking the spuds an' I lifts the lid off to give 'em a prong and I 'ears, quite suddin again, "Wot for!" Oh! I don't mean only the spuds and the kid – I mean – I mean,' she hiccoughed – 'you know what I mean, Mr Jo.'

'I know,' said Jo, scratching his head.

'Trouble with me is,' she leaned across the table, 'he left me too much alone. When the coach stopped coming, sometimes he'd go away days, sometimes he'd go away weeks, and leave me ter look after the store. Back 'e'd come – pleased as Punch. "Oh, 'allo," 'e'd say. "'Ow are you gettin' on? Come and give us a kiss." Sometimes I'd turn a bit nasty, and then 'e'd go off again, and if I took it all right, 'e'd wait till 'e could twist me round 'is finger, then 'e'd say, "Well, so long, I'm off," and do you think I could keep 'im? – not me!'

'Mumma,' bleated the kid, 'I made a picture of them on the 'ill, an' you an' me an' the dog down below.'

'Shut your mouth!' said the woman.

A vivid flash of lightning played over the room – we heard the mutter of thunder.

'Good thing that's broke loose,' said Jo. 'I've 'ad it in me 'ead for three days.'

'Where's your old man now?' asked Jim slowly.

The woman blubbered and dropped her head on to the table. 'Jim, 'e's gone shearin' and left me alone again,' she wailed.

' 'Ere, look out for the glasses,' said Jo. 'Cheer-o, 'ave another drop. No good cryin' over spilt 'usbands! You, Jim, you blasted cuckoo!'

'Mr Jo,' said the woman, drying her eyes on her jacket frill, 'you're a gent, an' if I was a secret woman I'd place any confidence in your 'ands. I don't mind if I do 'ave a glass on that.'

Every moment the lightning grew more vivid and the thunder sounded nearer. Jim and I were silent – the kid never moved from her bench. She poked her tongue out and blew on her paper as she drew.

'It's the loneliness,' said the woman, addressing Jo – he made sheep's eyes at her – 'and bein' shut up 'ere like a broody 'en.' He reached his hand across the table and held hers, and though the position looked most uncomfortable when they wanted to pass the water and whisky, their hands stuck together as though glued. I pushed back my chair and went over to the kid, who immediately sat flat down on her artistic achievements and made a face at me.

'You're not to look,' said she.

'Oh, come on, don't be nasty!' Jim came over to us, and we were just drunk enough to wheedle the kid into showing us. And those drawings of hers were extraordinary and repulsively vulgar. The creations of a lunatic with a lunatic's cleverness. There was no doubt about it, the kid's mind was diseased. While she showed them to us, she worked herself up into a mad excitement, laughing and trembling, and shooting out her arms.

'Mumma,' she yelled. 'Now I'm going to draw them what you told me I never was to – now I am.'

The woman rushed from the table and beat the child's head with the flat of her hand.

'I'll smack you with yer clothes turned up if yer dare say that again,' she bawled.

Jo was too drunk to notice, but Jim caught her by the arm. The kid did not utter a cry. She drifted over to the window and began picking flies from the treacle paper.

We returned to the table – Jim and I sitting one side, the woman and Jo, touching shoulders, the other. We listened to the thunder, saying stupidly, 'That was a near one,' 'There it goes again,' and Jo, at a heavy hit, 'Now we're off,' 'Steady on the brake,' until rain began to fall, sharp as cannon shot on the iron roof.

'You'd better doss here for the night,' said the woman.

'That's right,' assented Jo, evidently in the know about this move.

'Bring up yer things from the tent. You two can doss in the store along with the kid – she's used to sleep in there and won't mind you.'

'Oh, Mumma, I never did,' interrupted the kid.

'Shut yer lies! An' Mr Jo can 'ave this room.'

It sounded a ridiculous arrangement, but it was useless to attempt to cross them, they were too far gone. While the woman sketched the plan of action, Jo sat, abnormally solemn and red, his eyes bulging, and pulling at his moustache.

'Give us a lantern,' said Jim, 'I'll go down to the paddock.' We two went together. Rain whipped in our faces, the land was light as though a bush fire was raging. We behaved like two children let loose in the thick of an adventure, laughed and shouted to each other, and came back to the whare to find the kid already bedded in the counter of the store. The woman brought us a lamp. Jo took his bundle from Jim, the door was shut.

'Good night all,' shouted Jo.

Jim and I sat on two sacks of potatoes. For the life of us we could not stop laughing. Strings of onions and half-hams dangled from the ceiling – wherever we looked there were advertisements for 'Camp Coffee' and tinned meats. We pointed at them, tried to read them aloud – overcome with laughter and hiccoughs. The kid in the counter stared at us. She threw off her blanket and scrambled to the floor, where she stood in her grey flannel nightgown rubbing one leg against the other. We paid no attention to her.

'Wot are you laughing at?' she said uneasily.

'You!' shouted Jim. 'The red tribe of you, my child.'

She flew into a rage and beat herself with her hands. 'I won't be laughed at, you curs – you.' He swooped down upon the child and swung her on to the counter.

'Go to sleep, Miss Smarty – or make a drawing – here's a pencil – you can use Mumma's account book.'

Through the rain we heard Jo creak over the boarding of the next room – the sound of a door being opened – then shut to.

'It's the loneliness,' whispered Jim.

'One hundred and twenty-five different ways – alas! my poor brother!'

The kid tore out a page and flung it at me.

'There you are,' she said. 'Now I done it ter spite Mumma for shutting me up 'ere with you two. I done the one she told me I never ought to. I done the one she told me she'd shoot me if I did. Don't care! Don't care!'

The kid had drawn the picture of the woman shooting at a man with a rook rifle and then digging a hole to bury him in.

She jumped off the counter and squirmed about on the floor biting her nails.

Jim and I sat till dawn with the drawing beside us. The rain ceased, the little kid fell asleep, breathing loudly. We got up, stole out of the whare, down into the paddock. White clouds floated over a pink sky – a chill wind blew; the air smelled of wet grass. Just as we swung into the saddle Jo came out of the whare – he motioned to us to ride on.

'I'll pick you up later,' he shouted.

A bend in the road, and the whole place disappeared.

(1911)

Ole Underwood

To Anne Estelle Rice

DOWN THE WINDY HILL STALKED Ole Underwood. He carried a
black umbrella in one hand, in the other a red and white spotted
handkerchief knotted into a lump. He wore a black peaked cap like a
pilot; gold rings gleamed in his ears and his little eyes snapped like
two sparks. Like two sparks they glowed in the smoulder of his
bearded face. On one side of the hill grew a forest of pines from the
road right down to the sea. On the other side short tufted grass and
little bushes of white manuka flower. The pine trees roared like
waves in their topmost branches, their stems creaked like the timber
of ships; in the windy air flew the white manuka flower. 'Ah-k!'
shouted Ole Underwood, shaking his umbrella at the wind bearing
down upon him, beating him, half strangling him with his black cape.
'Ah-k!' shouted the wind a hundred times as loud, and filled his
mouth and nostrils with dust. Something inside Ole Underwood's
breast beat like a hammer. One, two – one, two – never stopping,
never changing. He couldn't do anything. It wasn't loud. No, it
didn't make a noise – only a thud. One, two – one, two – like
someone beating on an iron in a prison, someone in a secret place –
bang – bang – bang – trying to get free. Do what he would, fumble at
his coat, throw his arms about, spit, swear, he couldn't stop the noise.
Stop! Stop! Stop! Stop! Ole Underwood began to shuffle and run.

Away below, the sea heaving against the stone walls, and the little
town just out of its reach close packed together, the better to face the
grey water. And up on the other side of the hill the prison with high
red walls. Over all bulged the grey sky with black web-like clouds
streaming.

Ole Underwood slackened his pace as he neared the town, and
when he came to the first house he flourished his umbrella like a
herald's staff and threw out his chest, his head glancing quickly from
right to left. They were ugly little houses leading into the town,
built of wood – two windows and a door, a stumpy veranda and a

green mat of grass before. Under one veranda yellow hens huddled out of the wind. 'Shoo!' shouted Ole Underwood, and laughed to see them fly, and laughed again at the woman who came to the door and shook a red, soapy fist at him. A little girl stood in another yard untwisting some rags from a clothes-line. When she saw Ole Underwood she let the clothes-prop fall and rushed screaming to the door, beating it screaming 'Mumma – Mumma!' That started the hammer in Ole Underwood's heart. Mum-ma – Mum-ma! He saw an old face with a trembling chin and grey hair nodding out of the window as they dragged him past. Mumma – Mum-ma! He looked up at the big red prison perched on the hill and he pulled a face as if he wanted to cry.

At the corner in front of the pub some carts were pulled up, some men sat in the porch of the pub drinking and talking. Ole Underwood wanted a drink. He slouched into the bar. It was half full of old and young men in big coats and top-boots with stock-whips in their hands. Behind the counter a big girl with red hair pulled the beer handles and cheeked the men. Ole Underwood sneaked to one side, like a cat. Nobody looked at him, only the men looked at each other, one or two of them nudged. The girl nodded and winked at the fellow she was serving. He took some money out of his knotted handkerchief and slipped it on to the counter. His hand shook. He didn't speak. The girl took no notice; she served everybody, went on with her talk, and then as if by accident shoved a mug towards him. A great big jar of red pinks stood on the bar counter. Ole Underwood stared at them as he drank and frowned at them. Red – red – red – red! beat the hammer. It was very warm in the bar and quiet as a pond, except for the talk and the girl. She kept on laughing. Ha! Ha! That was what the men liked to see, for she threw back her head and her great breasts lifted and shook to her laughter.

In one corner sat a stranger. He pointed at Ole Underwood. 'Cracked!' said one of the men. 'When he was a young fellow, thirty years ago, a man 'ere done in 'is woman, and 'e foun' out an' killed 'er. Got twenty years in quod up on the 'ill. Came out cracked.'

''Oo done 'er in?' asked the man.

'Dunno. 'E dunno, nor nobody. 'E was a sailor till 'e marrid 'er. Cracked!' The man spat and smeared the spittle on the floor, shrugging his shoulders. ''E's 'armless enough.'

Ole Underwood heard; he did not turn, but he shot out an old claw and crushed up the red pinks. 'Uh-Uh! You ole beast! Uh! You ole swine!' screamed the girl, leaning across the counter and banging him with a tin jug. 'Get art! Get art! Don' you never come 'ere no more!' Somebody kicked him: he scuttled like a rat.

He walked past the Chinamen's shops. The fruit and vegetables were all piled up against the windows. Bits of wooden cases, straw and old newspapers were strewn over the pavement. A woman flounced out of a shop and slushed a pail of slops over his feet. He peered in at the windows, at the Chinamen sitting in little groups on old barrels playing cards. They made him smile. He looked and looked, pressing his face against the glass and sniggering. They sat still with their long pigtails bound round their heads and their faces yellow as lemons. Some of them had knives in their belts, and one old man sat by himself on the floor plaiting his long crooked toes together. The Chinamen didn't mind Ole Underwood. When they saw him they nodded. He went to the door of a shop and cautiously opened it. In rushed the wind with him, scattering the cards. 'Ya-Ya! Ya-Ya!' screamed the Chinamen, and Ole Underwood rushed off, the hammer beating quick and hard. Ya-Ya! He turned a corner out of sight. He thought he heard one of the Chinks after him, and he slipped into a timber-yard. There he lay panting . . .

Close by him, under another stack, there was a heap of yellow shavings. As he watched them they moved and a little grey cat unfolded herself and came out waving her tail. She trod delicately over to Ole Underwood and rubbed against his sleeve. The hammer in Ole Underwood's heart beat madly. It pounded up into his throat, and then it seemed to half stop and beat very, very faintly. 'Kit! Kit! Kit!' That was what she used to call the little cat he brought her off the ship – 'Kit! Kit! Kit!' – and stoop down with the saucer in her hands. 'Ah! my God! my Lord!' Ole Underwood sat up and took the kitten in his arms and rocked to and fro, crushing it against his face. It was warm and soft, and it mewed faintly. He buried his eyes in its fur. My God! My Lord! He tucked the little cat in his coat and stole out of the wood-yard and slouched down towards the wharves. As he came near the sea, Ole Underwood's nostrils expanded. The mad wind smelled of tar and ropes and slime and salt. He crossed the railway line, he crept behind the wharf-sheds and along a little cinder path that threaded through a patch of rank fennel to some stone drainpipes carrying the sewage into the sea. And he stared up at the wharves and at the ships with flags flying, and suddenly the old, old lust swept over Ole Underwood. 'I will! I will! I will!' he muttered.

He tore the little cat out of his coat and swung it by its tail and flung it out to the sewer opening. The hammer beat loud and strong. He tossed his head, he was young again. He walked on to the wharves, past the wool-bales, past the loungers and the loafers to the extreme end of the wharves. The sea sucked against the wharf-poles as though it drank something from the land. One ship was loading wool. He heard a crane rattle and the shriek of a whistle. So he came to the little ship lying by herself with a bit of a plank for a gangway, and no sign of anybody – anybody at all. Ole Underwood looked once back at the town, at the prison perched like a red bird, at the black webby clouds trailing. Then he went up the gangway and on to the slippery deck. He grinned, and rolled in his walk, carrying high in his hand the red and white handkerchief. His ship! Mine! Mine! Mine! beat the hammer. There was a door latched open on the lee-side, labelled 'State-room'. He peered in. A man lay sleeping on a bunk – his bunk – a great big man in a seaman's coat with a long, fair beard and hair on the red pillow. And looking down upon him from the wall there shone her picture – his woman's picture – smiling and smiling at the big sleeping man.

(1912)

The Little Girl

To the little girl he was a figure to be feared and avoided. Every morning before going to business he came into the nursery and gave her a perfunctory kiss, to which she responded with 'Goodbye, father.' And oh, the glad sense of relief when she heard the noise of the buggy growing fainter and fainter down the long road!

In the evening, leaning over the banisters at his homecoming, she heard his loud voice in the hall. 'Bring my tea into the smoking-room . . . Hasn't the paper come yet? Have they taken it into the kitchen again? Mother, go and see if my paper's out there – and bring me my slippers.'

'Kezia,' mother would call to her, 'if you're a good girl you can come down and take off father's boots.' Slowly the girl would slip down the stairs, holding tightly to the banisters with one hand – more slowly still, across the hall, and push open the smoking-room door.

By that time he had his spectacles on and looked at her over them in a way that was terrifying to the little girl.

'Well, Kezia, get a move on and pull off these boots and take them outside. Been a good girl today?'

'I d-d-don't know, father.'

'You d-d-don't know? If you stutter like that mother will have to take you to the doctor.'

She never stuttered with other people – had quite given it up – but only with father, because then she was trying so hard to say the words properly.

'What's the matter? What are you looking so wretched about? Mother, I wish you would teach this child not to appear on the brink of suicide . . . Here, Kezia, carry my teacup back to the table – carefully; your hands jog like an old lady's. And try to keep your handkerchief in your pocket, *not* up your sleeve.'

'Y-y-yes, father.'

On Sundays she sat in the same pew with him in church, listening while he sang in a loud, clear voice, watching while he made little notes during the sermon with the stump of a blue pencil on the back of an envelope – his eyes narrowed to a slit – one hand beating a silent tattoo on the pew ledge. He said his prayers so loudly she was certain God heard him above the clergyman.

He was so big – his hands and his neck, especially his mouth when he yawned. Thinking about him alone in the nursery was like thinking about a giant.

On Sunday afternoons grandmother sent her down to the drawing-room, dressed in her brown velvet, to have a 'nice talk with father and mother'. But the little girl always found mother reading *The Sketch* and father stretched out on the couch, his handkerchief on his face, his feet propped on one of the best sofa pillows, and so soundly sleeping that he snored.

She, perched on the piano-stool, gravely watched him until he woke and stretched, and asked the time – then looked at her.

'Don't stare so, Kezia. You look like a little brown owl.'

One day, when she was kept indoors with a cold, the grandmother told her that father's birthday was next week, and suggested she should make him a pin-cushion for a present out of a beautiful piece of yellow silk.

Laboriously, with a double cotton, the little girl stitched three sides. But what to fill it with? That was the question. The grandmother was out in the garden, and she wandered into mother's bedroom to look for 'scraps.' On the bed-table she discovered a great many sheets of fine paper, gathered them up, shredded them into tiny pieces, and stuffed her case, then sewed up the fourth side.

That night there was a hue and cry over the house. Father's great speech for the Port Authority had been lost. Rooms were ransacked – servants questioned. Finally mother came into the nursery.

'Kezia, I suppose you didn't see some papers on a table in our room?'

'Oh yes,' she said. 'I tore them up for my s'prise.'

'*What!*' screamed mother. 'Come straight down to the dining-room this instant.'

And she was dragged down to where father was pacing to and fro, hands behind his back.

'Well?' he said sharply.

Mother explained.

He stopped and stared in a stupefied manner at the child.

'Did you do that?'

'N-n-no,' she whispered.

'Mother, go up to the nursery and fetch down the damned thing – see that the child's put to bed this instant.'

Crying too much to explain, she lay in the shadowed room watching the evening light sift through the venetian blinds and trace a sad little pattern on the floor.

Then father came into the room with a ruler in his hands.

'I am going to whip you for this,' he said.

'Oh, no, no!' she screamed, cowering down under the bedclothes. He pulled them aside.

'Sit up,' he commanded, 'and hold out your hands. You must be taught once and for all not to touch what does not belong to you.'

'But it was for your b-b-birthday.'

Down came the ruler on her little, pink palms.

Hours later, when the grandmother had wrapped her in a shawl and rocked her in the rocking-chair, the child cuddled close to her soft body.

'What did Jesus make fathers for?' she sobbed.

'Here's a clean hanky, darling, with some of my lavender water on it. Go to sleep, pet; you'll forget all about it in the morning. I tried to explain to father, but he was too upset to listen tonight.'

But the child never forgot. Next time she saw him she whipped both hands behind her back, and a red colour flew into her cheeks.

The Macdonalds lived in the next-door house. Five children there were. Looking through a hole in the vegetable garden fence the little girl saw them playing 'tag' in the evening. The father with the baby Mac on his shoulders, two little girls hanging on to his coat tails, ran round and round the flower beds, shaking with laughter. Once she saw the boys turn the hose on him – *turn the hose on him* – and he made a great grab at them, tickling them until they got hiccoughs.

Then it was she decided there were different sorts of fathers.

Suddenly, one day, mother became ill, and she and grandmother drove into town in a closed carriage.

The little girl was left alone in the house with Alice, the 'general'. That was all right in the daytime, but while Alice was putting her to bed she grew suddenly afraid.

'What'll I do if I have nightmare?' she asked. 'I *often* have night-mare, and then grannie takes me into her bed – I can't stay in the dark – it all gets "whispery" . . . What'll I do if I do?'

'You just go to sleep, child,' said Alice, pulling off her socks and whacking them against the bedrail, 'and don't you holler out and wake your poor pa.'

But the same old nightmare came – the butcher with a knife and a rope who grew nearer and nearer, smiling that dreadful smile, while she could not move, could only stand still, crying out, 'Grandma, grandma!' She woke shivering, to see father beside her bed, a candle in his hand.

'What's the matter?' he said.

'Oh, a butcher – a knife – I want grannie.' He blew out the candle, bent down and caught up the child in his arms, carrying her along the passage to the big bedroom. A newspaper was on the bed – a half-smoked cigar balanced against his reading-lamp. He pitched the paper on the floor, threw the cigar into the fireplace, then carefully tucked up the child. He lay down beside her. Half asleep still, still with the butcher's smile all about her, it seemed she crept close to him, snuggled her head under his arm, held tightly to his pyjama jacket.

Then the dark did not matter; she lay still.

'Here, rub your feet against my legs and get them warm,' said father.

Tired out, he slept before the little girl. A funny feeling came over her. Poor father! Not so big, after all – and with no one to look after him . . . He was harder than the grandmother, but it was a nice hardness . . . And every day he had to work and was too tired to be a Mr Macdonald . . . She had torn up all his beautiful writing . . . She stirred suddenly, and sighed.

'What's the matter?' asked father. 'Another dream?'

'Oh,' said the little girl, 'my head's on your heart; I can hear it going. What a big heart you've got, father dear.'

                                                        (1912)

Millie

MILLIE STOOD leaning against the veranda until the men were out of
sight. When they were far down the road Willie Cox turned round
on his horse and waved. But she didn't wave back. She nodded her
head a little and made a grimace. Not a bad young fellow, Willie
Cox, but a bit too free and easy for her taste. Oh, my word! it was hot.
Enough to fry your hair!

Millie put her handkerchief over her head and shaded her eyes
with her hand. In the distance along the dusty road she could see
the horses, like brown spots dancing up and down, and when she
looked away from them and over the burnt paddocks she could see
them still – just before her eyes, jumping like mosquitoes. It was half-
past two in the afternoon. The sun hung in the faded blue sky like a
burning mirror, and away beyond the paddocks the blue mountains
quivered and leapt like the sea.

Sid wouldn't be back until half-past ten. He had ridden over to the
township with four of the boys to help hunt down the young fellow
who'd murdered Mr Williamson. Such a dreadful thing! And Mrs
Williamson left all alone with all those kids. Funny! she couldn't
think of Mr Williamson being dead! He was such a one for a joke.
Always having a lark. Willie Cox said they found him in the barn,
shot bang through the head, and the young English 'johnny' who'd
been on the station learning farming – disappeared. Funny! she
couldn't think of anyone shooting Mr Williamson, and him so
popular and all. My word! when they caught that young man! Well,
you couldn't be sorry for a young fellow like that. As Sid said, if he
wasn't strung up where would they all be? A man like that doesn't
stop at one go. There was blood all over the barn. And Willie Cox
said he was that knocked out he picked a cigarette up out of the blood
and smoked it. My word! he must have been half dotty.

Millie went back into the kitchen. She put some ashes on the stove
and sprinkled them with water. Languidly, the sweat pouring down
her face, and dropping off her nose and chin, she cleared away the

dinner, and going into the bedroom, stared at herself in the fly-specked mirror, and wiped her face and neck with a towel. She didn't know what was the matter with herself that afternoon. She could have a good cry – just for nothing – and then change her blouse and have a good cup of tea. Yes, she felt like that!

She flopped down on the side of the bed and stared at the coloured print on the wall opposite, *Garden Party at Windsor Castle*. In the foreground emerald lawns planted with immense oak trees, and in their grateful shade a muddle of ladies and gentlemen and parasols and little tables. The background was filled with the towers of Windsor Castle, flying three Union Jacks, and in the middle of the picture the old Queen, like a tea-cosy with a head on top of it. 'I wonder if it really looked like that.' Millie stared at the flowery ladies, who simpered back at her. 'I wouldn't care for that sort of thing. Too much side. What with the Queen an' one thing an' another.'

Over the packing-case dressing-table there was a large photograph of her and Sid, taken on their wedding day. Nice picture that – if you *do* like. She was sitting down in a basket chair, in her cream cashmere and satin ribbons, and Sid, standing with one hand on her shoulder, looking at her bouquet. And behind them there were some fern trees and a waterfall, and Mount Cook in the distance, covered with snow. She had almost forgotten her wedding day; time did pass so, and if you hadn't anyone to talk things over with, they soon dropped out of your mind. 'I wunner why we never had no kids . . . ' She shrugged her shoulders – gave it up. 'Well, *I've* never missed them. I wouldn't be surprised if Sid had, though. He's softer than me.'

And then she sat quiet, thinking of nothing at all, her red swollen hands rolled in her apron, her feet stuck out in front of her, her little head with the thick screw of dark hair drooped on her chest. *Tick-tick* went the kitchen clock, the ashes clinked in the grate, and the venetian blind knocked against the kitchen window. Quite suddenly Millie felt frightened. A queer trembling started inside her – in her stomach – and then spread all over to her knees and hands. 'There's somebody about.' She tiptoed to the door and peered into the kitchen. Nobody there; the veranda doors were closed, the blinds were down, and in the dusky light the white face of the clock shone, and the furniture seemed to bulge and breathe . . . and listen, too. The clock – the ashes – and the venetian – and then again – something else, like steps in the back yard. 'Go an' see what it is, Millie Evans.'

She darted to the back door, opened it, and at the same moment someone ducked behind the wood pile. 'Who's that?' she cried, in a loud, bold voice. 'Come out o' that! I seen yer. I know where y'are. I got my gun. Come out from behind of that wood stack!' She was not frightened any more. She was furiously angry. Her heart banged like a drum. 'I'll teach you to play tricks with a woman,' she yelled, and she took a gun from the kitchen corner, and dashed down the veranda steps, across the glaring yard to the other side of the wood stack. A young man lay there, on his stomach, one arm across his face. 'Get up! You're shamming!' Still holding the gun she kicked him in the shoulders. He gave no sign. 'Oh, my God, I believe he's dead.' She knelt down, seized hold of him, and turned him over on his back. He rolled like a sack. She crouched back on her haunches, staring; her lips and nostrils fluttered with horror.

He was not much more than a boy, with fair hair and a growth of fair down on his lips and chin. His eyes were open, rolled up, showing the whites, and his face was patched with dust caked with sweat. He wore a cotton shirt and trousers, with sandshoes on his feet. One of the trousers was stuck to his leg with a patch of dark blood. 'I *can't*,' said Millie, and then, 'You've got to.' She bent over and felt his heart. 'Wait a minute,' she stammered, 'wait a minute,' and she ran into the house for brandy and a pail of water. 'What are you going to do, Millie Evans? Oh, I don't know. I never seen anyone in a dead faint before.' She knelt down, put her arm under the boy's head and poured some brandy between his lips. It spilled down both sides of his mouth. She dipped a corner of her apron in the water and wiped his face and his hair and his throat, with fingers that trembled. Under the dust and sweat his face gleamed, white as her apron, and thin, and puckered in little lines. A strange dreadful feeling gripped Millie Evans' bosom – some seed that had never flourished there, unfolded and struck deep roots and burst into painful leaf. 'Are yer coming round? Feeling all right again?' The boy breathed sharply, half choked, his eyelids quivered, and he moved his head from side to side. 'You're better,' said Millie, smoothing his hair. 'Feeling fine now again, ain't yer?' The pain in her bosom half suffocated her. 'It's no good you crying, Millie Evans. You got to keep your head.' Quite suddenly he sat up and leaned against the wood pile, away from her, staring on the ground. 'There now!' cried Millie Evans, in a strange, shaking voice.

The boy turned and looked at her, still not speaking, but his eyes were so full of pain and terror that she had to shut her teeth and clench her hands to stop from crying. After a long pause he said, in the little voice of a child talking in his sleep, 'I'm hungry.' His lips quivered. She scrambled to her feet and stood over him. 'You come right into the house and have a sit-down meal,' she said. 'Can you walk?' 'Yes,' he whispered, and swaying he followed her across the glaring yard to the veranda. At the bottom step he paused, looking at her again. 'I'm not coming in,' he said. He sat on the veranda step in the little pool of shade that lay round the house. Millie watched him. 'When did yer last 'ave anything to eat?' He shook his head. She cut a chunk off the greasy corned beef and a round of bread plastered with butter; but when she brought it he was standing up, glancing round him, and paid no attention to the plate of food. 'When are they coming back?' he stammered.

At that moment she knew. She stood, holding the plate, staring. He was Harrison. He was the English johnny who'd killed Mr Williamson. 'I know who you are,' she said, very slowly, 'yer can't fox me. That's who you are. I must have been blind in me two eyes not to 'ave known from the first.' He made a movement with his hands as though that was all nothing. 'When are they coming back?' And she meant to say, 'Any minute. They're on their way now.' Instead she said to the dreadful, frightened face, 'Not till 'arf-past ten.' He sat down, leaning against one of the veranda poles. His face broke up into little quivers. He shut his eyes, and tears streamed down his cheeks. 'Nothing but a kid. An' all them fellows after 'im. 'E don't stand any more of a chance than a kid would.' 'Try a bit of beef,' said Millie. 'It's the food you want. Somethink to steady your stomach.' She moved across the veranda and sat down beside him, the plate on her knees. ''Ere – try a bit.' She broke the bread and butter into little pieces, and she thought, 'They won't ketch him. Not if I can 'elp it. Men is all beasts. I don't care wot 'e's done, or wot 'e 'asn't done. See 'im through, Millie Evans. 'E's nothink but a sick kid.'

* * *

Millie lay on her back, her eyes wide open, listening. Sid turned over, hunched the quilt round his shoulders, muttered 'Good night, ole girl.' She heard Willie Cox and the other chap drop their clothes on to the kitchen floor, and then their voices, and Willie Cox saying, 'Lie down, Gumboil. Lie down, yer little devil,' to his dog. The house dropped quiet. She lay and listened. Little pulses tapped in her body, listening, too. It was hot. She was frightened to move because of Sid. ''E must get off. 'E must. I don't care anythink about justice an' all the rot they've bin spoutin' tonight,' she thought savagely. ''Ow are yer to know what anythink's like till yer *do* know. It's all rot.' She strained to the silence. He ought to be moving . . . Before there was a sound from outside, Willie Cox's Gumboil got up and padded sharply across the kitchen floor and sniffed at the back door. Terror started up in Millie. 'What's that dog doing? Uh! What a fool that young fellow is with a dog 'anging about. Why don't 'e lie down an' sleep.' The dog stopped, but she knew it was listening.

Suddenly, with a sound that made her cry out in horror the dog started barking and rushing to and fro. 'What's that? What's up?' Sid flung out of bed. 'It ain't nothink. It's only Gumboil. Sid, Sid!' She clutched his arm, but he shook her off. 'My Christ, there's somethink up. My God!' Sid flung into his trousers. Willie Cox opened the back door. Gumboil in a fury darted out into the yard, round the corner of the house. 'Sid, there's someone in the paddock,' roared the other chap. 'What is it – what's that?' Sid dashed out on to the front veranda. ''Ere, Millie, take the lantin. Willie, some skunk's got 'old of one of the 'orses.' The three men bolted out of the house, and at the same moment Millie saw Harrison dash across the paddock on Sid's horse and down the road. 'Millie, bring that blasted lantin.' She ran in her bare feet, her nightdress flicking her legs. They were after him in a flash. And at the sight of Harrison in the distance, and the three men hot after, a strange mad joy smothered everything else. She rushed into the road – she laughed and shrieked and danced in the dust, jigging the lantern. 'A – ah! Arter 'im, Sid! A – a – a – h! Ketch him, Willie. Go it! Go it! A – ah, Sid! Shoot 'im down. Shoot 'im!'

(1913)

Pension Séguin

THE SERVANT who opened the door was twin sister to that efficient and hideous creature bearing a soup tureen into the *First French Picture*. Her round red face shone like freshly washed china. She had a pair of immense bare arms to match, and a quantity of mottled hair arranged in a sort of bow. I stammered in a ridiculous, breathless fashion, as though a pack of Russian wolves were behind me, rather than five flights of beautifully polished French stairs.

'Have you a room?' The servant girl did not know. She would ask Madame. Madame was at dinner.

'Will you come in, please?'

Through the dark hall, guarded by a large black stove that had the appearance of a headless cat with one red all-seeing eye in the middle of its stomach, I followed her into the salon.

'Please to sit down,' said the servant girl, closing the door behind her. I heard her list slippers shuffle along the corridor, the sound of another door opening – a little clamour – instantly suppressed. Silence followed.

The salon was long and narrow, with a yellow floor dotted with white mats. White muslin curtains hid the windows: the walls were white, decorated with pictures of pale ladies drifting down cypress avenues to forsaken temples, and moons rising over boundless oceans. You would have thought that all the long years of Madame's virginity had been devoted to the making of white mats – that her childish voice had lisped its numbers in crochet-work stitches. I did not dare to begin counting them. They rained upon me from every possible place, like impossible snowflakes. Even the piano stool was buttoned into one embroidered with P.F.

I had been looking for a resting-place all the morning. At the start I flew up innumerable stairs as though they were major scales – the most cheerful things in the world – but after repeated failures the scales had resolved into the minor, and my heart, which was quite cast down by this time, leapt up again at these signs and tokens of virtue and sobriety. 'A woman with such sober passions,' thought I, 'is bound to be quiet and clean, with few babies and a much absent husband. Mats are not the sort of things that lend themselves in their making to cheerful singing. Mats are essentially the fruits of pious solitude. I shall certainly take a room here.' And I began to dream of unpacking my clothes in a little white room, and getting into a kimono and lying on a white bed, watching the curtains float out from the windows in the delicious autumn air that smelled of apples and honey . . . until the door opened and a tall, thin woman in a lilac pinafore came in, smiling in a vague fashion.

'Madame Séguin?'

'Yes, Madame.'

I repeated the familiar story. A quiet room, removed from any church bells, or crowing cocks, or little boys' schools, or railway stations.

'There are none of such things anywhere near here,' said Madame, looking very surprised. 'I have a very beautiful room to let, and quite unexpectedly. It has been occupied by a young gentleman from Buenos Aires whose father died, unfortunately, and implored him to return home immediately. Quite natural, indeed.'

'Oh, very!' said I, hoping that the Hamlet-like apparition was at rest again and would not invade my solitude to make certain of his son's obedience.

'If Madame will follow me.'

Down a dark corridor, round a corner I felt my way. I wanted to ask Madame if this was where Buenos Aires *père* appeared unto his son, but I did not dare to.

'Here – you see. Quite away from everything,' said Madame.

I have always viewed with a proper amount of respect and abhorrence those penetrating spirits who are not susceptible to appearances? What is there to believe in except appearances? I have nearly always found that they are the only things worth enjoying at all, and if ever an innocent child lays its head upon my knee and begs for the truth of the matter, I shall tell it the story of my one and only nurse, who, knowing my horror of gooseberry jam, spread a coat of apricot over the top of the jam jar. As long as I believed it apricot I was happy, and learning wisdom, I contrived to eat the apricot and leave the gooseberry behind. 'So, you see, my little innocent creature,' I shall end, 'the great thing to learn in this life is to be content with appearances, and shun the vulgarities of the grocer and philosopher.'

Bright sunlight streamed through the windows of the delightful room. There was an alcove for the bed, a writing-table was placed against the window, a couch against the wall. And outside the window I looked down upon an avenue of gold and red trees and up at a range of mountains white with fresh fallen snow.

'One hundred and eighty francs a month,' murmured Madame, smiling at nothing, but seeming to imply by her manner, 'Of course this has nothing to do with the matter.' I said, 'That is too much. I cannot afford more than one hundred and fifty francs.'

'But,' explained Madame, 'the size! the alcove! And the extreme rarity of being overlooked by so many mountains.'

'Yes,' I said.

'And then the food. There are four meals a day, and breakfast in your room if you wish it.'

'Yes,' I said, more feebly.

'And my husband a Professor at the Conservatoire – that again is so rare.'

Courage is like a disobedient dog, once it starts running away it flies all the faster for your attempts to recall it.

'One hundred and sixty,' I said.

'If you agree to take it for two months I will accept,' said Madame, very quickly. I agreed.

Marie helped to unstrap my boxes. She knelt on the floor, grinning and scratching her big red arms.

'Ah, how glad I am Madame has come,' she said. 'Now we shall have some life again. Monsieur Arthur, who lived in this room – he was a gay one. Singing all day and sometimes dancing. Many a time Mademoiselle Ambatielos would be playing and he'd dance for an hour without stopping.'

'Who is Mademoiselle Ambatielos?' I asked.

'A young lady studying at the Conservatoire,' said Marie, sniffing in a very friendly fashion. 'But she gives lessons too. Ah, *mon Dieu*, sometimes when I am dusting in her room I think her fingers will drop off. She plays all day long. But I like that – that's life, noise is. That's what I say. You'll hear her soon. Up and down she goes!' said Marie, with extreme heartiness.

'But,' I cried, loathing Marie, 'how many other people are staying here?'

Marie shrugged. 'Nobody to speak of. There's the Russian gentleman, a priest he is, and Madame's three children – and that's all. The children are lively enough,' she said, filling the washstand pitcher, 'but then there's the baby – the boy! Ah, you'll know about him, poor little one, soon enough!' She was so detestable I would not ask her anything further.

I waited until she was gone, and leaned against the windowsill, watching the sun deepen in the trees until they seemed full and trembling with gold, and wondering what was the matter with the mysterious baby.

All through the afternoon Mademoiselle Ambatielos and the piano warred with the *Appassionata* Sonata. They shattered it to bits and re-made it to their heart's desire – they unpicked it – and tried it in various styles. They added a little touch – caught up something. Finally they decided that the only thing of importance was the loud pedal. The mysterious baby, hidden behind heaven knows how many doors, cried with such curious persistence that I had to strain my ears, wondering if it was a baby or an engine or a far-off whistle. At dusk Marie, accompanied by the two little girls, brought me a lamp. My appearance disturbed these charming children to such an extent that they rushed up and down the corridor in a frenzied state for half an hour afterwards, bumping themselves against the walls, and shrieking with derisive laughter.

At eight the gong sounded for supper. I was hungry. The corridor was filled with the warm, strong smell of cooked meat. 'Well,' I thought, 'at any rate, judging by the smell, the food must be good.' And feeling very frightened I entered the dining-room.

. Two rows of faces turned to watch me. M. Séguin introduced me, rapped on the table with the soup spoon, and the two little girls, impudent and scornful, cried, '*Bon soir, Madame*,' while the baby, half washed away by his afternoon's performance, emptied his cup of milk over his head while Madame Séguin showed me my seat. In the confusion caused by this last episode, and by his being carried away by Marie, screaming and spitting with rage, I sat down next to the Russian priest and opposite Mademoiselle Ambatielos. M. Séguin took a loaf of bread from a three-legged basket at his elbow and carved it against his chest. Soup was served – with vermicelli letters of the alphabet floating in it. These were last straws to the little Séguins' table manners.

'Maman, Yvonne's got more letters than me.'

'Maman, Hélène keeps taking my letters out with her spoon.'

'Children! Children! Quiet, quiet!' said Madame Séguin gently. 'No, don't do it.'

Hélène seized Yvonne's plate and pulled it towards her.

'Stop,' said M. Séguin, who was like a rat, with spectacles all misted over with soup steam. 'Hélène, leave the table. Go to Marie.' Exit Hélène, with her apron over her head.

Soup was followed by chestnuts and Brussels sprouts. All the time the Russian priest, who wore a pale blue tie with a buttoned frock-coat and a moustache fierce as a Gogol novel, kept up a flow of conversation with Mademoiselle Ambatielos. She looked very young. She was stout, with a high firm bust decorated with a spray of artificial roses. She never ceased touching the roses or her blouse or hair, or looking at her hands – with a smile trembling on her mouth and her blue eyes wide and staring. She seemed half intoxicated with her fresh young body.

'I saw you this morning when you didn't see me,' said the priest.

'You didn't.'

'I did.'

'He didn't, did he, Madame?'

Madame Séguin smiled, and carried away the chestnuts, bringing back a dish of pears.

'I hope you will come into the salon after dinner,' she said to me. 'We always chat a little – we are such a family party.' I smiled, wondering why pears should follow chestnuts.

'I must apologise for baby,' she went on. 'He is so nervous. But he spends his day in a room at the other end of the apartment to you. You will not be troubled. Only think of it! He passes whole days banging his little head against the floor and walls. The doctors cannot understand it at all.'

M. Séguin pushed back his chair, said grace. I followed desperately into the salon. 'I expect you have been admiring my mats,' said Madame Séguin, with more animation than she had hitherto shown. 'People always imagine they are the product of my industry. But, alas, no! They are all made by my friend, Madame Kummer, who has the pension on the first floor.'

(1913)

Violet

I met a young virgin
Who sadly did moan . . .

THERE IS A VERY unctuous and irritating English proverb to the effect that 'Every cloud has a silver lining'. What comfort can it be to one steeped to the eyebrows in clouds to ponder over their linings, and what an unpleasant picture-postcard seal it sets upon one's tragedy – turning it into a little ha'penny monstrosity with a moon in the left-hand corner like a vainglorious threepenny bit! Nevertheless, like most unctuous and irritating things, it is true. The lining woke me after my first night at the Pension Séguin and showed me over the feather bolster a room bright with sunlight as if every golden-haired baby in heaven were pelting the earth with buttercup posies. 'What a charming fancy!' I thought. 'How much prettier than the proverb! It sounds like a day in the country with Katharine Tynan.'

And I saw a little picture of myself and Katharine Tynan being handed glasses of milk by a red-faced woman with an immensely fat apron, while we discussed the direct truth of proverbs as opposed to the fallacy of playful babies. But in such a case imaginary I was ranged on the side of the proverbs. 'There's a lot of sound sense in 'em,' said that coarse being. 'I admire the way they put their collective foot down upon the female attempt to embroider everything. "The pitcher that goes too often to the well gets broken." *Also gut.* Not even a loophole for a set of verses to a broken pitcher. No possible chance of the well being one of those symbolic founts to which all hearts in the form of pitchers are carried. The only proverb I disapprove of,' went on this impossible creature, pulling a spring onion from the garden bed and chewing on it, 'is the one about a bird in the hand. I naturally prefer birds in bushes.' 'But,' said Katharine Tynan, tender and brooding, as she lifted a little green fly from her milk glass, 'but if you were Saint Francis, the bird would not *mind* being in your hand. It would *prefer* the white nest of your fingers to any bush.'

I jumped out of bed and ran over to the window and opened it wide and leaned out. Down below in the avenue a wind shook and swung the trees; the scent of leaves was on the lifting air. The houses lining the avenue were small and white. Charming, chaste-looking little houses, showing glimpses of lace and knots of ribbon, for all the world like country children in a row, about to play 'Nuts and May'. I began to imagine an adorable little creature named Yvette who lived in one and all of these houses . . . She spends her morning in a white lace boudoir cap, worked with daisies, sipping chocolate from a Sèvres cup with one hand, while a faithful attendant polishes the little pink nails of the other. She spends the afternoon in her tiny white and gold boudoir, curled up, a Persian kitten on her lap, while her ardent, beautiful lover leans over the back of the sofa, kissing and kissing again that thrice fascinating dimple on her left shoulder . . . When one of the balcony windows opened, and a stout servant swaggered out with her arms full of rugs and carpet strips. With a gesture expressing fury and disgust she flung them over the railing, disappeared, re-appeared again with a long-handled cane broom and fell upon the wretched rugs and carpets. Bang! Whack! Whack! Bang! Their feeble, pitiful jigging inflamed her to ever greater effort. Clouds of dust flew up round her, and when one little rug escaped and flopped down to the avenue below, like a fish, she leaned over the balcony shaking her fist and the broom at it.

Lured by the noise, an old gentleman came to a window opposite and cast an eye of approval upon the industrious girl and yawned in the face of the lovely day. There was an air of detachment and deliberation about the way he carefully felt over the muscles of his arms and legs, pressed his throat, coughed, and shot a jet of spittle out of the window. Nobody seemed more surprised at this last feat than he. He seemed to regard it as a small triumph in its way, buttoning his immense stomach into a white piqué waistcoat with every appearance of satisfaction. Away flew my charming Yvette in a black and white check dress, an alpaca apron and a market basket over her arm.

I dressed, ate a roll and drank some tepid coffee, feeling very sobered. I thought how true it was that the world was a delightful place if it were not for the people, and how more than true it was that people were not worth troubling about, and that wise men should set their affections upon nothing smaller than cities, heavenly or otherwise, and countrysides which are always heavenly.

With these reflections, both pious and smug, I put on my hat, groped my way along the dark passage, and ran down the five flights of stairs into the Rue St Léger. There was a garden on the opposite side of the street, through which one walked to the University and the more pretentious avenues fronting the Place du Théâtre. Although autumn was well advanced, not a leaf had fallen from the trees, the little shrubs and bushes were touched with pink and crimson, and against the blue sky the trees stood sheathed in gold. On stone benches nursemaids in white cloaks and stiff white caps chattered and wagged their heads like a company of cockatoos, and, up and down, in the sun, some genteel babies bowled hoops with a delicate air. What peculiar pleasure it is to wander through a strange city and amuse oneself as a child does, playing a solitary game!

'*Pardon, Madame, mais voulez-vous . . .* ' and then the voice faltered and cried my name as though I had been given up for lost times without number; as though I had been drowned in foreign seas, and burnt in American hotel fires, and buried in a hundred lonely graves. 'What on *earth* are you doing here?' Before me, not a day changed, not a hairpin altered, stood Violet Burton. I was flattered beyond measure at this enthusiasm, and pressed her cold, strong hand, and said 'Extraordinary!'

'But what are you *here* for?'

' . . . Nerves.'

'Oh, impossible, I really can't believe that.'

'It is perfectly true,' I said, my enthusiasm waning. There is nothing more annoying to a woman than to be suspected of nerves of iron.

'Well, you certainly don't *look* it,' said she, scrutinising me, with that direct English frankness that makes one feel as though sitting in the glare of a window at breakfast-time.

'What are *you* here for?' I said, smiling graciously to soften the glare. At that she turned and looked across the lawns, and fidgeted with her umbrella like a provincial actress about to make a confession.

'I' – in a quiet affected voice – 'I came here to forget . . . But,' facing me again and smiling energetically, 'don't let's talk about that. Not yet. I can't explain. Not until I know you all over again.' Very solemnly – 'Not until I am sure you are to be trusted.'

'Oh, don't trust me, Violet!' I cried. 'I'm not to be trusted. I wouldn't if I were you.' She frowned and stared.

'What a terrible thing to say. You can't be in earnest.'

'Yes, I am. There's nothing I adore talking about so much as another person's secret.' To my surprise, she came to my side and put her arm through mine.

'Thank you,' she said gratefully. 'I think it's awfully good of you to take me into your confidence like that. Awfully. And even if it were true . . . but no, it can't be true, otherwise you wouldn't have told me. I mean it can't be psychologically true of the same nature to be frank and dishonourable at the same time. Can it? But then . . . I don't know. I suppose it is possible. Don't you find that the Russian novelists have made an upheaval of all your conclusions?' We walked, *bras dessus bras dessous*, down the sunny path.

'Let's sit down,' said Violet. 'There's a fountain quite near this bench. I often come here. You can hear it all the time.' The faint noise of the water sounded like a half-forgotten tune, half sly, half laughing.

'Isn't it wonderful!' breathed Violet. 'Like weeping in the night.'

'Oh, Violet,' said I, terrified at this turn. 'Wonderful things don't weep in the night. They sleep like tops and know nothing more till again it is day.'

She put her arm over the back of the bench and crossed her legs.

'Why do you persist in denying your emotions? Why are you ashamed of them?' she demanded.

'I'm not. But I keep them tucked away, and only produce them very occasionally, like special little pots of jam, when the people whom I love come to tea.'

'There you are again! Emotions and jam! Now, I'm absolutely different. I live on mine. Sometimes I wish I didn't – but then again I would rather suffer through them – suffer intensely, I mean; go down into the depths with them, for the sake of that wonderful upward swing on to the pinnacles of happiness.' She edged nearer to me.

'I wish I could think where I get my nature from,' she went on. 'Father and mother are absolutely different. I mean – they're quite normal – quite commonplace.' I shook my head and raised my eyebrows. 'But it is no use fighting it. It has beaten me. Absolutely – once and for all.' A pause, inadequately filled by the sly, laughing water. 'Now,' said Violet impressively, 'you know what I meant when I said I came here to forget.'

'But I assure you I don't, Violet. How can you expect me to be so subtle? I quite understand that you don't wish to tell me until you know me better. Quite!'

She opened her eyes and her mouth.

'I *have* told you! I mean – not straight out. Not in so many words. But then – how could I? But when I told you of my emotional nature, and that I had been in the depths and swept up to the pinnacles . . . surely, surely you realised that I was telling you, symbolically. What else can you have thought?'

No young girl ever performs such gymnastic feats by herself. Yet in my experience I had always imagined that the depths followed the pinnacles. I ventured to suggest so.

'They do,' said Violet gloomily. 'You see them, if you look, before and after.'

'Like the people in Shelley's *Skylark*,' said I.

Violet looked vague, and I repented. But I did not know how to sympathise, and I had no idea of the relative sizes.

'It was in the summer,' said Violet. 'I had been most frightfully depressed. I don't know what it was. For one thing I felt as though I could not make up my mind to anything. I felt so terribly useless – that I had no place in the scheme of things – and worst of all, nobody who understood me . . . It may have been what I was reading at the time . . . but I don't think . . . not entirely. Still, one never knows. Does one? And then I met . . . Mr Farr, at a dance – '

'Oh, call him by his Christian name, Violet. You can't go on telling me about Mr Farr and you . . . on the heights.'

'Why on earth not? Very well – I met – Arthur. I think I must have been mad that evening. For one thing there had been a bother about going. Mother didn't want me to, because she said there wouldn't be anybody to see me home. And I was frightfully keen. I must have had a presentiment, I think. Do you believe in presentiments? . . . I don't know, we can't be certain, can we? Anyhow, I went. And *he* was there.' She turned a deep scarlet and bit her lip. Oh, I really began to like Violet Burton – to like her very much indeed.

'Go on,' I said.

'We danced together seven times and we talked the whole time. The music was very slow – we talked of everything. You know . . . about books and theatres and all that sort of thing at first, and then – about our souls.'

' . . . What?'

'I said – our souls. He understood me *absolutely*. And after the seventh dance . . . No, I must tell you the first thing he ever said to me. He said, "Do you believe in Pan?" Quite quietly. Just like that. And then he said, "I knew you did." Wasn't that extraor-din-ary!

After the seventh dance we sat out on the landing. And . . . shall I go on?'

'Yes, go on.'

'He said, "I think I must be mad. I want to kiss you," – and – I let him.'

'Do go on.'

'I simply can't tell you what I felt like. Fancy! I'd never kissed out of the family before. I mean – of course – never a man. And then he said: "I must tell you – I am engaged." '

'Well?'

'What else is there? Of course I simply rushed upstairs and tumbled everything over in the dressing-room and found my coat and went home. And next morning I made Mother let me come here. I thought,' said Violet, 'I thought I would have died of shame.'

'Is that all?' I cried. 'You can't mean to say that's all?'

'What else could there be? What on earth did you expect? How extraordinary you are – staring at me like that!'

And in the long pause I heard again the little fountain, half sly, half laughing – at me, I thought, not at Violet.

(1913)

Bains Turcs

'THIRD STOREY – to the left, Madame,' said the cashier, handing me a pink ticket. 'One moment – I will ring for the elevator.' Her black satin skirt swished across the scarlet and gold hall, and she stood among the artificial palms, her white neck and powdered face topped with masses of gleaming orange hair – like an over-ripe fungus bursting from a thick, black stem. She rang and rang. 'A thousand pardons, Madame. It is disgraceful. A new attendant. He leaves this week.' With her fingers on the bell she peered into the cage as though she expected to see him, lying on the floor, like a dead bird. 'It is disgraceful.' There appeared from nowhere a tiny figure disguised in a peaked cap and dirty white cotton gloves. 'Here you are!' she scolded. 'Where have you been? What have you been doing?' For answer the figure hid its face behind one of the white cotton gloves and sneezed twice. 'Ugh! Disgusting! Take Madame to the third storey!' The midget stepped aside, bowed, entered after me and clashed the gates to. We ascended, very slowly, to an accompaniment of sneezes and prolonged, half-whistling sniffs. I asked the top of the patent-leather cap: 'Have you a cold?' 'It is the air, Madame,' replied the creature, speaking through its nose with a restrained air of great relish, 'one is never dry here. Third floor – *if* you please,' sneezing over my ten-centime tip.

I walked along a tiled corridor decorated with advertisements for lingerie and bust improvers – was allotted a tiny cabin and a blue print chemise and told to undress and find the Warm Room as soon as possible. Through the matchboard walls and from the corridor sounded cries and laughter and snatches of conversation.

'Are you ready?'

'Are you coming out now?'

'Wait till you see me!'

'Berthe – Berthe!'

'One moment! One moment! Immediately!'

I undressed quickly and carelessly, feeling like one of a troupe of little schoolgirls let loose in a swimming-bath.

The Warm Room was not large. It had terracotta painted walls with a fringe of peacocks, and a glass roof through which one could see the sky, pale and unreal as a photographer's background screen. Some round tables strewn with shabby fashion journals, a marble basin in the centre of the room, filled with yellow lilies, and on the long, towel-enveloped chairs a number of ladies, apparently languid as the flowers . . . I lay back with a cloth over my head, and the air, smelling of jungles and circuses and damp washing, made me begin to dream . . . Yes, it might have been very fascinating to have married an explorer . . . and lived in a jungle, as long as he didn't shoot anything or take anything captive. I detest performing beasts. Oh . . . those circuses at home . . . the tent in the paddock and the children swarming over the fence to stare at the wagons and at the clown making up, with his glass stuck on the wagon wheel – and the steam organ playing 'The Honeysuckle and the Bee' much too fast . . . over and over. I know what this air reminds me of – a game of follow-my-leader among the clothes hung out to dry . . .

The door opened. Two tall blonde women in red and white check gowns came in and took the chairs opposite mine. One of them carried a box of mandarins wrapped in silver paper and the other a manicure set. They were very stout, with gay, bold faces, and quantities of exquisite whipped fair hair.

Before sitting down they glanced round the room, looked the other women up and down, turned to each other, grimaced, whispered something, and one of them said, offering the box, 'Have a mandarin?' At that they started laughing – they lay back and shook, and each time they caught sight of each other broke out afresh.

'Ah, that was too good,' cried one, wiping her eyes very carefully, just at the corners. 'You and I, coming in here, quite serious, you know, very correct – and looking round the room – and – and as a result of our *careful* inspection – I offer you a mandarin. No, it's too funny. I must remember that. It's good enough for a music-hall. Have a mandarin?'

'But I cannot imagine,' said the other, 'why women look so hideous in Turkish baths – like beef-steaks in chemises. Is it the women – or is it the air? Look at that one, for instance – the skinny one, reading a book and sweating at the moustache – and those two over in the corner, discussing whether or not they ought to tell their non-existent babies how babies come – and . . . Heavens! Look at this one coming in. Take the box, dear. Have all the mandarins.'

The newcomer was a short, stout little woman with flat, white feet, and a black mackintosh cap over her hair. She walked up and down the room, swinging her arms, in affected unconcern, glancing contemptuously at the laughing women, and rang the bell for the attendant. It was answered immediately by Berthe, half naked and sprinkled with soapsuds. 'Well, what is it, Madame? I've no time . . .'

'Please bring me a hand towel,' said the Mackintosh Cap in German.

'Pardon? I do not understand. Do you speak French?'

'*Non*,' said the Mackintosh Cap.

'Ber-the!' shrieked one of the blonde women, 'have a mandarin. Oh, *mon Dieu*, I shall die of laughing.'

The Mackintosh Cap went through a pantomime of finding herself wet and rubbing herself dry. '*Verstehen Sie?*'

'*Mais non, Madame*,' said Berthe, watching with round eyes that snapped with laughter, and she left the Mackintosh Cap, winked at the blonde women, came over, felt them as though they had been a pair of prize poultry, said 'You are doing very well,' and disappeared again.

The Mackintosh Cap sat down on the edge of a chair, snatched a fashion journal, smacked over the crackling pages and pretended to read, while the blonde women leaned back eating the mandarins and throwing the peelings into the lily basin. A scent of fruit, fresh and penetrating, hung on the air. I looked round at the other women. Yes, they were hideous, lying back, red and moist, with dull eyes and lank hair, the only little energy they had vented in shocked prudery at the behaviour of the two blondes. Suddenly I discovered Mackintosh Cap staring at me over the top of her fashion journal, so intently that I took flight and went into the hot room. But in vain! Mackintosh Cap followed after and planted herself in front of me.

'I know,' she said, confident and confiding, 'that you can speak German. I saw it in your face just now. Wasn't that a scandal about the attendant refusing me a towel? I shall speak to the management about that, and I shall get my husband to write them a letter this evening. Things always come better from a man, don't they? No,' she said, rubbing her yellowish arms, 'I've never been in such a scandalous place – and four francs fifty to pay! Naturally, I shall not give a tip. You wouldn't, would you? Not after that scandal about a hand-towel . . . I've a great mind to complain about those women as well. Those two that keep on laughing and eating. Do you know who they are?' She shook her head. 'They're not respectable women – you can tell at a glance. At least I can, any married woman can. They're nothing but a couple of street women. I've never been so insulted in my life. Laughing at me, mind you! The great big fat pigs like that! And I haven't sweated at all properly, just because of them. I got so angry that the sweat turned in instead of out; it does in excitement, you know, sometimes, and now instead of losing my cold I wouldn't be surprised if I brought on a fever.'

I walked round the hot room in misery pursued by the Mackintosh Cap until the two blonde women came in, and seeing her, burst into another fit of laughter. To my rage and disgust Mackintosh Cap sidled up to me, smiled meaningly, and drew down her mouth. 'I don't care,' she said, in her hideous German voice. 'I shouldn't lower myself by paying any attention to a couple of street women. If my husband knew he'd never get over it. Dreadfully particular he is. We've been married six years. We come from Pfalzburg. It's a nice town. Four children I have living, and it was really to get over the shock of the fifth that we came here. The fifth,' she whispered, padding after me, 'was born, a fine healthy child, and it never breathed! Well, after nine months, a woman can't help being disappointed, can she?'

I moved towards the vapour room. 'Are you going in there?' she said. 'I wouldn't if I were you. Those two have gone in. They may think you want to strike up an acquaintance with them. You never know women like that.' At that moment they came out, wrapping themselves in the rough gowns, and passing Mackintosh Cap like disdainful queens. 'Are you going to take your chemise off in the vapour room?' asked she. 'Don't mind me, you know. Woman is woman, and besides, if you'd rather, I won't look at you. I know – I used to be like that. I wouldn't mind betting,' she went on savagely, 'those filthy women had a good look at each other. Pooh! women like that. You can't shock them. And don't they look dreadful? Bold, and all that false hair. That manicure box one of them had was fitted up with gold. Well, I don't suppose it was real, but I think it was disgusting to bring it. One might at least cut one's nails in private, don't you think? I *cannot* see,' she said, 'what men see in such women. No, a husband and children and a home to look after, that's what a woman needs. That's what my husband says. Fancy one of these hussies peeling potatoes or choosing the meat! Are you going already?'

I flew to find Berthe, and all the time I was soaped and smacked and sprayed and thrown in a cold-water tank I could not get out of my mind the ugly, wretched figure of the little German with a good husband and four children, railing against the two fresh beauties who had never peeled potatoes nor chosen the right meat. In the ante-room I saw them once again. They were dressed in blue. One was pinning on a bunch of violets, the other buttoning a pair of ivory suède gloves. In their charming feathered hats and furs they stood talking. 'Yes, there they are,' said a voice at my elbow.

And there was Mackintosh Cap, transformed, in a blue and white check blouse and crochet collar, with the little waist and large hips of the German woman and a terrible bird nest, which Pfalzburg doubt-less called *Reisehut*, on her head. 'How do you suppose they can afford clothes like that? The horrible, low creatures. No, they're enough to make a young girl think twice.' And as the two walked out of the ante-room, Mackintosh Cap stared after them, her sallow face all mouth and eyes, like the face of a hungry child before a forbidden table.

(1913)

Something Childish but Very Natural

WHETHER HE HAD FORGOTTEN what it felt like, or his head had really grown bigger since the summer before, Henry could not decide. But his straw hat hurt him: it pinched his forehead and started a dull ache in the two bones just over the temples. So he chose a corner seat in a third-class 'smoker', took off his hat and put it in the rack with his large black cardboard portfolio and his Aunt B.'s Christmas-present gloves. The carriage smelt horribly of wet india-rubber and soot. There were ten minutes to spare before the train went, so Henry decided to go and have a look at the book-stall. Sunlight darted through the glass roof of the station in long beams of blue and gold; a little boy ran up and down carrying a tray of primroses; there was something about the people – about the women especially – something idle and yet eager. The most thrilling day of the year, the first real day of Spring had unclosed its warm delicious beauty even to London eyes. It had put a spangle in every colour and a new tone in every voice, and city folks walked as though they carried real live bodies under their clothes with real live hearts pumping the stiff blood through.

Henry was a great fellow for books. He did not read many nor did he possess above half a dozen. He looked at all in the Charing Cross Road during lunch-time and at any odd time in London; the quantity with which he was on nodding terms was amazing. By his clean neat handling of them and by his nice choice of phrase when discussing them with one or another bookseller you would have thought that he had taken his pap with a tome propped before his nurse's bosom. But you would have been quite wrong. That was only Henry's way with everything he touched or said. That afternoon it was an anthology of English poetry, and he turned over the pages until a title struck his eye – *Something Childish But Very Natural!*

Had I but two little wings,
And were a little feathery bird,
To you I'd fly, my dear,
But thoughts like these are idle things,
And I stay here.

But in my sleep to you I fly,
I'm always with you in my sleep,
The world is all one's own,
But then one wakes and where am I?
All, all alone.

Sleep stays not though a monarch bids,
So I love to wake at break of day,
For though my sleep be gone,
Yet while 'tis dark one shuts one's lids,
And so, dreams on.

He could not have done with the little poem. It was not the words so much as the whole air of it that charmed him! He might have written it lying in bed, very early in the morning, and watching the sun dance on the ceiling. 'It is *still*, like that,' thought Henry. 'I am sure he wrote it when he was half-awake some time, for it's got a smile of a dream on it.' He stared at the poem and then looked away and repeated it by heart, missed a word in the third verse and looked again and again, until he became conscious of shouting and shuffling and he looked up to see the train moving slowly.

'God's thunder!' Henry dashed forward. A man with a flag and a whistle had his hand on a door. He clutched Henry somehow . . . Henry was inside with the door slammed, in a carriage that wasn't a 'smoker', that had not a trace of his straw hat or the black portfolio or his Aunt B.'s Christmas-present gloves. Instead, in the opposite corner, close against the wall, there sat a girl. Henry did not dare to look at her, but he felt certain she was staring at him. 'She must think I'm mad,' he thought, 'dashing into a train without even a hat, and in the evening, too.' He felt so funny. He didn't know how to sit or sprawl. He put his hands in his pockets and tried to appear quite indifferent and frown at a large photograph of Bolton Abbey. But feeling her eyes on him he gave her just the tiniest glance. Quick she looked away out of the window, and then Henry, careful of her slightest movement, went on looking. She sat pressed against the window, her cheek and shoulder half hidden by a long wave of marigold-coloured hair. One little hand in a grey cotton glove held a leather case on her lap with the initials E.M. on it. The other hand she had slipped through the window-strap, and Henry noticed a silver bangle on the wrist with a Swiss cow-bell and a silver shoe and a fish. She wore a green coat and a hat with a wreath round it. All this Henry saw while the title of the new poem persisted in his brain – *Something Childish But Very Natural*. 'I suppose she goes to some school in London,' thought Henry. 'She might be in an office. Oh no, she is too young. Besides, she'd have her hair up if she was. It isn't even down her back.' He could not keep his eyes off that beautiful waving hair. ' "My eyes are like two drunken bees . . . " Now, I wonder if I read that or made it up?'

That moment the girl turned round and, catching his glance, she blushed. She bent her head to hide the red colour that flew in her cheeks, and Henry, terribly embarrassed, blushed too. 'I shall have to speak – have to – have to!' He started putting up his hand to raise the hat that wasn't there. He thought that funny; it gave him confidence.

'I'm – I'm most awfully sorry,' he said, smiling at the girl's hat. 'But I can't go on sitting in the same carriage with you and not explaining why I dashed in like that, without my hat even. I'm sure I gave you a fright, and just now I was staring at you – but that's only an awful fault of mine; I'm a terrible starer! If you'd like me to explain – how I got in here – not about the staring, of course,' – he gave a little laugh – 'I will.'

For a minute she said nothing, then in a low, shy voice – 'It doesn't matter.'

The train had flung behind the roofs and chimneys. They were swinging into the country, past little black woods and fading fields and pools of water shining under an apricot evening sky. Henry's heart began to thump and beat to the beat of the train. He couldn't leave it like that. She sat so quiet, hidden in her fallen hair. He felt that it was absolutely necessary that she should look up and understand him – understand him at least. He leant forward and clasped his hands round his knees.

'You see I'd just put all my things – a portfolio – into a third-class "smoker" and was having a look at the book-stall,' he explained.

As he told the story she raised her head. He saw her grey eyes under the shadow of her hat and her eyebrows like two gold feathers. Her lips were faintly parted. Almost unconsciously he seemed to absorb the fact that she was wearing a bunch of primroses and that her throat was white – the shape of her face wonderfully delicate against all that burning hair. 'How beautiful she is! How simply beautiful she is!' sang Henry's heart, and swelled with the words, bigger and bigger and trembling like a marvellous bubble – so that he was afraid to breathe for fear of breaking it.

'I hope there was nothing valuable in the portfolio,' said she, very grave.

'Oh, only some silly drawings that I was taking back from the office,' answered Henry airily. 'And – I was rather glad to lose my hat. It had been hurting me all day.'

'Yes,' she said, 'it's left a mark,' and she nearly smiled.

Why on earth should those words have made Henry feel so free suddenly and so happy and so madly excited? What was happening between them? They said nothing, but to Henry their silence was alive and warm. It covered him from his head to his feet in a trembling wave. Her marvellous words, 'It's made a mark,' had in some mysterious fashion established a bond between them. They could not be utter strangers to each other if she spoke so simply and so naturally. And now she was really smiling. The smile danced in her eyes, crept over her cheeks to her lips and stayed there. He leant back. The words flew from him – 'Isn't life wonderful!'

At that moment the train dashed into a tunnel. He heard her voice raised against the noise. She leant forward.

'I don't think so. But then I've been a fatalist for a long time now' – a pause – 'months.'

They were shattering through the dark. 'Why?' called Henry.

'Oh . . .'

Then she shrugged, and smiled and shook her head, meaning she could not speak against the noise. He nodded and leant back. They came out of the tunnel into a sprinkle of lights and houses. He waited for her to explain. But she got up and buttoned her coat and put her hands to her hat, swaying a little. 'I get out here,' she said. That seemed quite impossible to Henry.

The train slowed down and the lights outside grew brighter. She moved towards his end of the carriage.

'Look here!' he stammered. 'Shan't I see you again?' He got up too, and leant against the rack with one hand. 'I *must* see you again.' The train was stopping.

She said breathlessly, 'I come down from London every evening.'

'You – you – you do – really?' His eagerness frightened her. He was quick to curb it. Shall we or shall we not shake hands? raced through his brain. One hand was on the door-handle, the other held the little bag. The train stopped. Without another word or glance she was gone.

2

Then came Saturday – a half-day at the office – and Sunday between. By Monday evening Henry was quite exhausted. He was at the station far too early, with a pack of silly thoughts at his heels as it were driving him up and down. 'She didn't say she came by this train!' 'And supposing I go up and she cuts me.' 'There may be somebody with her.' 'Why do you suppose she's ever thought of you again?' 'What are you going to say if you do see her?' He even prayed, 'Lord, if it be Thy will, let us meet.'

But nothing helped. White smoke floated against the roof of the station – dissolved and came again in swaying wreaths. Of a sudden, as he watched it, so delicate and so silent, moving with such mysterious grace above the crowd and the scuffle, he grew calm. He felt very tired – he only wanted to sit down and shut his eyes – she was not coming – a forlorn relief breathed in the words. And then he saw her quite near to him walking towards the train with the same little leather case in her hand. Henry waited. He knew, somehow, that she had seen him, but he did not move until she came close to him and said in her low, shy voice – 'Did you get them again?'

'Oh yes, thank you, I got them again,' and with a funny half-gesture he showed her the portfolio and the gloves. They walked side by side to the train and into an empty carriage. They sat down opposite to each other, smiling timidly but not speaking, while the train moved slowly, and slowly gathered speed and smoothness. Henry spoke first.

'It's so silly,' he said, 'not knowing your name.' She put back a big piece of hair that had fallen on her shoulder, and he saw how her hand in the grey glove was shaking. Then he noticed that she was sitting very stiffly with her knees pressed together – and he was, too – both of them trying not to tremble so. She said, 'My name is Edna.'

'And mine is Henry.'

In the pause they took possession of each other's names and turned them over and put them away, a shade less frightened after that.

'I want to ask you something else now,' said Henry. He looked at Edna, his head a little on one side. 'How old are you?'

'Over sixteen,' she said, 'and you?'

'I'm nearly eighteen . . .'

'Isn't it hot?' she said suddenly, and pulled off her grey gloves and put her hands to her cheeks and kept them there. Their eyes were not frightened – they looked at each other with a sort of desperate calmness. If only their bodies would not tremble so stupidly! Still half hidden by her hair, Edna said: 'Have you ever been in love before?'

'No, never! Have you?'

'Oh, never in all my life.' She shook her head. 'I never even thought it possible.'

His next words came in a rush. 'Whatever have you been doing since last Friday evening? Whatever did you do all Saturday and all Sunday and today?'

But she did not answer – only shook her head and smiled and said, 'No, you tell *me*.'

'I?' cried Henry – and then he found he couldn't tell her either. He couldn't climb back to those mountains of days, and he had to shake his head too.

'But it's been agony,' he said, smiling brilliantly – 'agony.' At that she took away her hands and started laughing, and Henry joined her. They laughed until they were tired.

'It's so – so extraordinary,' she said. 'So suddenly, you know, and I feel as if I'd known you for years.'

'So do I . . .' said Henry. 'I believe it must be the Spring. I believe I've swallowed a butterfly – and it's fanning its wings just here.' He put his hand on his heart.

'And the really extraordinary thing is,' said Edna, 'that I had made up my mind that I didn't care for – men at all. I mean all the girls at College – '

'Were you at College?'

She nodded. 'A training college, learning to be a secretary.' She sounded scornful.

'I'm in an office,' said Henry. 'An architect's office – such a funny little place up one hundred and thirty stairs. We ought to be building nests instead of houses, I always think.'

'Do you like it?'

'No, of course I don't. I don't want to do anything, do you?'

'No, I hate it . . . And,' she said, 'my mother is a Hungarian – I believe that makes me hate it even more.'

That seemed to Henry quite natural. 'It would,' he said.

'Mother and I are exactly alike. I haven't a thing in common with my father; he's just . . . a little man in the City – but mother has got wild blood in her and she's given it to me. She hates our life just as much as I do.' She paused and frowned. 'All the same, we don't get on a bit together – that's funny – isn't it? But I'm absolutely alone at home.'

Henry was listening – in a way he was listening, but there was something else he wanted to ask her. He said, very shyly, 'Would you – would you take off your hat?'

She looked startled. 'Take off my hat?'

'Yes – it's your hair. I'd give anything to see your hair properly.'

She protested. 'It isn't really . . .'

'Oh, it *is*,' cried Henry, and then, as she took off the hat and gave her head a little toss, 'Oh, Edna! it's the loveliest thing in the world.'

'Do you like it?' she said, smiling and very pleased. She pulled it round her shoulders like a cape of gold. 'People generally laugh at it. It's such an absurd colour.' But Henry would not believe that. She leaned her elbows on her knees and cupped her chin in her hands. 'That's how I often sit when I'm angry and than I feel it burning me up . . . Silly?'

'No, no, not a bit,' said Henry. 'I knew you did. It's your sort of weapon against all the dull horrid things.'

'However did you know that? Yes, that's just it. But however did you know?'

'Just knew,' smiled Henry. 'My God!' he cried, 'what fools people are! All the little pollies that you know and that I know. Just look at you and me. Here we are – that's all there is to be said. I know about you and you know about me – we've just found each other – quite simply – just by being natural. That's all life is – something childish and very natural. Isn't it?'

'Yes – yes,' she said eagerly. 'That's what I've always thought.'

'It's people that make things so – silly. As long as you can keep away from them you're safe and you're happy.'

'Oh, I've thought that for a long time.'

'Then you're just like me,' said Henry. The wonder of that was so great that he almost wanted to cry. Instead he said very solemnly: 'I believe we're the only two people alive who think as we do. In fact, I'm sure of it. Nobody understands me. I feel as though I were living in a world of strange beings – do you?'

'Always.'

'We'll be in that loathsome tunnel again in a minute,' said Henry. 'Edna! can I – just touch your hair?'

She drew back quickly. 'Oh no, please don't,' and as they were going into the dark she moved a little away from him.

3

'Edna! I've bought the tickets. The man at the concert hall didn't seem at all surprised that I had the money. Meet me outside the gallery doors at three, and wear that cream blouse and the corals – will you? I love you. I don't like sending these letters to the shop. I always feel those people with "Letters received" in their window keep a kettle in their back parlour that would steam open an elephant's ear of an envelope. But it really doesn't matter, does it, darling? Can you get away on Sunday? Pretend you are going to spend the day with one of the girls from the office, and let's meet at some little place and walk or find a field where we can watch the daisies uncurling. I do love you, Edna. But Sundays without you are simply impossible. Don't get run over before Saturday, and don't eat anything out of a tin or drink anything from a public fountain. That's all, darling.'

'My dearest, yes, I'll be there on Saturday – and I've arranged about Sunday too. That is one great blessing. I'm quite free at home. I have just come in from the garden. It's such a lovely evening. Oh, Henry, I could sit and cry, I love you so tonight. Silly – isn't it? I either feel so happy I can hardly stop laughing or else so sad I can hardly stop crying, and both for the same reason. But we are so young to have found each other, aren't we? I am sending you a violet. It is quite warm. I wish you were here now, just for a minute even. Good-night, darling. – I am, Edna.'

4

'Safe,' said Edna, 'safe! And excellent places, aren't they, Henry?'

She stood up to take off her coat and Henry made a movement to help her. 'No – no – it's off.' She tucked it under the seat. She sat down beside him. 'Oh, Henry, what have you got there? Flowers?'

'Only two tiny little roses.' He laid them in her lap.

'Did you get my letter all right?' asked Edna, unpinning the paper.

'Yes,' he said, 'and the violet is growing beautifully. You should see my room. I planted a little piece of it in every corner and one on my pillow and one in the pocket of my pyjama jacket.'

She shook her hair at him. 'Henry, give me the programme.'

'Here it is – you can read it with me. I'll hold it for you.'

'No, let me have it.'

'Well, then, I'll read it for you.'

'No, you can have it after.'

'Edna,' he whispered.

'Oh, please don't,' she pleaded. 'Not here – the people.'

Why did he want to touch her so much and why did she mind? Whenever he was with her he wanted to hold her hand or take her arm when they walked together, or lean against her – not hard – just lean lightly so that his shoulder should touch her shoulder – and she wouldn't even have that. All the time that he was away from her he was hungry, he craved the nearness of her. There seemed to be comfort and warmth breathing from Edna that he needed to keep him calm. Yes, that was it. He couldn't get calm with her because she wouldn't let him touch her. But she loved him. He knew that. Why did she feel so curiously about it? Every time he tried to or even asked for her hand she shrank back and looked at him with pleading, frightened eyes as though he wanted to hurt her. They could say anything to each other. And there wasn't any question of their belonging to each other. And yet he couldn't touch her. Why, he couldn't even help her off with her coat. Her voice dropped into his thoughts.

'Henry!' He leaned to listen, setting his lips. 'I want to explain something to you. I will – I will – I promise – after the concert.'

'All right.' He was still hurt.

'You're not sad, are you?' she said.

He shook his head.

'Yes, you are, Henry.'

'No, really not.' He looked at the roses lying in her hands.

'Well, are you happy?'

'Yes. Here comes the orchestra.'

It was twilight when they came out of the hall. A blue net of light hung over the streets and houses, and pink clouds floated in a pale sky. As they walked away from the hall Henry felt they were very little and alone. For the first time since he had known Edna his heart was heavy.

'Henry!' She stopped suddenly and stared at him. 'Henry, I'm not coming to the station with you. Don't – don't wait for me. Please, please leave me.'

'My God!' cried Henry, and started, 'what's the matter – Edna – darling – Edna, what have I done?'

'Oh, nothing – go away,' and she turned and ran across the street into a square and leaned up against the square railings – and hid her face in her hands.

'Edna – Edna – my little love – you're crying. Edna, my baby girl!'

She leaned her arms along the railings and sobbed distractedly.

'Edna – stop – it's all my fault. I'm a fool – I'm a thundering idiot. I've spoiled your afternoon. I've tortured you with my idiotic mad bloody clumsiness. That's it. Isn't it, Edna? For God's sake.'

'Oh,' she sobbed, 'I do hate hurting you so. Every time you ask me to let – let you hold my hand or – or kiss me I could kill myself for not doing it – for not letting you. I don't know why I don't even.' She said wildly, 'It's not that I'm frightened of you – it's not that – it's only a feeling, Henry, that I can't understand myself even. Give me your handkerchief, darling.' He pulled it from his pocket. 'All through the concert I've been haunted by this, and every time we meet I know it's bound to come up. Somehow I feel if once we did that – you know – held each other's hands and kissed, it would be all changed – and I feel we wouldn't be free like we are – we'd be doing something secret. We wouldn't be children any more . . . silly, isn't it? I'd feel awkward with you, Henry, and I'd feel shy, and I do so feel that just because you and I are you and I, we don't need that sort of thing.' She turned and looked at him, pressing her hands to her cheeks in the way he knew so well, and behind her as in a dream he saw the sky and half a white moon and the trees of the square with their unbroken buds. He kept twisting, twisting up in his hands the concert programme. 'Henry! You do understand me – don't you?'

'Yes, I think I do. But you're not going to be frightened any more, are you?' He tried to smile. 'We'll forget, Edna. I'll never mention it again. We'll bury the bogy in this square – now – you and I – won't we?'

'But,' she said, searching his face – 'will it make you love me less?'

'Oh no,' he said. 'Nothing could – nothing on earth could do that.'

5

London became their playground. On Saturday afternoons they explored. They found their own shops where they bought cigarettes and sweets for Edna – and their own tea-shop with their own table – their own streets – and one night when Edna was supposed to be at a lecture at the Polytechnic they found their own village. It was the name that made them go there. 'There's white geese in that name,' said Henry, telling it to Edna. 'And a river and little low houses with old men sitting outside them – old sea captains with wooden legs winding up their watches, and there are little shops with lamps in the windows.'

It was too late for them to see the geese or the old men, but the river was there and the houses and even the shops with lamps. In one a woman sat working a sewing-machine on the counter. They heard the whirring hum and they saw her big shadow filling the shop. 'Too full for a single customer,' said Henry. 'It is a perfect place.'

The houses were small and covered with creepers and ivy. Some of them had worn wooden steps leading up to the doors. You had to go down a little flight of steps to enter some of the others; and just across the road – to be seen from every window – was the river, with a walk beside it and some high poplar trees.

'This is the place for us to live in,' said Henry. 'There's a house to let, too. I wonder if it would wait if we asked it. I'm sure it would.'

'Yes, I would like to live there,' said Edna. They crossed the road and she leaned against the trunk of a tree and looked up at the empty house with a dreamy smile.

'There is a little garden at the back, dear,' said Henry, 'a lawn with one tree on it and some daisy bushes round the wall. At night the stars shine in the tree like tiny candles. And inside there are two rooms downstairs and a big room with folding doors upstairs and above that an attic. And there are eight stairs to the kitchen – very dark, Edna. You are rather frightened of them, you know. "Henry, dear, would you mind bringing the lamp? I just want to make sure that Euphemia has raked out the fire before we go to bed." '

'Yes,' said Edna. 'Our bedroom is at the very top – that room with the two square windows. When it is quiet we can hear the river flowing and the sound of the poplar trees far, far away, rustling and flowing in our dreams, darling.'

'You're not cold – are you?' he said suddenly.

'No – no, only happy.'

'The room with the folding doors is yours.' Henry laughed. 'It's a mixture – it isn't a room at all. It's full of your toys and there's a big blue chair in it where you sit curled up in front of the fire with the flames in your curls – because though we're married you refuse to put your hair up and only tuck it inside your coat for the church service. And there's a rug on the floor for me to lie on, because I'm so lazy. Euphemia – that's our servant – only comes in the day. After she's gone we go down to the kitchen and sit on the table and eat an apple, or perhaps we make some tea, just for the sake of hearing the kettle sing. That's not joking. If you listen to a kettle right through it's like an early morning in Spring.'

'Yes, I know,' she said. 'All the different kinds of birds.'

A little cat came through the railings of the empty house and into the road. Edna called it and bent down and held out her hands – 'Kitty! Kitty!' The little cat ran to her and rubbed against her knees.

'If we're going for a walk just take the cat and put it inside the front door,' said Henry, still pretending. 'I've got the key.'

They walked across the road and Edna stood stroking the cat in her arms while Henry went up the steps and pretended to open the door.

He came down again quickly. 'Let's go away at once. It's going to turn into a dream.'

The night was dark and warm. They did not want to go home. 'What I feel so certain of is,' said Henry, 'that we ought to be living there now. We oughtn't to wait for things. What's age? You're as old as you'll ever be and so am I. You know,' he said, 'I have a feeling often and often that it's dangerous to wait for things – that if you wait for things they only go further and further away.'

'But, Henry – money! You see we haven't any money.'

'Oh, well – perhaps if I disguised myself as an old man we could get a job as caretakers in some large house – that would be rather fun. I'd make up a terrific history of the house if anyone came to look over it, and you could dress up and be the ghost moaning and wringing your hands in the deserted picture gallery, to frighten them off. Don't you ever feel that money is more or less accidental – that if one really wants things it's either there or it doesn't matter?'

She did not answer that – she looked up at the sky and said, 'Oh dear, I don't want to go home.'

'Exactly – that's the whole trouble – and we oughtn't to go home. We ought to be going back to the house and find an odd saucer to give the cat the dregs of the milk-jug in. I'm not really laughing – I'm not even happy. I'm lonely for you, Edna – I would give anything to lie down and cry' . . . and he added limply, 'with my head in your lap and your darling cheek in my hair.'

'But, Henry,' she said, coming closer, 'you have faith, haven't you? I mean you are absolutely certain that we shall have a house like that and everything we want – aren't you?'

'Not enough – that's not enough. I want to be sitting on those very stairs and taking off these very boots this very minute. Don't you? Is faith enough for you?'

'If only we weren't so young . . .' she said miserably. 'And yet,' she sighed, 'I'm sure I don't feel very young – I feel twenty at least.'

6

Henry lay on his back in the little wood. When he moved the dead leaves rustled beneath him, and above his head the new leaves quivered like fountains of green water steeped in sunlight. Somewhere out of sight Edna was gathering primroses. He had been so full of dreams that morning that he could not keep pace with her delight in the flowers. 'Yes, love, you go and come back for me. I'm too lazy.' She had thrown off her hat and knelt down beside him, and by and by her voice and her footsteps had grown fainter. Now the wood was silent except for the leaves, but he knew that she was not far away and he moved so that the tips of his fingers touched her pink jacket. Ever since waking he had felt so strangely that he was not really awake at all, but just dreaming. The time before Edna was a dream, and now he and she were dreaming together and somewhere in some dark place another dream waited for him. 'No, that can't be true because I can't ever imagine the world without us. I feel that we two together mean something that's got to be there just as naturally as trees or birds or clouds.' He tried to remember what it had felt like without Edna, but he could not get back to those days. They were hidden by her; Edna with the marigold hair and strange, dreamy smile filled him up to the brim. He breathed her; he ate and drank her. He walked about with a shining ring of Edna keeping the world away or touching whatever it lighted on with its own beauty. 'Long after you have stopped laughing,' he told her, 'I can hear your laugh running up and down my veins – and yet – are we a dream?' And suddenly he saw himself and Edna as two very small children walking through the streets, looking through windows, buying things and playing with them, talking to each other, smiling – he saw even their gestures and the way they stood, so often, quite still, face to face – and then he rolled over and pressed his face in the leaves – faint with longing. He wanted to kiss Edna, and to put his arms round her and press her to him and feel her cheek hot against his kiss, and kiss her until he'd no breath left and so stifle the dream.

'No, I can't go on being hungry like this,' said Henry, and jumped up and began to run in the direction she had gone. She had wandered a long way. Down in a green hollow he saw her kneeling, and when she saw him she waved and said – 'Oh, Henry – such beauties! I've never seen such beauties. Come and look.' By the time he had reached her he would have cut off his hand rather than spoil her happiness. How strange Edna was that day! All the time she talked to

Henry her eyes laughed; they were sweet and mocking. Two little spots of colour like strawberries glowed on her cheeks and 'I wish I could feel tired,' she kept saying. 'I want to walk over the whole world until I die. Henry – come along. Walk faster – Henry! If I start flying suddenly, you'll promise to catch hold of my feet, won't you? Otherwise I'll never come down.' And 'Oh,' she cried, 'I am so happy. I'm so frightfully happy!' They came to a weird place, covered with heather. It was early afternoon and the sun streamed down upon the purple.

'Let's rest here a little,' said Edna, and she waded into the heather and lay down. 'Oh, Henry, it's so lovely. I can't see anything except the little bells and the sky.'

Henry knelt down by her and took some primroses out of her basket and made a long chain to go round her throat. 'I could almost fall asleep,' said Edna. She crept over to his knees and lay hidden in her hair just beside him. 'It's like being under the sea, isn't it, dearest, so sweet and so still?'

'Yes,' said Henry, in a strange, husky voice. 'Now I'll make you one of violets.' But Edna sat up. 'Let's go in,' she said.

They came back to the road and walked a long way. Edna said, 'No, I couldn't walk over the world – I'm tired now.' She trailed on the grass edge of the road. 'You and I are tired, Henry! How much further is it?'

'I don't know – not very far,' said Henry, peering into the distance. Then they walked in silence.

'Oh,' she said at last, 'it really is too far, Henry, I'm tired and I'm hungry. Carry my silly basket of primroses.' He took them without looking at her.

At last they came to a village and a cottage with a notice 'Teas Provided'.

'This is the place,' said Henry. 'I've often been here. You sit on the little bench and I'll go and order the tea.' She sat down on the bench, in the pretty garden all white and yellow with spring flowers. A woman came to the door and leaned against it watching them eat. Henry was very nice to her, but Edna did not say a word. 'You haven't been here for a long spell,' said the woman.

'No – the garden's looking wonderful.'

'Fair,' said she. 'Is the young lady your sister?' Henry nodded Yes, and took some jam.

'There's a likeness,' said the woman. She came down into the garden and picked a head of white jonquils and handed it to

Edna. 'I suppose you don't happen to know anyone who wants a cottage,' said she. 'My sister's taken ill and she left me hers. I want to let it.'

'For a long time?' asked Henry politely.

'Oh,' said the woman vaguely, 'that depends.'

Said Henry, 'Well – I might know of somebody – could we go and look at it?'

'Yes, it's just a step down the road, the little one with the apple trees in front – I'll fetch you the key.'

While she was away Henry turned to Edna and said, 'Will you come?' She nodded.

They walked down the road and in through the gate and up the grassy path between the pink and white trees. It was a tiny place – two rooms downstairs and two rooms upstairs. Edna leaned out of the top window, and Henry stood at the doorway. 'Do you like it?' he asked.

'Yes,' she called, and then made a place for him at the window. 'Come and look. It's so sweet.'

He came and leant out of the window. Below them were the apple trees tossing in a faint wind that blew a long piece of Edna's hair across his eyes. They did not move. It was evening – the pale green sky was sprinkled with stars. 'Look!' she said – 'stars, Henry.'

'There will be a moon in two T's,' said Henry.

She did not seem to move and yet she was leaning against Henry's shoulder; he put his arm round her – 'Are all those trees down there – apple?' she asked in a shaky voice.

'No, darling,' said Henry. 'Some of them are full of angels and some of them are full of sugar almonds – but evening light is awfully deceptive.' She sighed. 'Henry – we mustn't stay here any longer.'

He let her go and she stood up in the dusky room and touched her hair. 'What has been the matter with you all day?' she said – and then did not wait for an answer but ran to him and put her arms round his neck, and pressed his head into the hollow of her shoulder. 'Oh,' she breathed, 'I do love you. Hold me, Henry.' He put his arms round her, and she leaned against him and looked into his eyes. 'Hasn't it been terrible, all today?' said Edna. 'I knew what was the matter and I've tried every way I could to tell you that I wanted you to kiss me – that I'd quite got over the feeling.'

'You're perfect, perfect, perfect,' said Henry.

7

'The thing is,' said Henry, 'how am I going to wait until evening?' He took his watch out of his pocket, went into the cottage and popped it into a china jar on the mantelpiece. He'd looked at it seven times in one hour, and now he couldn't remember what time it was. Well, he'd look once again. Half-past four. Her train arrived at seven. He'd have to start for the station at half-past six. Two hours more to wait. He went through the cottage again – downstairs and upstairs. 'It looks lovely,' he said. He went into the garden and picked a round bunch of white pinks and put them in a vase on the little table by Edna's bed. 'I don't believe this,' thought Henry. 'I don't believe this for a minute. It's too much. She'll be here in two hours and we'll walk home, and then I'll take that white jug off the kitchen table and go across to Mrs Biddie's and get the milk, and then come back, and when I come back she'll have lighted the lamp in the kitchen and I'll look through the window and see her moving about in the pool of lamplight. And then we shall have supper, and after supper (Bags I washing up!) I shall put some wood on the fire and we'll sit on the hearth-rug and watch it burning. There won't be a sound except the wood and perhaps the wind will creep round the house once . . . And then we shall light our candles and she will go up first with her shadow on the wall beside her, and she will call out, Good-night, Henry – and I shall answer – Good-night, Edna. And then I shall dash upstairs and jump into bed and watch the tiny bar of light from her room brush my door, and the moment it disappears will shut my eyes and sleep until morning. Then we'll have all tomorrow and tomorrow and tomorrow night. Is she thinking all this, too? Edna, come quickly!

> Had I but two little wings,
> And were a little feathery bird,
> To you I'd fly, my dear –

'No, no, dearest . . . Because the waiting is a sort of Heaven, too, darling. If you can understand that. Did you ever know a cottage could stand on tiptoe. This one is doing it now.'

He was downstairs and sat on the doorstep with his hands clasped round his knees. That night when they found the village – and Edna said, 'Haven't you faith, Henry?' 'I hadn't then. Now I have,' he said, 'I feel just like God.'

He leaned his head against the lintel. He could hardly keep his eyes open, not that he was sleepy, but . . . for some reason . . . and a long time passed.

Henry thought he saw a big white moth flying down the road. It perched on the gate. No, it wasn't a moth. It was a little girl in a pinafore. What a nice little girl, and he smiled in his sleep, and she smiled, too, and turned in her toes as she walked. 'But she can't be living here,' thought Henry. 'Because this is ours. Here she comes.'

When she was quite close to him she took her hand from under her pinafore and gave him a telegram and smiled and went away. There's a funny present! thought Henry, staring at it. 'Perhaps it's only a make-believe one, and it's got one of those snakes inside it that fly up at you.' He laughed gently in the dream and opened it very carefully. 'It's just a folded paper.' He took it out and spread it open.

The garden became full of shadows – they spun a web of darkness over the cottage and the trees and Henry and the telegram. But Henry did not move.

(1914)

An Indiscreet Journey

I

SHE IS LIKE St Anne. Yes, the concierge is the image of St Anne, with that black cloth over her head, the wisps of grey hair hanging, and the tiny smoking lamp in her hand. Really very beautiful, I thought, smiling at St Anne, who said severely: 'Six o'clock. You have only just got time. There is a bowl of milk on the writing-table.' I jumped out of my pyjamas and into a basin of cold water like any English lady in any French novel. The concierge, persuaded that I was on my way to prison cells and death by bayonets, opened the shutters and the cold clear light came through. A little steamer hooted on the river; a cart with two horses at a gallop flung past. The rapid swirling water; the tall black trees on the far side, grouped together like negroes conversing. Sinister, very, I thought, as I buttoned on my age-old Burberry. (That Burberry was very significant. It did not belong to me. I had borrowed it from a friend. My eye lighted upon it hanging in her little dark hall. The very thing! The perfect and adequate disguise – an old Burberry. Lions have been faced in a Burberry. Ladies have been rescued from open boats in mountainous seas wrapped in nothing else. An old Burberry seems to me the sign and the token of the undisputed venerable traveller, I decided, leaving my purple peg-top with the real seal collar and cuffs in exchange.)

'You will never get there,' said the concierge, watching me turn up the collar. 'Never! Never!' I ran down the echoing stairs – strange they sounded, like a piano flicked by a sleepy housemaid – and on to the Quai. 'Why so fast, *ma mignonne?*' said a lovely little boy in coloured socks, dancing in front of the electric lotus buds that curve over the entrance to the Métro. Alas! there was not even time to blow him a kiss. When I arrived at the big station I had only four minutes to spare, and the platform entrance was crowded and packed with soldiers, their yellow papers in one hand and big untidy bundles. The Commissaire of Police stood on one side, a Nameless Official on the other. Will he let me pass? Will he? He was an old man with a fat swollen face covered with big warts. Horn-rimmed spectacles squatted on his nose. Trembling, I made an effort. I conjured up my sweetest early-morning smile and handed it with the papers. But the delicate thing fluttered against the horn spectacles and fell. Nevertheless, he let me pass, and I ran, ran in and out among the soldiers and up the high steps into the yellow-painted carriage.

'Does one go direct to X.?' I asked the collector who dug at my ticket with a pair of forceps and handed it back again. 'No, Mademoiselle, you must change at X.Y.Z.'

'At – ?'

'X.Y.Z.'

Again I had not heard. 'At what time do we arrive there, if you please?'

'One o'clock.' But that was no good to me. I hadn't a watch. Oh, well – later.

Ah! the train had begun to move. The train was on my side. It swung out of the station, and soon we were passing the vegetable gardens, passing the tall, blind houses to let, passing the servants beating carpets. Up already and walking in the fields, rosy from the rivers and the red-fringed pools, the sun lighted upon the swinging train and stroked my muff and told me to take off that Burberry. I was not alone in the carriage. An old woman sat opposite, her skirt turned back over her knees, a bonnet of black lace on her head. In her fat hands, adorned with a wedding and two mourning rings, she held a letter. Slowly, slowly she sipped a sentence, and then looked up and out of the window, her lips trembling a little, and then another sentence, and again the old face turned to the light, tasting it. . . . Two soldiers leaned out of the window, their heads nearly touching – one of them was whistling, the other had his coat fastened with some rusty safety-pins. And now there were soldiers everywhere working on the railway line, leaning against trucks or standing hands on hips, eyes fixed on the train as though they expected at least one camera at every window. And now we were passing big wooden sheds like rigged-up dancing halls or seaside pavilions, each flying a flag. In and out of them walked the Red Cross men; the wounded sat against the walls sunning themselves. At all the bridges, the crossings, the stations, a *petit soldat*, all boots and bayonet. Forlorn and desolate he looked, like a little comic picture waiting for the joke to be written underneath. Is there really such a thing as war? Are all these laughing voices really going to the war? These dark woods lighted so mysteriously by the white stems of the birch and the ash – these watery fields with the big birds flying over – these rivers green and blue in the light – have battles been fought in places like these?

What beautiful cemeteries we are passing! They flash gay in the sun. They seem to be full of cornflowers and poppies and daisies. How can there be so many flowers at this time of the year? But they are not flowers at all. They are bunches of ribbons tied on to the soldiers' graves.

I glanced up and caught the old woman's eye. She smiled and folded the letter. 'It is from my son – the first we have had since October. I am taking it to my daughter-in-law.'

'. . . ?'

'Yes, very good,' said the old woman, shaking down her skirt and putting her arm through the handle of her basket. 'He wants me to send him some handkerchiefs and a piece of stout string.'

What is the name of the station where I have to change? Perhaps I shall never know. I got up and leaned my arms across the window rail, my feet crossed. One cheek burned as in infancy on the way to the seaside. When the war is over I shall have a barge and drift along these rivers with a white cat and a pot of mignonette to bear me company.

Down the side of the hill filed the troops, winking red and blue in the light. Far away, but plainly to be seen, some more flew by on bicycles. But really, *ma France adorée*, this uniform is ridiculous. Your soldiers are stamped upon your bosom like bright irreverent transfers.

The train slowed down, stopped . . . Everybody was getting out except me. A big boy, his sabots tied to his back with a piece of string, the inside of his tin wine cup stained a lovely impossible pink, looked very friendly. Does one change here perhaps for X.? Another whose kepi had come out of a wet paper cracker swung my suitcase to earth. What darlings soldiers are! '*Merci bien, Monsieur, vous êtes tout à fait aimable* . . .' 'Not this way,' said a bayonet. 'Not this,' said another. So I followed the crowd. 'Your passport, Mademoiselle . . .' '*We, Sir Edward Grey* . . .' I ran through the muddy square and into the buffet.

A green room with a stove jutting out and tables on each side. On the counter, beautiful with coloured bottles, a woman leans, her breasts in her folded arms. Through an open door I can see a kitchen, and the cook in a white coat breaking eggs into a bowl and tossing the shells into a corner. The blue and red coats of the men who are eating hang upon the walls. Their short swords and belts are piled upon chairs. Heavens! what a noise. The sunny air seemed all broken up and trembling with it. A little boy, very pale, swung from table to table, taking the orders, and poured me out a glass of purple coffee. *Ssssh*, came from the eggs. They were in a pan. The woman rushed from behind the counter and began to help the boy. *Toute de suite, tout' suite!* she chirruped to the loud impatient voices. There came a clatter of plates and the pop-pop of corks being drawn.

Suddenly in the doorway I saw someone with a pail of fish – brown speckled fish, like the fish one sees in a glass case, swimming through forests of beautiful pressed seaweed. He was an old man in a tattered jacket, standing humbly, waiting for someone to attend to him. A thin beard fell over his chest, his eyes under the tufted eyebrows were bent on the pail he carried. He looked as though he had escaped from some holy picture, and was entreating the soldiers' pardon for being there at all . . .

But what could I have done? I could not arrive at X. with two fishes hanging on a straw; and I am sure it is a penal offence in France to throw fish out of railway-carriage windows, I thought, miserably climbing into a smaller, shabbier train. Perhaps I might have taken them to – *ah, mon Dieu* – I had forgotten the name of my uncle and aunt again! Buffard, Buffon – what was it? Again I read the unfamiliar letter in the familiar handwriting.

MY DEAR NIECE,
Now that the weather is more settled, your uncle and I would be charmed if you would pay us a little visit. Telegraph me when you are coming. I shall meet you outside the station if I am free. Otherwise our good friend, Madame Grinçon, who lives in the little toll-house by the bridge, *juste en face de le gare*, will conduct you to our home. *Je vous embrasse bien tendrement.*

JULIE BOIFFARD

A visiting card was enclosed: *M. Paul Boiffard.*

Boiffard – of course that was the name. *Ma tante Julie et mon oncle Paul* – suddenly they were there with me, more real, more solid than any relations I had ever known. I saw *tante Julie* bridling, with the soup-tureen in her hands, and *oncle Paul* sitting at the table with a red and white napkin tied round his neck. Boiffard – Boiffard – I must remember the name. Supposing the Commissaire Militaire should ask me who the relations were I was going to and I muddled the name – Oh, how fatal! Buffard – no, Boiffard. And then for the first time, folding Aunt Julie's letter, I saw scrawled in a corner of the empty back page: *Venez vite, vite*. Strange impulsive woman! My heart began to beat . . .

'Ah, we are not far off now,' said the lady opposite. 'You are going to X, Mademoiselle?'

'*Oui, Madame.*'

'I also . . . You have been there before?'

'No, Madame. This is the first time.'

'Really, it is a strange time for a visit.'

I smiled faintly, and tried to keep my eyes off her hat. She was quite an ordinary little woman, but she wore a black velvet toque, with an incredibly surprised looking seagull camped on the very top of it. Its round eyes, fixed on me so inquiringly, were almost too much to bear. I had a dreadful impulse to shoo it away, or to lean forward and inform her of its presence . . .

'*Excusez-moi, Madame*, but perhaps you have not remarked there is an *espèce de* seagull *couché sur votre chapeau.*'

Could the bird be there on purpose? I must not laugh . . . I must not laugh. Had she ever looked at herself in a glass with that bird on her head?

'It is very difficult to get into X. at present, to pass the station,' she said, and she shook her head with the seagull at me. 'Ah, such an affair. One must sign one's name and state one's business.'

'Really, is it as bad as all that?'

'But naturally. You see the whole place is in the hands of the military, and' – she shrugged – 'they have to be strict. Many people do not get beyond the station at all. They arrive. They are put in the waiting-room, and there they remain.'

Did I or did I not detect in her voice a strange, insulting relish?

'I suppose such strictness is absolutely necessary,' I said coldly, stroking my muff.

'Necessary,' she cried. 'I should think so. Why, Mademoiselle, you cannot imagine what it would be like otherwise! You know what women are like about soldiers' – she raised a final hand – 'mad, completely mad. But – ' and she gave a little laugh of triumph – 'they could not get into X. *Mon Dieu*, no! There is no question about that.'

'I don't suppose they even try,' said I.

'Don't you?' said the seagull.

Madame said nothing for a moment. 'Of course the authorities are very hard on the men. It means instant imprisonment, and then – off to the firing-line without a word.'

'What are *you* going to X. for?' said the seagull. 'What on earth are *you* doing here?'

'Are you making a long stay in X., Mademoiselle?'

She had won, she had won. I was terrified. A lamp-post swam past the train with the fatal name upon it. I could hardly breathe – the train had stopped. I smiled gaily at Madame and danced down the steps to the platform . . .

It was a hot little room, completely furnished, with two colonels seated at two tables. They were large grey-whiskered men with a touch of burnt red on their cheeks. Sumptuous and omnipotent they looked. One smoked what ladies love to call a heavy Egyptian cigarette, with a long creamy ash, the other toyed with a gilded pen. Their heads rolled on their tight collars, like big over-ripe fruits. I had a terrible feeling, as I handed my passport and ticket, that a soldier would step forward and tell me to kneel. I would have knelt without question.

'What's this?' said God I, querulously. He did not like my passport at all. The very sight of it seemed to annoy him. He waved a dissenting hand at it, with a '*Non, je ne peux pas manger ça*' air.

'But it won't do. It won't do at all, you know. Look – read for yourself,' and he glanced with extreme distaste at my photograph, and then with even greater distaste his pebble eyes looked at me.

'Of course the photograph is deplorable,' I said, scarcely breathing with terror, 'but it has been *visé*d and *visé*d.'

He raised his big bulk and went over to God II.

'Courage!' I said to my muff and held it firmly, 'Courage!'

God II held up a finger to me, and I produced Aunt Julie's letter and her card. But he did not seem to feel the slightest interest in her. He stamped my passport idly, scribbled a word on my ticket, and I was on the platform again.

'That way – you pass out that way.'

Terribly pale, with a faint smile on his lips, his hand at salute, stood the little corporal. I gave no sign, I am sure I gave no sign. He stepped behind me.

'And then follow me as though you do not see me,' I heard him half whisper, half sing.

How fast he went, through the slippery mud towards a bridge. He had a postman's bag on his back, a paper parcel and the *Matin* in his hand. We seemed to dodge through a maze of policemen, and I could not keep up at all with the little corporal who began to whistle.

From the toll-house 'our good friend, Madame Grinçon,' her hands wrapped in a shawl, watched our coming, and against the toll-house there leaned a tiny faded cab. *Montez vite, vite!* said the little corporal, hurling my suitcase, the postman's bag, the paper parcel and the *Matin* on to the floor.

'A-ie! A-ie! Do not be so mad. Do not ride yourself. You will be seen,' wailed 'our good friend, Madame Grinçon.'

'*Ah, je m'en f—*' said the little corporal.

The driver jerked into activity. He lashed the bony horse and away we flew, both doors, which were the complete sides of the cab, flapping and banging.

'*Bon jour, mon amie.*'

'*Bon jour, mon ami.*'

And then we swooped down and clutched at the banging doors. They would not keep shut. They were fools of doors.

'Lean back, let me do it!' I cried. 'Policemen are as thick as violets everywhere.'

At the barracks the horse reared up and stopped. A crowd of laughing faces blotted the window.

'*Prends ça, mon vieux,*' said the little corporal, handing the paper parcel.

'It's all right,' called someone.

We waved, we were off again. By a river, down a strange white street, with little houses on either side, gay in the late sunlight.

'Jump out as soon as he stops again. The door will be open. Run straight inside. I will follow. The man is already paid. I know you will like the house. It is quite white. And the room is white too, and the people are – '

'White as snow.'

We looked at each other. We began to laugh. 'Now,' said the little corporal.

Out I flew and in at the door. There stood, presumably, my Aunt Julie. There in the background hovered, I supposed, my Uncle Paul.

'*Bon jour, Madame!*' '*Bon jour, Monsieur!*'

'It is all right, you are safe,' said my Aunt Julie. Heavens, how I loved her! And she opened the door of the white room and shut it upon us. Down went the suitcase, the postman's bag, the *Matin*. I threw my passport up into the air, and the little corporal caught it.

2

What an extraordinary thing. We had been there to lunch and to dinner each day; but now in the dusk and alone I could not find it. I clop-clopped in my borrowed *sabots* through the greasy mud, right to the end of the village, and there was not a sign of it. I could not even remember what it looked like, or if there was a name painted on the outside, or any bottles or tables showing at the window. Already the village houses were sealed for the night behind big wooden shutters. Strange and mysterious they looked in the ragged drifting light and thin rain, like a company of beggars perched on the hill-side, their bosoms full of rich unlawful gold. There was nobody about but the soldiers. A group of wounded stood under a lamp-post, petting a mangy, shivering dog. Up the street came four big boys singing:

> *Dodo, mon homme, fais vit' dodo . . .*

and swung off down the hill to their sheds behind the railway station. They seemed to take the last breath of the day with them. I began to walk slowly back.

'It must have been one of these houses. I remember it stood far back from the road – and there were no steps, not even a porch – one seemed to walk right through the window.' And then quite suddenly the waiting-boy came out of just such a place. He saw me and grinned cheerfully, and began to whistle through his teeth.

'*Bon soir, mon petit.*'

'*Bon soir, Madame.*' And he followed me up the café to our special table, right at the far end by the window, and marked by a bunch of violets that I had left in a glass there yesterday.

'You are two?' asked the waiting-boy, flicking the table with a red and white cloth. His long swinging steps echoed over the bare floor. He disappeared into the kitchen and came back to light the lamp that hung from the ceiling under a spreading shade, like a haymaker's hat. Warm light shone on the empty place that was really a barn, set out with dilapidated tables and chairs. Into the middle of the room a black stove jutted. At one side of it there was a table with a row of bottles on it, behind which Madame sat and took the money and made entries in a red book. Opposite her desk a door led into the kitchen. The walls were covered with a creamy paper patterned all over with green and swollen trees – hundreds and hundreds of trees reared their mushroom heads to the ceiling. I began to wonder who had chosen the paper and why. Did Madame think it was beautiful,

or that it was a gay and lovely thing to eat one's dinner at all
seasons in the middle of a forest . . . On either side of the clock there
hung a picture: one, a young gentleman in black tights wooing a
pear-shaped lady in yellow over the back of a garden seat, *Premier
Rencontre*; two, the black and yellow in amorous confusion, *Triomphe
d'Amour*.

The clock ticked to a soothing lilt, *C'est ça, c'est ça.* In the kitchen
the waiting-boy was washing up. I heard the ghostly chatter of the
dishes.

And years passed. Perhaps the war is long since over – there is no
village outside at all – the streets are quiet under the grass. I have an
idea this is the sort of thing one will do on the very last day of all – sit
in an empty café and listen to a clock ticking until –

Madame came through the kitchen door, nodded to me and took
her seat behind the table, her plump hands folded on the red book.
Ping went the door. A handful of soldiers came in, took off their
coats and began to play cards, chaffing and poking fun at the pretty
waiting-boy, who threw up his little round head, rubbed his thick
fringe out of his eyes and cheeked them back in his broken voice.
Sometimes his voice boomed up from his throat, deep and harsh, and
then in the middle of a sentence it broke and scattered in a funny
squeaking. He seemed to enjoy it himself. You would not have been
surprised if he had walked into the kitchen on his hands and brought
back your dinner turning a catherine-wheel.

Ping went the door again. Two more men came in. They sat at
the table nearest Madame, and she leaned to them with a birdlike
movement, her head on one side. Oh, they had a grievance! The
Lieutenant was a fool – nosing about – springing out at them –
and they'd only been sewing on buttons. Yes, that was all – sewing
on buttons, and up comes this young spark. 'Now then, what are
you up to?' They mimicked the idiotic voice. Madame drew down
her mouth, nodding sympathy. The waiting-boy served them with
glasses. He took a bottle of some orange-coloured stuff and put it on
the table edge. A shout from the card-players made him turn sharply,
and crash! over went the bottle, spilling on the table, the floor –
smash! to tinkling atoms. An amazed silence. Through it the drip-
drip of the wine from the table on to the floor. It looked very strange
dropping so slowly, as though the table were crying. Then there
came a roar from the card-players. 'You'll catch it, my lad! That's the
style! Now you've done it! . . . *Sept, huit, neuf.*' They started playing
again. The waiting-boy never said a word. He stood, his head bent,

his hands spread out, and then he knelt and gathered up the glass, piece by piece, and soaked the wine up with a cloth. Only when Madame cried cheerfully, 'You wait until *he* finds out,' did he raise his head.

'He can't say anything, if I pay for it,' he muttered, his face jerking, and he marched off into the kitchen with the soaking cloth.

'*Il pleure de colère*,' said Madame delightedly, patting her hair with her plump hands.

The café slowly filled. It grew very warm. Blue smoke mounted from the tables and hung about the haymaker's hat in misty wreaths. There was a suffocating smell of onion soup and boots and damp cloth. In the din the door sounded again. It opened to let in a weed of a fellow, who stood with his back against it, one hand shading his eyes.

'Hullo! you've got the bandage off?'

'How does it feel, *mon vieux?*'

'Let's have a look at them.'

But he made no reply. He shrugged and walked unsteadily to a table, sat down and leant against the wall. Slowly his hand fell. In his white face his eyes showed, pink as a rabbit's. They brimmed and spilled, brimmed and spilled. He dragged a white cloth out of his pocket and wiped them.

'It's the smoke,' said someone. 'It's the smoke tickles them up for you.'

His comrades watched him a bit, watched his eyes fill again, again brim over. The water ran down his face, off his chin on to the table. He rubbed the place with his coat-sleeve, and then, as though forgetful, went on rubbing, rubbing with his hand across the table, staring in front of him. And then he started shaking his head to the movement of his hand. He gave a loud strange groan and dragged out the cloth again.

'*Huit, neuf, dix*,' said the card-players.

'*P'tit*, some more bread.'

'Two coffees.'

'*Un Picon!*'

The waiting-boy, quite recovered, but with scarlet cheeks, ran to and fro. A tremendous quarrel flared up among the card-players, raged for two minutes, and died in flickering laughter. 'Ooof!' groaned the man with the eyes, rocking and mopping. But nobody paid any attention to him except Madame. She made a little grimace at her two soldiers.

'*Mais vous savez, c'est un peu dégoûtant, ça,*' she said severely.

'*Ah, oui, Madame,*' answered the soldiers, watching her bent head and pretty hands, as she arranged for the hundredth time a frill of lace on her lifted bosom.

'*V'là, Monsieur!*' cawed the waiting-boy over his shoulder to me. For some silly reason I pretended not to hear, and I leaned over the table smelling the violets, until the little corporal's hand closed over mine.

'Shall we have *un peu de charcuterie* to begin with?' he asked tenderly.

3

'In England,' said the blue-eyed soldier, 'you drink whisky with your meals. *N'est-ce pas, Mademoiselle?* A little glass of whisky neat before eating. Whisky and soda with your *bifteks*, and after, more whisky with hot water and lemon.'

'Is it true that?' asked his great friend who sat opposite, a big red-faced chap with a black beard and large moist eyes and hair that looked as though it had been cut with a sewing-machine.

'Well, not quite true,' said I.

'*Si, si,*' cried the blue-eyed soldier. 'I ought to know. I'm in business. English travellers come to my place, and it's always the same thing.'

'Bah, I can't stand whisky,' said the little corporal. 'It's too disgusting the morning after. Do you remember, *ma fille*, the whisky in that little bar at Montmartre?'

'*Souvenir tendre,*' sighed Blackbeard, putting two fingers in the breast of his coat and letting his head fall. He was very drunk.

'But I know something that you've never tasted,' said the blue-eyed soldier, pointing a finger at me, 'something really good.' *Cluck* he went with his tongue. '*E-patant!* And the curious thing is that you'd hardly know it from whisky except that it's' – he felt with his hand for the word – 'finer, sweeter perhaps, not so sharp, and it leaves you feeling gay as a rabbit next morning.'

'What is it called?'

'Mirabelle!' He rolled the word round his mouth, under his tongue. 'Ah-ha, that's the stuff.'

'I could eat another mushroom,' said Blackbeard. 'I would like another mushroom very much. I am sure I could eat another mushroom if Mademoiselle gave it to me out of her hand.'

'You ought to try it,' said the blue-eyed soldier, leaning both hands on the table and speaking so seriously that I began to wonder how much more sober he was than Blackbeard. 'You ought to try it, and tonight. I would like you to tell me if you don't think it's like whisky.'

'Perhaps they've got it here,' said the little corporal, and he called the waiting-boy. *'P'tit!'*

'Non, Monsieur,' said the boy, who never stopped smiling. He served us with dessert plates painted with blue parrots and horned beetles.

'What is the name for this in English?' said Blackbeard, pointing. I told him 'Parrot.'

'Ah, *mon Dieu!* . . . Pair-rot . . . ' He put his arms round his plate. 'I love you, *ma petite* pair-rot. You are sweet, you are blonde, you are English. You do not know the difference between whisky and mirabelle.'

The little corporal and I looked at each other, laughing. He squeezed up his eyes when he laughed, so that you saw nothing but the long curly lashes.

'Well, I know a place where they do keep it,' said the blue-eyed soldier. *'Café des Amis.* We'll go there – I'll pay – I'll pay for the whole lot of us.' His gesture embraced thousands of pounds.

But with a loud whirring noise the clock on the wall struck half-past eight; and no soldier is allowed in a café after eight o'clock at night.

'It is fast,' said the blue-eyed soldier. The little corporal's watch said the same. So did the immense turnip that Blackbeard produced and carefully deposited on the head of one of the horned beetles.

'Ah, well, we'll take the risk,' said the blue-eyed soldier, and he thrust his arms into his immense cardboard coat. 'It's worth it,' he said. 'It's worth it. You just wait.'

Outside, stars shone between wispy clouds and the moon fluttered like a candle flame over a pointed spire. The shadows of the dark plume-like trees waved on the white houses. Not a soul to be seen. No sound to be heard but the *Hsh! Hsh!* of a far-away train, like a big beast shuffling in its sleep.

'You are cold,' whispered the little corporal. 'You are cold, *ma fille.'*

'No, really not.'

'But you are trembling.'

'Yes, but I'm not cold.'

'What are the women like in England?' asked Blackbeard. 'After the war is over I shall go to England. I shall find a little English woman and marry her – and her pair-rot.' He gave a loud choking laugh.

'Fool!' said the blue-eyed soldier, shaking him; and he leant over to me. 'It is only after the second glass that you really taste it,' he whispered. 'The second little glass and then – ah! – then you know.'

Café des Amis gleamed in the moonlight. We glanced quickly up and down the road. We ran up the four wooden steps, and opened the ringing glass door into a low room lighted with a hanging lamp, where about ten people were dining. They were seated on two benches at a narrow table.

'Soldiers!' screamed a woman, leaping up from behind a white soup-tureen – a scrag of a woman in a black shawl. 'Soldiers! At this hour! Look at that clock, look at it.' And she pointed to the clock with the dripping ladle.

'It's fast,' said the blue-eyed soldier. 'It's fast, Madame. And don't make so much noise, I beg of you. We will drink and we will go.'

'Will you?' she cried, running round the table and planting herself in front of us. 'That's just what you won't do. Coming into an honest woman's house this hour of the night – making a scene – getting the police after you. Ah, no! Ah, no! It's a disgrace, that's what it is.'

'Sh!' said the little corporal, holding up his hand. Dead silence. In the silence we heard steps passing.

'The police,' whispered Blackbeard, winking at a pretty girl with rings in her ears, who smiled back at him, saucy. 'Sh!'

The faces lifted, listening. 'How beautiful they are!' I thought. 'They are like a family party having supper in the New Testament . . .' The steps died away.

'Serve you very well right if you had been caught,' scolded the angry woman. 'I'm sorry on your account that the police didn't come. You deserve it – you deserve it.'

'A little glass of mirabelle and we will go,' persisted the blue-eyed soldier.

Still scolding and muttering she took four glasses from the cupboard and a big bottle. 'But you're not going to drink in here. Don't you believe it.' The little corporal ran into the kitchen. 'Not there! Not there! Idiot!' she cried. 'Can't you see there's a window there, and a wall opposite where the police come every evening to . . .'

'Sh!' Another scare.

'You are mad and you will end in prison – all four of you,' said the woman. She flounced out of the room. We tiptoed after her into a dark smelling scullery, full of pans of greasy water, of salad leaves and meat-bones.

'There now,' she said, putting down the glasses. 'Drink and go!'

'Ah, at last!' The blue-eyed soldier's happy voice trickled through the dark. 'What do you think? Isn't it just as I said? Hasn't it got a taste of excellent – *ex-cellent* whisky?'

(1915)

Spring Pictures

I

IT IS RAINING. Big soft drops splash on the people's hands and cheeks; immense warm drops like melted stars. 'Here are roses! Here are lilies! Here are violets!' caws the old hag in the gutter. But the lilies, bunched together in a frill of green, look more like faded cauliflowers. Up and down she drags the creaking barrow. A bad, sickly smell comes from it. Nobody wants to buy. You must walk in the middle of the road, for there is no room on the pavement. Every single shop brims over; every shop shows a tattered frill of soiled lace and dirty ribbon to charm and entice you. There are tables set out with toy cannons and soldiers and Zeppelins and photograph frames complete with ogling beauties. There are immense baskets of yellow straw hats piled up like pyramids of pastry, and strings of coloured boots and shoes so small that nobody could wear them. One shop is full of little squares of mackintosh, blue ones for girls and pink ones for boys with *Bébé* printed in the middle of each . . .

'Here are lilies! Here are roses! Here are pretty violets!' warbles the old hag, bumping into another barrow. But this barrow is still. It is heaped with lettuces. Its owner, a fat old woman, sprawls across, fast asleep, her nose in the lettuce roots . . . Who is ever going to buy anything here . . . ? The sellers are women. They sit on little canvas stools, dreamy and vacant-looking. Now and again one of them gets up and takes a feather duster, like a smoky torch, and flicks it over a thing or two and then sits down again. Even the old man in tangerine spectacles with a balloon of a belly, who turns the revolving stand of 'comic' postcards round and round, cannot decide . . .

Suddenly, from the empty shop at the corner a piano strikes up, and a violin and flute join in. The windows of the shop are scrawled over – *New Songs. First Floor. Entrance Free*. But the windows of the first floor being open, nobody bothers to go up. They hang about grinning as the harsh voices float out into the warm rainy air. At the doorway there stands a lean man in a pair of burst carpet slippers. He has stuck a feather through the broken rim of his hat; with what an air he wears it! The feather is magnificent. It is gold epaulettes, frogged coat, white kid gloves, gilded cane. He swaggers under it and the voice rolls off his chest, rich and ample.

'Come up! Come up! Here are the new songs! Each singer is an artiste of European reputation. The orchestra is famous and second to none. You can stay as long as you like. It is the chance of a lifetime, and once missed never to return!' But nobody moves. Why should they? They know all about those girls – those famous artistes. One is dressed in cream cashmere and one in blue. Both have dark crimped hair and a pink rose pinned over the ear . . . They know all about the pianist's button boots – the left foot – the pedal foot – burst over the bunion on his big toe. The violinist's bitten nails, the long, far too long cuffs of the flute player – all these things are as old as the new songs.

For a long time the music goes on and the proud voice thunders. Then somebody calls down the stairs and the showman, still with his grand air, disappears. The voices cease. The piano, the violin and the flute dribble into quiet. Only the lace curtain gives a wavy sign of life from the first floor.

It is raining still; it is getting dusky . . . Here are roses! Here are lilies! Who will buy my violets? . . .

2

Hope! You misery – you sentimental, faded female! Break your last string and have done with it. I shall go mad with your endless thrumming; my heart throbs to it and every little pulse beats in time. It is morning. I lie in the empty bed – the huge bed big as a field and as cold and unsheltered. Through the shutters the sunlight comes up from the river and flows over the ceiling in trembling waves. I hear from outside a hammer tapping and far below in the house a door swings open and shuts. Is this my room? Are those my clothes folded over an armchair? Under the pillow, sign and symbol of a lonely woman, ticks my watch. The bell jangles. Ah! At last! I leap out of bed and run to the door. Play faster – faster – Hope!

'Your milk, Mademoiselle,' says the concierge, gazing at me severely.

'Ah, thank you,' I cry, gaily swinging the milk bottle. 'No letters for me?'

'Nothing, Mademoiselle.'

'But the postman – he has called already?'

'A long half-hour ago, Mademoiselle.'

Shut the door. Stand in the little passage a moment. Listen – listen for her hated twanging. Coax her – court her – implore her to play just once that charming little thing for one string only. In vain.

3

Across the river, on the narrow stone path that fringes the bank, a woman is walking. She came down the steps from the Quay, walking slowly, one hand on her hip. It is a beautiful evening; the sky is the colour of lilac and the river of violet leaves. There are big bright trees along the path full of trembling light, and the boats, dancing up and down, send heavy curls of foam rippling almost to her feet. Now she has stopped. Now she has turned suddenly. She is leaning up against a tree, her hands over her face; she is crying. And now she is walking up and down wringing her hands. Again she leans against the tree, her back against it, her head raised and her hands clasped as though she leaned against someone dear. Round her shoulders she wears a little grey shawl; she covers her face with the ends of it and rocks to and fro.

But one cannot cry for ever, so at last she becomes serious and quiet, patting her hair into place, smoothing her apron. She walks a step or two. No, too soon, too soon! Again her arms fly up – she runs back – again she is blotted against the tall tree. Squares of gold light show in the houses; the street lamps gleam through the new leaves; yellow fans of light follow the dancing boats. For a moment she is a blur against the tree, white, grey and black, melting into the stones and the shadows. And then she is gone.

(1915)

Late at Night

(Virginia is seated by the fire. Her outdoor things are thrown on a chair; her boots are faintly steaming in the fender.)

Virginia (*laying the letter down*): I don't like this letter at all – not at all. I wonder if he means it to be so snubbing – or if it's just his way. (*Reads.*) 'Many thanks for the socks. As I have had five pairs sent me lately, I am sure you will be pleased to hear I gave yours to a friend in my company.' No; it can't be my fancy. He must have meant it; it is a dreadful snub.

Oh, I wish I hadn't sent him that letter telling him to take care of himself. I'd give anything to have that letter back. I wrote it on a Sunday evening too – that was so fatal. I never ought to write letters on Sunday evenings – I always let myself go so. I can't think why Sunday evenings always have such a funny effect on me. I simply yearn to have someone to write to – or to love. Yes, that's it; they make me feel sad and full of love. Funny, isn't it!

I must start going to church again; it's fatal sitting in front of the fire and thinking. There are the hymns, too; one can let oneself go so safely in the hymns. (*She croons*) 'And then for those our Dearest and our Best' – (*but her eye lights on the next sentence in the letter*). 'It was most kind of you to have knitted them yourself.' Really! Really, that is too much! Men are abominably arrogant! He actually imagines that I knitted them myself. Why, I hardly know him; I've only spoken to him a few times. Why on earth should I knit him socks? He must think I am far gone to throw myself at his head like that. For it certainly is throwing oneself at a man's head to knit him socks – if he's almost a stranger. Buying him an odd pair is a different matter altogether. No; I shan't write to him again – that's definite. And, besides, what would be the use? I might get really keen on him and he'd never care a straw for me. Men don't.

I wonder why it is that after a certain point I always seem to repel people. Funny, isn't it! They like me at first; they think me un-common, or original; but then immediately I want to show them –

even give them a hint – that I like them, they seem to get frightened and begin to disappear. I suppose I shall get embittered about it later on. Perhaps they know somehow that I've got so much to give. Perhaps it's that that frightens them. Oh, I feel I've got such boundless, boundless love to give to somebody – I would care for somebody so utterly and so completely – watch over them – keep everything horrible away – and make them feel that if ever they wanted anything done I lived to do it. If only I felt that somebody wanted me, that I was of use to somebody, I should become a different person. Yes; that is the secret of life for me – to feel loved, to feel wanted, to know that somebody leaned on me for everything absolutely – for ever. And I am strong, and far, far richer than most women. I am sure that most women don't have this tremendous yearning to – express themselves. I suppose that's it – to come into flower, almost. I'm all folded and shut away in the dark and nobody cares. I suppose that is why I feel this tremendous tenderness for plants and sick animals and birds – it's one way of getting rid of this wealth, this burden of love. And then, of course, they are so helpless – that's another thing. But I have a feeling that if a man were really in love with you he'd be just as helpless too. Yes, I am sure that men are very helpless . . .

I don't know why, I feel inclined to cry tonight. Certainly not because of this letter; it isn't half important enough. But I keep wondering if things will ever change or if I shall go on like this until I am old – just wanting and wanting. I'm not as young as I was even now. I've got lines and my skin isn't a bit what it used to be. I never was really pretty, not in the ordinary way, but I did have lovely skin and lovely hair – and I walked well. I only caught sight of myself in a glass today – stooping and shuffling along . . . I looked dowdy and elderly. Well, no; perhaps not quite as bad as that; I always exaggerate about myself. But I'm faddy about things now – that's a sign of age, I'm sure. The wind – I can't bear being blown about in the wind now; and I hate having wet feet. I never used to care about those things – I used almost to revel in them – they made me feel so *one* with Nature in a way. But now I get cross and I want to cry and I yearn for something to make me forget. I suppose that's why women take to drink. Funny, isn't it!

The fire is going out. I'll burn this letter. What's it to me? Pooh! I don't care. What is it to me? The five other women can send him socks! And I don't suppose he was a bit what I imagined. I can just hear him saying, 'It was most kind of you, to have knitted them yourself.' He has a fascinating voice. I think it was his voice that attracted me to him – and his hands; they looked so strong – they were such man's hands. Oh, well, don't sentimentalise over it; burn it! . . . No, I can't now – the fire's gone out. I'll go to bed. I wonder if he really meant to be snubbing. Oh, I am tired. Often when I go to bed now I want to pull the clothes over my head – and just cry. Funny, isn't it!

(1917)

Two Tuppenny Ones, Please

Lady. Yes, there is, dear; there's plenty of room. If the lady next to me would move her seat and sit opposite . . . Would you mind? So that my friend may sit next to me . . . Thank you so much! Yes, dear, both the cars on war work; I'm getting quite used to buses. Of course, if we go to the theatre, I phone Cynthia. She's still got one car. Her chauffeur's been called up . . . Ages ago . . . Killed by now, I think. I can't quite remember. I don't like her new man at all. I don't mind taking any reasonable risk, but he's so obstinate – he charges everything he sees. Heaven alone knows what would happen if he rushed into something that wouldn't swerve aside. But the poor creature's got a withered arm, and something the matter with one of his feet, I believe she told me. I suppose that's what makes him so careless. I mean – well! . . . Don't you know! . . .

Friend. . . . ?

Lady. Yes, she's sold it. My dear, it was far too small. There were only ten bedrooms, you know. There were only ten bedrooms in that house. Extraordinary! One wouldn't believe it from the outside – would one? And with the governesses and the nurses – and so on. All the menservants had to sleep out . . . You know what that means.

Friend. . . . !!

Conductor. Fares, please. Parse your fares along.

Lady. How much is it? Tuppence, isn't it? Two tuppenny ones, please. Don't bother – I've got some coppers, somewhere or other.

Friend. . . . !

Lady. No, it's all right. I've got some – if only I can find them.

Conductor. Parse your fares, please.

Friend. . . . !

Lady. Really? So I did. I remember now. Yes, I paid coming. Very well, I'll let you, just this once. War time, my dear.

Conductor. 'Ow far do you want ter go?

Lady. To the Boltons.

Conductor. Another 'a'penny each.

Lady. No – oh no! I only paid tuppence coming. Are you quite sure?

Conductor (*savagely*). Read it on the board for yourself.

Lady. Oh, very well. Here's another penny. (*To friend*): Isn't it extraordinary how disobliging these men are? After all, he's paid to do his job. But they are nearly all alike. I've heard these motor buses affect the spine after a time. I suppose that's it . . . You've heard about Teddie – haven't you?'

Friend. . . .

Lady. He's got his . . . He's got his . . . Now what is it? Whatever can it be? How ridiculous of me!

Friend. . . . ?

Lady. Oh no! He's been a Major for ages.

Friend. . . . ?

Lady. Colonel? Oh no, my dear, it's something much higher than that. Not his company – he's had his company a long time. Not his battalion . . .

Friend. . . . ?

Lady. Regiment! Yes, I believe it is his regiment. But what I was going to say is he's been made a . . . Oh, how silly I am! What's higher than a Brigadier-General? Yes, I believe that's it. Chief of Staff. Of course, Mrs T.'s frightfully gratified.

Friend. . . .

Lady. Oh, my dear, everybody goes over the top nowadays. Whatever his position may be. And Teddy is such a sport, I really don't see how . . . Too dreadful – isn't it!

Friend. . . . ?

Lady. Didn't you know? She's at the War Office, and doing very well. I believe she got a rise the other day. She's something to do with notifying the deaths or finding the missing. I don't know exactly what it is. At any rate, she says it is too depressing for words, and she has to read the most heart-rending letters from parents, and so on. Happily, they're a very cheery little group in her room – all officers' wives, and they make their own tea, and get cakes in turn from Stewart's. She has one afternoon a week off, when she shops or has her hair waved. Last time she and I went to see Yvette's Spring Show.

Friend. . . . ?

Lady. No, not really. I'm getting frightfully sick of these coat-frocks, aren't you? I mean, as I was saying to her, what is the use of paying an enormous price for having one made by Yvette when you can't really tell the difference, in the long run, between it and one of those cheap ready-made ones. Of course, one has the satisfaction for oneself of knowing that the material is good, and so on – but it looks nothing. No; I advised her to get a good coat and skirt. For, after all, a good coat and skirt always tells. Doesn't it?

Friend. . . . !

Lady. Yes, I didn't tell her that – but that's what I had in mind. She's much too fat for those coat-frocks. She goes out far too much at the hips. I half ordered a rather lovely indefinite blue one for myself, trimmed with the new lobster red . . . I've lost my good Kate, you know.

Friend. . . . !

Lady. Yes, isn't it annoying! Just when I got her more or less trained. But she went off her head, like they all do nowadays, and decided that she wanted to go into munitions. I told her when she gave notice that she would go on the strict understanding that if she got a job (which, I think, is highly improbable) she was not to come back and disturb the other servants.

Conductor (*savagely*). Another penny each, if you're going on.

Lady. Oh, we're there. How extraordinary! I never should have noticed . . .

Friend. . . . ?

Lady. Tuesday? Bridge on Tuesday? No, dear, I'm afraid I can't manage Tuesday. I trot out the wounded every Tuesday, you know. I let cook take them to the Zoo or some place like that – don't you know. Wednesday – I'm perfectly free on Wednesday.

Conductor. It'll be Wednesday before you get off the bus if you don't 'urry up.

Lady. That's quite enough, my man.

Friend. . . . !!

(1917)

The Black Cap

(A lady and her husband are seated at breakfast. He is quite calm, reading the newspaper and eating; but she is strangely excited, dressed for travelling, and only pretending to eat.)

She. Oh, if you should want your flannel shirts, they are on the right-hand bottom shelf of the linen press.

He (*at a board meeting of the Meat Export Company*). No.

She. You didn't hear what I said. I said if you should want your flannel shirts, they are on the right-hand bottom shelf of the linen press.

He (*positively*). I quite agree!

She. It does seem rather extraordinary that on the very morning that I am going away you cannot leave the newspaper alone for five minutes.

He (*mildly*). My dear woman, I don't want you to go. In fact, I have asked you not to go. I can't for the life of me see . . .

She. You know perfectly well that I am only going because I absolutely must. I've been putting it off and putting it off, and the dentist said last time . . .

He. Good! Good! Don't let's go over the ground again. We've thrashed it out pretty thoroughly, haven't we?

Servant. Cab's here, m'm.

She. Please put my luggage in.

Servant. Very good, m'm.

(She gives a tremendous sigh)

He. You haven't got too much time if you want to catch that train.

She. I know. I'm going. (*In a changed tone.*) Darling, don't let us part like this. It makes me feel so wretched. Why is it that you always seem to take a positive delight in spoiling my enjoyment?

He. I don't think going to the dentist is so positively enjoyable.

She. Oh, you know that's not what I mean. You're only saying that to hurt me. You know you are begging the question.

He (*laughing*). And you are losing your train. You'll be back on Thursday evening, won't you?

She (*in a low, desperate voice*). Yes, on Thursday evening. Goodbye, then. (*Comes over to him, and takes his head in her hands.*) Is there anything really the matter? Do at least look at me. Don't you – care – at – all?

He. My darling girl! This is like an exit on the cinema.

She (*letting her hands fall*). Very well. Goodbye. (*Gives a quick tragic glance round the dining-room and goes.*)

(On the way to the station)

She. How strange life is! I didn't think I should feel like this at all. All the glamour seems to have gone, somehow. Oh, I'd give anything for the cab to turn round and go back. The most curious thing is that I feel if he really had made me believe he loved me it would have been much easier to have left him. But that's absurd. How strong the hay smells. It's going to be a very hot day. I shall never see these fields again. Never! never! But in another way I am glad that it happened like this; it puts me so finally, absolutely in the right for ever! He doesn't want a woman at all. A woman has no meaning for him. He's not the type of man to care deeply for anybody except himself. I've become the person who remembers to take the links out of his shirts before they go to the wash – that is all! And that's not enough for me. I'm young – I'm too proud. I'm not the type of woman to vegetate in the country and rave over 'our' own lettuces . . .

What you have been trying to do, ever since you married me, is to make me submit, to turn me into your shadow, to rely on me so utterly that you'd only to glance up to find the right time printed on me somehow, as if I were a clock. You have never been curious about me; you never wanted to explore my soul. No; you wanted me to settle down to your peaceful existence. Oh! how your blindness has outraged me – how I hate you for it! I am glad – thankful – thankful to have left you! I'm not a green girl; I am not conceited, but I do know my powers. It's not for nothing that I've always longed for riches and passion and freedom and felt that they were mine by right. (*She leans against the buttoned back of the cab and murmurs.*) 'You are a Queen. Let mine be the joy of giving you your kingdom.' (*She smiles at her little royal hands.*) I wish my heart didn't beat so hard. It really hurts me. It tires me so and excites me so. It's like someone in a dreadful hurry beating against a door . . . This cab is only crawling along; we shall never be at the station at this rate. Hurry! Hurry! My love, I am coming as quickly as ever I can. Yes, I am suffering just like you. It's dreadful, isn't it unbearable – this last half-hour without each other . . . Oh, God! the horse has begun to walk again. Why doesn't he beat the great strong brute of a thing . . . Our wonderful life! We shall travel all over the world together. The whole world shall be ours because of our love. Oh, be patient! I am coming as fast as I possibly can . . . Ah, now it's downhill; now we really are going faster. (*An old man attempts to cross the road.*) Get out of my way, you old fool! He deserves to be run over . . . Dearest – dearest; I am nearly there. Only be patient!

(*At the station*)

Put it in a first-class smoker . . . There's plenty of time after all. A full ten minutes before the train goes. No wonder he's not here. I mustn't appear to be looking for him. But I must say I'm disappointed. I never dreamed of being the first to arrive. I thought he would have been here and engaged a carriage and bought papers and flowers . . . How curious! I absolutely saw in my mind a paper of pink carnations . . . He knows how fond I am of carnations. But pink ones are not my favourites. I prefer dark red or pale yellow. He really will be late if he doesn't come now. The guard has begun to shut the doors. Whatever can have happened? Something dreadful. Perhaps at the last moment he has shot himself . . . I could not bear the thought of ruining your life . . . But you are not ruining my life. Ah, where are you? I shall have to get into the carriage . . . Who is this? That's not him! It can't be – yes, it is. What on earth has he got on his head? A black cap. But how awful! He's utterly changed. What can he be wearing a black cap for? I wouldn't have known him. How absurd he looks coming towards me, smiling, in that appalling cap!

He. My darling, I shall never forgive myself. But the most absurd, tragic-comic thing happened. (*They get into the carriage.*) I lost my hat. It simply disappeared. I had half the hotel looking for it. Not a sign! So finally, in despair, I had to borrow this from another man who was staying there. (*The train moves off.*) You're not angry. (*Tries to take her in his arms.*)

She. Don't! We're not even out of the station yet.

He (*ardently*). Great God! What do I care if the whole world were to see us? (*Tries to take her in his arms.*) My wonder! My joy!

She. Please don't! I hate being kissed in trains.

He (*profoundly hurt*). Oh, very well. You *are* angry. It's serious. You can't get over the fact that I was late. But if you only knew the agony I suffered . . .

She. How can you think I could be so small-minded? I am not angry at all.

He. Then why won't you let me kiss you?

She (*laughing hysterically*). You look so different somehow – almost a stranger.

He (*jumps up and looks at himself in the glass anxiously, and fatuously, she decides*). But it's all right, isn't it?

She. Oh, quite all right; perfectly all right. Oh, oh, oh! (*She begins to laugh and cry with rage.*)

(*They arrive*)

She (*while he gets a cab*). I must get over this. It's an obsession. It's incredible that anything should change a man so. I must tell him. Surely it's quite simple to say: Don't you think now that you are in the city you had better buy yourself a hat? But that will make him realise how frightful the cap has been. And the extraordinary thing is that he doesn't realise it himself. I mean if he has looked at himself in the glass, and doesn't think that cap too ridiculous, how different our points of view must be . . . How deeply different! I mean, if I had seen him in the street I would have said I could not possibly love a man who wore a cap like that. I couldn't even have got to know him. He isn't my style at all. (*She looks round.*) Everybody is smiling at it. Well, I don't wonder! The way it makes his ears stick out, and the way it makes him have no back to his head at all.

He. The cab is ready, my darling. (*They get in.*)

He (*tries to take her hand*). The miracle that we two should be driving together, so simply, like this.

(*She arranges her veil*)

He (*tries to take her hand, very ardent*). I'll engage one room, my love.

She. Oh no! Of course you must take two.

He. But don't you think it would be wiser not to create suspicion?

She. I must have my own room. (*To herself.*) You can hang your cap *behind your own door!* (*She begins to laugh hysterically.*)

He. Ah! thank God! My queen is her happy self again!

(*At the hotel*)

Manager. Yes, sir, I quite understand. I think I've got the very thing for you, sir. Kindly step this way. (*He takes them into a small sitting-room, with a bedroom leading out of it.*) This would suit you nicely, wouldn't it? And if you liked, we could make you up a bed on the sofa.

He. Oh, admirable! Admirable!

(*The Manager goes*)

She (*furious*). But I told you I wanted a room to myself. What a trick to play upon me! I told you I did not want to share a room. How dare you treat me like this? (*She mimics.*) Admirable! Admirable! I shall never forgive you for that!

He (*overcome*). Oh, God, what is happening! I don't understand – I'm in the dark. Why have you suddenly, on this day of days, ceased to love me? What have I done? Tell me!

She (*sinks on the sofa*). I'm very tired. If you do love me, please leave me alone. I – I only want to be alone for a little.

He (*tenderly*). Very well. I shall try to understand. I do begin to understand. I'll go out for half an hour, and then, my love, you may feel calmer. (*He looks round, distracted.*)

She. What is it?

He. My heart – you are sitting on my cap. (*She gives a positive scream and moves into the bedroom. He goes. She waits a moment, and then puts down her veil, and takes up her suitcase.*)

(*In the taxi*)

She. Yes, Waterloo. (*She leans back.*) Ah, I've escaped – I've escaped! I shall just be in time to catch the afternoon train home. Oh, it's like a dream – I'll be home before supper. I'll tell him that the city was too hot or the dentist away. What does it matter? I've a right to my own home . . . It will be wonderful driving up from the station; the fields will smell so delicious. There is cold fowl for supper left over from yesterday, and orange jelly . . . I have been mad, but now I am sane again. Oh, my husband!

(1917)

A Suburban Fairy Tale

MR AND MRS B. sat at breakfast in the cosy red dining-room of their 'snug little crib just under half-an-hour's run from the City'.

There was a good fire in the grate – for the dining-room was the living-room as well – the two windows overlooking the cold empty garden patch were closed, and the air smelled agreeably of bacon and eggs, toast and coffee. Now that this rationing business was really over Mr B. made a point of a thoroughly good tuck-in before facing the very real perils of the day. He didn't mind who knew it – he was a true Englishman about his breakfast – he had to have it; he'd cave in without it, and if you told him that these Continental chaps could get through half the morning's work he did on a roll and a cup of coffee – you simply didn't know what you were talking about.

Mr B. was a stout youngish man who hadn't been able – worse luck – to chuck his job and join the Army; he'd tried for four years to get another chap to take his place, but it was no go. He sat at the head of the table reading the *Daily Mail*. Mrs B. was a youngish plump little body, rather like a pigeon. She sat opposite, preening herself behind the coffee set and keeping an eye of warning love on little B. who perched between them, swathed in a napkin and tapping the top of a soft-boiled egg.

Alas! Little B. was not at all the child that such parents had every right to expect. He was no fat little trot, no dumpling, no firm little pudding. He was undersized for his age, with legs like macaroni, tiny claws, soft, soft hair that felt like mouse fur and big wide-open eyes. For some strange reason everything in life seemed the wrong size for Little B. – too big and too violent. Everything knocked him over, took the wind out of his feeble sails and left him gasping and frightened. Mr and Mrs B. were quite powerless to prevent this; they could only pick him up after the mischief was done – and try to set him going again. And Mrs B. loved him as only weak children are loved – and when Mr B. thought what a marvellous little chap he was too – thought of the spunk of the little man, he – well he – by George – he . . .

'Why aren't there two kinds of eggs?' said Little B. 'Why aren't there little eggs for children and big eggs like what this one is for grown-ups?'

'Scotch hares,' said Mr B. 'Fine Scotch hares for 5s. 3d. How about getting one, old girl?'

'It would be a nice change, wouldn't it?' said Mrs B. 'Jugged.'

And they looked across at each other and there floated between them the Scotch hare in its rich gravy with stuffing balls and a white pot of red-currant jelly accompanying it.

'We might have had it for the weekend,' said Mrs B. 'But the butcher has promised me a nice little sirloin and it seems a pity' . . . Yes, it did, and yet . . . Dear me, it was very difficult to decide. The hare would have been such a change – on the other hand, could you beat a really nice little sirloin?

'There's hare soup, too,' said Mr B., drumming his fingers on the table. 'Best soup in the world!'

'O-oh!' cried Little B. so suddenly and sharply that it gave them quite a start – 'Look at the whole lot of sparrows flown on to our lawn' – he waved his spoon. 'Look at them,' he cried. 'Look!' And while he spoke, even though the windows were closed, they heard a loud shrill cheeping and chirping from the garden.

'Get on with your breakfast like a good boy, do,' said his mother, and his father said, 'You stick to the egg, old man, and look sharp about it.'

'But look at them – look at them all hopping,' he cried. 'They don't keep still not for a minute. Do you think they're hungry, father?'

Cheek-a-cheep-cheep-cheek! cried the sparrows.

'Best postpone it perhaps till next week,' said Mr B., 'and trust to luck they're still to be had then.'

'Yes, perhaps that would be wiser,' said Mrs B.

Mr B. picked another plum out of his paper.

'Have you bought any of those controlled dates yet?'

'I managed to get two pounds yesterday,' said Mrs B.

'Well, a date pudding's a good thing,' said Mr B. And they looked across at each other and there floated between them a dark round pudding covered with creamy sauce. 'It would be a nice change, wouldn't it?' said Mrs B.

Outside on the grey frozen grass the funny eager sparrows hopped and fluttered. They were never for a moment still. They cried, flapped their ungainly wings. Little B., his egg finished, got down, took his bread and marmalade to eat at the window.

'Do let us give them some crumbs,' he said. 'Do open the window, father, and throw them something. Father, *please*!'

'Oh, don't nag, child,' said Mrs B., and his father said – 'Can't go opening windows, old man. You'd get your head bitten off.'

'But they're hungry,' cried Little B., and the sparrows' little voices were like ringing of little knives being sharpened. *Cheek-a-cheep-cheep-cheek!* they cried.

Little B. dropped his bread and marmalade inside the china flower-pot in front of the window. He slipped behind the thick curtains to see better, and Mr and Mrs B. went on reading about what you could get now without coupons – no more ration books after May – a glut of cheese – a glut of it – whole cheeses revolved in the air between them like celestial bodies.

Suddenly as Little B. watched the sparrows on the grey frozen grass, they grew, they changed, still flapping and squeaking. They turned into tiny little boys, in brown coats, dancing, jigging out-side, up and down outside the window squeaking, 'Want something to eat, want something to eat!' Little B. held with both hands to the curtain. 'Father,' he whispered, 'Father! They're not sparrows. They're little boys. Listen, Father!' But Mr and Mrs B would not hear. He tried again. 'Mother,' he whispered. 'Look at the little boys. They're not sparrows, Mother!' But nobody noticed his nonsense.

'All this talk about famine,' cried Mr B., 'all a Fake, all a Blind.'

With white shining faces, their arms flapping in the big coats, the little boys danced. 'Want something to eat, want something to eat.'

'Father,' muttered Little B. 'Listen, Father! Mother, listen, please!'

'Really!' said Mrs B. 'The noise those birds are making! I've never heard such a thing.'

'Fetch me my shoes, old man,' said Mr B.

Cheek-a-cheep-cheep-cheek! said the sparrows.

Now where had that child go to? 'Come and finish your nice cocoa, my pet,' said Mrs B.

Mr B. lifted the heavy cloth and whispered, 'Come on, Rover,' but no little dog was there.

'He's behind the curtain,' said Mrs B.

'He never went out of the room,' said Mr B.

Mrs B. went over to the window and Mr B. followed. And they looked out. There on the grey frozen grass, with a white, white face, the little boy's thin arms flapping like wings, in front of them all, the smallest, tiniest was Little B. Mr and Mrs B. heard his voice above all the voices. 'Want something to eat, want something to eat.'

Somehow, somehow, they opened the window. 'You shall! All of you. Come in *at once*. Old man! Little man!'

But it was too late. The little boys were changed into sparrows again, and away they flew – out of sight – out of call.

(1917)

Carnation

ON THOSE HOT DAYS Eve – curious Eve – always carried a flower. She snuffed it and snuffed it, twirled it in her fingers, laid it against her cheek, held it to her lips, tickled Katie's neck with it, and ended, finally, by pulling it to pieces and eating it, petal by petal.

'Roses are delicious, my dear Katie,' she would say, standing in the dim cloak-room, with a strange decoration of flowery hats on the hat pegs behind her – 'but carnations are simply divine! They taste like – like – ah well!' And away her little thin laugh flew, fluttering among those huge, strange flower heads on the wall behind her. (But how cruel her little thin laugh was! It had a long sharp beak and claws and two bead eyes, thought fanciful Katie.)

Today it was a carnation. She brought a carnation to the French class, a deep, deep red one, that looked as though it had been dipped in wine and left in the dark to dry. She held it on the desk before her, half shut her eyes and smiled.

'Isn't it a darling?' said she. But –

'*Un peu de silence, s'il vous plaît*,' came from M. Hugo. Oh, bother! It was too hot! Frightfully hot! Grilling simply!

The two square windows of the French Room were open at the bottom and the dark blinds drawn half-way down. Although no air came in, the blind cord swung out and back and the blind lifted. But really there was not a breath from the dazzle outside.

Even the girls, in the dusky room, in their pale blouses, with stiff butterfly-bow hair ribbons perched on their hair, seemed to give off a warm, weak light, and M. Hugo's white waistcoat gleamed like the belly of a shark.

Some of the girls were very red in the face and some were white. Vera Holland had pinned up her black curls *à la japonaise* with a penholder and a pink pencil; she looked charming. Francie Owen pushed her sleeves nearly up to the shoulders, and then she inked the little blue vein in her elbow, shut her arm together, and then looked to see the mark it made; she had a passion for inking herself; she always had a face drawn on her thumb nail, with black, forked hair. Sylvia Mann took off her collar and tie, took them off simply, and laid them on the desk beside her, as calm as if she were going to wash her hair in her bedroom at home. She *had* a nerve! Jennie Edwards tore a leaf out of her notebook and wrote 'Shall we ask old Hugo-Wugo to give us a thrippenny vanilla on the way home!!!' and passed it across to Connie Baker, who turned absolutely purple and nearly burst out crying. All of them lolled and gaped, staring at the round clock, which seemed to have grown paler, too; the hands scarcely crawled.

'*Un peu de silence, s'il vous plaît*,' came from M. Hugo. He held up a puffy hand. 'Ladies, as it is so 'ot we will take no more notes today, but I will read you' – and he paused and smiled a broad, gentle smile – 'a little French poetry.'

'Go – od God!' moaned Francie Owen.

M. Hugo's smile deepened. 'Well, Mees Owen, you need not attend. You can paint yourself. You can 'ave my red ink as well as your black one.'

How well they knew the little blue book with red edges that he tugged out of his coat-tail pocket! It had a green silk marker embroidered in forget-me-nots. They often giggled at it when he handed the book round. Poor old Hugo-Wugo! He adored reading poetry. He would begin, softly and calmly, and then gradually his voice would swell and vibrate and gather itself together, then it would be pleading and imploring and entreating, and then rising, rising triumphant, until it burst into light, as it were, and then – gradually again, it ebbed, it grew soft and warm and calm and died down into nothingness.

The great difficulty was, of course, if you felt at all feeble, not to get the most awful fit of the giggles. Not because it was funny, really, but because it made you feel uncomfortable, queer, silly, and some-how ashamed for old Hugo-Wugo. But – oh dear – if he was going to inflict it on them in this heat . . . !

'Courage, my pet,' said Eve, kissing the languid carnation.

He began, and most of the girls fell forward, over the desks, their heads on their arms, dead at the first shot. Only Eve and Katie sat upright and still. Katie did not know enough French to understand, but Eve sat listening, her eyebrows raised, her eyes half veiled, and a smile that was like the shadow of her cruel little laugh, like the wing shadows of that cruel little laugh fluttering over her lips. She made a warm, white cup of her fingers – the carnation inside. Oh, the scent!

554 SOMETHING CHILDISH AND OTHER STORIES

It floated across to Katie. It was too much. Katie turned away to the dazzling light outside the window.

Down below, she knew, there was a cobbled courtyard with stable buildings round it. That was why the French Room always smelled faintly of ammonia. It wasn't unpleasant; it was even part of the French language for Katie – something sharp and vivid and – and – biting!

Now she could hear a man clatter over the cobbles and the jing-jang of the pails he carried. And now *Hoo-hor-her! Hoo-hor-her!* as he worked the pump and a great gush of water followed. Now he was flinging the water over something, over the wheels of a carriage perhaps. And she saw the wheel, propped up, clear of the ground, spinning round, flashing scarlet and black, with great drops glancing off it. And all the while he worked the man kept up a high, bold whistling that skimmed over the noise of the water as a bird skims over the sea. He went away – he came back again leading a cluttering horse.

Hoo-hor-her! Hoo-hor-her! came from the pump. Now he dashed the water over the horse's legs and then swooped down and began brushing.

She *saw* him simply – in a faded shirt, his sleeves rolled up, his chest bare, all splashed with water – and as he whistled, loud and free, and as he moved, swooping and bending, Hugo-Wugo's voice began to warm, to deepen, to gather together, to swing, to rise – somehow or other to keep time with the man outside (Oh, the scent of Eve's carnation!) until they became one great rushing, rising, triumphant thing, bursting into light, and then –

The whole room broke into pieces.

'Thank you, ladies,' cried M. Hugo, bobbing at his high desk, over the wreckage.

And 'Keep it, dearest,' said Eve. '*Souvenir tendre*,' and she popped the carnation down the front of Katie's blouse.

(1917)

See-Saw

SPRING. As the people leave the road for the grass their eyes become fixed and dreamy like the eyes of people wading in the warm sea. There are no daisies yet, but the sweet smell of the grass rises, rises in tiny waves the deeper they go. The trees are in full leaf. As far as one can see there are fans, hoops, tall rich plumes of various green. A light wind shakes them, blowing them together, blowing them free again; in the blue sky floats a cluster of tiny white clouds like a brood of ducklings. The people wander over the grass – the old ones inclined to puff and waddle after their long winter snooze; the young ones suddenly linking hands and making for that screen of trees in the hollow or the shelter of that clump of dark gorse tipped with yellow – walking very fast, almost running, as though they had heard some lovely little creature caught in the thicket crying to them to be saved.

On the top of a small green mound there is a very favourite bench. It has a young chestnut growing beside it shaped like a mushroom. Below the earth has crumbled, fallen away, leaving three or four clayey hollows – caves – caverns – and in one of them two little people had set up house with a minute pickaxe, an empty match-box, a blunted nail and a shovel for furniture. He had red hair cut in a deep fringe, light-blue eyes, a faded pink smock and brown button shoes. Her flowery curls were caught up with a yellow ribbon and she wore two dresses – her this week's underneath and her last week's on top. This gave her rather a bulky air.

'If you don't get me no sticks for my fire,' said she, 'there won't be no dinner.' She wrinkled her nose and looked at him severely. 'You seem to forget I've got a fire to make.' He took it very easy, balancing on his toes – 'Well – where's I to find any sticks?'

'Oh,' said she – flinging up her hands – 'anywhere of course – ' And then she whispered just loud enough for him to hear, 'they needn't be real ones – *you* know.'

'Ooh,' he breathed. And then he shouted in a loud distinct tone: 'Well, I'll just go an' get a few sticks.'

He came in a moment with an armful.

'Is that a whole pennorth?' said she, holding out her skirts for them.

'Well,' said he, 'I don't know, because I had them give to me by a man that was moving.'

'Perhaps they're bits of what was broke,' said she. 'When we moved, two of the pictures was broken and my Daddy lit the fire with them, and my Mummy said – she said – ' a tiny pause – 'soldier's manners!'

'What's that?' said he.

'Good *gracious!*' She made great eyes at him. 'Don't you *know*?'

'No,' said he. 'What does it mean?'

She screwed up a bit of her skirt, scrunched it, then looked away – 'Oh, don't bother me, child,' said she.

He didn't care. He took the pickaxe and hacked a little piece out of the kitchen floor.

'Got a newspaper?'

He plucked one out of the air and handed it to her. *Ziz, ziz, ziz!* She tore it into three pieces – knelt down and laid the sticks over. 'Matches, please.' The real box was a triumph, and the blunted nails. But funny – *Zip, zip, zip*, it wouldn't light. They looked at each other in consternation.

'Try the other side,' said she. *Zip.* 'Ah! that's better.' There was a great glow – and they sat down on the floor and began to make the pie.

To the bench beside the chestnut came two fat old babies and plumped themselves down. She wore a bonnet trimmed with lilac and tied with lilac velvet strings; a black satin coat and a lace tie – and each of her hands, squeezed into black kid gloves, showed a morsel of purplish flesh. The skin of his swollen old face was tight and glazed – and he sat down clasping his huge soft belly as though careful not to jolt or alarm it.

'Very hot,' said he, and he gave a low, strange trumpeting cry with which she was evidently familiar, for she gave no sign. She looked into the lovely distance and quivered: 'Nellie cut her finger last night.'

'Oh, did she?' said the old snorter. Then – 'How did she do that?'

'At dinner,' was the reply, 'with a knife.'

They both looked ahead of them – panting – then, 'Badly?'

The weak worn old voice, the old voice that reminded one some-how of a piece of faintly smelling dark lace, said, 'Not very badly.'

Again he gave that low strange cry. He took off his hat, wiped the rim and put it on again.

The voice beside him said with a spiteful touch: 'I think it was carelessness' – and he replied, blowing out his cheeks: 'Bound to be!'

But then a little bird flew on to a branch of the young chestnut above them – and shook over the old heads a great jet of song.

He took off his hat, heaved himself up, and beat in its direction in the tree. Away it flew.

'Don't want bird muck falling on us,' said he, lowering his belly carefully – carefully again.

The fire was made.

'Put your hand in the oven,' said she, 'an' see if it's hot.'

He put his hand in, but drew it out again with a squeak, and danced up and down. 'It's ever so hot,' said he.

This seemed to please her very much. She, too, got up and went over to him and touched him with a finger.

'Do you like playing with me?' And he said, in his small solid way, 'Yes, I do.' At that she flung away from him and cried, 'I'll never be done if you keep on bothering me with these questions.'

As she poked the fire he said: 'Our dog's had kittens.'

'Kittens!' She sat back on her heels – 'Can a dog have kittens?'

'Of course they can,' said he. 'Little ones, you know.'

'But cats have kittens,' cried she. 'Dogs don't, dogs have – ' she stopped, stared – looked for the word – couldn't find it – it was gone. 'They have – '

'*Kittens*,' cried he. 'Our dog's been an' had two.'

She stamped her foot at him. She was pink with exasperation. 'It's *not* kittens,' she wailed, 'it's – '

'It is – it is – it is – ' he shouted, waving the shovel.

She threw her top dress over her head and began to cry. 'It's not – it's – it's . . . '

Suddenly, without a moment's warning, he lifted his pinafore and made water.

At the sound she emerged.

'Look what you've been an' done,' said she, too appalled to cry any more. 'You've put out my fire.'

'Ah, never mind. Let's move. You can take the pickaxe and the match-box.'

They moved to the next cave. 'It's much nicer here,' said he. 'Off you go,' said she, 'and get me some sticks for my fire.'

The two old babies above began to rumble, and obedient to the sign they got up without a word and waddled away.

(1917)

This Flower

But I tell you, my lord fool, out of this nettle, danger,
we pluck this flower, safety.

As SHE LAY THERE, looking up at the ceiling, she had her moment –
yes, she had her moment! And it was not connected with anything
she had thought or felt before, not even with those words the doctor
had scarcely ceased speaking. It was single, glowing, perfect; it was
like – a pearl, too flawless to match with another . . . Could she
describe what happened? Impossible. It was as though, even if she
had not been conscious (and she certainly had not been conscious all
the time) that she was fighting against the stream of life – the stream
of life indeed! – she had suddenly ceased to struggle. Oh, more than
that! She had yielded, yielded absolutely, down to every minutest
pulse and nerve, and she had fallen into the bright bosom of the
stream and it had borne her . . . She was part of her room – part of the
great bouquet of southern anemones, of the white net curtains that
blew in stiff against the light breeze, of the mirrors, the white silky
rugs; she was part of the high, shaking, quivering clamour, broken
with little bells and crying voices that went streaming by outside –
part of the leaves and the light.

Over. She sat up. The doctor had reappeared. This strange little
figure with his stethoscope still strung round his neck – for she had
asked him to examine her heart – squeezing and kneading his freshly
washed hands, had told her . . .

It was the first time she had ever seen him. Roy, unable, of course,
to miss the smallest dramatic opportunity, had obtained his rather
shady Bloomsbury address from the man in whom he always confided everything, who, although he'd never met her, knew 'all
about them'.

'My darling,' Roy had said, 'we'd better have an absolutely unknown man just in case it's – well, what we don't either of us want it
to be. One can't be too careful in affairs of this sort. Doctors *do* talk.
It's all damned rot to say they don't.' Then, 'Not that I care a straw

who on earth knows. Not that I wouldn't – if you'd have me – blazon it on the skies, or take the front page of the *Daily Mirror* and have our two names on it, in a heart, you know – pierced by an arrow.'

Nevertheless, of course, his love of mystery and intrigue, his passion for 'keeping our secret beautifully' (his phrase!) had won the day, and off he'd gone in a taxi to fetch this rather sodden-looking little man.

She heard her untroubled voice saying, 'Do you mind not mentioning anything of this to Mr King? If you'd tell him that I'm a little run down and that my heart wants a rest. For I've been complaining about my heart.'

Roy had been really *too* right about the kind of man the doctor was. He gave her a strange, quick, leering look, and taking off the stethoscope with shaking fingers he folded it into his bag that looked somehow like a broken old canvas shoe.

'Don't you worry, my dear,' he said huskily. 'I'll see you through.'

Odious little toad to have asked a favour of! She sprang to her feet, and picking up her purple cloth jacket, went over to the mirror. There was a soft knock at the door, and Roy – he really did look pale, smiling his half-smile – came in and asked the doctor what he had to say.

'Well,' said the doctor, taking up his hat, holding it against his chest and beating a tattoo on it, 'all I've got to say is that Mrs – h'm – Madam wants a bit of a rest. She's a bit run down. Her heart's a bit strained. Nothing else wrong.'

In the street a barrel-organ struck up something gay, laughing, mocking, gushing, with little trills, shakes, jumbles of notes.

> That's *all* I got to say, to say,
> That's *all* I got to say,

it mocked. It sounded so near she wouldn't have been surprised if the doctor were turning the handle.

She saw Roy's smile deepen; his eyes took fire. He gave a little 'Ah!' of relief and happiness. And just for one moment he allowed himself to gaze at her without caring a jot whether the doctor saw or not, drinking her up with that gaze she knew so well, as she stood tying the pale ribbons of her camisole and drawing on the little purple cloth jacket. He jerked back to the doctor, 'She shall go away. She shall go away to the sea at once,' said he, and then, terribly anxious, 'What about her food?' At that, buttoning her jacket in the long mirror, she couldn't help laughing at him.

'That's all very well,' he protested, laughing back delightfully at her and at the doctor. 'But if I didn't manage her food, doctor, she'd never eat anything but caviare sandwiches and – and white grapes. About wine – oughtn't she to have wine?'

Wine would do her no harm.

'Champagne,' pleaded Roy. How he was enjoying himself!

'Oh, as much champagne as she likes,' said the doctor, 'and a brandy and soda with her lunch if she fancies it.'

Roy loved that; it tickled him immensely.

'Do you hear that?' he asked solemnly, blinking and sucking in his cheeks to keep from laughing. 'Do you fancy a brandy and soda?'

And, in the distance, faint and exhausted, the barrel-organ:

> A brandy and so-da,
> A brandy and soda, please!
> A brandy and soda, please!

The doctor seemed to hear that, too. He shook hands with her, and Roy went with him into the passage to settle his fee.

She heard the front door close and then – rapid, rapid steps along the passage. This time he simply burst into her room, and she was in his arms, crushed up small while he kissed her with warm quick kisses, murmuring between them, 'My darling, my beauty, my delight. You're mine, you're safe.' And then three soft groans. 'Oh! Oh! Oh! the relief!' Still keeping his arms round her he leant his head against her shoulder as though exhausted. 'If you knew how frightened I've been,' he murmured. 'I thought we were in for it this time. I really did. And it would have been so – fatal – so fatal!'

(1919)

The Wrong House

'TWO PURL – TWO PLAIN – woolinfrontoftheneedle – and knit two together.' Like an old song, like a song that she had sung so often that only to breathe was to sing it, she murmured the knitting pattern. Another vest was nearly finished for the mission parcel.

'It's your vests, Mrs Bean, that are so acceptable. Look at these poor little mites without a shred!' And the churchwoman showed her a photograph of repulsive little black objects with bellies shaped like lemons . . .

'Two purl – two plain.' Down dropped the knitting on to her lap; she gave a great long sigh, stared in front of her for a moment and then picked the knitting up and began again. What did she think about when she sighed like that? Nothing. It was a habit. She was always sighing. On the stairs, particularly, as she went up and down, she stopped, holding her dress up with one hand, the other hand on the banister, staring at the steps – sighing.

'Woolinfrontoftheneedle . . .' She sat at the dining-room window facing the street. It was a bitter autumn day; the wind ran in the street like a thin dog; the houses opposite looked as though they had been cut out with a pair of ugly steel scissors and pasted on to the grey paper sky. There was not a soul to be seen.

'Knit two together!' The clock struck three. Only three? It seemed dusk already; dusk came floating into the room, heavy, powdery dusk settling on the furniture, filming over the mirror. Now the kitchen clock struck three – two minutes late – for *this* was the clock to go by and *not* the kitchen clock. She was alone in the house. Dollicas was out shopping; she had been gone since a quarter to two. Really, she got slower and slower! What did she *do* with the time? One cannot spend more than a certain time buying a chicken . . . And oh, that habit of hers of dropping the stove-rings when she made up the fire! And she set her lips, as she had set her lips for the past thirty-five years, at that habit of Dollicas'.

There came a faint noise from the street, a noise of horses' hooves. She leaned further out to see. Good gracious! It was a funeral. First the glass coach, rolling along briskly with the gleaming, varnished coffin inside (but no wreaths), with three men in front and two standing at the back, then some carriages, some with black horses, some with brown. The dust came bowling up the road, half hiding the procession. She scanned the houses opposite to see which had the blinds down. What horrible-looking men, too! laughing and joking. One leaned over to one side and blew his nose with his black glove – horrible! She gathered up the knitting, hiding her hands in it. Dollicas surely would have known . . . There, they were passing . . . It was the other end . . .

What was this? What was happening? What could it mean? Help, God! Her old heart leaped like a fish and then fell as the glass coach drew up outside her door, as the outside men scrambled down from the front, swung off the back, and the tallest of them, with a glance of surprise at the windows, came quickly, stealthily, up the garden path.

'No!' she groaned. But yes, the blow fell, and for the moment it struck her down. She gasped, a great cold shiver went through her, and stayed in her hands and knees. She saw the man withdraw a step, and again – that puzzled glance at the blinds – and then –

'No!' she groaned, and stumbling, catching hold of things, she managed to get to the door before the blow fell again. She opened it, her chin trembled, her teeth clacked; somehow or other she brought out, 'The wrong house!'

Oh! he was shocked. As she stepped back she saw behind him the black hats clustered at the gate. 'The wrong 'ouse!' he muttered. She could only nod. She was shutting the door again when he fished out of the tail of his coat a black, brass-bound notebook and swiftly opened it. 'No 20 Shuttleworth Crescent?'

'S – street! Crescent round the corner.' Her hand lifted to point, but shook and fell.

He was taking off his hat as she shut the door and leaned against it, whimpering in the dusky hall, 'Go away! Go away!'

Clockety-clock-clock. Cluk! Cluk! Clockety-clock-cluk! sounded from outside, and then a faint *Cluk! Cluk!* and then silence. They were gone. They were out of sight. But still she stayed leaning against the door, staring into the hall, staring at the hall-stand that was like a great lobster with hat-pegs for feelers. But she thought of nothing; she did not even think of what had happened. It was as if she had fallen into a cave whose walls were darkness . . .

She came to herself with a deep inward shock, hearing the gate bang and quick, short steps crunching the gravel; it was Dollicas hurrying round to the back door. Dollicas must not find her there; and wavering, wavering like a candle-flame, back she went into the dining-room to her seat by the window.

Dollicas was in the kitchen. *Klang!* went one of the iron rings into the fender. Then her voice, 'I'm just putting on the tea-kettle, 'm.' Since they had been alone she had got into the way of shouting from one room to another. The old woman coughed to steady herself. 'Please bring in the lamp,' she cried.

'The lamp!' Dollicas came across the passage and stood in the doorway. 'Why, it's only just on four, 'm.'

'Never mind,' said Mrs Bean dully. 'Bring it in!' And a moment later the elderly maid appeared, carrying the gentle lamp in both hands. Her broad soft face had the look it always had when she carried anything, as though she walked in her sleep. She set it down on the table, lowered the wick, raised it, and then lowered it again. Then she straightened up and looked across at her mistress.

'Why, 'm, whatever's that you're treading on?'

It was the mission vest.

'T't! T't!' As Dollicas picked it up she thought, 'The old lady has been asleep. She's not awake yet.' Indeed the old lady looked glazed and dazed, and when she took up the knitting she drew out a needle of stitches and began to unwind what she had done.

'Don't forget the mace,' she said. Her voice sounded thin and dry. She was thinking of the chicken for that night's supper. And Dollicas understood and answered, 'It's a lovely young bird!' as she pulled down the blind before going back to her kitchen . . .

(1919)

Sixpence

CHILDREN ARE unaccountable little creatures. Why should a small boy like Dicky, good as gold as a rule, sensitive, affectionate, obedient, and marvellously sensible for his age, have moods when, without the slightest warning, he suddenly went 'mad dog', as his sisters called it, and there was no doing anything with him?

'Dicky, come here! Come here, sir, at once! Do you hear your mother calling you? Dicky!'

But Dicky wouldn't come. Oh, he heard right enough. A clear, ringing little laugh was his only reply. And away he flew; hiding, running through the uncut hay on the lawn, dashing past the wood-shed, making a rush for the kitchen garden, and there dodging, peering at his mother from behind the mossy apple trunks, and leaping up and down like a wild Indian.

It had begun at tea-time. While Dicky's mother and Mrs Spears, who was spending the afternoon with her, were quietly sitting over their sewing in the drawing-room, this, according to the servant girl, was what had happened at the children's tea. They were eating their first bread and butter as nicely and quietly as you please, and the servant girl had just poured out the milk and water, when Dicky had suddenly seized the bread plate, put it upside down on his head, and clutched the bread knife.

'Look at me!' he shouted.

His startled sisters looked, and before the servant girl could get there, the bread plate wobbled, slid, flew to the floor, and broke into shivers. At this awful point the little girls lifted up their voices and shrieked their loudest.

'Mother, come and look what he's done!'

'Dicky's broke a great big plate!'

'Come and stop him, mother!'

You can imagine how mother came flying. But she was too late. Dicky had leapt out of his chair, run through the french windows on to the veranda, and, well – there she stood – popping her thimble on and off, helpless. What could she do? She couldn't chase after the child. She couldn't stalk Dicky among the apples and damsons. That would be too undignified. It was more than annoying, it was exasperating. Especially as Mrs Spears, Mrs Spears of all people, whose two boys were so exemplary, was waiting for her in the drawing-room.

'Very well, Dicky,' she cried, 'I shall have to think of some way of punishing you.'

'I don't care,' sounded the high little voice, and again there came that ringing laugh. The child was quite beside himself . . .

'Oh, Mrs Spears, I don't know how to apologise for leaving you by yourself like this.'

'It's quite all right, Mrs Bendall,' said Mrs Spears, in her soft, sugary voice, and raising her eyebrows in the way she had. She seemed to smile to herself as she stroked the gathers. 'These little things will happen from time to time. I only hope it was nothing serious.'

'It was Dicky,' said Mrs Bendall, looking rather helplessly for her only fine needle. And she explained the whole affair to Mrs Spears. 'And the worst of it is, I don't know how to cure him. Nothing when he's in that mood seems to have the slightest effect on him.'

Mrs Spears opened her pale eyes. 'Not even a whipping?' said she.

But Mrs Bendall, threading her needle, pursed up her lips. 'We never have whipped the children,' she said. 'The girls never seem to have needed it. And Dicky is such a baby, and the only boy. Somehow . . .'

'Oh, my dear,' said Mrs Spears, and she laid her sewing down. 'I don't wonder Dicky has these little outbreaks. You don't mind my saying so? But I'm sure you make a great mistake in trying to bring up children without whipping them. Nothing really takes its place. And I speak from experience, my dear. I used to try gentler measures' – Mrs Spears drew in her breath with a little hissing sound – 'soaping the boys' tongues, for instance, with yellow soap, or making them stand on the table for the whole of Saturday afternoon. But no, believe me,' said Mrs Spears, 'there is nothing, there is nothing like handing them over to their father.'

Mrs Bendall in her heart of hearts was dreadfully shocked to hear of that yellow soap. But Mrs Spears seemed to take it so much for granted, that she did too.

'Their father,' she said. 'Then you don't whip them yourself?'

'Never.' Mrs Spears seemed quite shocked at the idea. 'I don't think it's the mother's place to whip the children. It's the duty of the father. And, besides, he impresses them so much more.'

'Yes, I can imagine that,' said Mrs Bendall faintly.

'Now my two boys,' Mrs Spears smiled kindly, encouragingly, at Mrs Bendall, 'would behave just like Dicky if they were not afraid to. As it is . . . '

'Oh, your boys are perfect little models,' cried Mrs Bendall.

They were. Quieter, better-behaved little boys, in the presence of grown-ups, could not be found. In fact, Mrs Spears' callers often made the remark that you never would have known that there was a child in the house. There wasn't – very often.

In the front hall, under a large picture of fat, cheery old monks fishing by the riverside, there was a thick, dark horse-whip that had belonged to Mr Spears' father. And for some reason the boys preferred to play out of sight of this, behind the dog-kennel or in the tool-house, or round about the dustbin.

'It's such a mistake,' sighed Mrs Spears, breathing softly, as she folded her work, 'to be weak with children when they are little. It's such a sad mistake, and one so easy to make. It's so unfair to the child. That is what one has to remember. Now Dicky's little escapade this afternoon seemed to me as though he'd done it on purpose. It was the child's way of showing you that he needed a whipping.'

'Do you really think so?' Mrs Bendall was a weak little thing, and this impressed her very much.

'I do; I feel sure of it. And a sharp reminder now and then,' cried Mrs Spears in quite a professional manner, 'administered by the father, will save you so much trouble in the future. Believe me, my dear.' She put her dry, cold hand over Mrs Bendall's.

'I shall speak to Edward the moment he comes in,' said Dicky's mother firmly.

The children had gone to bed before the garden gate banged, and Dicky's father staggered up the steep concrete steps carrying his bicycle. It had been a bad day at the office. He was hot, dusty, tired out.

But by this time Mrs Bendall had become quite excited over the new plan, and she opened the door to him herself.

'Oh, Edward, I'm so thankful you have come home,' she cried.

'Why, what's happened?' Edward lowered the bicycle and took off his hat. A red angry pucker showed where the brim had pressed. 'What's up?'

'Come – come into the drawing-room,' said Mrs Bendall, speaking very fast. 'I simply can't tell you how naughty Dicky has been. You have no idea – you can't have at the office all day – how a child of that age can behave. He's been simply dreadful. I have no control over him – none. I've tried everything, Edward, but it's all no use. The only thing to do,' she finished breathlessly, 'is to whip him – is for you to whip him, Edward.'

In the corner of the drawing-room there was a what-not, and on the top shelf stood a brown china bear with a painted tongue. It seemed in the shadow to be grinning at Dicky's father, to be saying, 'Hooray, this is what you've come home to!'

'But why on earth should I start whipping him?' said Edward, staring at the bear. 'We've never done it before.'

'Because,' said his wife, 'don't you see, it's the only thing to do. I can't control the child . . . ' Her words flew from her lips. They beat round him, beat round his tired head. 'We can't possibly afford a nurse. The servant girl has more than enough to do. And his naughtiness is beyond words. You don't understand, Edward; you can't, you're at the office all day.'

The bear poked out his tongue. The scolding voice went on. Edward sank into a chair.

'What am I to beat him with?' he said weakly.

'Your slipper, of course,' said his wife. And she knelt down to untie his dusty shoes.

'Oh, Edward,' she wailed, 'you've still got your cycling clips on in the drawing-room. No, really – '

'Here, that's enough.' Edward nearly pushed her away. 'Give me that slipper.' He went up the stairs. He felt like a man in a dark net. And now he wanted to beat Dicky. Yes, damn it, he wanted to beat something. My God, what a life! The dust was still in his hot eyes, his arms felt heavy.

He pushed open the door of Dicky's slip of a room. Dicky was standing in the middle of the floor in his night-shirt. At the sight of him Edward's heart gave a warm throb of rage.

'Well, Dicky, you know what I've come for,' said Edward.

Dicky made no reply.

'I've come to give you a whipping.'

No answer.

'Lift up your night-shirt.'

At that Dicky looked up. He flushed a deep pink. 'Must I?' he whispered.

'Come on, now. Be quick about it,' said Edward, and, grasping the slipper, he gave Dicky three hard slaps.

'There, that'll teach you to behave properly to your mother.'

Dicky stood there, hanging his head.

'Look sharp and get into bed,' said his father.

Still he did not move. But a shaking voice said, 'I've not done my teeth yet, Daddy.'

'Eh, what's that?'

Dicky looked up. His lips were quivering, but his eyes were dry. He hadn't made a sound or shed a tear. Only he swallowed and said huskily, 'I haven't done my teeth, Daddy.'

But at the sight of that little face Edward turned, and, not knowing what he was doing, he bolted from the room, down the stairs, and out into the garden. Good God! What had he done? He strode along and hid in the shadow of the pear tree by the hedge. Whipped Dicky – whipped his little man with a slipper – and what the devil for? He didn't even know. Suddenly he barged into his room – and there was the little chap in his night-shirt. Dicky's father groaned and held on to the hedge. And he didn't cry. Never a tear. If only he'd cried or got angry. But that 'Daddy'! And again he heard the quivering whisper. Forgiving like that without a word. But he'd never forgive himself – never. Coward! Fool! Brute! And suddenly he remembered the time when Dicky had fallen off his knee and sprained his wrist while they were playing together. He hadn't cried then, either. And that was the little hero he had just whipped.

Something's got to be done about this, thought Edward. He strode back to the house, up the stairs, into Dicky's room. The little boy was lying in bed. In the half-light his dark head, with the square fringe, showed plain against the pale pillow. He was lying quite still, and even now he wasn't crying. Edward shut the door and leaned against it. What he wanted to do was to kneel down by Dicky's bed and cry himself and beg to be forgiven. But, of course, one can't do that sort of thing. He felt awkward, and his heart was wrung.

'Not asleep yet, Dicky?' he said lightly.

'No, Daddy.'

Edward came over and sat on his boy's bed, and Dicky looked at him through his long lashes.

'Nothing the matter, little chap, is there?' said Edward, half whispering.

'No-o, Daddy,' came from Dicky.

Edward put out his hand, and carefully he took Dicky's hot little paw.

'You – you mustn't think any more of what happened just now, little man,' he said huskily. 'See? That's all over now. That's forgotten. That's never going to happen again. See?'

'Yes, Daddy.'

'So the thing to do now is to buck up, little chap,' said Edward, 'and to smile.' And he tried himself an extraordinary trembling apology for a smile. 'To forget all about it – to – eh? Little man . . . Old boy . . . '

Dicky lay as before. This was terrible. Dicky's father sprang up and went over to the window. It was nearly dark in the garden. The servant girl had run out, and she was snatching, twitching some white clothes off the bushes and piling them over her arm. But in the boundless sky the evening star shone, and a big gum tree, black against the pale glow, moved its long leaves softly. All this he saw, while he felt in his trouser pocket for his money. Bringing it out, he chose a new sixpence and went back to Dicky.

'Here you are, little chap. Buy yourself something,' said Edward softly, laying the sixpence on Dicky's pillow.

But could even that – could even a whole sixpence – blot out what had been?

(1921)

Poison

THE POST WAS VERY LATE. When we came back from our walk after lunch it still had not arrived.

'*Pas encore, Madame,*' sang Annette, scurrying back to her cooking.

We carried our parcels into the dining-room. The table was laid. As always, the sight of the table laid for two – for two people only – and yet so finished, so perfect, there was no possible room for a third, gave me a queer, quick thrill as though I'd been struck by that silver lightning that quivered over the white cloth, the brilliant glasses, the shadow bowl of freesias.

'Blow the old postman! Whatever can have happened to him?' said Beatrice. 'Put those things down, dearest.'

'Where would you like them . . . ?'

She raised her head; she smiled her sweet, teasing smile.

'Anywhere – Silly.'

But I knew only too well that there was no such place for her, and I would have stood holding the squat liqueur bottle and the sweets for months, for years, rather than risk giving another tiny shock to her exquisite sense of order.

'Here – I'll take them.' She plumped them down on the table with her long gloves and a basket of figs. 'The Luncheon Table. Short story by – by – ' She took my arm. 'Let's go on to the terrace – ' and I felt her shiver. '*Ça sent,*' she said faintly, '*de la cuisine . . .*'

I had noticed lately – we had been living in the south for two months – that when she wished to speak of food, or the climate, or, playfully, of her love for me, she always dropped into French.

We perched on the balustrade under the awning. Beatrice leaned over gazing down – down to the white road with its guard of cactus spears. The beauty of her ear, just her ear, the marvel of it was so great that I could have turned from regarding it to all that sweep of glittering sea below and stammered: 'You know – her ear! She has ears that are simply the most . . . '

She was dressed in white, with pearls round her throat and lilies-of-the-valley tucked into her belt. On the third finger of her left hand she wore one pearl ring – no wedding-ring.

'Why should I, *mon ami*? Why should we pretend? Who could possibly care?'

And of course I agreed, though privately, in the depths of my heart, I would have given my soul to have stood beside her in a large, yes, a large, fashionable church, crammed with people, with old reverend clergymen, with *The Voice that breathed o'er Eden*, with palms and the smell of scent, knowing there was a red carpet and confetti outside, and somewhere, a wedding-cake and champagne and a satin shoe to throw after the carriage – if I could have slipped our wedding-ring on to her finger.

Not because I cared for such horrible shows, but because I felt it might possibly perhaps lessen this ghastly feeling of absolute freedom, *her* absolute freedom, of course.

Oh, God! What torture happiness was – what anguish! I looked up at the villa, at the windows of our room hidden so mysteriously behind the green straw blinds. Was it possible that she ever came moving through the green light and smiling that secret smile, that languid, brilliant smile that was just for me? She put her arm round my neck; the other hand softly, terribly, brushed back my hair.

'Who are you?' Who was she? She was – Woman.

. . . On the first warm evening in spring, when lights shone like pearls through the lilac air and voices murmured in the fresh-flowering gardens, it was she who sang in the tall house with the tulle curtains. As one drove in the moonlight through the foreign city hers was the shadow that fell across the quivering gold of the shutters. When the lamp was lighted, in the newborn stillness her steps passed your door. And she looked out into the autumn twilight, pale in her furs, as the automobile swept by . . .

In fact, to put it shortly, I was twenty-four at the time. And when she lay on her back, with the pearls slipped under her chin, and sighed 'I'm thirsty, dearest. *Donne-moi un orange*,' I would gladly, willingly, have dived for an orange into the jaws of a crocodile – if crocodiles ate oranges.

> Had I two little feathery wings
> And were a little feathery bird . . .

sang Beatrice.

I seized her hand. 'You wouldn't fly away?'

'Not far. Not further than the bottom of the road.'

'Why on earth there?'

She quoted: ' "He cometh not, she said . . . " '

'Who? The silly old postman? But you're not expecting a letter.'

'No, but it's maddening all the same. Ah!' Suddenly she laughed and leaned against me. 'There he is – look – like a blue beetle.'

And we pressed our cheeks together and watched the blue beetle beginning to climb.

'Dearest,' breathed Beatrice. And the word seemed to linger in the air, to throb in the air like the note of a violin.

'What is it?'

'I don't know,' she laughed softly. 'A wave of – a wave of affection, I suppose.'

I put my arm round her. 'Then you wouldn't fly away?'

And she said rapidly and softly: 'No! No! Not for worlds. Not really. I love this place. I've loved being here. I could stay here for years, I believe. I've never been so happy as I have these last two months, and you've been so perfect to me, dearest, in every way.'

This was such bliss – it was so extraordinary, so unprecedented, to hear her talk like this that I had to try to laugh it off.

'Don't! You sound as if you were saying goodbye.'

'Oh, nonsense, nonsense. You mustn't say such things even in fun!' She slid her little hand under my white jacket and clutched my shoulder. 'You've been happy, haven't you?'

'Happy? Happy? Oh, God – if you knew what I feel at this moment . . . Happy! My Wonder! My Joy!'

I dropped off the balustrade and embraced her, lifting her in my arms. And while I held her lifted I pressed my face in her breast and muttered: 'You *are* mine?' And for the first time in all the desperate months I'd known her, even counting the last month of – surely – Heaven – I believed her absolutely when she answered: 'Yes, I am yours.'

The creek of the gate and the postman's steps on the gravel drew us apart. I was dizzy for the moment. I simply stood there, smiling, I felt, rather stupidly. Beatrice walked over to the cane chairs.

'You go – go for the letters,' said she.

I – well – I almost reeled away. But I was too late. Annette came running. '*Pas de lettres*,' said she.

My reckless smile in reply as she handed me the paper must have surprised her. I was wild with joy. I threw the paper up into the air and sang out: 'No letters, darling!' as I came over to where the beloved woman was lying in the long chair.

For a moment she did not reply. Then she said slowly as she tore off the newspaper wrapper: ' "The world forgetting, *by* the world forgot." '

There are times when a cigarette is just the very one thing that will carry you over the moment. It is more than a confederate, even; it is a secret, perfect, little friend who knows all about it and understands absolutely. While you smoke you look down at it – smile or frown, as the occasion demands; you inhale deeply and expel the smoke in a slow fan. This was one of those moments. I walked over to the magnolia and breathed my fill of it. Then I came back and leaned over her shoulder. But quickly she tossed the paper away on to the stone.

'There's nothing in it,' said she. 'Nothing. There's only some poison trial. Either some man did or didn't murder his wife, and twenty thousand people have sat in court every day and two million words have been wired all over the world after each proceeding.'

'Silly world!' said I, flinging into another chair. I wanted to forget the paper, to return, but cautiously, of course, to that moment before the postman came. But when she answered I knew from her voice the moment was over for now. Never mind. I was content to wait – five hundred years, if need be – now that I knew.

'Not so very silly,' said Beatrice. 'After all, it isn't only morbid curiosity on the part of the twenty thousand.'

'What is it, darling?' Heavens knows I didn't care.

'Guilt!' she cried. 'Guilt! Didn't you realise that? They're fascinated like sick people are fascinated by anything – any scrap of news about their own case. The man in the dock may be innocent enough, but the people in court are nearly all of them poisoners. Haven't you ever thought' – she was pale with excitement – 'of the amount of poisoning that goes on? It's the exception to find married people who don't poison each other – married people and lovers. Oh,' she cried, 'the number of cups of tea, glasses of wine, cups of coffee that are just tainted. The number I've had myself, and drunk, either knowing or not knowing – and risked it. The only reason why so many couples' – she laughed – '*survive*, is because the one is frightened of giving the other the fatal dose. That dose takes nerve! But it's bound to come sooner or later.

There's no going back once the first little dose has been given. It's the beginning of the end, really – don't you agree? Don't you see what I mean?'

She didn't wait for me to answer. She unpinned the lilies-of-the-valley and lay back, drawing them across her eyes.

'Both my husbands poisoned me,' said Beatrice. 'My first husband gave me a huge dose almost immediately, but my second was really an artist in his way. Just a tiny pinch, now and again, cleverly disguised – Oh, so cleverly! – until one morning I woke up and in every single particle of me, to the ends of my fingers and toes, there was a tiny grain. I was just in time . . . '

I hated to hear her mention her husbands so calmly, especially today. It hurt. I was going to speak, but suddenly she cried mournfully: 'Why! Why should it have happened to me? What have I done? Why have I been all my life singled out by . . . It's a conspiracy.'

I tried to tell her it was because she was too perfect for this horrible world – too exquisite, too fine. It frightened people. I made a little joke.

'But I – I haven't tried to poison you.'

Beatrice gave a queer small laugh and bit the end of a lily stem.

'You!' said she. 'You wouldn't hurt a fly!'

Strange. That hurt, though. Most horribly.

Just then Annette ran out with our *apéritifs*. Beatrice leaned forward and took a glass from the tray and handed it to me. I noticed the gleam of the pearl on what I called her pearl finger. How could I be hurt at what she said?

'And you,' I said, taking the glass, 'You've never poisoned anybody.'

That gave me an idea; I tried to explain. 'You – you do just the opposite. What is the name for one like you who, instead of poisoning people, fills them – everybody, the postman, the man who drives us, our boatman, the flower-seller, me – with new life, with something of her own radiance, her beauty, her – '

Dreamily she smiled; dreamily she looked at me.

'What are you thinking of – my lovely darling?'

'I was wondering,' she said, 'whether, after lunch, you'd go down to the post-office and ask for the afternoon letters. Would you mind, dearest? Not that I'm expecting one – but – I just thought, perhaps – it's silly not to have the letters if they're there. Isn't it? Silly to wait till tomorrow.' She twirled the stem of the glass in her fingers. Her beautiful head was bent. But I lifted my glass and drank, sipped rather – sipped slowly, deliberately, looking at that dark head and thinking of – postmen and blue beetles and farewells that were not farewells and . . .

Good God! Was it fancy? No, it wasn't fancy. The drink tasted chill, bitter, *queer*.

(1921)

IN A GERMAN PENSION

First published in 1911

INTRODUCTORY NOTE

In a German Pension was Katherine Mansfield's first book. It was published in 1911, when she was twenty-one. The sketches and stories which compose it first appeared in *The New Age* during the previous two years.

In a German Pension met with a considerable success on its appearance. It ran quickly into three editions. Then the publisher defaulted and was made bankrupt. The stereotyped plates disappeared into the void, and with them all hope of royalties.

Katherine Mansfield was not very disappointed. She quickly became indifferent to the book; then hostile. It represented for her a phase of youthful bitterness and crude cynicism which she desired to disown for ever. How alien to herself she considered it may be judged from the fact that at the outbreak of the war with Germany, when one or two publishers made her attractive offers for the right of republishing it, she steadily refused, although she badly needed money. At that moment, in the general detestation of all things German, there is no dobt that the book would have achieved a very great popular success; at that moment, and indeed at most other times of her life, £500 would have been untold wealth to Katherine Mansfield. But nothing would induce her to make £500 by republishing *In a German Pension*, partly because she thought the book itself unworthy, but even more, as I remember, because she thought it unworthy of herself to take advantage of the odium into which Germany had fallen.

There followed a long period during which Katherine Mansfield wrote much and published nothing. Not until the publication of 'Prelude' in 1917 was the silence broken. When *Bliss* appeared in 1920 and achieved immediate success, she was once more urged to allow *In a German Pension* to be reissued. I passed the request on to her. This was her reply:

'I cannot have *The German Pension* reprinted under any circumstances. It is far too immature, and I don't even acknowledge it today. I mean I don't "hold" by it. I can't go foisting that kind of stuff on the public. *It's not good enough*. But if you send me the note that refers to it, I will reply and offer a new book by May 1. But I could not for a moment entertain republishing the *Pension*. It's positively juvenile, and besides that, it's not what I mean; it's a lie. Oh no, never!'

To which I replied that an author, having once deliberately printed a book, could not disown it in that way; and that the reason why she felt so acutely about her first book was that she had waited so long before publishing her second. In fact it was not merely a good book, but a truly remarkable one to have written at nineteen. Moreover, by refusing to republish it, she could not annihilate it. *In a German Pension* was, irrevocably, in existence. She replied:

'Very well, Isabel, about the *Pension*. But I must write an introduction saying it is early, early work, or just that it was written between certain years, because you know, Betsy, it's nothing to be proud of. If you didn't advise me I should drop it overboard. But of course I'll do the other thing, and certainly it airs one's name. But why isn't it better? It makes me simply hang my head. I'll have to forge ahead and get another decent one written, that's all . . . '

But Katherine Mansfield never did write the introduction.

J. M. M.

Germans at Meat

BREAD SOUP WAS PLACED upon the table. 'Ah,' said the Herr Rat, leaning upon the table as he peered into the tureen, 'that is what I need. My *magen* has not been in order for several days. Bread soup, and just the right consistency. I am a good cook myself' – he turned to me.

'How interesting,' I said, attempting to infuse just the right amount of enthusiasm into my voice.

'Oh yes – when one is not married it is necessary. As for me, I have had all I wanted from women without marriage.' He tucked his napkin into his collar and blew upon his soup as he spoke. 'Now at nine o'clock I make myself an English breakfast, but not much. Four slices of bread, two eggs, two slices of cold ham, one plate of soup, two cups of tea – that is nothing to you.'

He asserted the fact so vehemently that I had not the courage to refute it.

All eyes were suddenly turned upon me. I felt I was bearing the burden of the nation's preposterous breakfast – I who drank a cup of coffee while buttoning my blouse in the morning.

'Nothing at all,' cried Herr Hoffmann from Berlin. 'Ach, when I was in England in the morning I used to eat.'

He turned up his eyes and his moustache, wiping the soup drippings from his coat and waistcoat.

'Do they really eat so much?' asked Fräulein Stiegelauer. 'Soup and baker's bread and pig's flesh, and tea and coffee and stewed fruit, and honey and eggs, and cold fish and kidneys, and hot fish and liver? All the ladies eat, too, especially the ladies.'

'Certainly. I myself have noticed it, when I was living in a hotel in Leicester Square,' cried the Herr Rat. 'It was a good hotel, but they could not make tea – now – '

'Ah, that's one thing I *can* do,' said I, laughing brightly. 'I can make very good tea. The great secret is to warm the teapot.'

'Warm the teapot,' interrupted the Herr Rat, pushing away his soup plate. 'What do you warm the teapot for? Ha! ha! that's very good! One does not eat the teapot, I suppose?'

He fixed his cold blue eyes upon me with an expression which suggested a thousand premeditated invasions.

'So that is the great secret of your English tea? All you do is to warm the teapot.'

I wanted to say that was only the preliminary canter, but could not translate it, and so was silent.

The servant brought in veal, with sauerkraut and potatoes.

'I eat sauerkraut with great pleasure,' said the Traveller from North Germany, 'but now I have eaten so much of it that I cannot retain it. I am immediately forced to – '

'A beautiful day,' I cried, turning to Fräulein Stiegelauer. 'Did you get up early?'

'At five o'clock I walked for ten minutes in the wet grass. Again in bed. At half-past five I fell asleep, and woke at seven, when I made an "overbody" washing! Again in bed. At eight o'clock I had a cold-water poultice, and at half past eight I drank a cup of mint tea. At nine I drank some malt coffee, and began my "cure". Pass me the sauerkraut, please. You do not eat it?'

'No, thank you. I still find it a little strong.'

'Is it true,' asked the Widow, picking her teeth with a hairpin as she spoke, 'that you are a vegetarian?'

'Why, yes; I have not eaten meat for three years.'

'Im – possible! Have you any family?'

'No.'

'There now, you see, that's what you're coming to! Who ever heard of having children upon vegetables? It is not possible. But you never have large families in England now; I suppose you are too busy with your suffragetting. Now I have had nine children, and they are all alive, thank God. Fine, healthy babies – though after the first one was born I had to – '

'How *wonderful*!' I cried.

'Wonderful,' said the Widow contemptuously, replacing the hair-pin in the knob which was balanced on the top of her head. 'Not at all! A friend of mine had four at the same time. Her husband was so pleased he gave a supper-party and had them placed on the table. Of course she was very proud.'

'Germany,' boomed the Traveller, biting round a potato which he had speared with his knife, 'is the home of the Family.'

Followed an appreciative silence.

The dishes were changed for beef, red currants and spinach. They wiped their forks upon black bread and started again.

'How long are you remaining here?' asked the Herr Rat.

'I do not know exactly. I must be back in London in September.'

'Of course you will visit München?'

'I am afraid I shall not have time. You see, it is important not to break into my "cure".'

'But you *must* go to München. You have not seen Germany if you have not been to München. All the Exhibitions, all the Art and Soul life of Germany are in München. There is the Wagner Festival in August, and Mozart and a Japanese collection of pictures – and there is the beer! You do not know what good beer is until you have been to München. Why, I see fine ladies every afternoon, but fine ladies, I tell you, drinking glasses so high.' He measured a good washstand pitcher in height, and I smiled.

'If I drink a great deal of München beer I sweat so,' said Herr Hoffmann. 'When I am here, in the fields or before my baths, I sweat, but I enjoy it; but in the town it is not at all the same thing.'

Prompted by the thought, he wiped his neck and face with his dinner napkin and carefully cleaned his ears.

A glass dish of stewed apricots was placed upon the table.

'Ah, fruit!' said Fräulein Stiegelauer, 'that is so necessary to health. The doctor told me this morning that the more fruit I could eat the better.'

She very obviously followed the advice.

Said the Traveller: 'I suppose you are frightened of an invasion, too, eh? Oh, that's good. I've been reading all about your English play in a newspaper. Did you see it?'

'Yes.' I sat upright. 'I assure you we are not afraid.'

'Well, then, you ought to be,' said the Herr Rat. 'You have got no army at all – a few little boys with their veins full of nicotine poisoning.'

'Don't be afraid,' Herr Hoffmann said. 'We don't want England. If we did we would have had her long ago. We really do not want you.'

He waved his spoon airily, looking across at me as though I were a little child whom he would keep or dismiss as he pleased.

'We certainly do not want Germany,' I said.

'This morning I took a half bath. Then this afternoon I must take a knee bath and an arm bath,' volunteered the Herr Rat; 'then I do my exercises for an hour, and my work is over. A glass of wine and a couple of rolls with some sardines – '

They were handed cherry cake with whipped cream.

'What is your husband's favourite meat?' asked the Widow.

'I really do not know,' I answered.

'You really do not know? How long have you been married?'

'Three years.'

'But you cannot be in earnest! You would not have kept house as his wife for a week without knowing that fact.'

'I really never asked him; he is not at all particular about his food.'

A pause. They all looked at me, shaking their heads, their mouths full of cherry stones.

'No wonder there is a repetition in England of that dreadful state of things in Paris,' said the Widow, folding her dinner napkin. 'How can a woman expect to keep her husband if she does not know his favourite food after three years?'

'*Mahlzeit!*'

'*Mahlzeit!*'

I closed the door after me.

The Baron

'WHO IS HE?' I said. 'And why does he sit always alone, with his back to us, too?'

'Ah!' whispered the Frau Oberregierungsrat, 'he is a *Baron*.'

She looked at me very solemnly, and yet with the slightest possible contempt – a 'fancy-not-recognising-that-at-the-first-glance' expression.

'But, poor soul, he cannot help it,' I said. 'Surely that unfortunate fact ought not to debar him from the pleasures of intellectual intercourse.'

If it had not been for her fork I think she would have crossed herself.

'Surely you cannot understand. He is one of the First Barons.'

More than a little unnerved, she turned and spoke to the Frau Doktor on her left.

'My omelette is empty – *empty*,' she protested, 'and this is the third I have tried!'

I looked at the First of the Barons. He was eating salad – taking a whole lettuce leaf on his fork and absorbing it slowly, rabbit-wise – a fascinating process to watch.

Small and slight, with scanty black hair and beard and yellow-toned complexion, he invariably wore black serge clothes, a rough linen shirt, black sandals, and the largest black-rimmed spectacles that I had ever seen.

The Herr Oberlehrer, who sat opposite me, smiled benignantly.

'It must be very interesting for you, *gnadige Frau*, to be able to watch . . . of course this is a *very fine house*. There was a lady from the Spanish Court here in the summer; she had a liver. We often spoke together.'

I looked gratified and humble.

'Now, in England, in your "boarding 'ouse", one does not find the First Class, as in Germany.'

'No, indeed,' I replied, still hypnotised by the Baron, who looked like a little yellow silkworm.

'The Baron comes every year,' went on the Herr Oberlehrer, 'for his nerves. He has never spoken to any of the guests – *yet*! A smile crossed his face. I seemed to see his visions of some splendid upheaval of that silence – a dazzling exchange of courtesies in a dim future, a splendid sacrifice of a newspaper to this Exalted One, a '*danke schön*' to be handed down to future generations.

At that moment the postman, looking like a German army officer, came in with the mail. He threw my letters into my milk pudding, and then turned to a waitress and whispered. She retired hastily. The manager of the pension came in with a little tray. A picture postcard was deposited on it, and reverently bowing his head, the manager of the pension carried it to the Baron.

Myself, I felt disappointed that there was not a salute of twenty-five guns.

At the end of the meal we were served with coffee. I noticed the Baron took three lumps of sugar, putting two in his cup and wrapping up the third in a corner of his pocket-handkerchief. He was always the first to enter the dining-room and the last to leave; and in a vacant chair beside him he placed a little black leather bag.

In the afternoon, leaning from my window, I saw him pass down the street, walking tremulously and carrying the bag. Each time he passed a lamp-post he shrank a little, as though expecting it to strike him, or maybe the sense of plebeian contamination . . .

I wondered where he was going, and why he carried the bag. Never had I seen him at the Casino or the Bath Establishment. He looked forlorn, his feet slipped in his sandals. I found myself pitying the Baron.

That evening a party of us were gathered in the salon discussing the day's *kur* with feverish animation. The Frau Oberregierungsrat sat by me knitting a shawl for her youngest of nine daughters, who was in that very interesting, frail condition . . . 'But it is bound to be quite satisfactory,' she said to me. 'The dear married a banker – the desire of her life.'

There must have been eight or ten of us gathered together, we who were married exchanging confidences as to the underclothing and peculiar characteristics of our husbands, the unmarried discussing the over-clothing and peculiar fascinations of Possible Ones.

'I knit them myself,' I heard the Frau Lehrer cry, 'of thick grey wool. He wears one a month, with two soft collars.'

'And then,' whispered Fräulein Lisa, 'he said to me, "Indeed you please me. I shall, perhaps, write to your mother." '

Small wonder that we were a little violently excited, a little expostulatory.

Suddenly the door opened and admitted the Baron.

Followed a complete and deathlike silence.

He came in slowly, hesitated, took up a toothpick from a dish on the top of the piano, and went out again.

When the door was closed we raised a triumphant cry! It was the first time he had ever been known to enter the salon. Who could tell what the Future held?

Days lengthened into weeks. Still we were together, and still the solitary little figure, head bowed as though under the weight of the spectacles, haunted me. He entered with the black bag, he retired with the black bag – and that was all.

At last the manager of the pension told us the Baron was leaving the next day.

'Oh,' I thought, 'surely he cannot drift into obscurity – be lost without one word! Surely he will honour the Frau Oberregierungsrat of the Frau Feldleutnantswitwe *once* before he goes.'

In the evening of that day it rained heavily. I went to the post office, and as I stood on the steps, umbrellaless, hesitating before plunging into the slushy road, a little, hesitating voice seemed to come from under my elbow.

I looked down. It was the First of the Barons with the black bag and an umbrella. Was I mad? Was I sane? He was asking me to share the latter. But I was exceedingly nice, a trifle diffident, appropriately reverential. Together we walked through the mud and slush.

Now, there is something peculiarly intimate in sharing an umbrella.

It is apt to put one on the same footing as brushing a man's coat for him – a little daring, naive.

I longed to know why he sat alone, why he carried the bag, what he did all day. But he himself volunteered some information.

'I fear,' he said, 'that my luggage will be damp. I invariably carry it with me in this bag – one requires so little – for servants are untrustworthy.'

'A wise idea,' I answered. And then: 'Why have you denied us the pleasure – '

'I sit alone that I may eat more,' said the Baron, peering into the dusk; 'my stomach requires a great deal of food. I order double portions, and eat them in peace.'

Which sounded finely Baronial.

'And what do you do all day?'

'I imbibe nourishment in my room,' he replied, in a voice that closed the conversation and almost repented of the umbrella.

When we arrived at the pension there was very nearly an open riot.

I ran half way up the stairs, and thanked the Baron audibly from the landing.

He distinctly replied: 'Not at all!'

It was very friendly of the Herr Oberlehrer to have sent me a bouquet that evening, and the Frau Oberregierungsrat asked me for my pattern of a baby's bonnet!

*   *   *

Next day the Baron was gone.
Sic transit gloria German mundi.

The Sister of the Baroness

'THERE ARE TWO new guests arriving this afternoon,' said the manager of the pension, placing a chair for me at the breakfast table. 'I have only received the letter acquainting me with the fact this morning. The Baroness von Gall is sending her little daughter – the poor child is dumb – to make the "cure". She is to stay with us a month, and then the Baroness herself is coming.'

'Baroness von Gall,' cried the Frau Doktor, coming into the room and positively scenting the name. 'Coming here? There was a picture of her only last week in "Sport and Salon". She is a friend of the court: I have heard that the Kaiserin says *du* to her. But this is delightful! I shall take my doctor's advice and spend an extra six weeks here. There is nothing like young society.'

'But the child is dumb,' ventured the manager apologetically.

'Bah! What does that matter? Afflicted children have such pretty ways.'

Each guest who came into the breakfast-room was bombarded with the wonderful news. 'The Baroness von Gall is sending her little daughter here; the Baroness herself is coming in a month's time.' Coffee and rolls took on the nature of an orgy. We positively scintillated. Anecdotes of the High Born were poured out, sweetened and sipped: we gorged on scandals of High Birth generously buttered.

'They are to have the room next to yours,' said the manager, addressing me. 'I was wondering if you would permit me to take down the portrait of the Kaiserin Elizabeth from above your bed to hang over their sofa.'

'Yes, indeed, something homelike' – the Frau Oberregierungsrat patted my hand – 'and of no possible significance to you.'

I felt a little crushed. Not at the prospect of losing that vision of diamonds and blue velvet bust, but at the tone – placing me outside the pale – branding me as a foreigner.

We dissipated the day in valid speculations. Decided it was too warm to walk in the afternoon, so lay down on our beds, mustering in great force for afternoon coffee. And a carriage drew up at the door. A tall young girl got out, leading a child by the hand. They entered the hall, were greeted and shown to their room. Ten minutes later she came down with the child to sign the visitors' book. She wore a black, closely fitting dress, touched at throat and wrists with white frilling. Her brown hair, braided, was tied with a black bow – unusually pale, with a small mole on her left cheek.

'I am the Baroness von Gall's sister,' she said, trying the pen on a piece of blotting-paper, and smiling at us deprecatingly. Even for the most jaded of us life holds its thrilling moments. Two Baronesses in two months! The manager immediately left the room to find a new nib.

To my plebeian eyes that afflicted child was singularly unattractive. She had the air of having been perpetually washed with a blue bag, and hair like grey wool – dressed, too, in a pinafore so stiffly starched that she could only peer at us over the frill of it – a social barrier of a pinafore – and perhaps it was too much to expect a noble aunt to attend to the menial consideration of her niece's ears. But a dumb niece with unwashed ears struck me as a most depressing object.

They were given places at the head of the table. For a moment we all looked at one another with an eena-deena-dina-do expression. Then the Frau Oberregierungsrat: 'I hope you are not tired after your journey.'

'No,' said the sister of the Baroness, smiling into her cup.

'I hope the dear child is not tired,' said the Frau Doktor.

'Not at all.'

'I expect, I hope you will sleep well tonight,' the Herr Oberlehrer said reverently.

'Yes.'

The poet from Munich never took his eyes off the pair. He allowed his tie to absorb most of his coffee while he gazed at them exceedingly soulfully.

Unyoking Pegasus, thought I. Death spasms of his Odes to Solitude! There were possibilities in that young woman for an inspiration, not to mention a dedication, and from that moment his suffering temperament took up its bed and walked.

They retired after the meal, leaving us to discuss them at leisure.

'There is a likeness,' mused the Frau Doktor. 'Quite. What a manner she has. Such reserve, such a tender way with the child.'

'Pity she has the child to attend to,' exclaimed the student from Bonn. He had hitherto relied upon three scars and a ribbon to produce an effect, but the sister of a Baroness demanded more than these.

Absorbing days followed. Had she been one whit less beautifully born we could not have endured the continual conversation about her, the songs in her praise, the detailed account of her movements. But she graciously suffered our worship and we were more than content.

The poet she took into her confidence. He carried her books when we went walking, he jumped the afflicted one on his knee – poetic licence, this – and one morning brought his notebook into the salon and read to us.

'The sister of the Baroness has assured me she is going into a convent,' he said. (That made the student from Bonn sit up.) 'I have written these few lines last night from my window in the sweet night air – '

'Oh, your *delicate* chest,' commented the Frau Doktor.

He fixed a stony eye on her, and she blushed.

'I have written these lines:

> Ah, will you to a convent fly,
>   So young, so fresh, so fair?
> Spring like a doe upon the fields
>   And find your beauty there.

Nine verses equally lovely commanded her to equally violent action. I am certain that had she followed his advice not even the remainder of her life in a convent would have given her time to recover her breath.

'I have presented her with a copy,' he said. 'And today we are going to look for wild flowers in the wood.'

The student from Bonn got up and left the room. I begged the poet to repeat the verses once more. At the end of the sixth verse I saw from the window the sister of the Baroness and the scarred youth disappearing through the front gate, which enabled me to thank the poet so charmingly that he offered to write me out a copy.

But we were living at too high pressure in those days. Swinging from our humble pension to the high walls of palaces, how could we help but fall? Late one afternoon the Frau Doktor came upon me in the writing-room and took me to her bosom.

'She has been telling me all about her life,' whispered the Frau Doktor. 'She came to my bedroom and offered to massage my arm.

You know, I am the greatest martyr to rheumatism. And, fancy now, she has already had six proposals of marriage. Such beautiful offers that I assure you I wept – and every one of noble birth. My dear, the most beautiful was in the wood. Not that I do not think a proposal should take place in a drawing-room – it is more fitting to have four walls – but this was a private wood. He said, the young officer, she was like a young tree whose branches had never been touched by the ruthless hand of man. Such delicacy!' She sighed and turned up her eyes.

'Of course it is difficult for you English to understand when you are always exposing your legs on cricket-fields, and breeding dogs in your back gardens. The pity of it! Youth should be like a wild rose. For myself I do not understand how your women ever get married at all.'

She shook her head so violently that I shook mine too, and a gloom settled round my heart. It seemed we were really in a very bad way. Did the spirit of romance spread her rose wings only over aristocratic Germany?

I went to my room, bound a pink scarf about my hair, and took a volume of Morike's lyrics into the garden. A great bush of purple lilac grew behind the summer-house. There I sat down, finding a sad significance in the delicate suggestion of half mourning. I began to write a poem myself.

> They sway and languish dreamily,
> And we, close pressed, are kissing there.

It ended! 'Close pressed' did not sound at all fascinating. Savoured of wardrobes. Did my wild rose then already trail in the dust? I chewed a leaf and hugged my knees. Then – magic moment – I heard voices from the summer-house, the sister of the Baroness and the student from Bonn.

Second-hand was better than nothing; I pricked up my ears.

'What small hands you have,' said the student from Bonn. 'They are like white lilies lying in the pool of your black dress.' This certainly sounded the real thing. Her high-born reply was what interested me. Sympathetic murmur only.

'May I hold one?'

I heard two sighs – presumed they held – he had rifled those dark waters of a noble blossom.

'Look at my great fingers beside yours.'

'But they are beautifully kept,' said the sister of the Baroness shyly.

The minx! Was love then a question of manicure?

'How I should adore to kiss you,' murmured the student. 'But you know I am suffering from severe nasal catarrh, and I dare not risk giving it to you. Sixteen times last night did I count myself sneezing. And three different handkerchiefs.'

I threw Morike into the lilac bush, and went back to the house. A great automobile snorted at the front door. In the salon great commotion. The Baroness was paying a surprise visit to her little daughter. Clad in a yellow mackintosh she stood in the middle of the room questioning the manager. And every guest the pension contained was grouped about her, even the Frau Doktor, presumably examining a timetable, as near to the august skirts as possible.

'But where is my maid?' asked the Baroness.

'There was no maid,' replied the manager, 'save for your gracious sister and daughter.'

'Sister!' she cried sharply. 'Fool, I have no sister. My child travelled with the daughter of my dressmaker.'

Tableau grandissimo!

Frau Fischer

FRAU FISCHER was the fortunate possessor of a candle factory somewhere on the banks of the Eger, and once a year she ceased from her labours to make a 'cure' in Dorschausen, arriving with a dress-basket neatly covered in a black tarpaulin and a hand-bag. The latter contained amongst her handkerchiefs, eau de Cologne, toothpicks, and a certain woollen muffler very comforting to the *magen*, samples of her skill in candle-making, to be offered up as tokens of thanksgiving when her holiday time was over.

Four of the clock one July afternoon she appeared at the Pension Muller. I was sitting in the arbour and watched her bustling up the path followed by the red-bearded porter with her dress-basket in his arms and a sunflower between his teeth. The widow and her five innocent daughters stood tastefully grouped upon the steps in appropriate attitudes of welcome; and the greetings were so long and loud that I felt a sympathetic glow.

'What a journey!' cried the Frau Fischer. 'And nothing to eat in the train – nothing solid. I assure you the sides of my stomach are flapping together. But I must not spoil my appetite for dinner – just a cup of coffee in my room. Bertha,' turning to the youngest of the five, 'how changed! What a bust! Frau Hartmann, I congratulate you.'

Once again the Widow seized Frau Fischer's hands. 'Kathi, too, a splendid woman; but a little pale. Perhaps the young man from Nürnberg is here again this year. How you keep them all I don't know. Each year I come expecting to find you with an empty nest. It's surprising.'

Frau Hartmann, in an ashamed, apologetic voice: 'We are such a happy family since my dear man died.'

'But these marriages – one must have courage; and after all, give them time, they all make the happy family bigger – thank God for that . . . Are there many people here just now?'

'Every room engaged.'

Followed a detailed description in the hall, murmured on the stairs, continued in six parts as they entered the large room (windows opening upon the garden) which Frau Fischer occupied each successive year. I was reading the *Miracles of Lourdes*, which a Catholic priest – fixing a gloomy eye upon my soul – had begged me to digest; but its wonders were completely routed by Frau Fischer's arrival. Not even the white roses upon the feet of the Virgin could flourish in that atmosphere.

' . . . It was a simple shepherd-child who pastured her flocks upon the barren fields . . . '

Voices from the room above: 'The washstand has, of course, been scrubbed over with soda.'

' . . . Poverty-stricken, her limbs with tattered rags half covered . . . '

'Every stick of the furniture has been sunning in the garden for three days. And the carpet we made ourselves out of old clothes. There is a piece of that beautiful flannel petticoat you left us last summer.'

' . . . Deaf and dumb was the child; in fact, the population considered her half idiot . . . '

'Yes, that is a new picture of the Kaiser. We have moved the thorn-crowned one of Jesus Christ out into the passage. It was not cheerful to sleep with. Dear Frau Fischer, won't you take your coffee out in the garden?'

'That is a very nice idea. But first I must remove my corsets and my boots. Ah, what a relief to wear sandals again. I am needing the "cure" very badly this year. My nerves! I am a mass of them. During the entire journey I sat with my handkerchief over my head, even while the guard collected the tickets. Exhausted!'

She came into the arbour wearing a black and white spotted dressing-gown, and a calico cap peaked with patent leather, followed by Kathi, carrying the little blue jugs of malt coffee. We were formally introduced. Frau Fischer sat down, produced a perfectly clean pocket handkerchief and polished her cup and saucer, then lifted the lid of the coffee-pot and peered in at the contents mournfully.

'Malt coffee,' she said. 'Ah, for the first few days I wonder how I can put up with it. Naturally, absent from home one must expect much discomfort and strange food. But as I used to say to my dear husband: with a clean sheet and a good cup of coffee I can find my happiness anywhere. But now, with nerves like mine, no sacrifice is too terrible for me to make. What complaint are you suffering from? You look exceedingly healthy!'

I smiled and shrugged my shoulders.

'Ah, that is so strange about you English. You do not seem to enjoy discussing the functions of the body. As well speak of a railway train and refuse to mention the engine. How can we hope to understand anybody, knowing nothing of their stomachs? In my husband's most severe illness – the poultices – '

She dipped a piece of sugar in her coffee and watched it dissolve.

'Yet a young friend of mine who travelled to England for the funeral of his brother told me that women wore bodices in public restaurants no waiter could help looking into as he handed the soup.'

'But only German waiters,' I said. 'English ones look over the top of your head.'

'There,' she cried, 'now you see your dependence on Germany. Not even an efficient waiter can you have by yourselves.'

'But I prefer them to look over your head.'

'And that proves that you must be ashamed of your bodice.'

I looked out over the garden full of wall-flowers and standard rose trees growing stiffly like German bouquets, feeling I did not care one way or the other. I rather wanted to ask her if the young friend had gone to England in the capacity of waiter to attend the funeral baked meats, but decided it was not worth it. The weather was too hot to be malicious, and who could be uncharitable, victimised by the flapping sensations which Frau Fischer was enduring until six-thirty? As a gift from heaven for my forbearance, down the path towards us came the Herr Rat, angelically clad in a white silk suit. He and Frau Fischer were old friends. She drew the folds of her dressing-gown together, and made room for him on the little green bench.

'How cool you are looking,' she said; 'and if I may make the remark – what a beautiful suit!'

'Surely I wore it last summer when you were here? I brought the silk from China – smuggled it through the Russian customs by swathing it round my body. And such a quantity: two dress lengths for my sister-in-law, three suits for myself, a cloak for the house-keeper of my flat in Munich. How I perspired! Every inch of it had to be washed afterwards.'

'Surely you have had more adventures than any man in Germany. When I think of the time that you spent in Turkey with a drunken guide who was bitten by a mad dog and fell over a precipice into a field of attar of roses, I lament that you have not written a book.'

'Time – time. I am getting a few notes together. And now that you are here we shall renew our quiet little talks after supper. Yes? It is necessary and pleasant for a man to find relaxation in the company of women occasionally.'

'Indeed I realise that. Even here your life is too strenuous – you are so sought after – so admired. It was just the same with my dear husband. He was a tall, beautiful man, and sometimes in the evening he would come down into the kitchen and say: "Wife, I would like to be stupid for two minutes." Nothing rested him so much then as for me to stroke his head.'

The Herr Rat's bald pate glistening in the sunlight seemed symbolical of the sad absence of a wife.

I began to wonder as to the nature of these quiet little after-supper talks. How could one play Delilah to so shorn a Samson?

'Herr Hoffmann from Berlin arrived yesterday,' said the Herr Rat.

'That young man I refuse to converse with. He told me last year that he had stayed in France in an hotel where they did not have serviettes; what a place it must have been! In Austria even the cabmen have serviettes. Also I have heard that he discussed "free love" with Bertha as she was sweeping his room. I am not accustomed to such company. I had suspected him for a long time.'

'Young blood,' answered the Herr Rat genially. 'I have had several disputes with him – you have heard them – is it not so?' turning to me.

'A great many,' I said, smiling.

'Doubtless you too consider me behind the times. I make no secret of my age; I am sixty-nine; but you must have surely observed how impossible it was for him to speak at all when I raised my voice.'

I replied with the utmost conviction, and, catching Frau Fischer's eye, suddenly realised I had better go back to the house and write some letters.

It was dark and cool in my room. A chestnut tree pushed green boughs against the window. I looked down at the horsehair sofa so openly flouting the idea of curling up as immoral, pulled the red pillow on to the floor and lay down. And barely had I got comfortable when the door opened and Frau Fischer entered.

'The Herr Rat had a bathing appointment,' she said, shutting the door after her. 'May I come in? Pray do not move. You look like a little Persian kitten. Now, tell me something really interesting about your life. When I meet new people I squeeze them dry like a sponge. To begin with – you are married.'

I admit the fact.

'Then, dear child, where is your husband?'

I said he was a sea-captain on a long and perilous voyage.

'What a position to leave you in – so young and so unprotected.'

She sat down on the sofa and shook her finger at me playfully.

'Admit, now, that you keep your journeys secret from him. For what man would think of allowing a woman with such a wealth of hair to go wandering in foreign countries? Now, supposing that you lost your purse at midnight in a snowbound train in North Russia?'

'But I haven't the slightest intention – ' I began.

'I don't say that you have. But when you said goodbye to your dear man I am positive that you had no intention of coming here. My dear, I am a woman of experience, and I know the world. While he is away you have a fever in your blood. Your sad heart flies for comfort to these foreign lands. At home you cannot bear the sight of that empty bed – it is like widowhood. Since the death of my dear husband I have never known an hour's peace.'

'I like empty beds,' I protested sleepily, thumping the pillow.

'That cannot be true because it is not natural. Every wife ought to feel that her place is by her husband's side – sleeping or waking. It is plain to see that the strongest tie of all does not yet bind you. Wait until a little pair of hands stretches across the water – wait until he comes into harbour and sees you with the child at your breast.'

I sat up stiffly.

'But I consider child-bearing the most ignominious of all professions,' I said.

For a moment there was silence. Then Frau Fischer reached down and caught my hand.

'So young and yet to suffer so cruelly,' she murmured. 'There is nothing that sours a woman so terribly as to be left alone without a man, especially if she is married, for then it is impossible for her to accept the attention of others – unless she is unfortunately a widow. Of course, I know that sea-captains are subject to terrible temptations, and they are as inflammable as tenor singers – that is why you must present a bright and energetic appearance, and try and make him proud of you when his ship reaches port.'

This husband that I had created for the benefit of Frau Fischer became in her hands so substantial a figure that I could no longer see myself sitting on a rock with seaweed in my hair, awaiting that phantom ship for which all women love to suppose they hunger. Rather I saw myself pushing a perambulator up the gangway, and counting up the missing buttons on my husband's uniform jacket.

'Handfuls of babies, that is what you are really in need of,' mused

Frau Fischer. 'Then, as the father of a family he cannot leave you. Think of his delight and excitement when he saw you!'

The plan seemed to me something of a risk. To appear suddenly with handfuls of strange babies is not generally calculated to raise enthusiasm in the heart of the average British husband. I decided to wreck my virgin conception and send him down somewhere off Cape Horn.

Then the dinner-gong sounded.

'Come up to my room afterwards,' said Frau Fischer. 'There is still much that I must ask you.'

She squeezed my hand, but I did not squeeze back.

Frau Brechenmacher Attends a Wedding

GETTING READY was a terrible business. After supper Frau Brechenmacher packed four of the five babies to bed, allowing Rosa to stay with her and help to polish the buttons of Herr Brechenmacher's uniform. Then she ran over his best shirt with a hot iron, polished his boots, and put a stitch or two into his black satin necktie.

'Rosa,' she said, 'fetch my dress and hang it in front of the stove to get the creases out. Now, mind, you must look after the children and not sit up later than half-past eight, and not touch the lamp – you know what will happen if you do.'

'Yes, Mamma,' said Rosa, who was nine and felt old enough to manage a thousand lamps. 'But let me stay up – the "Bub" may wake and want some milk.'

'Half-past eight!' said the Frau. 'I'll make the father tell you too.'

Rosa drew down the corners of her mouth.

'But . . . but . . . '

'Here comes the father. You go into the bedroom and fetch my blue silk handkerchief. You can wear my black shawl while I'm out – there now!'

Rosa dragged it off her mother's shoulders and wound it carefully round her own, tying the two ends in a knot at the back. After all, she reflected, if she had to go to bed at half past eight she would keep the shawl on. Which resolution comforted her absolutely.

'Now, then, where are my clothes?' cried Herr Brechenmacher, hanging his empty letter-bag behind the door and stamping the snow out of his boots. 'Nothing ready, of course, and everybody at the wedding by this time. I heard the music as I passed. What are you doing? You're not dressed. You can't go like that.'

'Here they are – all ready for you on the table, and some warm water in the tin basin. Dip your head in. Rosa, give your father the towel. Everything ready except the trousers. I haven't had time to shorten them. You must tuck the ends into your boots until we get there.'

'*Nu,*' said the Herr, 'there isn't room to turn. I want the light. You go and dress in the passage.'

Dressing in the dark was nothing to Frau Brechenmacher. She hooked her skirt and bodice, fastened her handkerchief round her neck with a beautiful brooch that had four medals to the Virgin dangling from it, and then drew on her cloak and hood.

'Here, come and fasten this buckle,' called Herr Brechenmacher. He stood in the kitchen puffing himself out, the buttons on his blue uniform shining with an enthusiasm which nothing but official buttons could possibly possess. 'How do I look?'

'Wonderful,' replied the little Frau, straining at the waist buckle and giving him a little pull here, a little tug there. 'Rosa, come and look at your father.'

Herr Brechenmacher strode up and down the kitchen, was helped on with his coat, then waited while the Frau lighted the lantern.

'Now, then – finished at last! Come along.'

'The lamp, Rosa,' warned the Frau, slamming the front door behind them.

Snow had not fallen all day; the frozen ground was slippery as an ice-pond. She had not been out of the house for weeks past, and the day had so flurried her that she felt muddled and stupid – felt that Rosa had pushed her out of the house and her man was running away from her.

'Wait, wait!' she cried.

'No. I'll get my feet damp – you hurry.'

It was easier when they came into the village. There were fences to cling to, and leading from the railway station to the *Gasthaus* a little path of cinders had been strewn for the benefit of the wedding guests.

The *Gasthaus* was very festive. Lights shone out from every window, wreaths of fir twigs hung from the ledges. Branches decorated the front doors, which swung open, and in the hall the landlord voiced his superiority by bullying the waitresses, who ran about continually with glasses of beer, trays of cups and saucers, and bottles of wine.

'Up the stairs – up the stairs!' boomed the landlord. 'Leave your coats on the landing.'

Herr Brechenmacher, completely overawed by this grand manner, so far forgot his rights as a husband as to beg his wife's pardon for jostling her against the banisters in his efforts to get ahead of everybody else.

Herr Brechenmacher's colleagues greeted him with acclamation as he entered the door of the *Festsaal*, and the Frau straightened her brooch and folded her hands, assuming the air of dignity becoming to the wife of a postman and the mother of five children. Beautiful indeed was the *Festsaal*. Three long tables were grouped at one end, the remainder of the floor space cleared for dancing. Oil lamps, hanging from the ceiling, shed a warm, bright light on the walls decorated with paper flowers and garlands; shed a warmer, brighter light on the red faces of the guests in their best clothes.

At the head of the centre table sat the bride and bridegroom, she in a white dress trimmed with stripes and bows of coloured ribbon, giving her the appearance of an iced cake all ready to be cut and served in neat little pieces to the bridegroom beside her, who wore a suit of white clothes much too large for him and a white silk tie that rose halfway up his collar. Grouped about them, with a fine regard for dignity and precedence, sat their parents and relations; and perched on a stool at the bride's right hand a little girl in a crumpled muslin dress with a wreath of forget-me-nots hanging over one ear. Everybody was laughing and talking, shaking hands, clinking glasses, stamping on the floor – a stench of beer and perspiration filled the air.

Frau Brechenmacher, following her man down the room after greeting the bridal party, knew that she was going to enjoy herself. She seemed to fill out and become rosy and warm as she sniffed that familiar festive smell. Somebody pulled at her skirt, and, looking down, she saw Frau Rupp, the butcher's wife, who pulled out an empty chair and begged her to sit beside her.

'Fritz will get you some beer,' she said. 'My dear, your skirt is open at the back. We could not help laughing as you walked up the room with the white tape of your petticoat showing!'

'But how frightful!' said Frau Brechenmacher, collapsing into her chair and biting her lip.

'Na, it's over now,' said Frau Rupp, stretching her fat hands over the table and regarding her three mourning rings with intense enjoyment; 'but one must be careful, especially at a wedding.'

'And such a wedding as this,' cried Frau Ledermann, who sat on the other side of Frau Brechenmacher. 'Fancy Theresa bringing that child with her. It's her own child, you know, my dear, and it's going to live with them. That's what I call a sin against the Church for a free-born child to attend its own mother's wedding.'

The three women sat and stared at the bride, who remained very still, with a little vacant smile on her lips, only her eyes shifting uneasily from side to side.

'Beer they've given it, too,' whispered Frau Rupp, 'and white wine and an ice. It never did have a stomach; she ought to have left it at home.'

Frau Brechenmacher turned round and looked towards the bride's mother. She never took her eyes off her daughter, but wrinkled her brown forehead like an old monkey, and nodded now and again very solemnly. Her hands shook as she raised her beer mug, and when she had drunk she spat on the floor and savagely wiped her mouth with her sleeve. Then the music started and she followed Theresa with her eyes, looking suspiciously at each man who danced with her.

'Cheer up, old woman,' shouted her husband, digging her in the ribs; 'this isn't Theresa's funeral.' He winked at the guests, who broke into loud laughter.

'I *am* cheerful,' mumbled the old woman, and beat upon the table with her fist, keeping time to the music, proving she was not out of the festivities.

'She can't forget how wild Theresa has been,' said Frau Ledermann. 'Who could – with the child there? I heard that last Sunday evening Theresa had hysterics and said that she would not marry this man. They had to get the priest to her.'

'Where is the other one?' asked Frau Brechenmacher. 'Why didn't he marry her?'

The woman shrugged her shoulders.

'Gone – disappeared. He was a traveller, and only stayed at their house two nights. He was selling shirt buttons – I bought some myself, and they were beautiful shirt buttons – but what a pig of a fellow! I can't think what he saw in such a plain girl – but you never know. Her mother says she's been like fire ever since she was sixteen!'

Frau Brechenmacher looked down at her beer and blew a little hole in the froth.

'That's not how a wedding should be,' she said; 'it's not religion to love two men.'

'Nice time she'll have with this one,' Frau Rupp exclaimed. 'He was lodging with me last summer and I had to get rid of him. He never changed his clothes once in two months, and when I spoke to him of the smell in his room he told me he was sure it floated up from the shop. Ah, every wife has her cross. Isn't that true, my dear?'

Frau Brechenmacher saw her husband among his colleagues at the next table. He was drinking far too much, she knew – gesticulating wildly, the saliva spluttering out of his mouth as he talked.

'Yes,' she assented, 'that's true. Girls have a lot to learn.'

Wedged in between these two fat old women, the Frau had no hope of being asked to dance. She watched the couples going round and round; she forgot her five babies and her man and felt almost like a girl again. The music sounded sad and sweet. Her roughened hands clasped and unclasped themselves in the folds of her skirt. While the music went on she was afraid to look anybody in the face, and she smiled with a little nervous tremor round the mouth.

'But, my God,' Frau Rupp cried, 'they've given that child of Theresa's a piece of sausage. It's to keep her quiet. There's going to be a presentation now – your man has to speak.'

Frau Brechenmacher sat up stiffly. The music ceased, and the dancers took their places again at the tables.

Herr Brechenmacher alone remained standing – he held in his hands a big silver coffee-pot. Everybody laughed at his speech, except the Frau; everybody roared at his grimaces, and at the way he carried the coffee-pot to the bridal pair, as if it were a baby he was holding.

She lifted the lid, peeped in, then shut it down with a little scream and sat biting her lips. The bridegroom wrenched the pot away from her and drew forth a baby's bottle and two little cradles holding china dolls. As he dandled these treasures before Theresa the hot room seemed to heave and sway with laughter.

Frau Brechenmacher did not think it funny. She stared round at the laughing faces, and suddenly they all seemed strange to her. She wanted to go home and never come out again. She imagined that all these people were laughing at her, more people than there were in the room even – all laughing at her because they were so much stronger than she was.

* * *

They walked home in silence. Herr Brechenmacher strode ahead, she stumbled after him. White and forsaken lay the road from the railway station to their house – a cold rush of wind blew her hood from her face, and suddenly she remembered how they had come home together the first night. Now they had five babies and twice as much money; *but* –

'Na, what is it all for?' she muttered, and not until she had reached home, and prepared a little supper of meat and bread for her man did she stop asking herself that silly question.

Herr Brechenmacher broke the bread into his plate, smeared it round with his fork and chewed greedily.

'Good?' she asked, leaning her arms on the table and pillowing her breast against them.

'But fine!'

He took a piece of the crumb, wiped it round his plate edge, and held it up to her mouth. She shook her head.

'Not hungry,' she said.

'But it is one of the best pieces, and full of the fat.'

He cleared the plate; then pulled off his boots and flung them into a corner.

'Not much of a wedding,' he said, stretching out his feet and wriggling his toes in the worsted socks.

'N-no,' she replied, taking up the discarded boots and placing them on the oven to dry.

Herr Brechenmacher yawned and stretched himself, and then looked up at her, grinning.

'Remember the night that we came home? You were an innocent one, you were.'

'Get along! Such a time ago I forget.' Well she remembered.

'Such a clout on the ear as you gave me . . . But I soon taught you.'

'Oh, don't start talking. You've too much beer. Come to bed.'

He tilted back in his chair, chuckling with laughter.

'That's not what you said to me that night. God, the trouble you gave me!'

But the little Frau seized the candle and went into the next room. The children were all soundly sleeping. She stripped the mattress off the baby's bed to see if he was still dry, then began unfastening her blouse and skirt.

'Always the same,' she said – 'all over the world the same; but, God in heaven – but *stupid*.'

Then even the memory of the wedding faded quite. She lay down on the bed and put her arm across her face like a child who expected to be hurt as Herr Brechenmacher lurched in.

The Modern Soul

'GOOD EVENING,' said the Herr Professor, squeezing my hand; 'wonderful weather! I have just returned from a party in the wood. I have been making music for them on my trombone. You know, these pine trees provide most suitable accompaniment for a trombone! They are sighing delicacy against sustained strength, as I remarked once in a lecture on wind instruments in Frankfort. May I be permitted to sit beside you on this bench, *gnadige Frau*?'

He sat down, tugging at a white-paper package in the tail pocket of his coat.

'Cherries,' he said, nodding and smiling. 'There is nothing like cherries for producing free saliva after trombone playing, especially after Grieg's "*Ich Liebe Dich*". Those sustained blasts on "*liebe*" make my throat as dry as a railway tunnel. Have some?' He shook the bag at me.

'I prefer watching you eat them.'

'Ah, ha!' He crossed his legs, sticking the cherry bag between his knees, to leave both hands free. 'Psychologically I understood your refusal. It is your innate feminine delicacy in preferring etherealised sensations . . . Or perhaps you do not care to eat the worms. All cherries contain worms. Once I made a very interesting experiment with a colleague of mine at the university. We bit into four pounds of the best cherries and did not find one specimen without a worm. But what would you? As I remarked to him afterwards – dear friend, it amounts to this: if one wishes to satisfy the desires of nature one must be strong enough to ignore the facts of nature . . . The conversation is not out of your depth? I have so seldom the time or opportunity to open my heart to a woman that I am apt to forget.'

I looked at him brightly.

'See what a fat one!' cried the Herr Professor. 'That is almost a mouthful in itself; it is beautiful enough to hang from a watch-chain.' He chewed it up and spat the stone an incredible distance – over the garden path into the flower bed. He was proud of the feat. I saw it. 'The quantity of fruit I have eaten on this bench,' he sighed; 'apricots, peaches and cherries. One day that garden bed will become an orchard grove, and I shall allow you to pick as much as you please, without paying me anything.'

I was grateful, without showing undue excitement.

'Which reminds me' – he hit the side of his nose with one finger – 'the manager of the pension handed me my weekly bill after dinner this evening. It is almost impossible to credit. I do not expect you to believe me – he has charged me extra for a miserable little glass of milk I drink in bed at night to prevent insomnia. Naturally, I did not pay. But the tragedy of the story is this: I cannot expect the milk to produce somnolence any longer; my peaceful attitude of mind towards it is completely destroyed. I know I shall throw myself into a fever in attempting to plumb this want of generosity in so wealthy a man as the manager of a pension. Think of me tonight,' – he ground the empty bag under his heel – 'think that the worst is happening to me as your head drops asleep on your pillow.'

Two ladies came on the front steps of the pension and stood, arm in arm, looking over the garden. The one, old and scraggy, dressed almost entirely in black bead trimming and a satin reticule; the other, young and thin, in a white gown, her yellow hair tastefully garnished with mauve sweet peas.

The Professor drew in his feet and sat up sharply, pulling down his waistcoat.

'The Godowskas,' he murmured. 'Do you know them? A mother and daughter from Vienna. The mother has an internal complaint and the daughter is an actress. Fräulein Sonia is a very modern soul. I think you would find her most sympathetic. She is forced to be in attendance on her mother just now. But what a temperament! I have once described her in her autograph album as a tigress with a flower in the hair. Will you excuse me? Perhaps I can persuade them to be introduced to you.'

I said, 'I am going up to my room.' But the Professor rose and shook a playful finger at me. 'Na,' he said, 'we are friends, and, therefore, I shall speak quite frankly to you. I think they would consider it a little "marked" if you immediately retired to the house at their approach, after sitting here alone with me in the twilight. You know this world. Yes, you know it as I do.'

I shrugged my shoulders, remarking with one eye that while the Professor had been talking the Godowskas had trailed across the lawn towards us. They confronted the Herr Professor as he stood up.

'Good evening,' quavered Frau Godowska. 'Wonderful weather! It has given me quite a touch of hay fever!' Fräulein Godowska said nothing. She swooped over a rose growing in the embryo orchard, then stretched out her hand with a magnificent gesture to the Herr Professor. He presented me.

'This is my little English friend of whom I have spoken. She is the stranger in our midst. We have been eating cherries together.'

'How delightful,' sighed Frau Godowska. 'My daughter and I have often observed you through the bedroom window. Haven't we, Sonia?'

Sonia absorbed my outward and visible form with an inward and spiritual glance, then repeated the magnificent gesture for my benefit. The four of us sat on the bench, with that faint air of excitement of passengers established in a railway carriage on the *qui vive* for the train whistle. Frau Godowska sneezed. 'I wonder if it is hay fever,' she remarked, worrying the satin reticule for her handkerchief, 'or would it be the dew. Sonia, dear, is the dew falling?'

Fräulein Sonia raised her face to the sky, and half closed her eyes. 'No, mamma, my face is quite warm. Oh, look, Herr Professor, there are swallows in flight; they are like a little flock of Japanese thoughts – *nicht wahr?*'

'Where?' cried the Herr Professor. 'Oh yes, I see, by the kitchen chimney. But why do you say "Japanese"? Could you not compare them with equal veracity to a little flock of German thoughts in flight?' He rounded on me. 'Have you swallows in England?'

'I believe there are some at certain seasons. But doubtless they have not the same symbolical value for the English. In Germany – '

'I have never been to England,' interrupted Fräulein Sonia, 'but I have many English acquaintances. They are so cold!' She shivered.

'Fish-blooded,' snapped Frau Godowska. 'Without soul, without heart, without grace. But you cannot equal their dress materials. I spent a week in Brighton twenty years ago, and the travelling cape I bought there is not yet worn out – the one you wrap the hot-water bottle in, Sonia. My lamented husband, your father, Sonia, knew a great deal about England. But the more he knew about it the oftener he remarked to me, "England is merely an island of beef flesh swimming in a warm gulf sea of gravy." Such a brilliant way of putting things. Do you remember, Sonia?'

'I forget nothing, mamma,' answered Sonia.

Said the Herr Professor: 'That is the proof of your calling, *gnadiges*

Fräulein. Now I wonder – and this is a very interesting speculation – is memory a blessing or – excuse the word – a curse?'

Frau Godowska looked into the distance, then the corners of her mouth dropped and her skin puckered. She began to shed tears.

'*Ach Gott!* Gracious lady, what have I said?' exclaimed the Herr Professor.

Sonia took her mother's hand. 'Do you know,' she said, 'tonight it is stewed carrots and nut tart for supper. Suppose we go in and take our places,' her sidelong, tragic stare accusing the Professor and me the while.

I followed them across the lawn and up the steps. Frau Godowska was murmuring, 'Such a wonderful, beloved man'; with her disengaged hand Fräulein Sonia was arranging the sweet pea 'garniture'.

* * *

'A concert for the benefit of afflicted Catholic infants will take place in the salon at eight-thirty p.m. Artists: Fräulein Sonia Godowska, from Vienna; Herr Professor Windberg and his trombone; Frau Oberlehrer Weidel, and others.'

This notice was tied round the neck of the melancholy stag's head in the dining-room. It graced him like a red and white dinner bib for days before the event, causing the Herr Professor to bow before it and say 'good appetite' until we sickened of his pleasantry and left the smiling to be done by the waiter, who was paid to be pleasing to the guests.

On the appointed day the married ladies sailed about the pension dressed like upholstered chairs, and the unmarried ladies like draped muslin dressing-table covers. Frau Godowska pinned a rose in the centre of her reticule; another blossom was tucked in the mazy folds of a white antimacassar thrown across her breast. The gentlemen wore black coats, white silk ties and ferny buttonholes tickling the chin.

The floor of the salon was freshly polished, chairs and benches arranged, and a row of little flags strung across the ceiling – they flew and jigged in the draught with all the enthusiasm of family washing. It was arranged that I should sit beside Frau Godowska, and that the Herr Professor and Sonia should join us when their share of the concert was over.

'That will make you feel quite one of the performers,' said the Herr Professor genially. 'It is a great pity that the English nation is so unmusical. Never mind! Tonight you shall hear something – we have discovered a nest of talent during the rehearsals.'

'What do you intend to recite, Fräulein Sonia?'

She shook back her hair. 'I never know until the last moment. When I come on the stage I wait for one moment and then I have the sensation as though something struck me here,' – she placed her hand upon her collar brooch – 'and . . . words come!'

'Bend down a moment,' whispered her mother. 'Sonia, love, your skirt safety-pin is showing at the back. Shall I come outside and fasten it properly for you, or will you do it yourself?'

'Oh, mamma, please don't say such things,' Sonia flushed and grew very angry. 'You know how sensitive I am to the slightest unsympathetic impression at a time like this . . . I would rather my skirt dropped off my body –'

'Sonia – my heart!'

A bell tinkled.

The waiter came in and opened the piano. In the heated excitement of the moment he entirely forgot what was fitting, and flicked the keys with the grimy table napkin he carried over his arm. The Frau Oberlehrer tripped on the platform followed by a very young gentleman, who blew his nose twice before he hurled his handkerchief into the bosom of the piano.

> Yes, I know you have no love for me,
> And no forget-me-not.
> No love, no heart, and no forget-me-not.

sang the Frau Oberlehrer, in a voice that seemed to issue from her forgotten thimble and have nothing to do with her.

'*Ach*, how sweet, how delicate,' we cried, clapping her soothingly. She bowed as though to say, 'Yes, isn't it?' and retired, the very young gentleman dodging her train and scowling.

The piano was closed, an armchair was placed in the centre of the platform. Fräulein Sonia drifted towards it. A breathless pause. Then, presumably, the winged shaft struck her collar brooch. She implored us not to go into the woods in trained dresses, but rather as lightly draped as possible, and bed with her among the pine needles. Her loud, slightly harsh voice filled the salon. She dropped her arms over the back of the chair, moving her lean hands from the wrists. We were thrilled and silent. The Herr Professor, beside me, abnormally serious, his eyes bulging, pulled at his moustache ends. Frau Godowska adopted that peculiarly detached attitude of the proud parent. The only soul who remained untouched by her appeal was the waiter, who leaned idly against the wall of the salon and cleaned his nails with the edge of a programme. He was 'off duty' and intended to show it.

'What did I say?' shouted the Herr Professor under cover of tumultuous applause, 'tem-per-ament! There you have it. She is a flame in the heart of a lily. I know I am going to play well. It is my turn now. I am inspired. Fräulein Sonia' – as that lady returned to us, pale and draped in a large shawl – 'you are my inspiration. Tonight you shall be the soul of my trombone. Wait only.'

To right and left of us people bent over and whispered admiration down Fräulein Sonia's neck. She bowed in the grand style.

'I am always successful,' she said to me. 'You see, when I act I *am*. In Vienna, in the plays of Ibsen we had so many bouquets that the cook had three in the kitchen. But it is difficult here. There is so little magic. Do you not feel it? There is none of that mysterious perfume which floats almost as a visible thing from the souls of the Viennese audiences. My spirit starves for want of that.' She leaned forward, chin on hand. 'Starves,' she repeated.

The Professor appeared with his trombone, blew into it, held it up to one eye, tucked back his shirt cuffs and wallowed in the soul of Sonia Godowska. Such a sensation did he create that he was recalled to play a Bavarian dance, which he acknowledged was to be taken as a breathing exercise rather than an artistic achievement. Frau Godowska kept time to it with a fan.

Followed the very young gentleman who piped in a tenor voice that he loved somebody, 'with blood in his heart and a thousand pains'. Fräulein Sonia acted a poison scene with the assistance of her mother's pill vial and the armchair replaced by a *chaise longue*; a young girl scratched a lullaby on a young fiddle; and the Herr Professor performed the last sacrificial rites on the altar of the afflicted children by playing the National Anthem.

'Now I must put mamma to bed,' whispered Fräulein Sonia. 'But afterwards I must take a walk. It is imperative that I free my spirit in the open air for a moment. Would you come with me as far as the railway station and back?'

'Very well, then, knock on my door when you're ready.'

Thus the modern soul and I found ourselves together under the stars.

'What a night!' she said. 'Do you know that poem of Sappho about her hands in the stars . . . I am curiously sapphic. And this is so remarkable – not only am I sapphic, I find in all the works of all the greatest writers, especially in their unedited letters, some touch, some sign of myself – some resemblance, some part of myself, like a thousand reflections of my own hands in a dark mirror.'

'But what a bother,' said I.

'I do not know what you mean by "bother"; is it rather the curse of my genius . . . ' She paused suddenly, staring at me. 'Do you know my tragedy?' she asked.

I shook my head.

'My tragedy is my mother. Living with her I live with the coffin of my unborn aspirations. You heard that about the safety-pin tonight. It may seem to you a little thing, but it ruined my three first gestures. They were – '

'Impaled on a safety-pin,' I suggested.

'Yes, exactly that. And when we are in Vienna I am the victim of moods, you know. I long to do wild, passionate things. And mamma says, "Please pour out my mixture first." Once I remember I flew into a rage and threw a washstand jug out of the window. Do you know what she said? "Sonia, it is not so much throwing things out of windows, if only you would – " '

'Choose something smaller?' said I.

'No . . . "tell me about it beforehand." Humiliating! And I do not see any possible light out of this darkness.'

'Why don't you join a touring company and leave your mother in Vienna?'

'What! Leave my poor, little, sick, widowed mother in Vienna! Sooner than that I would drown myself. I love my mother as I love nobody else in the world – nobody and nothing! Do you think it is impossible to love one's tragedy? "Out of my great sorrows I make my little songs," that is Heine or myself.'

'Oh, well, that's all right,' I said cheerfully.

'But it is not all right!'

I suggested we should turn back. We turned.

'Sometimes I think the solution lies in marriage,' said Fräulein Sonia. 'If I find a simple, peaceful man who adores me and will look after mamma – a man who would be for me a pillow – for genius cannot hope to mate – I shall marry him . . . You know the Herr Professor has paid me very marked attentions.'

'Oh, Fräulein Sonia,' I said, very pleased with myself, 'why not marry him to your mother?' We were passing the hairdresser's shop at the moment. Fräulein Sonia clutched my arm.

'You, you,' she stammered. 'The cruelty. I am going to faint.

Mamma to marry again before I marry – the indignity. I am going to faint here and now.'

I was frightened. 'You can't,' I said, shaking her. 'Come back to the pension and faint as much as you please. But you can't faint here. All the shops are closed. There is nobody about. Please don't be so foolish.'

'Here and here only!' She indicated the exact spot and dropped quite beautifully, lying motionless.

'Very well,' I said, 'faint away; but please hurry over it.'

She did not move. I began to walk home, but each time I looked behind me I saw the dark form of the modern soul prone before the hairdresser's window. Finally I ran, and rooted out the Herr Professor from his room. 'Fräulein Sonia has fainted,' I said crossly.

'*Du lieber Gott*! Where? How?'

'Outside the hairdresser's shop in the Station Road.'

'Jesus and Maria! Has she no water with her?' – he seized his carafe – 'nobody beside her?'

'Nothing.'

'Where is my coat? No matter, I shall catch a cold on the chest. Willingly, I shall catch one . . . You are ready to come with me?'

'No,' I said; 'you can take the waiter.'

'But she must have a woman. I cannot be so indelicate as to attempt to loosen her stays.'

'Modern souls oughtn't to wear them,' said I. He pushed past me and clattered down the stairs.

* * *

When I came down to breakfast next morning there were two places vacant at table. Fräulein Sonia and Herr Professor had gone off for a day's excursion in the woods.

I wondered.

At Lehmann's

CERTAINLY SABINA did not find life slow. She was on the trot from early morning until late at night. At five o'clock she tumbled out of bed, buttoned on her clothes, wearing a long-sleeved alpaca pinafore over her black frock, and groped her way downstairs into the kitchen.

Anna, the cook, had grown so fat during the summer that she adored her bed because she did not have to wear her corsets there, but could spread as much as she liked, roll about under the great mattress, calling upon Jesus and Holy Mary and Blessed Anthony himself that her life was not fit for a pig in a cellar.

Sabina was new to her work. Pink colour still flew in her cheeks; there was a little dimple on the left side of her mouth that even when she was most serious, most absorbed, popped out and gave her away. And Anna blessed that dimple. It meant an extra half-hour in bed for her; it made Sabina light the fire, turn out the kitchen and wash endless cups and saucers that had been left over from the evening before. Hans, the scullery boy, did not come until seven. He was the son of the butcher – a mean, undersized child very much like one of his father's sausages, Sabina thought. His red face was covered with pimples, and his nails indescribably filthy. When Herr Lehmann himself told Hans to get a hairpin and clean them he said they were stained from birth because his mother had always got so inky doing the accounts – and Sabina believed him and pitied him.

Winter had come very early to Mindelbau. By the end of October the streets were banked waist-high with snow, and the greater number of the 'Cure Guests', sick unto death of cold water and herbs, had departed in nothing approaching peace. So the large salon was shut at Lehmann's and the breakfast-room was all the accommodation the café afforded. Here the floor had to be washed over, the tables rubbed, coffee-cups set out, each with its little china platter of sugar, and newspapers and magazines hung on their hooks along the walls before Herr Lehmann appeared at seven-thirty and opened business.

As a rule his wife served in the shop leading into the café, but she had chosen the quiet season to have a baby, and, a big woman at the best of times, she had grown so enormous in the process that her husband told her she looked unappetising, and had better remain upstairs and sew.

Sabina took on the extra work without any thought of extra pay. She loved to stand behind the counter, cutting up slices of Anna's marvellous chocolate-spotted confections, or doing up packets of sugar almonds in pink and blue striped bags.

'You'll get varicose veins, like me,' said Anna. 'That's what the Frau's got, too. No wonder the baby doesn't come! All her swelling's got into her legs.' And Hans was immensely interested.

During the morning business was comparatively slack. Sabina answered the shop bell, attended to a few customers who drank a liqueur to warm their stomachs before the midday meal, and ran upstairs now and again to ask the Frau if she wanted anything. But in the afternoon six or seven choice spirits played cards, and everybody who was anybody drank tea or coffee.

'Sabina . . . Sabina . . . '

She flew from one table to the other, counting out handfuls of small change, giving orders to Anna through the 'slide', helping the men with their heavy coats, always with that magical child air about her, that delightful sense of perpetually attending a party.

'How is the Frau Lehmann?' the women would whisper.

'She feels rather low, but as well as can be expected,' Sabina would answer, nodding confidentially.

Frau Lehmann's bad time was approaching. Anna and her friends referred to it as her 'journey to Rome', and Sabina longed to ask questions, yet, being ashamed of her ignorance, was silent, trying to puzzle it out for herself. She knew practically nothing except that the Frau had a baby inside her, which had to come out – very painful indeed. One could not have one without a husband – that she also realised. But what had the man got to do with it? So she wondered as she sat mending tea towels in the evening, head bent over her work, light shining on her brown curls. Birth – what was it? wondered Sabina. Death – such a simple thing. She had a little picture of her dead grandmother dressed in a black silk frock, tired hands clasping the crucifix that dragged between her flattened breasts, mouth curiously tight, yet almost secretly smiling. But the grandmother had been born once – that was the important fact.

As she sat there one evening, thinking, the Young Man entered the café, and called for a glass of port wine. Sabina rose slowly. The long

day and the hot room made her feel a little languid, but as she poured
out the wine she felt the Young Man's eyes fixed on her, looked
down at him and dimpled.

'It's cold out,' she said, corking the bottle.

The Young Man ran his hands through his snow-powdered hair
and laughed.

'I wouldn't call it exactly tropical,' he said, 'But you're very snug in
here – look as though you've been asleep.'

Very languid felt Sabina in the hot room, and the Young
Man's voice was strong and deep. She thought she had never
seen anybody who looked so strong – as though he could take
up the table in one hand – and his restless gaze wandering over
her face and figure gave her a curious thrill deep in her body,
half pleasure, half pain . . . She wanted to stand there, close
beside him, while he drank his wine. A little silence followed. Then
he took a book out of his pocket, and Sabina went back to her
sewing. Sitting there in the corner, she listened to the sound of the
leaves being turned and the loud ticking of the clock that hung over
the gilt mirror. She wanted to look at him again – there was
a something about him, in his deep voice, even in the way his
clothes fitted. From the room above she heard the heavy dragging
sound of Frau Lehmann's footsteps, and again the old thoughts
worried Sabina. If she herself should one day look like that –
feel like that! Yet it would be very sweet to have a little baby to
dress and jump up and down.

'Fräulein – what's your name – what are you smiling at?' called the
Young Man.

She blushed and looked up, hands quiet in her lap, looked across
the empty tables and shook her head.

'Come here, and I'll show you a picture,' he commanded.

She went and stood beside him. He opened the book, and Sabina
saw a coloured sketch of a naked girl sitting on the edge of a great,
crumpled bed, a man's opera hat on the back of her head.

He put his hand over the body, leaving only the face exposed, then
scrutinised Sabina closely.

'Well?'

'What do you mean?' she asked, knowing perfectly well.

'Why, it might be your own photograph – the face, I mean – that's
as far as I can judge.'

'But the hair's done differently,' said Sabina, laughing. She threw
back her head, and the laughter bubbled in her round white throat.

'It's rather a nice picture, don't you think?' he asked. But she was looking at a curious ring he wore on the hand that covered the girl's body, and only nodded.

'Ever seen anything like it before?'

'Oh, there's plenty of those funny ones in the illustrated papers.'

'How would you like to have your picture taken that way?'

'Me? I'd never let anybody see it. Besides, I haven't got a hat like that!'

'That's easily remedied.'

Again a little silence, broken by Anna throwing up the slide.

Sabina ran into the kitchen.

'Here, take this milk and egg up to the Frau,' said Anna. 'Who've you got in there?'

'Got such a funny man! I think he's a little gone here,' tapping her forehead.

Upstairs in the ugly room the Frau sat sewing, a black shawl round her shoulders, her feet encased in red woollen slippers. The girl put the milk on a table by her, then stood, polishing a spoon on her apron.

'Nothing else?'

'Na,' said the Frau, heaving up in her chair. 'Where's my man?'

'He's playing cards over at Snipold's. Do you want him?'

'Dear heaven, leave him alone. I'm nothing. I don't matter . . . And the whole day waiting here.'

Her hand shook as she wiped the rim of the glass with her fat finger.

'Shall I help you to bed?'

'You go downstairs, leave me alone. Tell Anna not to let Hans grub the sugar – give him one on the ear.'

'Ugly – ugly – ugly,' muttered Sabina, returning to the café where the Young Man stood coat-buttoned, ready for departure.

'I'll come again tomorrow,' said he. 'Don't twist your hair back so tightly; it will lose all its curl.'

'Well, you are a funny one,' she said. 'Good night.'

By the time Sabina was ready for bed Anna was snoring. She brushed out her long hair and gathered it in her hands . . . Perhaps it would be a pity if it lost all its curl. Then she looked down at her straight chemise, and drawing it off, sat down on the side of the bed.

'I wish,' she whispered, smiling sleepily, 'there was a great big looking-glass in this room.'

Lying down in the darkness, she hugged her little body.

'I wouldn't be the Frau for one hundred marks – not for a thousand marks. To look like that.'

And half-dreaming, she imagined herself heaving up in her chair with the port wine bottle in her hand as the Young Man entered the café.

Cold and dark the next morning. Sabina woke, tired, feeling as though something heavy had been pressing under her heart all night. There was a sound of footsteps shuffling along the passage. Herr Lehmann! She must have overslept herself. Yes, he was rattling the door-handle.

'One moment, one moment,' she called, dragging on her stockings.

'Bina, tell Anna to go to the Frau – but quickly. I must ride for the nurse.'

'Yes, yes!' she cried. 'Has it come?'

But he had gone, and she ran over to Anna and shook her by the shoulder.

'The Frau – the baby – Herr Lehmann for the nurse,' she stuttered.

'Name of God!' said Anna, flinging herself out of bed.

No complaints today. Importance – enthusiasm in Anna's whole bearing.

'You run downstairs and light the oven. Put on a pan of water' – speaking to an imaginary sufferer as she fastened her blouse – 'Yes, yes, I know – we must be worse before we are better – I'm coming – patience.'

It was dark all that day. Lights were turned on immediately the café opened, and business was very brisk. Anna, turned out of the Frau's room by the nurse, refused to work, and sat in a corner nursing herself, listening to sounds overhead. Hans was more sympathetic than Sabina. He also forsook work, and stood by the window, picking his nose.

'But why must I do everything?' said Sabina, washing glasses. 'I can't help the Frau; she oughtn't to take such a time about it.'

'Listen,' said Anna, 'they've moved her into the back bedroom above here, so as not to disturb the people. That was a groan – that one!'

'Two small beers,' shouted Herr Lehmann through the slide.

'One moment, one moment.'

At eight o'clock the café was deserted. Sabina sat down in the corner without her sewing. Nothing seemed to have happened to the Frau. A doctor had come – that was all.

'Ach,' said Sabina. 'I think no more of it. I listen no more. Ach, I would like to go away – I hate this talk. I will not hear it. No, it is too much.' She leaned both elbows on the table – cupped her face in her hands and pouted.

But the outer door suddenly opening, she sprang to her feet and laughed. It was the Young Man again. He ordered more port, and brought no book this time.

'Don't go and sit miles away,' he grumbled. 'I want to be amused. And here, take my coat. Can't you dry it somewhere? – snowing again.'

'There's a warm place – the ladies' cloak-room,' she said. 'I'll take it in there – just by the kitchen.'

She felt better, and quite happy again.

'I'll come with you,' he said. 'I'll see where you put it.'

And that did not seem at all extraordinary. She laughed and beckoned to him.

'In here,' she cried. 'Feel how warm. I'll put more wood on that oven. It doesn't matter, they're all busy upstairs.'

She knelt down on the floor, and thrust the wood into the oven, laughing at her own wicked extravagance.

The Frau was forgotten, the stupid day was forgotten. Here was someone beside her laughing, too. They were together in the little warm room stealing Herr Lehmann's wood. It seemed the most exciting adventure in the world. She wanted to go on laughing – or burst out crying – or – or – catch hold of the Young Man.

'What a fire,' she shrieked, stretching out her hands.

'Here's a hand; pull up,' said the Young Man. 'There, now, you'll catch it tomorrow.'

They stood opposite to each other, hands still clinging. And again that strange tremor thrilled Sabina.

'Look here,' he said roughly, 'are you a child, or are you playing at being one?'

'I – I –'

Laughter ceased. She looked up at him once, then down at the floor, and began breathing like a frightened little animal.

He pulled her closer still and kissed her mouth.

'Na, what are you doing?' she whispered.

He let go her hands, he placed his on her breasts, and the room seemed to swim round Sabina. Suddenly, from the room above, a frightful, tearing shriek.

She wrenched herself away, tightened herself, drew herself up.
'Who did that – who made that noise?'

* * *

In the silence the thin wailing of a baby.
'Achk!' shrieked Sabina, rushing from the room.

The Luft Bad

I THINK IT MUST BE the umbrellas which make us look ridiculous.

When I was admitted into the enclosure for the first time, and saw my fellow-bathers walking about very nearly 'in their nakeds', it struck me that the umbrellas gave a distinctly 'Little Black Sambo' touch.

Ridiculous dignity in holding over yourself a green cotton thing with a red parroquet handle when you are dressed in nothing larger than a handkerchief.

There are no trees in the 'Luft Bad.' It boasts a collection of plain, wooden cells, a bath shelter, two swings and two odd clubs – one, presumably the lost property of Hercules or the German army, and the other to be used with safety in the cradle.

And there in all weathers we take the air – walking, or sitting in little companies talking over each other's ailments and measurements and ills that flesh is heir to.

A high wooden wall compasses us all about; above it the pine trees look down a little superciliously, nudging each other in a way that is peculiarly trying to a debutante. Over the wall, on the right side, is the men's section. We hear them chopping down trees and sawing through planks, dashing heavy weights to the ground, and singing part songs. Yes, they take it far more seriously.

On the first day I was conscious of my legs, and went back into my cell three times to look at my watch, but when a woman with whom I had played chess for three weeks cut me dead, I took heart and joined a circle.

We lay curled on the ground while a Hungarian lady of immense proportions told us what a beautiful tomb she had bought for her second husband.

'A vault it is,' she said, 'with nice black railings. And so large that I can go down there and walk about. Both their photographs are there, with two very handsome wreaths sent me by my first husband's brother. There is an enlargement of a family group photograph, too, and an illuminated address presented to my first husband on his marriage. I am often there; it makes such a pleasant excursion for a fine Saturday afternoon.'

She suddenly lay down flat on her back, took in six long breaths, and sat up again.

'The death agony was dreadful,' she said brightly; 'of the second, I mean. The "first" was run into by a furniture wagon, and had fifty marks stolen out of a new waistcoat pocket, but the "second" was dying for sixty-seven hours. I never ceased crying once – not even to put the children to bed.'

A young Russian, with a 'bang' curl on her forehead, turned to me. 'Can you do the "Salome" dance?' she asked. 'I can.'

'How delightful,' I said.

'Shall I do it now? Would you like to see me?'

She sprang to her feet, executed a series of amazing contortions for the next ten minutes, and then paused, panting, twisting her long hair.

'Isn't that nice?' she said. 'And now I am perspiring so splendidly. I shall go and take a bath.'

Opposite to me was the brownest woman I have ever seen, lying on her back, her arms clasped over her head.

'How long have you been here today?' she was asked.

'Oh, I spend the day here now,' she answered. 'I am making my own "cure", and living entirely on raw vegetables and nuts, and each day I feel my spirit is stronger and purer. After all, what can you expect? The majority of us are walking about with pig corpuscles and oxen fragments in our brain. The wonder is the world is as good as it is. Now I live on the simple, provided food' – she pointed to a little bag beside her – 'a lettuce, a carrot, a potato, and some nuts are ample, rational nourishment. I wash them under the tap and eat them raw, just as they come from the harmless earth – fresh and uncontaminated.'

'Do you take nothing else all day?' I cried.

'Water. And perhaps a banana if I wake in the night.' She turned round and leaned on one elbow. 'You over-eat yourself dreadfully,' she said, 'shamelessly! How can you expect the Flame of the Spirit to burn brightly under layers of superfluous flesh?'

I wished she would not stare at me, and thought of going to look at my watch again when a little girl wearing a string of coral beads joined us.

'The poor Frau Hauptmann cannot join us today,' she said, 'she has come out in spots all over on account of her nerves. She was very excited yesterday after having written two postcards.'

'A delicate woman,' volunteered the Hungarian, 'but pleasant. Fancy, she has a separate plate for each of her front teeth! But she has no right to let her daughters wear such short sailor suits. They sit about on benches, crossing their legs in a most shameless manner. What are you going to do this afternoon, Fräulein Anna?'

'Oh,' said the Coral Necklace, 'the Herr Oberleutnant has asked me to go with him to Landsdorf. He must buy some eggs there to take home to his mother. He saves a penny on eight eggs by knowing the right peasants to bargain with.'

'Are you an American?' said the Vegetable Lady, turning to me.

'No.'

'Then you are an Englishwoman?'

'Well, hardly – '

'You must be one of the two; you cannot help it. I have seen you walking alone several times. You wear your – '

I got up and climbed on to the swing. The air was sweet and cool, rushing past my body. Above, white clouds trailed delicately through the blue sky. From the pine forest streamed a wild perfume, the branches swayed together, rhythmically, sonorously. I felt so light and free and happy – so childish! I wanted to poke my tongue out at the circle on the grass, who, drawing close together, were whispering meaningly.

'Perhaps you do not know,' cried a voice from one of the cells, 'to swing is very upsetting for the stomach? A friend of mine could keep nothing down for three weeks after exciting herself so.'

I went to the bath shelter and was hosed.

As I dressed, someone tapped on the wall.

'Do you know,' said a voice, 'there is a man who *lives* in the Luft Bad next door? He buries himself up to the armpits in mud and refuses to believe in the Trinity.'

The umbrellas are the saving grace of the Luft Bad. Now when I go, I take my husband's 'storm' gamp and sit in a corner, hiding behind it.

Not that I am in the least ashamed of my legs.

A Birthday

ANDREAS BINZER woke slowly. He turned over on the narrow bed and stretched himself – yawned – opening his mouth as widely as possible and bringing his teeth together afterwards with a sharp 'click'. The sound of that click fascinated him; he repeated it quickly several times, with a snapping movement of the jaws. What teeth! he thought. Sound as a bell, every man jack of them. Never had one out, never had one stopped. That comes of no tomfoolery in eating, and a good regular brushing night and morning. He raised himself on his left elbow and waved his right arm over the side of the bed to feel for the chair where he put his watch and chain overnight. No chair was there – of course, he'd forgotten, there wasn't a chair in this wretched spare room. Had to put the confounded thing under his pillow. 'Half-past eight, Sunday, breakfast at nine – time for the bath' – his brain ticked to the watch. He sprang out of bed and went over to the window. The venetian blind was broken, hung fan-shaped over the upper pane . . . 'That blind must be mended. I'll get the office boy to drop in and fix it on his way home tomorrow – he's a good hand at blinds. Give him twopence and he'll do it as well as a carpenter . . . Anna could do it herself if she was all right. So would I, for the matter of that, but I don't like to trust myself on rickety step-ladders.' He looked up at the sky: it shone, strangely white, unflecked with cloud; he looked down at the row of garden strips and back-yards. The fence of these gardens was built along the edge of a gully, spanned by an iron suspension bridge, and the people had a wretched habit of throwing their empty tins over the fence into the gully. Just like them, of course! Andreas started counting the tins, and decided, viciously, to write a letter to the papers about it and sign it – sign it in full.

The servant girl came out of their back door into the yard, carrying his boots. She threw one down on the ground, thrust her hand into the other, and stared at it, sucking in her cheeks.

Suddenly she bent forward, spat on the toecap, and started polishing with a brush rooted out of her apron pocket . . . 'Slut of a girl! Heaven knows what infectious disease may be breeding now in that boot. Anna must get rid of that girl – even if she has to do without one for a bit – as soon as she's up and about again. The way she chucked one boot down and then spat upon the other! She didn't care whose boots she'd got hold of. *She* had no false notions of the respect due to the master of the house.' He turned away from the window and switched his bath towel from the washstand rail, sick at heart. 'I'm too sensitive for a man – that's what's the matter with me. Have been from the beginning, and will be to the end.'

There was a gentle knock at the door and his mother came in. She closed the door after her and leant against it. Andreas noticed that her cap was crooked, and a long tail of hair hung over her shoulder. He went forward and kissed her.

'Good morning, mother; how's Anna?'

The old woman spoke quickly, clasping and unclasping her hands.

'Andreas, please go to Doctor Erb as soon as you are dressed.'

'Why,' he said, 'is she bad?'

Frau Binzer nodded, and Andreas, watching her, saw her face suddenly change; a fine network of wrinkles seemed to pull over it from under the skin surface.

'Sit down on the bed a moment,' he said. 'Been up all night?'

'Yes. No, I won't sit down, I must go back to her. Anna has been in pain all night. She wouldn't have you disturbed before because she said you looked so run down yesterday. You told her you had caught a cold and been very worried.'

Straightway Andreas felt that he was being accused.

'Well, she made me tell her, worried it out of me; you know the way she does.'

Again Frau Binzer nodded.

'Oh yes, I know. She says, is your cold better, and there's a warm undervest for you in the left-hand corner of the big drawer.'

Quite automatically Andreas cleared his throat twice.

'Yes,' he answered. 'Tell her my throat certainly feels looser. I suppose I'd better not disturb her?'

'No, and besides, *time*, Andreas.'

'I'll be ready in five minutes.'

They went into the passage. As Frau Binzer opened the door of the front bedroom, a long wail came from the room.

That shocked and terrified Andreas. He dashed into the bathroom, turned on both taps as far as they would go, cleaned his teeth and pared his nails while the water was running.

'Frightful business, frightful business,' he heard himself whispering. 'And I can't understand it. It isn't as though it were her first – it's her third. Old Schafer told me, yesterday, his wife simply "dropped" her fourth. Anna ought to have had a qualified nurse. Mother gives way to her. Mother spoils her. I wonder what she meant by saying I'd worried Anna yesterday. Nice remark to make to a husband at a time like this. Unstrung, I suppose – and my sensitiveness again.'

When he went into the kitchen for his boots, the servant girl was bent over the stove, cooking breakfast. 'Breathing into that, now, I suppose,' thought Andreas, and was very short with the servant girl. She did not notice. She was full of terrified joy and importance in the goings on upstairs. She felt she was learning the secrets of life with every breath she drew. Had laid the table that morning saying, 'Boy,' as she put down the first dish, 'Girl,' as she placed the second – it had worked out with the salt spoon to 'Boy'. 'For two pins I'd tell the master that, to comfort him, like,' she decided. But the Master gave her no opening.

'Put an extra cup and saucer on the table,' he said; 'the doctor may want some coffee.'

'The doctor, sir?' The servant girl whipped a spoon out of a pan, and spilt two drops of grease on the stove. 'Shall I fry something extra?' But the master had gone, slamming the door after him. He walked down the street – there was nobody about at all – dead and alive this place on a Sunday morning. As he crossed the suspension bridge a strong stench of fennel and decayed refuse streamed from the gulley, and again Andreas began concocting a letter. He turned into the main road. The shutters were still up before the shops. Scraps of newspaper, hay, and fruit skins strewed the pavement; the gutters were choked with the leavings of Saturday night. Two dogs sprawled in the middle of the road, scuffling and biting. Only the public-house at the corner was open; a young barman slopped water over the doorstep.

Fastidiously, his lips curling, Andreas picked his way through the water. 'Extraordinary how I am noticing things this morning. It's partly the effect of Sunday. I loathe a Sunday when Anna's tied by the leg and the children are away. On Sunday a man has the right to expect his family. Everything here's filthy, the whole place might be down with the plague, and will be, too, if this street's not swept away.

I'd like to have a hand on the government ropes.' He braced his shoulders. 'Now for this doctor.'

'Doctor Erb is at breakfast,' the maid informed him. She showed him into the waiting-room, a dark and musty place, with some ferns under a glass-case by the window. 'He says he won't be a minute, please, sir, and there is a paper on the table.'

'Unhealthy hole,' thought Binzer, walking over to the window and drumming his fingers on the glass fern-shade. 'At breakfast, is he? That's the mistake I made: turning out early on an empty stomach.'

A milk cart rattled down the street, the driver standing at the back, cracking a whip; he wore an immense geranium flower stuck in the lapel of his coat. Firm as a rock he stood, bending back a little in the swaying cart. Andreas craned his neck to watch him all the way down the road, even after he had gone, listening for the sharp sound of those rattling cans.

'H'm, not much wrong with him,' he reflected. 'Wouldn't mind a taste of that life myself. Up early, work all over by eleven o'clock, nothing to do but loaf about all day until milking time.' Which he knew was an exaggeration, but he wanted to pity himself.

The maid opened the door, and stood aside for Doctor Erb. Andreas wheeled round; the two men shook hands.

'Well, Binzer,' said the doctor jovially, brushing some crumbs from a pearl-coloured waistcoat, 'son and heir becoming importunate?'

Up went Binzer's spirits with a bound. Son and heir, by Jove! He was glad to have to deal with a man again. And a sane fellow this, who came across this sort of thing every day of the week.

'That's about the measure of it, Doctor,' he answered, smiling and picking up his hat. 'Mother dragged me out of bed this morning with imperative orders to bring you along.'

'Gig will be round in a minute. Drive back with me, won't you? Extraordinary, sultry day; you're as red as a beetroot already.'

Andreas affected to laugh. The doctor had one annoying habit – imagined he had the right to poke fun at everybody simply because he was a doctor. 'The man's riddled with conceit, like all these professionals,' Andreas decided.

'What sort of night did Frau Binzer have?' asked the doctor. 'Ah, here's the gig. Tell me on the way up. Sit as near the middle as you can, will you, Binzer? Your weight tilts it over a bit one side – that's the worst of you successful business men.'

'Two stone heavier than I, if he's a pound,' thought Andreas. 'The man may be all right in his profession – but heaven preserve me.'

'Off you go, my beauty.' Doctor Erb flicked the little brown mare. 'Did your wife get any sleep last night?'

'No; I don't think she did,' answered Andreas shortly. 'To tell you the truth, I'm not satisfied that she hasn't a nurse.'

'Oh, your mother's worth a dozen nurses,' cried the doctor, with immense gusto. 'To tell you the truth, I'm not keen on nurses – too raw – raw as rump-steak. They wrestle for a baby as though they were wrestling with Death for the body of Patroclus . . . Ever seen that picture by an English artist. Leighton? Wonderful thing – full of sinew!'

'There he goes again,' thought Andreas, 'airing off his knowledge to make a fool of me.'

'Now your mother – she's firm – she's capable. Does what she's told with a fund of sympathy. Look at these shops we're passing – they're festering sores. How on earth this government can tolerate – '

'They're not so bad – sound enough – only want a coat of paint.'

The doctor whistled a little tune and flicked the mare again.

'Well, I hope the young shaver won't give his mother too much trouble,' he said. 'Here we are.'

A skinny little boy, who had been sliding up and down the back seat of the gig, sprang out and held the horse's head. Andreas went straight into the dining-room and left the servant girl to take the doctor upstairs. He sat down, poured out some coffee, and bit through half a roll before helping himself to fish. Then he noticed there was no hot plate for the fish – the whole house was at sixes and sevens. He rang the bell, but the servant girl came in with a tray holding a bowl of soup and a hot plate.

'I've been keeping them on the stove,' she simpered.

'Ah, thanks, that's very kind of you.' As he swallowed the soup his heart warmed to this fool of a girl.

'Oh, it's a good thing Doctor Erb has come,' volunteered the servant girl, who was bursting for want of sympathy.

'H'm, h'm,' said Andreas.

She waited a moment, expectantly, rolling her eyes, then in full loathing of menkind went back to the kitchen and vowed herself to sterility.

Andreas cleared the soup bowl, and cleared the fish. As he ate, the room slowly darkened. A faint wind sprang up and beat the tree branches against the window. The dining-room looked over the breakwater of the harbour, and the sea swung heavily in rolling waves. Wind crept round the house, moaning drearily.

'We're in for a storm. That means I'm boxed up here all day. Well, there's one blessing; it'll clear the air.' He heard the servant girl rushing importantly round the house, slamming windows. Then he caught a glimpse of her in the garden, unpegging tea towels from the line across the lawn. She was a worker, there was no doubt about that. He took up a book, and wheeled his armchair over to the window. But it was useless. Too dark to read; he didn't believe in straining his eyes, and gas at ten o'clock in the morning seemed absurd. So he slipped down in the chair, leaned his elbows on the padded arms and gave himself up, for once, to idle dreaming. 'A boy? Yes, it was bound to be a boy this time . . . ' 'What's your family, Binzer?' 'Oh, I've two girls and a boy!' A very nice little number. Of course he was the last man to have a favourite child, but a man needed a son. 'I'm working up the business for my son! Binzer & Son! It would mean living very tight for the next ten years, cutting expenses as fine as possible; and then – '

A tremendous gust of wind sprang upon the house, seized it, shook it, dropped, only to grip the more tightly. The waves swelled up along the breakwater and were whipped with broken foam. Over the white sky flew tattered streamers of grey cloud.

Andreas felt quite relieved to hear Doctor Erb coming down the stairs; he got up and lit the gas.

'Mind if I smoke in here?' asked Doctor Erb, lighting a cigarette before Andreas had time to answer. 'You don't smoke, do you? No time to indulge in pernicious little habits!'

'How is she now?' asked Andreas, loathing the man.

'Oh, well as can be expected, poor little soul. She begged me to come down and have a look at you. Said she knew you were worrying.' With laughing eyes the doctor looked at the breakfast-table. 'Managed to peck a bit, I see, eh?'

'Hoo-wih!' shouted the wind, shaking the window-sashes.

'Pity – this weather,' said Doctor Erb.

'Yes, it gets on Anna's nerves, and it's just nerve she wants.'

'Eh, what's that?' retorted the doctor. 'Nerve! Man alive! She's got twice the nerve of you and me rolled into one. Nerve! she's nothing but nerve. A woman who works as she does about the house and has three children in four years thrown in with the dusting, so to speak!'

He pitched his half-smoked cigarette into the fireplace and frowned at the window.

'Now *he's* accusing me,' thought Andreas. 'That's the second time this morning – first mother and now this man taking advantage of my sensitiveness.' He could not trust himself to speak, and rang the bell for the servant girl.

'Clear away the breakfast things,' he ordered. 'I can't have them messing about on the table till dinner!'

'Don't be hard on the girl,' coaxed Doctor Erb. 'She's got twice the work to do today.'

At that Binzer's anger blazed out.

'I'll trouble you, Doctor, not to interfere between me and my servants!' And he felt a fool at the same moment for not saying 'servant'.

Doctor Erb was not perturbed. He shook his head, thrust his hands into his pockets, and began balancing himself on toe and heel.

'You're jagged by the weather,' he said wryly, 'nothing else. A great pity – this storm. You know climate has an immense effect upon birth. A fine day perks a woman – gives her heart for her business. Good weather is as necessary to a confinement as it is to a washing day. Not bad – that last remark of mine – for a professional fossil, eh?'

Andreas made no reply.

'Well, I'll be getting back to my patient. Why don't you take a walk, and clear your head? That's the idea for you.'

'No,' he answered, 'I won't do that; it's too rough.'

He went back to his chair by the window. While the servant girl cleared away he pretended to read . . . then his dreams! It seemed years since he had had the time to himself to dream like that – he never had a breathing space. Saddled with work all day, and couldn't shake it off in the evening like other men. Besides, Anna was interested – they talked of practically nothing else together. Excellent mother she'd make for a boy; she had a grip of things.

Church bells started ringing through the windy air, now sounding as though from very far away, then again as though all the churches in the town had been suddenly transplanted into their street. They stirred something in him, those bells, something vague and tender. Just about that time Anna would call him from the hall. 'Andreas, come and have your coat brushed. I'm ready.' Then off they would go, she hanging on his arm, and looking up at him. She certainly was a little thing. He remembered once saying when they were engaged, 'Just as high as my heart,' and she had jumped on to a stool and pulled his head down, laughing. A kid in those days, younger than her children in nature, brighter, more 'go' and 'spirit' in her. The way she'd run down the road to meet him after business! And the way she laughed when they were looking for a house. By Jove! that laugh of hers! At the memory he grinned, then grew suddenly grave. Marriage certainly changed a woman far more than it did a man. Talk about sobering down. She had lost all her go in two months! Well, once this boy business was over she'd get stronger. He began to plan a little trip for them. He'd take her away and they'd loaf about together somewhere. After all, dash it, they were young still. She'd got into a groove; he'd have to force her out of it, that's all.

He got up and went into the drawing-room, carefully shut the door and took Anna's photograph from the top of the piano. She wore a white dress with a big bow of some soft stuff under the chin, and stood, a little stiffly, holding a sheaf of artificial poppies and corn in her hands. Delicate she looked even then; her masses of hair gave her that look. She seemed to droop under the heavy braids of it, and yet she was smiling. Andreas caught his breath sharply. She was his wife – that girl. Posh! it had only been taken four years ago. He held it close to him, bent forward and kissed it. Then rubbed the glass with the back of his hand. At that moment, fainter than he had heard in the passage, more terrifying, Andreas heard again that wailing cry. The wind caught it up in mocking echo, blew it over the house-tops, down the street, far away from him. He flung out his arms, 'I'm so damnably helpless,' he said, and then, to the picture, 'Perhaps it's not as bad as it sounds; perhaps it is just my sensitiveness.' In the half light of the drawing-room the smile seemed to deepen in Anna's portrait, and to become secret, even cruel. 'No,' he reflected, 'that smile is not at all her happiest expression – it was a mistake to let her have it taken smiling like that. She doesn't look like my wife – like the mother of my son.' Yes, that was it, she did not look like the mother of a son who was going to be a partner in the firm. The picture got on his nerves; he held it in different lights, looked at it from a distance, sideways, spent, it seemed to Andreas afterwards, a whole lifetime trying to fit it in. The more he played with it the deeper grew his dislike of it. Thrice he carried it over to the fireplace and decided to chuck it behind the Japanese umbrella in the grate; then he thought it absurd to waste an expensive frame. There was no good in beating about the bush. Anna looked like a stranger – abnormal, a freak – it might be a picture taken just before or after death.

Suddenly he realised that the wind had dropped, that the whole house was still, terribly still. Cold and pale, with a disgusting feeling that spiders were creeping up his spine and across his face, he stood in the centre of the drawing-room, hearing Doctor Erb's footsteps descending the stairs.

He saw Doctor Erb come into the room; the room seemed to change into a great glass bowl that spun round, and Doctor Erb seemed to swim through this glass bowl towards him, like a goldfish in a pearl-coloured waistcoat.

'My beloved wife has passed away!' He wanted to shout it out before the doctor spoke.

'Well, she's hooked a boy this time!' said Doctor Erb. Andreas staggered forward.

'Look out. Keep on your pins,' said Doctor Erb, catching Dinzer's arm, and murmuring, as he felt it, 'Flabby as butter.'

A glow spread all over Andreas. He was exultant.

'Well, by God! Nobody can accuse *me* of not knowing what suffering is,' he said.

The Child-Who-Was-Tired

She was just beginning to walk along a little white road with tall black trees on either side, a little road that led to nowhere, and where nobody walked at all, when a hand gripped her shoulder, shook her, slapped her ear.

'Oh, oh, don't stop me,' cried the Child-Who-Was-Tired. 'Let me go.'

'Get up, you good-for-nothing brat,' said a voice; 'get up and light the oven or I'll shake every bone out of your body.'

With an immense effort she opened her eyes, and saw the Frau standing by, the baby bundled under one arm. The three other children who shared the same bed with the Child-Who-Was-Tired, accustomed to brawls, slept on peacefully. In a corner of the room the Man was fastening his braces.

'What do you mean by sleeping like this the whole night through – like a sack of potatoes? You've let the baby wet his bed twice.'

She did not answer, but tied her petticoat string, and buttoned on her plaid frock with cold, shaking fingers.

'There, that's enough. Take the baby into the kitchen with you, and heat that cold coffee on the spirit lamp for the master, and give him the loaf of black bread out of the table drawer. Don't guzzle it yourself or I'll know.'

The Frau staggered across the room, flung herself on to her bed, drawing the pink bolster round her shoulders.

It was almost dark in the kitchen. She laid the baby on the wooden settle, covering him with a shawl, then poured the coffee from the earthenware jug into the saucepan, and set it on the spirit lamp to boil.

'I'm sleepy,' nodded the Child-Who-Was-Tired, kneeling on the floor and splitting the damp pine logs into little chips. 'That's why I'm not awake.'

The oven took a long time to light. Perhaps it was cold, like herself, and sleepy . . . Perhaps it had been dreaming of a little white road with black trees on either side, a little road that led to nowhere.

Then the door was pulled violently open and the Man strode in.

'Here, what are you doing, sitting on the floor?' he shouted. 'Give me my coffee. I've got to be off. Ugh! You haven't even washed over the table.'

She sprang to her feet, poured his coffee into an enamel cup, and gave him bread and a knife, then, taking a wash rag from the sink, smeared over the black linoleumed table.

'Swine of a day – swine's life,' mumbled the Man, sitting by the table and staring out of the window at the bruised sky, which seemed to bulge heavily over the dull land. He stuffed his mouth with bread and then swilled it down with the coffee.

The Child drew a pail of water, turned up her sleeves, frowning the while at her arms, as if to scold them for being so thin, so much like little stunted twigs, and began to mop over the floor.

'Stop sousing about the water while I'm here,' grumbled the Man. 'Stop the baby snivelling; it's been going on like that all night.'

The Child gathered the baby into her lap and sat rocking him.

'Ts – ts – ts,' she said. 'He's cutting his eye teeth, that's what makes him cry so. *And* dribble – I never seen a baby dribble like this one.' She wiped his mouth and nose with a corner of her skirt. 'Some babies get their teeth without you knowing it,' she went on, 'and some take on this way all the time. I once heard of a baby that died, and they found all its teeth in its stomach.'

The Man got up, unhooked his cloak from the back of the door, and flung it round him.

'There's another coming,' said he.

'What – a tooth!' exclaimed the Child, startled for the first time that morning out of her dreadful heaviness, and thrusting her finger into the baby's mouth.

'No,' he said grimly, 'another baby. Now, get on with your work; it's time the others got up for school.' She stood a moment quite silently, hearing his heavy steps on the stone passage, then the gravel walk, and finally the slam of the front gate.

'Another baby! Hasn't she finished having them *yet*?' thought the Child. 'Two babies getting eye teeth – two babies to get up for in the night – two babies to carry about and wash their little piggy clothes!' She looked with horror at the one in her arms, who, seeming to understand the contemptuous loathing of her tired glance, doubled his fists, stiffened his body, and began violently screaming.

'Ts – ts – ts.' She laid him on the settle and went back to her floor-washing. He never ceased crying for a moment, but she got quite used to it and kept time with her broom. Oh, how tired she was! Oh, the heavy broom handle and the burning spot just at the back of her neck that ached so, and a funny little fluttering feeling just at the back of her waistband, as though something were going to break.

The clock struck six. She set the pan of milk in the oven, and went into the next room to wake and dress the three children. Anton and Hans lay together in attitudes of mutual amity which certainly never existed out of their sleeping hours. Lena was curled up, her knees under her chin, only a straight, standing-up pigtail of hair showing above the bolster.

'Get up,' cried the Child, speaking in a voice of immense authority, pulling off the bedclothes and giving the boys sundry pokes and digs. 'I've been calling you this last half-hour. It's late, and I'll tell on you if you don't get dressed this minute.'

Anton awoke sufficiently to turn over and kick Hans on a tender part, whereupon Hans pulled Lena's pigtail until she shrieked for her mother.

'Oh, do be quiet,' whispered the Child. 'Oh, do get up and dress. You know what will happen. There – I'll help you.'

But the warning came too late. The Frau got out of bed, walked in a determined fashion into the kitchen, returning with a bundle of twigs in her hand fastened together with a strong cord. One by one she laid the children across her knee and severely beat them, expending a final burst of energy on the Child-Who-Was-Tired, then returned to bed, with a comfortable sense of her maternal duties in good working order for the day. Very subdued, the three allowed themselves to be dressed and washed by the Child, who even laced the boys' boots, having found through experience that if left to themselves they hopped about for at least five minutes to find a comfortable ledge for their foot, and then spat on their hands and broke the bootlaces.

While she gave them their breakfast they became uproarious, and the baby would not cease crying. When she filled the tin kettle with milk, tied on the rubber teat, and, first moistening it herself, tried with little coaxing words to make him drink, he threw the bottle on to the floor and trembled all over.

'Eye teeth!' shouted Hans, hitting Anton over the head with his empty cup; 'he's getting the evil-eye teeth, I should say.'

'Smarty!' retorted Lena, poking out her tongue at him, and then, when he promptly did the same, crying at the top of her voice, 'Mother, Hans is making faces at me!'

'That's right,' said Hans, 'go on howling, and when you're in bed tonight I'll wait till you're asleep, and then I'll creep over and take a little tiny piece of your arm and twist and twist it until – ' He leant over the table making the most horrible faces at Lena, not noticing that Anton was standing behind his chair until the little boy bent over and spat on his brother's shaven head.

'Oh, weh! Oh, weh!'

The Child-Who-Was-Tired pushed and pulled them apart, muffled them into their coats, and drove them out of the house.

'Hurry, hurry! the second bell's rung,' she urged, knowing perfectly well she was telling a story, and rather exulting in the fact. She washed up the breakfast things, then went down to the cellar to look out the potatoes and beetroot.

Such a funny, cold place the coal cellar! With potatoes banked on one corner, beetroot in an old candle box, two tubs of sauerkraut, and a twisted mass of dahlia roots – that looked as real as though they were fighting one another, thought the Child.

She gathered the potatoes into her skirt, choosing big ones with few eyes because they were easier to peel, and bending over the dull heap in the silent cellar, she began to nod.

'Here, you, what are you doing down there?' cried the Frau, from the top of the stairs. 'The baby's fallen off the settle, and got a bump as big as an egg over his eye. Come up here, and I'll teach you!'

'It wasn't me – it wasn't me!' screamed the Child, beaten from one side of the hall to the other, so that the potatoes and beetroot rolled out of her skirt.

The Frau seemed to be as big as a giant, and there was a certain heaviness in all her movements that was terrifying to anyone so small.

'Sit in the corner, and peel and wash the vegetables, and keep the baby quiet while I do the washing.'

Whimpering she obeyed, but as to keeping the baby quiet, that was impossible. His face was hot, little beads of sweat stood all over his head, and he stiffened his body and cried. She held him on her knees, with a pan of cold water beside her for the cleaned vegetables and the 'ducks' bucket' for the peelings.

'Ts – ts – ts!' she crooned, scraping and boring, 'there's going to be another soon, and you can't both keep on crying. Why don't you go to sleep, baby? I would, if I were you. I'll tell you a dream. Once upon a time there was a little white road – '

She shook back her head, a great lump ached in her throat and then the tears ran down her face on to the vegetables.

'That's no good,' said the Child, shaking them away. 'Just stop crying until I've finished this, baby, and I'll walk you up and down.'

But by that time she had to peg out the washing for the Frau. A wind had sprung up. Standing on tiptoe in the yard, she almost felt she would be blown away. There was a bad smell coming from the ducks' coop, which was half full of manure water, but away in the meadow she saw the grass blowing like little green hairs. And she remembered having heard of a child who had once played for a whole day in just such a meadow with real sausages and beer for her dinner – and not a little bit of tiredness. Who had told her that story? She could not remember, and yet it was so plain.

The wet clothes flapped in her face as she pegged them; danced and jigged on the line, bulged out and twisted. She walked back to the house with lagging steps, looking longingly at the grass in the meadow.

'What must I do now, please?' she said.

'Make the beds and hang the baby's mattress out of the window, then get the wagon and take him for a little walk along the road. In front of the house, mind – where I can see you. Don't stand there, gaping! Then come in when I call you and help me cut up the salad.'

When she had made the beds the Child stood and looked at them. Gently she stroked the pillow with her hand, and then, just for one moment, let her head rest there. Again the smarting lump in her throat, the stupid tears that fell and kept on falling as she dressed the baby and dragged the little wagon up and down the road.

A man passed, driving a bullock wagon. He wore a long, queer feather in his hat, and whistled as he passed. Two girls with bundles on their shoulders came walking out of the village – one wore a red handkerchief about her head and one a blue. They were laughing and holding each other by the hand. Then the sun pushed by a heavy fold of grey cloud and spread a warm yellow light over everything.

'Perhaps,' thought the Child-Who-Was-Tired, 'if I walked far enough up this road I might come to a little white one, with tall black trees on either side – a little road – '

'Salad, salad!' cried the Frau's voice from the house.

Soon the children came home from school, dinner was eaten, the Man took the Frau's share of pudding as well as his own, and the three children seemed to smear themselves all over with whatever they ate. Then more dish-washing and more cleaning and baby-minding. So the afternoon dragged coldly through.

Old Frau Grathwohl came in with a fresh piece of pig's flesh for the Frau, and the Child listened to them gossiping together.

'Frau Manda went on her "journey to Rome" last night, and brought back a daughter. How are you feeling?'

'I was sick twice this morning,' said the Frau. 'My insides are all twisted up with having children too quickly.'

'I see you've got a new help,' commented old Mother Grathwohl.

'Oh, dear Lord' – the Frau lowered her voice – 'don't you know her? She's the free-born one – daughter of the waitress at the railway station. They found her mother trying to squeeze her head in the wash-hand jug, and the child's half silly.'

'Ts – ts – ts!' whispered the 'free-born' one to the baby.

As the day drew in the Child-Who-Was-Tired did not know how to fight her sleepiness any longer. She was afraid to sit down or stand still. As she sat at supper the Man and the Frau seemed to swell to an immense size as she watched them, and then become smaller than dolls, with little voices that seemed to come from outside the window. Looking at the baby, it suddenly had two heads, and then no head. Even his crying made her feel worse. When she thought of the nearness of bedtime she shook all over with excited joy. But as eight o'clock approached there was the sound of wheels on the road, and presently in came a party of friends to spend the evening.

Then it was: 'Put on the coffee.' 'Bring me the sugar tin.' 'Carry the chairs out of the bedroom.' 'Set the table.'

And, finally, the Frau sent her into the next room to keep the baby quiet.

There was a little piece of candle burning in the enamel bracket. As she walked up and down she saw her great big shadow on the wall like a grown-up person with a grown-up baby. Whatever would it look like when she carried two babies so!

'Ts – ts – ts!' Once upon a time she was walking along a little white road, with oh! such great big black trees on either side.

'Here you!' called the Frau's voice, 'bring me my new jacket from behind the door.' And as she took it into the warm room one of the women said, 'She looks like an owl. Such children are seldom right in their heads.'

'Why don't you keep that baby quiet?' said the Man, who had just drunk enough beer to make him feel very brave and master of his house.

'If you don't keep that baby quiet you'll know why later on.'

They burst out laughing as she stumbled back into the bedroom.

'I don't believe Holy Mary could keep him quiet,' she murmured. 'Did Jesus cry like this when He was little? If I was not so tired perhaps I could do it; but the baby just knows that I want to go to sleep. And there is going to be another one.'

She flung the baby on the bed, and stood looking at him with terror.

From the next room there came the jingle of glasses and the warm sound of laughter.

And she suddenly had a beautiful marvellous idea.

She laughed for the first time that day, and clapped her hands.

'Ts – ts – ts!' she said, 'lie there, silly one; you *will* go to sleep. You'll not cry any more or wake up in the night. Funny, little, ugly baby.'

He opened his eyes, and shrieked loudly at the sight of the Child-Who-Was-Tired. From the next room she heard the Frau call out to her.

'One moment – he is almost asleep,' she cried.

And then gently, smiling, on tiptoe, she brought the pink bolster from the Frau's bed and covered the baby's face with it, pressed with all her might as he struggled, 'like a duck with its head off, wriggling', she thought.

She heaved a long sigh, then fell back on to the floor, and was walking along a little white road with tall black trees on either side, a little road that led to nowhere, and where nobody walked at all – nobody at all.

The Advanced Lady

'Do you think we might ask her to come with us,' said Fräulein Elsa, retying her pink sash ribbon before my mirror. 'You know, although she is so intellectual, I cannot help feeling convinced that she has some secret sorrow. And Lisa told me this morning, as she was turning out my room, that she remains hours and hours by herself, writing; in fact Lisa says she is writing a book! I suppose that is why she never cares to mingle with us, and has so little time for her husband and the child.'

'Well, *you* ask her,' said I. 'I have never spoken to the lady.'

Elsa blushed faintly. 'I have only spoken to her once,' she confessed. 'I took her a bunch of wild flowers, to her room, and she came to the door in a white gown, with her hair loose. Never shall I forget that moment. She just took the flowers, and I heard her – because the door was not quite properly shut – I heard her, as I walked down the passage, saying "Purity, fragrance, the fragrance of purity and the purity of fragrance!" It was wonderful!'

At that moment Frau Kellermann knocked at the door.

'Are you ready?' she said, coming into the room and nodding to us very genially. 'The gentlemen are waiting on the steps, and I have asked the Advanced Lady to come with us.'

'Na, how extraordinary!' cried Elsa. 'But this moment the *gnadige Frau* and I were debating whether – '

'Yes, I met her coming out of her room and she said she was charmed with the idea. Like all of us, she has never been to Schlingen. She is downstairs now, talking to Herr Erchardt. I think we shall have a delightful afternoon.'

'Is Fritzi waiting too?' asked Elsa.

'Of course he is, dear child – as impatient as a hungry man listening for the dinner bell. Run along!'

Elsa ran, and Frau Kellermann smiled at me significantly. In the past she and I had seldom spoken to each other, owing to the fact that her 'one remaining joy' – her charming little Karl – had never succeeded in kindling into flame those sparks of maternity which are supposed to glow in great numbers upon the altar of every respectable female heart; but, in view of a premeditated journey together, we became delightfully cordial.

'For us,' she said, 'there will be a double joy. We shall be able to watch the happiness of these two dear children, Elsa and Fritz. They only received the letters of blessing from their parents yesterday morning. It is a very strange thing, but whenever I am in the company of newly-engaged couples I blossom. Newly-engaged couples, mothers with first babies, and normal deathbeds have precisely the same effect on me. Shall we join the others?'

I was longing to ask her why normal deathbeds should cause anyone to burst into flower, and said, 'Yes, do let us.'

We were greeted by the little party of 'cure guests' on the pension steps, with those cries of joy and excitement which herald so pleasantly the mildest German excursion. Herr Erchardt and I had not met before that day, so, in accordance with strict pension custom, we asked each other how long we had slept during the night, had we dreamed agreeably, what time we had got up, was the coffee fresh when we had appeared at breakfast, and how had we passed the morning. Having toiled up these stairs of almost national politeness we landed, triumphant and smiling, and paused to recover breath.

'And now,' said Herr Erchardt, 'I have a pleasure in store for you. The Frau Professor is going to be one of us for the afternoon. Yes,' nodding graciously to the Advanced Lady. 'Allow me to introduce you to each other.'

We bowed very formally, and looked each other over with that eye which is known as 'eagle' but is far more the property of the female than that most unoffending of birds. 'I think you are English?' she said. I acknowledged the fact. 'I am reading a great many English books just now – rather, I am studying them.'

'*Nu*,' cried Herr Erchardt. 'Fancy that! What a bond already! I have made up my mind to know Shakespeare in his mother tongue before I die, but that you, Frau Professor, should be already immersed in those wells of English thought!'

'From what I have read,' she said, 'I do not think they are very deep wells.'

He nodded sympathetically.

'No,' he answered, 'so I have heard . . . But do not let us embitter our excursion for our little English friend. We will speak of this another time.'

'*Nu*, are we ready?' cried Fritz, who stood, supporting Elsa's elbow in his hand, at the foot of the steps. It was immediately discovered that Karl was lost.

'Ka – rl, Karl – chen!' we cried. No response.

'But he was here one moment ago,' said Herr Langen, a tired, pale youth, who was recovering from a nervous breakdown due to much philosophy and little nourishment. 'He was sitting here, picking out the works of his watch with a hairpin!'

Frau Kellermann rounded on him. 'Do you mean to say, my dear Herr Langen, you did not stop the child!'

'No,' said Herr Langen, 'I've tried stopping him before now.'

'Da, that child has such energy; never is his brain at peace. If he is not doing one thing, he is doing another!'

'Perhaps he has started on the dining-room clock now,' suggested Herr Langen, abominably hopeful.

The Advanced Lady suggested that we should go without him. 'I never take my little daughter for walks,' she said. 'I have accustomed her to sitting quietly in my bedroom from the time I go out until I return!'

'There he is – there he is,' piped Elsa, and Karl was observed slithering down a chestnut tree, very much the worse for twigs.

'I've been listening to what you said about me, mumma,' he confessed while Frau Kellermann brushed him down. 'It was not true about the watch. I was only looking at it, and the little girl never stays in the bedroom. She told me herself she always goes down to the kitchen, and – '

'Da, that's enough!' said Frau Kellermann.

We marched *en masse* along the station road. It was a very warm afternoon, and continuous parties of 'cure guests', who were giving their digestions a quiet airing in pension gardens, called after us, asked if we were going for a walk, and cried '*Herr Gott* – happy journey' with immense ill-concealed relish when we mentioned Schlingen.

'But that is eight kilometres,' shouted one old man with a white beard, who leaned against a fence, fanning himself with a yellow handkerchief.

'Seven and a half,' answered Herr Erchardt shortly.

'Eight,' bellowed the sage.

'Seven and a half!'

'Eight!'

'The man is mad,' said Herr Erchardt.

'Well, please let him be mad in peace,' said I, putting my hands over my ears.

'Such ignorance must not be allowed to go uncontradicted,' said he, and turning his back on us, too exhausted to cry out any longer, he held up seven and a half fingers.

'Eight!' thundered the greybeard, with pristine freshness.

We felt very sobered, and did not recover until we reached a white signpost which entreated us to leave the road and walk through the field path – without trampling down more of the grass than was necessary. Being interpreted, it meant 'single file', which was distressing for Elsa and Fritz. Karl, like a happy child, gambolled ahead, and cut down as many flowers as possible with the stick of his mother's parasol – followed the three others – then myself – and the lovers in the rear. And above the conversation of the advance party I had the privilege of hearing these delicious whispers.

Fritz: 'Do you love me?' Elsa: '*Nu* – yes.' Fritz passionately: 'But how much?' To which Elsa never replied – except with 'How much do *you* love *me*?'

Fritz escaped that truly Christian trap by saying, 'I asked you first.'

It grew so confusing that I slipped in front of Frau Kellermann – and walked in the peaceful knowledge that she was blossoming and I was under no obligation to inform even my nearest and dearest as to the precise capacity of my affections. 'What right have they to ask each other such questions the day after letters of blessing have been received?' I reflected. 'What right have they even to question each other? Love which becomes engaged and married is a purely affirmative affair – they are usurping the privileges of their betters and wisers!'

The edges of the field frilled over into an immense pine forest – very pleasant and cool it looked. Another signpost begged us to keep to the broad path for Schlingen and deposit waste paper and fruit peelings in wire receptacles attached to the benches for the purpose. We sat down on the first bench, and Karl with great curiosity explored the wire receptacle.

'I love woods,' said the Advanced Lady, smiling pitifully into the air. 'In a wood my hair already seems to stir and remember something of its savage origin.'

'But speaking literally,' said Frau Kellermann, after an appreciative pause, 'there is really nothing better than the air of pine trees for the scalp.'

'Oh, Frau Kellermann, please don't break the spell,' said Elsa.

The Advanced Lady looked at her very sympathetically. 'Have you, too, found the magic heart of Nature?' she said.

That was Herr Langen's cue. 'Nature has no heart,' said he, very bitterly and readily, as people do who are over-philosophised and underfed. 'She creates that she may destroy. She eats that she may spew up and she spews up that she may eat. That is why we, who are forced to eke out an existence at her trampling feet, consider the world mad, and realise the deadly vulgarity of production.'

'Young man,' interrupted Herr Erchardt, 'you have never lived and you have never suffered!'

'Oh, excuse me – how can you know?'

'I know because you have told me, and there's an end of it. Come back to this bench in ten years' time and repeat those words to me,' said Frau Kellermann, with an eye upon Fritz, who was engaged in counting Elsa's fingers with passionate fervour – 'and bring with you your young wife, Herr Langen, and watch, perhaps, your little child playing with – ' She turned towards Karl, who had rooted an old illustrated paper out of the receptacle and was spelling over an advertisement for the enlargement of Beautiful Breasts.

The sentence remained unfinished. We decided to move on. As we plunged more deeply into the wood our spirits rose – reaching a point where they burst into song – on the part of the three men – '*O Welt, wie bist du wunderbar!*' – the lower part of which was piercingly sustained by Herr Langen, who attempted quite unsuccessfully to infuse satire into it in accordance with his – 'world outlook'. They strode ahead and left us to trail after them – hot and happy.

'Now is the opportunity,' said Frau Kellermann. 'Dear Frau Professor, do tell us a little about your book.'

'Ach, how did you know I was writing one?' she cried playfully.

'Elsa, here, had it from Lisa. And never before have I personally known a woman who was writing a book. How do you manage to find enough to write down?'

'That is never the trouble,' said the Advanced Lady – she took Elsa's arm and leaned on it gently. 'The trouble is to know where to stop. My brain has been a hive for years, and about three months ago the pent-up waters burst over my soul, and since then I am writing all day until late into the night, still ever finding fresh inspirations and thoughts which beat impatient wings about my heart.'

'Is it a novel?' asked Elsa shyly.

'Of course it is a novel,' said I.

'How can you be so positive?' said Frau Kellermann, eyeing me severely.

'Because nothing but a novel could produce an effect like that.'

'Ach, don't quarrel,' said the Advanced Lady sweetly. 'Yes, it is a novel – upon the Modern Woman. For this seems to me the woman's hour. It is mysterious and almost prophetic, it is the symbol of the true advanced woman: not one of those violent creatures who deny their sex and smother their frail wings under . . . under – '

'The English tailor-made?' from Frau Kellermann.

'I was not going to put it like that. Rather, under the lying garb of false masculinity!'

'Such a subtle distinction!' I murmured.

'Whom then,' asked Fräulein Elsa, looking adoringly at the Advanced Lady – 'whom then do you consider the true woman?'

'She is the incarnation of comprehending Love!'

'But my dear Frau Professor,' protested Frau Kellermann, 'you must remember that one has so few opportunities for exhibiting Love within the family circle nowadays. One's husband is at business all day, and naturally desires to sleep when he returns home – one's children are out of the lap and in at the university before one can lavish anything at all upon them!'

'But Love is not a question of lavishing,' said the Advanced Lady. 'It is the lamp carried in the bosom touching with serene rays all the heights and depths of – '

'Darkest Africa,' I murmured flippantly.

She did not hear.

'The mistake we have made in the past – as a sex,' said she, 'is in not realising that our gifts of giving are for the whole world – we are the glad sacrifice of ourselves!'

'Oh!' cried Elsa rapturously, and almost bursting into gifts as she breathed – 'how I know that! You know ever since Fritz and I have been engaged, I share the desire to give to everybody, to share everything!'

'How extremely dangerous,' said I.

'It is only the beauty of danger, or the danger of beauty' said the Advanced Lady – 'and there you have the ideal of my book – that woman is nothing but a gift.'

I smiled at her very sweetly. 'Do you know,' I said, 'I, too, would like to write a book, on the advisability of caring for daughters, and taking them for airings and keeping them out of kitchens!'

I think the masculine element must have felt these angry vibrations: they ceased from singing, and together we climbed out of the wood, to see Schlingen below us, tucked in a circle of hills, the white houses shining in the sunlight, 'for all the world like eggs in a bird's nest', as Herr Erchardt declared. We descended upon Schlingen and demanded sour milk with fresh cream and bread at the Inn of the Golden Stag, a most friendly place, with tables in a rose-garden where hens and chickens ran riot – even flopping upon the disused tables and pecking at the red checks on the cloths. We broke the bread into the bowls, added the cream, and stirred it round with flat wooden spoons, the landlord and his wife standing by.

'Splendid weather!' said Herr Erchardt, waving his spoon at the landlord, who shrugged his shoulders.

'What! You don't call it splendid!'

'As you please,' said the landlord, obviously scorning us.

'Such a beautiful walk,' said Fräulein Elsa, making a free gift of her most charming smile to the landlady.

'I never walk,' said the landlady; 'when I go to Mindelbau my man drives me – I've more important things to do with my legs than walk them through the dust!'

'I like these people,' confessed Herr Langen to me. 'I like them very, very much. I think I shall take a room here for the whole summer.'

'Why?'

'Oh, because they live close to the earth, and therefore despise it.'

He pushed away his bowl of sour milk and lit a cigarette. We ate, solidly and seriously, until those seven and a half kilometres to Mindelbau stretched before us like an eternity. Even Karl's activity became so full fed that he lay on the ground and removed his leather waistbelt. Elsa suddenly leaned over to Fritz and whispered, who on hearing her to the end and asking her if she loved him, got up and made a little speech.

'We – we wish to celebrate our betrothal by – by – asking you all to drive back with us in the landlord's cart – if – it will hold us!'

'Oh, what a beautiful, noble idea!' said Frau Kellermann, heaving a sigh of relief that audibly burst two hooks.

'It is my little gift,' said Elsa to the Advanced Lady, who by virtue of three portions almost wept tears of gratitude.

Squeezed into the peasant cart and driven by the landlord, who showed his contempt for mother earth by spitting savagely every now and again, we jolted home again, and the nearer we came to Mindelbau the more we loved it and one another.

'We must have many excursions like this,' said Herr Erchardt to me, 'for one surely gets to know a person in the simple surroundings of the open air – one *shares* the same joys – one feels friendship. What is it your Shakespeare says? One moment, I have it. "The friends thou hast, and their adoption tried – grapple them to thy soul with hoops of steel!" '

'But,' said I, feeling very friendly towards him, 'the bother about my soul is that it refuses to grapple anybody at all – and I am sure that the dead weight of a friend whose adoption it had tried would kill it immediately. Never yet has it shown the slightest sign of a hoop!'

He bumped against my knees and excused himself and the cart.

'My dear little lady, you must not take the quotation literally. Naturally, one is not physically conscious of the hoops; but hoops there are in the soul of him or her who loves his fellow-men . . . Take this afternoon, for instance. How did we start out? As strangers you might almost say, and yet – all of us – how have we come home?'

'In a cart,' said the only remaining joy, who sat upon his mother's lap and felt sick.

We skirted the field that we had passed through, going round by the cemetery. Herr Langen leaned over the edge of the seat and greeted the graves. He was sitting next to the Advanced Lady – inside the shelter of her shoulder. I heard her murmur: 'You look like a little boy with your hair blowing about in the wind.' Herr Langen, slightly less bitter – watched the last graves disappear. And I heard her murmur: 'Why are you so sad? I too am very sad sometimes – but – you look young enough for me to dare to say this – I – too – know of much joy!'

'What do you know?' said he.

I leaned over and touched the Advanced Lady's hand. 'Hasn't it been a nice afternoon?' I said questioningly. 'But you know, that theory of yours about women and Love – it's as old as the hills – oh, older!'

From the road a sudden shout of triumph. Yes, there he was again – white beard, silk handkerchief and undaunted enthusiasm.

'What did I say? Eight kilometres – it is!'

'Seven and a half!' shrieked Herr Erchardt.

'Why, then, do you return in carts? Eight kilometres it must be.'

Herr Erchardt made a cup of his hands and stood up in the jolting cart while Frau Kellermann clung to his knees. 'Seven and a half!'

'Ignorance must not go uncontradicted!' I said to the Advanced Lady.

The Swing of the Pendulum

THE LANDLADY knocked at the door.

'Come in,' said Viola.

'There is a letter for you,' said the landlady, 'a special letter' – she held the green envelope in a corner of her dingy apron.

'Thanks.' Viola, kneeling on the floor, poking at the little dusty stove, stretched out her hand. 'Any answer?'

'No; the messenger has gone.'

'Oh, all right!' She did not look the landlady in the face; she was ashamed of not having paid her rent, and wondered grimly, without any hope, if the woman would begin to bluster again.

'About this money owing to me – ' said the landlady.

'Oh, the Lord – off she goes!' thought Viola, turning her back on the woman and making a grimace at the stove.

'It's settle – or it's go!' The landlady raised her voice; she began to bawl. 'I'm a landlady, I am, and a respectable woman, I'll have you know. I'll have no lice in my house, sneaking their way into the furniture and eating up everything. It's cash – or out you go before twelve o'clock tomorrow.'

Viola felt rather than saw the woman's gesture. She shot out her arm in a stupid helpless way, as though a dirty pigeon had suddenly flown at her face. 'Filthy old beast! Ugh! And the smell of her – like stale cheese and damp washing.'

'Very well!' she answered shortly; 'it's cash down or I leave tomorrow. All right: don't shout.'

It was extraordinary – always before this woman came near her she trembled in her shoes – even the sound of those flat feet stumping up the stairs made her feel sick, but once they were face to face she felt immensely calm and indifferent, and could not understand why she even worried about money, nor why she sneaked out of the house on tiptoe, not even daring to shut the door after her in case the landlady should hear and shout something terrible, nor why she spent nights pacing up and down her room – drawing up sharply before the mirror and saying to a tragic reflection: 'Money, money, money!' When she was alone her poverty was like a huge dream-mountain on which her feet were fast rooted – aching with the ache of the size of the thing – but if it came to definite action, with no time for imaginings, her dream-mountain dwindled into a beastly 'hold-your-nose' affair, to be passed as quickly as possible, with anger and a strong sense of superiority.

The landlady bounced out of the room, banging the door, so that it shook and rattled as though it had listened to the conversation and fully sympathised with the old hag.

Squatting on her heels, Viola opened the letter. It was from Casimir.

I shall be with you at three o'clock this afternoon – and must be off again this evening. All news when we meet. I hope you are happier than I. – CASIMIR.

'Huh! how kind!' she sneered; 'how condescending. Too good of you, really!' She sprang to her feet, crumbling the letter in her hands. 'And how are you to know that I shall stick here awaiting your pleasure until three o'clock this afternoon?' But she knew she would; her rage was only half sincere. She longed to see Casimir, for she was confident that this time she would make him understand the situation . . . 'For, as it is, it's intolerable – intolerable!' she muttered.

It was ten o'clock in the morning of a grey day curiously lighted by pale flashes of sunshine. Searched by these flashes her room looked tumbled and grimed. She pulled down the window-blinds – but they gave a persistent, whitish glare which was just as bad. The only thing of life in the room was a jar of hyacinths given her by the landlady's daughter: it stood on the table exuding a sickly perfume from its plump petals; there were even rich buds unfolding, and the leaves shone like oil.

Viola went over to the washstand, poured some water into the enamel basin, and sponged her face and neck. She dipped her face into the water, opened her eyes, and shook her head from side to side – it was exhilarating. She did it three times. 'I suppose I could drown myself if I stayed under long enough,' she thought. 'I wonder how long it takes to become unconscious? . . . Often read of women drowning in a bucket. I wonder if any air enters by the ears – if the basin would have to be as deep as a bucket?' She experimented – gripped the washstand with both hands and slowly sank her head into the water, when again there was a knock on the door. Not the landlady this time – it must be Casimir. With her face and hair dripping, with her petticoat bodice unbuttoned, she ran and opened it.

A strange man stood against the lintel – seeing her, he opened his eyes very wide and smiled delightfully. 'Excuse me – does Fräulein Schafer live here?'

'No; never heard of her.' His smile was so infectious, she wanted to smile too – and the water had made her feel so fresh and rosy.

The strange man appeared overwhelmed with astonishment. 'She doesn't?' he cried. 'She is out, you mean!'

'No, she's not living here,' answered Viola.

'But – pardon – one moment.' He moved from the door lintel, standing squarely in front of her. He unbuttoned his greatcoat and drew a slip of paper from the breast pocket, smoothing it in his gloved fingers before handing it to her.

'Yes, that's the address, right enough, but there must be a mistake in the number. So many lodging-houses in this street, you know, and so big.'

Drops of water fell from her hair on to the paper. She burst out laughing. 'Oh, *how* dreadful I must look – one moment!' She ran back to the washstand and caught up a towel. The door was still open . . . After all, there was nothing more to be said. Why on earth had she asked him to wait a moment? She folded the towel round her shoulders, and returned to the door, suddenly grave. 'I'm sorry; I know no such name' in a sharp voice.

Said the strange man: 'Sorry, too. Have you been living here long?'

'Er – yes – a long time.' She began to close the door slowly.

'Well – good morning, thanks so much. Hope I haven't been a bother.'

'Good morning.'

She heard him walk down the passage and then pause – lighting a cigarette. Yes – a faint scent of delicious cigarette smoke penetrated her room. She sniffed at it, smiling again. Well, that had been a fascinating interlude! He looked so amazingly happy: his heavy clothes and big buttoned gloves; his beautifully brushed hair . . . and that smile . . . 'Jolly' was the word – just a well-fed boy with the world for his playground. People like that did one good – one felt 'made over' at the sight of them. *Sane* they were – so sane and solid. You could depend on them never having one mad impulse from the day they were born until the day they died. And Life was in league with them – jumped them on her knee – quite rightly, too. At that moment she noticed Casimir's letter, crumpled up on the floor – the smile faded. Staring at the letter she began braiding her hair – a dull feeling of rage crept through her – she seemed to be braiding it into her brain, and binding it, tightly, above her head . . . Of course that had been the mistake all along. What had? Oh, Casimir's frightful seriousness. If she had been happy when they first met she never would have looked at him – but they had been like two patients in the same hospital ward – each finding comfort in the sickness of the other – sweet foundation for a love episode! Misfortune had knocked their heads together: they had looked at each other, stunned with the conflict and sympathised . . . 'I wish I could step outside the whole affair and just judge it – then I'd find a way out. I certainly was in love with Casimir . . . Oh, be sincere for once.' She flopped down on the bed and hid her face in the pillow. 'I was not in love. I wanted somebody to look after me – and keep me until my work began to sell – and he kept bothers with other men away. And what would have happened if he hadn't come along? I would have spent my wretched little pittance, and then – Yes, that was what decided me, thinking about that "then". He was the only solution. And I believed in him then. I thought his work had only to be recognised once, and he'd roll in wealth. I thought perhaps we might be poor for a month – but he said, if only he could have me, the stimulus . . . Funny, if it wasn't so damned tragic! Exactly the contrary has happened – he hasn't had a thing published for months – neither have I – but then I didn't expect to. Yes, the truth is, I'm hard and bitter, and I have neither faith nor love for unsuccessful men. I always end by despising them as I despise Casimir. I suppose it's the savage pride of the female who likes to think the man to whom she has given herself must be a very great chief indeed. But to stew in this disgusting house while Casimir scours the land in the hope of finding one editorial open door – it's humiliating. It's changed my whole nature. I wasn't born for poverty – I only flower among really jolly people, and people who never are worried.'

The figure of the strange man rose before her – would not be dismissed. 'That was the man for me, after all is said and done – a man without a care – who'd give me everything I want and with whom I'd always feel that sense of life and of being in touch with the world. I never wanted to fight – it was thrust on me. Really, there's a fount of happiness in me that is drying up, little by little, in this hateful existence. I'll be dead if this goes on – and' – she stirred in the bed and flung out her arms – 'I want passion, and love, and adventure – I yearn for them. Why should I stay here and rot? – I am rotting!' she cried, comforting herself with the sound of her breaking voice. 'But if I tell Casimir all this when he comes this afternoon, and he says, "Go" – as he certainly will – that's another thing I loathe about him – he's under my thumb – what should I do then – where should I go to?' There was nowhere. 'I don't want to work – or carve out my own path. I want ease and any amount of nursing in the lap of luxury. There is only one thing I'm fitted for, and that is to be a great courtesan.' But she did not know how to go about it. She was frightened to go into the streets – she heard of such awful things happening to those women – men with diseases – or men who didn't pay – besides, the idea of a strange man every night – no, that was out of the question. 'If I'd the clothes I would go to a really good hotel and find some wealthy man . . . like the strange man this morning. He would be ideal. Oh, if I only had his address – I am sure I would fascinate him. I'd keep him laughing all day – I'd make him give me unlimited money . . . ' At the thought she grew warm and soft. She began to dream of a wonderful house, and of presses full of clothes and of perfumes. She saw herself stepping into carriages – looking at the strange man with a mysterious, voluptuous glance – she practised the glance, lying on the bed – and never another worry, just drugged with happiness. That was the life for her. Well, the thing to do was to let Casimir go on his wild-goose chase that evening, and while he was away – What! Also – please to remember – there was the rent to be paid before twelve next morning, and she hadn't the money for a square meal. At the thought of food she felt a sharp twinge in her stomach, a sensation as though there were a hand in her stomach, squeezing it dry. She was terribly hungry – all Casimir's fault – and that man had lived on the fat of the land ever since he was born. He looked as though he could order a magnificent dinner. Oh, why hadn't she played her cards better? – he'd been sent by Providence – and she'd snubbed him. 'If I had that time over again, I'd be safe by now.' And instead of the ordinary man who had spoken with her at the door her mind created a brilliant, laughing image, who would treat her like a queen . . . 'There's only one thing I could not stand – that he should be coarse or vulgar. Well, he wasn't – he was obviously a man of the world, and the way he apologised . . . I have enough faith in my own power and beauty to know I could make a man treat me just as I wanted to be treated.' . . . It floated into her dreams – that sweet scent of cigarette smoke. And then she remembered that she had heard nobody go down the stone stairs. Was it possible that the strange man was still there? . . . The thought was too absurd – Life didn't play tricks like that – and yet – she was quite conscious of his nearness. Very quietly she got up, unhooked from the back of the door a long white gown, buttoned it on – smiling slyly. She did not know what was going to happen. She only thought: 'Oh, what fun!' and that they were playing a delicious game – this strange man and she. Very gently she turned the door-handle, screwing up her face and biting her lip as the lock snapped back. Of course, there he was – leaning against the banister rail. He wheeled round as she slipped into the passage.

'*Da*,' she muttered, folding her gown tightly around her, 'I must go downstairs and fetch some wood. Brr! The cold!'

'There isn't any wood,' volunteered the strange man. She gave a little cry of astonishment, and then tossed her head.

'You again,' she said scornfully, conscious the while of his merry eye, and the fresh, strong smell of his healthy body.

'The landlady shouted out there was no wood left. I just saw her go out to buy some.'

'Story – story!' she longed to cry. He came quite close to her, stood over her and whispered: 'Aren't you going to ask me to finish my cigarette in your room?'

She nodded. 'You may if you want to!'

In that moment together in the passage a miracle had happened. Her room was quite changed – it was full of sweet light and the scent of hyacinth flowers. Even the furniture appeared different – exciting. Quick as a flash she remembered childish parties when they had played charades, and one side had left the room and come in again to act a word – just what she was doing now. The strange man went over to the stove and sat down in her armchair. She did not want him to talk or come near her – it was enough to see him in the room, so secure and happy. How hungry she had been for the nearness of someone like that – who knew nothing at all about her – and made no demands – but just lived. Viola ran over to the table and put her arms round the jar of hyacinths.

'Beautiful! Beautiful!' she cried – burying her head in the flowers – and sniffing greedily at the scent. Over the leaves she looked at the man and laughed.

'You are a funny little thing,' said he lazily.

'Why? Because I love flowers?'

'I'd far rather you loved other things,' said the strange man slowly. She broke off a little pink petal and smiled at it.

'Let me send you some flowers,' said the strange man. 'I'll send you a roomful if you'd like them.'

His voice frightened her slightly. 'Oh no, thanks – this one is quite enough for me.'

'No, it isn't' – in a teasing voice.

'What a stupid remark!' thought Viola, and looking at him again he did not seem quite so jolly. She noticed that his eyes were set too closely together – and they were too small. Horrible thought, that he should prove stupid.

'What do you do all day?' she asked hastily.

'Nothing.'

'Nothing at all?'

'Why should I do anything?'

'Oh, don't imagine for one moment that I condemn such wisdom – only it sounds too good to be true!'

'What's that?' – he craned forward. 'What sounds too good to be true?' Yes – there was no denying it – he looked silly.

'I suppose the searching after Fräulein Schafer doesn't occupy all your days.'

'Oh no' – he smiled broadly – 'that's very good! By Jove! no. I drive a good bit – are you keen on horses?'

She nodded. 'Love them.'

'You must come driving with me – I've got a fine pair of greys. Will you?'

'Pretty I'd look perched behind greys in my one and only hat,' thought she. Aloud: 'I'd love to.' Her easy acceptance pleased him.

'How about tomorrow?' he suggested. 'Suppose you have lunch with me tomorrow and I take you driving.'

After all – this was just a game. 'Yes, I'm not busy tomorrow,' she said.

A little pause – then the strange man patted his leg. 'Why don't you come and sit down?' he said.

She pretended not to see and swung on to the table. 'Oh, I'm all right here.'

'No, you're not' – again the teasing voice. 'Come and sit on my knee.'

'Oh no,' said Viola very heartily, suddenly busy with her hair.

'Why not?'

'I don't want to.'

'Oh, come along' – impatiently.

She shook her head from side to side. 'I wouldn't dream of such a thing.'

At that he got up and came over to her. 'Funny little puss cat!' He put up one hand to touch her hair.

'Don't,' she said – and slipped off the table. 'I – I think it's time you went now.' She was quite frightened now – thinking only: 'This man must be got rid of as quickly as possible.'

'Oh, but you don't want me to go?'

'Yes, I do – I'm very busy.'

'Busy. What does the pussy cat do all day?'

'Lots and lots of things!' She wanted to push him out of the room and slam the door on him – idiot – fool – cruel disappointment.

'What's she frowning for?' he asked. 'Is she worried about anything?' Suddenly serious: 'I say – you know, are you in any financial difficulty? Do you want money? I'll give it to you if you like!'

'Money! Steady on the brake – don't lose your head!' – so she spoke to herself.

'I'll give you two hundred marks if you'll kiss me.'

'Oh, boo! What a condition! And I don't want to kiss you – I don't like kissing. Please go!'

'Yes – you do! – yes, you do.' He caught hold of her arms above the elbows. She struggled, and was quite amazed to realise how angry she felt.

'Let me go – immediately!' she cried – and he slipped one arm round her body, and drew her towards him – like a bar of iron across her back – that arm.

'Leave me alone! I tell you. Don't be mean! I didn't want this to happen when you came into my room. How dare you?'

'Well, kiss me and I'll go!'

It was too idiotic – dodging that stupid, smiling face.

'I won't kiss you! – you brute! – I won't!' Somehow she slipped out of his arms and ran to the wall – stood back against it – breathing quickly.

'Get out!' she stammered. 'Go on now, clear out!'

At that moment, when he was not touching her, she quite enjoyed herself. She thrilled at her own angry voice. 'To think I should talk to a man like that!' An angry flush spread over his face – his lips curled back, showing his teeth – just like a dog, thought Viola. He made a rush at her, and held her against the wall – pressed upon her with all the weight of his body. This time she could not get free.

'I won't kiss you. I won't. Stop doing that! Ugh! you're like a dog – you ought to find lovers round lamp-posts – you beast – you fiend!'

He did not answer. With an expression of the most absurd determination he pressed ever more heavily upon her. He did not even look at her – but rapped out in a sharp voice: 'Keep quiet – keep quiet.'

'Gar – r! Why are men so strong?' She began to cry. 'Go away – I don't want you, you dirty creature. I want to murder you. Oh, my God! if I had a knife.'

'Don't be silly – come and be good!' He dragged her towards the bed.

'Do you suppose I'm a light woman?' she snarled, and swooping over she fastened her teeth in his glove.

'*Ach*! don't do that – you are hurting me!'

She did not let go, but her heart said, 'Thank the Lord I thought of this.'

'Stop this minute – you vixen – you bitch.' He threw her away from him. She saw with joy that his eyes were full of tears. 'You've really hurt me,' he said in a choking voice.

'Of course I have. I meant to. That's nothing to what I'll do if you touch me again.'

The strange man picked up his hat. 'No thanks,' he said grimly. 'But I'll not forget this – I'll go to your landlady.'

'Pooh!' She shrugged her shoulders and laughed. 'I'll tell her you forced your way in here and tried to assault me. Who will she believe? – with your bitten hand. You go and find your Schafers.'

A sensation of glorious, intoxicating happiness flooded Viola. She rolled her eyes at him. 'If you don't go away this moment I'll bite you again,' she said, and the absurd words started her laughing. Even when the door was closed, hearing him descending the stairs, she laughed, and danced about the room.

What a morning! Oh, chalk it up. That was her first fight, and she'd won – she'd conquered that beast – all by herself. Her hands were still trembling. She pulled up the sleeve of her gown – great red marks on her arms. 'My ribs will be blue. I'll be blue all over,' she reflected. 'If only that beloved Casimir could have seen us.' And the feeling of rage and disgust against Casimir had totally disappeared. How could the poor darling help not having any money? It was her fault as much as his, and he, just like her, was apart from the world,

fighting it, just as she had done. If only three o'clock would come.
She saw herself running towards him and putting her arms round his
neck. 'My blessed one! Of course we are bound to win. Do you love
me still? Oh, I have been horrible lately.'

A Blaze

'MAX, YOU SILLY DEVIL, you'll break your neck if you go careering down the slide that way. Drop it, and come to the Club House with me and get some coffee.'

'I've had enough for today. I'm damp all through. There, give us a cigarette, Victor, old man. When are you going home?'

'Not for another hour. It's fine this afternoon, and I'm getting into decent shape. Look out, get off the track; here comes Fräulein Winkel. Damned elegant the way she manages her sleigh!'

'I'm cold all through. That's the worst of this place – the mists – it's a damp cold. Here, Forman, look after this sleigh – and stick it somewhere so that I can get it without looking through a hundred and fifty others tomorrow morning.'

They sat down at a small round table near the stove and ordered coffee. Victor sprawled in his chair, patting his little brown dog Bobo and looking, half laughingly, at Max.

'What's the matter, my dear? Isn't the world being nice and pretty?'

'I want my coffee, and I want to put my feet into my pocket – they're like stones . . . Nothing to eat, thanks – the cake is like underdone india-rubber here.'

Fuchs and Wistuba came and sat at their table. Max half turned his back and stretched his feet out to the oven. The three other men all began talking at once – of the weather – of the record slide – of the fine condition of the Wald See for skating.

Suddenly Fuchs looked at Max, raised his eyebrows and nodded across to Victor, who shook his head.

'Baby doesn't feel well,' he said, feeding the brown dog with broken lumps of sugar, 'and nobody's to disturb him – I'm nurse.'

'That's the first time I've ever known him off colour,' said Wistuba. 'I've always imagined he had the better part of this world that could not be taken away from him. I think he says his prayers to the dear Lord for having spared him being taken home in seven basketsful tonight. It's a fool's game to risk your all that way and leave the nation desolate.'

'Dry up,' said Max. 'You ought to be wheeled about on the snow in a perambulator.'

'Oh, no offence, I hope. Don't get nasty. How's your wife, Victor?'

'She's not at all well. She hurt her head coming down the slide with Max on Sunday. I told her to stay at home all day.'

'I'm sorry. Are you other fellows going back to the town or stopping on here?'

Fuchs and Victor said they were stopping – Max did not answer, but sat motionless while the men paid for their coffee and moved away. Victor came back a moment and put a hand on his shoulder.

'If you're going right back, my dear, I wish you'd look Elsa up and tell her I won't be in till late. And feed with us tonight at Limpold, will you? And take some hot grog when you get in.'

'Thanks, old fellow, I'm all right. Going back now.'

He rose, stretched himself, buttoned on his heavy coat and lighted another cigarette.

From the door Victor watched him plunging through the heavy snow – head bent – hands thrust in his pockets – he almost appeared to be running through the heavy snow towards the town.

*   *   *

Someone came stamping up the stairs – paused at the door of her sitting- room, and knocked.

'Is that you, Victor?' she called.

'No, it is I . . . can I come in?'

'Of course. Why, what a Santa Claus! Hang your coat on the landing and shake yourself over the banisters. Had a good time?'

The room was full of light and warmth. Elsa, in a white velvet tea-gown, lay curled up on the sofa – a book of fashions on her lap, a box of creams beside her.

The curtains were not yet drawn before the windows and a blue light shone through, and the white boughs of the trees sprayed across.

A woman's room – full of flowers and photographs and silk pillows – the floor smothered in rugs – an immense tiger-skin under the piano – just the head protruding – sleepily savage.

'It was good enough,' said Max. 'Victor can't be in till late. He told me to come up and tell you.'

He started walking up and down – tore off his gloves and flung them on the table.

'Don't do that, Max,' said Elsa, 'you get on my nerves. And I've got a headache today; I'm feverish and quite flushed . . . Don't I look flushed?'

He paused by the window and glanced at her a moment over his shoulder.

'No,' he said, 'I didn't notice it.'

'Oh, you haven't looked at me properly, and I've got a new tea-gown on, too.' She pulled her skirts together and patted a little place on the couch.

'Come along and sit by me and tell me why you're being naughty.'

But, standing by the window, he suddenly flung his arm across his eyes.

'Oh,' he said, 'I can't. I'm done – I'm spent – I'm smashed.'

Silence in the room. The fashion-book fell to the floor with a quick rustle of leaves. Elsa sat forward, her hands clasped in her lap; a strange light shone in her eyes, a red colour stained her mouth.

Then she spoke very quietly.

'Come over here and explain yourself. I don't know what on earth you are talking about.'

'You do know – you know far better than I. You've simply played with Victor in my presence that I may feel worse. You've tormented me – you've led me on – offering me everything and nothing at all. It's been a spider-and-fly business from first to last – and I've never for one moment been ignorant of that – and I've never for one moment been able to withstand it.'

He turned round deliberately.

'Do you suppose that when you asked me to pin your flowers into your evening gown – when you let me come into your bedroom when Victor was out while you did your hair – when you pretended to be a baby and let me feed you with grapes – when you have run to me and searched in all my pockets for a cigarette – knowing perfectly well where they were kept – going through every pocket just the same – I knowing too – I keeping up the farce – do you suppose that now you have finally lighted your bonfire you are going to find it a peaceful and pleasant thing – you are going to prevent the whole house from burning?'

She suddenly turned white and drew in her breath sharply.

'Don't talk to me like that. You have no right to talk to me like that. I am another man's wife.'

'Hum,' he sneered, throwing back his head, 'that's rather late in the game, and that's been your trump card all along. You only love

Victor on the cat-and-cream principle – you a poor little starved kitten that he's given everything to, that he's carried in his breast, never dreaming that those little pink claws could tear out a man's heart.'

She stirred, looking at him with almost fear in her eyes.

'After all' – unsteadily – 'this is my room; I'll have to ask you to go.'

But he stumbled towards her, knelt down by the couch, burying his head in her lap, clasping his arms round her waist.

'And I *love* you – I love you; the humiliation of it – I adore you. Don't – don't – just a minute let me stay here – just a moment in a whole life – Elsa! Elsa!'

She leant back and pressed her head into the pillows.

Then his muffled voice: 'I feel like a savage. I want your whole body. I want to carry you away to a cave and love you until I kill you – you can't understand how a man feels. I kill myself when I see you – I'm sick of my own strength that turns in upon itself, and dies, and rises new born like a Phoenix out of the ashes of that horrible death. Love me just this once, tell me a lie, *say* that you do – you are always lying.'

Instead, she pushed him away – frightened.

'Get up,' she said; 'suppose the servant came in with the tea?'

'Oh, ye gods!' He stumbled to his feet and stood staring down at her.

'You're rotten to the core and so am I. But you're heathenishly beautiful.'

The woman went over to the piano – stood there – striking one note – her brows drawn together. Then she shrugged her shoulders and smiled.

'I'll make a confession. Every word you have said is true. I can't help it. I can't help seeking admiration any more than a cat can help going to people to be stroked. It's my nature. I'm born out of my time. And yet, you know, I'm not a *common* woman. I like men to adore me – to flatter me – even to make love to me – but I would never give myself to any man. I would never let a man kiss me . . . even.'

'It's immeasurably worse – you've no legitimate excuse. Why, even a prostitute has a greater sense of generosity!'

'I know,' she said, 'I know perfectly well – but I can't help the way I'm built . . . Are you going?'

He put on his gloves.

'Well,' he said, 'what's going to happen to us now?'

Again she shrugged her shoulders.

'I haven't the slightest idea. I never have – just let things occur.'

*   *   *

'All alone?' cried Victor. 'Has Max been here?'

'He only stayed a moment, and wouldn't even have tea. I sent him home to change his clothes . . . He was frightfully boring.'

'You poor darling, your hair's coming down. I'll fix it, stand still a moment . . . so you were bored?'

'Um – m – frightfully . . . Oh, you've run a hairpin right into your wife's head – you naughty boy!'

She flung her arms round his neck and looked up at him, half laughing, like a beautiful, loving child.

'God! What a woman you are,' said the man. 'You make me so infernally proud – dearest, that I . . . I tell you!'